D1087891

ANOTHER
THREE-ACT SPECIAL

3 Complete Mystery
Novels
in
One Volume

NGAIO MARSH

Another Three-Act Special

3 COMPLETE MYSTERY NOVELS

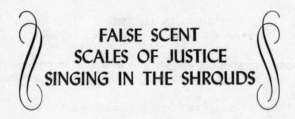

FALSE SCENT
SCALES OF JUSTICE
SINGING IN THE SHROUDS

Little, Brown and Company
Boston   **Toronto**

FALSE SCENT

For Jemima with love

Contents

CHAPTER ONE   Pardoner's Place.   9:00 A.M.

When she died it was as if all the love she had inspired in so many people suddenly blossomed. She had never, of course, realized how greatly she was loved, never known that she was to be carried by six young men who would ask to perform this last courtesy: to bear her on their strong shoulders, so gently and with such dedication.

Quite insignificant people were there: her old Ninn, the family nurse, with a face like a boot, grimly crying. And Florence, her dresser, with a bunch of primroses, because of all flowers they were the ones she had best loved to see on her make-up table. And George, the stage doorkeeper at the Unicorn, sober as sober and telling anyone who would listen to him that there, if you liked, had been a great lady. Pinky Cavendish in floods and Maurice, very Guardee, with a stiff upper lip. Crowds of people whom she herself would have scarcely remembered but upon whom, at some time, she had bestowed the gift of her charm.

All the Knights and Dames, of course, and the Management, and Timon Gantry, the great producer, who had so often directed her. Bertie Saracen, who had created her dresses since the days when she was a bit-part actress and who had, indeed, risen to his present eminence in the wake of her mounting fame. But it was not for her fame that they had come to say goodbye to her. It was because, quite simply, they had loved her.

And Richard? Richard was there, white and withdrawn. And—this was an afterthought—and, of course, Charles.

Miss Bellamy paused, bogged down in her own fantasy. Enjoyable tears started from her eyes. She often indulged herself with plans for her

funeral and she never failed to be moved by them. The only catch was
the indisputable fact that she wouldn't live to enjoy it. She would be,
as it were, cheated of her own obsequies and she felt there was some
injustice in this.

But perhaps, after all, she *would* know. Perhaps she would hover ambiguously over the whole show, employing her famous gift for making a
party go without seeming to do anything about it. Perhaps—? Feeling
slightly uncomfortable, she reminded herself of her magnificent constitu-
tion and decided to think about something else.

There was plenty to think about. The new play. Her role: a fat part if
ever she saw one. The long speech about keeping the old chin up and
facing the future with a wry smile. Richard hadn't put it quite like that
and she did sometimes wish he would write more simply. Perhaps she
would choose her moment and suggest to him that a few homely phrases
would do the trick much more effectively than those rather involved,
rather *arid* sentences that were so bloody difficult to memorize. What
was wanted—the disreputable word "gimmick" rose to the surface and
was instantly slapped down—what was wanted, when all was said and
done, was the cosy human touch: a vehicle for her particular genius. She
believed in humanity. Perhaps this morning would be the right occasion
to talk to Richard. He would, of course, be coming to wish her many
happy returns. Her birthday! That had to be thought of selectively and
with a certain amount of care. She must at all costs exclude that too easy
little sum whose answer would provide her age. She had, quite literally
and by dint of a yogi-like discipline, succeeded in forgetting it. Nobody
else that mattered knew, except Florence, who was utterly discreet and
Old Ninn, who, one must face it, was getting a bit garrulous, especially
when she'd taken her glass or two of port. Please God she wouldn't forget
herself this afternoon.

After all it was how you felt and how you looked that mattered. She
lifted her head from the pillows and turned it. There, across the room,
she was, reflected in the tall glass above her dressing-table. Not bad, she
thought, not half bad, even at that hour and with no make-up. She
touched her face here and there, manipulating the skin above the temples
and at the top of the jawline. To lift or not to lift? Pinky Cavendish was
all for it and said that nowadays there was no need for the stretched look.
But what about her famous triangular smile? Maintaining the lift, she
smiled. The effect was still triangular.

She rang her bell. It was rather touching to think of her little household, oriented to her signal. Florence, Cooky, Gracefield, the parlourmaid, the housemaid and the odd woman: all ready in the kitchen and
full of plans for the Great Day. Old Ninn, revelling in her annual holiday,

sitting up in bed with her *News of the World* or perhaps putting the final touch to the bed-jacket she had undoubtedly knitted and which would have to be publicly worn for her gratification. And, of course, Charles. It was curious how Miss Bellamy tended to leave her husband out of her meditations, because, after all, she was extremely fond of him. She hurriedly inserted him. He would be waiting for Gracefield to tell him she was awake and had rung. Presently he would appear, wearing a pink scrubbed look and that plum-coloured dressing-gown that did so little to help.

She heard a faint chink and a subdued rumble. The door opened and Florence came in with her tray.

"Top of the morning, dear," said Florence. "What's it feel like to be eighteen again?"

"You old fool," Miss Bellamy said and grinned at her. "It feels fine."

Florence built pillows up behind her and set the tray across her knees. She then drew back the curtains and lit the fire. She was a pale, small woman with black dyed hair and sardonic eyes. She had been Miss Bellamy's dresser for twenty-five years and her personal maid for fifteen. "Three rousing cheers," she said, "it's a handsome-looking morning."

Miss Bellamy examined her tray. The basket-ends were full of telegrams, a spray of orchids lay across the plate and beside it a parcel in silver wrapping tied with pink ribbon.

"What's all this?" she asked, as she had asked for her last fifteen birthdays, and took up the parcel.

"The flowers are from the Colonel. He'll be bringing his present later on, as per usual, I suppose."

"I wasn't talking about the flowers," Miss Bellamy said and opened the parcel. "Florrie! Florrie, *darling!*"

Florence clattered the firearms. "Might as well get in early," she muttered, "or it'd never be noticed."

It was a chemise, gossamer fine and exquisitely embroidered.

"Come *here!*" Miss Bellamy said, fondly bullying.

Florence walked over to the bed and suffered herself to be kissed. Her face became crimson. For a moment she looked at her employer with a devotion that was painful in its intensity and then turned aside, her eyes filmed with unwilling tears.

"But it's out of this world!" Miss Bellamy marvelled, referring to the chemise. "That's all! It's just *made* my day for me." She shook her head slowly from side to side, lost in wonderment. "I can't wait," she said and, indeed, she was very pleased with it.

"There's the usual mail," Florence grunted. "More, if anything."

"Truly?"

"Outside on the trolley. Will I fetch it in here?"

"After my bath, darling, may we?"

Florence opened drawers and doors, and began to lay out the clothes her mistress had chosen to wear. Miss Bellamy, who was on a strict diet, drank her tea, ate her toast, and opened her telegrams, awarding each of them some pleased ejaculation. "Darling, Bertie! Such a sweet muddled little message. And a cable, Florrie, from the Bantings in New York. Heaven of them!"

"That show's folding, I'm told," Florence said, "and small wonder. Dirty *and* dull, by all accounts. You mustn't be both."

"You don't know anything about it," Miss Bellamy absent-mindedly observed. She was staring in bewilderment at the next telegram. "This," she said, "isn't true. It's just not true. My dear Florrie, *will* you listen." Modulating her lovely voice, Miss Bellamy read it aloud, " 'Her birth was of the womb of morning dew and her conception of the joyous prime.' "

"Disgusting," said Florence.

"I call it rather touching. But who in the wide world is Octavius Browne?"

"Search me, love." Florence helped Miss Bellamy into a negligée designed by Bertie Saracen, and herself went into the bathroom. Miss Bellamy settled down to some preliminary work on her face.

There was a tap on the door connecting her room with her husband's and he came in. Charles Templeton was sixty years old, big and fair with a heavy belly. His eyeglass dangled over his dark red dressing-gown; his hair, thin and babyishly fine, was carefully brushed; and his face, which had the florid colouring associated with heart disease, was freshly shaved. He kissed his wife's hand and forehead and laid a small parcel before her. "A very happy birthday to you, Mary, my dear," he said. Twenty years ago, when she married him, she had told him that his voice was charming. If it was so still, she no longer noticed it or, indeed, listened very attentively to much that he said.

But she let her birthday gaiety play about him and was enchanted with her present, a diamond and emerald bracelet. It was, even for Charles, quite exceptionally magnificent, and for a fleeting moment she remembered that he, as well as Florence and Old Ninn, knew her age. She wondered if there was any intention of underlining this particular anniversary. There were some numerals that by their very appearance—stodgy and rotund—wore an air of horrid maturity. Five, for instance. She pulled her thoughts up short and showed him the telegram. "I should like to know what in the world you make of that," she said and went into the bathroom, leaving the door open. Florence came back and began to make the bed with an air of standing none of its nonsense.

"Good morning, Florence," Charles Templeton said. He put up his eyeglass and walked over to the bow window with the telegram.

"Good morning, sir," Florence woodenly rejoined. Only when she was alone with her mistress did she allow herself the freedom of the dressing-room.

"Did you," Miss Bellamy shouted from her bath, "ever see anything quite like it?"

"But it's delightful," he said, "and how very nice of Octavius."

"You don't mean to say you know who he is?"

"Octavius Browne? Of course I do. He's the old boy down below in the Pegasus Bookshop. Up at the House, but a bit before my time. Delightful fellow."

"Blow me down flat!" Miss Bellamy ejaculated, splashing luxuriously. "You mean that dim little place with a fat cat in the window."

"That's it. He specializes in pre-Jacobean literature."

"Does that account for the allusion to wombs and conceptions? Of *what* can he be thinking, poor Mr. Browne?"

"It's a quotation," Charles said, letting his eyeglass drop. "From Spenser. I bought a very nice Spenser from him last week. No doubt he supposes you've read it."

"Then, of course, I must pretend I have. I shall call on him and thank him. Kind Mr. Browne!"

"They're great friends of Richard's."

Miss Bellamy's voice sharpened a little. "Who? *They?*"

"Octavius Browne and his niece. A good-looking girl." Charles glanced at Florence and after a moment's hesitation added, "She's called Anelida Lee."

Florence cleared her throat.

"Not true!" The voice in the bathroom gave a little laugh. "A-nelly-da! It sounds like a face cream."

"It's Chaucerian."

"I suppose the cat's called Piers Plowman."

"No. He's out of the prevailing period. He's called Hodge."

"I've never heard Richard utter her name."

Charles said; "She's on the stage, it appears."

"Oh, *God!*"

"In that new club theatre behind Walton Street. The Bonaventure."

"You need say no more, my poor Charles. One knows the form."

Charles was silent and the voice asked impatiently, "Are you still there?"

"Yes, my dear."

"How do you know Richard's so thick with them?"

"I meet him there occasionally," Charles said, and added lightly, "I'm thick with them too, Mary."

There was a further silence and then the voice, delightful and gay, shouted, "Florrie! Bring me *you know what.*"

Florence picked up her own offering and went into the bathroom.

Charles Templeton stared through the window at a small London square, brightly receptive of April sunshine. He could just see the flower-woman at the corner of Pardoner's Row, sitting in a galaxy of tulips. There were tulips everywhere. His wife had turned the bow window into an indoor garden and had filled it with them and with a great mass of early-flowering azaleas, brought up in the conservatory and still in bud. He examined these absent-mindedly and discovered among them a tin with a spray-gun mechanism. The tin was labelled 'Slaypest' and bore alarming captions about the lethal nature of its contents. Charles peered at them through his eyeglass.

"Florence," he said, "I don't think this stuff ought to be left lying about."

"Just what I tell her," Florence said, returning.

"There are all sorts of warnings. It shouldn't be used in enclosed places. *Is* it used like that?"

"It won't be for want of my telling her if it is."

"Really, I *don't* like it. Could you lose it?"

"I'd get the full treatment meself if I did," Florence grunted.

"Nevertheless," Charles said, "I think you should do so."

Florence shot a resentful look at him and muttered under her breath.

"What did you say?" he asked.

"I said it wasn't so easy. She knows. She can read. I've told her." She glowered at him and then said, "I take my orders from her. Always have and always will."

He waited for a moment. "Quite so," he said. "But all the same—" and hearing his wife's voice, put the spray-gun down, gave a half-sigh and turned to confront the familiar room.

Miss Bellamy came into it wearing Florence's gift. There was a patch of sunshine in the room and she posed in it, expectant, unaware of its disobliging candour.

"Look at my smashing shift!" she cried. "Florrie's present! A new birthday suit."

She had "made an entrance," comic-provocative, skilfully French-farcical. She had no notion at all of the disservice she had done herself.

The voice that she had once called charming said, "Marvellous. How kind of Florence."

He was careful to wait a little longer before he said, "Well, darling,

I shall leave you to your mysteries," and went down to his solitary breakfast.

2

There was no particular reason why Richard Dakers should feel uplifted that morning; indeed, there were many formidable reasons why he should not. Nevertheless, as he made his way by bus and on foot to Pardoner's Place, he did experience, very strongly, that upward kick of the spirit which lies in London's power of bestowal. He sat in the front seat at the prow of the bus and felt like a figurehead, cleaving the tide of the King's Road, masterfully above it, yet gloriously of it. The Chelsea shops were full of tulips and when, leaving the bus, he walked to the corner of Pardoner's Row, there was his friend the flower-woman with buckets of them, still pouted up in buds.

"Morning, dear," said the flower-woman. "Duck of a day, innit?"

"It's a day for the gods," Richard agreed, "and your hat fits you like a halo, Mrs. Tinker."

"It's me straw," Mrs. Tinker said. "I usually seem to change to me straw on the second Sat in April."

"Aphrodite on her cockleshell couldn't say fairer. I'll take two dozen of the yellows."

She wrapped them up in green paper. "Ten bob to you," said Mrs. Tinker.

"Ruin!" Richard ejaculated, giving her eleven shillings. "Destitution! But what the hell!"

"That's right, dear, we don' care, do we? Tulips, lady? Lovely tulips."

Carrying his tulips and with his dispatch case tucked under his arm, Richard entered Pardoner's Place and turned right. Three doors along he came to the Pegasus, a bow-fronted Georgian house that had been converted by Octavius Browne into a bookshop. In the window, tilted and open, lay a first edition of Beijer and Duchartre's *Premières Comédies Italiennes*. A little further back, half in shadow, hung a Negro marionette, very grand in striped silks. And in the watery depths of the interior Richard could just make out the shapes of the three beautifully polished old chairs, the lovely table and the vertical strata of rows and rows of books. He could see, too, the figure of Anelida Lee moving about among her uncle's treasures, attended by Hodge, their cat. In the mornings Anelida, when not rehearsing at her club theatre, helped her uncle. She hoped that she was learning to be an actress. Richard, who knew a good deal about it, was convinced that already she was one.

He opened the door and went in.

Anelida had been dusting and wore her black smock, an uncompromising garment. Her hair was tied up in a white scarf. He had time to reflect that there was a particular beauty that most pleased when it was least adorned and that Anelida was possessed of it.

"Hullo," he said. "I've brought you some tulips. Good morning, Hodge." Hodge stared at him briefly, jerked his tail, and walked away.

"How lovely! But it's not *my* birthday."

"Never mind. It's because it's a nice morning and Mrs. Tinker was wearing her straw."

"I couldn't be better pleased," said Anelida. "Will you wait while I get a pot for them? There's a green jug."

She went into a room at the back. He heard a familiar tapping noise on the stairs. Her uncle Octavius came down, leaning on his black stick. He was a tall man of about sixty-three with a shock of grey hair and a mischievous face. He had a trick of looking at people out of the corners of his eyes as if inviting them to notice what a bad boy he was. He was rather touchy, immensely learned and thin almost to transparency.

"Good morning, my dear Dakers," he said, and seeing the tulips, touched one of them with the tip of a bluish finger. "Ah," he said, "'Art could not feign more simple grace, Nor Nature take a line away.' How very lovely and so pleasantly uncomplicated by any smell. We have found something for you, by the way. Quite nice and I hope in character, but it may be a little too expensive. You must tell us what you think."

He opened a parcel on his desk and stood aside for Richard to look at the contents.

"A tinsel picture, as you see," he said, "of Madame Vestris *en travesti* in jockey's costume." He looked sideways at Richard. "Beguiling little breeches, don't you think? Do you suppose it would appeal to Miss Bellamy?"

"I don't see how it could fail."

"It's rare-ish. The frame's contemporary. I'm afraid it's twelve guineas."

"It's mine," Richard said. "Or rather, it's Mary's."

"You're sure? Then, if you'll excuse me for a moment, I'll get Nell to make a birthday parcel of it. There's a sheet of Victorian tinsel somewhere. Nell, my dear! Would you—?"

He tapped away and presently Anelida returned with the green jug and his parcel, beautifully wrapped.

Richard put his hand on his dispatch case. "What do you suppose is in there?" he asked.

"Not—not *the* play? Not *Husbandry in Heaven*?"

"Hot from the typist." He watched her thin hands arrange the tulips. "Anelida, I'm going to show it to Mary."

"You couldn't choose a better day," she said warmly, and when he didn't answer, "What's the matter?"

"There isn't a part for her in it," he blurted out.

After a moment she said, "Well, no. But does that matter?"

"It might. If, of course, it ever comes to production. And, by the way, Timmy Gantry's seen it and makes agreeable noises. All the same, it's tricky about Mary."

"But why? I don't see—"

"It's not all that easy to explain," he mumbled.

"You've already written a new play for her and she's delighted with it, isn't she? This is something quite different."

"And better? You've read it."

"Immeasurably better. In another world. Everybody must see it."

"Timmy Gantry likes it."

"Well, there you are! It's special. Won't she see that?"

He said: "Anelida, dear, you don't really know the theatre yet, do you? Or the way actors tick over?"

"Well, perhaps I don't. But I know how close you are to each other and how wonderfully she understands you. You've told me."

"That's just it," Richard said and there followed a long silence.

"I don't believe," he said at last, "that I've ever told you exactly what she and Charles did?"

"No," she agreed. "Not exactly. But—"

"My parents, who were Australians, were friends of Mary's. They were killed in a car smash on the Grande Corniche when I was rising two. They were staying with Mary at the time. There was no money to speak of. She had me looked after by her own old nanny, the celebrated Ninn, and then, after she had married Charles, they took me over completely. I owe everything to her. I like to think that, in a way, the plays have done something to repay. And now—you see what I go and do."

Anelida finished her tulips and looked directly at him. "I'm sure it'll work out," she said gently. "All very fine, I daresay, for me to say so, but you see, you've talked so much about her, I almost feel I know her."

"I very much want you to know her. Indeed, this brings me to the main object of my pompous visit. Will you let me call for you at six and take you to see her? There's a party of sorts at half-past which I hope may amuse you, but I'd like you to meet her first. Will you, Anelida?"

She waited too long before she said, "I don't think I can. I'm—I've booked myself up."

"I don't believe you. Why won't you come?"

"But I can't. It's her birthday and it's special to her and her friends.

You can't go hauling in an unknown female. *And* an unknown actress, to boot."

"Of course I can."

"It wouldn't be comely."

"What a fantastic word! And why the hell do you suppose it wouldn't be comely for the two people I like best in the world to meet each other?"

Anelida said, "I didn't know—"

"Yes, you did," he said crossly. "You must have."

"We scarcely know each other."

"I'm sorry you feel like that about it."

"I only meant—well, in point of time—"

"Don't hedge."

"Now, look here—"

"I'm sorry. Evidently I've taken too much for granted."

While they stared aghast at the quarrel that between them they had somehow concocted, Octavius came tapping back. "By the way," he said happily, "I yielded this morning to a romantic impulse, Dakers. I sent your patroness a birthday greeting: one among hundreds, no doubt. The allusion was from Spenser. I hope she won't take it amiss."

"How very nice of you, sir," Richard said loudly. "She'll be enchanted. She loves people to be friendly. Thank you for finding the picture."

And forgetting to pay for it, he left hurriedly in a miserable frame of mind.

3

Mary Bellamy's house was next door to the Pegasus Bookshop, but Richard was too rattled to go in. He walked round Pardoner's Place trying to sort out his thoughts. He suffered one of those horrid experiences, fortunately rare, in which the victim confronts himself as a stranger in an abrupt perspective. The process resembles that of pseudo-scientific films in which the growth of a plant, by mechanical skulduggery, is reduced from seven weeks to as many minutes and the subject is seen wavering, extending, elongating itself in response to some irresistible force until it breaks into its pre-ordained fluorescence.

The irresistible force in Richard's case had undoubtedly been Mary Bellamy. The end-product, after twenty-seven years of the treatment, was two successful West End comedies, a third in the bag, and (his hand tightened on his dispatch case) a serious play.

He owed it all, as he had so repeatedly told her, to Mary. Well, perhaps not quite all. Not the serious play.

He had almost completed his round of the little Place and, not wanting to pass the shop window, turned back. Why in the world had he gone grand and huffy when Anelida refused to meet Mary? And why *did* she refuse? Any other girl in Anelida's boots, he thought uneasily, would have jumped at that sort of invitation: the great Mary Bellamy's birthday party. A tiny, handpicked group from the topmost drawer in the London theatre. *The* Management. *The* producer. Any other girl—He fetched up short, not liking himself very much, conscious that if he followed his thoughts to their logical conclusion he would arrive at an uncomfortable position. What sort of man, he would have to ask himself, was Richard Dakers? Reality would disintegrate and he would find himself face-to-face with a stranger. It was a familiar experience and one he didn't enjoy. He shook himself free of it, made a sudden decision, walked quickly to the house and rang the bell.

Charles Templeton breakfasted in his study on the ground floor. The door was open and Richard saw him there, reading his *Times*, at home among his six so judiciously chosen pieces of *chinoiserie*, his three admirable pictures, his few distinguished chairs and lovely desk. Charles was fastidious about his surroundings and extremely knowledgeable. He could wait, sometimes for years, for the acquisition of a single treasure.

Richard went in. "Charles!" he said. "How are you?"

"Hullo, old boy. Come to make your devotions?"

"Am I the first?"

"The first in person. There are the usual massive offerings in kind. Mary'll be delighted to see you."

"I'll go up," Richard said, but still hovered. Charles lowered his newspaper. How often, Richard wondered, had he seen him make that gesture, dropping his eyeglass and vaguely smiling. Richard, still involved in the aftermath of his moment of truth, if that was its real nature, asked himself what he knew of Charles. How used he was to that even courtesy, that disengagement! What of Charles in other places? What of the reputedly implacable man of affairs who had built his own fortune? Or of the lover Charles must have been five and twenty years ago? Impossible to imagine, Richard thought, looking vaguely at an empty niche in the wall.

He said, "Hullo! Where's the T'ang musician?"

"Gone," Charles said.

"Gone! Where? Not broken?"

"Chipped. The peg of her lute. Gracefield did it, I think. I've given her to Maurice Warrender."

"But—even so—I mean, so often they're not absolutely perfect and you —it was your treasure."

"Not now," Charles said. "I'm a perfectionist, you know."

"That's what you say!" Richard exclaimed warmly. "But I bet it was because Maurice always coveted her. You're so absurdly generous."

"Oh nonsense," Charles said and looked at his paper. Richard hesitated. He heard himself say,

"Charles, do I ever say thank you? To you and Mary?"

"My dear fellow, what for?"

"For everything." He took refuge in irony. "For befriending the poor orphan boy, you know, among other things."

"I sincerely hope you're not making a vicarious birthday resolution."

"It just struck me."

Charles waited for a moment and then said, "You've given us a tremendous interest and very much pleasure." He again hesitated as if assembling his next sentence. "Mary and I," he said at last, "look upon you as an achievement. And now, do go and make your pretty speeches to her."

"Yes," Richard said. "I'd better, hadn't I? See you later."

Charles raised his newspaper and Richard went slowly upstairs, wishing, consciously, for perhaps the first time in his life, that he was not going to visit Miss Bellamy.

She was in her room, dressed and enthroned among her presents. He slipped into another gear as he took her to his heart in a birthday embrace and then held her at arm's length to tell her how lovely she looked.

"Darling, darling, darling!" she cried joyously. "How *perfect* of you to come. I've been hoping and hoping!"

It occurred to him that it would have been strange indeed if he hadn't performed this time-honoured observance, but he kissed her again and gave her his present.

It was early in the day and her reservoir of enthusiasm scarcely tapped. She was able to pour a freshet of praise over his tinsel picture and did so with many cries of gratitude and wonder. Where, she asked, where, *where* had he discovered the *one*, the *perfect* present?

It was an opening Richard had hoped for, but he found himself a little apprehensive nevertheless.

"I found it," he said, "at the Pegasus—or rather Octavius Browne found it for me. He says it's rare-ish."

Her triangular smile didn't fade. Her eyes continued to beam into his, her hands to press his hands.

"Ah yes!" she cried gaily. "The old man in the bookshop! Believe it or not, darling, he sent me a telegram about my conception. Too sweet, but a little difficult to acknowledge."

"He's very donnish," Richard said. She made a comic face at him. "He *was*, in fact, a don, but he found himself out of sympathy with angry young men and set up a bookshop instead."

She propped up her tinsel picture on the dressing-table and gazed at it through half-closed eyes. "Isn't there a daughter or something? I seem to have heard—"

"A niece," Richard said. Maddeningly, his mouth had gone dry.

"Ought I," she asked, "to nip downstairs and thank him? One never quite knows with that sort of person."

Richard kissed her hand. "Octavius," he said, "is not that sort of person, darling. Do nip down. He'll be enchanted. And Mary—"

"What, my treasure?"

"I thought perhaps you might be terribly kind and ask them for a drink. If you find them pleasant, that is."

She sat at her dressing-table and examined her face in the glass. "I wonder," she said, "if I *really* like that new eyeshade." She took up a heavy Venetian glass scent-spray and used it lavishly. "I hope someone gives me some really superlative scent," she said. "This is almost gone." She put it down. "For a drink?" she said "When? Not today, of course."

"*Not* today, you think?"

She opened her eyes very wide. "My dear, we'd only embarrass them."

"Well," he murmured, "see how you feel about it."

She turned back to the glass and said nothing. He opened his dispatch case and took out his typescript.

"I've brought something," he said, "for you to read. It's a surprise, Mary." He laid it on the dressing-table. "There."

She looked at the cover page. "*Husbandry in Heaven.* A play by Richard Dakers."

"Dicky? Dicky, darling, *what* is all this?"

"Something I've kept for today," he said and knew at once that he'd made a mistake. She gave him that special luminous gaze that meant she was deeply moved. "Oh Dicky!" she whispered. "For me? My *dear!*"

He was panic-stricken.

"But when?" she asked him, slowly shaking her head in bewilderment. "When did you *do* it? With all the other work? I don't understand. I'm flabbergasted, Dicky!"

"I've been working on it for some time. It's—it's quite a different thing. Not a comedy. You may hate it."

"Is it the great one—at last?" she whispered. "The one that we always knew would happen? And all by yourself, Dicky? Not even with poor stupid, old, loving me to listen?"

She was saying all the things he would least have chosen for her to say. It was appalling.

"For all I know," he said, "it may be frighteningly bad. I've got to that state where one just can't tell. Anyway, don't let's burden the great day with it."

"You couldn't have given me anything else that would make me half so happy." She stroked the typescript with both eloquent, not very young hands. "I'll shut myself away for an hour before lunch and wolf it up."

"Mary," he said desperately. "Don't be so sanguine about it. It's not your sort of play."

"I won't hear a word against it. You've written it for *me*, darling."

He was hunting desperately for some way of telling her he had done nothing of the sort when she said gaily, "All right! We'll see. I won't tease you. What were we talking about? Your funnies in the bookshop? I'll pop in this morning and see what I think of them, shall I? Will that do?"

Before he could answer two voices, one elderly and uncertain and the other a fluting alto, were raised outside in the passage:

"*Happy birthday to you. Happy birthday to you.*
Happy birthday, dear Mary,
Happy birthday to you."

The door opened to admit Colonel Warrender and Mr. Bertie Saracen.

4

Colonel Warrender was sixty years old, a bachelor and a cousin of Charles Templeton, whom, in a leaner, better-looking way, he slightly resembled. He kept himself fit, was well dressed and wore a moustache so neatly managed that it looked as if it had been ironed on his face. His manner was pleasant and his bearing soldierly.

Mr. Bertie Saracen was also immaculate, but more adventurously so. The sleeves of his jacket were narrower and displayed a great deal of pinkish cuff. He had a Berlin-china complexion, wavy hair, blue eyes and wonderfully small hands. His air was gay and insouciant. He too was a bachelor and most understandably so.

They made a comic entrance together: Warrender good-naturedly self-conscious, Bertie Saracen revelling in his act of prima ballerina. He chasséd to right and left, holding aloft his votive offering and finally laid it at Miss Bellamy's feet.

"God, what a fool I must look!" he exclaimed. "Take it, darling, quickly or we'll kill the laugh."

A spate of greetings broke out and an examination of gifts: from Warrender, who had been abroad, gloves of Grenoble, and from Bertie a miniature group of five bathing beauties and a photographer all made of balsa wood and scraps of cotton. "It's easily the nicest present you'll get," he said. "And now I must enjoy a good jeer at all the others."

He flitted about the room, making little darts at them. Warrender, a rather silent man, generally believed to entertain a long-standing and blameless adoration of Mary Bellamy, had a word with Richard, who liked him.

"Rehearsals started yet?" he asked. "Mary tells me she's delighted with her new part."

"Not yet. It's the mixture as before," Richard rejoined.

Warrender gave him a brief look. "Early days to settle into a routine, isn't it?" he said surprisingly. "Leave that to the old hands, isn't it?" He had a trick of ending his remarks with this colloquialism.

"I'm trying, on the side, to break out in a rash of serious writing."

"Are you? Good. Afford to take risks, I'd have thought."

"How pleasant," Richard exclaimed, "to hear somebody say that!"

Warrender looked at his shoes. "Never does," he said, "to let yourself be talked into things. Not that I know anything about it."

Richard thought with gratitude: "That's exactly the kind of thing I wanted to be told," but was prevented from saying so by the entrance of Old Ninn.

Old Ninn's real name was Miss Ethel Plumtree, but she was given the courtesy title of "Mrs." She had been Mary Bellamy's nurse, and from the time of his adoption by Mary and Charles, Richard's also. Every year she emerged from retirement for a fortnight to stay with her former charge. She was small, scarlet-faced and fantastically opinionated. Her age was believed to be eighty-one. Nannies being universally accepted as character parts rather than people in their own right, Old Ninn was the subject of many of Mary Bellamy's funniest stories. Richard sometimes wondered if she played up to her own legend. In her old age she had developed a liking for port and under its influence made great mischief among the servants and kept up a sort of guerrilla warfare with Florence, with whom, nevertheless, she was on intimate terms. They were united, Miss Bellamy said, in their devotion to herself.

Wearing a cerise shawl and a bold floral print, for she adored bright colours, Old Ninn trudged across the room with the corners of her mouth turned down and laid a tissue paper parcel on the dressing-table.

"Happy birthday, m'," she said. For so small a person she had an alarmingly deep voice.

A great fuss was made over her. Bertie Saracen attempted Mercutian badinage and called her Nurse Plumtree. She ignored him and addressed herself exclusively to Richard.

"We don't see much of you these days," she said, and by the sour look she gave him, proclaimed her affection.

"I've been busy, Ninn."

"Still making up your plays, by all accounts."

"That's it."

"You always were a fanciful boy. Easy to see, you've never grown out of it."

Mary Bellamy had unwrapped the parcel and disclosed a knitted bed-jacket of sensible design. Her thanks were effusive, but Old Ninn cut them short.

"Four-ply," she said. "You require warmth when you're getting on in years and the sooner you face the fact the more comfortable you'll find yourself. Good morning, sir," Ninn added, catching sight of Warrender. "I dare say you'll bear me out. Well, I won't keep you."

With perfect composure she trudged away, leaving a complete silence behind her.

"Out of this world!" Bertie said with a shrillish laugh. "Darling Mary, here I am *sizzling* with decorative fervour. *When* are we to tuck up our sleeves and lay all our plots and plans?"

"Now, darling, if you're ready. Dicky, treasure, will you and Maurice be able to amuse yourselves? We'll scream if we want any help. Come along, Bertie."

She linked her arm in his. He sniffed ecstatically. "You smell," he said, "like all, but *all*, of King Solomon's wives *and* concubines. In spring. *En avant!*"

They went downstairs. Warrender and Richard were left together in a room that still retained the flavour of her personality, as inescapably potent as the all-pervasive aftermath of her scent.

It was an old established custom that she and Bertie arranged the house for her birthday party. Her drawing-room was the first on the left on the ground floor. It was a long Georgian saloon with a door into the hall and with folding doors leading into the dining-room. This, in its turn opened both into the hall and into the conservatory, which was her especial pride. Beyond the conservatory lay a small formal garden. When all the doors were open an impressive vista was obtained. Bertie himself had "done" the décor and had used a wealth of old French brocades. He had painted bunches of misty cabbage roses in the recesses above the doors and in the wall panels, and had found some really distinguished chandeliers. This year the flowers were to be all white and yellow. He settled down with the greatest efficiency and determination to his task, borrowing one of Gracefield's, the butler's, aprons for the purpose. Miss Bellamy tied herself into a modish confection with a flounced bib, put on washleather gloves, and wandered happily about her conservatory, snipping off deadheads and re-arranging groups of flowerpots. She was an enthusiastic gardener. They shouted at each other from room to room, exchanging theatre shop, and breaking every now and then into stage cockney: "Whatseye, dear?" and "Coo! You wouldn't credit it!" this mode of communication being sacred to the occasion. They enjoyed themselves enormously while from under Bertie's clever fingers emerged bouquets of white and gold and wonderful garlands for the table. In this setting, Miss Bellamy was at her best.

They had been at it for perhaps half an hour and Bertie had retired to the flower-room when Gracefield ushered in Miss Kate Cavendish, known to her intimates as Pinky.

Pinky was younger than her famous contemporary and less distinguished. She had played supporting roles in many Bellamy successes and their personal relationship, not altogether to her satisfaction, resembled their professional one. She had an amusing face, dressed plainly and well, and possessed the gifts of honesty and direct thinking. She was, in fact, a charming woman.

"I'm in a tizzy," she said. "High as a rocket, darling, and in a minute I'll tell you why. Forty thousand happy returns, Mary, and may your silhouette never grow greater. Here's my offering."

It was a flask of a new scent by a celebrated maker and was called Formidable. "I got it smuggled over from Paris," she said. "It's not here yet. A lick on either lobe, I'm told, and the satellites reel in their courses."

Miss Bellamy insisted on opening it. She dabbed the stopper on her wrists and sniffed. "Pinky," she said solemnly, "it's *too* much! Darling, it opens the *floodgates!* Honestly!"

"It's good, isn't it?"

"Florrie shall put it into my spray. At once. Before Bertie can get at it. You know what he is."

"Is Bertie here?" Pinky asked quickly.

"He's in the flower-room."

"Oh."

"Why? Have you fallen out with him?"

"Far from it," Pinky said. "Only—well it's just that I'm not really meant to let my cat out of its bag as yet and Bertie's involved. But I really am, I fear, more than a little tiddly."

"*You!* I thought you never touched a thing in the morning."

"Nor I do. But this is an occasion, Mary. I've been drinking with the Management. Only two small ones, but on an empty tum: Bingo!"

Miss Bellamy said sharply, "*With the Management?*"

"That gives you pause, doesn't it?"

"And Bertie's involved?"

Pinky laughed rather wildly and said, "If I don't tell somebody I'll spontaneously combust, so I'm going to tell you. Bertie can lump it, bless him, because why, after all, shouldn't I be audibly grateful."

Mary Bellamy looked fixedly at her friend for a moment and then said, "Grateful?"

"All right. I know I'm incoherent. Here it comes. Darling: I'm to have the lead in Bongo Dillon's new play. At the Unicorn. Opening in September. Swear you won't breathe it, but it's true and it's settled and the contract's mine for the signing. My first lead, Mary. Oh God, I'm so happy."

A hateful and all too-familiar jolt under the diaphragm warned Miss Bellamy that she had been upset. Simultaneously she knew that somehow or another she must run up a flag of welcome, must show a responsive warmth, must override the awful, menaced, slipping feeling, the nausea of the emotions that Pinky's announcement had churned up.

"Sweetie-pie!" she said. "How wonderful!" It wasn't, she reflected, much cop as an expression of delighted congratulation from an old chum, but Pinky was too excited to pay any attention. She went prancing on about the merits of her contract, the glories of the role, the nice behaviour of the Management (Miss Bellamy's Management, as she sickeningly noted), and the feeling that at last this was going to be It. All this gave Miss Bellamy a breather. She began to make fairly appropriate responses. Presently when Pinky drew breath, she was able to say with the right touch of down-to-earth honesty:

"Pinky, this is going to be your Great Thing."

"I know it! I feel it myself," Pinky said soberly and added, "Please God, I'll have what it takes. Please God, I will."

"My dear, you will," she rejoined and for the life of her couldn't help adding, "Of course, I haven't read the play."

"The *purest* Bongo! Comedy with a twist. You know? Though I says it as shouldn't, it's right up my cul-de-sac. Bongo says he had me in mind all the time he was writing it."

Miss Bellamy laughed. "Darling! We do know our Bongo, don't we? The number of plays he's said he'd written for me and when one looked at them—!"

With one of her infuriating moments of penetration, Pinky said, "Mary! Be pleased for me."

"But, sweetie, *naturally* I'm pleased. It sounds like a wonderful bit of luck and I hope with all my heart it works out."

"Of course, I know it means giving up my part in Richard's new one for you. But, face it, there wasn't much in it for me, was there? And nothing was really settled, so I'm not letting the side down, am I?"

Miss Bellamy couldn't help it. "My dear," she said with a kindly laugh, "we'll lose no sleep over that little problem: the part'll cast itself in two seconds."

"Exactly!" Pinky cried happily and Miss Bellamy felt one of her rare onsets of rage begin to stir. She said:

"But you were talking about Bertie, darling. Where does he come in?"

"Aha!" Pinky said maddeningly and shook her finger.

At this juncture Gracefield, the butler, arrived with a drinks tray. Miss Bellamy controlled herself. "Come on," she said, "I'm going to break my rule, too. We *must* have a drink on this, darling."

"No, no, no!"

"Yes, yes, yes. A teeny one. Pink for Pinky?"

She stood between Pinky and the drinks and poured out one stiff and one negligible gin-and-bitters. She gave the stiff one to Pinky.

"To your wonderful future, darling," she said. "Bottoms up!"

"Oh *dear!*" Pinky said. "I shouldn't."

"Never mind."

They drank.

"And Bertie?" Miss Bellamy asked presently. "Come on. You know I'm as silent as the grave."

The blush that long ago had earned Pinky her nickname appeared in her cheeks. "This really *is* a secret," she said. "Deep and deadly. But I'm sure he won't mind my telling *you*. You see, it's a part that has to be dressed up to the hilt—five changes and all of them grand as grand. Utterly beyond me and my little woman in Bayswater. Well! Bertie, being so much mixed up with the Management, has heard all about it, and do you know, darling, he's offered, *entirely* of his own accord, to do my clothes. Designs, materials, making—*everything* from Saracen. And all completely free-ers. *Isn't* that kind?"

Wave after wave of fury chased each other like electrical frequencies through Miss Bellamy's nerves and brain. She had time to think: "I'm going to throw a temperament and it's bad for me," and then she arrived at the point of climax.

The explosion was touched off by Bertie himself, who came tripping back with a garland of tuberoses twined round his person. When he saw Pinky he stopped short, looked from her to Miss Bellamy and turned rather white.

"Bertie," Pinky said. "I've split on you."

"How could you!" he said. "Oh Pinky, how could you!"

Pinky burst into tears.

"I don't know!" she stammered. "I didn't mean to, Bertie darling. Forgive me. I was high."

"Stay me with flagons!" he said in a small voice. Miss Bellamy, employing a kind of enlargement of herself that was technically one of her most telling achievements, crossed to him and advanced her face to within four inches of his own.

"You rat, Bertie," she said quietly. "You little, two-timing, double-crossing, dirty rat."

And she wound her hands in his garland, tore it off him and threw it in his face.

CHAPTER TWO   # Preparation for a Party

Mary Bellamy's temperaments were of rare occurrence but formidable in the extreme and frightening to behold. They were not those regulation theatre tantrums that seem to afford pleasure both to observer and performer; on the contrary they devoured her like some kind of migraine and left her exhausted. Their onset was sudden, their duration prolonged and their sequel incalculable.

Bertie and Pinky, both familiar with them, exchanged looks of despair. Miss Bellamy had not raised her voice, but a kind of stillness seemed to have fallen on the house. They themselves spoke in whispers. They also, out of some impulse of helpless unanimity, said the same thing at the same time.

"Mary!" they said. "Listen! Don't!"

They knew very well that they had better have held their tongues. Their effort, feeble though it was, served only to inflame her. With an assumption of calmness that was infinitely more alarming than raging hysteria she set about them, concentrating at first on Bertie.

"I wonder," she said, "what it feels like to be you. I wonder if you enjoy your own cunning. I expect you do, Bertie. I expect you rather pride yourself on your talent for cashing in on other people's generosity. On mine, for instance."

"Mary, *darling!* Please!"

"Let us," she continued, trembling slightly, "look at this thing quite calmly and objectively, shall we? I'm afraid it will not be a delicious experience, but it has to be faced."

Gracefield came in, took one look at his mistress and went out again. He had been with the family for some time.

"I am the last woman in the world," Miss Bellamy explained, "to remind people of their obligations. The last. However—"

She began to remind Bertie of his obligations. Of the circumstances under which she had discovered him—she did not, to his evident relief, say how many years ago—of how she had given him his first chance; of how, since then, he had never looked back; of how there had been an agreement—"gentlemen's," she added bitterly—that he would never design for another leading lady in the Management without first consulting her. He opened his mouth, but was obliged without utterance to shut it again. Had he not, she asked, risen to his present position entirely on the wings of her patronage? Besieged as she was by the importunities of the great fashion houses, had she not stuck resolutely to him through thick and thin? And now—

She executed a gesture, Siddons-like in its tragic implications, and began to pace to and fro while Pinky and Bertie hastily made room for her to do so. Her glance lighting for a moment on Pinky she began obliquely to attack her.

"I imagine," she said, still to Bertie, "that I shall not be accused of lack of generosity. I am generally said, I think, to be a good friend. Faithful and just," she added, perhaps with some obscure recollection of Mark Antony. "Over and over again, for friendship's sake, I've persuaded the Management to cast actresses who were unable to give me adequate support."

"Now, look here . . . !" Pinky began warmly.

"—Over and over again. Timmy said, only the other day: 'Darling, you're sacrificing yourself on the altar of your personal loyalties!' He's said, over and over again, that he wouldn't for anybody else under the sun accept the casting as it stood. Only for me . . ."

"What casting?" Pinky demanded. Miss Bellamy continued to address herself exclusively to Bertie.

"Only for me, Timmy said, would he dream of taking into any production of his an artist whose spiritual home was weekly rep. in the ham-counties."

"Timmy," Pinky said dangerously, "is producing my play. It's entirely due to him and the author that I've got the part. They told the Management they wanted me."

Bertie said, "I happen to know that's perfectly true."

"Conspiracy!" Miss Bellamy shouted so loudly and suddenly that the others jumped in unison. She was ravaged by a terrible vision of Bertie, Pinky and Timmy all closeted with the Management and agreeing to say nothing to her of their plots and plans. In a Delphic fury she outlined this scene. Bertie, who had been moodily disengaging himself from the remnants of his garland, showed signs of fight. He waited his chance and cut in.

"Speaking," he began, "as a two-timing, double-crossing rat, which God knows I am *not*, I take leave to assure you, darling Mary, that you're wrecking yourself for nothing. I'm doing Pinky's gowns out of friendliness and my name isn't going to appear and I must say I'd have thought . . ."

He was allowed to get no further.

"It's not," Miss Bellamy said, "what you've done, both of you, but the revolting way you've done it. If you'd come to me in the first instance and said . . ." Then followed an exposition of what they should have said and of the generous response they would have enjoyed if they'd said it. For a moment it looked as if the row was going to degenerate into an aimless and repetitive wrangle. It would probably have done so if Pinky had not said abruptly:

"Now, look here, Mary! It's about time you faced up to yourself. You know jolly well that anything you've done for either of us has been paid back with interest. I know you've had a lot to do with my getting on the Management's short list and I'm grateful, but I also know that it's suited you very well to have me there. I'm a good foil to you. I know all your gimmicks. How you like to be fed lines. And when you dry, as nowadays you very often do, I can fill in like nobody's business. In the gentle art of letting myself be upstaged, cheated out of points and fiddled into nonentity, I've done you proud and you'll find I'm damn hard to replace."

"My *God!* My *God!* that I should have to listen to this!"

"As for Bertie . . ."

"Never mind, Pinky," he said quickly.

"I do mind. It's true you gave Bertie his start, but what hasn't he done for you? Your décor! Your clothes! Face it, Mary, without the Saracen Concealed Curve you'd be the Grand Old Lady of the Hip Parade."

Bertie gave a hysterical hoot of laughter and looked terrified.

"The truth is," Pinky said, "you want it both ways, Mary. You want to boss everybody and use everybody for your own ends and at the same time you want us all to wallow in your wake saying how noble and generous and wonderful you are. You're a cannibal, Mary, and it's high time somebody had the guts to tell you so."

A dead silence followed this unexampled speech.

Miss Bellamy walked to the door and turned. It was a movement with which they were familiar.

"After this," she said very slowly, dead-panning her voice to a tortured monotone, "there is only one thing for me to do and much as it hurts me, I shall do it. I shall see the Management. Tomorrow."

She opened the door. They had a brief glimpse of Charles, Warrender and Richard, irresolute in the hall, before she swept out and shut the door behind her.

The room seemed very quiet after she had gone.

"Bertie," Pinky said at last, "if I've done you any harm I'm desperately sorry. I was high. I'll never, never forgive myself."

"That's all right, dear."

"You're so *kind*. Bertie—do you think she'll—do you think she can . . . ?"

"She'll try, dear. She'll try."

"It took everything I've got, I promise you, to give battle. Honestly, Bertie, she frightened me. She looked murderous."

"Horrid, wasn't it?"

Pinky stared absently at the great flask of the scent called Formidable. A ray of sunshine had caught it and it shone golden.

"What are *you* going to do?" she asked.

Bertie picked up a handful of tuberoses from the carpet. "Get on with me bloody flowers, dear," he said. "Get on with me bloody flowers."

2

Having effected her exit, Miss Bellamy swept like a sirocco past Richard, Warrender and her husband and continued upstairs. In her bedroom she encountered Florence, who said, "What have *you* been doing to yourself?"

"You shut up," Miss Bellamy shouted and slammed the door.

"Whatever it is, it's no good to you. Come on, dear. What's the story?"

"Bloody treachery's the story. Shut up. I don't want to tell you. My God, what friends I've got! My God, what friends!"

She strode about the room and made sounds of outrage and defeat. She flung herself on the bed and pummelled it.

Florence said, "You know what'll be the end of this—party and all."

Miss Bellamy burst into tears. "I haven't," she sobbed, "a friend in the world. Not in the whole wide world. Except Dicky."

A spasm of something that might have been chagrin twitched at Florence's mouth. "Him!" she said under her breath.

Miss Bellamy abandoned herself to a passion of tears. Florence went into the bathroom and returned with sal volatile.

"Here," she said. "Try this. Come along now, dear."

"I don't want that muck. Give me one of my tablets."

"Not now."

"Now!"

"You know as well as I do, the doctor said only at night."

"I don't care what he said. Get me one."

She turned her head and looked up at Florence. "Did you hear what I said?"

"There aren't any left. I was going to send out."

Miss Bellamy said through her teeth, "I've had enough of this. You think you can call the tune here, don't you? You think you're indispensable. You never made a bigger mistake. You're not indispensable and the sooner you realize it, the better for you. Now, get out."

"You don't mean that."

"Get out!"

Florence stood quite still for perhaps ten seconds and then left the room.

Miss Bellamy stayed where she was. Her temperament, bereft of an audience, gradually subsided. Presently she went to her dressing-table, dealt with her face and gave herself three generous shots from her scent-spray. At the fourth, it petered out. The bottle was empty. She made an exasperated sound, stared at herself in the glass and for the first time since the onset of her rage, began to think collectedly.

At half-past twelve she went down to call on Octavius Browne and Anelida Lee.

Her motives in taking this action were mixed. In the first place her temperament, having followed the classic pattern of diminishing returns, had finally worked itself out and had left her restless. She was unwilling to stay indoors. In the second, she wanted very badly to prove to herself how grossly she had been misjudged by Pinky and Bertie, and could this be better achieved than by performing an act of gracious considera-tion towards Richard? In the third place, she was burningly anxious to set her curiosity at rest in the matter of Anelida Lee.

On her way down she looked in at the drawing-room. Bertie, evidently, had finished the flowers and gone. Pinky had left a note saying she was sorry if she'd been too upsetting but not really hauling down her flag an inch. Miss Bellamy blew off steam to Charles, Richard and Warrender without paying much attention to their reactions. They withdrew, dis-mayed, to Charles's study from whence came the muted sound of inter-mittent conversation. Superbly dressed and gloved she let herself out and after pausing effectively for a moment in the sunshine, turned into the Pegasus.

Octavius was not in the shop. Anelida, having completed her cleaning, had a smudge across her cheek and grubby hands. She had cried a little after Richard went out in a huff and there had been no time to repair the damage. She was not looking her best.

Miss Bellamy was infinitely relieved.

She was charming to Anelida. Her husband and Richard Dakers, she said, had talked so much about the shop: it was so handy for them, funny old bookworms that they were, to have found one practically on the doorstep. She understood that Anelida was hoping to go on the stage. Anelida replied that she was working at the Bonaventure. With every appearance of infinite generosity Miss Bellamy said that, unlike most of her friends, she thought the little experimental club theatres performed a very useful function in showing plays that otherwise would never see the light of day. Anelida was quiet, well-mannered and, Miss Bellamy supposed, much overcome by the honour that was being paid her. That was the kindest interpretation to put upon her somewhat ungushing response. "Not much temperament *there*," Miss Bellamy thought and from her this was not a complimentary assessment. She grew more and more cordial.

Octavius returned from a brief shopping expedition and was a success. On being introduced by Anelida—quite prettily, Miss Bellamy had to admit—he uncovered his dishevelled head and smiled so broadly that his face looked rather like a mask of comedy.

"But what a pleasure!" he said, shaping his words with exquisite precision. "May we not exclaim 'Hic ver assiduum' since April herself walks in at our door?"

Miss Bellamy got the general trend of this remark and her spirits rose. She thanked him warmly for his telegram and he at once looked extremely pleased with himself. "Your husband and your ward," he said, "told us of the event and I thought, you know, of the many delicious hours you have given us and of how meagre a return is the mere striking together of one's hands." He looked sideways at her. "An old fogey's impulse," he said and waved it aside. He made her a little bow and put his head on one side. Anelida wished he wouldn't.

"It was *heaven* of you," said Miss Bellamy. "So much pleasure it gave, you can't think! And what's more I haven't thanked you for finding that *perfect* picture for Dicky to give me, nor," she improvised on the spur of the moment, "for that heavenly copy of . . ." Maddeningly, she had forgotten the author of Charles's purchase and of the quotation in the telegram. She marked time with a gesture indicating ineffable pleasure and then mercifully remembered. "Of Spenser," she cried.

"You admired the Spenser? I'm very glad."

"So much. And now," she continued with an enchanting air of diffidence, "I'm going to ask you something that you'll think quite preposterous. I've come with an invitation. You are, I know, *great* friends of my ward's—of Dicky's—and I, like you, am a creature of impulse. I want you both—*please*—to come to my little party this evening. Drinks and a handful of ridiculous chums at half-past six. Now, please be very sweet and spoil me on my birthday. Please, say yes."

Octavius turned quite pink with gratification. He didn't hear his niece who came near to him and said hurriedly, "Unk, I don't think we . . ."

"I have never," Octavius said, "in my life attended a theatrical party. It is something quite outside my experience. Really it's extraordinarily kind of you to think of inviting us. My niece, no doubt, is an initiate. Though not at such an exalted level, I think, Nelly, my love?"

Anelida had begun to say, "It's terribly kind . . ." but Miss Bellamy was already in full spate. She had taken Octavius impulsively by the hands and was beaming into his face. "You will? Now, *isn't* that *big* of you? I *was* so afraid I might be put in my place or that you would be booked up. And I'm *not!* And you *aren't!* Isn't that wonderful!"

"We are certainly free," Octavius said. "Anelida's theatre is not open on Monday evenings. She had offered to help me with our new catalogue. I shall be enchanted."

"Wonderful!" Miss Bellamy gaily repeated. "And now I must run. *Au revoir*, both of you. Till this evening!"

She did, almost literally, run out of the shop filled with a delicious sense of having done something altogether charming. "Kind!" she thought. "That's what I've been. Kind as kind. Dicky will be so touched. And when he sees that *rather* dreary *rather* inarticulate girl in his own setting —well, if there *has* been anything, it'll peter out on the spot."

She saw the whole thing in a gratifying flash of clairvoyance: the last fumes of temperament subsided in the sunshine of her own loving-kindness. She returned to the house and found Richard in the hall.

"Darling!" she cried. "All settled! I've seen your buddies and asked them. The old fuddy-duddy's heaven, isn't he? Out of this world. And the girl's the nicest little thing. Are you pleased?"

"But," Richard said, amazed. "Are they . . . ? Did Anelida say they'd come?"

"My dear, you don't imagine, do you, that a bit-part fill-in at the Bonaventure is going to turn down an invitation to my birthday party!"

"It's not a bit-part," Richard said. "They're doing *Pygmalion* and she's playing Eliza."

"Poor child."

He opened his mouth and shut it again.

"There's something," Miss Bellamy said, "so endlessly depressing about those clubs. Blue jeans, beards and a snack-bar, no doubt." He didn't answer and she said kindly, "Well! We mustn't let them feel too lost, must we? I'll tell Maurice and Charles to be kind. And now, sweetie, I'm off to keep my date with the Great Play."

Richard said hurriedly, "There's something I wanted to alter . . . Could we . . ."

"Darling! You're such heaven when you panic. I'll read it and then I'll put it in your study. Blessings!"

"Mary—Mary, thank you so much."

She kissed him lightly and almost ran upstairs to read his play and to telephone Pinky and Bertie. She would tell them that she couldn't bear to think of any cloud of dissonance overshadowing her birthday and she would add that she expected them at six-thirty. That would show them how ungrudging she could be. "After all," she thought, "they'll be in a tizzy because if I *did* do my stuff with the Management . . ." Reassured on all counts she went into her room.

Unfortunately, neither Bertie nor Pinky was at home, but she left messages. It was now one o'clock. Half an hour before luncheon in which to relax and skim through Richard's play. Everything was going, in the event, very well. "I'll put me boots up," she said to herself in stage cockney and did so on the chaise-longue in the bow window of her room. She noticed that once again the azaleas were infected and reminded herself to spray them with Slaypest. She turned her attention, now growing languid, to the play. *Husbandry in Heaven.* Not a very good title, she thought. Wasn't it a quotation from something? The dialogue seemed to be quite unlike Dicky: a bit Sloane Square, in fact. The sort of dialogue that is made up of perfectly understandable phrases that taken together add up to a kind of egg-headed Goon show. Was it or was it not in verse? She read Dicky's description of the leading woman.

"*Mimi comes on. She might be nineteen or twenty-nine. Her beauty is bone-deep. Seductive without luxury. Virginal and dangerous.*" "Hum!" thought Miss Bellamy. "*Hodge comes out of the Prompt corner. Wolf-whistles. Gestures unmistakably and with feline intensity.*"

Now, why had that line stirred up some obscure misgivings? She turned the pages. It was certainly an enormously long part.

"*Mimi: Can this be April, then, or have I, so early in the day, misinterpreted my directive?*"

"Hell!" thought Miss Bellamy.

But she read one or two of the lines aloud and decided that they might have something. As she flipped over the pages she became more and more satisfied that Dicky had tried to write a wonderful part for her. Different. It wouldn't do, of course, but at least the loving intention was there.

The typescript tipped over and fell across her chest. Her temperaments always left her tired. Just before she dropped off she suffered one of those mysterious jolts that briefly galvanize the body. She had been thinking about Pinky. It may be fanciful to suppose that her momentary discomfort was due to a spasm of hatred rather than to any physical cause. However that may be, she fell at last into an unenjoyable doze.

Florence came in. She had the flask of scent called Formidable in her hands. She tip-toed across the room, put it on the dressing-table and stood for a moment looking at Miss Bellamy. Beyond the chaise-longue in the bay window were ranks of tulips and budding azaleas and among them stood the tin of Slaypest. To secure it, Florence had to lean across her mistress. She did so, delicately, but Miss Bellamy, at that moment, stirred. Florence drew back and tip-toed out of the room.

Old Ninn was on the landing. She folded her arms and stared up at Florence.

"Asleep," Florence said, with a jerk of her head. "Gone to bye-byes."

"Always the same after tantrums," said Old Ninn. She added woodenly, "She'll be the ruin of that boy."

"She'll be the ruin of herself," said Florence, "if she doesn't watch her step."

3

When Miss Bellamy had gone, Anelida, in great distress, turned to her uncle. Octavius was humming a little Elizabethan catch and staring at himself in a Jacobean looking-glass above his desk.

"Captivating!" he said. "Enchanting! Upon my word, Nell, it must be twenty years since a pretty woman made much of me. I feel, I promise you, quite giddily inclined. And the whole thing—so spontaneous: so touchingly impulsive! We have widened our horizon, my love."

"Unk," Anelida said rather desperately, "you can't think, my poor blessing, what a muddle you've made."

"A *muddle?*" He looked plaintively at her and she knew she was in for trouble. "What do you mean? I accept an invitation, most graciously extended by a charming woman. Pray where is the muddle?" She didn't answer and he said, "There are certain matters, of course, to be considered. I do not, for instance, know what clothes are proper, nowadays, for cocktail parties. In my day one would have worn . . ."

"It's not a matter of clothes."

"No? In any case, you shall instruct me."

"I've already told Richard I can't go to the party."

"Nonsense, my dear. Of course we can go," Octavius said. "What are you thinking of?"

"It's so hard to explain, Unky. It's just that—well, it's partly because of me being in the theatre only so very much at the bottom of the ladder —less than the dust, you know, beneath Miss B.'s chariot wheels. I'd be like a corporal in the officers' mess."

"That," said Octavius, reddening with displeasure, "seems to me to be a false analogy, if you'll forgive me for saying so, Nelly. And, my dear, when one quotes it is pleasant to borrow from reputable sources. The *Indian Love Lyrics*, in my undergraduate days, were the scourge of the drawing-rooms."

"I'm sorry."

"It would be extremely uncivil to refuse so kind an invitation," Octavius said, looking more and more like a spoilt and frustrated child. "I *want* to accept it. What is the matter with you, Anelida?"

"The truth is," Anelida said rather desperately, "I don't quite know where I am with Richard Dakers."

Octavius stared at her and experienced a moment of truth. "Now that I consider it," he said huffily, "I realize that Dakers is paying his addresses to you. I wonder that it hasn't occurred to me before. Have you taken against him?"

To her dismay Anelida found herself on the brink of tears. "No!" she cried. "No! Nothing like that—really. I mean—I mean I just don't know . . ." She looked helplessly at Octavius. He was, she knew, hovering on the edge of one of his rare fits of temper. His vanity had been tickled by Miss Bellamy. He had almost strutted and preened before her. Anelida, who loved him very much, could have shaken him.

"Never mind," she said. "It's not worth another thought. But I'm sorry, darling, if you're put out over your lovely party."

"I *am* put out," Octavius said crossly. "I want to go."

"And you shall go. I'll do your tie and make you look beautiful."

"My dear," Octavius said, "it is you who would have looked beautiful. It would have been a great pleasure to take you. I should have been proud."

"Oh hell!" said Anelida. She rushed at him and gave him an exasperated hug. He was much puzzled and hit her gently several times on the shoulder blades.

The shop door opened.

"Here," Octavius said over the top of Anelida's head, "*is* Dakers."

Coming from the sunshine into the dark shop, Richard had been given a confused impression of Anelida collaring Octavius in a high tackle. He waited for her to emerge, which she did after some fumbling with her uncle's handkerchief.

Octavius said, "If you'll excuse me, Nell. Really, one *must* get on with one's job." He nodded to Richard and limped away into his back room.

Richard was careful not to look at Anelida. "I came," he said, "first to apologize."

"Not at all. I expect I behaved badly."

"And to say how very glad I am. Mary told me you had decided for the party."

"It was terribly kind of her to come. Unk was bewitched."

"We are being polite to each other, aren't we?"

"Better than flying into rages."

"May I call for you?"

"There's no need. Really. You'll be busy with the party. Unk will be proud to escort me. He said so."

"So he well might." Richard now looked directly at Anelida. "You've been crying," he said, "and your face is dirty. Like a little girl's. Smudged."

"All right. All right. I'm going to tidy it up."

"Shall I?"

"No."

"How old are you, Anelida?"

"Nineteen. Why?"

"I'm twenty-eight."

"You've done very well," Anelida said politely, "for your age. Famous dramatist."

"Playwright."

"I think with the new one you may allow yourself to be a dramatist."

"My God, you've got a cheek," he said thoughtfully. After a moment he said, "Mary's reading it. Now."

"Was she pleased about it?"

"For the wrong reason. She thinks I wrote it for her."

"But—how could she? Still, she'll soon find out."

"As I mentioned before, you don't really know much as yet about theatre people."

Anelida said, to her own astonishment, "But I do know I can act."

"Yes," he agreed. "Of course you do. You're a good actress."

"You haven't seen me."

"That's what you think."

"Richard!"

"At least I've surprised you into calling me by my name."

"But when did you see me?"

"It slipped out. It's part of a deep-laid plan. You'll find out."

"When?"

"At the party. I'm off, now. Au revoir, dear Anelida."

When he had gone, Anelida sat perfectly still for quite a long time. She was bewildered, undecided and piercingly happy.

Richard, however, returned to the house with his mind made up. He went straight to Charles Templeton's study. He found Charles and Maurice Warrender there, rather solemn over a decanter of sherry. When he came in they both looked self-conscious.

"We were just talking about you," Charles said. "Have whatever it is you do have at this hour, Dicky. Lager?"

"Please. I'll get it. Should I make myself scarce so that you can go on talking about me?"

"No, no."

"We'd finished," Warrender said, "I imagine. Hadn't we, Charles?"

"I suppose we had."

Richard poured out his lager. "As a matter of fact," he said, "I sidled in with the idea of boring you with a few observations under that very heading."

Warrender muttered something about taking himself off. "Not unless you have to, Maurice," Richard said. "It arises, in a way, out of what you said this morning." He sat down and stared at his beer mug. "This is going to be difficult," he said.

They waited, Warrender looking owlish, Charles, as always, politely attentive.

"I suppose it's a question of divided allegiances," Richard said at last. "Partly that, anyway." He went on, trying to put what he wanted to say as objectively as might be. He knew that he was floundering and almost at once began to regret his first impulse.

Charles kept turning his elderly freckled hand and looking at it. Warrender sipped his sherry and shot an occasional, almost furtive, glance at Richard.

Presently Charles said, "Couldn't we come to the point?"

"I wish I could," Richard rejoined. "I'm making a mess of this, I know."

"May I have a go at it? Is this what you're trying to tell us? You think you can write a different kind of play from the sort of thing that suits Mary. You have, in fact, written one. You think it's the best thing you've done, but you're afraid Mary won't take kindly to the idea of your making a break. You've shown it to her and she's reading it now. You're afraid that she'll take it for granted that you see her in the lead. Right, so far?"

"Yes. That's it."

"But," Warrender demanded unexpectedly, "she won't like this play, what!"

"I don't think she'll like it."

"Isn't that your answer?" Charles said. "If she doesn't like it you can offer it elsewhere?"

"It isn't," Richard said, "as simple as that." And looking at these two men, each old enough to be his father, each with thirty years' experience of Mary Bellamy, he saw that he was understood.

"There's been one row already this morning," he said. "A snorter."

Warrender shot a look at Charles. "I don't know if I'm imagining it," he said, "but I've fancied the rows come a bit oftener these days, isn't it?"

Charles and Richard were silent.

Warrender said, "Fellow's got to live his own life. My opinion. Worst thing that can happen to a man's getting himself bogged down in a mistaken loyalty. Seen it happen. Man in my regiment. Sorry business."

Charles said, "We all have our mistaken loyalties."

There was a further silence.

Richard said violently, "But—I owe everything to her. The ghastly things I began to write at school. The first shamingly hopeless plays. Then the one that rang the bell. *She* made the Management take it. We talked everything over. Everything. And now—suddenly—I don't want to. I—don't—want—to. Why? *Why?*"

"Very well," Charles said. Richard looked at him in surprise, but he went on very quietly. "Writing plays is your business. You understand it. You're an expert. You should make your own decisions."

"Yes. But Mary . . ."

"Mary holds a number of shares in companies that I direct, but I don't consult her about their policy or confine my interests to those companies only."

"Surely it's not the same thing."

"Isn't it?" Charles said placidly. "I think it is. Sentiment," he added, "can be a disastrous guide in such matters. Mary doesn't understand your change of policy—the worst reason in the world for mistrusting it. She is guided almost entirely by emotion."

Warrender said, "Think *she's* changed? Sorry, Charles, I've no kind of business to ask."

"She has changed," her husband said. "One does."

"You can see," Richard said, "what happened with Pinky and Bertie. How much more will she mind with me! Was there anything so terrible about what they did? The truth is, of course, that they didn't confide in her because they didn't know how she'd take it. Well—you saw how she took it."

"I suppose," Warrender began dimly, "as a woman gets older . . ." He faded out in a bass rumble.

"Charles," Richard said, "you may consider this a monstrous suggestion, but have you thought, lately, that there might be anything—anything . . ."

"Pathological?" Charles said.

"It's so unlike her to be vindictive. *Isn't it?*" He appealed to both of them. "Well, my God, *isn't* it?"

To his astonishment they didn't answer immediately. Presently Charles said with a suggestion of pain in his voice: "The same thing has occurred to me. I—I asked Frank Harkness about it. He's looked after us both for years, as you know. He thinks she's been a bit nervy for some time, I gather, like many women of her—well, of her age. He thinks the high-pressure atmosphere of the theatre may have increased the tension. I got the impression he was understating his case. I don't mind telling you," Charles added unhappily, "it's been worrying me for some time. These—these ugly scenes."

Warrender muttered, "Vindictive," and looked as if he regretted it.

Richard cried out, "Her kindness! I've always thought she had the kindest eyes I'd ever seen in a woman."

Warrender, who seemed this morning to be bent on speaking out of character, did so now. "People," he said, "talk about eyes and mouths as if they had something to do with the way other people think and behave. Only bits of the body, aren't they? Like navels and knees and toenails. Arrangements."

Charles glanced at him with amusement. "My dear Maurice, you terrify me. So you discount our old friends the generous mouth, the frank glance, the open forehead. I wonder if you're right."

"Right or wrong," Richard burst out, "it doesn't get me any nearer a decision."

Charles put down his sherry and put up his eyeglass. "If I were you, Dicky," he said, "I should go ahead."

"Hear, hear!"

"Thank you, Maurice. Yes. I should go ahead. Offer your play in what you believe to be the best market. If Mary's upset it won't be for long, you know. You must keep a sense of perspective, my dear boy."

Colonel Warrender listened to this with his mouth slightly open and a glaze over his eyes. When Charles had finished Warrender looked at his watch, rose and said he had a telephone call to make before luncheon. "I'll do it from the drawing-room if I may," he said. He glared at Richard. "Stick to your guns, isn't it?" he said. "Best policy." And went out.

Richard said, "I've always wondered: just how simple *is* Maurice?"

"It would be the greatest mistake," Charles said, "to underrate him."

4

In their houses and flats, all within a ten-mile radius of Pardoner's Place, the guests for Mary Bellamy's birthday party made ready to present themselves. Timon (Timmy) Gantry, the famous director, made few preparations for such festivities. He stooped from his inordinate height to the cracked glass on his bathroom wall in order to brush his hair, which he kept so short that the gesture was redundant. He had changed into a suit which he was in the habit of calling his "decent blue," and as a concession to Miss Bellamy, wore a waistcoat instead of a plum-coloured pullover. He looked rather like a retired policeman whose enthusiasm had never dwindled. He sang a snatch from *Rigoletto,* an opera he had recently directed, and remembered how much he disliked cocktail parties.

"Bell-a-*me*-a, you're a hell of a bore," he sang, improvising to the tune of "Bella Figlia." And it was true, he reflected. Mary was becoming more and more of a tiresome girl. It would probably be necessary to quarrel with her before her new play went on. She was beginning to jib at the physical demands made upon her by his production methods. He liked to keep his cast moving rather briskly through complicated, almost fugal, patterns and Mary was not as sound in the wind as she used to be. Nor in the temper, he reflected. He rather thought that this play would be his last production for her.

"For she's not my, not my cuppa tea at all," he sang.

This led him to think of her influence on other people, particularly on Richard Dakers. "She's a succuba," he chanted. "She's an o—ogress. She devours young men alive. Nasty Mary!" He was delighted that Richard showed signs of breaking loose with his venture into serious dramatic writing. He had read *Husbandry in Heaven* to Gantry while it was still in manuscript. Gantry always made up his mind at once about a play and he did so about this one.

"If you go on writing slip-slop for Mary when you've got this sort of stuff under your thatch," he had said, "you deserve to drown in it. Parts of this thing are bloody awful and must come out. Other parts need a rewrite. Fix them and I'm ready to produce the piece."

Richard had fixed them.

Gantry shoved his birthday present for Miss Bellamy into his pocket. It was a bit of pinchbeck he'd picked up for five bob on a street stall. He bought his presents in an inverse ratio to the monetary situation of the recipients and Miss Bellamy was rich.

As he strode along in the direction of Knightsbridge, he thought with increasing enthusiasm about *Husbandry in Heaven* and of what he would do with it if he could persuade the Management to take it.

"The actors," he promised himself, "shall skip like young rams."

At Hyde Park Corner he began to sing again. At the corner of Wilton Place a chauffeur-driven car pulled up alongside him. The Management in the person of Mr. Montague Marchant, exquisitely dressed, with a gardenia in his coat, leaned from the window. His face and his hair were smooth, fair and pale, and his eyes wary.

"Timmy!" Mr. Marchant shouted. "*Look* at you! *So* purposeful! Such *devouring* strides! Come in, do, for God's sake, and let us support each other on our approach to the shrine."

Gantry said, "I wanted to see you." He doubled himself up like a camel and got into the car. It was his custom to plunge directly into whatever matter concerned him at the moment. He presented his ideas with the same ruthless precipitancy that he brought to his work in the theatre. It was a deceptive characteristic, because in Gantry impulse was subordinate to design.

He drew in his breath with an authoritative gasp. "Listen!" he said. "I have a proposition."

All the way along Sloane Street and into the King's Road he thrust Richard's play at Marchant. He was still talking, very eloquently, as they turned up Pardoner's Row. Marchant listened with the undivided though guarded attention that the Management brought to bear only on the utterances of the elect.

"You will do this," Gantry said as the car turned into Pardoner's Place, "not for me and not for Dicky. You will do it because it's going to be a Thing for the Management. Mark my words. Here we are. Oh misery, *how* I abominate grand parties!"

"I'd have you remember," Marchant said as they went in, "that I commit myself to nothing, Timmy."

"Naturally, my dear man. But naturally. You *will* commit yourself, however, I promise you. You will."

"Mary, *darling!*" they both exclaimed and were swallowed up by the party.

Pinky and Bertie had arranged to go together. They came to this decision after a long gloomy post-luncheon talk in which they weighed the dictates of proper pride against those of professional expediency.

"Face it, sweetie-pie," Bertie had said, "if we *don't* show up she'll turn plug-ugly again and go straight to the Management. You know what a fuss Monty makes about personal relationships. 'A happy theatre is a successful theatre.' Nobody—but *nobody* can afford to cut up rough. He loathes internal strife."

Pinky, who was feeling the effects of her morning excesses, sombrely agreed. "God knows," she said, "that at this juncture I can ill afford to get myself the reputation of being difficult. After all my contract isn't signed, Bertie."

"It's as clear as daylight; magnanimity must be our watchword."

"I'll be blowed if I crawl."

"We shan't have to, dear. A pressure of the hand and a long, long gaze into the eyeballs will carry us through."

"I resent having to."

"Never mind. Rise above. Watch me. I'm a past master at it. Gird up the loins, dear, such as they are, and remember you're an actress." He giggled. "Looked at in the right way it'll be rather fun."

"What shall I wear?"

"Black, and no jewelry. She'll be clanking."

"I hate being at enmity, Bertie. What a beastly profession ours is. In some ways."

"It's a jungle, darling. Face it—it's a jungle."

"You," Pinky said rather enviously, "don't seem to be unduly perturbed, I must say."

"My poorest girl, little do you know. I'm quaking."

"Really? But could she actually do you any damage?"

"Can the boa constrictor," Bertie said, "consume the rabbit?"

Pinky had thought it better not to press this matter any further. They had separated and gone to their several flats, where in due course they make ready for the party.

Anelida and Octavius also made ready. Octavius, having settled for a black coat, striped trousers and the complementary details that he considered appropriate to these garments, had taken up a good deal of his niece's attention. She had managed to have a bath and was about to dress when, for the fourth time, he tapped at her door and presented himself before her, looking anxious and unnaturally tidy. "My hair," he said. "Having no unguent, I used a little olive oil. Do I smell like a salad?"

She reassured him, gave his coat a brush and begged him to wait for her in the shop. He had old-fashioned ideas about punctuality and had begun to fret. "It's five-and-twenty minutes to seven. We were asked for half-past six, Nelly."

"That means seven at the earliest, darling. Just take a furtive leer through the window and you'll see when people begin to come. And please, Unk, we can't go while I'm still in my dressing-gown, can we, now?"

"No, no, of course not. Half-past six *for* a quarter-to-seven? Or seven? I see. I see. In that case . . ."

He pottered downstairs.

Anelida thought, "It's a good thing I've had some practice in quick changes." She did her face and hair, and she put on a white dress that had been her one extravagance of the year, a large white hat with a black velvet crown, and new gloves. She looked in the glass, forcing herself to adopt the examining attitude she used in the theatre. "And it might as well be a first night," she thought, "the way I'm feeling." Did Richard like white? she wondered.

Heartened by the certainty of her dress being satisfactory and her hat becoming, Anelida began to daydream along time-honoured lines: She and Octavius arrived at the party. There was a sudden hush. Monty Marchant, the Management in person, would ejaculate to Timon Gantry, the great producer, "Who are they?" and Timon Gantry, with the abrupt grasp which all actors, whether they had heard it or not, liked to imitate, would reply, "I don't know, but by God, I'm going to find out." The ranks would part as she and Octavius, escorted by Miss Bellamy, moved down the room to the accompaniment of a discreet murmur. They would be the cynosure of all eyes. What was a cynosure and why was it never mentioned except in reference to eyes? All eyes on Anelida Lee. And there, wrapt in admiration, would be Richard . . .

At this point Anelida stopped short, was stricken with shame, had a good laugh at herself and became the prey of her own nerves.

She went to her window and looked down into Pardoner's Place. Cars were now beginning to draw up at Miss Bellamy's house. Here came a large black one with a very smart chauffeur. Two men got out. Anelida's inside somersaulted. The one with the gardenia *was* Monty Marchant and that incredibly tall, that unmistakably shabby figure *was* the greatest of all directors, Timon Gantry.

"Whoops!" Anelida said. "None of your nonsense, Cinderella." She counted sixty and then went downstairs.

Octavius was seated at his desk, reading, and Hodge was on his knee. They both looked extraordinarily smug.

"Have you come over calm?" Anelida asked.

"What? Calm? Yes," Octavius said. "Perfectly, thank you. I have been reading *The Gull's Hornbook*."

"Have you been up to something, Unk?"

He rolled his eyes round at her. "Up to something? I? What can you mean?"

"You look as if butter wouldn't melt on your whiskers."

"Really? I wonder why. Should we go?"

He displaced Hodge, who was moulting. Anelida was obliged to fetch the clothesbrush again.

"I wouldn't change you," she said, "for the Grand Cham of Tartary. Come on, darling, let's go."

5

Miss Bellamy's preparation for the party occupied the best part of ninety minutes and had something of the character of a Restoration salon, with Florence, truculently unaware of this distinction, in the role of abigail.

It followed the after-luncheon rest and, in its early stages, was conducted in the strictest privacy. She lay on her bed. Florence, unspeaking and tight-mouthed, darkened the room and produced from the bathroom sundry bottles and pots. She removed the make-up from her mistress's face, put wet pads over her eyes and began to apply a layer of greenish astringent paste. Miss Bellamy attempted to make conversation and was unsuccessful. At last she demanded impatiently, "What's the matter with *you?* Gone upstage?" Florence was silent. "Oh for heaven's *sake!*" Miss Bellamy ejaculated. "You're not holding out on me because of this morning, are you?"

Florence slapped a layer across Miss Bellamy's upper lip. "That stuff's stinging me," Miss Bellamy mumbled with difficulty. "You haven't mixed it properly."

Florence completed the mask. From behind it Miss Bellamy attempted to say, "All right, you can go to hell and sulk there," but remembering she was not supposed to speak, lay fuming. She heard Florence go out of the room. Ten minutes later she returned, stood for some time looking down on the greenish, blinded face and then set about removing the mask.

The toilet continued in icy silence, proceeding through its manifold and exacting routines. The face was scrutinized like a microscope slide. The hair was drilled. The person was subjected to masterful but tactful discipline. That which, unsubjected, declared itself centrally, was forced to make a less aggressive re-appearance above the seventh rib where it was trapped, confined and imperceptibly distributed. And throughout these intimate manipulations, Florence and Miss Bellamy maintained an absolute and inimical silence. Only when they had been effected did Miss Bellamy open her door to her court.

In the past, Pinky and Bertie had attended: the former vaguely in the role of confidante, the latter to advise about the final stages of the ritual. Today they had not presented themselves and Miss Bellamy was illogically resentful. Though her initial fury had subsided, it lay like a sediment at the bottom of her thoughts and it wouldn't take much, she realized, to stir it up.

Charles was the first to arrive and found her already dressed. She wore crimson chiffon, intricately folded and draped with loose panels that floated tactfully past her waist and hips. The décolletage plunged and at its lowest point contained orchids and diamonds. Diamonds appeared again at intervals in the form of brooches and clips, flashed in stalactites from her ears and encircled her neck and wrist in a stutter of brilliance. She was indeed magnificent.

"Well?" she said and faced her husband.

"My dear!" said Charles gently. "I'm overwhelmed."

Something in his voice irritated her. "You don't like it," she said. "What's the matter with it?"

"It's quite superb. Dazzling."

Florence had opened the new bottle of scent and was pouring it into the Venetian glass atomizer. The air was thickened with effluvium so strong that it almost gave the impression of being visible. Charles made the slightest of grimaces.

"Do you think I'm overdressed, Charles?" Miss Bellamy demanded.

"I have implicit faith in your judgment," he said. "And you look glorious."

"Why did you make a face?"

"It's that scent. I find it a bit too much. It's—well . . ."

"Well! What is it?"

"I fancy indecent is the word I'm groping for."

"It happens to be the most exclusive perfume on the market."

"I don't much like the word 'perfume,' but in this case it seems to be entirely appropriate."

"I'm sorry," she said in a high voice, "that you find my choice of words non-U."

"My dear Mary . . . !"

Florence screwed the top on the atomizer and placed it, with the three-quarters emptied bottle, on the dressing-table. She then retired to the bathroom.

Charles Templeton took his wife's hands in his and kissed them. "Ah!" he said. "That's your usual scent."

"The last dregs."

"I'll give you some more."

She made as if to pull her hands away, but he folded them between his own.

"Do something for me," he said. "Will you? I never ask you."

"My dear Charles!" she exclaimed impatiently. "What?"

"Don't use that stuff. It's vulgar, Mary. The room stinks of it already."

She stared at him with a kind of blank anger. His skin was mottled.

The veins showed on his nose and his eyes were watery. It was an elderly face, and not very handsome.

"Don't be ridiculous," she said and withdrew her hands.

Warrender tapped on the door and came in. When he saw Miss Bellamy he ejaculated "What!" several times and was so clearly bowled over that her ill-humour modulated into a sort of petulant gratification. She made much of him and pointedly ignored her husband.

"You are the most fabulous, heavenly sweetie-pie," she said and kissed his ear.

He turned purple and said, "By George!"

Charles had walked over to the window. The tin of Slaypest was still there. At the same moment Florence re-entered the room. Charles indicated the tin. Florence cast up her eyes.

He said, "Mary, you do leave the windows open, don't you, when you use this stuff on your plants?"

"Oh for heaven's *sake!*" she exclaimed. "Have you got a secret Thing about sprays? You'd better get yourself psychoed, my poor Charles."

"It's dangerous. I took the trouble to buy a textbook on these things and what it has to say is damn disquieting. I showed it to Maurice. Read it yourself, my dear, if you don't believe me. Ask Maurice. You don't think she ought to monkey about with it, do you, Maurice?"

Warrender picked up the tin and stared at the label with its red skull and crossbones and intimidating warning. "Shouldn't put this sort of stuff on the market," he said. "My opinion."

"Exactly. Let Florence throw it out, Mary."

"Put it down!" she shouted. "My God, Charles, what a bore you can be when you set your mind to it."

Suddenly she thrust the scent atomizer into Warrender's hands. "Stand there, darling," she said. "Far enough away for it not to make rivers or stain my dress. Just a delicious mist. Now! Spray madly."

Warrender did as he was told. She stood in the redolent cloud with her chin raised and her arms extended.

"Go on, Maurice," she said, shutting her eyes in a kind of ecstasy. "Go on."

Charles said, very quietly, "My God!"

Warrender stared at him, blushed scarlet, put down the scent-spray and walked out of the room.

Mary and Charles looked at each other in silence.

The whole room reeked of Formidable.

CHAPTER THREE   **Birthday Honours**

Mr. and Mrs. Charles Templeton stood just inside their drawing-room door. The guests, on their entry, encountered a bevy of press photographers, while a movie outfit was established at the foot of the stairs, completely blocking the first flight. New arrivals smiled or looked thoughtful as the flash lamps discovered them. Then, forwarded by the parlourmaid in the hall to Gracefield on the threshold, they were announced and, as it were, passed on to be neatly fielded by their hosts.

It was not an enormous party—perhaps fifty, all told. It embraced the elite of the theatre world and it differed in this respect from other functions of its size. It was a little as if the guests gave rattling good performances of themselves arriving at a cocktail party. They did this to music, for Miss Bellamy, in an alcove of her great saloon, had stationed a blameless instrumental trio.

Although, in the natural course of events, they met each other very often, there was a tendency among the guests to express astonishment, even rapture, at this particular encounter. Each congratulated Miss Bellamy on her birthday and her superb appearance. Some held her at arm's length the better to admire. Some expressed bewilderment and others a sort of matey reverence. Then in turn they shook hands with Charles and by the particular pains the nice ones took with him, they somehow established the fact that he was not quite of their own world.

When Pinky and Bertie arrived, Miss Bellamy greeted them with magnanimity.

"So glad," she said to both of them, "that you decided to come." The kiss that accompanied this greeting was tinctured with forbearance and what passed with Miss Bellamy for charity. It also, in some ineffable manner, seemed to convey a threat. They were meant to receive it like a sacrament and (however reluctantly) they did so, progressing on the conveyor belt of hospitality to Charles, who was markedly cordial to both of them.

They passed on down the long drawing-room and were followed by two Dames, a Knight, three distinguished commoners, another Knight and his Lady, Montague Marchant and Timon Gantry.

Richard, filling his established role of a sort of unofficial son of the house, took over the guests as they came his way. He was expected to pilot them through the bottleneck of the intake and encourage them to move to the dining-room and conservatory. He also helped the hired barman and the housemaid with the drinks until Gracefield and the parlourmaid were able to carry on. He was profoundly uneasy. He had been out to lunch and late returning and had had no chance to speak to Mary before the first guests appeared. But he knew that all was not well. There were certain only too unmistakable signs, of which a slight twitch in Mary's triangular smile was the most ominous, "There's been another temperament," Richard thought, and he fancied he saw confirmation of this in Charles, whose hands were not quite steady and whose face was unevenly patched.

The rooms filled up. He kept looking towards the door and thinking he saw Anelida.

Timon Gantry came up to him. "I've been talking to Monty," he said. "Have you got a typescript for him?"

"Timmy, how kind of you! Yes, of course."

"Here?"

"Yes. Mary's got one. She said she'd leave it in my old room upstairs."

"*Mary!* Why?"

"I always show her my things."

Gantry looked at him for a moment, gave his little gasp and then said, "I see I must speak frankly. Will Mary think you wrote the part for her?"

Richard said, "I—that was not my intention . . ."

"Because you'd better understand at once, Dicky, that I wouldn't dream of producing this play with Mary in the lead. Nor would I dream of advising the Management to back it with Mary in the lead. Nor could it be anything but a disastrous flop with Mary in the lead. Is that clear?"

"Abundantly," Richard said.

"Moreover," Gantry said, "I should be lacking in honesty and friendship if I didn't tell you it was high time you cut loose from those particular apron strings. Thank you, I would prefer whisky and water."

Richard, shaken, turned aside to get it. As he made his way back to Gantry he was aware of one of those unaccountable lulls that sometimes fall across the insistent din of a cocktail party. Gantry, inches taller than anyone else in the room, was looking across the other guests towards the door. Several of them also had turned in the same direction, so that it was past the backs of heads and through a gap between shoulders that Richard first saw Anelida and Octavius come in.

It was not until a long time afterwards that he realized his first reaction had been one of simple gratitude to Anelida for being, in addition to everything else, so very beautiful.

He heard Timon Gantry say, "Monty, look." Montague Marchant had come up to them.

"I am looking," he said. "Hard."

And indeed they all three looked so hard at Anelida that none of them saw the smile dry out on Mary Bellamy's face and then reappear as if it had been forcibly stamped there.

Anelida shook hands with her hostess, expected, perhaps, some brief return of the morning's excessive cordiality, heard a voice say, "So kind of you to come," and witnessed the phenomenon of the triangular smile. Followed by Octavius, she moved on to Charles. And then she was face to face with Richard, who, as quickly as he could, had made his way down the room to meet them.

"Well?" Timon Gantry said.

"Well," Marchant repeated. "What is it?"

"It's an actress."

"Any good?"

"I'll answer that one," Gantry said, "a little later."

"Are you up to something?"

"Yes."

"What, for God's sake?"

"Patience, patience."

"I sometimes wonder, Timmy, why we put up with you."

"You needn't. You put up with me, dear boy, because I give the Management its particular brand of prestige."

"So you say."

"True?"

"I won't afford you the ignoble satisfaction of saying so."

"All the same, to oblige me, stay where you are."

He moved towards the group of three that was slowly making its way down the drawing-room.

Marchant continued to look at Anelida.

When Richard met Anelida and took her hand he found, to his astonishment, he was unable to say to her any of the things that for the last ten years he had so readily said to lovely ladies at parties. The usual procedure would have been to kiss her neatly on the cheek, tell her she looked marvellous and then pilot her by the elbow about the room. If she was his lady of the moment, he would contrive to spend a good deal of time in her company and they would probably dine somewhere after the party. How the evening then proceeded would depend upon a number of circumstances, none of which seemed to be entirely appropriate to Anelida. Richard felt, unexpectedly, that his nine years seniority were more like nineteen.

Octavius had found a friend. This was Miss Bellamy's physician, Dr. Harkness, a contemporary of Octavius's Oxford days and up at the House with him. They could be left together, happily reminiscent, and Anelida could be given her dry Martini and introduced to Pinky and Bertie, who were tending to hunt together through the party.

Bertie said rapidly, "I *do* congratulate you. *Do* swear to me on your *sacred* word of honour, *never* to wear anything but white and always, but *always* with your clever hat. *Ever!*"

"You mustn't take against Bertie," Pinky said kindly. "It's really a smashing compliment, coming from him."

"I'll bear it in mind," Anelida said. It struck her that they were both behaving rather oddly. They kept looking over her shoulder as if somebody or something behind her exerted a strange attraction over them. They did this so often that she felt impelled to follow their gaze and did so. It was Mary Bellamy at whom they had been darting their glances. She had moved further into the room and stood quite close, surrounded by a noisy group of friends. She herself was talking. But to Anelida's embarrassment she found Miss Bellamy's eyes looked straight into her own, coldly and searchingly. It was not, she was sure, a casual or accidental affair. Miss Bellamy had been watching her and the effect was disconcerting. Anelida turned away only to meet another pair of eyes, Timon Gantry's. And beside him yet another pair, Montague Marchant's, speculative, observant. It was like an inversion of her ridiculous daydream and she found it disturbing. "The cynosure of all eyes indeed! With a difference," thought Anelida.

But Richard was beside her, not looking at her, his arm scarcely touching hers, but *there*, to her great content. Pinky and Bertie talked with peculiar energy, making a friendly fuss over Anelida but conveying, nevertheless, a singular effect of nervous tension.

Presently Richard said, "Here's somebody else who would like to meet you, Anelida." She looked up at a brick-coloured Guardee face and a pair of surprised blue eyes. "Colonel Warrender," Richard said.

After his bumpy fashion, Warrender made conversation. "Everybody always shouts at these things, isn't it? Haven't got up to pitch yet but will, of course. You're on the stage, isn't it?"

"Just."

"Jolly good! What d'you think of Dicky's plays?"

Anelida wasn't yet accustomed to hearing Richard called Dicky or to being asked that sort of question in that sort of way.

She said, "Well—immensely successful, of course."

"Oh!" he said. "Successful! Awfully successful! 'Course. And I like 'em, you know. I'm his typical audience—want something gay and 'musing, with a good part for Mary. Not up to intellectual drama. Point is, though, is *he* satisfied? What d'you think? Wasting himself or not? What?"

Anelida was greatly taken aback and much exercised in her mind. Did this elderly soldier know Richard very intimately or did all Richard's friends plunge on first acquaintance into analyses of each other's inward lives for the benefit of perfect strangers? And did Warrender know about *Husbandry in Heaven?*

Again she had the feeling of being closely watched.

She said, "I hope he'll give us a serious play one of these days and I shouldn't have thought he'll be really satisfied until he does."

"Ah!" Warrender exclaimed, as if she'd made a dynamic observation. "There you are! Jolly good! Keep him up to it. Will you?"

"I!" Anelida cried in a hurry. She was about to protest that she was in no position to keep Richard up to anything, when it occurred to her, surprisingly, that Warrender might consider any such disclaimer an affectation.

"But does he need 'keeping up'?" she asked.

"Oh Lord, yes!" he said. "What with one thing and another. You must know all about that."

Anelida reminded herself she had only drunk half a dry Martini, so she couldn't possibly be under the influence of alcohol. Neither, she would have thought, was Colonel Warrender. Neither, apparently, was Miss Bellamy or Charles Templeton or Miss Kate Cavendish or Mr. Bertie Saracen. Nor, it would seem, was Mr. Timon Gantry, to whom, suddenly, she was being introduced by Richard.

"Timmy," Richard was saying. "Here is Anelida Lee."

To Anelida it was like meeting a legend.

"Good evening," the so-often mimicked voice was saying. "What is there for us to talk about? I know. You shall tell me precisely why you make that 'throw-it-over-your-shoulder' gesture in your final speech and whether it is your own invention or a bit of producer's whimsy."

"Is it wrong?" Anelida demanded. She then executed the mime that is known in her profession as a double-take. Her throat went dry, her eyes started and she crammed the knuckle of her gloved hand between her separated teeth. "You haven't *seen* me!" she cried.

"But I have. With Dicky Dakers."

"Oh my God!" whispered Anelida, and this was not an expression she was in the habit of using.

"Look out. You'll spill your drink. Shall we remove a little from this barnyard cacophony? The conservatory seems at the moment to be unoccupied."

Anelida disposed of her drink by distractedly swallowing it. "Come along," Gantry said. He took her by the elbow and piloted her towards the conservatory. Richard, as if by sleight-of-hand, had disappeared. Octavius was lost to her.

"Good evening, Bunny. Good evening, my dear Paul. Good evening, Tony," Gantry said with the omniscience of M. de Charlus. Celebrated faces responded to these greetings and drifted astern. They were in the conservatory and for the rest of her life the smell of freesias would carry Anelida back to it.

"There!" Gantry said, releasing her with a little pat. "Now then."

"Richard didn't tell me. Nobody said you were in front."

"Nobody knew, dear. We came in during the first act and left before the curtain. I preferred it."

She remembered, dimly, that this kind of behaviour was part of his legend.

"Why are you fussed?" Gantry inquired. "Are you ashamed of your performance?"

"No," Anelida said truthfully, and she added in a hurry, "I know it's very bad in patches."

"How old are you?"

"Nineteen."

"What else have you played?"

"Only bits at the Bonaventure."

"No *dra-mat-ic ac-ad-emy?*" he said, venomously spitting out the consonants. "No agonizing in devoted little groups? No *depicting?* No going to bed with Stanislavsky and rising with Method?"

Anelida, who was getting her second wind, grinned at him.

"I admire Stanislavsky," she said. "Intensely."

"Very well. Very well. Now, attend to me. I am going to tell you about your performance."

He did so at some length and in considerable detail. He was waspish, didactic, devastating and overwhelmingly right. For the most part she listened avidly and in silence, but presently she ventured to ask for elucidation. He answered, and seemed to be pleased.

"Now," he said, "those are all the things that were amiss with your performance. You will have concluded that I wouldn't have told you about them if I didn't think you were an actress. Most of your mistakes were technical. You will correct them. In the meantime I have a suggestion to make. Just that. No promises. It's in reference to a play that may never go into production. I believe you have already read it. You will do so again, if you please, and to that end you will come to the Unicorn at ten o'clock next Thursday morning. Hi! Monty!"

Anelida was getting used to the dreamlike situation in which she found herself. It had, in its own right, a kind of authenticity. When the Management, that bourne to which all unknown actresses aspired, appeared before her in the person of Montague Marchant, she was able to make a reasonable response. How pale was Mr. Marchant, how matt his surface, how immense his aplomb! He talked of the spring weather, of the flowers in the conservatory and, through some imperceptible gradation, of the theatre. She was, he understood, an actress.

"She's playing Eliza Doolittle," Gantry remarked.

"Of course. Nice notices," Marchant murmured and tidily smiled at her. She supposed he must have seen them.

"I've been bullying her about the performance," Gantry continued.

"What a bad man!" Marchant said lightly. "Isn't he?"

"I suggest you take a look at it."

"Now, you see, Miss Lee, he's trying to bully me."

"You mustn't let him," Anelida said.

"Oh, I'm well up to his tricks. Are you liking Eliza?"

"Very much indeed. It's a great stroke of luck for me to try my hand at her."

"How long is your season?"

"Till Sunday. We change every three weeks."

"God, yes. Club policy."

"That's it."

"I see no good reason," Gantry said, "for fiddling about with this conversation. You know the part I told you about in Dicky's new play? She's going to read it for me. In the meantime, Monty, my dear, you're going to look at the piece and then pay a call on the Bonaventure." He suddenly displayed the cockeyed charm for which he was famous. "No promises made, no bones broken. Just a certain amount of very kind trouble taken because you know I wouldn't ask it idly. Come, Monty, do say you will."

"I seem," Marchant said, "to be cornered," and it was impossible to tell whether he really minded.

Anelida said, "It's asking altogether too much—please *don't* be cornered."

"I shall tell you quite brutally if I think you've wasted my time."

"Yes, of course."

"Ah, Dicky!" Marchant said. "May I inquire if you're a party to this conspiracy?"

Richard was there again, beside her. "Conspiracy?" he said. "I'm up to my neck in it. Why?"

Gantry said, "The cloak-and-dagger business is all mine, however. Dicky's a puppet."

"Aren't we all!" Marchant said. "I need another drink. So, I should suppose, do you."

Richard had brought them. "Anelida," he asked, "what have they been cooking?"

For the third time, Anelida listened to her own incredible and immediate future.

"I've turned bossy, Richard," Gantry said. "I've gone ahead on my own. This child's going to take a running jump at reading your wench in *Heaven*. Monty's going to have a look at the play and see her Eliza. I tell him he'll be pleased. Too bad if you think she can't make it." He looked at Anelida and a very pleasant smile broke over his face. He flipped the brim of her hat with a thumb and forefinger. "Nice hat," he said.

Richard's hand closed painfully about her arm. "Timmy!" he shouted. "You're a *splendid* fellow! *Timmy!*"

"The author, at least," Marchant said drily, "would appear to be pleased."

"In that case," Gantry proposed, "let's drink to the unknown quantity. To your bright eyes, Miss Potential."

"I may as well go down gracefully," Marchant said. "To your Conspiracy, Timmy. In the person of Anelida Lee."

They had raised their glasses to Anelida when a voice behind them said, "I don't enjoy conspiracies in my own house, Monty, and I'm afraid I'm not mad about what I've heard of this one. Do let me in on it, won't you?"

It was Miss Bellamy.

2

Miss Bellamy had not arrived in the conservatory unaccompanied. She had Colonel Warrender in attendance upon her. They had been followed by Charles Templeton, Pinky Cavendish and Bertie Saracen. These three had paused by Gracefield to replenish their glasses and then moved from the dining-room into the conservatory, leaving the door open. Gracefield, continuing his round, was about to follow them. The conglomerate of voices in the rooms behind had mounted to its extremity, but above it, high-pitched, edged with emotion, a single voice rang out: Mary Bellamy's. There, in the conservatory she was, for all to see. She faced Anelida and leant slightly towards her.

"No, no, no, my dear. That, really is not quite good enough."

A sudden lull, comparable to that which follows the lowering of house-lights in a crowded theatre, was broken by the more distant babble in the further room and by the inconsequent, hitherto inaudible, excursions of the musicians. Heads were turned towards the conservatory. Warrender came to the door. Gracefield found himself moved to one side; Octavius was there, face to face with Warrender. Gantry's voice said:

"Mary. This won't do."

"I think," Octavius said, "if I may, I would like to go to my niece."

"Not yet," Warrender said. "Do you mind?" He shut the door and cut off the voices in the conservatory.

For a moment the picture beyond the glass walls was held. Mary Bellamy's lips worked. Richard faced her and was speaking. So were Charles and Gantry. It was like a scene from a silent film. Then, with a concerted movement, the figures of Gantry, Charles, Richard and Warrender, their backs to their audience, hid Miss Bellamy and Anelida.

"Ah, there you are, Occy!" a jovial, not quite sober voice exclaimed. "I was going to ask you, old boy. D'you remember . . ."

It was Octavius's old acquaintance, Dr. Harkness, now rather tight. As if he had given a signal, everybody began to talk again very loudly indeed. Charles broke from the group and came through the glass door, shutting it quickly behind him. He put his hand on Octavius's arm.

"It's all right, Browne, I assure you," he said. "It's nothing. Dicky is taking care of her. Believe me, it's all right." He turned to Gracefield. "Tell them to get on with it," he said. "At once."

Gracefield gave his butler's inclination and moved away.

Octavius said, "But all the same I would prefer to join Anelida."

Charles looked at him. "How would you have liked," he said, "to have spent the greater part of your life among aliens?"

Octavius blinked. "My dear Templeton," he said, "I don't know. But if you'll forgive me I find myself in precisely that situation at the moment and I should still like to go to my niece."

"Here she is now."

The door had opened again and Anelida had come through with Richard. They were both very white. Again a single voice was heard. Miss Bellamy's. "Do you suppose for one moment that I'm taken in . . ." and again Warrender shut the door.

"Well, Nelly darling," Octavius said. "I promised to remind you that we must leave early. Are you ready?"

"Quite ready," Anelida said. She turned to Charles Templeton and offered him her hand. "I'm so sorry," she said. "We'll slip out under our own steam."

"I'm coming," Richard announced grimly.

"So there's nothing," Charles said, "to be done?"

"I'm afraid we must go," Octavius said.

"We're running late as it is," Anelida agreed. Her voice, to her own astonishment, was steady. "Goodbye," she said, and to Richard, "No, don't come."

"I am coming."

Octavius put his hand on her shoulder and turned her towards the end of the room.

As he did so a cascade of notes sounded from a tubular gong. The roar of voices again died down, the musicians stood up and began to play that inevitable, that supremely silly air:

Happy birthday *to* you,
Happy birthday *to* you . . .

The crowd in the far room surged discreetly through into the dining-room, completely blocking the exit. Richard muttered, "This way. Quick," and propelled them towards a door into the hall. Before they could reach it, it opened to admit a procession: the maids, Gracefield with magnums of champagne, Florence, Cooky, in a white hat and carrying an enormously ornate birthday cake, and Old Ninn. They walked to the central table and moved ceremoniously to their appointed places. The cake was set down. Led by Dr. Harkness the assembly broke into applause.

"Now," Richard said.

And at last they were out of the room and in the hall. Anelida was conscious for the first time of her own heartbeat. It thudded in her throat and ears. Her mouth was dry and she trembled.

Octavius, puzzled and disturbed, touched her arm. "Nelly, my love," he said, "shall we go?"

"Yes," Anelida said and turned to Richard. "Don't come any further. Goodbye."

"I'm coming with you. I've got to."

"Please not."

He held her by the wrist. "I don't insult you with apologies, Anelida, but I do beg you to be generous and let me talk to you."

"Not now. Please, Richard, not now."

"Now. You're cold and you're trembling. Anelida!" He looked into her face and his own darkened. "Never again shall she speak to you like that. Do you hear me, Anelida? Never again." She drew away from him.

The door opened. Pinky and Bertie came through. Pinky made a dramatic pounce at Anelida and laid her hand on her arm. "Darling!" she cried incoherently. "Forget it! Nothing! God, what a scene!" She turned distractedly to the stairs, found herself cut off by the cinema unit and doubled back into the drawing-room. The camera men began to move their equipment across the hall.

"*Too* much!" Bertie said. "No! *Too* much." He disappeared in the direction of the men's cloakroom.

Timon Gantry came out. "Dicky," he said, "push off. I want a word with this girl. You won't do any good while you're in this frame of mind. Off!"

He took Anelida by the shoulders. "Listen to me," he said. "You will rise above. You will not let this make the smallest difference. Go home, now, and sort yourself out. I shall judge you by this and I shall see you on Thursday. Understood?" He gave her a firm little shake and stood back.

Warrender appeared, shutting the door behind him. He glared wretchedly at Anelida and barked, "Anything I can do—realize how distressed . . . Isn't it?"

Octavius said, "Very kind. I don't think, however . . ."

Richard announced loudly, "I'll never forgive her for this. Never."

Anelida thought, "If I don't go now I'll break down." She heard her own voice, "Don't give it another thought. Come along, Unk."

She turned and walked out of the house into the familiar square, and Octavius followed her.

"Richard," Warrender said, "I must have a word with you, boy. Come in here."

"No," Richard said, and he too went out into the square.

Gantry stood for a moment looking after him.

"I find myself," he observed, "unable, any longer, to tolerate Mary Bellamy."

A ripple of applause broke out in the dining-room. Miss Bellamy was about to cut her birthday cake.

3

Miss Bellamy was a conscientious, able and experienced actress. Her public appearances were the result of hard work as well as considerable talent, and if one principle above all others could be said to govern them, it was that which is roughly indicated in the familiar slogan "The show must go on." It was axiomatic with Miss Bellamy that whatever disrupting influences might attend her, even up to the moment when her hand was on the offstage doorknob, they would have no effect whatsoever upon her performance.

They had none on the evening of her fiftieth birthday. She remained true to type.

When the procession with the cake appeared in the dining-room beyond the glass wall of the conservatory, she turned upon the persons with whom she had been doing battle and uttered the single and strictly professional order: "Clear!"

They had done so. Pinky, Bertie, Warrender and Gantry had all left her. Charles had already gone. Only Marchant remained, according, as it were, to the script. It had been arranged that he escort Miss Bellamy and make the birthday speech. They stood together in the conservatory, watching. Gracefield opened the champagne. There was a great deal of laughter and discreet skirmishing among the guests. Glasses were distributed and filled. Gracefield and the maids returned to their appointed places. Everybody looked towards the conservatory.

"This," Marchant said, "is it. You'd better bury the temperament, sweetie, for the time being." He opened the door, adding blandly as he did so, "Bitch into them, dear."

"The hell I will," said Miss Bellamy. She shot one malevolent glance at him, stepped back, collected herself, parted her lips in their triangular smile and made her entrance.

The audience, naturally, applauded.

Marchant, who had his own line in smiles, fingered his bow-tie and then raised a deprecating hand.

"Mary, darling," he said, pitching his voice, "and everybody! Please!"

A press photographer's lamp flashed.

Marchant's speech was short, graceful, bland, and for the most part, highly appreciated. He made the point, an acceptable one to his audience, that nobody really understood the people of their wonderful old profession but they themselves. The ancient classification of "rogues and vagabonds" was ironically recapitulated. The warmth, the dedication, the loyalties were reviewed and a brief but moving reference was made to "our wonderful Mary's happy association with, he would not say Marchant and Company, but would use a more familiar and he hoped affectionate phrase—the 'Management.'" He ended by asking them all to raise their glasses and drink "to Mary."

Miss Bellamy's behaviour throughout was perfect. She kept absolutely still and even the most unsympathetic observer would scarcely have noticed that she was anything but oblivious of her audience. She was, in point of fact, attentive to it and was very well aware of the absence of Richard, Pinky, Bertie, Warrender and Gantry—to say nothing of Anelida and Octavius. She also noticed that Charles, a late arrival in his supporting role of consort, looked pale and troubled. This irritated her. She saw that Old Ninn, well to the fore, was scarlet in the face, a sure sign of intemperance. No doubt there had been port-drinking parties with

Florence and Gracefield and further noggins on her own account. Infuriating of Old Ninn! Outrageous of Richard, Pinky, Bertie, Maurice and Timon to absent themselves from the speech! Intolerable, that on her birthday she should be subjected to slight after slight and deception after deception: culminating, my God, in their combined treachery over that bony girl from the bookshop! It was time to give Monty a look of misty gratitude. They were drinking her health.

She replied, as usual, very briefly. The suggestion was of thoughts too deep for words and the tone whimsical. She ended by making a special reference to the cake and said that on this occasion Cooky, if that were possible, had excelled herself and she called attention to the decorations.

There was a round of applause, during which Gantry, Pinky, Bertie and Warrender edged in through the far doorway. Miss Bellamy was about to utter her peroration, but before she could do so, Old Ninn loudly intervened. "What's a cake without candles?" said Old Ninn.

A handful of guests laughed, nervously and indulgently. The servants looked scandalized and apprehensive.

"Fifty of them," Old Ninn proclaimed. "Oh, wouldn't they look lovely!" and broke into a disreputable chuckle.

Miss Bellamy took the only possible action. She topped Old Ninn's lines by snatching up the ritual knife and plunging it into the heart of the cake. The gesture, which may have had something of the character of a catharsis, was loudly applauded.

The press photographer's lamps flashed.

The ceremony followed its appointed course. The cake was cut up and distributed. Glasses were refilled and the guests began to talk again at the tops of their voices. It was time for her to open the presents, which had already been deposited on a conveniently placed table in the drawing-room. When that had been done they would go and the party would be over. But it would take a considerable time and all her resources. In the meantime, there was Old Ninn, purple-faced, not entirely steady on her pins and prepared to continue her unspeakable act for the benefit of anyone who would listen to her.

Miss Bellamy made a quick decision. She crossed to Old Ninn, put her arm about her shoulders and gaily laughing, led her towards the door into the hall. In doing so she passed Warrender, Pinky, Bertie and Timon Gantry. She ignored them, but shouted to Monty Marchant that she was going to powder her nose. Charles was in the doorway. She was obliged to stop for a moment. He said under his breath, "You've done a terrible thing." She looked at him with contempt.

"You're in my way. I want to go out."

"I can't allow you to go on like this."

"Get *out!*" she whispered and thrust towards him. In that overheated room her scent engulfed him like a fog.

He said loudly, "At least don't use any more of that stuff. At least don't do that. Mary, listen to me!"

"I think you must be mad."

They stared at each other. He stood aside and she went out, taking Old Ninn with her. In the hall she said, "Ninn, go to your room and lie down. Do you hear me!"

Old Ninn looked her fully in the face, drew down the corners of her mouth, and keeping a firm hold on the banister, plodded upstairs.

Neither she nor Charles had noticed Florence, listening avidly, a pace or two behind them. She moved away down the hall and a moment later Richard came in by the front door. When he saw Miss Bellamy he stopped short.

"Where have you been?" she demanded.

"I've been trying, not very successfully, to apologize to my friends."

"They've taken themselves off, it appears."

"Would you have expected them to stay?"

"I should have thought them capable of anything."

He looked at her with a sort of astonishment and said nothing.

"I've got to speak to you," she said between her teeth.

"Have you? I wonder what you can find to say."

"Now."

"The sooner the better. But shouldn't you—" he jerked his head at the sounds beyond the doors, "be in there?"

"*Now.*"

"Very well."

"Not here."

"Wherever you like, Mary."

"In my room."

She had turned to the stairs when a press photographer, all smiles, emerged from the dining-room.

"Miss Bellamy, could I have a shot? By the door? With Mr. Dakers perhaps? It's an opportunity. Would you mind?"

For perhaps five seconds, she hesitated. Richard said something under his breath.

"It's a bit crowded in there. We'd like to run a full-page spread," said the photographer and named his paper.

"But of course," said Miss Bellamy.

Richard watched her touch her hair and re-do her mouth. Accustomed though he was to her professional technique he was filled with amazement. She put away her compact and turned brilliantly to the photographer. "Where?" she asked him.

"In the entrance I thought. Meeting Mr. Dakers."

She moved down the hall to the front door. The photographer dodged round her. "Not in the full glare," she said, and placed herself.

"Mr. Dakers?" said the photographer.

"Isn't it better as it is?" Richard muttered.

"Don't pay any attention to him," she said with ferocious gaiety. "Come along, Dicky."

"There's a new play on the skids, isn't there? If Mr. Dakers could be showing it to you, perhaps? I've brought something in case."

He produced a paperbound quarto of typescript, opened it and put it in her hands.

"Just as if you'd come to one of those sure-fire laugh lines," the photographer said. "Pointing it out to him, you know? Right, Mr. Dakers?"

Richard, nauseated, said, "I'm photocatastrophic. Leave me out."

"No!" said Miss Bellamy. Richard shook his head.

"You're too modest," said the photographer. "Just a little this way. Grand."

She pointed to the opened script. "And the great big smile," he said. The bulb flashed. "Wonderful. *Thank* you," and he moved away.

"And now," she said through her teeth, "I'll talk to you."

Richard followed her upstairs. On the landing they passed Old Ninn, who watched them go into Miss Bellamy's room. After the door had shut she stood outside and waited.

She was joined there by Florence, who had come up by the back stairway. They communicated in a series of restrained gestures and brief whispers.

"You all right, Mrs. Plumtree?"

"Why not!" Ninn countered austerely.

"You look flushed," Florence observed drily.

"The heat in those rooms is disgraceful."

"Has She come up?"

"In there."

"Trouble?" Florence asked, listening. Ninn said nothing. "It's him, isn't it? Mr. Richard? What's *he* been up to?"

"Nothing," Ninn said, "that wouldn't be a credit to him, Floy, and I'll thank you to remember it."

"Oh, dear," Florence said rather acidly. "He's a man like the rest of them."

"He's better than most."

In the bedroom Miss Bellamy's voice murmured, rose sharply and died. Richard's, scarcely audible, sounded at intervals. Then both together, urgent and expostulatory, mounted to some climax and broke off. There followed a long silence during which the two women stared at each other, and then a brief unexpected sound.

"What was that!" Florence whispered.

"Was she laughing?"

"It's left off now."

Ninn said nothing. "Oh well," Florence said, and had moved away when the door opened.

Richard came out, white to the lips. He walked past without seeing them, paused at the stairhead and pressed the palms of his hands against his eyes. They heard him fetch his breath with a harsh sound that might have been a sob. He stood there for some moments like a man who had lost his bearings and then struck his closed hand twice on the newel post and went quickly downstairs.

"What did I tell you," Florence said. She stole nearer to the door. It was not quite shut. "Trouble," she said.

"None of his making."

"How do you know?"

"The same way," Ninn said, "that I know how to mind my own business."

Inside the room, perhaps beyond it, something crashed.

They stood there, irresolute, listening.

4

At first Miss Bellamy had not been missed. Her party had reverted to its former style, a little more confused by the circulation of champagne. It spread through the two rooms and into the conservatory and became noisier and noisier. Everybody forgot about the ceremony of opening the birthday presents. Nobody noticed that Richard, too, was absent.

Gantry edged his way towards Charles, who was in the drawing-room, and stooped to make himself heard.

"Dicky," he said, "has made off."

"Where to?"

"I imagine to do the best he can with the girl and her uncle."

Charles looked at him with something like despair. "There's nothing to be done," he said, "nothing. It was shameful."

"Where is she?"

"I don't know. Isn't she in the next room?"

"I don't know," Gantry said.

"I wish to God this show was over."

"She ought to get on with the present-opening. They won't go till she does."

Pinky had come up. "Where's Mary?" she said.

"We don't know," Charles said. "She ought to be opening her presents."

"She won't miss her cue, my dear, you may depend upon it. Don't you feel it's time?"

"I'll find her," Charles said. "Get them mustered if you can, Gantry, will you?"

Bertie Saracen joined them, flushed and carefree. "What goes on?" he inquired.

"We're waiting for Mary."

"She went upstairs for running repairs," Bertie announced and giggled. "I *am* a poet and *don't* I know it!" he added.

"Did you see her?" Gantry demanded.

"I heard her tell Monty. She's not uttering to poor wee me."

Monty Marchant edged towards them. "Monty, ducky," Bertie cried, "your speech was too poignantly right. Live forever! *Oh*, I'm so tiddly."

Marchant said, "Mary's powdering her nose, Charles. Should we do a little shepherding?"

"I thought so."

Gantry mounted a stool and used his director's voice, "Attention, the cast!" It was a familiar summons and was followed by an obedient hush. "To the table, please, everybody, and clear an entrance. Last act, ladies and gentlemen. Last act, please!"

They did so at once. The table with its heaped array of parcels had already been moved forward by Gracefield and the maids. The guests ranged themselves at both sides like a chorus in grand opera, leaving a passage to the principal door.

Charles said, "I'll just see . . ." and went into the hall. He called up the stairs, "Oh, Florence! Tell Miss Bellamy we're ready, will you?" and came back. "Florence'll tell her," he said.

There was a longish, expectant pause. Gantry drew in his breath with a familiar hiss.

"*I'll* tell her," Charles said, and started off for the door.

Before he could reach it they all heard a door slam and running steps on the stairway. There was a relieved murmur and little indulgent laughter.

"First time Mary's ever missed an entrance," someone said.

The steps ran across the hall. An irregular flutter of clapping broke out and stopped.

A figure appeared in the entrance and paused there.

It was not Mary Bellamy but Florence.

Charles said, "Florence! Where's Miss Mary?"

Florence, breathless, mouthed at him. "Not coming."

"Oh God!" Charles ejaculated. "Not *now!*"

As if to keep the scene relentlessly theatrical, Florence cried out in a shrill voice,

"A doctor. For Christ's sake. Quick. Is there a doctor in the house!"

CHAPTER FOUR   # Catastrophe

It might be argued that the difference between high tragedy and melodrama rests in the indisputable fact that the latter is more true to nature. People, even the larger-than-life people of the theatre, tend at moments of tension to express themselves not in unexpected or memorable phrases but in clichés.

Thus, when Florence made her entrance, one or two voices in her audience cried out, "My God, what's happened?" Bertie Saracen cried out shrilly, "Does she mean Mary?" and somebody whose identity remained a secret said in an authoritative British voice, "Quiet, everybody. No need to panic," as if Florence had called for a fireman rather than a physician.

The only person to remain untouched was Dr. Harkness, who was telling a long, inebriated story to Monty Marchant and whose voice droned on indecently in a far corner of the dining-room.

Florence stretched out a shaking hand towards Charles Templeton. "Oh, for Christ's sake, sir!" she stammered. "Oh, for Christ's sake, come quick."

"—And this chap said to the other chap . . ." Dr. Harkness recounted.

Charles said, "Good God, what's the matter! Is it . . . ?"

"It's her, sir. Come quick."

Charles thrust her aside, ran from the room and pelted upstairs.

"A doctor!" Florence said. "My God, a doctor!"

It was Marchant who succeeded in bringing Dr. Harkness into focus. "You're wanted," he said. "Upstairs. Mary."

"Eh? Bit of trouble?" Dr. Harkness asked vaguely.

"Something's happened to Mary."

Timon Gantry said, "Pull yourself together, Harkness. You've got a patient."

Dr. Harkness had forgotten to remove his smile, but a sort of awareness now overtook him. "Patient?" he said. "Where? Is it Charles?"

"Upstairs. Mary."

"Good gracious!" said Dr. Harkness. "Very good. I'll come." He rocked slightly on his feet and remained stationary.

Maurice Warrender said to Florence, "Is it bad?"

Her hand to her mouth she nodded her head up and down like a mandarin.

Warrender took a handful of ice from a wine-cooler and suddenly thrust it down the back of Dr. Harkness's collar. "Come on," he said. Harkness let out a sharp oath. He swung round as if to protest, lost his balance and fell heavily.

Florence screamed.

"I'm a'right," Dr. Harkness said from the floor. "Tripped over something. Silly!"

Warrender and Gantry got him to his feet. "I'm all *right!*" he repeated angrily. "Gimme some water, will you?"

Gantry tipped some out of the ice bucket. Dr. Harkness swallowed it down noisily and shuddered. "Beastly stuff," he said. "Where's this patient?"

From the stairhead, Charles called in an unrecognizable voice, "Harkness! *Harkness!*"

"Coming," Warrender shouted. Harkness, gasping, was led out.

Florence looked wildly round the now completely silent company, wrung her hands and followed them.

Timon Gantry said, "More ice, perhaps," picked up the wine-cooler and overtook them on the stairs.

The party was left in suspension.

In Mary Bellamy's bedroom all the windows were open. An evening breeze stirred the curtains and the ranks of tulips. Dr. Harkness knelt beside a pool of rose-coloured chiffon from which protruded, like rods, two legs finished with high-heeled shoes and two naked arms whose clenched hands glittered with diamonds. Diamonds were spattered across the rigid plane of the chest and shone through a hank of disarranged hair. A length of red chiffon lay across the face and this was a good thing.

Dr. Harkness had removed his coat. His ice-wet shirt stuck to his spine. His ear was laid against the place from which he had pulled away the red chiffon.

He straightened up, looked closely into the face, re-veiled it and got to his feet.

"I'm afraid there's nothing whatever to be done," he said.

Charles said, "There must be. You don't know. There must be. Try. Try something. My God, try!"

Warrander, in his short-stepped, square-shouldered way, walked over to Harkness and looked down for a moment.

"No good," he said. "Have to face it. What?"

Charles sat on the bed and rubbed his freckled hand across his mouth. "I can't believe it's happened," he said. "It's—*there*—it's *happened*. And I can't believe it."

Florence burst noisily into tears.

Dr. Harkness turned to her. "You," he said. "Florence, isn't it? Try to control yourself, there's a good girl. Did you find her like this?"

Florence nodded and sobbed out something indistinguishable.

"But she was . . ." Harkness glanced at Charles. "Conscious?"

Florence said, "Not to know me. Not to speak," and broke down completely.

"Were the windows open?"

Florence shook her head.

"Did you open them?"

She shook her head again, "I didn't think to—I got such a wicked shock—I didn't think . . ."

"I opened them," Charles said.

"First thing to be done," Warrender muttered.

Gantry, who from the time of his entry had stood motionless near the door, joined the others. "But what *was* it?" he asked. "What happened?"

Warrender said unevenly, "Perfectly obvious. She used that bloody spray thing there. I said it was dangerous. Only this morning."

"What thing?"

Warrender stooped. The tin of Slaypest lay on its side close to the clenched right hand. A trickle of dark fluid stained the carpet. "This," he said.

"Better leave it," Dr. Harkness said sharply.

"What?"

"Better leave it where it is." He looked at Gantry. "It's some damned insecticide. For plants. The tin's smothered in warnings."

"We told her," Warrender said. "Look at it."

"I said don't touch it."

Warrender straightened up. The blood had run into his face. "Sorry," he said, and then, "Why not?"

"You're a bit too ready with your hands. I'm wet as hell and half frozen."

"You were tight. Best cure, my experience."

They eyed each other resentfully. Dr. Harkness looked at Charles, who sat doubled up with his hands on his chest. He went to him. "Not too good?" he said. Timon Gantry put a hand on Charles's shoulder.

"I'm going to take you to your room, old boy. Next door, isn't it?"

"Yes," Dr. Harkness said. "But not just yet. In a minute. Good idea." He turned to Florence. "Do you know where Mr. Templeton keeps his tablets? Get them, will you? And you might bring some aspirin at the same time. Run along, now." Florence went into the dressing-room. He sat beside Charles on the bed and took his wrist. "Steady does it," he said and looked at Gantry. "Brandy."

"I know where it is," Warrender said, and went out.

Gantry said, "What about that mob downstairs?"

"They can wait." He held the wrist a little longer and then laid Charles's hand on his knee, keeping his own over it. "We'll move you in a moment. You must let other people think for you. It's been a bad thing."

"I can't . . ." Charles said. "I can't . . ." and fetched his breath in irregular, tearing sighs.

"Don't try to work things out. Not just yet. Ah, here's Florence. Good. Now then, one of these."

He gave Charles a tablet. Warrender came back with brandy. "This'll help," Dr. Harkness said. They waited in silence.

"I'm all right," Charles said presently.

"Fine. Now, an arm each and take it steady. His room's next door. Lie down, Charles, won't you?"

Charles nodded and Warrender moved towards him. "No," Charles said quite strongly, and turned to Gantry. "I'm all right," he repeated, and Gantry very efficiently supported him through the door into his dressing-room.

Warrender stood for a moment, irresolute, and then lifted his chin and followed them.

"Get him a hot bottle," Harkness said to Florence.

When she'd gone he swallowed three aspirins, took up the bedside telephone and dialled a number.

"This is Dr. Frank Harkness. I'm speaking from Number 2 Pardoner's Place. Mr. Charles Templeton's house. There's been an accident. A fatality. Some sort of pest killer. Mrs. Templeton. Yes. About fifty people —a party. Right. I'll wait."

As he replaced the receiver Gantry came back. He stopped short when he saw Harkness. "What now?" he asked.

"I've telephoned the police."

"The *police!*"

"In cases like this," Harkness said, "one notifies the police."

"Anybody would think . . ."

"Anybody will think anything," Dr. Harkness grunted. He turned back the elaborate counterpane and the blankets under it. "I don't want to call the servants," he said, "and that woman's on the edge of hysteria. This sheet'll do." He pulled it off, bundled it up and threw it to Gantry. "Cover her up, old boy, will you?"

Gantry turned white round the mouth. "I don't like this sort of thing," he said. "I've produced it often enough, but I've never faced the reality." And he added with sudden violence, "Cover her up yourself."

"All right. All right," sighed Dr. Harkness. He took the sheet, crossed the room and busied himself with masking the body. The breeze from the open windows moved the sheet, as if, fantastically, it was stirred by what it covered.

"May as well shut them, now," Dr. Harkness said and did so. "Can you straighten the bed at least?" he asked. Gantry did his best with the bed.

"Right," said Dr. Harkness, putting on his coat. "Does this door lock? Yes. Will you come?"

As they went out Gantry said, "Warrender's crocked up. Charles didn't seem to want him, so he flung a sort of poker-backed, stiff-lipped, Blimp-type temperament and made his exit. I don't know where he's gone, but in his way," Gantry said, "he's wonderful. Terrifyingly ham, but wonderful. He's upset, though."

"Serve him bloody well right. It won't be his fault if I escape pneumonia. My *head!*" Dr. Harkness said, momentarily closing his eyes.

"You were high."

"Not so high I couldn't come down."

Old Ninn was on the landing. Her face had bleached round its isolated patches of crimson. She confronted Dr. Harkness.

"What's she done to herself?" asked Old Ninn.

Dr. Harkness once more summoned up his professional manner. He bent over her. "You've got to be very sensible and good, Nanny," he said, and told her briefly what had happened.

She looked fixedly into his face throughout the recital and at the end said, "Where's Mr. Templeton?"

Dr. Harkness indicated the dressing-room.

"Who's looking after him?"

"Florence was getting him a hot bottle."

"Her!" Ninn said with a brief snort, and without another word stumped to the door. She gave it a smart rap and let herself in.

"Wonderful character," Gantry murmured.

"Remarkable."

They turned towards the stairs. As they did so a figure moved out of the shadows at the end of the landing, but they did not notice her. It was Florence.

"And now, I suppose," Dr. Harkness said as they went downstairs, "for the mob."

"Get rid of them?" Gantry asked.

"Not yet. They're meant to wait. Police orders."

"But . . ."

"Matter of form."

Gantry said, "At least we can boot the press off, can't we?"

"Great grief, I'd forgotten that gang!"

"Leave them to me."

The press was collected about the hall. A light flashed as Gantry and Harkness came down, and a young man who had evidently just arrived advanced hopefully. "Mr. Timon Gantry? I wonder if you could . . ."

Gantry, looking down from his great height, said, "I throw you one item. And one only. Miss Mary Bellamy was taken ill this evening and died some minutes ago."

"Doctor er . . . ? Could you . . . ?"

"The cause," Dr. Harkness said, "is at present undetermined. She collapsed and did not recover consciousness."

"Is Mr. Templeton . . . ?"

"No," they said together. Gantry added, "And that is all, gentlemen. Good evening to you."

Gracefield appeared from the back of the hall, opened the front door and said, "Thank you, gentlemen. If you will step outside."

They hung fire. A car drew up in the Place. From it emerged a heavily built man, wearing a bowler hat and a tidy overcoat. He walked into the house.

"Inspector Fox," he said.

2

It has been said of Mr. Fox that his arrival at any scene of disturbance has the effect of a large and almost silent vacuum cleaner.

Under his influence the gentlemen of the press were tidied out into Pardoner's Place, where they lingered restively for a long time. The guests, some of whom were attempting to leave, found themselves neatly mustered in the drawing-room. The servants waited quietly in the hall. Mr. Fox and Dr. Harkness went upstairs. A constable appeared and stood inside the front door.

"I locked the door," Dr. Harkness said, with the air of a schoolboy hoping for praise. He produced the key.

"Very commendable, Doctor," said Fox comfortably.

"Nothing's been moved. The whole thing speaks for itself."

"Quite so. Very sad."

Fox laid his bowler on the bed, knelt by the sheet and turned it back. "Strong perfume," he said. He drew out his spectacles, placed them and looked closely into the dreadful face.

"You can see for yourself," Dr. Harkness said. "Traces of the stuff all over her."

"Quite so," Fox repeated. "Very profuse."

He contemplated the Slaypest but did not touch it. He rose and made a little tour of the room. He had very bright eyes for a middle-aged person.

"If it's convenient, sir," he said, "I'll have a word with Mr. Templeton."

"He's pretty well knocked out. His heart's dicky. I made him lie down."

"Perhaps you'd just have a little chat with him yourself, Doctor. Would you be good enough to say I won't keep him more than a minute? No need to disturb him; I'll come to his room. Where would it be?"

"Next door."

"Nice and convenient. I'll give you a minute with him and then I'll come in. Thank you, Doctor."

Dr. Harkness looked sharply at him, but he was restoring his spectacles to their case and had turned to contemplate the view from the window.

"Pretty square, this," said Mr. Fox.

Dr. Harkness went out.

Fox quietly locked the door and went to the telephone. He dialled a number and asked for an extension.

"Mr. Alleyn?" he said. "Fox, here. It's about this case in Pardoner's Place. There are one or two little features . . ."

3

When Superintendent Alleyn had finished speaking to Inspector Fox, he went resignedly into action. He telephoned his wife with the routine information that he would not after all be home for dinner, summoned Detective Sergeants Bailey and Thompson with their impedimenta, rang the police surgeon, picked up his homicide bag and went whistling to the car. "A lady of the theatre," he told his subordinates, "appears to have looked upon herself as a common or garden pest and sprayed herself out of this world. She was mistaken as far as her acting was concerned. Miss Mary Bellamy. A comedienne of the naughty darling school and not a beginner. It's Mr. Fox's considered opinion that somebody done her in."

When they arrived at 2 Pardoner's Place, the tidying-up process had considerably advanced. Fox had been shown the guest list with addresses. He had checked it, politely dismissed those who had stayed throughout in what he called the reception area and mildly retained the persons who had left it "prior," to quote Mr. Fox, "to the unfortunate event." These were Timon Gantry, Pinky Cavendish, and Bertie Saracen, who were closeted in Miss Bellamy's boudoir on the ground floor. Hearing that Colonel Warrender was a relation, Mr. Fox suggested that he join Charles Templeton, who had now come down to his study. Showing every sign of reluctance but obedient to authority, Warrender did so. Dr. Harkness had sent out for a corpse-reviver for himself and gloomily occupied a chair in the conservatory. Florence having been interviewed and Old Ninn briefly surveyed, they had retired to their sitting-room in the top story. Gracefield, the maids and the hired men had gone a considerable way towards removing the debris.

Under a sheet from her own bed on the floor of her locked room, Miss Bellamy began to stiffen.

Alleyn approached the front door to the renewed activity of the camera men. One of them called out, "Give us a break, won't you, Super?"

"All in good time," he said.

"What d'you know, Mr. Alleyn?"

"Damn all," Alleyn said and rang the bell.

He was admitted by Fox. "Sorry you've been troubled, sir," Fox said.

"I daresay. What *is* all this?"

Fox told him in a few neatly worded sentences.

"All right," Alleyn said. "Let's have a look, shall we?"

They went upstairs to Miss Bellamy's bedroom.

He knelt by the body. "Did she *bathe* in scent?" he wondered.

"Very strong, isn't it, sir?"

"Revolting. The whole room stinks of it." He uncovered the head and shoulders. "I see."

"Not very nice," Fox remarked.

"Not very." Alleyn was silent for a moment or two. "I saw her a week ago," he said, "on the last night of that play of Richard Dakers's that's been running so long. It was a flimsy, conventional comedy, but she filled it with her own kind of gaiety. And now—to this favour is she come."

He looked more closely. "Could the stuff have blown back in her face? But you tell me they say the windows were shut?"

"That's right."

"The face and chest are quite thickly spattered."

"Exactly. I wondered," Fox said, "if the spray-gun mechanism on the Slaypest affair was not working properly and she turned it towards her to see."

"And it *did* work? Possible, I suppose. But she'd stop at once, and look at her. Just look, Fox. There's a fine spray such as she'd get if she held the thing at arm's length and didn't use much pressure. And over that there are great blotches and runnels of the stuff, as if she'd held it close to her face and pumped it like mad."

"People do these things."

"They do. As a theory I don't fancy it. Nobody's handled the Slaypest tin? Since the event?"

"They say not," Fox said.

"Bailey'll have to go over it for dabs, of course. Damn this scent. You can't get a whiff of anything else."

Alleyn bent double and advanced his nose to the tin of Slaypest. "I know this stuff," he said. "It's about as highly concentrated as they come, and in my opinion shouldn't be let loose on the public for all the warnings on the label. The basic ingredient seems to be hexa-ethyl-tetra-phosphate."

"You don't say," Fox murmured.

"It's a contact poison and very persistent." He replaced the sheet, got up and examined the bank of growing plants in the bay window. "Here it is again. They've got thrips and red spider." He stared absently at Fox. "So what does she do, Br'er Fox? She comes up here in the middle of her own party wearing her best red wisp of tulle and all her diamonds and sets about spraying her azaleas."

"Peculiar," Fox said. "What I thought."

"Very rum indeed."

He wandered to the dressing-table. The central drawer was pulled out. Among closely packed ranks of boxes and pots was an open powder bowl. A piece of cotton-wool coloured with powder lay on the top of the table near a lipstick that had been imperfectly shut. Nearby was a bunch of Parma violets, already wilting.

"She *did* have a fiddle with her face," Alleyn pointed out. "She's got a personal maid, you say. The woman that found her."

"Florence."

"All right. Well, Florence would have tidied up any earlier goes at the powder and paint. And she'd have done something about these violets.

Where do *they* come in? So this poor thing walks in, pulls out the drawer, does her running repairs and I should say from the smell, has a lavish whack at her scent." He sniffed the atomizer. "That's it. Quarter full and stinks like a civet cat, and here's the bottle it came from, empty. 'Formidable.' Expensive maker. 'Abominable' would be more like it. How women can use such muck passes my understanding."

"I rather fancy it," said Mr. Fox. "It's intriguing."

Alleyn gave him a look. "If we're to accept what appears to be the current explanation, she drenches her azaleas with hexa-ethyl-tetra-phosphate and then turns the spray-gun full in her own face and kills herself. D'you believe that?"

"Not when you put it like that."

"Nor I. Bailey and Thompson are down below and Dr. Curtis is on his way. Get them up here. We'll want the complete treatment. Detailed pictures of the body and the room, tell Thompson. And Bailey'll need to take her prints and search the spray-gun, the dressing-table and anything else that may produce dabs, latent or otherwise. We don't know what we're looking for, of course." The bathroom door was open and he glanced in. "Even this place reeks of scent. What's that on the floor? Broken picture." He looked more closely. "Rather nice tinsel picture. Madame Vestris, I fancy. Corner of the washbasin freshly chipped. Somebody's tramped broken glass over the floor. Did she drop her pretty picture? And why in the bathroom? Washing the glass? Or what? We won't disturb it." He opened the bathroom cupboard. "The things they take!" he muttered. "The tablets. For insomnia. One with water on retiring. The unguents! The lotions! Here's some muck like green clay. Lifting mask. 'Apply with spatula and leave on for ten minutes. Do not move lips or facial muscles during treatment.' Here *is* the spatula with some nice fresh dabs. Florence's, no doubt. And in the clothes basket, a towel with greenish smears. She had the full treatment before the party. Sal volatile bottle by the handbasin. Did someone try to force sal volatile down her throat?"

"Not a chance, I should say, sir."

"She must have taken it earlier in the day. Why? Very fancy loo, tarted up with a quilted cover, good Lord! All right, Fox. Away we go. I'd better see the husband."

"He's still in his study with a Colonel Warrender, who seems to be a relative. Mr. Templeton had a heart-attack after the event. The doctor says he's subject to them. Colonel Warrender and Mr. Gantry took him into his dressing-room there, and then the Colonel broke up and went downstairs. Mr. Templeton was still lying in there when I came up, but I suggested the Colonel should take him down to the study. They didn't seem to fancy the move, but I wanted to clear the ground. It's awkward," Mr. Fox said, "having people next door to the body."

Alleyn went into the dressing-room, leaving the door open. "Change of atmosphere," Fox heard him remark. "Very masculine. Very simple. Very good. Who gave him a hot bottle?"

"Florence. The doctor says the old nurse went in later, to take a look at him. By all accounts she's a bossy old cup-of-tea and likes her drop of port wine."

"This," Alleyn said, "is the house of a damn rich man. And woman, I suppose."

"He's a big name in the City, isn't he?"

"He is indeed. C. G. Templeton. He brought off that coup with Eastland Transport two years ago. Reputation of being an implacable chap to run foul of."

"The servants seem to fancy him. The cook says he must have everything just so. One slip and you're out. But well-liked. He's taken this very hard. Very shaky when I saw him but easy to handle. The Colonel was tougher."

"Either of them strike you as being the form for a woman-poisoner?"

"Not a bit like it," Fox said cheerfully.

"They tell me you never know."

"That's right. So they say."

They went out. Fox locked the door. "Not that it makes all that difference," he sighed. "The keys on this floor are interchangeable. As usual. However," he added, brightening, "I've taken the liberty of removing all the others."

"You'll get the sack one of these days. Come on." They went downstairs.

"The remaining guests," Fox said, "are in the second room on the right. They're the lot who were with deceased up to the time she left the conservatory and the only ones who went outside the reception area before the speeches began. And, by the way, sir, up to the time the speeches started, there was a photographer and a moving camera unit blocking the foot of the stairs and for the whole period a kind of bar with a man mixing drinks right by the back stairs. I've talked to the man concerned and he says nobody but the nurse and Florence went up while he was on duty. This is deceased's sitting-room. Or boudoir. The study is the first on the right."

"Where's the quack?"

"In the glasshouse with a hangover. Shall I stir him up?"

"Thank you."

They separated. Alleyn tapped on the boudoir door and went in.

Pinky sat in an armchair with a magazine, Timon Gantry was finishing a conversation on the telephone, and Bertie, petulant and flushed, was reading a rare edition of *'Tis Pity She's a Whore.* When they saw Alleyn the two men got up and Pinky put down her magazine as if she was ashamed of it.

Alleyn introduced himself. "This is just to say I'm very sorry to keep you waiting about."

Gantry said, "It's damned awkward. I've had to tell people over the telephone."

"There's no performance involved, is there?"

"No. But there's a new play going into rehearsal. Opening in three weeks. One has to cope."

"Of course," Alleyn said, "one does, indeed," and went out.

"What a superb-looking man," Bertie said listlessly, and returned to his play.

Warrender and Charles had the air of silence about them. It was not, Alleyn fancied, the kind of silence that falls naturally between two cousins united in a common sorrow; they seemed at odds with each other. He could have sworn his arrival was a relief rather than an annoyance. He noticed that the study, like the dressing-room, had been furnished and decorated by a perfectionist with restraint, judgment and a very great deal of money. There was a kind of relationship between the reserve of these two men and the setting in which he found them. He thought that they had probably been sitting there for a long time without speech. A full decanter and two untouched glasses stood between them on a small and exquisite table.

Charles began to rise. Alleyn said, "Please, don't move," and he sank heavily back again. Warrender stood up. His eyes were red and his face patched with uneven colour.

"Bad business, this," he said. "What?"

"Yes," Alleyn said. "Very bad." He looked at Charles. "I'm sorry, sir, that at the moment we're not doing anything to make matters easier."

With an obvious effort Charles said, "Sit down, won't you? Alleyn, isn't it? I know your name, of course."

Warrender pushed a chair forward.

"Will you have a drink?" Charles asked.

"No, thank you very much. I won't trouble you longer than I can help. There's a certain amount of unavoidable business to be got through. There will be an inquest and, I'm afraid, a post-mortem. In addition to that we're obliged to check, as far as we're able, the events leading to the accident. All this, I know, is very distressing and I'm sorry."

Charles lifted a hand and let it fall.

Warrender said, "Better make myself scarce."

"No," Alleyn said. "I'd be glad if you waited a moment."

Warrender was looking fixedly at Alleyn. He tapped himself above the heart and made a very slight gesture towards Charles. Alleyn nodded.

"If I may," he said to Charles, "I'll ask Colonel Warrender to give me an account of the period before your wife left the party and went up to her room. If, sir, you would like to amend or question or add to anything he says, please do so."

Charles said, "Very well. Though God knows what difference it can make."

Warrender straightened his back, touched his Brigade-of-Guards tie, and made his report, with the care and, one would have said, the precision of experience.

He had, he said, been near to Mary Bellamy from the time she left her post by the door and moved through her guests towards the conservatory. She had spoken to one group after another. He gave several names. She had then joined a small party in the conservatory.

Alleyn was taking notes. At this point there was a pause. Warrender was staring straight in front of him. Charles had not moved.

"Yes?" Alleyn said.

"She stayed in there until the birthday cake was brought in," Warrender said.

"And the other people in her group stayed there too?"

"No," Charles said. "I came out and—I spoke to two of our guests who —who were leaving early."

"Yes? Did you return?"

He said wearily, "I told Gracefield, our butler, to start the business with the cake. I stayed in the main rooms until they brought it in."

Alleyn said, "Yes. And then . . . ?"

"They came in with the cake," Warrender said. "And she came out and Marchant—her management is Marchant & Company—Marchant gave the birthday speech."

"And did the other people in the conservatory come out?"

"Yes."

"With Miss Bellamy?"

Warrender said, "Not with her."

"After her?"

"No. Before. Some of them. I expect all of them except Marchant."

"You yourself, sir? What did you do?"

"I came out before she did."

"Did you stay in the main rooms?"

"No," he said. "I went into the hall for a moment." Alleyn waited.

"To say goodbye," Warrender said, "to the two people who were leaving early."

"Oh yes. Who were they?"

"Feller called Browne and his niece."

"And having done that you returned?"

"Yes," he said.

"To the conservatory?"

"No. To the dining-room. That's where the speech was made."

"Had it begun when you returned?"

Still looking straight before him, Warrender said, "Finished. She was replying."

"Really? You stayed in the hall for some time then?"

"Longer," he said, "than I'd intended. Didn't realize the ceremony had begun, isn't it."

"Do you remember who the other people were? The ones who probably came out before Miss Bellamy from the conservatory?"

"Miss Cavendish and Saracen. And Timon Gantry, the producer-man. Your second-in-command went over all this and asked them to stay."

"I'd just like, if you don't mind, to sort it out for myself. Anyone else? The two guests who left early, for instance. Were they in the conservatory party?"

"Yes."

"And left . . . ?"

"First," Warrender said loudly.

"So you caught them up in the hall. What were they doing in the hall, sir?"

"Talking. Leaving. I don't know exactly."

"You don't remember to whom they were talking?"

"I cannot," Charles said, "for the very life of me see why these two comparative strangers, who were gone long before anything happened, should be of the remotest interest to you."

Alleyn said quickly, "I know it sounds quite unreasonable, but they do at the moment seem to have been the cause of other people's behaviour."

He saw that for some reason this observation had disturbed Warrender. He looked at Alleyn as if the latter had said something outrageous and penetrating.

"You see," Alleyn explained, "in order to establish accident, one does have to make a formal inquiry into the movements of those persons who were nearest to Miss Bellamy up to the *time* of the accident."

"Oh!" Warrender said flatly. "Yes. Possibly."

"But—Mary—my wife—was *there*. Still *there*! Radiant. *There*, seen by everybody—I can't imagine . . ." Charles sank back in his chair. "Never mind," he murmured. "Go on."

Warrender said, "Browne and his niece had, I think, been talking to Saracen and Miss Cavendish. When I came into the hall . . . They were —saying goodbye to Gantry."

"I see. And nobody else was concerned in this leavetaking? In the hall?"

There was a long silence. Warrender looked as if somebody had tapped him smartly on the back of the head. His eyes started and he turned to Charles, who leant forward, grasping the arms of his chair.

"My God!" Warrender said. "Where is he? What's become of him? *Where's Richard!*"

<h1 style="text-align:center">4</h1>

Alleyn had been trained over a long period of time to distinguish between simulated and involuntary reactions in human behaviour. He was perhaps better equipped than many of his colleagues in this respect, being fortified by an instinct that he was particularly careful to mistrust. It seldom let him down. He thought now that, whereas Charles Templeton was quite simply astounded by his own forgetfulness, Warrender's reaction was much less easily defined. Alleyn had a notion that Warrender's reticence was of the formidable kind which conceals nothing but the essential.

It was Warrender, now, who produced an explanation.

"Sorry," he said. "Just remembered something. Extraordinary we should have forgotten. We're talking about Richard Dakers."

"The playwright?"

"That's the man. He's—you may not know this—he was . . ." Warrender boggled inexplicably and looked at his boots. "He's—he was my cousin's—he was the Templetons' ward."

For the first time since Alleyn had entered the room, Charles Templeton looked briefly at Warrender.

"Does he know about this catastrophe?" Alleyn asked.

"No," Warrender said, "he can't know. Be a shock."

Alleyn began to ask about Richard Dakers and found that they were both unwilling to talk about him. When had he last been seen? Charles remembered he had been in the conservatory. Warrender, pressed, admitted that Richard was in the hall, when Browne and his niece went away. Odd, Alleyn thought, that, as the climax of the party approached, no less than five of Miss Bellamy's most intimate friends should turn their backs on her to say goodbye to two people whom her husband had described as comparative strangers. He hinted as much.

Warrender glanced at Charles and then said, "Point of fact they're friends of Richard Dakers. His guests in a way. Naturally he wanted to see them off."

"And having done so, he returned for the speeches and the cake-cutting ceremony?"

"I—ah . . . Not exactly," Warrender said.

"No?"

"No. Ah, speaking out of school, isn't it, but I rather fancy there's an attraction. He—ah—he went out—they live in the next house."

"Not," Alleyn ejaculated, "*Octavius* Browne of the Pegasus?"

"Point of fact, yes," Warrender said, looking astonished.

"And Mr. Dakers went out with them?"

"After them."

"But you think he meant to join them?"

"Yes," he said woodenly.

"And is perhaps with them still?"

Warrender was silent.

"Wouldn't he mind missing the ceremony?" Alleyn asked.

Warrender embarked on an incomprehensible spate of broken phrases.

"If he's there," Charles said to Alleyn, "he ought to be told."

"I'll go," Warrender said and moved to the door.

Alleyn said, "One minute, if you please."

"What?"

"Shall we just see if he *is* there? It'll save trouble, won't it? May I use the telephone?"

He was at the telephone before they could reply and looking up the number.

"I know Octavius quite well," he said pleasantly. "Splendid chap, isn't he?"

Warrender looked at him resentfully. "If the boy's there," he said, "I'd prefer to tell him about this myself."

"Of course," Alleyn agreed heartily. "Ah, here we are." He dialled a number. They heard a voice at the other end.

"Hullo," Alleyn said. "Is Mr. Richard Dakers there by any chance?"

"No," the voice said. "I'm sorry. He left some time ago."

"Really? How long would you say?"

The voice replied indistinguishably.

"I see. Thank you so much. Sorry to have bothered you."

He hung up. "He was only with them for a very short time," he said. "He must have left, it seems, before this thing happened. They imagined he came straight back here."

Warrender and Templeton were, he thought, at peculiar pains not to look at each other or at him. He said lightly, "Isn't that a little odd? Wouldn't you suppose he'd be sure to attend the birthday speeches?"

Perhaps each of them waited for the other to reply. After a moment Warrender barked out two words. "Lovers' tiff?" he suggested.

"You think it might be that?"

"I think," Warrender said angrily, "that whatever it was it's got nothing to do with this—this tragedy. Good Lord, why should it!"

"I really do assure you," Alleyn said, "that I wouldn't worry you about these matters if I didn't think it was necessary."

"Matter of opinion," Warrender said.

"Yes. A matter of opinion and mine may turn out to be wrong."

He could see that Warrender was on the edge of some outburst and was restrained, it appeared, only by the presence of Charles Templeton.

"Perhaps," Alleyn said, "we might just make quite sure that Mr. Dakers didn't, in fact, come back. After all, it was a biggish party. Might he not have slipped in, unnoticed, and gone out again for some perfectly explainable reason? The servants might have noticed. If you would . . ."

Warrender jumped at this. "Certainly! I'll come out with you." And after a moment, "D'you mind, Charles?"

With extraordinary vehemence Charles said, "Do what you like. If he comes back I don't want to see him. I . . ." He passed an unsteady hand across his eyes. "Sorry," he said, presumably to Alleyn. "This has been a bit too much for me."

"We'll leave you to yourself," Alleyn said. "Would you like Dr. Harkness to come in?"

"No. No. No. If I might be left alone. That's all."

"Of course."

They went out. The hall was deserted except for the constable who waited anonymously in a corner. Alleyn said, "Will you excuse me for a moment?" and went to the constable.

"Anybody come in?" he asked under his breath.

"No, sir."

"Keep the press out, but admit anyone else and don't let them go again. Take the names and say there's been an accident in the vicinity and we're doing a routine check."

"Very good, sir."

Alleyn returned to Warrender. "No one's come in," he said. "Where can we talk?"

Warrender glanced at him. "Not here," he muttered, and led the way into the deserted drawing-room, now restored to order but filled with the flower-shop smell of Bertie Saracen's decorations and the faint reek of cigarette smoke and alcohol. The connecting doors into the dining-room were open and beyond them, in the conservatory, Dr. Harkness could be seen, heavily asleep in a canvas chair and under observation by Inspector Fox. When Fox saw them he came out and shut the glass door. "He's down to it," he said, "but rouseable. I thought I'd leave him as he is till required."

Warrender turned on Alleyn. "Look here!" he demanded. "What *is* all this? Are you trying to make out there's been any—any . . ." he boggled, "any hanky-panky?"

"We can't take accident as a matter-of-course."

"Why not? Clear as a pikestaff."

"Our job," Alleyn said patiently, "is to collect all the available information and present it to the coroner. At the moment we are not drawing any conclusions. Come, sir," he said, as Warrender still looked mulish, "I'm sure that, as a soldier, you'll recognize the position. It's a matter of procedure. After all, to be perfectly frank about it, a great many suicides as well as homicides have been rigged to look like accidents."

"Either suggestion's outrageous."

"And will, we hope, soon turn out to be so."

"But, good God, is there anything at all to make you suppose . . ." He stopped and jerked his hands ineloquently.

"Suppose what?"

"That it could be—either? Suicide—or murder?"

"Oh, yes," Alleyn said. "Could be. Could be."

"What? What evidence . . . ?"

"I'm afraid I'm not allowed to discuss details."

"Why the hell not?"

"God bless my soul!" Alleyn exclaimed. "Do *consider*. Suppose it was murder—for all I know you might have done it. You can't expect me to make you a present of what may turn out to be the police case against you."

"I think you must be dotty," said Colonel Warrender profoundly.

"Dotty or sane, I must get on with my job. Inspector Fox and I propose to have a word with those wretched people we've cooped up over the way. Would you rather return to Mr. Templeton, sir?"

"My God, no!" he ejaculated with some force and then looked hideously discomfited.

"Why not?" Alleyn asked coolly. "Have you had a row with him?"

"No!"

"Well, I'm afraid it's a case of returning to him or staying with me."

"I . . . God damn it, I'll stick to you."

"Right. Here we go, then."

Bertie, Pinky and Timon Gantry seemed hardly to have moved since he last saw them. Bertie was asleep in his chair and resembled an over-dressed baby. Pinky had been crying. Gantry now was reading *'Tis Pity She's a Whore.* He laid it aside and rose to his feet.

"I don't want to be awkward," Gantry said, "but I take leave to ask why the hell we're being mewed up in this interminable and intolerable fashion."

He used what was known in the theatre as the Terrifying Tone. He moved towards Alleyn, who was almost his own height.

"This room," Bertie faintly complained as he opened his eyes, "would appear to be inhabited by angry giants."

"You're being mewed up," Alleyn said with some evidence of tough-ness, "because of death. Death, for your information, with what are known as unexplained features. I don't know how much longer you'll be here. If you're hungry, we shall arrange for food to be sent in. If you're stuffy, you may walk in the garden. If you want to talk, you may use the telephone, and the usual offices are last on the right at the far end of the hall."

There was an appreciable pause.

"And the worst of it is, Timmy angel," Bertie said, "you can't tell him the casting's gone wrong and you'll let him know if he's wanted."

Pinky was staring at Alleyn. "I never," she muttered, "could have thought to see the day."

There can be no dictator whose discomfiture will not bring some slight degree of pleasure, to his most ardent disciples. Bertie and Pinky, in-voluntarily, had given this reaction. There was a suggestion of repressed glee.

Gantry gave them the sort of look he would have thrown at an in-attentive actor. They made their faces blank.

He drew in his breath. "So be it," he said. "One submits. Naturally. Perhaps one would prefer to know a little more, but elucidation is evi-dently *not* an ingredient of the Yardly mystique."

From his ramrod station inside the door, Warrender said, "Foul play. What it amounts to. They're suggesting foul play."

"Oh my God!" cried Pinky and Bertie in unison. They turned sheet-white and began to talk at the tops of their voices. Fox took out his notebook.

Alleyn raised his hand and they petered out. "It doesn't," he said crossly, "amount to anything of the sort. The situation is precisely as I have tried to define it. There are unexplained discrepancies. They may add up to accident, suicide or homicide, and I know no better than any one of you what the answer will be. And now, if you please, we will try to arrive at a few possibly unimportant facts."

To his surprise he found himself supported.

Timon Gantry said, "We're being emotional and tedious. Pay no attention. Your facts?"

Alleyn said patiently, "Without any overtones or suggestions of criminal intention, I would rather like to trace exactly the movements of the group of people who were in conversation with Miss Bellamy during the last ten minutes or so of her life. You have all heard, *ad nauseam*, I daresay, of police routine. This is an example of it. I know you were all with her in the conservatory. I know each one of you, before the climax of her party, came out into the hall with the intention, Colonel Warrender tells me, of saying goodbye to two comparative strangers, who for some reason that has not yet been divulged, were leaving just before this climax. Among you was Mr. Richard Dakers, Miss Bellamy's ward. Mr. Dakers left the house on the heels of those two guests. His reason for doing so may well be personal and, from my point of view, completely uninteresting. *But I've got to clear him up.* Now, then. Any of you know why they left and why he left?"

"Certainly," Gantry said promptly. "He's catched with Anelida Lee. No doubt he wanted to see more of her."

"At that juncture? All right!" Alleyn added quickly. "We leave that one, do we? We take it that there was nothing remarkable about Octavius Browne and his niece sweeping out of the party, do we, and that it was the most natural thing in the world for Miss Bellamy's ward to turn his back on her and follow them? Do we? Or do we?"

"Oh Lord, Lord, *Lord!*" Bertie wavered. "The way you put things."

Pinky said, "I *did* hear the uncle remind her that they had to leave early."

"Did he say why?"

"No."

"Had any of you met them before?"

Silence.

"None of you? Why did you all feel it necessary to go into the hall to say goodbye to them?"

Pinky and Bertie looked at each other out of the corners of their eyes and Warrender cleared his throat. Gantry appeared to come to a decision.

"I don't usually discuss this sort of thing outside the theatre," he said, "but under the circumstances I suppose I'd better tell you. I've decided to hear Miss Lee read the leading role in . . ." he hesitated fractionally, "in a new play."

"Really? Wonderful luck for her," Alleyn said. "What play?"

"*Oops!*" Bertie said involuntarily.

"It's called *Husbandry in Heaven.*"

"By . . . ?"

Warrender barked, "Does it matter?"

"Not that I know," Alleyn murmured. "Why should it? Let's find out."

Pinky said boldly, "I don't see a bit why it should matter. We all heard about it."

"Did you?" Alleyn asked. "When? At the party?"

She blushed scarlet. "Yes. It was mentioned there."

"In the conservatory?"

Bertie said in a hurry, "Mentioned. Just mentioned."

"And we haven't had the author's name yet, have we?"

Pinky said, "It's a new play by Dicky Dakers, isn't it, Timmy?"

"Yes, dear," Gantry agreed and refrained with some difficulty, Alleyn thought, from casting his eyes up to heaven. "In the hall I had a word with her about reading the part for me," he said.

"Right. And," Alleyn pursued, "might that not explain why Dakers also wanted to have a further word with Miss Lee?"

They agreed feverishly.

"Strange," he continued, "that this explanation didn't occur to any of you."

Bertie laughed musically. "Weren't we sillies?" he asked. "Fancy!"

"Perhaps you *all* hurtled into the hall in order to offer your congratulations to Miss Lee?"

"That's right!" Bertie cried, opening his eyes very wide. "So we did! And anyway," he added, "I wanted the loo. That was really why I came out. Anything else was purely incidental. I'd forgotten."

"Well," Alleyn remarked, "since you're all so bad at remembering your motives I suppose I'd better go on cooking them up for you."

Pinky Cavendish made a quick expostulatory movement with her hands. "Yes?" Alleyn asked her. "What is it?"

"Nothing. Not really. Only—I wish you wouldn't make one feel shabby," Pinky said.

"Do I? I'm sorry about that."

"Look!" she said. "We're all of us shocked and horrified about Mary. She was our friend—a great friend. No, Timmy, please let me. She was tricky and temperamental and exacting and she said and did things that we'd rather forget about now. The important thing to remember is that one way or another, at one time or another, we've all loved her. You couldn't help it," Pinky said, "or I couldn't. Perhaps I should only speak for myself."

Alleyn asked gently, "Are you trying to tell me that you are protecting her memory?"

"You might put it like that," Pinky said.

"Nonsense, dear," Gantry said impatiently. "It doesn't arise."

Alleyn decided to dig a little further.

"The farewells being accomplished," he said, "and the two guests departed, what did you all do? Miss Cavendish?"

"Oh dear! What *did* I do? I know! I tried to nip upstairs, but the cameramen were all over the bottom steps so I returned to the party."

"Mr. Saracen?"

"The gents. Downstairs. Last, as you've observed, on the right. Then I beetled back, bright as a button, for the speeches."

"Mr. Gantry?"

"I returned to the drawing-room, heard the speeches, and helped Templeton clear the way for the . . ." he jibbed for a moment, "for what would have been the last scene. The opening of the presents."

"Colonel Warrender?"

Warrender was staring at some part of the wall above Alleyn's head. "Went back," he said.

"Where?"

"To the party."

"Oo!" Bertie said.

"Yes, Mr. Saracen?"

"Nothing," Bertie said hurriedly. "Pay no attention."

Alleyn looked round at them all. "Tell me," he said, "hasn't Richard Dakers, up till now, written his plays exclusively for Miss Bellamy? Light comedies? *Husbandry in Heaven* doesn't suggest a light comedy."

He knew by their silence that he had struck home. Pinky's face alone would have told him as much. It was already too late when Warrender said defensively, "No need to put all his eggs in one basket, isn't it?"

"Exactly," Gantry agreed.

"Did Miss Bellamy hold this view?"

"I still fail to understand . . ." Warrender began, but Bertie Saracen cried out in a sort of rage:

"I really *don't* see, I don't for the *life* of me see why we should fiddle and fuss and fabricate! Honestly! It's all very well to be nice about poor Mary's memory and Dicky's dilemma and everybody madly loving everybody else, but sooner or later Mr. Alleyn's going to find out and then we'll all look peculiar and I for one *won't* and I'm sorry, Timmy, but I'm going to spill beans and unbag cats galore and announce in a ringing head tone that Mary minded like *hell* and that she made a scene in the conservatory and insulted the girl and Dicky left in a rage and why not, because suppose somebody *did* do something frightful to Mary, it couldn't be Dicky because Dicky flounced out of the house while Mary was still fighting fit and cutting her cake. And one other thing. I don't know why Colonel Warrender should go all cagey and everything but he didn't go straight back to the party. He went out. At the front door. I *saw* him on my way back from the loo. Now then!"

He had got to his feet and stood there, blinking, but defiant.

Gantry said, "*Oh*, well!" and flung up his hands.

Pinky said, "I'm on Bertie's side."

But Warrender, purple in the face, advanced upon Bertie.

"Don't touch me!" Bertie shouted angrily.

"You little rat!" Warrender said and seized his arm.

Bertie gave an involuntary giggle. "That's what she called me," he said.

"Take," Warrender continued between his teeth, "that damned impertinent grin off your face and hold your tongue, sir, or by God I'll give you something to make you."

He grasped Bertie with his left hand. He had actually drawn back his right and Alleyn had moved in, when a voice from the door said: "*Will somebody be good enough to tell me what goes on in this house?*"

Warrender lowered his hand and let Bertie go, Gantry uttered a short oath and Pinky, a stifled cry. Alleyn turned.

A young man with a white face and distracted air confronted him in the doorway.

"Thank God!" Bertie cried. "Dicky!"

CHAPTER FIVE   ## Questions of Adherence

The most noticeable thing about Richard Dakers was his agitation. He was pale, his face was drawn and his hands were unsteady. During the complete silence that followed Bertie's ejaculation, Richard stood where he was, his gaze fixed with extraordinary concentration upon Colonel Warrender. Warrender, in his turn, looked at him with, as far as his soldierly blueprint of a face could express anything, the same kind of startled attention. In a crazy sort of way, each might have been the reflection of the other.

Warrender said, "Can I have a word with you, old boy? Shall we . . . ?"

"No!" Richard said quickly and then, "I'm sorry. I don't understand. What's that damned bobby doing in the hall? What's happened? Where's everybody? Where's Mary?"

Alleyn said, "One moment," and went to him. "You're Mr. Richard

Dakers, aren't you? I'm from Scotland Yard—Alleyn. . . . At the moment I'm in charge of a police inquiry here. Shall we find somewhere where I can tell you why?"

"I'll tell him," Warrender said.

"I think not," Alleyn rejoined and opened the door. "Come along," he said and looked at the others. "You will stay here, if you please."

Richard put his hand to his head. "Yes. All right. But—why?" Perhaps out of force of habit he turned to Timon Gantry. "Timmy?" he said. "What *is* this?"

Gantry said, "We must accept authority, Dicky. Go with him."

Richard stared at him in amazement and walked out of the room, followed by Alleyn and Fox.

"In here, shall we?" Alleyn suggested and led the way into the deserted drawing-room.

There, he told Richard, as briefly as possible and without emphasis, what had happened. Richard listened distractedly, making no interruption but once or twice wiping his hand over his face as if a cobweb lay across it. When Alleyn had finished he said haltingly, "Mary? It's happened to Mary? How can I possibly believe it?"

"It *is* hard, isn't it?"

"But—*how? How* did it happen? With the plant spray?"

"It seems so."

"But she's used it over and over again. For a long time. Why did it happen now?" He had the air, often observable in people who have suffered a shock, of picking over the surface of the matter and distractedly examining the first thing he came upon. "Why now?" he repeated and appeared scarcely to attend to the answer.

"That's one of the things we've got to find out."

"Of course," Richard said, more, it seemed, to himself than to Alleyn, "it *is* dangerous. We were always telling her." He shook his head impatiently. "But—I don't see—she went to her room just after the speeches and . . ."

"Did she? How do you know?"

Richard said quickly, "Why, because . . ." and then, if possible, turned whiter than he had been before. He looked desperately at Alleyn, seemed to hover on the edge of an outburst and then said, "She must have. You say she was found there."

"Yes. She was found there."

"But why? Why would she use the plant spray at that moment? It sounds so crazy."

"I know. Very strange."

Richard beat his hands together. "I'm sorry," he said, "I can't get hold of myself. I'm sorry."

Looking at him, Alleyn knew that he was in that particular state of emotional unbalance when he would be most vulnerable to pressure. He was a nice-looking chap, Alleyn thought. It was a sensitive face and yet, obscurely, it reminded him of one much less sensitive. But whose?

He said, "You yourself have noticed two aspects of this tragic business that are difficult to explain. Because of them and because of normal police procedure I have to check as fully as possible the circumstances surrounding the event."

"Do you?" Richard asked vaguely and then seemed to pull himself together. "Yes. Very well. What circumstances?"

"I'm told you left the house before the birthday speeches. Is that right?"

Unlike the others, Richard appeared to feel no resentment or suspicion. "I?" he said. "Oh, yes, I think I did. I don't think they'd started. The cake had just been taken in."

"Why did you leave, Mr. Dakers?"

"I wanted to talk to Anelida," he said at once and then: "Sorry. You wouldn't know. Anelida Lee. She lives next door and . . ." He stopped.

"I do know that Miss Lee left early with her uncle. But it must have been a very important discussion, mustn't it? To take you away at that juncture?"

"Yes. It was. To me. It was private," Richard added. "A private matter."

"A long discussion?"

"It didn't happen."

"Not?"

"She wasn't—available." He produced a palpable understatement. "She wasn't—feeling well."

"You saw her uncle?"

"Yes."

"Was it about her part in your play—*Husbandry in Heaven*, isn't it? —that you wanted to talk to her?"

Richard stared at him and for the first time seemed to take alarm. "Who told you about that?" he demanded.

"Timon Gantry."

"He did!" Richard exclaimed and then, as if nothing could compete with the one overriding shock, added perfunctorily, "How extraordinary." But he was watching Alleyn now with a new awareness. "It was partly to do with that," he muttered.

Alleyn decided to fire point-blank. "Was Miss Bellamy displeased with the plans for this new play?" he asked. Richard's hands made a sharp involuntary movement which was at once checked. His voice shook.

"I told you this was a private matter," he said. "It is entirely private."

"I'm afraid there is very little room for privacy in a police inquiry."

Richard surprised him by suddenly crying out, "You *think she did it herself!* She didn't! I can't believe it! Never!"

"Is there any reason why she should?"

"No! My God, no! *No!*"

Alleyn waited for a little, visited, as was not unusual with him, by a distaste for this particular aspect of his job.

He said, "What did you do when Miss Lee couldn't receive you?"

Richard moved away from him, his hands thrust down in his pockets. "I went for a walk," he said.

"Now, look here," Alleyn said, "you must see that this is a very odd story. Your guardian, as I believe Miss Bellamy was, reaches the top moment of her birthday party. You leave her cold, first in pursuit of Miss Lee and then to go for a stroll round Chelsea. Are you telling me that you've been strolling ever since?"

Without turning, Richard nodded.

Alleyn walked round him and looked him full in the face.

"Mr. Dakers," he said. "Is that the truth? It's now five to nine. Do you give me your word that from about seven o'clock when you left this house you didn't return to it until you came in, ten minutes ago?"

Richard, looking desperately troubled, waited for so long that to Alleyn the scene became quite unreal. The two of them were fixed in the hiatus-like figures in a suspended film sequence.

"Are you going to give me an answer?" Alleyn said at last.

"I—I—don't—think—I did actually—just after—she was . . ." A look of profound astonishment came into Richard's face. He crumpled into a faint at Alleyn's feet.

2

"He'll do," Dr. Harkness said, relinquishing Richard's pulse. He straightened up and winced a little in the process. "You say he's been walking about on an empty stomach and two or three drinks. The shock coming on top of it did the trick for him, I expect. In half an hour he won't be feeling any worse than I do and that's medium to bloody awful. Here he comes."

Richard had opened his eyes. He stared at Dr. Harkness and then frowned. "Lord, I'm sorry," he said. "I passed out, didn't I?"

"You're all right," Dr. Harkness said. "Where's this sal volatile, Gracefield?"

Gracefield presented it on a tray. Richard drank it down and let his head fall back. They had put him on a sofa there in the drawing-room. "I was talking to somebody," he said. "That man—God, yes! Oh God."

"It's all right," Alleyn said, "I won't worry you. We'll leave you to yourself for a bit."

He saw Richard's eyes dilate. He was looking past Alleyn towards the door. "Yes," he said loudly. "I'd rather be alone."

"What is all this?"

It was Warrender. He shut the door behind him and went quickly to the sofa. "What the devil have you done to him? Dicky, old boy . . ."

"No!" Richard said with exactly the same inflexion as before. Warrender stood above him. For a moment, apparently, they looked at each other. Then Richard said, "I forgot that letter you gave me to post. I'm sorry."

Alleyn and Fox moved, but Warrender anticipated them, stooping over Richard and screening him.

"If you don't mind," Richard said, "I'd rather be by myself. I'm all right."

"And I'm afraid," Alleyn pointed out, "that I must remind you of instructions, Colonel Warrender. I asked you to stay with the others. Will you please go back to them?"

Warrender stood like a rock for a second or two and then, without another word, walked out of the room. On a look from Alleyn, Fox followed him.

"We'll leave you," Alleyn said. "Don't get up."

"No," Dr. Harkness said. "Don't. I'll ask them to send you in a cup of tea. Where's that old Nanny of yours? She can make herself useful. Can you find her, Gracefield?"

"Very good, sir," Gracefield said.

Alleyn, coolly picking up Richard's dispatch case, followed Gracefield into the hall.

"Gracefield."

Gracefield, frigid, came to a halt.

"I want one word with you. I expect this business has completely disorganized your household and I'm afraid it can't be helped. But I think it may make things a little easier in your department if you know what the form will be."

"Indeed, sir?"

"In a little while a mortuary van will come. It will be better if we keep everybody out of the way at that time. I don't want to worry Mr. Templeton more than I can help, but I shall have to interview people and it would suit us all if we could find some place that would serve as an office for the purpose. Is that possible?"

"There is Mr. Richard's old study, sir, on the first floor. It is unoccupied."

"Splendid. Where exactly?"

"The third on the right along the passage, sir."

"Good." Alleyn glanced at the pallid and impassive face. "For your information," he said, "it's a matter of clearing up the confusion that unfortunately always follows accidents of this sort. The further we can get, now, the less publicity at the inquest. You understand?"

"Quite so, sir," said Gracefield with a slight easing of manner.

"Very well. And I'm sorry you'll be put to so much trouble."

Gracefield's hand curved in classic acceptance. There was a faint crackle.

"Thank you, Gracefield."

"Thank you very much, sir," said Gracefield. "I will inform Mrs. Plumtree and then ascertain if your room is in order." He inclined his head and mounted the stairs.

Alleyn raised a finger and the constable by the front door came to him.

"What happened," he asked, "about Mr. Dakers? As quick and complete as you can."

"He arrived, sir, about three minutes after you left your instructions, according to which I asked for his name and let on it was because of an accident. He took it up it was something about a car. He didn't seem to pay much attention. He was very excited and upset. He went upstairs and was there about eight to ten minutes. You and Mr. Fox were with the two gentlemen and the lady in that little room, sir. When he came down he had a case in his hand. He went to the door to go out and I advised him it couldn't be done. He still seemed very upset, sir, and that made him more so. He said, 'Good God, what is all this?' and went straight to the room where you were, sir."

"Good. Thank you. Keep going."

"Sir," said the constable.

"And Philpott."

"Sir?"

"We've sent for another man. In the meantime I don't want any of the visitors in the house moving about from room to room. Get them all together in the drawing-room and keep them there, including Colonel Warrender and Mr. Templeton, if he's feeling fit enough. Mr. Dakers can stay where he is. Put the new man on the door and you keep observation in the dining-room. We can't do anything about the lavatory, I suppose,

but everywhere else had better be out of bounds. If Colonel Warrender
wants to go to the lavatory, you go with him."

"Sir."

"And ask Mr. Fox to join me upstairs."

The constable moved off.

A heavy thumping announced the descent of Old Ninn. She came
down one step at a time. When she got to the bottom of the stairs and
saw Alleyn she gave him a look and continued on her way. Her face
was flaming and her mouth drawn down. For a small person she ema-
nated an astonishingly heavy aura of the grape.

"Mrs. Plumtree?" Alleyn asked.

"Yes," said Old Ninn. She halted and looked into his face. Her eyes,
surprisingly, were tragic.

"You're going to look after Mr. Richard, aren't you?"

"What's he been doing to himself?" she asked, as if Richard had been
playing roughly and had barked his knee.

"He fainted. The doctor thinks it was shock."

"Always takes things to heart," Old Ninn said.

"Did you bring him up?"

"From three months." She continued to look fixedly at Alleyn. "He
was a good child," she said, as if he was abusing Richard, "and he's
grown into a good man. No harm in him and never was."

"An orphan?" Alleyn ventured.

"Father and mother killed in a motor accident."

"How very sad."

"You don't," Old Ninn said, "feel the want of what you've never had."

"And of course Miss Bellamy—Mrs. Templeton—took him over."

"She," Old Ninn said, "was a different type of child altogether. If you'll
excuse me I'll see what ails him." But she didn't move at once. She said
very loudly, "Whatever it is it'll be no discredit to him," and then
stumped heavily and purposefully on to her charge.

Alleyn waited for a moment, savouring her observations. There has
been one rather suggestive remark, he thought.

Dr. Harkness came out of the drawing-room, looking very wan.

"He's all right," he said, "and I wish I could say as much for myself.
The secondary effects of alcoholic indulgence are the least supportable.
By the way, can I go out to the car for my bag? It's just opposite the
house. Charles Templeton's my patient, you know, and I'd like to run
him over. Just in case. He's had a bad knock over this."

"Yes, of course," Alleyn said and nodded to the constable at the door.
"Before you go, though—was Mrs. Templeton your patient too?"

"She was," Harkness agreed and looked wary.

"Would you have expected anything like this? Supposing it to be a case of suicide?"

"No. I wouldn't."

"Not subject to fits of depression? No morbid tendencies? Nothing like that?"

Harkness looked at his hands. "It wasn't an equable disposition," he said carefully. "Far from it. She had 'nervous' spells. The famous theatrical temperament, you know."

"No more than that?" Alleyn persisted.

"Well—I don't like discussing my patients and never do, of course, but . . ."

"I think you may say the circumstances warrant it."

"I suppose so. As a matter of fact I have been a bit concerned. The temperaments had become pretty frequent and increasingly violent. Hysteria, really. Partly the time of life, but she was getting over that. There was some occasion for anxiety. One or two little danger signals. One was keeping an eye on her. But nothing suicidal. On the contrary. What's more, you can take my word for it she was the last woman on earth to disfigure herself. The last."

"Yes," Alleyn said. "That's a point, isn't it? I'll see you later."

"I suppose you will," Harkness said disconsolately, and Alleyn went upstairs. He found that Miss Bellamy's room now had the familiar look of any area given over to police investigation: something between an improvised laboratory and a photographer's studio with its focal point that unmistakable sheeted form on the floor.

Dr. Curtis, the police surgeon, had finished his examination of the body. Sergeant Bailey squatted on the bathroom floor employing the tools of his trade upon the tinsel picture, and as Alleyn came in, Sergeant Thompson, whistling between his teeth, uncovered Mary Bellamy's terrible face and advanced his camera to within a few inches of it. The bulb flashed.

Fox was seated at the dressing-table completing his notes.

"Well, Curtis?" Alleyn asked.

"Well, now," Dr. Curtis said. "It's quite a little problem, you know. I can't see a verdict of accident, Alleyn, unless the coroner accepts the idea of her presenting this spray-gun thing at her own face and pumping away like mad at it to see how it works. The face is pretty well covered with the stuff. It's in the nostrils and mouth and all over the chest and dress."

"Suicide?"

"I don't see it. Have to be an uncommon determined effort. Any motive?"

"Not so far, unless you count a suspected bout of tantrums, but I don't yet know about that. I don't see it, either. Which leaves us with homicide. See here, Curtis. Suppose I picked up that tin of Slaypest, pointed it at you and fell to work on the spray-gun—what'd you do?"

"Dodge."

"And if I chased you up?"

"Either collar you low or knock it out of your hands or bolt, yelling blue murder."

"Exactly. But wouldn't the immediate reaction, particularly in a woman, be to throw up her arms and hide her face?"

"I think it might, certainly. Yes."

"Yes," said Fox, glancing up from his notes.

"It wasn't hers. There's next to nothing on the hands and arms. And look," Alleyn went on, "at the actual character of the spray. Some of it's fine, as if delivered from a distance. Some, on the contrary, is so coarse that it's run down in streaks. Where's the answer to that one?"

"I don't know," said Dr. Curtis.

"How long would it take to kill her?"

"Depends on the strength. This stuff is highly concentrated. Hexa-ethyl-tetra-phosphate of which the deadly ingredient is TEPP: tetra-ethyl-pyro-phosphate. Broken down, I'd say, with some vehicle to reduce the viscosity. The nozzle's a very fine job: designed for indoor use. In my opinion the stuff shouldn't be let loose on the market. If she got some in the mouth, and it's evident she did, it might only be a matter of minutes. Some recorded cases mention nausea and convulsions. In others, the subject has dropped down insensible and died a few seconds later."

Fox said, "When the woman—Florence—found her, she was on the floor in what Florence describes as a sort of fit."

"I'll see Florence next," Alleyn said.

"And when Dr. Harkness and Mr. Templeton arrived she was dead," Fox concluded.

"Where *is* Harkness?" Dr. Curtis demanded. "He's pretty damn casual, isn't he? He ought to have shown up at once."

"He was flat-out with a hangover among the exotics in the conservatory," Alleyn said. "I stirred him up to look at Mr. Richard Dakers, who was in a great tizzy before he knew there was anything to have a tizzy about. When I talked to him he fainted."

"What a mob!" Curtis commented in disgust.

"Curtis, if you've finished here I think you'll find your colleague in reasonably working order downstairs."

"He'd better be. Everything is fixed now. I'll do the p.m. tonight."

"Good. Fox, you and I had better press on. We've got an office. Third on the right from here."

They found Gracefield outside the door looking scandalized.

"I'm very sorry, I'm sure, sir," he said, "but the keys on this landing appear to have been removed. If you require to lock up . . ."

"'T, 't!" Fox said and dived in his pocket. "Thoughtless of me! Try this one."

Gracefield coldly accepted it. He showed Alleyn into a small pleasantly furnished study and left Fox to look after himself, which he did very comfortably.

"Will there be anything further, sir?" Gracefield asked Alleyn.

"Nothing. This will do admirably."

"Thank you, sir."

"Here," Fox said, "are the other keys. They're interchangeable, which is why I took the liberty of removing them."

Gracefield received them without comment and retired.

"I always seem to hit it off better," Fox remarked, "with the female servants."

"No doubt they respond more readily to your unbridled body-urge," said Alleyn.

"That's one way of putting it, Mr. Alleyn," Fox primly conceded.

"And the other is that I tipped that antarctic monument. Never mind. You'll have full play in a minute with Florence. Take a look at this room. It was Mr. Richard Dakers's study. I suppose he now inhabits a bachelor flat somewhere, but he was adopted and brought up by the Templetons. Here you have his boyhood, adolescence and early maturity in microcosm. The usual school groups on one wall. Note the early dramatic interest. On the other three, his later progress. O.U.D.S. Signed photographs of lesser lights succeeded by signed photographs of greater ones. Sketches from unknown designers followed by the full treatment from famous designers and topped up by Saracen. The last is for a production that opened three years ago and closed last week. Programme of Command Performance. Several framed photographs of Miss Mary Bellamy, signed with vociferous devotion. One small photograph of Mr. Charles Templeton. A calendar on the desk to support the theory that he left the house a year ago. Books from E. Nesbit to Samuel Beckett. *Who's Who in the Theatre* and *Spotlight* and cast an eye at this one, will you?"

He pulled out a book and showed it to Fox. "*Handbook of Poisons by a Medical Practitioner*. Bookplate: '*Ex Libris* C. H. Templeton.' Let's see if the medical practitioner has anything to say about pest killers. Here we are. Poisons of Vegetable Origin. Tobacco. Alkaloid of." He read for a moment or two. "Rather scanty. Only one case quoted. Gentleman who swallowed nicotine from a bottle and died quietly in thirty seconds after heaving a deep sigh. Warnings about agricultural use of. And here are the newer concoctions including HETP and TEPP. Exceedingly deadly and to be handled with the greatest care. Ah, well!"

He replaced the book.

"That'll be the husband's," Fox said. "Judging by the bookplate."

"The husband's. Borrowed by the ward and accessible to all and sundry. For what it's worth. Well, Foxkin, that about completes our tour of the room. Tabloid history of the tastes and career of Richard Dakers. Hullo! Look here, Fox."

He was stooping over the writing desk and had opened the blotter.

"This looks fresh," he said. "Green ink. Ink on desk dried up and anyway, blue."

There was a small Georgian glass above the fireplace. Alleyn held the blotting-paper to it and they looked at the reflected image:

"I   e   ck to   y at it w u d e o se my   te ding I   n't
    n ven a   rible shock   that I   t get t   rted   t t I'm
sure t ll e   ter if we do t me t. I c t hin clea   now   ut at
    ast I now I'll n   for e your tr ment of An   d this after on
I   ould   ave been told everything from the beginning. R."

Alleyn copied this fragmentary message on a second sheet of paper, carried the blotter back to the desk and very carefully removed the sheet in question.

"We'll put the experts on to this," he said, "but I'm prepared to take a sporting chance on the result, Br'er Fox. Are you?"

"I'd give it a go, Mr. Alleyn."

"See if you can find Florence, will you? I'll take a flying jump while you're at it."

Fox went out. Alleyn put his copy of the message on the desk and looked at it.

The correct method of deciphering and completing a blotting-paper impression is by measurement, calculation and elimination but occasionally, for persons with a knack, the missing letters start up vividly in the mind and the scientific method is thus accurately anticipated. When he was on his game, Alleyn possessed this knack and he now made use of it. Without allowing himself any second thoughts, he wrote rapidly within the copy and stared with disfavour at the result. He then opened Richard Dakers's dispatch case and found it contained a typescript of a play, *Husbandry in Heaven*. He flipped the pages over and came across some alterations in green ink and in the same hand as the letter.

"Miss Florence Johnson," said Fox, opening the door and standing aside with something of the air of a large sporting dog retrieving a bird. Florence, looking not unlike an apprehensive fowl, came in.

Alleyn saw an unshapely little woman, with a pallid, tear-stained face and hair so remorselessly dyed that it might have been a raven wig. She wore that particular air of disillusionment that is associated with the Cockney and she reeked of backstage.

"The Superintendent," Fox told her, "just wants to hear the whole story like you told it to me. Nothing to worry about."

"Of course not," Alleyn said. "Come and sit down. We won't keep you long."

Florence looked as if she might prefer to stand, but compromised by sitting on the edge of the chair Fox had pushed forward.

"This has been a sad business for you," Alleyn said.

"That's right," Florence said woodenly.

"And I'm sure you must want to have the whole thing cleared up as soon and as quietly as possible."

"Clear enough, isn't it? She's dead. You can't have it much clearer than that."

"You can't indeed. But you see it's our job to find out why."

"Short of seeing it happen you wouldn't get much nearer, would you? If you can read, that is."

"You mean the tin of Slaypest?"

"Well, it wasn't perfume," Florence said impertinently. "They put that in bottles." She shot a glance at Alleyn and seemed to undergo a slight change of temper. Her lips trembled and she compressed them. "It wasn't all that pleasant," she said. "Seeing what I seen. Finding her like that. You'd think I might be let alone."

"So you will be if you behave like a sensible girl. You've been with her a long time, haven't you?"

"Thirty years, near enough."

"You must have got along very well to have stayed together all that time."

Florence didn't answer and he waited. At last she said, "I knew her ways."

"And you were fond of her?"

"She was all right. Others might have their own ideas. I knew 'er. Inside out. She'd talk to me like she wouldn't to others. She was all right."

It was, Alleyn thought, after its fashion, a tribute.

He said, "Florence, I'm going to be very frank indeed with you. Suppose it wasn't an accident. You'd want to know, wouldn't you?"

"It's no good you thinking she did it deliberate. She never! Not she. Wouldn't."

"I didn't mean suicide."

Florence watched him for a moment. Her mouth, casually but emphatically painted, narrowed into a scarlet thread.

"If you mean murder," she said flatly, "that's different."

"You'd want to know," he repeated. "Wouldn't you?"

The tip of her tongue showed for a moment in the corner of her mouth. "That's right," she said.

"So do we. Now, Inspector Fox has already asked you about this, but never mind, I'm asking you again. I want you to tell me in as much detail as you can remember just what happened from the time when Miss Bellamy dressed for her party up to the time you entered her room and found her—as you did find her. Let's start with the preparations, shall we?"

She was a difficult subject. She seemed to be filled with some kind of resentment and everything had to be dragged out of her. After luncheon, it appeared, Miss Bellamy rested. At half-past four Florence went in to her. She seemed to be "much as usual."

"She hadn't been upset by anything during the day?"

"Nothing," Florence muttered, after a further silence, "to matter."

"I only ask," Alleyn said, "because there's a bottle of sal volatile left out in the bathroom. Did you give her sal volatile at any stage?"

"This morning."

"What was the matter, this morning? Was she faint?"

Florence said, "Overexcited."

"About what?"

"I couldn't say," Florence said, and shut her mouth like a trap.

"Very well," he said patiently. "Let's get on with the preparation for the party. Did you give her a facial treatment of some kind?"

She stared at him. "That's correct," she said. "A mask."

"What did she talk about, Florence?"

"Nothing. You don't with that stuff over your face. Can't."

"And then?"

"She made up and dressed. The two gentlemen came in and I went out."

"That would be Mr. Templeton and—who?"

"The Colonel."

"Did either of them bring her Parma violets?"

She stared at him. "Vi'lets? Them? No. She didn't like vi'lets."

"There's a bunch on her dressing-table."

"I never noticed," she said. "I don't know anything about vi'lets. There wasn't any when I left the room."

"And you saw her again—when?"

"At the party."

"Well, let's hear about it."

For a second or two he thought she was going to keep mum. She had the least eloquent face he had ever seen. But she began to speak as if somebody had switched her on. She said that from the time she left her mistress and during the early part of the cocktail party she had been with Mrs. Plumtree in their little sitting-room. When the gong sounded they went down to take their places in the procession. After the speeches were over Old Ninn had dropped her awful brick about candles. Florence recounted the incident with detachment, merely observing that Old Ninn was, in fact, very old and sometimes forgot herself. "Fifty candles," Florence said grimly. "What a remark to pass!" It was the only piece of comment, so far, that she had proffered. She had realized, Alleyn gathered, that her mistress had been upset and thinking she might be wanted had gone into the hall. She heard her mistress speak for a moment to Mr. Templeton, something about him asking her not to use her scent. Up to here Florence's statement had been about as emotional as a grocery list, but at this point she appeared to boggle. She looked sideways at Alleyn, seemed to lose her bearings and came to a stop.

Alleyn said, "That's all perfectly clear so far. Then did Miss Bellamy and the nanny—Mrs. Plumtree, isn't it?—go upstairs together?"

Florence, blankly staring, said, "No."

"They didn't? What happened exactly?"

Ninn, it appeared, had gone first.

"Why? What delayed Miss Bellamy?"

"A photographer come butting in."

"He took a photograph of her, did he?"

"That's right. By the front door."

"Alone?"

"*He* came in. The chap wanted him in too."

"Who?"

Her hands ground together in her lap. After waiting for a moment he asked, "Don't you want to answer that one?"

"I want to know," Florence burst out, "if it's murder. If it's murder I don't care who it was, I want to see 'er righted. Never mind who! You can be mistaken in people, as I often told her. Them you think nearest and dearest are likely as not the ones that you didn't ought to trust. What I told her. Often and often."

How vindictive, Alleyn wondered, was Florence? Of what character, precisely, was her relationship with her mistress? She was looking at him now, guardedly but with a kind of arrogance. "What I want to know," she repeated, "is it murder?"

He said, "I believe it may be."

She muttered, "You ought to know: being trained to it. They tell you the coppers always know."

From what background had Florence emerged nearly thirty years ago into Miss Bellamy's dressing-room? She was speaking now like a Bermondsey girl. Fly and wary. Her voice, hitherto negative and respectable, had ripened into strong Cockney.

Alleyn decided to take a long shot. He said, "I expect you know Mr. Richard Dakers very well, don't you?"

"Hardly help meself, could I?"

"No, indeed. He was more like a son than a ward to her, I daresay."

Florence stared at him out of two eyes that closely resembled, and were about as eloquent as, boot-buttons.

"Acted like it," she said. "If getting nothing but the best goes for anything. And taking it as if it was 'is right."

"Well," Alleyn said lightly, "he's repaid her with two very successful plays, hasn't he?"

"Them! What'd they have been without her? See another actress in the lead! Oh dear! What a change! She *made* them, he couldn't have touched it on 'is own. She'd have breathed life into a corpse," Florence said and then looked sick.

Alleyn said, "Mr. Dakers left the house before the speeches, I understand?"

"He did. What a way to behave!"

"But he came back, didn't he?"

"He's back now," she said quickly. "You seen 'im, didn't you?" Gracefield, evidently, had talked.

"I don't mean now. I mean between the time he first left before the speeches and the time when he returned about half an hour ago. Wasn't there another visit in between?"

"That's right," she said under her breath.

"After the birthday speech?"

"That's right."

"Take the moment we're discussing. Mrs. Plumtree had gone upstairs, Miss Bellamy was in the hall. You had come out to see if she needed you." He waited for a moment and then took his gamble. "Did he walk in at the front door? At that moment?"

He thought she was going to say "No"; she seemed to be struggling with some kind of doubt. Then she nodded.

"Did he speak to Miss Bellamy?" She nodded again.

"What about, do you know?"

"I didn't catch. I was at the other end of the hall."

"What happened then?"

"They were photographed and then they went upstairs."

"And you?"

"I went up. By the back stairs," said Florence.

"Where to?"

"I went along to the landing."

"And did you go in to her?"

"Mrs. Plumtree was on the landing," Florence said abruptly. Alleyn waited. "They was talking inside—him and the Lady. So I didn't disturb her."

"And you could hear them talking?"

She said angrily, "What say we could? We weren't snooping, if that's what you mean. We didn't hear a word. She laughed—once."

"And then?"

"He came out and went downstairs."

"And did you go in to Miss Bellamy?"

"No," Florence said loudly.

"Why not?"

"I didn't reckon she'd want me."

"But why?"

"I didn't reckon she would."

"Had you," he asked without emphasis, "had a row of some sort with Miss Bellamy?"

She went very white. "What are you getting at?" she demanded and then, "I told you. I understood her. Better than anyone."

"And there'd been no trouble betweeen you?"

"No!" she said loudly.

He decided not to press this point. "So what did you do?" he asked. "You and Mrs. Plumtree?"

"Stayed where we was. Until . . ."

"Yes?"

"Until we heard something."

"What was that?"

"Inside her room. Something. Kind of a crash."

"What was it, do you think?"

"I wouldn't know. I was going in to see, whether or no, when I heard Mr. Templeton in the hall. Calling. I go down to the half-landing," Florence continued, changing her tense for the narrative present. "He calls up, they're waiting for her. So I go back to fetch her. And . . ." for the first time her voice trembled. "And I walk in."

"Yes," Alleyn said. "Before we go on, Florence, will you tell me this? Did Mr. Richard at this time seem at all upset?"

"That's right," she said, again with that air of defiance.

"When he arrived?" She nodded. "I see. And when he came out of Miss Bellamy's room?"

And now there was no mistaking Florence's tone. It was one of pure hatred.

"'Im? 'E looked ghasterly. 'E looked," said Florence, "like death."

3

As if, by this one outburst, she had bestowed upon herself some kind of emotional bloodletting, Florence returned to her earlier manner—cagey, grudging, implicitly resentful. Alleyn could get no more from her about Richard Dakers's behaviour. When he suggested, obliquely, that perhaps Old Ninn might be more forthcoming, Florence let fall a solitary remark. "Her!" she said. "You won't get her to talk. Not about him!" and refused to elaborate.

He had learned to recognize the point at which persistence defeats its own end. He took her on to the time where she entered the bedroom and discovered her mistress. Here, Florence exhibited a characteristic attitude towards scenes of violence. It was, he thought, as if she recognized in her own fashion their epic value and was determined to do justice to the current example.

When she went into the room, Mary Bellamy was on her knees, her hands to her throat and her eyes starting. She had tried to speak but had succeeded only in making a terrible retching noise. Florence had attempted to raise her, to ask her what had happened, but her mistress, threshing about on the floor, had been as unresponsive to these ministrations as an animal in torment. Florence had thought she heard the word "doctor." Quite beside herself, she had rushed out of the room and downstairs. "Queer," she said. That was what she had felt. "Queer." It was "queer" that at such a moment she should concern herself with Miss Bellamy's non-appearance at her party. It was "queer" that a hackneyed theatre phrase should occur to her in such a crisis but it had and she remembered using it, "Is there a doctor in the house?" though, of course, she knew, really, that Dr. Harkness was one of the guests. On the subject of Dr. Harkness she was violent.

"Him! Nice lot of help he give, I *don't* think! Silly with what he'd taken and knew it. Couldn't make up his mind where he was or what he was wanted for till the Colonel shoved ice down his neck. Even then he was stupid-like and had to be pushed upstairs. For all we know," Florence said, "'e might of saved 'er. For all we know! But when 'e got there it was over and in my opinion 'e's got it on 'is conscience for the rest of 'is days. And that's no error. Dr. Harkness!"

Alleyn asked her to describe, in detail, the state of the room when she first went into it. She remembered nothing but her mistress and when he pressed her to try, he thought she merely drew on what she saw after she returned.

He said, "We've almost finished, but there's one question I must ask you. Do you know of anyone who had cause to wish for her death?"

She thought this over, warily. "There's plenty," she said, "that was jealous of her and there's some that acted treacherous. Some that called themselves friends."

"In the profession?" Alleyn ventured.

"Ah! Miss Kate Cavendish, who'd never have got further than Brighton Pier in the off-season without the Lady hadn't looked after 'er! Mr. Albert Smith, pardon the slip, I should of said Saracen. But for her 'e'd of stuck behind 'is counter in the Manchester department. Look what she done for them and how do they pay 'er back? Only this morning!"

"What happened this morning?"

"Sauce and treachery was what happened."

"That doesn't really answer my question, does it?"

She stood up. "It's all the answer you'll get. You know your own business best, I suppose. But if she's been murdered, there's only one that had the chance. Why waste your time?"

"Only one?" Alleyn said. "Do you really think so?"

For the first time she looked frightened, but her answer was unexpected. "I don't want what I've said to go no further," she said with a look at Fox, who had been quietly taking notes. "I don't fancy being quoted, particularly in some quarters. There's some that'd turn very nasty if they knew what I said."

"Old Ninn?" Alleyn suggested. "For one?"

"Smart," Florence said with spirit, "aren't you? All right. Her for one. She's got her fancy like I had mine. Only mine," Florence said, and her voice was desolate, "mine's gone where it won't come back, and that's the difference." A spasm of something that might have been hatred crossed her face and she cried out with violence, "I'll never forgive her! Never. I'll be even with her no matter what comes out of it, see if I'm not. Clara Plumtree!"

"But what did she do?"

He thought she was going to jib, but suddenly it all came out. It had happened, she said, after the tragedy. Charles Templeton had been taken to his dressing-room and Ninn had appeared on the landing while Florence was taking him a hot bottle. Florence herself had been too agitated to tell her what had happened in any detail. She had given Mr. Templeton the bottle and left him. He was terribly distressed and wanted to be left alone. She had returned to the landing and seen Dr. Harkness and Timon Gantry come out of the bedroom and speak to Mrs. Plumtree, who had then gone into the dressing-room. Florence herself had been consumed with a single overwhelming desire.

"I wanted to see after *her*. I wanted to look after my Lady. I knew what she'd have liked me to do for her. The way they'd left her! The way she looked! I wasn't going to let them see her like that and take her away like that. I knew her better than anybody. She'd have wanted her old Floy to look after her."

She gave a harsh sob but went on very doggedly. She had gone to the bedroom door and found it locked. This, Alleyn gathered, had roused a kind of fury in her. She had walked up and down the landing in an agony of frustration and had then remembered the communicating door between the bedroom and dressing-room. So she had stolen to the door from the landing into the dressing-room and had opened it very carefully, not wishing to disturb Mr. Templeton. She had found herself face to face with Mrs. Plumtree.

It must, Alleyn thought, have been an extraordinary scene. The two women had quarrelled in whispers. Florence had demanded to be allowed to go through into the bedroom. Mrs. Plumtree had refused. Then Florence had told her what she wanted to do.

"I told her! I told her I was the only one to lay my poor girl out and make her look more like herself. She said I couldn't. She said she wasn't to be touched by doctor's orders. *Doctor's orders!* I'd of pulled her away and gone through. I'd got me hands on 'er to do it, but it was too late."

She turned to Fox. "He'd come in. He was coming upstairs. She said, 'That's the police. D'you want to get yourself locked up?' I had to give over and I went to my room."

"I'm afraid she was right, Florence."

"*Are* you! That shows how much you know! *I* wasn't to touch the body! Me! Me, that loved her. All right! So what was Clara Plumtree doing in the bedroom? Now!"

"What!" Fox ejaculated. "In the bedroom? Mrs. Plumtree?"

"Ah!" Florence cried out in a kind of triumph. "Her! She'd been in there herself and let her try and deny it!"

Alleyn said, "How do you know she'd been in the bedroom?"

"How? Because I heard the tank filling and the basin tap running in the bathroom beyond. She'd been in there doing what it was my right to do. Laying her hands on my poor girl."

"But why do you suppose this? Why?"

Her lips trembled and she rubbed her hand across them. "Why! Why! I'll tell you why. Because she smelt of that scent. Smelt of it, I tell you, so strong it would sicken you. So if you're going to lock anybody up, you can start on Clara Plumtree."

Her mouth twisted. Suddenly she burst into tears and blundered out of the room.

Fox shut the door after her and removed his spectacles. "A tartar," he observed.

"Yes," Alleyn agreed. "A faithful, treacherous, jealous, pigheaded tartar. You never know how they'll cut up in a crisis. Never. And I fancy, for our pains, we've got a brace of them in this party."

As if to confirm this opinion there was a heavy single bang on the door. It swung violently open and there, on the threshold, was Old Ninn Plumtree with P. C. Philpott, only less red-faced than herself, towering in close attendance.

"Lay a finger on me, young man," Old Ninn was saying, "and I'll make a public example of you."

"I'm sure I'm very sorry, sir," said Philpott. "The lady insists on seeing you and short of taking her in charge I don't seem to be able to prevent it."

"All right, Philpott," Alleyn said. "Come in, Ninn. Come in."

She did so. Fox resignedly shut the door. He put a chair behind Ninn, but she disregarded it. She faced Alleyn over her own folded arms. To look in his face she was obliged to tilt her own acutely backwards and in doing so gave out such an astonishingly potent effluvium that she might have been a miniature volcano smouldering with port and due to erupt. Her voice was sepulchral and her manner truculent.

"I fancied," she said, "I knew a gentleman when I saw one and I hope you're not going to be a disappointment. Don't answer me back. I prefer to form my own opinion."

Alleyn did not answer her back.

"That Floy," Old Ninn continued, "has been at you. A bad background, if ever there was one. What's bred in the child comes out in the woman. Don't believe a word of what she tells you. What's she been saying about the boy?"

"About Mr. Dakers?"

"Certainly. A man to you, seem he may; to me who knows him inside out, he's a boy. Twenty-eight and famous, I daresay, but no more harm in him than there ever has been, which is never. Sensitive and fanciful, yes. Not practical, granted. Vicious, fiddle! Now. What's that Floy been putting about?"

"Nothing very terrible, Ninn."

"Did she say he was ungrateful? Or bad-mannered?"

"Well . . ."

"He's nothing of the sort. What else?"

Alleyn was silent. Old Ninn unfolded her arms. She laid a tiny gnarled paw on Alleyn's hand. "Tell me what else," she said, glaring into his face, "I've got to know. Tell me."

"*You* tell *me*," he said and put his hand over hers. "What was the matter between Mr. Richard and Mrs. Templeton? It's better I should know. What was it?"

She stared at him. Her lips moved but no sound came from them.

"You saw him," Alleyn said, "when he came out of her room. What was the matter? Florence told us . . ."

"*She* told you! *She* told you that!"

"I'd have found out, you know. Can you clear it up for us? Do, if you can."

She shook her head in a very desolate manner. Her eyes were glazed with tears and her speech had become uncertain. He supposed she had fortified herself with an extra glass before tackling him and it was now taking full effect.

"I can't say," she said indistinctly. "I don't know. One of her tantrums. A tyrant from the time she could speak. The boy's never anything but good and patient." And after a moment she added quite briskly, "Doesn't take after *her* in that respect. More like the father."

Fox looked up from his notes. Alleyn remained perfectly still. Old Ninn rocked very slightly on her feet and sat down.

"Mr. Templeton?" Alleyn said.

She nodded two or three times with her eyes shut. "You may well say so," she murmured, "you—may—well . . ." Her voice trailed into silence and she dozed.

Fox opened his mouth and Alleyn signalled him and he shut it again. There was a considerable pause. Presently Old Ninn gave a slight snore, moved her lips and opened her eyes.

Alleyn said, "Does Mr. Richard know about his parentage?"

She looked fixedly at him. "Why shouldn't he?" she said. "They were both killed in a motor accident and don't you believe anything you're told to the contrary. Name of Dakers." She caught sight of Fox and his notebook. "Dakers," she repeated and spelt it out for him.

"Thank you very much," said Fox.

Alleyn said, "Did you think Mr. Richard looked very much upset when he came out of her room?"

"She had the knack of upsetting him. He takes things to heart."

"What did he do?"

"Went downstairs. Didn't look at me. I doubt if he saw me."

"Florence," Alleyn said, "thought he looked like death."

Ninn got to her feet. Her little hands clutched at his arm. "What's she mean? What's she been hinting? Why didn't she say what I heard? After she went downstairs? I told her. Why didn't she tell you?"

"What did you hear?"

"She knows! I told her. I didn't think anything of it at the time and now she won't admit it. Trying to lay the blame on the boy. She's a wicked girl and always has been."

"What did you hear?"

"I heard the Lady using that thing. The poison thing. Hissing. *Heard* it! She killed herself," Ninn said. "Why, we'll never know and the sin's on her head forever. She killed herself."

4

There was a long pause during which Ninn showed signs of renewed instability. Fox put his arm under hers. "Steady does it," he said comfortably.

"That's no way to talk," she returned sharply and sat down again.

"Florence," Alleyn said, "tells us Miss Bellamy was incapable of any such thing."

The mention of Florence instantly restored her.

"Florence said this and Florence said that," she barked. "And did Florence happen to mention she fell out with her lady and as good as got her notice this morning? Did she tell you that?"

"No," Alleyn murmured, "she didn't tell us that."

"Ah! There you are, you see!"

"What did you do after Mr. Richard left the room and went downstairs? After Florence had gone and after you'd heard the spray?"

She had shut her eyes again and he had to repeat his questions. "I retired," she said with dignity, "to my room."

"When did you hear of the catastrophe?"

"There was a commotion. Floy with a hot bottle on the landing having hysterics. I couldn't get any sense out of her. Then the doctor came out and told me."

"And after that, what did you do?"

He could have sworn that she made a considerable effort to collect herself and that his question had alarmed her. "I don't remember," she said and then added, "Went back to my room." She had opened her eyes and was watching him very warily.

"Are you sure, Ninn? Didn't you have a look at Mr. Templeton in the dressing-room?"

"I've forgotten. I might have. I believe I did. You can't think of everything," she added crossly.

"How was he? How did you find him?"

"How would you expect him to be?" she countered. "Very low. Didn't speak. Upset. Naturally. With his trouble, it might have been the death of him. The shock and all."

"How long were you in the dressing-room?"

"I don't remember. Till the police came and ordered everybody about."

"Did you," Alleyn asked her, "go into the bedroom?"

She waited for a long time. "No," she said at last.

"Are you sure? You didn't go through into the bathroom or begin to tidy the room?"

"No."

"Or touch the body?"

"I didn't go into the bedroom."

"And you didn't let Florence go in either?"

"What's she been telling you?"

"That she wanted to go in and that you—very properly—told her that the doctor had forbidden it."

"She was hysterical. She's a silly girl. Bad in some ways."

"Did Mr. Templeton go into the bedroom?"

"He had occasion," she said with great dignity, "to pass through it in order to make use of the convenience. That is not forbidden, I hope?"

"Naturally not."

"Very well then," she stifled a hiccough and rose. "I'm going to bed," she said loudly, and as there was nothing further to be collected from her, they let her out.

Fox offered assistance but was rebuffed. She tacked rapidly towards the door.

He opened it quickly.

There, on the landing, looking remarkably uncomfortable, was Richard Dakers.

5

He had been caught, it was evident, in the act of moving away from the door. Now, he stood stock-still, an uncomfortable smile twitching at the corner of his mouth. Old Ninn stopped short when she saw him, appeared to get her bearings and went up to him.

"Ninn," he said, looking past her at Alleyn and speaking with most unconvincing jauntiness, "what *have* you been up to!"

She stared into his face. "Speak up for yourself," she said. "They'll put upon you if you don't."

"Hadn't you better go to bed? You're not yourself, you know."

"Exactly," Ninn said with hauteur. "I'm going."

She made off at an uncertain gait towards the backstairs. Alleyn said, "Mr. Dakers, what are you doing up here?"

"I wanted to get into my room."

"I'm afraid we're occupying it at the moment. But if there's anything you need . . ."

"Oh God!" Richard cried out. "Is there to be no end to these indignities? No! No, there's nothing I need. Not now. I wanted to be by myself in my room where I could make some attempt to think."

"You had it all on your own in the drawing-room," Fox said crossly. "Why couldn't you think down there? How did you get past the man on duty, sir?"

"He was coping with a clutch of pressmen at the front door and I nipped up the back stairs."

"Well," Alleyn said, "you'd better nip down again to where you came from and if you're sick of the drawing-room, you can join the party next door. Unless, of course, you'd like to stay and tell us your real object in coming up here."

Richard opened his mouth and shut it again. He then turned on his heels and went downstairs. He was followed by Fox, who returned looking portentous. "I gave that chap in the hall a rocket," he said. "They don't know the meaning of keeping observation these days. Mr. Dakers is back in the drawing-room. Why do you reckon he broke out, sir?"

"I think," Alleyn said, "he may have remembered the blotting-paper."

"Ah, there is that. May be. Mrs. Plumtree wasn't bad value, though, was she?"

"Not bad. But none of it proves anything, of course," Alleyn said. "Not a damn thing."

"Floy getting the sack's interesting. If true."

"It may be a recurrent feature of their relationship, for all we know. What about the sounds they both heard in the bedroom?"

"Do we take it," Fox asked, "that Floy's crash came before Mrs. Plumtree's hiss?"

"I suppose so. Yes."

"And that Florence retired after the crash?"

"While Ninn remained for the hiss. Precisely."

"The inference being," Fox pursued, "that as soon as Mr. Dakers left her, the lady fell with a deafening crash on the four-pile carpet."

"And then sprayed herself all over with Slaypest."

"Quite so, Mr. Alleyn."

"I prefer a less dramatic reading of the evidence."

"All the same, it doesn't look very pleasant for Mr. Dakers." And as Alleyn didn't reply, "D'you reckon Mrs. Plumtree was talking turkey when she let out about his parentage?"

"I think it's at least possible that she believes it."

"Born," Fox speculated, "out of wedlock and the parents subsequently married?"

"Your guess is as good as mine. Wait a bit." He took down the copy of *Who's Who in the Theatre*. "Here we are. Bellamy. Sumptuous entry. Birth, not given. Curtis says fifty. Married 1932, Charles Gavin Templeton. Now, where's the playwright? Dakers, Richard. Very conservative entry. Born 1931. Educated Westminster and Trinity. List of three plays. That's all. Could be, Foxkin. I suppose we can dig it out if needs must."

Fox was silent for a moment. "There is this," he then said. "Mrs. Plumtree was alone on the landing after Florence went downstairs?"

"So it seems."

"And she says she heard deceased using the Slaypest. What say she went in and used it herself? On deceased."

"All right. Suppose she did. Why?"

"Because of the way deceased treated her ward or son or whatever he is? Went in and let her have it and then made off before Florence came back."

"Do you like it?"

"Not much," Fox grunted. "What about this story of Mrs. Plumtree going into the bedroom and rearranging the remains?"

"She didn't. The body was as Harkness and Gantry left it. Unless Harkness is too much hungover to notice."

"It might be something quite slight."

"What, for pity's sake?"

"God knows," Fox said. "Could *you* smell scent on Mrs. P.?"

"I could smell nothing but rich old tawny port on Mrs. P."

"Might be a blind for the perfume. Ah, forget it!" Fox said disgustedly. "It's silly. How about this crash they heard after Mr. Dakers left the room?"

"Oh that. That was the lady pitching Madame Vestris into the bathroom."

"Why?"

"Professional jealousy? Or perhaps it was his birthday present to her and she was taking it out on the Vestris."

"Talk about conjecture! We do nothing else," Fox grumbled. "All right. So what's the next step, sir?"

"We've got to clear the ground. We've got to check, for one thing, Mr. Bertie Saracen's little outburst. And the shortest way with that one, I suppose, is to talk to Anelida Lee."

"Ah, yes. You know the young lady, don't you, Mr. Alleyn?"

"I've met her in her uncle's bookshop. She's a charming girl. I know Octavius quite well. I tell you what, Foxkin, you go round the camp, will you? Talk to the butler. Talk to the maids. Pick up anything that's offering on the general set-up. Find out the pattern of the day's events. Furious Floy suggested a dust-up of some sort with Saracen and Miss Cavendish. Get the strength of it. And see if you can persuade the staff to feed the troops. Hullo—what's that?"

He went out into the passage and along to the landing. The door of Miss Bellamy's room was open. Dr. Curtis and Dr. Harkness stood just inside it watching the activities of two white-coated men. They had laid Miss Bellamy's body on a stretcher and had neatly covered it in orthodox sheeting. P. C. Philpott from the half-landing said, "O.K. chaps," and the familiar progress started. They crossed the landing, changed the angle of their burden and gingerly began the descent. Thus Miss Bellamy made her final journey downstairs. Alleyn heard a subdued noise somewhere above him. He moved to a position from which he could look up the narrower flight of stairs to the second-floor landing. Florence was there, scarcely to be seen in the shadows, and the sound he had heard was of her sobbing.

Alleyn followed the stretcher downstairs. He watched the mortuary van drive away, had a final word with his colleagues, and went next door to call on Octavius Browne.

Octavius, after hours, used his shop as his sitting-room. With the curtains drawn, the lamp on his reading table glowing and the firelight shining on his ranks of books, the room was enchanting. So, in his way, was Octavius, sunk deep in a red morocco chair with his book in his hand and his cat on his knee.

He had removed his best suit and, out of habit, had changed into old grey trousers and a disreputable but becoming velvet coat. For about an hour after Richard Dakers left (Anelida having refused to see him), Octavius had been miserable. Then she had come down, looking pale but familiar, saying she was sorry she'd been tiresome. She had kissed the top of his head and made him an omelette for his supper and had settled in her usual Monday night place on the other side of the fireplace

behind a particularly large file in which she was writing up their catalogue. Once, Octavius couldn't resist sitting up high in order to look at
her and as usual she made a hideous face at him and he made one back
at her, which was a private thing they did on such occasions. He was reassured but not entirely so. He had a very deep affection for Anelida,
but he was one of those people in whom the distress of those they love
begets a kind of compassionate irritation. He liked Anelida to be gay
and dutiful and lovely to look at; when he suspected that she had been
crying he felt at once distressed and helpless and the sensation bored him
because he didn't understand it.

When Alleyn rang the bell Anelida answered it. He saw, at once, that
she had done her eyes up to hide the signs of tears.

Many of Octavius's customers were also his friends and it was not unusual for them to call after hours. Anelida supposed that Alleyn's was
that sort of visit and so did Octavius, who was delighted to see him.
Alleyn sat down between them, disliking his job.

"You look so unrepentantly cosy and Dickensian," he said, "both of
you, that I feel like an interloper."

"My dear Alleyn, I do hope your allusion is not to that other and unspeakable little Nell and her drooling grandparent. No, I'm sure it's not.
You are thinking of *Bleak House*, perhaps, and your fellow-investigator's
arrival at his friend's fireside. I seem to remember, though, that his visit
ended uncomfortably in an arrest. I hope you've left *your* manacles at
the Yard."

Alleyn said, "As a matter of fact, Octavius, I *am* here on business,
though not, I promise, to take either of you into custody."

"Really? How very intriguing! A bookish reference perhaps? Some
malefactor with a flair for the collector's item?"

"I'm afraid not," Alleyn said. "It's a serious business, Octavius, and
indirectly it concerns you both. I believe you were at Miss Mary Bellamy's
birthday party this evening, weren't you?"

Anelida and her uncle both made the same involuntary movement of
their hands. "Yes," Octavius said. "For a short time. We were."

"When did you arrive?"

"At seven. We were asked," Octavius said, "for six-thirty, but Anelida
informed me it is the 'done thing' nowadays to be late."

"We waited," Anelida said, "till other people had begun to stream in."

"So you kept an eye on the earlier arrivals?"

"A bit. I did. They were rather intimidating."

"Did you by any chance see anybody go in with a bunch of Parma
violets?"

Octavius jerked his leg. "Damn you, Hodge," he ejaculated and added mildly, "He makes bread on one's thigh. Unconscionable feline, be gone."

He cuffed the cat and it leapt indignantly to the floor.

Alleyn said, "I know you left early. I believe I know why."

"Mr. Alleyn," Anelida said. "What's happened? Why are you talking like this?"

Alleyn said, "It *is* a serious matter."

"Has Richard . . . ?" she began and stopped. "What are you trying to tell us?"

"He's all right. He's had a shock but he's all right."

"My dear Alleyn . . ."

"Unk," she said, "we'd better just listen."

And Alleyn told them, carefully and plainly, what had happened. He said nothing of the implications.

"I wonder," he ended, "that you haven't noticed the comings and goings outside."

"Our curtains are drawn, as you see," Octavius said. "We had no occasion to look out. Had we, Nelly?"

Anelida said, "This will hurt Richard more than anything else that has ever happened to him." And then with dismay, "I wouldn't see him when he came in. I turned him away. He won't forgive me and I won't forgive myself."

"My darling child, you had every cause to behave as you did. She was an enchanting creature but evidently not always prettily behaved," Octavius said. "I always think," he added, "that one does a great disservice to the dead when one praises them inaccurately. *Nil nisi*, if you will, but at least let the *bonum* be authentic."

"I'm not thinking of her!" she cried out. "I'm thinking of Richard."

"Are you, indeed, my pet?" he said uncomfortably.

Anelida said, "I'm sorry, Mr. Alleyn. This is bad behaviour, isn't it? You must put it down to the well-known hysteria of theatre people."

"I put it down to the natural result of shock," Alleyn said, "and believe me, from what I've seen of histrionic behaviour, yours is in the last degree conservative. You must be a beginner."

"How right you are!" she said and looked gratefully at him.

The point had been reached where he should tell them of the implications and he was helped by Octavius, who said, "But why, my dear fellow, are you concerned in all this? Do the police in cases of accident . . ."

"That's just it," Alleyn said. "They do. They have to make sure."

He explained why they had to make sure. When he said that he must know exactly what had happened in the conservatory, Anelida turned so pale that he wondered if she, too, was going to faint. But she waited for a moment, taking herself in hand, and then told him, very directly, what had happened.

Timon Gantry, Montague and Richard had been talking to her about her reading the leading role in *Husbandry in Heaven*. Mary Bellamy had come in, unnoticed by them, and had heard enough to make her realize what was afoot.

"She was very angry," Anelida said steadily. "She thought of it as a conspiracy and she accused me of—of—" Her voice faltered but in a moment she went on. "She said I'd been setting my cap at Richard to further my own ends in the theatre. I don't remember everything she said. They all tried to stop her, but that seemed to make her more angry. Kate Cavendish and Bertie Saracen had come in with Mr. Templeton. When she saw them she attacked them as well. It was something about another new production. She accused them, too, of conspiracy. I could see Unk on the other side of the glass door, like somebody you want very badly in a nightmare and can't reach. And then Mr. Templeton went out and spoke to him. And then I went out. And Unk behaved perfectly. And we came home."

"Beastly experience," Alleyn said. "For both of you."

"Oh horrid," Octavius agreed. "And *very* puzzling. She was, to meet, you know, so perfectly enchanting. One is quite at a loss . . . !" He rumpled his hair.

"Poor Unky!" Anelida said.

"Was Colonel Warrender in the conservatory?"

"That is Templeton's cousin, isn't it? One sees the likeness," said Octavius. "Yes, he was. He came into the hall and tried to say something pleasant, poor man."

"So did the others," Anelida said. "I'm afraid I wasn't as responsive as I ought to have been. I—we just walked out."

"And Richard Dakers walked out after you?"

"Yes," she said. "He did. And I went off to my room and wouldn't see him. Which is so awful."

"So what did he do?" Alleyn asked Octavius.

"Do? Dakers? He was in a great taking-on. I felt sorry for him. Angry, you know, with *her*. He said a lot of hasty, unpleasant things which I feel sure he didn't mean."

"What sort of things?"

"Oh!" Octavius said. "It was, as far as I recollect, to the effect that Mrs. Templeton had ruined his life. All very extravagant and ill-considered. I was sorry to hear it."

"Did he say what he meant to do when he left here?"

"Yes, indeed. He said he was going back to have it out with her. Though how he proposed to do anything of the sort in the middle of a party, one can't imagine. I went to the door with him, trying to calm him down, and I saw him go into the house."

"And that was the last you saw of him?"

"In point of fact, yes. The telephone rang at that moment. It's in the back room as you'll remember. I answered it and when I returned here I thought for a moment he had done so, too. I suppose because he was so much in my mind."

Anelida made a small ejaculation, but her uncle went on:

"A ludicrous mistake. It was dark in here by then—very—and he was standing in silhouette against the windows. I said, 'My dear chap, what now?' or something of that sort, and he turned and then, of course, I saw it was Colonel Warrender, you know."

"What had *he* come for?" Anelida asked rather desperately.

"Well, my dear, I suppose on behalf of his cousin and to repeat his vicarious apologies and to attempt an explanation. I felt it much better to make as little of the affair as possible. After all we don't *know* Warrender and in any case it was really nothing to do with him. He meant very well, no doubt. I was, I hope, perfectly civil, but I got rid of him in a matter of seconds."

"Yes," Alleyn said. "I see. To sidetrack for a moment, I suppose you're by way of being an authority on Victorian tinsel pictures, aren't you? Do you go in for them? I seem to remember . . ."

"How *very* odd!" Octavius exclaimed. "My dear fellow, I sold one this morning to young Dakers, as a birthday present for—oh, well, there you are!—for his guardian."

"Madam Vestris?"

"You saw it then? Charming, isn't it?"

"Yes," Alleyn said. "Charming."

Anelida had been watching Alleyn, as he was well aware, very closely. She now asked him the question he had expected.

"Mr. Alleyn," Anelida said. "Do you think it was not an accident?"

He gave her the inevitable answer. "We don't know. We're not sure."

"But what do you believe? In your heart? I must know. I won't do anything silly or make a nuisance of myself. Do you believe she was murdered?"

Alleyn said, "I'm afraid I do, Anelida."

"Have you told Richard?"

"Not in so many words."

"But he guessed?"

"I don't know," Alleyn said carefully, "what he thought. I've left him to himself for a little."

"Why?"

"He's had a very bad shock. He fainted."

She looked steadily at him and then with a quick collected movement rose to her feet.

"Unk," she said, "don't wait up for me and don't worry."

"My dear girl," he said, in a fluster, "what do you mean? Where are you going?"

"To Richard," she said. "Where else? Of course to Richard."

CHAPTER SIX   **On the Scent**

When Anelida rang the bell at 2 Pardoner's Place, it was answered, almost at once, by a policeman.

She said, "It's Miss Lee. I've been talking to Superintendent Alleyn. He knows I'm here and I think is probably coming himself in a moment. I want to speak to Mr. Richard Dakers."

The policeman said, "I see, Miss. Well, now, if you'll wait a moment I'll just find out whether that'll be all right. Perhaps you'd take a chair."

"No, thank you. I want to see him at once, please."

"I'll ascertain . . ." he had begun rather austerely when Alleyn himself arrived.

"Sir?"

"Yes, all right. Is Mr. Dakers still in the drawing-room? Good." Alleyn looked at Anelida. "Come along," he said. She lifted her chin and went to him.

She was in a state of mind she had never before experienced. It was as if her thoughts and desires and behaviour had been abruptly simplified and were governed by a single intention. She knew that somewhere within herself she must be afraid, but she also knew that fear, as things had turned out, was inadmissible.

She followed Alleyn across the hall. He said, "Here you are," and opened a door. She went from the hall into the drawing-room.

Immediately inside the door was a tall leather screen. She walked round it and there, staring out of a window, was Richard. Anelida moved a little towards him and halted. This gave her time to realize how very much she liked the shape of his head and at once she felt an immense tenderness for him and even a kind of exultation. In a second, she would speak his name, she would put herself absolutely on his side.

"Richard," she said.

He turned. She noticed that his face had bleached, not conventionally, over the cheekbone, but at the temples and down the jaw-line.

"Anelida?"

"I had to come. I'm trying to make up for my bad behaviour. Here, you see, I am."

He came slowly to her and when he took her hands in his, did so doubtfully. "I can't believe my luck," he said. "I thought I'd lost you quite irrevocably. Cause enough, God knows."

"On the contrary, I assure you."

He broke into an uncertain smile. "The things you say! Such grand phrases!" His hands tightened on hers. "You know what's happened, don't you? About Mary?"

"Yes. Richard, I'm so terribly sorry. And what a hopeless phrase *that* is!"

"I shouldn't let you stay. It's not the place for you. This is a nightmare of a house."

"Do you want me? Am I any good, being here?"

"I love you." He lifted her hands to his face. "Ah no! Why did I tell you! This isn't the time."

"Are you all right now—to talk, I mean? To talk very seriously?"

"I'm all right. Come over here."

They sat together on the sofa, Richard still holding her hands. "He told us you fainted," said Anelida.

"Alleyn? Has he been worrying you?"

"Not really. But it's because of what he did say that I'm here. And because—Richard, when I wouldn't see you and you went away—did you come back here?"

"Yes," he said. "I did."

"Did you see her?"

He looked down at their clasped hands. "Yes."

"Where?"

"In her room. Only for a few minutes. I—left her there."

"Was anyone else with you?"

"Good God, no!" he cried out.

"And then? Then what?"

"I went away. I walked for heaven knows how long. When I came back—it was like this."

There was a long silence. At last Richard said very calmly, "I know what you're trying to tell me. They think Mary has been murdered and they wonder if I'm their man. Isn't it?"

Anelida leant towards him and kissed him. "That's it," she said. "At least, I think so. We'll get it tidied up and disposed of in no time. But I think that's it."

"It seems," he said, "so fantastic. Too fantastic to be frightening. You mustn't be frightened. You must go away, my darling heart, and leave me to—to do something about it."

"I'll go when I think it'll make things easier for you. Not before."

"I love you so much. I should be telling you how much, not putting this burden upon you."

"They may not leave me with you for long. You must remember exactly what happened. Where you went. Who may have seen you. And Richard, you must tell them what she was doing when you left."

He released her hands and pressed the palms of his own to his eyes. "She was laughing," he said.

"Laughing? They'll want to know why, won't they? What you both said to make her laugh."

"Never!" he said violently. "Never!"

"But—they'll ask you."

"They can ask and ask and ask again. Never!"

"You must!" she said desperately. "Think! It's what one always reads— that innocent people hold out on the police and muddle everything up and put themselves in the wrong. Richard, think what they'll find out anyway! That she spoke as she did to me, that you were angry, that you said you'd never forgive her. Everyone in the hall heard you. Colonel Warrender . . ."

"He!" Richard said bitterly. "He won't talk. He daren't."

"What do you mean?"

"It doesn't matter."

"Oh!" she cried out. "You are frightening me! What's going to happen when they ask you about it? What'll they think when you won't tell them!"

"They can think what they like." He got up and began to walk about the room. "Too much has happened. I can't get it into perspective. You don't know what it's like. I've no right to load it on to you."

"Don't *talk* like that," Anelida said desperately. "I love you. It's my right to share."

"You're so young."

"I've got all the sense I'm ever likely to have."

"Darling!"

"Never mind about me! You needn't tell me anything you don't want to. It's what you're going to say to them that matters."

"I will tell you—soon—when I can."

"If it clears you they won't make any further to-do about it. That's all they'll worry about. Clearing it up. You must tell them what happened. Everything."

"I can't."

"My God, *why?*"

"Have you any doubts about me? Have you!"

She went to him. "You must know I haven't."

"Yes," he said. "I can see that."

They stared at each other. He gave an inarticulate cry and suddenly she was in his arms.

Gracefield came through the folding doors from the dining-room.

"Supper is served, sir," he said.

Alleyn rose from his uncomfortable seclusion behind the screen, slipped through the door into the hall, shut it soundlessly behind him and went up to their office.

2

"I've been talking," Mr. Fox remarked, "to a press photographer and the servants."

"And I," Alleyn said sourly, "have been eavesdropping on a pair of lovers. How low can you get? Next stop, with Polonius behind the arras in a bedroom."

"All for their good, I daresay," Fox observed comfortably.

"There is that. Fox, that blasted playwright is holding out on us. And on his girl for a matter of that. But I'm damned if I like him as a suspect."

"He seems," Fox considered, "a very pleasant young fellow."

"What the devil happened between him and Mary Bellamy when he came back? He won't tell his girl. He merely says the interview ended in Miss Bellamy laughing. We've got the reports from those two intensely prejudiced women, who both agree he looked ghastly. All right. He goes out. There's this crash Florence talked about. Florence goes down to the half-landing and Ninn hears a spray being used. Templeton comes out from the drawing-room to the foot of the stairs. He calls up to Florence to tell her mistress they're waiting for her. Florence goes up to the room and finds her mistress in her death throes. Dakers returns two hours after the death, comes up to this room, writes a letter and tries to go away. End of information. Next step: confront him with the letter?"

"Your reconstruction of it?"

"Oh," Alleyn said. "I fancy I can lay my hands on the original."

Fox looked at him with placid approval and said nothing.

"What did you get from your press photographer? And which photographer?" Alleyn asked.

"He was hanging about in the street and said he'd something to tell me. Put-up job to get inside, of course, but I thought I'd see what it was. He took a picture of deceased with Mr. Dakers in the background at twenty to eight by the hall clock. He saw them go upstairs together. Gives us an approximate time for the demise, for what it's worth."

"About ten minutes later. What did you extract from the servants?"

"Not a great deal. It seems the deceased wasn't all that popular with the staff, except Florence, who was hers, as the cook put it, body and soul. Gracefield held out on me for a bit, but he's taken quite a liking to you, sir, and I built on that with good results."

"What the hell have you been saying?"

"Well, Mr. Alleyn, you know as well as I do what snobs these high-class servants are."

Alleyn didn't pursue the subject.

"There was a dust-up," Fox continued, "this morning with Miss Cavendish and Mr. Saracen. Gracefield happened to overhear it." He repeated Gracefield's account, which had been detailed and accurate.

"According to Anelida Lee this row was revived in the conservatory," Alleyn muttered. "What were they doing here this morning?"

"Mr. Saracen had come to do the flowers, about which Gracefield spoke very sarcastically, and Miss Cavendish had brought the deceased that bottle of scent."

"What!" Alleyn said. "Not the muck on her dressing-table? Not Formidable? *This morning?*"

"That's right."

Alleyn slapped his hand down on Richard's desk and got up. "My God, what an ass I've been!" he said and then, sharply, "Who opened it?"

"She did. In the dining-room."

"And used it? Then?"

"Had a bit of a dab, Gracefield said. He happened to be glancing through the serving-hatch at the time."

"What became of it after that?"

"Florence took charge of it. I'm afraid," Fox said, "I'm not with you, Mr. Alleyn, in respect of the scent."

"My dear old boy, think! Think of the bottle."

"Very big," Fox said judiciously.

"Exactly. Very big. Well then . . . ?"

"Yes. Ah, yes," Fox said slowly and then, "Well, I'll be staggered!"

"And so you jolly well should. This could blow the whole damn case wide open again."

"Will I fetch them?"

"Do. And call on Florence, wherever she is. Get the whole story, Fox. Tactfully, as usual. Find out when the scent was decanted into the spray and when she used it. Watch the reactions, won't you? And see if there's anything in the Plumtree stories: about Richard Dakers's parentage and Florence being threatened with the sack."

Fox looked at his watch. "Ten o'clock," he said. "She may have gone to bed."

"That'll be a treat for you. Leave me your notes. Away you go."

While Fox was on this errand, Alleyn made a plot, according to information, of the whereabouts of Charles Templeton, the four guests, the servants and Richard Dakers up to the time when he himself arrived on the scene. Fox's spadework had been exhaustive, as usual, and a pretty complicated pattern emerged. Alleyn lifted an eyebrow over the result. How many of them had told the whole truth? Which of them had told a cardinal lie? He put a query against one name and was shaking his head over it when Fox returned.

"Bailey's finished with them," Fox said and placed on Richard's desk the scent-spray, the empty Formidable bottle and the tin of Slaypest.

"What'd he find in the way of dabs?"

"Plenty. All sorts, but none that you wouldn't expect. He's identified the deceased's. Florence says she and Mr. Templeton and Colonel Warrender all handled the exhibits during the day. She says the deceased got the Colonel to operate the spray on her, just before the party. Florence had filled it from the bottle."

"And how much was left in the bottle?"

"She thinks it was about a quarter-full. She *was* in bed," Fox added in a melancholy tone.

"That would tally," Alleyn muttered. "No sign of the bottle being knocked over and spilling, is there?"

"None."

Alleyn began to tap the Slaypest tin with his pencil. "About half-full. Anyone know when it was first used?"

"Florence reckons, a week ago. Mr. Templeton didn't like her using it and tried to get Florence to make away with it."

"Why didn't she?"

"No chance according to her. She went into a great taking-on and asked me if I was accusing her of murder."

"*Did* she get the sack, this morning?"

"When I asked her she went up like a rocket bomb, the story being that Mrs. Plumtree has taken against her and let out something that was told in confidence."

Alleyn put his head in his hands. "Oh *Lord!*" he said.

"You meet that kind of thing," Mr. Fox observed, "in middle-aged ladies. Florence says that when Miss Bellamy or Mrs. Templeton was out of humour, she would make out she was going to sack Florence, but there was nothing in it. She says she only told Mrs. Plumtree as a joke. I kind of nudged in a remark about Mr. Dakers's parentage, but she wasn't having any of that. She turned around and accused me of having a dirty mind and in the next breath had another go at Mrs. Plumtree. All the same," Mr. Fox added primly, "I reckon there's something in it. I reckon so from her manner. She appears to be very jealous of anybody who was near the deceased and that takes in Mr. Templeton, Mr. Dakers, Mrs. Plumtree and the Colonel."

"Good old Florrie," Alleyn said absent-mindedly.

"You know, sir," Fox continued heavily. "I've been thinking about the order of events. Take the latter part of the afternoon. Say, from when the Colonel used the scent-spray on deceased. What happened after *that*, now?"

"According to himself he went downstairs and had a quick one with Mrs. Templeton in the presence of the servants while Templeton and Dakers were closeted in the study. All this up to the time when the first guests began to come in. It looks good enough, but it's not cast iron."

"Whereas," Fox continued, "Florence and Mrs. Plumtree were upstairs. Either of them could have gone into Mrs. Templeton's room, and got up to the odd bit of hanky-panky, couldn't they, now?"

"The story is that they were together in their parlour until they went downstairs to the party. They're at daggers-drawn. Do you think that if one of them had popped out of the parlour the other would feel disposed to keep mum about it?"

"Ah. There is that, of course. But it might have been forgotten."

"Come off it, Foxkin."

"The same goes for Mr. Templeton and Mr. Dakers. They've said, independently of each other, that they were together in the study. I don't know how you feel about that one, Mr. Alleyn, but I'm inclined to accept it."

"So am I. Entirely."

"If we do accept all this, we've got to take it that the job was fixed after the guests began to arrive. Now, up to the row in the conservatory the three gentlemen were all in the reception rooms. The Colonel was in attendance on the deceased. Mr. Templeton was also with her receiving the guests and Mr. Dakers was on the lookout for his young lady."

"What's more, there was a press photographer near the foot of the stairs, a cinematographer half-way up, and a subsidiary bar at the foot of the backstairs with a caterer's man on duty throughout. He saw Florence and Ninn and nobody else go up. What's that leave us in the way of a roaring-hot suspect?"

"It means," Fox said, "either that one of those two women fixed it then . . ."

"But when? You mean before they met on the landing and tried to listen in on the famous scene?"

"I suppose I do. Yes. While the photograph was being taken."

"Yes?"

"Alternatively someone else went up before that."

"Again, when? It would have to be after the cinema unit moved away and before Mrs. Templeton left the conservatory and came out into the hall where she was photographed with Dakers glowering in the background. And it would have to be before she took him upstairs."

"Which restricts you to the entrance with the birthday cake and the speeches. I reckon someone could have slipped upstairs then."

"The general attention being focussed on the speakers and the stairs being clear? Yes. I agree with you. So far. But, see here, Fox; this expert didn't do the trick as simply as that. I'm inclined to think there was one more visit at least, more likely that there were two more, one before and one after the death. Tidying up, you know. If I'm right, there was a certain amount of tidying up."

"My God," Fox began with unwonted heat, "what are you getting at, Mr. Alleyn? It's tough enough as it is, d'you want to make it more difficult? What's the idea?"

"If it's any good it's going to make it easier. Much easier."

Alleyn stood up.

"You know, Br'er Fox," he said, "I can see only one explanation that really fits. Take a look at what's offering. Suicide? Leave her party, go up to her bedroom and spray herself to death? They all scout the notion and so do I. Accident? We've had it: the objection being the inappropriateness of the moment for her to horticult and the nature of the stains. Homicide? All right. What's the jury asked to believe? That she stood stock-still while her murderer pumped a deluge of Slaypest into her face at long and then at short range? Defending counsel can't keep a straight face over that one. But if, by any giddy chance, I'm on the right track, there's an answer that still admits homicide. Now, listen, while I check over and see if you can spot a weakness."

Mr. Fox listened placidly to a succinct argument, his gaze resting thoughtfully the while on the tin, the bottle, and the scent-spray.

"Yes," he said when Alleyn had finished. "Yes. It adds up, Mr. Alleyn. It fits. The only catch that I can see rests in the little difficulty of our having next-to-nothing to substantiate the theory."

Alleyn pointed a long finger at the exhibits. "We've got those," he said, "and it'll go damn hard if we don't rake up something else in the next half hour."

"Motive?"

"Motive unknown. It may declare itself. Opportunity's our bird, Fox. Opportunity, my boy."

"What's the next step?"

"I rather fancy shock tactics. They're all cooped up in the dining-room, aren't they?"

"All except Mr. Templeton. He's still in the study. When I looked in they were having supper. He'd ordered it for them. Cold partridge," Mr. Fox said rather wistfully. "A bit of a waste, really, as they didn't seem to have much appetite."

"We'll see if we can stimulate it," Alleyn said grimly, "with these," and waved his hand at the three exhibits.

3

Pinky Cavendish pushed her plate away and addressed herself firmly to her companions.

"I feel," she said, "completely unreal. It's not an agreeable sensation." She looked round the table. "Is there any reason why we don't say what's in all our minds? Here we sit, pretending to eat: every man-jack of us pea-green with worry but cutting the whole thing dead. I can't do with it. Not for another second. I'm a loquacious woman and I want to talk."

"Pinky," Timon Gantry said. "Your sense of timing! Never quite successfully co-ordinated, dear, is it?"

"But, *actually*," Bertie Saracen plaintively objected, "I do so feel Pinky's dead right. I mean we *are* all devastated and for my part, at least, terrified; but there's no *real* future, is there, in maintaining a *charnel-house* decorum? It can't improve anything, or can it? And it's so excessively wearing. Dicky, dear, you won't misunderstand me, will you? The hearts, I promise you, are utterly in their right place which, speaking for myself, is in the boots."

Richard, who had been talking in an undertone to Anelida, looked up. "Why not talk," he said, "if you can raise something that remotely resembles normal conversation."

Warrender darted a glance at him. "Of course," he said. "Entirely agree." But Richard wouldn't look at Warrender.

"Even abnormal conversation," Pinky said, "would be preferable to strangulated silence."

Bertie, with an air of relief, said, "Well then, everybody, let's face it. We're *not* being herded together in a"—he swallowed—"in a communal cell just out of constabular whimsy. Now *are* we?"

"No, Bertie," Pinky said, "we are not."

"Under hawklike supervision," Bertie added, "if Sergeant Philpott doesn't mind my mentioning it."

P. C. Philpott, from his post at the far end of the room, said, "Not at all, sir," and surreptitiously groped for his notebook.

"*Thank* you," Bertie said warmly. Gracefield and a maid came in and cleared the table in a deathly silence. When they had gone Bertie broke out again. "My God," he said. "Isn't it as clear as daylight that every one of us, except Anelida, is under suspicion for something none of us likes to mention?"

"I do," Pinky said. "I'm all for mentioning it, and indeed if I don't mention it I believe I'll go off like a geyser."

"No, you won't, dear," Gantry firmly intervened. He was sitting next to Pinky and looked down upon her with a cranelike tilt of his head. "You'll behave beautifully and not start any free-associating nonsense. This is not the time for it."

"Timmy darling, I'm sorry as sorry but I'm moved to defy you," Pinky announced with a great show of spirit. "In the theatre—never. Outside it and under threat of being accused of murder—yes. There!" she ejaculated. "I've said it! Murder. And aren't you all relieved?"

Bertie Saracen said at once, "Bless you, darling. Immeasurably."

Timon Gantry and Colonel Warrender simultaneously looked at the back of Philpott's head and then exchanged glances: two men, Anelida felt, of authority at the mercy of an uncontrollable situation.

"Very well, then," Pinky continued. "The police think Mary was murdered and presumably they think one of us murdered her. It sounds monstrous, but it appears to be true. The point is does anyone here agree with them?"

"I don't," Bertie said. He glanced at the serving-hatch and lowered his voice. "After all," he said uncomfortably, "we're not the only ones."

"If you mean the servants . . ." Richard said angrily.

"I don't mean anybody in particular," Bertie protested in a great hurry. "—It's quite unthinkable."

"To my mind," Pinky said, "the whole thing's out of this world. I don't and can't and won't believe it of anybody in the house."

"Heah, heah," Warrender ejaculated, lending a preposterously hearty note to the conversation. "Ridiculous idea," he continued loudly. "Alleyn's behaving altogether too damn highhandedly." He looked at Richard, hesitated and with an obvious effort said, "Don't you agree?"

Without turning his head, Richard said, "He knows his own business, I imagine."

There was a rather deadly little silence broken by Timon Gantry.

"For my part," Gantry said, "I feel the whole handling of the situation is so atrociously hard on Charles Templeton."

A guilty look came into their faces, Anelida noticed, as if they were ashamed of forgetting Charles. They made sympathetic noises and were embarrassed.

"What I resent," Pinky said suddenly, "is being left in the dark. *What* happened? *Why* the mystery? *Why not* accident? All we've been told is that poor Mary died of a dose of pest-killer. It's hideous and tragic and we're all shocked beyond words, but if we're being kept here under suspicion"—she brought her clenched fist down on the table—"*we've a right to know why!*"

She had raised her not inconsiderable voice to full projection point. None of them had heard the door from the hall open.

"Every right," Alleyn said, coming forward. "And I'm sorry that the explanation has been so long delayed."

The men had half-risen, but he lifted his hand and they sat back again. Anelida, for all her anxiety, had time to reflect that he was possessed of an effortless authority before which even Gantry, famous for this quality, became merely one of a controllable group. The attentive silence that descended upon them was of exactly the same kind as that which Gantry himself commanded at rehearsals. Even Colonel Warrender, though he raised his eyebrows, folded his arms and looked uncommonly portentous, found nothing to say.

"I think," Alleyn said, "that we will make this a round-the-table discussion." He sat in the vacant chair at the end of the table. "It gives one," he explained with a smile at Pinky Cavendish, "a spurious air of importance. We shall need five more chairs, Philpott."

P. C. Philpott placed them. Nobody spoke.

Fox came in from the hall bringing Florence and Old Ninn in his wake. Old Ninn was attired in a red flannel gown. Florence had evidently redressed herself rather sketchily and covered the deficiencies with an alpaca overall. Her hair was trapped in a tortuous system of tin curlers.

"Please sit down," Alleyn said. "I'm sorry about dragging you in again. It won't, I hope, be for long."

Florence and Ninn, both looking angry and extremely reluctant and each cutting the other dead, sat on opposite sides of the table, leaving empty chairs between themselves and their nearest neighbours.

"Where's Dr. Harkness, Fox?"

"Back in the conservatory, I believe, sir. We thought it better not to rouse him."

"I'm afraid we must do so now."

Curtains had been drawn across the conservatory wall. Fox disappeared behind them. Stertorous, unlovely and protesting noises were heard and presently he re-appeared with Dr. Harkness, now bloated with sleep and very tousled.

"Oh torment!" he said in a thick voice. "Oh hideous condition!"

"Would you," Alleyn asked, "be very kind and see if you think Mr. Templeton is up to joining us? If there's any doubt about it, we won't disturb him. He's in the study."

"Very well," said Dr. Harkness, trying to flatten his hair with both hands. "Never, never, never, any of you, chase up four whiskies with three glasses of champagne. Don't *do* it!" he added furiously as if somebody had shown signs of taking this action. He went out.

"We'll wait," Alleyn said composedly, "for Mr. Templeton," and arranged his papers.

Warrender cleared his throat. "Don't like the look of that sawbones," he said.

"Poor pet," Bertie sighed. "And yet I almost wish I were in his boots. A pitiable but *not* unenviable condition."

"Bad show!" Warrender said. "Fellar's on duty."

"Are you true?" Gantry asked suddenly, gazing at Warrender with a kind of devotion.

"I beg your pardon, sir?"

Gantry clasped his hands and said ecstatically, "One would never dare! Never! And yet people say one's productions tend towards caricature! You shall give them the lie in their teeth, Colonel. In your own person you shall refute them."

"I'm damned if I know what you're talking about, Gantry, but if you're trying to be abusive . . ."

" 'No abuse,' " Alleyn quoted unexpectedly. He was reading his notes. " 'No abuse in the world: no, faith, boys, none.' "

They stared at him. Gantry, thrown off his stride, looked round the table as if calling attention to Alleyn's eccentricity. Bertie leant towards him. "Formidable!" he murmured, indicating Alleyn.

"*What!*" Pinky ejaculated. "*What* did you say, dear?"

"Formidable!" Bertie repeated. "I said 'formidable.' Why? Oh God! Sorry!"

Warrender made some sort of exclamation.

"I was talking about Mr. Alleyn, dear," Bertie explained. "I said he was formidable."

"Oh!" Pinky said. "That! Sorry!"

"A misunderstanding," Alleyn remarked to his notes. "But don't let it put you off the scent. We're coming to that in a minute."

Pinky, greatly disconcerted, had opened her mouth to reply but was prevented by the appearance of Charles Templeton. He had come in with Dr. Harkness. He was a bad colour, seemed somehow to have shrunk and walked like the old man he actually was. But his manner was contained and he smiled faintly at them.

Alleyn got up and went to him. "He's all right," Dr. Harkness said. "He'll do. Won't you, Charles?"

"I'll do," Charles repeated. "Much better."

"Would you rather sit in a more comfortable chair?" Alleyn suggested. "As you see, we are making free with your dining-room table."

"Of course. I hope you've got everything you want. I'll join you."

He took the nearest chair. Richard had got up and now, gripping Charles's shoulders, leant over him. Charles turned his head and looked up at him. During that moment, Alleyn thought, he saw a resemblance.

Richard said, "Are you well enough for all this?"

"Yes, yes. Perfectly."

Richard returned to his place, Dr. Harkness and Fox took the two remaining seats, and the table was full.

Alleyn clasped his hands over his papers, said, "Well, now," and wishing, not for the first time, that he could find some other introductory formula, addressed himself to his uneasy audience.

Anelida thought, "Here we all sit like a committee meeting and the chairman thinks one of us is a murderer." Richard, very straight in his chair, looked at the table. When she stirred a little he reached for her hand, gripped it and let it go.

Alleyn was talking.

". . . I would like to emphasize that until the pathologist's report comes in, there can be no certainty, but in the meantime I think we must try to arrive at a complete pattern of events. There are a number of points still to be settled and to that end I have kept you so long and asked you to come here. Fox?"

Fox had brought a small case with him. He now opened it, produced the empty scent bottle and laid it on the table.

"Formidable," Alleyn said and turned to Pinky. "Your birthday present, wasn't it, and the cause, I think of your misunderstanding just now with Mr. Saracen."

Pinky said angrily, "What have you done with the scent? Sorry," she added. "It doesn't matter, of course. It's only that—well, it was full this morning."

"When you gave it to Miss Bellamy? In this room?"

"That's right."

Alleyn turned to Florence. "Can you help us?"

"I filled her spray from it," Florence said mulishly.

"That wouldn't account for the lot, Florry," Pinky pointed out.

"Was the spray empty?" Alleyn asked.

"Just about. She didn't mind mixing them."

"And how much was left in the bottle?"

"*He* asked me all this," Florence said, jerking her head at Fox.

"And now I do."

"About that much," she muttered, holding her thumb and forefinger an inch apart.

"About a quarter. And the spray was full?"

She nodded.

Fox, with the expertise of a conjuror, produced the scent-spray and placed it by the bottle.

"And only about 'that much,'" Alleyn pointed out, "is now in the spray. So we've got pretty well three-quarters of this large bottle of scent to account for, haven't we?"

"I fail utterly," Warrender began, "to see what you think you're driving at."

"Perhaps you can help. I understand, sir, that you actually used this thing earlier in the day."

"Not on myself, God damn it!" Warrender said and then shot an uneasy glance at Charles Templeton.

Gantry gave a snort of delight.

"On Miss Bellamy?" Alleyn suggested.

"Naturally."

"And did you happen to notice how much was left?"

"It was over three-quarters full. What!" Warrender demanded, appealing to Charles.

"I didn't notice," he said, and put his hand over his eyes.

"Do you mind telling me, sir, how you came to do this?"

"Not a bit. Why should I?" Warrender rejoined, and with every appearance of exquisite discomfort added, "She asked me to. Didn't she, Charles?"

He nodded.

Alleyn pressed for more detail and got an awkward account of the scene with a grudging confirmation from Florence and a leaden one from Charles.

"Did you use a great deal of the scent?" he asked.

"Fair amount. She *asked* me to," Warrender angrily repeated.

Charles shuddered and Alleyn said, "It's very strong, isn't it? Even the empty bottle seems to fill the room if one takes the stopper out."

"Don't!" Charles exclaimed. But Alleyn had already removed it. The smell, ponderable, sweet and improper, was disturbingly strong.

"Extraordinary!" Gantry said. "She only wore it for an afternoon and yet—the association."

"*Will* you be quiet, sir!" Warrender shouted. "My God, what sort of a cad do you call yourself? Can't you see . . ." He made a jerky, ineloquent gesture.

Alleyn replaced the stopper.

"Did you, do you think," he asked Warrender, "use so much that the spray could then accommodate what was left in the bottle?"

"I wouldn't have thought so."

"No," said Florence.

"And even if it was filled up again, the spray itself now only contains about that same amount. Which means, to insist on the point, that somehow or another three-quarters of the whole amount of scent has disappeared."

"That's impossible," Pinky said bluntly. "Unless it was spilt."

"No," Florence said again. Alleyn turned to her.

"And the spray and bottle were on the dressing-table when you found Miss Bellamy?"

"Must of been. I didn't stop," Florence said bitterly, "to tidy up the dressing-table."

"And the tin of Slaypest was on the floor?"

Fox placed the tin beside the other exhibits and they looked at it with horror.

"Yes?" Alleyn asked.

"Yes," said Warrender, Harkness and Gantry together, and Charles suddenly beat with his hand on the table.

"Yes, yes, *yes*," he said violently. "My God, must we have all this!"

"I'm very sorry, sir, but I'm afraid we must."

"Look here," Gantry demanded, "are you suggesting that—what the hell are you suggesting?"

"I suggest nothing," Alleyn said. "I simply want to try and clear up a rather odd state of affairs. Can anybody offer an explanation?"

"She herself—Mary—must have done something about it. Knocked it over perhaps."

"Which?" Alleyn asked politely. "The bottle or the spray?"

"I don't know," Gantry said irritably. "How should I? The spray, I suppose. And then filled it up."

"There's no sign of a spill, as Florence has pointed out."

"I know!" Bertie Saracen began. "You think it was used as a sort of blind to—to . . ."

"To what, Mr. Saracen?"

"Ah, no," Bertie said in a hurry. "I—thought—no, I was muddling. I don't know."

"I think I do," Pinky said and turned very white.

"Yes?" Alleyn said.

"I won't go on. I can't. It's not clear enough. Please."

She looked Alleyn straight in the eyes. "Mr. Alleyn," Pinky said. "If you prod and insist, you'll winkle out all sorts of odd bits of information about—about arguments and rows. Inside the theatre and out. Mostly inside. Like a good many other actresses, Mary did throw the odd temperament. She threw one," Pinky went on against an almost palpable surge of consternation among her listeners, "for a matter of that, this morning."

"*Pinky!*" Gantry warned her on a rising note.

"Timmy, why not? I daresay Mr. Alleyn already knows," she said wearily.

"How very wise you are," Alleyn exclaimed. "Thank you for it. Yes, we do know, in a piecemeal sort of way, as you've suggested, that there were ructions. We *have* winkled them out. We know, for instance, that there was a difference of opinion, on professional grounds, here in this room. This morning. We know it was resurrected with other controversial matters during the party. We know that you and Mr. Saracen were involved and when I say that, I'm quite sure you're both much too sensible to suppose I'm suggesting anything more. Fox and I speak only of facts. We'll be nothing but grateful if you can help us discard as many as possible of the awkward load of facts that we've managed to accumulate."

"All this," Gantry said, "sounds mighty fine. We're on foreign ground, Pinky, and may well make fools of ourselves. You watch your step, my girl."

"I don't believe you," she said, and still looking full at Alleyn, "What do you want to know?"

"First of all, what your particular row was about."

She said, "All right with you, Bertie?"

"Oh Christmas!" he said. "I suppose so."

"You're a fool, Bertie," Timon Gantry said angrily. "These things can't be controlled. You don't know where you'll fetch up."

"But then you see, Timmy dear, I never do," Bertie rejoined with a sad little giggle.

Gantry rounded on Pinky Cavendish. "You might care to remember that other people are involved."

"I don't forget, Timmy, I promise you." She turned to Alleyn. "This morning's row," she said, "was because I told Mary I was going to play the lead in a new play. She felt I was deserting her. Later on, during the party when we were all"—she indicated the conservatory—"in there, she brought it up again."

"And was still very angry?"

Pinky looked unhappily at Charles. "It was pretty hot while it lasted. Those sorts of dusts-up always were, with Mary."

"And you were involved, Mr. Saracen?"

"Not 'alf!" Bertie said and explained why.

"And you, Mr. Gantry?"

"Very well—yes. In so far as I am to produce the comedy."

"But you copped it both ways, Timmy," Bertie pointed out with some relish. "You were involved in the other one, too. About Dicky's 'different' play and Anelida being asked to do the lead. She was angrier about that than anything. She was livid."

"Mr. Alleyn knows," Anelida said and they looked uneasily at her.

"Never mind, dear," Gantry said rather bossily. "None of this need concern you. Don't get involved."

"She *is* involved," Richard said, looking at her. "With me. Permanently, I hope."

"*Really?*" Pinky cried out in her warmest voice and beamed at Anelida. "How lovely! Bertie! Timmy! Isn't that lovely! Dicky, *darling!* Anelida!"

They made enthusiastic noises. It was impossible, Anelida found, not to be moved by their friendliness, but it struck her as quite extraordinary that they could switch so readily to this congratulatory vein. She caught a look of—what? Surprise? Resignation? in Alleyn's eye and was astounded when he gave her the faintest shadow of a wink.

"Delightful though it is to refresh ourselves with this news," he said, "I'm afraid I must bring you back to the matter in hand. How did the row in the conservatory arise?"

Pinky and Bertie gave him a look in which astonishment mingled with reproach.

Richard said quickly, "Mary came into the conservatory while we were discussing the casting of my play, *Husbandry in Heaven.* I should have told her—warned her. I didn't and she felt I hadn't been frank about it."

"I'm sorry, but I shall have to ask you exactly what she said."

He saw at once that Pinky, Saracen and Gantry were going to refuse.

They looked quickly at one another and Gantry said rather off-handedly, "I imagine none of us remembers in any detail. When Mary threw a temperament she said all sorts of things that everybody knew she didn't mean."

"Did she, for instance, make threats of any sort?"

Gantry stood up. "For the last time," he said, "I warn you all that you're asking for every sort of trouble if you let yourselves be led into making ill-considered statements about matters that are entirely beside the point. For the last time I suggest that you consider your obligations to your profession and your careers. Keep your tongues behind your teeth or, by God, you'll regret it."

Bertie, looking frightened, said to Pinky, "He's right, you know. Or isn't he?"

"I suppose so," she agreed unhappily. "There is a limit—I suppose. All the same . . ."

"If ever you've trusted yourselves to my direction," Gantry said, "you'll do so now."

"All right." She looked at Alleyn. "Sorry."

Alleyn said, "Then I must ask Colonel Warrender and Mr. Templeton. Did Miss Bellamy utter threats of any sort?"

Warrender said, "In my opinion, Charles, this may be a case for a solicitor. One doesn't know what turn things may take. Meantime, wait and see, isn't it?"

"Very well," Charles said. "Very well."

"Mr. Dakers?" Alleyn asked.

"I'm bound by the general decision," Richard said, and Anelida, after a troubled look at him, added reluctantly:

"And I by yours."

"In that case," Alleyn said, "there's only one thing to be done. We must appeal to the sole remaining witness."

"Who the hell's that!" Warrender barked out.

"Will you see if you can get him, Fox? Mr. Montague Marchant," said Alleyn.

4

On Pinky and Bertie's part little attempt was made to disguise their consternation. It was obvious that they desired, more than anything else, an opportunity to consult together. Gantry, however, merely folded his arms, lay back in his chair and looked at the ceiling. He might have been waiting to rise in protest at a conference of Actors' Unity. Warrender, for his part, resembled a senior member at a club committee meeting. Charles fetched a heavy sigh and rested his head on his hand.

Fox went out of the room. As he opened the door into the hall a grandfather clock at the foot of the stairs was striking eleven. It provoked an involuntary exclamation from the persons Alleyn had brought together round the table. Several of them glanced in despair at their watches.

"In the meantime," Alleyn said, "shall we try to clear up the position of Mr. Richard Dakers?"

Anelida's heart suddenly thudded against her ribs as if drawing attention to its disregarded sovereignty. She had time to think: "I'm involved, almost without warning, in a monstrous situation. I'm committed, absolutely, to a man of whom I know next to nothing. It's a kind of dedication and I'm not prepared for it." She turned to look at Richard and, at once, knew that her allegiance, active or helpless, was irrevocable. "So this," Anelida thought in astonishment, "is what it's like to be in love."

Alleyn, aware of the immediate reactions, saw Old Ninn's hands move convulsively in her lap. He saw Florence look at her with a flash of something that might have been triumph and he saw the colour fade unevenly from Warrender's heavy face.

He went over the ground again up to the time of Richard's final return to the house.

"As you will see," he said, "there are blank passages. We don't know what passed between Mr. Dakers and Miss Bellamy in her room. We do know that, whatever it was, it seemed to distress him. We know he then went out and walked about Chelsea. We know he returned. We don't know why."

"I wanted," Richard said, "to pick up a copy of my play."

"Good. Why didn't you say so before?"

"I clean forgot," he said and looked astonished.

"Do you now remember what else you did?"

"I went up to my old study to get it."

"And did you do anything else while you were there?"

There was no answer. Alleyn said, "You wrote a letter, didn't you?"

Richard stared at him with a sort of horror. "How do you—why should you . . . ?" He made a small desperate gesture and petered out.

"To whom?"

"It was private. I prefer not to say."

"Where is it now? You've had no opportunity to post it."

"I—haven't got it."

"What have you done with it?"

"I got rid of it." Richard raised his voice. "I hope it's destroyed. It had nothing whatever to do with all this. I've told you it was private."

"If that's true I can promise you it will remain so. Will you tell me —in private—what it was about?"

Richard looked at him, hesitated, and then said, "I'm sorry. I can't."

Alleyn drew a folded paper from his pocket. "Will you read this, if you please? Perhaps you would rather take it to the light."

"I can . . . All right," Richard said. He took the paper, left the table and moved over to a wall lamp. The paper rustled as he opened it. He glanced at it, crushed it in his hand, strode to the far end of the table and flung it down in front of Warrender.

"Did you *have* to do this?" he said. "My God, what sort of a man are you!" He went back to his place beside Anelida.

Warrender, opening and closing his hands, sheet-white and speaking in an unrecognizable voice, said, "I don't understand. I've done nothing. What do you mean?"

His hand moved shakily towards the inside pocket of his coat. "No! It's not . . . It can't be."

"Colonel Warrender," Alleyn said to Richard, "has not shown me the letter. I came by its content in an entirely different way. The thing I have shown you is a transcription. The original, I imagine, is still in his pocket."

Warrender and Richard wouldn't look at each other. Warrender said, "Then how the hell . . ." and stopped.

"Evidently," Alleyn said, "the transcription is near enough to the original. I don't propose at the moment to make it generally known. I will only put it to you that when you, Mr. Dakers, returned the second time, you went to your study, wrote the original of this letter and subsequently, when you were lying on the sofa in the drawing-room, passed it to Colonel Warrender, saying, for my benefit, that you had forgotten to post it for him. Do you agree?"

"Yes."

"I suggest that it refers to whatever passed between you and Mrs. Templeton when you were alone with her in her room a few minutes before she died and that you wished to make Colonel Warrender read it. I'm still ready to listen to any statement you may care to make to me in private."

To Anelida the silence seemed interminable.

"Very well," Alleyn said. "We shall have to leave it for the time being."

None of them looked at Richard. Anelida suddenly and horribly remembered something she had once heard Alleyn tell her uncle. "You always know, in a capital charge, if the jury are going to bring in a verdict of guilty: they never look at the accused when they come back."

With a sense of doing something momentous she turned, looked Richard full in the face and found she could smile at him.

"It'll be all right," he said gently.

"All right!" Florence said bitterly. "It doesn't strike me as being all right, and I wonder you've the nerve to say so!"

As if Florence had put a match to her, Old Ninn exploded into fury. "You're a bad girl, Floy," she said, trembling very much and leaning across the table. "Riddled through and through with wickedness and jealousy and always have been."

"Thank you very much, I'm sure, Mrs. Plumtree," Florence countered with a shrill outbreak of laughter. "Everyone knows where your favour lies, Mrs. Plumtree, especially when you've had a drop of port wine. You wouldn't stop short of murder to back it up."

"Ninn," Richard said, before she could speak, "for the love of Mike, darling, shut up."

She reached out her small knotted hands to Charles Templeton. "You speak for him, sir. Speak for him."

Charles said gently, "You're making too much of this, Ninn. There's no need."

"There shouldn't be the need!" she cried. "And *she* knows it as well as I do." She appealed to Alleyn. "I've told you. *I've told you.* After Mr. Richard came out I heard her. That wicked woman, there, knows as well as I do." She pointed a gnarled finger at the spray-gun. "We heard her using that thing after everyone had warned her against it."

"How do you know it was the spray-gun, Ninn?"

"What else could it have been?"

Alleyn said, "It might have been her scent, you know."

"If it was! If it was, that makes no difference."

"I'm afraid it would," Alleyn said. "If the scent-spray had been filled up with Slaypest."

CHAPTER SEVEN **Re-entry of Mr. Marchant**

The scent-spray, the bottle and the Slaypest tin had assumed star-quality. There they stood in a neat row, three inarticulate objects, thrust into the spotlight. They might have been so many stagehands, yanked out of their anonymity and required to give an account of themselves before an unresponsive audience. They met with a frozen reception.

Timon Gantry was the first to speak. "Have you," he asked, "any argument to support your extraordinary assumption?"

"I have," Alleyn rejoined, "but I don't propose to advance it in detail. You might call it a *reductio ad absurdum*. Nothing else fits. One hopes," he added, "that a chemical analysis of the scent-spray will do something to support it. The supposition is based on a notion that while Mrs. Templeton had very little reason, after what seems to have been a stormy interview, to deluge her plants and herself with insecticide, she may more reasonably be pictured as taking up her scent-spray, and using that."

"Not full on her face," Bertie said unexpectedly. "She'd never use it on her face. Not directly. Not after she was made-up. Would she, Pinky? Pinky—would she?"

But Pinky was not listening to him. She was watching Alleyn.

"Well, anyway," Bertie said crossly. "She wouldn't."

"Oh yes she would, Mr. Saracen," Florence said tartly. "And did. Quite regular. Standing far enough off to get the fine spray only, which was what she done, as the Colonel and Mr. Templeton will bear me out, this afternoon."

"The point," Alleyn said, "is well taken, but it doesn't, I think, affect the argument. Shall we leave it for the time being? I'm following, by the way, a very unorthodox line over this inquiry and I see no reason for not telling you why. Severally, I believe you will all go on withholding information that may be crucial. Together I have hopes that you may find these tactics impracticable." And while they still gaped at him he added, "I may be wrong about this, of course, but it does seem to me that each of you, with one exception, is most mistakenly concealing something. I say mistakenly because I don't for a moment believe that there has been any collusion in this business. I believe that one of you, under pressure of an extraordinary emotional upheaval, has acted in a solitary and an extraordinary way. It's my duty to find out who this person is. So let's press on, shall we?" He looked at Charles. "There's a dictionary of poisons in Mr. Dakers's former study. I believe it belongs to you, sir."

Charles lifted a hand, saw that it trembled, and lowered it again. "Yes," he said. "I bought it a week ago. I wanted to look up plant sprays."

"Oh my goodness me!" Bertie ejaculated and stared at him. There was a general shocked silence.

"This specific spray?" Alleyn asked, pointing to the Slaypest.

"Yes. It gives the formula. I wanted to look it up."

"For God's sake, Charles," Warrender exclaimed, "why the devil can't you make yourself understood?" Charles said nothing and he waved his hands at Alleyn. "He was worried about the damned muck!" he said. "Told Mary. Showed it . . ."

"Yes?" Alleyn said as he came to a halt. "Showed it to whom?"

"To me, blast it! We'd been trying to persuade her not to use the stuff. Gave it to me to read."

"Did you read it?"

"'Course I did. Lot of scientific mumbo-jumbo but it showed how dangerous it was."

"What did you do with the book?"

"Do with it? I dunno. Yes, I do, though. I gave it to Florence. Asked her to get Mary to look at it. Didn't I, Florence?"

"I don't," said Florence, "remember anything about it, sir. You might have."

"Please try to remember," Alleyn said. "Did you, in fact, show the book to Mrs. Templeton?"

"Not me. She wouldn't have given me any thanks." She turned round in her chair and looked at Old Ninn. "I remember now. I showed it to Mrs. Plumtree. Gave it to her."

"Well, Ninn? What did you do with the book?"

Old Ninn glared at him. "Put it by," she said. "It was unwholesome."

"Where?"

"I don't recollect."

"In the upstairs study?"

"Might have been. I don't recollect."

"So much for the book," Alleyn said wryly and turned to Warrender. "You, sir, tell us that you actually used the scent-spray, lavishly, on Mrs. Templeton before the party. There were no ill-effects. What did you do after that?"

"Do? Nothing. I went out."

"Leaving Mr. and Mrs. Templeton alone together?"

"Yes. At least . . ." His eyes slewed round to look at her. "There was Florence."

"No, there wasn't. If you'll pardon my mentioning it, sir," Florence again intervened. "I left, just after you did, not being required any further."

"Do you agree?" Alleyn asked Charles Templeton. He drew his hand across his eyes.

"I? Oh yes. I think so."

"Do you mind telling me what happened then? Between you and your wife?"

"We talked for a moment or two. Not long."

"About?"

"I asked her not to use the scent. I'm afraid I was in a temper about it."

He glanced at Pinky. "I'm sorry, Pinky, I just—didn't like it. I expect my taste is hopelessly old-fashioned."

"That's all right, Charles. My God," Pinky added in a low voice, "I never want to smell it again, myself, as long as I live."

"Did Mrs. Templeton agree not to use it again?"

"No," he said at once. "She didn't. She thought me unreasonable."

"Did you talk about anything else?"

"About nothing that I care to recall."

"Is that final?"

"Final," Charles said.

"Did it concern, in some way, Mr. Dakers and Colonel Warrender?"

"Damn it!" Warrender shouted. "He's said he's not going to tell you, isn't it!"

"It did not concern them," Charles said.

"Where did you go when this conversation ended?"

"I went downstairs to my study. Richard came in at about that time and was telephoning. We stayed there until the first guests arrived."

"And you, Colonel Warrender? Where were you at this time? What did you do when you left the bedroom?"

"Ah—I was in the drawing-room. She—ah—Mary—came in. She wanted a re-arrangement of the tables. Gracefield and the other fella did it and she and I had a drink."

"Did she seem quite herself, did you think?"

"Rather nervy. Bit on edge."

"Why?"

"Been a trying day, isn't it?"

"Anything in particular?"

He glanced at Richard. "No," he said. "Nothing else."

Fox returned. "Mr. Marchant will be here in about a quarter of an hour, sir," he said.

There were signs of consternation from Pinky, Bertie and Timon Gantry.

"Right," Alleyn got up, walked to the far end of the table and picked up the crumpled paper that still lay where Richard had thrown it down. "I must ask Colonel Warrender and Mr. Dakers to give me a word or two in private. Perhaps we may use the study."

They both rose with the same abrupt movement and followed him from the room, stiffly erect.

He ushered them into the study and turned to Fox who had come into the hall.

"I'd better take this one solus, I think, Fox. Will you get the exhibits sent at once for analysis. Say it's first priority and we're looking for a trace of Slaypest in the scent-spray. They needn't expect to find more than a trace, I fancy. I want the result as soon as possible. Then go back to the party in there. See you later."

In Charles Templeton's study, incongruously friendly and comfortable, Warrender and Richard Dakers faced Alleyn, still not looking at each other.

Alleyn said, "I've asked you in here, without witnesses, to confirm or deny the conclusion I have drawn from the case-history, as far as it goes. Which is not by any means all the way. If I'm wrong, one or both of you can have a shot at knocking me down or hitting me across the face or performing any other of the conventional gestures. But I don't advise you to try."

They stared at him apparently in horrified astonishment.

"Well," he said, "here goes. My idea, such as it is, is based on this business of the letter, which, since you seem to accept my pot shot at it, runs like this."

He smoothed out the crumpled sheet of paper. "It's pieced together, by the way," he said, "from the impression left on the blotting-paper." He looked at Richard. "The original was written, I believe, by you to Mrs. Templeton when you returned, finally, to the house. I'm going to read this transcription aloud. If it's wrong anywhere, I hope you'll correct me."

Warrender said, "There's no need."

"Perhaps not. Would you prefer to show me the original?"

With an air of diffidence that sat very ill on him, Warrender appealed to Richard. "Whatever you say," he muttered.

Richard said, "Very well! Go on. Go on. Show him."

Warrender put his hand inside his coat and drew out an envelope. He dropped it on Charles Templeton's desk, crossed to the fireplace and stood there with his back turned to them.

Alleyn picked up the envelope. The word "Mary" was written on it in green ink. He took out the enclosure and laid his transcription beside it on the desk. As he read it through to himself the room seemed monstrously quiet. The fire settled in the grate. A car or two drove past and the clock in the hall told the half-hour.

"*I've come back,*" Alleyn read, "*to say that it would be no use my pretending I haven't been given a terrible shock and that I can't get it sorted out, but I'm sure it will be better if we don't meet. I can't think clearly now, but at least I know I'll never forgive your treatment of Anelida this afternoon. I should have been told everything from the beginning. R.*"

He folded the two papers and put them aside. "So they do correspond," he said. "And the handwriting is Mr. Dakers's."

Neither Richard nor Warrender moved or spoke.

"I think," Alleyn said, "that when you came back for the last time, you went up to your study and wrote this letter with the intention of putting it under her door. When you were about to do so you heard voices in the room, since two of my men were working there. So you came downstairs and were prevented from going out by the constable on duty. It was then that you came into the room where I was interviewing the others. The letter was in your breast pocket. You wanted to get rid of it and you wanted Colonel Warrender to know what was in it. So you passed it to him when you were lying on the sofa in the drawing-room. Do you agree?"

Richard nodded and turned away.

"This evening," Alleyn went on, "after Mr. Dakers left the Pegasus Bookshop, you, Colonel Warrender, also paid a call on Octavius Browne. Dusk had fallen but you were standing in the window when Octavius came in and seeing you against it he mistook you for his earlier visitor, who he thought must have returned. He was unable to say why he made this mistake, but I think I can account for it. Your heads are very much the same shape. The relative angles and distances from hairline to the top of the nose, from there to the tip and from the tip to the chin are almost identical. Seen in silhouette with the other features obliterated, your profiles must be strikingly alike. In full-face the resemblance disappears. Colonel Warrender has far greater width and a heavier jawline."

They were facing him now. He looked from one to the other.

"In these respects," he said, "Mr. Dakers, I think, takes after his mother."

2

"Well," Alleyn said at last, after a long silence, "I'm glad, at least, that it seems I am not going to be knocked down."

Warrender said, "I've nothing to say. Unless it's to point out that, as things have come about, I've had no opportunity to speak to"—he lifted his head—"to my son."

Richard said, "I don't want to discuss it. I should have been told from the beginning."

"Whereas," Alleyn said, "you were told, weren't you, by your mother this afternoon. You went upstairs with her when you returned from the Pegasus and she told you then."

"*Why!*" Warrender cried out. "Why, why, *why?*"

"She was angry," Richard said. "With me." He looked at Alleyn.

"You've heard or guessed most of it, apparently. She thought I'd conspired against her."

"Yes?"

"Well—that's all. That's how it was."

Alleyn waited. Richard drove his hands through his hair. "All right!" he cried out. "All right! I'll tell you. I suppose I've got to, haven't I? She accused me of ingratitude and disloyalty. I said I considered I owed her no more than I had already paid. I wouldn't have said that if she hadn't insulted Anelida. Then she came quite close to me and—it was horrible—I could see a nerve jumping under her cheek. She kept repeating that I owed her everything—everything, and that I'd insulted her by going behind her back. Then I said she'd no right to assume a controlling interest in either my friendships or my work. She said she had every right. And then it all came out. Everything. It happened because of our anger. We were both very angry. When she'd told me, she laughed as if she'd scored with the line of climax in a big scene. If she hadn't done that I might have felt some kind of compassion or remorse or something. I didn't. I felt cheated and sick and empty. I went downstairs and out into the streets and walked about trying to find an appropriate emotion. There was nothing but a sort of faint disgust." He moved away and then turned to Alleyn. "But I didn't murder my"—he caught his breath—"my brand-new mother. I'm not, it appears, that kind of bastard."

Warrender said, "For God's sake, Dicky!"

"Just for the record," Richard said, "*were* there two people called Dakers? A young married couple, killed in a car on the Riviera? Australians, I've always been given to understand."

"It's—it's a family name. My mother was a Dakers."

"I see," Richard said. "I just wondered. It didn't occur to you to marry her, evidently." He stopped short and a look of horror crossed his face. "I'm sorry! I'm sorry!" he cried out. "Forgive me, Maurice, it wasn't I who said that."

"My dear chap, of course I wanted to marry her. She wouldn't have it! She was at the beginning of her career. What could I give her? A serving ensign on a very limited allowance. She—naturally—she wasn't prepared to throw up her career and follow the drum."

"And—Charles?"

"He was in a different position. Altogether."

"Rich? Able to keep her in the style to which she would like to become accustomed?"

"There's no need," Warrender muttered, "to put it like that."

"Poor Charles!" Richard said and then suddenly, "Did he know?"

Warrender turned a painful crimson. "No," he said. "It was—it was all over by then."

"Did he believe in the Dakers story?"

"I think," Warrender said after a pause, "he believed everything Mary told him."

"Poor Charles!" Richard repeated, and then turned on Alleyn. "He's not going to be told? Not now! It'd kill him. There's no need—is there?"

"None," Alleyn said, "that I can see."

"And you!" Richard demanded of Warrender.

"Oh for God's sake, Dicky!"

"No. Naturally. Not you."

There was a long silence.

"I remember," Richard said at last, "that she once told me it was you who brought them together. What ambivalent roles you both contrived to play. Restoration comedy at its most elaborate."

Evidently they had forgotten Alleyn. For the first time they looked fully at each other.

"Funny," Richard said. "I have wondered if Charles was my father. Some pre-marital indiscretion, I thought it might have been. I fancied I saw a likeness—the family one, of course. You and Charles are rather alike, aren't you? I must say I never quite believed in the Dakers. But why did it never occur to me that she was my mother? It really was very clever of her to put herself so magnificently out of bounds."

"I don't know," Warrender exclaimed, "what to say to you. There's nothing I can say."

"Never mind."

"It need make no difference. To your work. Or to your marrying."

"I really don't know how Anelida will feel about it. Unless . . ." He turned, as if suddenly aware of him, to Alleyn. "Unless, of course, Mr. Alleyn is going to arrest me for matricide, which will settle everything very neatly, won't it?"

"I shouldn't," Alleyn said, "depend upon it. Suppose you set about clearing yourself if you can. Can you?"

"How the hell do I know? What am I supposed to have done?"

"It's more a matter of finding out what you couldn't have done. Where did you lunch? Here?"

"No. At the Garrick. It was a business luncheon."

"And after that?"

"I went to my flat and did some work. I'd got a typist in."

"Until when?"

"Just before six. I was waiting for a long-distance call from Edinburgh. I kept looking at the time because I was running late. I was meant to be here at six to organize the drinks. At last I fixed it up for the call to be transferred to this number. As it was I ran late and Mary—and she was coming downstairs. The call came through at a quarter to seven just as I arrived."

"Where did you take it?"

"Here in the study. Charles was there. He looked ill and I was worried about him. He didn't seem to want to talk. I kept getting cut off. It was important, and I had to wait. She—wasn't very pleased about that. The first people were arriving when I'd finished."

"So what did you do?"

"Went into the drawing-room with Charles and did my stuff."

"Had you brought her some Parma violets?"

"I? No. She hated violets."

"Did you see them in her room?"

"I didn't go up to her room. I've told you—I was here in the study."

"When had you last been in her room?"

"This morning."

"Did you visit it between then and the final time when you returned from the Pegasus and this disturbing scene took place?"

"I've told you. How could I? I . . ." His voice changed. "I was with Anelida until she left and I followed her into the Pegasus."

"Well," Alleyn said after a pause, "if all this is provable, and I don't see why it shouldn't be, you're in the clear."

Warrender gave a sharp outcry and turned quickly, but Richard said flatly, "I don't understand."

"If our reading of the facts is the true one, this crime was to all intents and purposes committed between the time (somewhere about six o'clock) when Mrs. Templeton was sprayed with scent by Colonel Warrender and the time fixed by a press photographer at twenty-five minutes to eight, when she returned to her room with you. She never left her room and died in it a few minutes after you had gone."

Richard flinched at the last phrase but seemed to have paid little attention to the earlier part. For the first time, he was looking at his father, who had turned his back to them.

"Colonel Warrender," Alleyn said, "why did you go to the Pegasus?"

Without moving he said, "Does it matter? I wanted to get things straight. With the gel."

"But you didn't see her?"

"No."

"Maurice," Richard said abruptly.

Colonel Warrender faced him.

"I call you that still," Richard went on. "I suppose it's not becoming, but I can't manage anything else. There are all sorts of adjustments to be arranged, aren't there? I know I'm not making this easy for either of us. You see one doesn't know how one's meant to behave. But I hope in time to do better: you'll have to give me time."

"I'll do that," Warrender said unevenly.

He made a slight movement as if to hold out his hand, glanced at Alleyn and withdrew it.

"I think," Alleyn said, "that I should get on with my job. I'll let you know when we need you."

And he went out, leaving them helplessly together.

In the hall he encountered Fox.

"Peculiar party in there," he said. "Boy meets father. Both heavily embarrassed. They manage these things better in France. What goes on at your end of the table?"

"I came out to tell you, sir. Mr. Templeton's come over very poorly again, and Dr. Harkness thinks he's had about as much as he can take. He's lying down in the drawing-room, but as soon as he can manage it the doctor wants to get him into bed. The idea is to make one up in his study and save the stairs. I thought the best thing would be to let those two—Florence and Mrs. Plumtree—fix it up. The doctor'll help him when the time comes."

"Yes. All right. What a hell of a party this is, by and large. All right. But they'll have to bung the mixed-up playwright and his custom-built poppa out of it. Where? Into mama-deceased's boudoir, I suppose. Or they can rejoin that goon-show round the dining-room table. I don't know. Nobody tells me a thing. What else?"

"None of them will own up to knowing anything about the Parma violets. They all say she had no time for violets."

"Blast and stink! Then who the devil put them on her dressing-table? The caterer in a fit of frustrated passion? Why the devil should we be stuck with a bunch of Parma violets wilting on our plates."

Like Scheherazade, Fox discreetly fell silent.

"Pardon me, sir, but did I hear you mention violets?"

It was Gracefield, wan in the countenance, who had emerged from the far end of the hall.

"You did indeed," Alleyn said warmly.

"If it is of any assistance, sir, a bunch of violets was brought in immediately prior to the reception. I admitted the gentleman myself, sir, and he subsequently presented them to madam on the first floor landing."

"You took his name, I hope, Gracefield?"

"Quite so, sir. It was the elderly gentleman from the bookshop. The name is Octavius Browne."

3

"And what the merry hell," Alleyn ejaculated when Gracefield had withdrawn, "did Octavius think he was up to, prancing about with violets at that hour of the day? Damnation, I'll have to find out, and Marchant's due any minute. Come on."

They went out at the front door. Light still glowed behind the curtains at the Pegasus.

"You hold the fort here, Fox, for five minutes. Let them get Templeton settled down in the study, and if Marchant turns up, keep him till I'm back. Don't put him in with that horde of extroverts in the dining-room. Save him up. What a go!"

He rang the bell and Octavius opened the door.

"You again!" he said. "How late! I thought you were Anelida."

"Well, I'm not and I'm sorry it's late, but you'll have to let me in."

"Very well," Octavius said, standing aside. "What's up, now?"

"Why," Alleyn asked, as soon as the door was shut, "did you take violets to Mrs. Templeton?"

Octavius blushed. "A man with a handcart," he said, "went past the window. They came from the Channel Islands."

"I don't give a damn where they came from. It's where they went to that matters. When did the cart go past?"

Octavius, disconcerted and rather huffy, was bustled into telling his story. Anelida had sent him downstairs while she got ready for the party. He was fretful because they'd been asked for half-past six and it was now twenty-five to seven and he didn't believe her story of the need to arrive late. He saw the handcart with the Parma violets and remembered that in his youth these flowers had been considered appropriate adjuncts to ladies of the theatre. So he went out and bought some. He then, Alleyn gathered, felt shy about presenting them in front of Anelida. The door of Miss Bellamy's house was open. The butler was discernible in the hall. Octavius mounted the steps. "After all," he said, "one preferred to give her the opportunity of attaching them in advance if she choose to do so."

He was in the act of handing them over to Gracefield when he heard a commotion on the first landing and a moment later Miss Bellamy shouted out at the top of her voice, "Which only shows how wrong you were. You can get out whenever you like, my friend, and the sooner the better."

For a moment Octavius was extremely flustered, imagining that he himself was thus addressed, but the next second she appeared above him on the stairs. She stopped short and gazed down at him in astonishment.

"A vision," Octavius said. "Rose-coloured or more accurately, geranium, but with the air, I must confess, of a Fury."

This impression, however, was almost at once dissipated. Miss Bellamy seemed to hesitate, Gracefield murmured an explanation which Octavius himself elaborated. "And then, you know," he said, "suddenly she was all graciousness. Overwhelmingly so. She"—he blushed again—"asked me to come up and I went. I presented my little votive offering. And then, in point of fact, she invited me into her room: a pleasing and Gallic informality. I was not unmoved by it. She laid the flowers on her dressing-table and told me she had just given an old bore the sack. Those were her words. I gathered that it was somebody who had been in her service for a long period. What did you say?"

"Nothing. Go on. You interest me strangely."

"Do I? Well. At that juncture there were sounds of voices downstairs —the door, naturally, remained open—and she said, 'Wait a moment, will you?' And left me."

"Well?" Alleyn said after a pause.

"Well, I did wait. Nothing happened. I bethought me of Nelly, who would surely be ready by now. Rightly or wrongly," Octavius said, with a sidelong look at Alleyn, "I felt that Nelly would be not entirely in sympathy with my impulsive little *sortie* and I was therefore concerned to return before I could be missed. So I went downstairs and there *she* was, speaking to Colonel Warrender in the drawing-room. They paid no attention to me. I don't think they saw me. Warrender, I thought, looked very much put out. There seemed nothing to do but go away. So I went. A curious and not unintriguing experience."

"Thank you, Octavius," Alleyn said, staring thoughtfully at him. "Thank you very much. And now I, too, must leave you. Good-night."

As he went out he heard Octavius saying rather fretfully that he supposed he might as well go to bed.

A very grand car had drawn up outside Miss Bellamy's house and Mr. Montague Marchant was climbing out of it. His blond head gleamed, his overcoat was impeccable and his face exceedingly pale.

"Wait," he said to his chauffeur.

Alleyn introduced himself. The anticipated remark was punctually delivered.

"This is a terrible business," said Mr. Marchant.

"Very bad," Alleyn said. "Shall we go in?"

Fox was in the hall.

"I just don't quite understand," Marchant said, "why I've been sent for. Naturally, we—her management—want to give every assistance but at the same time . . ." He waved his pearly gloves.

Alleyn said, "It's very simple. There are one or two purely business matters to be settled and it looks as if you are our sole authority."

"I should have thought . . ."

"Of course you would," Alleyn rejoined. "But there is some need for immediate action. Miss Bellamy has been murdered."

Marchant unsteadily passed his hand over the back of his head. "I don't believe you," he said.

"You may as well, because it happens to be true. Would you like to take your coat off? No? Then, shall we go in?"

Fox said, "We've moved into the drawing-room, sir, it being more comfortable. The doctor is with Mr. Templeton but will be coming in later."

"Where's Florence?"

"She helped Mrs. Plumtree with the bed-making and they're both waiting in the boudoir in case required."

"Right. In here, if you will, Mr. Marchant. I'll just have a look at the patient and then I'll join you."

He opened the door. After a moment's hesitation, Marchant went through and Fox followed him.

Alleyn went to the study, tapped on the door and went in.

Charles was in bed, looking very drawn and anxious. Dr. Harkness sat in a chair at a little distance, watching him. When he saw Alleyn he said, "We can't have any further upsets."

"I know," Alleyn rejoined and walked over to the bed. "I've only come in to inquire," he said.

Charles whispered, "I'm sorry about this. I'm all right. I could have carried on."

"There's no need. We can manage."

"There you are, Charles," Harkness said. "Stop fussing."

"But I want to know, Harkness! How can I stop fussing! My God, what a thing to say! I want to know what they're thinking and saying. I've a right to know. Alleyn, for God's sake tell me. You don't suspect—anyone close to her, do you? I can stand anything but that. Not—not the boy?"

"As things stand," Alleyn said, "there's no case against him."

"Ah!" Charles sighed and closed his eyes. "Thank God for that." He moved restlessly and his breath came short. "It's all these allusions and hints and evasions . . ." he began excitedly. "Why can't I be told things! Why not? Do you suspect *me!* Do you? Then for Christ's sake let's have it and be done with it."

Harkness came over to the bed. "This won't do at all," he said and to Alleyn, "Out."

"Yes, of course," Alleyn said and went out. He heard Charles panting, "But I *want* to talk to him," and Harkness trying to reassure him.

When Marchant went into the drawing-room Timon Gantry, Colonel Warrender, Pinky Cavendish and Bertie Saracen were sitting disconsolately in armchairs before a freshly tended fire. Richard and Anelida were together at some remove from the others and P. C. Philpott attended discreetly in the background. When Marchant came in, Pinky and Bertie made a little dash at him and Richard stood up. Marchant kissed Pinky with ritual solemnity, squeezed Bertie's arm, nodded at Gantry, and advanced upon Richard with soft extended hand.

"Dear boy!" he said. "What can one say! Oh my *dear* Dicky!"

Richard appeared to permit, rather than return, a long pressure of his hand. Marchant added a manly grip of his shoulder and moved on to acknowledge, more briefly, Anelida and Colonel Warrender. His prestige was unmistakable. He said any number of highly appropriate things. They listened to him dolefully and appeared to be relieved when at last Alleyn came in.

Alleyn said, "Before going any further, Mr. Marchant, I think I should make it quite clear that any questions I may put to you will be raised with the sole object of clearing innocent persons of suspicion and of helping towards the solution of an undoubted case of homicide. Mary Bellamy has been murdered; I believe by someone who is now in this house. You will understand that matters of personal consideration or professional reticence can't be allowed to obstruct an investigation of this sort. Any attempt to withhold information may have disastrous results. On the other hand information that turns out to be irrelevant, as yours, of course, may, will be entirely wiped out. Is that understood?"

Gantry said, "In my opinion, Monty, we should take legal advice." Marchant looked thoughtfully at him.

"You are at liberty to do so," Alleyn said. "You are also at liberty to refuse to answer to any or all questions until the arrival of your solicitor. Suppose you hear the questions and then decide."

Marchant examined his hands, lifted his gaze to Alleyn's face and said, "What are they?"

There was a restless movement among the others.

"First. What exactly was Mrs. Templeton's, or perhaps in this connection I should say Miss Bellamy's, position in the firm of Marchant & Company?"

Marchant raised his eyebrows. "A leading and distinguished artist who played exclusively for our management."

"Any business connection other than that?"

"Certainly," he said at once. "She had a controlling interest."

"*Monty!*" Bertie cried out.

"Dear boy, an examination of our shareholders list would give it."

"Has she held this position for some time?"

"Since 1956. Before that it was vested in her husband, but he transferred his holdings to her in that year."

"I had no idea he had financial interests in the theatre world."

"These were his only ones, I believe. After the war we were in considerable difficulties. Like many other managements we were threatened with a complete collapse. You may say that he saved us."

"In taking this action was he influenced by his wife's connection with the Management?"

"She brought the thing to his notice, but fundamentally I should say he believed in the prospect of our recovery and expansion. In the event he proved to be fully justified."

"Why did he transfer his share to her, do you know?"

"I don't know, but I can conjecture. His health is precarious. He's— he was—a devoted husband. He may have been thinking of death duties."

"Yes, I see."

Marchant said, "It's so warm in here," and unbuttoned his overcoat. Fox helped him out of it. He sat down, very elegantly and crossed his legs. The others watched him anxiously.

The door opened and Dr. Harkness came in. He nodded at Alleyn and said, "Better, but he's had as much as he can take."

"Anyone with him?"

"The old nurse. He'll settle down now. No more visits, mind."

"Right."

Dr. Harkness sat heavily on the sofa and Alleyn turned again to Marchant.

"Holding, as you say, a controlling interest," he said, "she must have been a power to reckon with, as far as other employees of the Management were concerned."

The lids drooped a little over Marchant's very pale eyes. "I really don't think I follow you," he said.

"She was, everyone agrees, a temperamental woman. For instance, this afternoon, we are told, she cut up very rough indeed. In the conservatory."

The heightened tension of his audience could scarcely have been more apparent if they'd all begun to twang like bowstrings, but none of them spoke.

"She would throw a temperament," Marchant said coolly, "if she felt the occasion for it."

"And she felt the occasion in this instance?"

"Quite so."

"Suppose, for the sake of argument, she had pressed for the severance of some long-standing connection with your management? Would she have carried her point?"

"I'm afraid I don't follow that either."

"I'll put it brutally. If she'd demanded that you sign no more contracts with, say, Mr. Gantry or Mr. Saracen or Miss Cavendish, would you have had to toe the line?"

"I would have talked softly and expected her to calm down."

"But if she'd stuck to it?" Alleyn waited for a moment and then took his risk. "Come," he said. "She did issue an ultimatum this afternoon."

Saracen scrambled to his feet. "There!" he shouted. "What did I tell you! Somebody's blown the beastly gaff and now we're to suffer for it. I *said* we should talk first, ourselves, and be frank and forthcoming and see how right I was!"

Gantry said, "For God's sake hold your tongue, Bertie."

"What do we get for holding our tongues?" He pointed to Warrender. "We get an outsider giving the whole thing away with both hands. I bet you, Timmy. I bet you anything you like."

"Utter balderdash!" Warrender exclaimed. "I don't know what you think you're talking about, Saracen."

"Oh pooh! You've told the Inspector or Commander or Great Panjandrum or whatever he is. You've *told* him."

"On the contrary," Gantry said, "you've told him yourself. You *fool*, Bertie."

Pinky Cavendish, in what seemed to be an agony of exasperation, cried out, "Oh *why*, for God's sake, can't we all admit we're no good at this sort of hedging! *I* can! Freely *and* without prejudice to the rest of you, if that's what you're all afraid of. And what's more, I'm going to. Look here, Mr. Alleyn, this is what happened to me in the conservatory. Mary accused me of conspiring against her and told Monty it was either her or me as far as the Management was concerned. Just that. And if it really came to the point I can assure you it'd be her and not me. You know, Monty, and we *all* know, that with her name and star-ranking, Mary was worth a damn sight more than me at the box-office *and* in the firm. All right! This very morning you'd handed me my first real opportunity with the Management. She was well able, if she felt like it, to cook my goose. But I'm no more capable of murdering her than I am of taking her place with her own particular public. And when you hear an actress admit that kind of thing," Pinky added, turning to Alleyn, "you can bet your bottom dollar she's talking turkey."

Alleyn said, "Produce this sort of integrity on the stage, Miss Cavendish, and nobody will be able to cook your goose for you." He looked round at Pinky's deeply perturbed audience. "Has anybody got anything to add to this?" he asked.

After a pause, Richard said, "Only that I'd like to endorse what Pinky said and to add that, as you and everybody else know, I was just as deeply involved as she. More so."

"Dicky darling!" Pinky said warmly. "No! Where you are now! Offer a comedy on the open market and watch the managements bay like ravenous wolves."

"Without Mary?" Marchant asked of nobody in particular.

"It's quite true," Richard said, "that I wrote specifically for Mary."

"Not always. And no reason," Gantry intervened, "why you shouldn't write now for somebody else." Once again he bestowed his most disarming smile on Anelida.

"Why not indeed!" Pinky cried warmly and laid her hand on Anelida's.

"Ah!" Richard said, putting his arm about her. "That's another story. Isn't it, darling?"

Wave after wave of unconsidered gratitude flowed through Anelida. "These are my people," she thought. "I'm in with them for the rest of my life."

"The fact remains, however," Gantry was saying to Alleyn, "that Bertie, Pinky and Richard all stood to lose by Mary's death. A point you might care to remember."

"Oh lawks!" Bertie said. "*Aren't* we all suddenly generous and noble-minded! Everybody loves everybody! Safety in numbers, or so they say. Or do they?"

"In this instance," Alleyn said, "they well might." He turned to Marchant. "Would you agree that, with the exception of her husband, yourself and Colonel Warrender, Miss Bellamy issued some kind of ultimatum against each member of the group in the conservatory?"

"Would I?" Marchant said easily. "Well, yes. I think I would."

"To the effect that it was either they or she and you could take your choice?"

"More or less," he murmured, looking at his fingernails.

Gantry rose to his enormous height and stood over Marchant.

"It would be becoming in you, Monty," he said dangerously, "if you acknowledged that as far as I enter into the picture the question of occupational anxiety does not arise. I choose my managements; they do not choose me."

Marchant glanced at him. "Nobody questions your prestige, I imagine, Timmy. I certainly don't."

"Or mine, I hope," said Bertie, rallying. "The offers I've turned down for the Management! Well, I mean to say! Face it, Monty dear, if Mary *had* bullied you into breaking off with Dicky and Timmy and Pinky and me, you'd have been in a very pretty pickle yourself."

"I am not," Marchant said, "a propitious subject for bullying."

"No," Bertie agreed. "Evidently." And there followed a deadly little pause. "I'd be obliged to everybody," he added rather breathlessly, "if they wouldn't set about reading horrors of any sort into what was an utterly unmeaningful little observation."

"In common," Warrender remarked, "with the rest of your conversation."

"Oh but what a catty big Colonel we've got!" Bertie said.

Marchant opened his cigarette case. "It seems," he observed, "incumbent on me to point out that, unlike the rest of you, I am ignorant of the circumstances. After Mary's death, I left this house at the request of" —he put a cigarette between his lips and turned his head slightly to look at Fox—"yes, at the request of this gentleman, who merely informed me that there had been a fatal accident. Throughout the entire time that Mary was absent until Florence made her announcement, I was in full view of about forty guests and those of you who had not left the drawing-room. I imagine I do *not* qualify for the star role." He lit his cigarette. "Or am I wrong?" he asked Alleyn.

"As it turns out, Monty," Gantry intervened, "you're dead wrong. It appears that the whole thing was laid on before Mary went to her room."

Marchant waited for a moment, and then said, "You astonish me."

"Fancy!" Bertie exclaimed and added in an exasperated voice, "I *do* wish, oh *how* I do wish, dearest Monty, that you would stop being a parody of your smooth little self and get down to tin-tacks (*why* tin-tacks, one wonders?) and admit that, like all the rest of us, you qualify for the homicide stakes."

"And what," Alleyn asked, "have you got to say to that, Mr. Marchant?"

An uneven flush mounted over Marchant's cheekbones. "Simply," he said, "that I think everybody has, most understandably, become overwrought by this tragedy and that, as a consequence, a great deal of nonsense is being bandied about on all hands. And, as an afterthought, that I agree with Timon Gantry. I prefer to take no further part in this discussion until I have consulted my solicitor."

"By all means," Alleyn said. "Will you ring him up? The telephone is over there in the corner."

Marchant leant a little further back in his chair. "I'm afraid that's quite out of the question," he said. "He lives in Buckinghamshire. I can't possibly call him up at this time of night."

"In that case you will give me your own address, if you please, and I shan't detain you any longer."

"My address is in the telephone book and I can assure you that you are not detaining me now nor are you likely to do so in the future." He half-closed his eyes. "I resent," he said, "the tone of this interview, but I prefer to keep observation—if that is the accepted police jargon—upon its sequel. I'll leave when it suits me to do so."

"You can't," Colonel Warrender suddenly announced in a parade-ground voice, "take that tone with the police, sir."

"Can't I?" Marchant murmured. "I promise you, my dear Colonel, I can take whatever tone I bloody well choose with whoever I bloody well like."

Into the dead silence that followed this announcement, there intruded a distant but reminiscent commotion. A door slammed and somebody came running up the hall.

"My *God*, what now!" Bertie Saracen cried out. With the exception of Marchant and Dr. Harkness they were all on their feet when Florence, grotesque in tin curling pins, burst into the room.

In an appalling parody of her fatal entrance she stood there, mouthing at them.

Alleyn strode over to her and took her by the wrist. "What is it?" he said. "Speak up."

And Florence, as if in moments of catastrophe she was in command of only one phrase, gabbled, "The doctor! Quick! For Christ's sake! Is the doctor in the house!"

CHAPTER EIGHT   # Pattern Completed

Charles Templeton lay face down, as if he had fallen forward, with his head toward the foot of the bed that had been made up for him in the study. One arm hung to the floor, the other was outstretched beyond the end of the bed. The back of his neck was empurpled under its margin of thin white hair. His pyjama jacket was dragged up, revealing an expanse of torso—old, white and flaccid. When Alleyn raised him and held him in a sitting position, his head lolled sideways, his mouth and eyes opened and a flutter of sound wavered in his throat. Dr. Harkness leant over him, pinching up the skin of his forearm to admit the needle. Fox hovered nearby. Florence, her knuckles clenched between her teeth, stood just inside the door. Charles seemed to be unaware of these four on-lookers; his gaze wandered past them, fixed itself in terror on the fifth; the short person who stood pressed back against the wall in shadow at the end of the room.

The sound in his throat was shaped with great difficulty into one word. "No!" it whispered. "No! No!"

Dr. Harkness withdrew the needle.

"What is it?" Alleyn said. "What do you want to tell us?"

The eyes did not blink or change their direction, but after a second or two they lost focus, glazed, and remained fixed. The jaw dropped, the body quivered and sank.

Dr. Harkness leant over it for some time and then drew back.

"Gone," he said.

Alleyn laid his burden down and covered it.

In a voice that they had not heard from him before, Dr. Harkness said, "He was all right ten minutes ago. Settled. Quiet. Something's gone wrong here and I've got to hear what it was." He turned on Florence. "Well?"

Florence, with an air that was half combative, half frightened, moved forward, keeping her eyes on Alleyn.

"Yes," Alleyn said, answering her look, "we must hear from you. You raised the alarm. What happened?"

"That's what I'd like to know!" she said at once. "I did the right thing, didn't I? I called the doctor. Now!"

"You'll do the right thing again, if you please, by telling me what happened before you called him."

She darted a glance at the small motionless figure in shadow at the end of the room and wetted her lips.

"Come on, now," Fox said. "Speak up."

Standing where she was, a serio-comic figure under her panoply of tin hair curlers, she did tell her story.

After Dr. Harkness had given his orders, she and—again that sidelong glance—she and Mrs. Plumtree had made up the bed in the study. Dr. Harkness had helped Mr. Templeton undress and had seen him into bed and they had all waited until he was settled down, comfortably. Dr. Harkness had left after giving orders that he was to be called if wanted. Florence had then gone to the pantry to fill a second hot-water bottle. This had taken some time as she had been obliged to boil a kettle. When she returned to the hall she had heard voices raised in the study. It seemed that she had paused outside the door. Alleyn had a picture of her, a hot-water bottle under her arm, listening avidly. She had heard Mrs.

Plumtree's voice but had been unable to distinguish any words. Then, she said, she had heard Mr. Templeton cry "No!" three times, just as he did before he died, only much louder; as if, Florence said, he was frightened. After that there had been a clatter and Mrs. Plumtree had suddenly become audible. She had shouted, Florence reported, at the top of her voice, "I'll put a stop to it," Mr. Templeton had given a loud cry and Florence had burst into the room.

"All right," Alleyn said. "And what did you find?"

A scene, it appeared, of melodrama. Mrs. Plumtree with the poker grasped and upraised, Mr. Templeton sprawled along the bed, facing her.

"And when they seen me," Florence said, "she dropped the poker in the hearth and he gasped 'Florrie, don't let 'er' and then he took a turn for the worse and I see he was very bad. So I said, 'Don't you touch 'im. Don't you dare,' and I fetched the doctor like you saw. And God's my witness," Florence concluded, "if she isn't the cause of his death! As good as if she'd struck him down, ill and all as he was, and which she'd of done if I hadn't come in when I did and which she'd do to me now if it wasn't for you gentlemen."

She stopped breathless. There was a considerable pause. "Well!" she demanded. "Don't you believe it? All right, then. Ask her. Go on. Ask her!"

"Everything in its turn," Alleyn said. "That will do from you for the moment. Stay where you are." He turned to the short motionless figure in the shadows. "Come along," he said. "You can't avoid it, you know. Come along."

She moved out into the light. Her small nose and the areas over her cheekbones were still patched with red, but otherwise her face was a dreadful colour. She said, automatically, it seemed, "You're a wicked girl, Floy."

"Never mind about that," Alleyn said. "Are *you* going to tell me what happened?"

She looked steadily up into his face. Her mouth was shut like a trap, but her eyes were terrified.

"Look here, Ninn," Dr. Harkness began very loudly. Alleyn raised a finger and he stopped short.

"Has Florence," Alleyn asked, "spoken the truth? I mean as to facts. As to what she saw and heard when she came back to this room?"

She nodded, very slightly.

"You had the poker in your hand. You dropped it when she came in. Mr. Templeton said, 'Florrie, don't let her.' That's true, isn't it?"

"Yes."

"And before she came in you had said, very loudly, to Mr. Templeton, 'I'll put a stop to it'? Did you say this?"

"Yes."

"What were you going to put a stop to?"

Silence.

"Was it something Mr. Templeton had said he would do?"

She shook her head.

For a lunatic second or two Alleyn was reminded of a panel game on television. He saw the Plumtree face in close-up; tight-lipped, inimical, giving nothing away, winning the round.

He looked at Fox. "Would you take Florence into the hall? You too, Dr. Harkness, if you will?"

"I'm not going," Florence said. "You can't make me."

"Oh yes, I can," Alleyn rejoined tranquilly, "but you'd be very foolish to put it to the test. Out you go, my girl."

Fox approached her. "You keep your hands off me!" she said.

"Now, now!" Fox rumbled cosily. He opened the door. For a moment she looked as if she would show fight and then, with a lift of her chin, she went out. Fox followed her.

Dr. Harkness said, "There are things to be done. I mean . . ." He gestured at the covered form on the bed.

"I know. I don't expect to be long. Wait for me in the hall, will you, Harkness?"

The door shut behind them.

For perhaps ten seconds Alleyn and that small, determined and miserable little woman looked at each other.

Then he said, "It's got to come out, you know. You've been trying to save him, haven't you?"

Her hands moved convulsively, and she looked in terror at the bed.

"No, no," Alleyn said. "Not there. I'm not talking about him. You didn't care about him. Your were trying to shield the boy, weren't you? You did what you did for Richard Dakers."

She broke into a passion of weeping and from then until the end of the case he had no more trouble with Ninn.

2

When it was over he sent her up to her room.

"Well," he said to Fox, "now for the final and far from delectable scene. We should, of course, have prevented all this, but I'm damned if I see how. We couldn't arrest on what we'd got. Unless they find some trace of Slaypest in the scent-spray my reading of the case will never be anything but an unsupported theory."

"They ought to be coming through with the result before long."

"You might ring up and see where they've got to."

Fox dialled a number. There was a tap at the door and Philpott looked in. He stared at the covered body on the bed.

"Yes," Alleyn said. "A death. Mr. Templeton."

"By violence, sir?"

"Not by physical violence. Heart disease. What is it, Philpott?"

"It's that lot in there, sir. They're getting very restive, especially Mr. Dakers and the Colonel. Wondering what was wrong with"—he looked again at the bed—"with him, sir."

"Yes. Will you ask Mr. Dakers and Colonel Warrender to go into the small sitting-room next door. I'll be there in a moment. Oh, and Philpott, I think you might ask Miss Lee to come too. And you may tell the others they will have very little longer to wait."

"Sir," said Philpott and withdrew.

Fox was talking into the telephone. "Yes. Yes. I'll tell him. He'll be very much obliged. Thank you."

He hung up. "They were just going to ring. They've found an identifiable trace inside the bulb of the scent-spray."

"Have they indeed? That provides the complete answer."

"So you were right, Mr. Alleyn."

"And what satisfaction," Alleyn said wryly, "is to be had out of that?"

He went to the bed and turned back the sheet. The eyes, unseeing, still stared past him. The imprint of a fear, already nonexistent, still disfigured the face. Alleyn looked down at it for a second or two. "What unhappiness!" he said and closed the eyes.

"He had a lot to try him," Fox observed with his customary simplicity.

"He had indeed, poor chap."

"So did they all, if it comes to that. She must have been a very vexing sort of lady. There'll have to be a p.m., Mr. Alleyn."

"Yes, of course. All right. I'll see these people next door."

He re-covered the face and went out.

Dr. Harkness and Florence were in the hall, watched over by a Yard reinforcement. Alleyn said, "I think you'd better come in with me, if you will, Harkness." And to Florence, "You'll stay where you are for the moment, if you please."

Harkness followed him into the boudoir.

It had been created by Bertie Saracen in an opulent mood and contrasted strangely with the exquisite austerity of the study. "Almost indecently *you*, darling!" Bertie had told Miss Bellamy and, almost indecently, it was so.

Its present occupants—Richard, Anelida and Warrender—were standing awkwardly in the middle of this room, overlooked by an enormous and immensely vivacious portrait in pastel of Mary Bellamy. Charles, photographed some twenty years ago, gazed mildly from the centre of an occasional table. To Alleyn there was something atrociously ironic in this circumstance.

Richard demanded at once: "What is it? What happened? Is Charles . . . ?"

"Yes," Alleyn said. "It's bad news. He collapsed a few minutes ago."

"But . . . ? You don't mean . . . ?"

"I'm afraid so."

Richard said, "Anelida! It's Charles. He means Charles has died. Doesn't he?"

"Why," she said fiercely, "must these things happen to you. *Why!*"

Dr. Harkness went up to him. "Sorry, old boy," he said, "I tried but it was no good. It might have happened any time during the last five years, you know."

Richard stared blankly at him. "My God!" he cried out. "You can't talk like that!"

"Steady, old chap. You'll realize, when you think it over. Any time."

"I don't believe you. It's because of everything else. It's because of Mary and . . ." Richard turned on Alleyn. "You'd no right to subject him to all this. It's killed him. You'd no right. If it hadn't been for you it needn't have happened."

Alleyn said very compassionately, "That may be true. He was in great distress. It may even be that for him this was the best solution."

"How dare you say that!" Richard exclaimed and then, "What do you mean?"

"Don't you think he'd pretty well got to the end of his tether? He'd lost the thing he most valued in life, hadn't he?"

"I—I want to see him."

Alleyn remembered Charles's face. "Then you shall," he promised, "presently."

"Yes," Harkness agreed quickly. "Presently."

"For the moment," Alleyn said, turning to Anelida, "I suggest that you take him up to his old room and give him a drink. Will you do that?"

"Yes," Anelida said. "That's the thing." She put her hand in Richard's. "Coming?"

He looked down at her. "I wonder," he said, "what on earth I should do without you, Anelida."

"Come on," she said, and they went out together.

Alleyn nodded to Harkness and he too went out.

An affected little French clock above the fireplace cleared its throat, broke into a perfect frenzy of silvery chimes and then struck midnight. Inspector Fox came into the room and shut the door.

Alleyn looked at Maurice Warrender.

"And now," he said, "there must be an end to equivocation. I must have the truth."

"I don't know what you mean," said Warrender, and could scarcely have sounded less convincing.

"I wonder why people always say that when they know precisely what one does mean. However, I'd better tell you. A few minutes ago, immediately after Charles Templeton died, I talked to the nanny, Mrs. Plumtree, who had been alone with him at the moment of his collapse. I told her that I believed she had uttered threats, that she had acted in this way because she thought Templeton was withholding information which would clear your son from suspicion of murder and that under the stress of this scene, Templeton suffered the heart attack from which he died. I told her your son was in no danger of arrest and she then admitted the whole story. I now tell you, too, that your son is in no danger. If you have withheld information for fear of incriminating him, you may understand that you have acted mistakenly."

Warrender seemed to be on the point of speaking but instead turned abruptly away and stood very still.

"You refused to tell me of the threats Mrs. Templeton uttered in the conservatory and I got them, after great difficulty it's true, from the other people who were there. When I asked you if you had quarrelled with Charles Templeton you denied it. I believe that, in fact, you *had* quarrelled with him and that it happened while you were together in the study before I saw you for the first time. For the whole of that interview you scarcely so much as looked at each other. He was obviously distressed by your presence and you were violently opposed to rejoining him there. I must ask you again. Had you quarrelled?"

Warrender muttered, "If you call it a quarrel."

"Was it about Richard Dakers?" Alleyn waited. "I think it was," he said, "but of course that's mere speculation and open, if you like, to contradiction."

Warrender squared his shoulders. "What's all this leading up to?" he demanded. "An arrest?"

"Surely you've heard of the usual warning. Come, sir, you did have a scene with Charles Templeton and I believe it was about Richard Dakers. Did you tell Templeton you were the father?"

"I did not," he said quickly.

"Did he know you were the father?"

"Not . . . We agreed from the outset that it was better that he shouldn't know. That nobody should know. Better on all counts."

"You haven't really answered my question, have you? Shall I put it this way? Did Templeton learn for the first time, this afternoon, that Dakers is your son?"

"Why should you suppose anything of the sort?"

"Your normal relationship appears to have been happy, yet at this time, when one would have expected you all to come together in your common trouble, he showed a vehement disinclination to see Dakers—or you."

Warrender made an unexpected gesture. He flung out his hands and lifted his shoulders. "Very well," he said.

"And *you* didn't tell him." Alleyn walked up to him and looked him full in the face. "She told him," he said. "Didn't she? Without consulting you, without any consideration for you or the boy. Because she was in one of those tantrums that have become less and less controllable. She made you spray that unspeakable scent over her in his presence, I suppose to irritate him. You went out and left them together. And she broke the silence of thirty years and told him."

"You can't possibly know."

"When she left the room a minute or two later she shouted at the top of her voice: 'Which only shows how wrong you were. You can get out whenever you like, my friend, and the sooner the better.' Florence had gone. You had gone. She was speaking to her husband. Did she tell you?"

"Tell *me!* What the hell . . ."

"Did she tell you what she'd said to Templeton?"

Warrender turned away to the fireplace, leant his arm on the shelf and hid his face.

"All right!" he stammered. "All right! What does it matter, now. All right."

"Was it during the party?"

He made some kind of sound, apparently in assent.

"Before or after the row in the conservatory?"

"After." He didn't raise his head and his voice sounded as if it didn't belong to him. "I tried to stop her attacking the girl."

"And that turned her against you? Yes, I see."

"I was following them, the girl and her uncle, and she whispered it. 'Charles knows about Dicky.' It was quite dreadful to see her look like that. I—I simply walked out—I . . ." He raised his head and looked at Alleyn. "It was indescribable."

"And your great fear after that was that she would tell the boy?"

He said nothing.

"As, of course, she did. Her demon was let loose. She took him up to her room and told him. They were, I daresay, the last words she spoke."

Warrender said, "You assume—you say these things—you . . ." and was unable to go on. His eyes were wet and bloodshot and his face grey. He looked quite old. "I don't know what's come over me," he said.

Alleyn thought he knew.

"It's not much cop," he said, "when a life's preoccupation turns out to have been misplaced. It seems to me that a man in such a position would rather see the woman dead than watch her turning into a monster."

"Why do you say these things to me. *Why!*"

"Isn't it so?"

With a strange parody of his habitual mannerism he raised a shaking hand to his tie and pulled at it.

"I understand," he said. "You've been very clever, I suppose."

"Not very, I'm afraid."

Warrender looked up at the beaming portrait of Mary Bellamy. "There's nothing left," he said. "Nothing. What do you want me to do?"

"I must speak to Dakers and then to those people in there. I think I must ask you to join us."

"Very well," Warrender said.

"Would you like a drink?"

"Thank you. If I may."

Alleyn looked at Fox who went out and returned with a tumbler and the decanter that Alleyn had seen on the table between Warrender and Charles at his first encounter with them.

"Whisky," Fox said. "If that's agreeable. Shall I pour it out, sir?"

Warrender took it neat and in one gulp. "I'm very much obliged to you," he said and straightened his back. The ghost of a smile distorted his mouth. "One more," he said, "and I shall be ready for anything, isn't it?"

Alleyn said, "I am going to have a word with Dakers before I see the others."

"Are you going to—to tell him?"

"I think it best to do so, yes."

"Yes. I see. Yes."

"When you are ready, Fox," Alleyn said and went out.

"He'll make it as easy as possible, sir," Fox said comfortably. "You may be sure of that."

"Easy!" said Warrender, and made a sound that might have been a laugh. "Easy!"

3

The persons sitting in the drawing-room were assembled there for the last time. In a few weeks Mary Bellamy's house would be transformed into the West End offices of a new venture in television, and a sedan chair for heaven knows what reason, would adorn the hall. Bertie Saracen's décor, taken over in toto, would be the background for the frenzied bandying about of new gimmicks and Charles Templeton's study a waiting-room for disengaged actors.

At the moment it had an air of stability. Most of its occupants, having exhausted each in his or her own kind their capacity for anxiety, anger or compassion, had settled down into apathy. They exchanged desultory remarks, smoked continuously and occasionally helped themselves, rather self-consciously, to the drinks that Gracefield had provided. P. C. Philpott remained alert in his corner.

It was Dr. Harkness who, without elaboration, announced Charles Templeton's death and that indeed shook them into a state of flabbergasted astonishment. When Richard came in, deathly pale, with Anelida, they all had to pull themselves together before they found anything at all to say to him. They did, indeed, attempt appropriate remarks, but it was clear to Anelida that their store of consolatory offerings was spent. However heartfelt their sympathy, they were obliged to fall back on their technique in order to express it. Pinky Cavendish broke into this unreal state of affairs by suddenly giving Richard a kiss and saying warmly, "It's no good, darling. There really is just literally nothing we can say or do, but we wish with all our hearts that there was, and Anelida must be your comfort. There!"

"Pinky," Richard said unevenly, "you really are no end of a darling. I'm afraid I can't—I can't . . . I'm sorry. I'm just not reacting much to anything."

"Exactly," Marchant said. "How well one understands. The proper thing, of course, would be for one to leave you to yourself, which unfortunately this Yard individual at the moment won't allow."

"He *did* send to say it wouldn't be long now," Bertie pointed out nervously.

"Do you suppose," Pinky asked, "that means he's going to arrest somebody?"

"Who can tell! Do you know *what?*" Bertie continued very rapidly and in an unnatural voice. "I don't mind betting every man jack of us is madly wondering what all the others think about him. Or her. I know I am. I keep saying to myself, '*Can* any of them think I darted upstairs instead of into the loo, and did it!' I suppose it's no use asking you all for a frank opinion is it? It would be taking an advantage."

"*I* don't think it of you," Pinky said at once. "I promise you, darling."

"Pinky! Nor I of you. Never for a moment. And I don't believe it of Anelida or Richard. Do you?"

"Never for a moment," she said firmly. "Absolutely not."

"Well," Bertie continued, inspired by Pinky's confidence, "I should like to know if any of you *does* suppose it might be me." Nobody answered. "I can't help feeling immensely gratified," Bertie said. "Thank you. Now. Shall I tell you which of you I think *could—just*—under *frightful* provocation—do something violent all of a sudden?"

"Me, I suppose," Gantry said. "I'm a hot-tempered man."

"Yes, Timmy dear, you! But *only* in boiling hot blood with one blind swipe, not really meaning to. And that doesn't seem to fit the bill at all. One wants a calculating iceberg of a person for this job, doesn't one?"

There followed a period of hideous discomfort, during which nobody looked at anybody else.

"An idle flight of speculation, I'm afraid, Bertie," said Marchant. "Would you be very kind and bring me a drink?"

"But of course," said Bertie, and did so.

Gantry glanced at Richard and said, "Obviously there's no connection —apart from the shock of Mary's death having precipitated it—between Charles's tragedy—and hers." Nobody spoke and he added half-angrily, "Well, *is* there! Harkness—you were there."

Dr. Harkness said quickly, "I don't know what's in Alleyn's mind."

"Where's that monumental, that superb old ham, the Colonel? Why's he gone missing all of a sudden?" Gantry demanded. "Sorry, Dicky, he's a friend of yours, isn't he?"

"He's . . . Yes," Richard said after a long pause. "He is. I think he's with Alleyn."

"Not," Marchant coolly remarked, "under arrest, one trusts."

"I believe not," Richard said. He turned his back on Marchant and sat beside Anelida on the sofa.

"Oh lud!" Bertie sighed, "how *wearing* has been this long, long day and how frightened in a vague sort of way I continue to feel. Never mind. *Toujours l'audace.*"

The handle of the door into the hall was heard to turn. Everybody looked up. Florence walked round the leather screen. "If you'll just wait, Miss," the constable said and retired. Philpott cleared his throat.

Richard said, "Come in, Floy. Come and sit down."

She glared stonily at him, walked into the farthest corner of the room and sat on the smallest chair. Pinky looked as if she'd like to say something friendly to her, but the impulse came to nothing and a heavy silence again fell upon the company.

It was broken by the same sound and a heavier tread. Bertie half-rose from his seat, gave a little cry of frustration and sank back again as Colonel Warrender made his entry, very erect and looking at no one in particular.

"We were just talking about you," said Bertie fretfully.

Richard stood up. "Come and join us," he said, and pushed a chair towards the sofa.

"Thank you, old boy," Warrender said awkwardly, and did so.

Anelida leant towards him and after a moment's hesitation put her hand on his knee. "I intend," she said under her breath, "to bully Richard into marrying me. Will you be on my side and give us your blessing?"

He drew his brows together and stared at her. He made an unsuccessful attempt to speak, hit her hand painfully hard with his own and ejaculated, "Clumsy ass. Hurt you, isn't it? Ah—Bless you."

"O.K." said Anelida and looked at Richard. "Now, you see, darling, you're sunk."

There was a sound of masculine voices in the hall, Pinky said, "Oh *dear!*" and Gantry, "Ah, for God's sake!" Marchant finished his drink quickly and P. C. Philpott rose to his feet. So, after a mulish second or two, did Florence.

This time it was Alleyn who came round the leather screen.

There was only one place in the room from which he could take them all in at one glance and that was the hearthrug. Accordingly, he went to it and stood there like the central figure in some ill-assembled conversation piece.

"I'm sorry," he said, "to have kept you hanging about. It was unavoidable and it won't be for much longer. Until a short time ago you were still, all of you, persons of importance. From the police point of view, I mean, of course. It was through you that we hoped to assemble the fragments and fit them into their pattern. The pattern is now complete and our uncomfortable association draws to its end. Tomorrow there will be an inquest and you will be required, most of you, to appear at it. The coroner's jury will hear your evidence and mine and one can only guess at what they will make of it. But you have all become too far involved for me to use any sort of evasion. Already some of you are suspecting others who are innocent. In my opinion this is one of those cases where the truth, at any cost, is less damaging in the long run, to vague, festering conjecture. For you all must know," Alleyn went on, "you *must* know even if you won't acknowledge it . . ."—his glance rested fleetingly on Richard—"that this has been a case of homicide."

He waited. Gantry said, "I don't accept that," but without much conviction.

"You will, I think, when I tell you that the Home Office analyst has found a trace of Slaypest in the bulb of the scent-spray."

"Oh," Gantry said faintly, as if Alleyn had made some quite unimportant remark. "I see. That's different."

"It's conclusive. It clears up all the extraneous matter. The professional rows, the threats that you were all so reluctant to admit, the evasions and half-lies. The personal bickerings and antagonisms. They are all tidied away by this single fact."

Marchant, whose hands were joined in front of his face, lifted his gaze for a moment to Alleyn. "You are not making yourself particularly clear," he said.

"I hope to do so. This one piece of evidence explains a number of indisputable facts. Here they are. The scent-spray was harmless when Colonel Warrender used it on Mrs. Templeton. At some time before she went up to her room with Mr. Dakers, enough Slaypest was transferred to the scent-spray to kill her. At some time after she was killed the scent-spray was emptied and washed out and the remaining scent from the original bottle was poured into it. I think there are two, possibly three, persons in the house at that time who could have committed these actions. They are all familiar with the room and its appointments and surroundings. The presence of any one of them in her room would, under normal circumstances, have been unremarkable."

A voice from outside the group violently demanded, "Where is she? Why hasn't she been brought down to face it?" And then, with satisfaction, "Has she been taken away? *Has* she?"

Florence advanced into the light.

Richard cried out, "What do you mean, Floy? Be quiet! You don't know what you're saying."

"*Where's Clara Plumtree?*"

"She will appear," Alleyn said, "if the occasion arises. And you *had* better be quiet, you know."

For a moment she looked as if she would defy him, but seemed to change her mind. She stood where she was and watched him.

"There is, however," Alleyn said, "a third circumstance. You will all remember that after the speeches you waited down here for Mrs. Templeton to take her part in the ceremony of opening the presents. Mr. Dakers had left her in her room, passing Florence and Mrs. Plumtree on his way downstairs. Mrs. Plumtree had then gone to her room, leaving Florence alone on the landing. Mr. Templeton went from here into the hall. From the foot of the stairs he saw Florence on the landing and called up to her that you were all waiting for her mistress. He then rejoined the party here. A minute or so later Florence ran downstairs into this room and, after a certain amount of confused ejaculation, made it known that her mistress was desperately ill. Mr. Templeton rushed upstairs. Dr. Harkness, after a short delay, followed. With Florence, Colonel Warrender and Mr. Gantry hard on his heels.

"They found Mrs. Templeton lying dead on the floor of her room. The overturned tin of Slaypest lay close beside her right hand. The scent-spray was on the dressing-table. That has been agreed to, but I am going to ask for a further confirmation."

Dr. Harkness said, "Certainly. That's how it was."

"You'd make a statement on oath to that effect?"

"I would." He looked at Gantry and Warrender. "Wouldn't you?" They said uneasily that they would.

"Well, Florence?" Alleyn asked.

"I said before: I didn't notice. I was too upset."

"But you don't disagree?"

"No," she admitted grudgingly.

"Very well. Now, you will see, I think, all of you, that the whole case turns on this one circumstance. The tin of Slaypest on the floor. The scent-spray and the empty bottle on the dressing-table."

"Isn't it awful?" Pinky said suddenly. "I know it must be childishly obvious, but I just can't bring myself to think."

"Can't you?" Gantry said grimly. "I can."

"Not having been involved in the subsequent discussions," Marchant remarked to nobody in particular, "the nicer points must be allowed, I hope, to escape me."

"Let me bring you up to date," Alleyn said. "There was poison in the scent-spray. Nobody, I imagine, will suggest that she put it there herself or that she used the Slaypest on herself. The sound of a spray in action was heard a minute or so before she died. By Ninn—Mrs. Plumtree."

"So she says," Florence interjected.

Alleyn went on steadily, "Mrs. Templeton was alone in her room. Very well. Having used the lethal scent-spray, did she replace it on the dressing-table and put the Slaypest on the floor?"

Florence said, "What did I tell you? Clara Plumtree! After I went. Say she *did* hear the thing being used. She done it! She went in and fixed it all. What did I tell you!"

"On your own evidence," Alleyn said, "and on that of Mr. Templeton, you were on the landing when he called up to you. You returned at once to the bedroom. Do you think that in those few seconds, Mrs. Plumtree, who moves very slowly, could have darted into the room, re-arranged the scent-spray, and Slaypest, darted out again and got out of sight?"

"She could've hid in the dressing-room. Like she done afterwards when she wouldn't let me in."

Alleyn said: "I'm afraid that won't quite do. Which brings me to the fourth point. I won't go into all the pathological details, but there is clear evidence that the spray was used in the normal way—at about arm's length and without undue pressure—and then at very close quarters and with maximum pressure. Her murderer, finding she was not dead, made sure that she would die. Mrs. Plumtree would certainly not have had an opportunity to do it. There is only one person who could have committed that act and the three other necessary acts as well. Only one."

"*Florence!*" Gantry cried out.

"No. Not Florence. Charles Templeton."

4

The drawing-room now seemed strangely deserted. Pinky Cavendish, Montague Marchant, Dr. Harkness, Bertie Saracen and Timon Gantry has all gone home. Charles Templeton's body had been carried away. Old Ninn was in her bed. Florence had retired to adjust her resentments and nurse her heartache as best she could. Mr. Fox was busy with routine arrangements. Only Alleyn, Richard, Anelida and Warrender remained in the drawing-room.

Richard said, "Ever since you told me and all through that last scene with them, I've been trying to see why. Why *should* he, having put up with so much for so long, do such a monstrous thing? It's—it's . . . I've always thought him—he was so . . ." Richard drove his fingers through his hair. "Maurice! You knew him. Better than any of us."

Warrender, looking at his clasped hands, muttered unhappily, "What's that word they use nowadays? Perfectionist?"

"But what do you . . . Yes. All right. He was a perfectionist, I suppose."

"Couldn't stand anything that wasn't up to his own standard. Look at those T'ang figures. Little lady with a flute and little lady with a lute. Lovely little creatures. Prized them more than anything else in the house. But when the parlourmaid or somebody knocked the end off one of the little lute pegs, he wouldn't have it. Gave it to me, by God!" said Warrender.

Alleyn said, "That's illuminating, isn't it?"

"But it's one thing to feel like that and another to—No!" Richard exclaimed, "it's a nightmare. You can't reduce it to that size. It's irreducible. Monstrous!"

"It's happened," Warrender said flatly.

"Mr. Alleyn," Anelida suggested, "would you tell us what you think? Would you take the things that led up to it out of their background and put them in order for us? Might that help, do you think, Richard?"

"I think it might, darling. If anything can."

"Well," Alleyn said, "shall I try? First of all, then, there's her personal history. There are the bouts of temperament that have increased in severity and frequency—to such a degree that they have begun to suggest a serious mental condition. You're all agreed about that, aren't you? Colonel Warrender?"

"I suppose so. Yes."

"What was she like thirty years ago, when he married her?"

Warrender looked at Richard. "Enchanting. Law unto herself. Gay. Lovely." He raised his hand and let it fall. "Ah, well! There it is. Never mind."

"Different? From these days?" Alleyn pursued.

"My God, yes!"

"So the musician's lute was broken? The perfect had become imperfect?"

"Very well. Go on."

"May we think back to yesterday, the day of the party? You must tell me if I'm all to blazes but this is how I see it. My reading, by the way, is pieced together from the statements Fox and I have collected from all of you and from the servants, who, true to form, knew more than any of you might suppose. Things began to go wrong quite early, didn't they? Wasn't it in the morning that she learnt for the first time that her . . ." He hesitated for a moment.

"It's all right," Richard said. "Anelida knows. Everything. She says she doesn't mind."

"Why on earth should I?" Anelida asked of the world at large. "We're not living in the reign of King Lear. In any case, Mr. Alleyn's talking about *Husbandry in Heaven* and me and how your mama didn't much fancy the idea that you'd taken up with me and still less the idea of my reading for the part."

"Which she'd assumed was written for her. That's it," Alleyn said. "That exacerbated a sense of being the victim of a conspiracy, which was set up by the scene in which she learnt that Miss Cavendish was to play the lead in another comedy and that Gantry and Saracen were in the 'plot.' She was a jealous, aging actress, abnormally possessive."

"But not always," Richard protested. "Not anything like always."

"Getting more so," Warrender muttered.

"Exactly. And perhaps because of that her husband, the perfectionist, may have transferred his ruling preoccupation from her to the young man whom he believed to be his son and on whom she was loath to relinquish her hold."

"But *did* he?" Richard cried out. "Maurice, did he think that?"

"She'd—let him assume it."

"I see. And in those days, as you've told us, he believed everything she said. I understand now," Richard said to Alleyn, "why you agreed that there was no need to tell him about me. He already knew, didn't he?"

"She herself," Alleyn went on, "told Colonel Warrender, after the flare-up in the conservatory, that she had disillusioned her husband."

"Did Charles," Richard asked Warrender, "say anything to you afterwards? Did he?"

"When we were boxed up together in the study. He hated my being there. It came out. He was . . ." Warrender seemed to search for an appropriate phrase. "I've never seen a man so angry," he said at last. "So sick with anger."

"Oh God!" Richard said.

"And then," Alleyn continued, "there was the row over the scent. He asked her not to use it. She made you, Colonel Warrender, spray it lavishly over her, in her husband's presence. You left the room. You felt, didn't you, that there was going to be a scene?"

"I shouldn't have done it. She could always make me do what she wanted," Warrender said. "I knew at the time but—isn't it?"

"Never mind," Richard said, and to Alleyn, "Was it then she told him?"

"I think it was at the climax of this scene. As he went out she was heard to shout after him, 'Which only shows how wrong you were. You can get out whenever you like, my friend, and the sooner the better.' She was not, as the hearer supposed, giving a servant the sack, she was giving it to him."

"And half an hour later," Richard said to Anelida, "there he was—standing beside her, shaking hands with her friends. I thought, when I was telephoning, he looked ill. I told you. He wouldn't speak."

"And then," Anelida said to Alleyn, "came the scene in the conservatory."

"Exactly. And, you see, he knew she had the power to make good her threats. Hard on the heels of the blow she had dealt him, he had to stand by and listen to her saying what she did say to all of you."

"Richard," Anelida said, "can you see? He'd loved her and he was watching her disintegrate. Anything to stop it!"

"I can see, darling, but I can't accept it. Not that."

"To put it very brutally," Alleyn said, "the treasured possession was not only hideously flawed, but possessed of a devil. She reeked of the scent he'd asked her not to wear. I don't think it would be too much to say that at that moment it symbolized for him the full horror of his feeling for her."

"D'you mean it was then he did it?" Warrender asked.

"Yes. Then. It must have been then. During all the movement and excitement just before the speeches. He went upstairs, emptied out some of the scent and filled up the atomizer with Slaypest. He returned during the speeches. As she left the drawing-room she came face to face with him. Florence heard him ask her not to use the scent."

Warrender gave an exclamation. "Yes?" Alleyn asked.

"Good God, d'you mean it was a—kind of gamble? If she did as he'd asked—like those gambles on suicide? Fella with a revolver. Half live, half blank cartridges."

"Exactly that. Only this time it was a gamble in murder." Alleyn looked at them. "It may seem strange that I tell you in detail so much that is painful and shocking. I do so because I believe that it is less damaging in the long run to know rather than to doubt."

"Of course it is," Anelida said quickly. "Richard, my dear, isn't it?"

"Yes," Richard said. "I expect it is. Yes, it is."

"Well, then," Alleyn said, "immediately after he'd spoken to her, you came in. The photographs were taken and you went upstairs together. You tackled her about her treatment of Anelida, didn't you?"

"It would be truer to say she attacked me. But, yes—we were both terribly angry. I've told you."

"And it ended in her throwing your parentage in your teeth?"

"It ended with that."

"When you'd gone she hurled your birthday present into the bathroom where it smashed to pieces. Instead of at once returning downstairs she went through an automatic performance. She powdered her face and painted her mouth. And then—well, then it happened. She used her scent-spray, holding it at arm's length. The windows were shut. It had an immediate effect, but not the effect he'd anticipated."

"What d'you mean?" Warrender asked.

"You've read the dictionary of poisons he bought. You may remember it gives a case of instant and painless death. But it doesn't always act in that way."

"He thought it would?"

"Probably. In this case, she became desperately ill. Florence came in and found her so. Do you remember what Charles Templeton said when Florence raised the alarm?"

Warrender thought for a moment. "Yes. I do. He said 'My God, not now!' I thought he meant 'Not a temperament at this juncture.'"

"Whereas he meant 'Not *now*. Not so soon.' He then rushed upstairs. There was some delay in getting Harkness under way, wasn't there?"

"Tight. Bad show. I put ice down his neck."

"And by the time you all arrived on the scene, the Slaypest was on the floor and the atomizer on the dressing-table. And she was dead. He had found her as Florence had left her. Whether she'd been able to say anything that showed she knew what he'd done is a matter of conjecture. Panic, terror, a determination to end it at all costs—we don't know. He *did* end it as quickly as he could and by the only means he had."

There was a long silence. Anelida broke it. "Perhaps," she said, "if it hadn't happened as it did, he would have changed his mind and not let it happen."

"Yes. It's possible, indeed. As it was he had to protect himself. He had to improvise. It must have been a nightmare. He'd had a bad heart-turn and had been settled down in his dressing-room. As soon as he was alone, he went through the communicating door, emptied the atomizer into the lavatory washed it out as best he could and poured in what was left of the scent."

"But how do you *know?*" Richard protested.

"As he returned, Old Ninn came into the dressing-room. She took it for granted he had been in the bathroom for the obvious reason. But later, when I developed my theory of the scent-spray, she remembered. She suspected the truth, particularly as he had smelt of Formidable. So strongly that when Florence stood in the open doorway of the dressing-room she thought it was Ninn, and that she had been attempting to do the service which Florence regarded as her own right."

"My poor old Ninn!" Richard cried.

"She, as you know, was not exactly at the top of her form. There had been certain potations, hadn't there? Florence, who in her anger and sorrow, was prepared to accuse anybody of anything, made some very damaging remarks about you."

"There's no divided allegiance," Richard said, "about Floy."

"Nor about Ninn. She was terrified. Tonight she went into the study after Templeton had been put to bed there and told him that if there was any chance of suspicion falling on you, she would tell her story. He was desperately ill but he made some kind of attempt to get at her. She made to defend herself. He collapsed and died."

Richard said, "One can't believe these things of people one has loved. For Charles to have died like that."

"Isn't it better?" Alleyn asked. "It *is* better. Because, as you know, we would have gone on. We would have brought him to trial. As it is, it's odds on that the coroner's jury will find it an accident. A rider will be added pointing out the dangers of indoor pest-killers. That's all."

"It is better," Anelida said, and after a moment, "Mightn't one say that he brought about his own retribution?" She turned to Richard and was visited by a feeling of great tenderness and strength. "We'll cope," she said, "with the future. Won't we?"

"I believe, we will, darling," Richard said. "We must, mustn't we?"

Alleyn said, "You've suffered a great shock and will feel it for some time. It's happened and can't be forgotten. But the hurt *will* grow less."

He saw that Richard was not listening to him. He had his arm about Anelida and had turned her towards him.

"You'll do," Alleyn said, unheeded.

He went up to Anelida and took her hand. "True," he said. "Believe me. He'll be all right. To my mind he has nothing to blame himself for. And that," Alleyn said, "is generally allowed to be a great consolation. Good-night."

5

Miss Bellamy's funeral was everything that she would have wished.

All the Knights and Dames, of course, and the Management and Timon Gantry, who had so often directed her. Bertie Saracen who had created her dresses since the days when she was a bit-part actress. Pinky Cavendish in floods, and Maurice, very Guardee, with a stiff upper lip.

Quite insignificant people, too: her old Ninn with a face like a boot and Florence with a bunch of primroses. Crowds of people whom she herself would have scarcely remembered, but upon whom, as a columnist in a woman's magazine put it, she had at some time bestowed the gift of her charm. And it was not for her fame, the celebrated clergyman pointed out in his address, that they had come to say goodbye to her. It was, quite simply, because they had loved her.

And Richard Dakers was there, very white and withdrawn, with a slim, intelligent-looking girl beside him.

Everybody.

Except, of course, her husband. It was extraordinary how little he was missed. The lady columnist could not, for the life of her, remember his name.

Charles Templeton had, as he would have wished, a private funeral.

SCALES OF JUSTICE

For Stella

ACKNOWLEDGMENTS

My most grateful thanks to Michael Godby, F.R.S., M.A. (Oxon.), for his learned advice in the matter of fish scales, to Eileen MacKay, to Eskdale Moloney and, as ever, to Vladimir and Anita Muling, without whom . . .

Contents

Cast of Characters

Nurse Kettle

Mr. Octavius Danberry-Phinn   *—of Jacob's Cottage*

Commander Syce   *—of Uplands*

Colonel Cartarette   *—of Hammer Farm*
Rose Cartarette   *—his daughter*
Kitty Cartarette   *—his wife*

Sir Harold Lacklander   *—of Nunspardon*
Lady Lacklander   *—his wife*
George Lacklander   *—their son*
Dr. Mark Lacklander   *—George's son*

Chief Detective-Inspector Alleyn ⎤
Inspector Fox | *of the C.I.D.,*
Detective-Sergeants Bailey and   }   *New Scotland Yard*
  Thompson |
Dr. Curtis, pathologist ⎦

Sergeant Oliphant ⎱   *—of the Swevenings*
P. C. Gripper   ⎰   *Constabulary*

Sir James Punston   *—Chief Constable of Barfordshire*

CHAPTER ONE   **Swevenings**

Nurse Kettle pushed her bicycle to the top of Watt's Hill and there paused. Sweating lightly, she looked down on the village of Swevenings. Smoke rose in cosy plumes from one or two chimneys; roofs cuddled into surrounding greenery. The Chyne, a trout stream, meandered through meadow and coppice and slid blamelessly under two bridges. It was a circumspect landscape. Not a *faux-pas*, architectural or horticultural, marred the seemliness of the prospect.

"Really," Nurse Kettle thought with satisfaction, "it is as pretty as a picture," and she remembered all the pretty pictures Lady Lacklander had made in irresolute water-colour, some from this very spot. She was reminded, too, of those illustrated maps that one finds in the Underground with houses, trees and occupational figures amusingly dotted about them. Seen from above like this, Swevenings resembled such a map. Nurse Kettle looked down at the orderly pattern of field, hedge, stream and land, and fancifully imposed upon it the curling labels and carefully naive figures that are proper to picture-maps.

From Watt's Hill, Watt's Lane ran steeply and obliquely into the valley. Between the lane and the Chyne was contained a hillside divided into three stripes, each garnished with trees, gardens and a house of considerable age. These properties belonged to three of the principal householders of Swevenings: Mr. Danberry-Phinn, Commander Syce and Colonel Cartarette.

Nurse Kettle's map, she reflected, would have a little picture of Mr. Danberry-Phinn at Jacob's Cottage surrounded by his cats, and one of Commander Syce at Uplands, shooting off his bow and arrow. Next door at Hammer Farm (only it wasn't a farm now but had been much converted) it would show Mrs. Cartarette in a garden chair with a cocktail-shaker, and Rose Cartarette, her stepdaughter, gracefully weeding. Her attention sharpened. There, in point of fact, deep down in the actual landscape, *was* Colonel Cartarette himself, a Lilliputian figure, moving along his rented stretch of the Chyne, east of Bottom Bridge, and followed at a respectful distance by his spaniel Skip. His creel was slung over his shoulder and his rod was in his hand.

"The evening rise," Nurse Kettle reflected; "he's after the Old 'Un," and she added to her imaginary map the picture of an enormous trout lurking near Bottom Bridge with a curly label above it bearing a legend: "The Old 'Un."

On the far side of the valley on the private golf course at Nunspardon Manor there would be Mr. George Lacklander, doing a solitary round with a glance (thought the gossip-loving Nurse Kettle) across the valley at Mrs. Cartarette. Lacklander's son, Dr. Mark, would be shown with his black bag in his hand and a stork, perhaps, quaintly flying overhead. And to complete, as it were, the gentry, there would be old Lady Lacklander, bog-bottomed on a sketching stool, and her husband, Sir Harold, on a bed of sickness, alas, in his great room, the roof of which, after the manner of pictorial maps, had been removed to display him.

In the map it would be demonstrated how Watt's Lane, wandering to the right and bending back again, neatly divided the gentry from what Nurse Kettle called the "ordinary folk." To the west lay the Danberry-Phinn, the Syce, the Cartarette and above all the Lacklander demesnes. Neatly disposed along the east margin of Watt's Lane were five conscientiously preserved thatched cottages, the village shop and across Monk's Bridge, the church and rectory and the Boy and Donkey.

And that was all. No Pulls-In for Carmen, no Olde Bunne Shoppes (which Nurse Kettle had learned to despise), no spurious half-timbering marred the perfection of Swevenings. Nurse Kettle, bringing her panting friends up to the top of Watt's Hill, would point with her little finger at the valley and observe triumphantly, " 'Where every prospect pleases,' " without completing the quotation, because in Swevenings not even Man was Vile.

With a look of pleasure on her shining and kindly face she mounted her bicycle and began to coast down Watt's Lane. Hedges and trees flew by. The road surface improved and on her left appeared the quickset hedge of Jacob's Cottage. From the far side came the voice of Mr. Octavius Danberry-Phinn.

"Adorable!" Mr. Danberry-Phinn was saying. "Queen of Delight! Fish!" He was answered by the trill of feline voices.

Nurse Kettle turned to the footpath, dexterously backpedalled, wobbled uncouthly and brought herself to anchor at Mr. Danberry-Phinn's gate.

"Good evening," she said, clinging to the gate and retaining her seat. She looked through the entrance cut in the deep hedge. There was Mr. Danberry-Phinn in his Elizabethan garden giving supper to his cats. In Swevenings, Mr. Phinn (he allowed his nearer acquaintances to neglect the hyphen) was generally considered to be more than a little eccentric, but Nurse Kettle was used to him and didn't find him at all disconcerting. He wore a smoking cap, tasselled, embroidered with beads and falling to pieces. On top of this was perched a pair of ready-made reading glasses, which he now removed and gaily waved at her.

"You appear," he said, "like some exotic deity mounted on an engine quaintly devised by Inigo Jones. Good evening to you, Nurse Kettle. Pray, what has become of your automobile?"

"She's having a spot of beauty treatment and a minor op'." Mr. Phinn flinched at this relentless breeziness, but Nurse Kettle, unaware of his reaction, carried heartily on, "And how's the world treating you? Feeding your kitties, I see."

"The Persons of the House," Mr. Phinn acquiesced, "now, as you observe, sup. Fatima," he cried, squatting on his plump haunches, "*Femme fatale*. Miss Paddy-Paws! A morsel more of haddock? Eat up, my heavenly felines." Eight cats of varying kinds responded but slightly to these overtures, being occupied with eight dishes of haddock. The ninth, a mother-cat, had completed her meal and was at her toilet. She blinked once at Mr. Phinn and with a tender and gentle expression stretched herself out for the accommodation of her three fat kittens.

"The celestial milk-bar is now open," Mr. Phinn pointed out with a wave of his hand.

Nurse Kettle chuckled obligingly. "No nonsense about *her*, at least," she said. "Pity some human mums I could name haven't got the same idea," she added with an air of professional candour. "Clever pussy!"

"The name," Mr. Phinn corrected tartly, "is Thomasina Twitchett, Thomasina modulating from Thomas and arising out of the usual mistake and Twitchett . . ." He bared his crazy-looking head. "*Hommage à la Divine Potter*. The boy-children are Ptolemy and Alexis. The girl-child who suffers from a marked mother-fixation is Edie."

"Edie?" Nurse Kettle repeated doubtfully.

"Edie Puss, of course," Mr. Phinn rejoined and looked fixedly at her.

Nurse Kettle, who knew that one must cry out against puns, ejaculated, "How you *dare! Honestly!*"

Mr. Phinn gave a short cackle of laughter and changed the subject.

"What errand of therapeutic mercy," he asked, "has set you darkling in the saddle? What pain and anguish wring which brow?"

"Well, I've one or two calls," said Nurse Kettle, "but the long and the short of me is that I'm on my way to spend the night at the big house. Relieving with the old gentleman, you know."

She looked across the valley to Nunspardon Manor.

"Ah, yes," said Mr. Phinn softly. "Dear me! May one enquire . . . ? Is Sir Harold . . . ?"

"He's seventy-five," said Nurse Kettle briskly, "and he's very tired. Still, you never know with cardiacs. He may perk up again."

"Indeed?"

"Oh, yes. We've got a day-nurse for him but there's no night-nurse to be had anywhere so I'm stop-gapping. To help Dr. Mark out, really."

"Dr. Mark Lacklander is attending his grandfather?"

"Yes. He had a second opinion but more for his own satisfaction than anything else. But there! Talking out of school! I'm ashamed of you, Kettle."

"I'm very discreet," said Mr. Phinn.

"So'm I, really. Well, I suppose I had better go on me way rejoicing."

Nurse Kettle did a tentative backpedal and started to wriggle her foot out of one of the interstices in Mr. Phinn's garden gate. He disengaged a sated kitten from its mother and rubbed it against his ill-shaven cheek.

"Is he conscious?" he asked.

"Off and on. Bit confused. There now! Gossiping again! Talking of gossip," said Nurse Kettle with a twinkle, "I see the Colonel's out for the evening rise."

An extraordinary change at once took place in Mr. Phinn. His face became suffused with purple, his eyes glittered and he bared his teeth in a canine grin.

"A hideous curse upon his sport," he said. "Where is he?"

"Just below the bridge."

"Let him venture a handspan above it and I'll report him to the authorities. What fly has he mounted? Has he caught anything?"

"I couldn't see," said Nurse Kettle, already regretting her part in the conversation, "from the top of Watt's Hill."

Mr. Phinn replaced the kitten.

"It is a dreadful thing to say about a fellow-creature," he said, "a shocking thing. But I do say advisedly and deliberately that I suspect Colonel Cartarette of having recourse to improper practices."

It was Nurse Kettle's turn to blush.

"I am sure I don't know to what you refer," she said.

"Bread! Worms!" said Mr. Phinn, spreading his arms. "Anything! Tickling, even! I'd put it as low as that."

"I'm sure you're mistaken."

"It is not my habit, Miss Kettle, to mistake the wanton extravagances of infatuated humankind. Look, if you will, at Cartarette's associates. Look, if your stomach is strong enough to sustain the experience, at Commander Syce."

"Good gracious me, what has the poor Commander done!"

"That man," Mr. Phinn said, turning pale and pointing with one hand to the mother-cat and with the other in the direction of the valley, "that intemperate filibuster, who divides his leisure between alcohol and the idiotic pursuit of archery, that wardroom cupid, my God, murdered the mother of Thomasina Twitchett."

"Not deliberately, I'm sure."

"How can you be sure?"

Mr. Phinn leant over his garden gate and grasped the handlebars of Nurse Kettle's bicycle. The tassel of his smoking cap fell over his face and he blew it impatiently aside. His voice began to trace the pattern of a much-repeated, highly relished narrative.

"In the cool of the evening Madame Thoms, for such was her name, was wont to promenade in the bottom meadow. Being great with kit, she presented a considerable target. Syce, flushed no doubt with wine, and flattering himself he cut the devil of a figure, is to be pictured upon his archery lawn. The instrument of destruction, a bow with the drawing-power, I am told, of sixty pounds, is in his grip and the lust of blood in his heart. He shot an arrow in the air," Mr. Phinn concluded, "and if you tell me that it fell to earth he knew not where, I shall flatly refuse to believe you. His target, his deliberate mark, I am persuaded, was my exquisite cat. Thomasina, my fur of furs, I am speaking of your mama."

The mother-cat blinked at Mr. Phinn and so did Nurse Kettle.

"I must *say*," she thought, "he really *is* a little off," and since she had a kind heart, she was filled with a vague pity for him.

"Living alone," she thought, "with only those cats. It's not to be wondered at, really."

She gave him her brightest professional smile and one of her standard valedictions.

"Ah, well," said Nurse Kettle, letting go her anchorage on the gate, "be good, and if you can't be good, be careful."

"Care," Mr. Danberry-Phinn countered with a look of real intemperance in his eye, "killed the cat. I am not likely to forget it. Good evening to you, Nurse Kettle."

2

Mr. Phinn was a widower, but Commander Syce was a bachelor. He lived next to Mr. Phinn in a Georgian house called Uplands, small and yet too big for Commander Syce, who had inherited it from an uncle. He was looked after by an ex-naval rating and his wife. The greater part of the grounds had been allowed to run to seed, but the kitchen-garden was kept up by the married couple and the archery lawn by Commander Syce himself. It overlooked the valley of the Chyne and was, apparently, his only interest. At one end in fine weather stood a target on an easel, and at the other on summer evenings, from as far away as Nunspardon, Commander Syce could be observed, in the classic pose, shooting a round from his sixty-pound bow. He was reputed to be a fine marksman, and it was noticed that however much his gait might waver, his stance, once he had opened his chest and stretched his bow, was that of a rock. He lived a solitary and aimless life. People would have inclined to be sorry for him if he had made any sign that he would welcome their sympathy. He did not do so and indeed at the smallest attempt at friendliness would sheer off, go about and make away as fast as possible. Although never seen in the bar, Commander Syce was a heroic supporter of the pub. Indeed, as Nurse Kettle pedalled up his overgrown drive, she encountered the lad from the Boy and Donkey pedalling down it with his bottle-carrier empty before him.

"There's the Boy," thought Nurse Kettle, rather pleased with herself for putting it that way, "and I'm very much afraid he's just paid a visit to the Donkey."

She, herself, had a bottle for Commander Syce, but it came from the chemist at Chyning. As she approached the house, she heard the sound of steps on the gravel and saw him limping away round the far end, his bow in his hand and his quiver girt about his waist. Nurse Kettle pedalled after him.

"Hi!" she called out brightly. "Good evening, Commander!"

Her bicycle wobbled and she dismounted.

Syce turned, hesitated for a moment and then came towards her.

He was a fairish, sunburned man who had run to seed. He still reeked of the navy and, as Nurse Kettle noticed when he drew nearer, of whisky. His eyes, blue and bewildered, stared into hers.

"Sorry," he said rapidly. "Good evening. I beg your pardon."

"Dr. Mark," she said, "asked me to drop in while I was passing and leave your prescription for you. There we are. The mixture as before."

He took it from her with a darting movement of his hand. "Most awfully kind," he said. "Frightfully sorry. Nothing urgent."

"No bother at all," Nurse Kettle rejoined, noticing the tremor of his hand. "I see you're going to have a shoot."

"Oh, yes. Yes," he said loudly, and backed away from her. "Well thank you, thank you, thank you."

"I'm calling in at Hammer. Perhaps you won't mind my trespassing. There's a footpath down to the right-of-way, isn't there?"

"Of course. Please do. Allow me."

He thrust his medicine into a pocket of his coat, took hold of her bicycle and laid his bow along the saddle and handlebars.

"Now *I'm* being the nuisance," said Nurse Kettle cheerfully. "Shall I carry your bow?"

He shied away from her and began to wheel the bicycle round the end of the house. She followed him, carrying the bow and talking in the comfortable voice she used for nervous patients. They came out on the archery lawn and upon a surprising and lovely view over the little valley of the Chyne. The trout stream shone like pewter in the evening light, meadows lay as rich as velvet on either side, the trees looked like pincushions, and a sort of heraldic glow turned the whole landscape into the semblance of an illuminated illustration to some forgotten romance. There was Major Cartarette winding in his line below Bottom Bridge and there up the hill on the Nunspardon golf course were old Lady Lacklander and her elderly son George, taking a postprandial stroll.

"*What* a clear evening," Nurse Kettle exclaimed with pleasure. "And *how* close everything looks. Do tell me, Commander," she went on, noticing that he seemed to flinch at this form of address, "with this bow of yours could you shoot an arrow into Lady Lacklander?"

Syce darted a look at the almost square figure across the little valley. He muttered something about a clout at two hundred and forty yards and limped on. Nurse Kettle, chagrined by his manner, thought, "What you need, my dear, is a bit of gingering up."

He pushed her bicycle down an untidy path through an overgrown shrubbery and she stumped after him.

"I have been told," she said, "that once upon a time you hit a mark you didn't bargain for, down there."

Syce stopped dead. She saw that beads of sweat had formed on the back of his neck. "Alcoholic," she thought. "Flabby. Shame. He must have been a fine man when he looked after himself."

"Great grief!" Syce cried out, thumping his fist on the seat of her bicycle. "You mean the bloody cat!"

"Well!"

"Great grief, it was an accident. I've told the old perisher! An accident! I *like* cats."

He swung round and faced her. His eyes were misted and his lips trembled. "I *like* cats," he repeated.

"We all make mistakes," said Nurse Kettle, comfortably.

He held his hand out for the bow and pointed to a little gate at the end of the path.

"There's the gate into Hammer," he said, and added with exquisite awkwardness, "I beg your pardon; I'm very poor company as you see. Thank you for bringing the stuff. Thank you, thank you."

She gave him the bow and took charge of her bicycle. "Dr. Mark Lacklander may be very young," she said bluffly, "but he's as capable a G.P. as I've come across in thirty years' nursing. If I were you, Commander, I'd have a good down-to-earth chinwag with him. Much obliged for the assistance. Good evening to you."

She pushed her bicycle through the gate into the well-tended coppice belonging to Hammer Farm and along a path that ran between herbaceous borders. As she made her way towards the house, she heard behind her at Uplands the twang of a bowstring and the "tock" of an arrow in a target.

"Poor chap," Nurse Kettle muttered, partly in a huff and partly compassionate. "Poor chap! Nothing to keep him out of mischief," and with a sense of vague uneasiness she wheeled her bicycle in the direction of the Cartarettes' rose garden, where she could hear the snip of garden secateurs and a woman's voice quietly singing.

"That'll be either *Mrs.*," thought Nurse Kettle, "or the stepdaughter. Pretty tune."

A man's voice joined in, making a second part.

> *Come away, come away, death,*
> *And in sad cypress let me be laid.*

The words, thought Nurse Kettle, were a trifle morbid, but the general effect was nice. The rose garden was enclosed behind quickset hedges and hidden from her, but the path she had taken led into it, and she must continue if she was to reach the house. Her rubber-shod feet made little sound on the flagstones, and the bicycle discreetly clicked along beside her. She had an odd feeling that she was about to break in on a scene of exquisite intimacy. She approached a green archway, and as she did so, the woman's voice broke off from its song and said, "That's my favourite of all."

"Strange," said a man's voice that fetched Nurse Kettle up with a jolt, "strange, isn't it, in a comedy, to make the love songs so sad! Don't you think so, Rose? Rose . . . Darling . . ."

Nurse Kettle tinkled her bicycle bell, passed through the green archway and looked to her right. She discovered Miss Rose Cartarette and Dr. Mark Lacklander gazing into each other's eyes with unmistakable significance.

3

Miss Cartarette had been cutting roses and laying them in the basket held by Dr. Lacklander. Dr. Lacklander blushed to the roots of his hair and said, "Good God! Good heavens! Good evening," and Miss Cartarette said, "Oh, hullo, Nurse. Good evening." She, too, blushed, but more delicately than Dr. Lacklander.

Nurse Kettle said, "Good evening, Miss Rose. Good evening, Doctor. Hope it's all right my taking the short cut." She glanced with decorum at Dr. Lacklander. "The child with the abscess," she said, in explanation of her own appearance.

"Ah, yes," Dr. Lacklander said. "I've had a look at her. It's your gardener's little girl, Rose."

They both began to talk to Nurse Kettle, who listened with an expression of good humour. She was a romantic woman and took pleasure in the look of excitement on Dr. Lacklander's face and of shyness on Rose's.

"Nurse Kettle," Dr. Lacklander said rapidly, "like a perfect angel, is going to look after my grandfather to-night. I don't know what we should have done without her."

"*And* by that same token," Nurse Kettle added, "I'd better go on me way rejoicing or I shall be late on duty."

They smiled and nodded at her. She squared her shoulders, glanced in a jocular manner at her bicycle and stumped off with it through the rose garden.

"Well," she thought, "if that's not a case, I've never seen young love before. Blow me down flat, but I never guessed! Fancy!"

As much refreshed by this incident as she would have been by a good strong cup of tea, she made her way to the gardener's cottage, her last port of call before going up to Nunspardon.

When her figure, stoutly clad in her District Nurse's uniform, had bobbed its way out of the enclosed garden, Rose Cartarette and Mark Lacklander looked at each other and laughed nervously.

Lacklander said, "She's a fantastically good sort, old Kettle, but at that particular moment I could have done without her. I mustn't stay, I suppose."

"Don't you want to see my papa?"

"Yes. But I shouldn't wait. Not that one can do anything much for the grandparent, but they like me to be there."

"I'll tell Daddy as soon as he comes in. He'll go up at once, of course."

"We'd be very grateful. Grandfather sets great store by his coming."

Mark Lacklander looked at Rose over the basket he carried and said unsteadily, "Darling."

"Don't," she said. "Honestly; don't."

"No? Are you warning me off, Rose? Is it all a dead loss?"

She made a small ineloquent gesture, tried to speak and said nothing.

"Well," Lacklander said, "I may as well tell you that I was going to ask if you'd marry me. I love you very dearly, and I thought we seemed to sort of suit. Was I wrong about that?"

"No," Rose said.

"Well, I know I wasn't. Obviously, we suit. So for pity's sake what's up? Don't tell me you love me like a brother, because I can't believe it."

"You needn't try to."

"Well, then?"

"I can't think of getting engaged, much less married."

"Ah!" Lacklander ejaculated. "Now, we're coming to it! This is going to be what I suspected. O, for God's sake let me get rid of this bloody basket! Here. Come over to the bench. I'm not going till I've cleared this up."

She followed him and they sat down together on a garden seat with the basket of roses at their feet. He took her by the wrist and stripped the heavy glove off her hand. "Now, tell me," he demanded, "do you love me?"

"You needn't bellow it at me like that. Yes, I do."

"Rose, darling! I was so panicked you'd say you didn't."

"Please listen, Mark. You're not going to agree with a syllable of this, but please listen."

"All right. I know what it's going to be, but . . . all right."

"You can see what it's like here. I mean the domestic set-up. You must have seen for yourself how much difference it makes to Daddy my being on tap."

"You are so funny when you use colloquialisms . . . a little girl shutting her eyes and firing off a pop-gun. All right; your father likes to have you about. So he well might and so he still would if we married. We'd probably live half our time at Nunspardon."

"It's much more than that." Rose hesitated. She had drawn away from him and sat with her hands pressed together between her knees. She wore a long house-dress. Her hair was drawn back into a knot at the base of her

neck, but a single fine strand had escaped and shone on her forehead.
She used very little make-up and could afford this economy for she was
a beautiful girl.

She said, "It's simply that his second marriage hasn't been a success.
If I left him now he'd really and truly have nothing to live for. Really."

"Nonsense," Mark said uneasily.

"He's never been able to do without me. Even when I was little. Nanny
and I and my governess all following the drum. So many countries and
journeys. And then after the war when he was given all those special
jobs—Vienna and Rome and Paris. I never went to school, because he
hated the idea of separation."

"All wrong, of course. Only half a life."

"No, no, no, that's not true, honestly. It was a wonderfully rich life.
I saw and heard and learnt all sorts of splendid things other girls miss."

"All the same . . ."

"No, honestly, it was grand."

"You should have been allowed to get under your own steam."

"It wasn't a case of being allowed! I was allowed almost anything I
wanted. And when I did get under my own steam just see what happened! He was sent with that mission to Singapore and I stayed in Grenoble and took a course at the university. He was delayed and delayed
. . . and I found out afterwards that he was wretchedly at a loose end.
And then . . . it was while he was there . . . he met Kitty."

Lacklander closed his well-kept doctor's hand over the lower half of
his face and behind it made an indeterminate sound.

"Well," Rose said, "it turned out as badly as it possibly could, and it
goes on getting worse, and if I'd been there I don't think it would have
happened."

"Why not? He'd have been just as likely to meet her. And even if he
hadn't, my heavenly and darling Rose, you cannot be allowed to think
of yourself as a twister of the tail of fate."

"If I'd been there . . ."

"Now *look* here!" said Lacklander. "Look at it like this. If you removed
yourself to Nunspardon as my wife, he and your stepmother might get together in a quick come-back."

"O, no," Rose said. "No, Mark. There's not a chance of that."

"How do you know? Listen. We're in love. I love you so desperately
much it's almost more than I can endure. I know I shall never meet anybody else who could make me so happy and, incredible though it may
seem, I don't believe you will either. I won't be put off, Rose. You shall
marry me and if your father's life here is too unsatisfactory, well, we'll

find some way of improving it. Perhaps if they part company he could come to us."

"Never! Don't you see! He couldn't bear it. He'd feel sort of extraneous."

"I'm going to talk to him. I shall tell him I want to marry you."

"No, Mark, darling! No . . . please . . ."

His hand closed momentarily over hers. Then he was on his feet and had taken up the basket of roses. "Good evening, Mrs. Cartarette," he said. "We're robbing your garden for my grandmother. You're very much ahead of us at Hammer with your roses."

Kitty Cartarette had turned in by the green archway and was looking thoughtfully at them.

4

The second Mrs. Cartarette did not match her Edwardian name. She did not look like a Kitty. She was so fair that without her make-up she would have seemed bleached. Her figure was well disciplined and her face had been skilfully drawn up into a beautifully cared-for mask. Her greatest asset was her acquired inscrutability. This, of itself, made a *femme fatale* of Kitty Cartarette. She had, as it were, been manipulated into a menace. She was dressed with some elaboration and, presumably because she was in the garden, she wore gloves.

"How nice to see you, Mark," she said. "I thought I heard your voices. Is this a professional call?"

Mark said, "Partly so at least. I ran down with a message for Colonel Cartarette, and I had a look at your gardener's small girl."

"How too kind," she said, glancing from Mark to her stepdaughter. She moved up to him and with her gloved hand took a dark rose from the basket and held it against her mouth.

"What a smell!" she said. "Almost improper, it's so strong. Maurice is not in, he won't be long. Shall we go up?"

She led the way to the house. Exotic wafts of something that was not roses drifted in her wake. She kept her torso rigid as she walked and slightly swayed her hips. "Very expensive," Mark Lacklander thought, "but not entirely exclusive. Why on earth did he marry her?"

Mrs. Cartarette's pin heels tapped along the flagstone path to a group of garden furniture heaped with cushions. A tray with a decanter and brandy glasses was set out on a white iron table. She let herself down on a swinging seat, put up her feet, and arranged herself for Mark to look at.

"Poorest Rose," she said, glancing at her stepdaughter, "you're wearing

such suitable gloves. Do cope with your scratchy namesakes for Mark.
A box perhaps."

"Please don't bother," Mark said. "I'll take them as they are."

"We can't allow that," Mrs. Cartarette murmured. "You doctors
mustn't scratch your lovely hands, you know."

Rose took the basket from him. He watched her go into the house
and turned abruptly at the sound of Mrs. Cartarette's voice.

"Let's have a little drink, shall we?" she said. "That's Maurice's pet
brandy and meant to be too wonderful. Give me an infinitesimal drop
and yourself a nice big one. I really prefer *crème de menthe*, but Maurice
and Rose think it a common taste, so I have to restrain my carnal appetite."

Mark gave her the brandy. "I won't, if you don't mind," he said. "I'm
by way of being on duty."

"Really? Who are you going to hover over, apart from the gardener's
child?"

"My grandfather," Mark said.

"How awful of me not to realize," she rejoined with the utmost composure. "How is Sir Harold?"

"Not so well this evening, I'm afraid. In fact I must get back. If I go by
the river path, perhaps I'll meet the Colonel."

"Almost sure to, I should think," she agreed indifferently, "unless he's
poaching for that fabled fish on Mr. Phinn's preserves, which, of course,
he's much too county to think of doing, whatever the old boy may say
to the contrary."

Mark said formally, "I'll go that way, then, and hope to see him."

She waved her rose at him in dismissal and held out her left hand in
a gesture that he found distressingly second-rate. He took it with his
own left and shook it crisply.

"Will you give your father a message from me?" she said. "I know how
worried he must be about your grandfather. Do tell him I wish so much
one could help."

The hand inside the glove gave his a sharp little squeeze and was withdrawn. "Don't forget," she said.

Rose came back with the flowers in a box. Mark thought, "I can't
leave her like this, half-way through a proposal, damn it." He said coolly,
"Come and meet your father. You don't take enough exercise."

"I live in a state of almost perpetual motion," she rejoined, "and I'm
not suitably shod or dressed for the river path."

Mrs. Cartarette gave a little laugh. "Poor Mark!" she murmured. "But
in any case, Rose, here *comes* your father."

Colonel Cartarette had emerged from a spinney half-way down the hill and was climbing up through the rough grass below the lawn. He was followed by his spaniel Skip, an old, obedient dog. The evening light had faded to a bleached greyness. Stivered grass, trees, lawns, flowers and the mildly curving thread of the shadowed trout stream joined in an announcement of oncoming night. Through this setting Colonel Cartarette moved as if he were an expression both of its substance and its spirit. It was as if from the remote past, through a quiet progression of dusks, his figure had come up from the valley of the Chyne.

When he saw the group by the lawn he lifted his hand in greeting. Mark went down to meet him. Rose, aware of her stepmother's heightened curiosity, watched him with profound misgiving.

Colonel Cartarette was a native of Swevenings. His instincts were those of a countryman and he had never quite lost his air of belonging to the soil. His tastes, however, were for the arts and his talents for the conduct of government services in foreign places. This odd assortment of elements had set no particular mark upon their host. It was not until he spoke that something of his personality appeared.

"Good evening, Mark," he called as soon as they were within comfortable earshot of each other. "My dear chap, what do you think! I've damned near bagged the Old 'Un."

"No!" Mark shouted with appropriate enthusiasm.

"I assure you! The Old 'Un! Below the bridge in his usual lurk, you know. I could see him. . . ."

And as he panted up the hill, the Colonel completed his classic tale of a magnificent strike, a Homeric struggle and a broken cast. Mark, in spite of his own preoccupations, listened with interest. The Old 'Un was famous in Swevenings: a trout of magnitude and cunning, the despair and desire of every rod in the district.

". . . so I lost him," the Colonel ended, opening his eyes very wide and at the same time grinning for sympathy at Mark. "What a thing! By Jove, if I'd got him I really believe old Phinn would have murdered me."

"Are you still at war, sir?"

"Afraid so. The chap's impossible, you know. Good God, he's accused me in so many words of poaching. Mad! How's your grandfather?"

Mark said, "He's failing pretty rapidly, I'm afraid. There's nothing we can do. It's on his account I'm here, sir," And he delivered his message.

"I'll come at once," the Colonel said. "Better drive round. Just give me a minute or two to clean up. Come round with me, won't you?"

But Mark felt suddenly that he could not face another encounter with Rose and said he would go home at once by the river path and would prepare his grandfather for the Colonel's arrival.

He stood for a moment looking back through the dusk towards the house. He saw Rose gather up the full skirt of her house-coat and run across the lawn, and he saw her father set down his creel and rod, take off his hat and wait for her, his bald head gleaming. She joined her hands behind his neck and kissed him. They went on towards the house arm-in-arm. Mrs. Cartarette's hammock had begun to swing to and fro.

Mark turned away and walked quickly down into the valley and across Bottom Bridge.

The Old 'Un, with Colonel Cartarette's cast in his jaw, lurked tranquilly under the bridge.

CHAPTER TWO **Nunspardon**

Sir Harold Lacklander watched Nurse Kettle as she moved about his room. Mark had given him something that had reduced his nightmare of discomfort and for the moment he seemed to enjoy the tragic self-importance that is the prerogative of the very ill. He preferred Nurse Kettle to the day-nurse. She was, after all, a native of the neighbouring village of Chyning, and this gave him the same satisfaction as the knowledge that the flowers on his table came out of the Nunspardon conservatories.

He knew now that he was dying. His grandson had not told him in so many words, but he had read the fact of death in the boy's face and in the behaviour of his own wife and son. Seven years ago he had been furious when Mark wished to become a doctor: a Lacklander and the only grandson. He had made it as difficult as he could for Mark. But he was glad now to have the Lacklander nose bending over him and the Lacklander hands doing the things doctors seemed to think necessary. He would have taken a sort of pleasure in the eminence to which approaching death had raised him if he had not been tormented by the most grievous of all ills. He had a sense of guilt upon him.

"Long time," he said. He used as few words as possible because with every one he uttered it was as if he squandered a measure of his dwindling capital. Nurse Kettle placed herself where he could see and hear her easily and said, "Doctor Mark says the Colonel will be here quite soon. He's been fishing."

"Luck?"

"I don't know. He'll tell you."

"Old 'Un."

"Ah," said Nurse Kettle comfortably, "they won't catch him in a hurry."

The wraith of a chuckle drifted up from the bed and was followed by an anxious sigh. She looked closely at the face that seemed during that day to have receded from its own bones.

"All right?" she asked.

The lacklustre eyes searched hers. "Papers?" the voice asked.

"I found them just where you said. They're on the table over there."

"Here."

"If it makes you feel more comfortable." She moved into the shadows at the far end of the great room and returned carrying a package, tied and sealed, which she put on his bedside table.

"Memoirs," he whispered.

"Fancy," said Nurse Kettle. "There must be a deal of work in them. I think it's lovely to be an author. And now I'm going to leave you to have a little rest."

She bent down and looked at him. He stared back anxiously. She nodded and smiled and then moved away and took up an illustrated paper. For a time there were no sounds in the great bedroom but the breathing of the patient and the rustle of a turned page.

The door opened. Nurse Kettle stood up and put her hands behind her back as Mark Lacklander came into the room. He was followed by Colonel Cartarette.

"All right, Nurse?" Mark asked quietly.

"Pretty much," she murmured. "Fretting. He'll be glad to see the Colonel."

"I'll just have a word with him first."

He walked down the room to the enormous bed. His grandfather stared anxiously up at him and Mark, taking the restless old hand in his, said at once, "Here's the Colonel, Grandfather. You're quite ready for him, aren't you?"

"Yes. Now."

"Right." Mark kept his fingers on his grandfather's wrist. Colonel Cartarette straightened his shoulders and joined him.

"Hullo, Cartarette," said Sir Harold so loudly and clearly that Nurse Kettle made a little exclamation. "Nice of you to come."

"Hullo, sir," said the Colonel, who was by twenty-five years the younger. "Sorry you're feeling so cheap. Mark says you want to see me."

"Yes." The eyes turned towards the bedside table. "Those things," he said. "Take them, will you? Now."

"They're the memoirs," Mark said.

"Do you want me to read them?" Cartarette asked, stooping over the bed.

"If you will." There was a pause. Mark put the package into Colonel Cartarette's hands. The old man's eyes watched in what seemed to be an agony of interest.

"I think," Mark said, "that Grandfather hopes you will edit the memoirs, sir."

"I'll . . . Of course," the Colonel said after an infinitesimal pause. "I'll be delighted; if you think you can trust me."

"Trust you. Implicitly. Implicitly. One other thing. Do you mind, Mark?"

"Of course not, Grandfather. Nurse, shall we have a word?"

Nurse Kettle followed Mark out of the room. They stood together on a dark landing at the head of a wide stairway.

"I don't think," Mark said, "that it will be much longer."

"Wonderful, though, how he's perked up for the Colonel."

"He'd set his will on it. I think," Mark said, "that he will now relinquish his life."

Nurse Kettle agreed. "Funny how they can hang on and funny how they will give up."

In the hall below a door opened and light flooded up the stairs. Mark looked over the banister and saw the enormously broad figure of his grandmother. Her hand flashed as it closed on the stair rail. She began heavily to ascend. He could hear her laboured breathing.

"Steady does it, Gar," he said.

Lady Lacklander paused and looked up. "Ha!" she said. "It's the doctor, is it?" Mark grinned at the sardonic overtone.

She arrived on the landing. The train of her old velvet dinner dress followed her, and the diamonds which every evening she absent-mindedly stuck about her enormous bosom burned and winked as it rose and fell.

"Good evening, Miss Kettle," she panted. "Good of you to come and help my poor old boy. How is he, Mark? Has Maurice Cartarette arrived? Why are you both closeted together out here?"

"The Colonel's here, Gar. Grandfather wanted to have a word privately with him, so Nurse and I left them together."

"Something about those damned memoirs," said Lady Lacklander vexedly. "I suppose, in that case, I'd better not go in."

"I don't think they'll be long."

There was a large Jacobean chair on the landing. He pulled it forward. She let herself down into it, shuffled her astonishingly small feet out of a pair of old slippers and looked critically at them.

"Your father," she said, "has gone to sleep in the drawing-room muttering that he would like to see Maurice." She shifted her great bulk towards Nurse Kettle. "Now, before you settle to your watch, you kind soul," she said, "you won't mind saving my mammoth legs a journey. Jog down to the drawing-room, rouse my lethargic son, tell him the Colonel's here and make him give you a drink and a sandwich. Um?"

"Yes, of course, Lady Lacklander," said Nurse Kettle and descended briskly. "Wanted to get rid of me," she thought, "but it was tactfully done."

"Nice woman, Kettle," Lady Lacklander grunted. "She knows I wanted to be rid of her. Mark, what is it that's making your grandfather unhappy?"

"Is he unhappy, Gar?"

"Don't hedge. He's worried to death. . . ." She stopped short. Her jewelled hands twitched in her lap. "He's troubled in his mind," she said, "and for the second occasion in our married life I'm at a loss to know why. Is it something to do with Maurice and the memoirs?"

"Apparently. He wants the Colonel to edit them."

"The first occasion," Lady Lacklander muttered, "was twenty years ago and it made me perfectly miserable. And now, when the time has come for us to part company . . . and it has come, child, hasn't it?"

"Yes, darling, I think so. He's very tired."

"I know. And I'm not. I'm seventy-five and grotesquely fat, but I have a zest for life. There are still," Lady Lacklander said with a change in her rather wheezy voice, "there are still things to be tidied up. George, for example."

"What's my poor papa doing that needs a tidying hand?" Mark asked gently.

"Your poor papa," she said, "is fifty and a widower and a Lacklander. Three ominous circumstances."

"Which can't be altered, even by you."

"They can, however, be . . . Maurice! What is it?"

Colonel Cararette had opened the door and stood on the threshold with the packages still under his arm.

"Can you come, Mark? Quickly."

Mark went past him into the bedroom. Lady Lacklander had risen and followed with more celerity than he would have thought possible. Colonel Cartarette stopped her in the doorway.

"My dear," he said, "wait a moment."

"Not a second," she said strongly. "Let me in, Maurice."

A bell rang persistently in the hall below. Nurse Kettle, followed by a tall man in evening clothes, came hurrying up the stairs.

Colonel Cartarette stood on the landing and watched them go in.

Lady Lacklander was already at her husband's bedside. Mark supported him with his right arm and with his left hand kept his thumb on a bell-push that lay on the bed. Sir Harold's mouth was open and he was fetching his breath in a series of half-yawns. There was a movement under the bedclothes that seemed to be made by a continuous flexion and extension of his leg. Lady Lacklander stood massively behind him and took both his hands between hers.

"I'm here, Hal," she said.

Nurse Kettle had appeared with a glass in her hand.

"Brandy," she said. "Old-fashioned but good."

Mark held it to his grandfather's open mouth. "Try," he said. "It'll help. Try."

The mouth closed over the rim.

"He's got a little," Mark said. "I'll give an injection."

Nurse Kettle took his place. Mark turned away and found himself face-to-face with his father.

"Can I do anything?" George Lacklander asked.

"Only wait here, if you will, Father."

"Here's George, Hal," Lady Lacklander said. "We're all here with you, my dear."

From behind the mask against Nurse Kettle's shoulder came a stutter, "Vic—Vic . . . Vic," as if the pulse that was soon to run down had become semi-articulate like a clock. They looked at each other in dismay.

"What is it?" Lady Lacklander asked. "What is it, Hal?"

"Somebody called Vic?" Nurse Kettle suggested brightly.

"There is nobody called Vic," said George Lacklander and sounded impatient. "For God's sake, Mark, can't you help him?"

"In a moment," Mark said from the far end of the room.

"Vic . . ."

"The vicar?" Lady Lacklander asked, pressing his hand and bending over him. "Do you want the vicar to come, Hal?"

His eyes stared up into hers. Something like a smile twitched at the corners of the gaping mouth. The head moved slightly.

Mark came back with the syringe and gave the injection. After a moment Nurse Kettle moved away. There was something in her manner that gave definition to the scene. Lady Lacklander and her son and grandson drew closer to the bed. She had taken her husband's hands again.

"What is it, Hal? What is it, my dearest?" she asked. "Is it the vicar?"

With a distinctness that astonished them he whispered, "After all, you never know," and with his gaze still fixed on his wife he then died.

2

On the late afternoon three days after his father's funeral, Sir George Lacklander sat in the study at Nunspardon going through the contents of the files and the desk. He was a handsome man with a look of conventional distinction. He had been dark but was now grizzled in the most becoming way possible with grey wings at his temples and a plume above his forehead. Inevitably, his mouth was firm and the nose above it appropriately hooked. He was, in short, rather like an illustration of an English gentleman in an American magazine. He had arrived at the dangerous age for such men, being now fifty years old and remarkably vigorous.

Sir Harold had left everything in apple-pie order, and his son anticipated little trouble. As he turned over the pages of his father's diaries, it occurred to him that as a family they richly deserved their too-much-publicized nicknames of "Lucky Lacklanders." How lucky, for instance, that the eighth baronet, an immensely wealthy man, had developed a passion for precious stones and invested in them to such an extent that they constituted a vast realizable fortune in themselves. How lucky that their famous racing stables were so phenomenally successful. How uniquely and fantastically lucky they had been in that no fewer than three times in the past century a Lacklander had won the most famous of all sweepstakes. It was true, of course, that he himself might be said to have had a piece of ill-fortune when his wife had died in giving birth to Mark, but as he remembered her, and he had to confess he no longer remembered her at all distinctly, she had been a disappointingly dull woman. Nothing like . . . But here he checked himself smartly and swept up his moustache with his thumb and forefinger. He was disconcerted when at this precise moment the butler came in to say that Colonel Cartarette had called and would like to see him. In a vague way the visit suggested a judgment. He took up a firm position on the hearthrug.

"Hullo, Maurice," he said when the Colonel came in. "Glad to see you." He looked self-consciously into the Colonel's face and with a changed voice said, "Anything wrong?"

"Well, yes," the Colonel said. "A hell of a lot actually. I'm sorry to bother you, George, so soon after your trouble and all that, but the truth is I'm so damned worried that I feel I've got to share my responsibility with you."

"Me!" Sir George ejaculated, apparently with relief and a kind of astonishment. The Colonel took two envelopes from his pocket and laid them on the desk. Sir George saw that they were addressed in his father's writing.

"Read the letter first," the Colonel said, indicating the smaller of the two envelopes. George gave him a wondering look. He screwed in his eyeglass, drew a single sheet of paper from the envelope, and began to read. As he did so, his mouth fell gently open and his expression grew increasingly blank. Once he looked up at the troubled Colonel as if to ask a question but seemed to change his mind and fell again to reading.

At last the paper dropped from his fingers and his monocle from his eye to his waistcoat.

"I don't," he said, "understand a word of it."

"You will," the Colonel said, "when you have looked at this." He drew a thin sheaf of manuscript out of the larger envelope and placed it before George Lacklander. "It will take you ten minutes to read. If you don't mind, I'll wait."

"My dear fellow! Do sit down. What am I thinking of? A cigar! A drink."

"No thank you, George. I'll smoke a cigarette. No, don't move. I've got one."

George gave him a wondering look, replaced his eyeglass and began to read again. As he did so, his face went through as many changes of expression as those depicted in strip-advertisements. He was a rubicund man, but the fresh colour drained out of his face. His mouth lost its firmness and his eyes their assurance. When he raised a sheet of manuscript, it quivered in his grasp.

Once, before he had read to the end, he did speak. "But it's not true," he said. "We've always known what happened. It was well known." He touched his lips with his fingers and read on to the end. When the last page had fallen on the others, Colonel Cartarette gathered them up and put them into their envelope.

"I'm damned sorry, George," he said. "God knows I didn't want to land you with all this."

"I can't see, now, why you've done it. Why bring it to me? Why do anything but throw it at the back of the fire?"

Cartarette said sombrely, "I see you haven't listened to me. I told you. I've thought it over very carefully. He's left the decision with me and I've decided I must publish . . ." he held up the long envelope . . . "this. I must, George. Any other course would be impossible."

"But have you thought what it will do to us? Have you thought? It . . . it's *un*thinkable. You're an old friend, Maurice. My father trusted you with this business because he thought of you as a friend. In a way," George added, struggling with an idea that was a little too big for him, "in a way he's bequeathed you our destiny."

"A most unwelcome legacy if it were so, but of course it's not. You're putting it altogether too high. I know, believe me, George, I know how painful and distressing this will be to you all, but I think the public will take a more charitable view than you might suppose."

"And since when," George demanded with a greater command of rhetoric than might have been expected of him, "since when have the Lacklanders stood cap-in-hand, waiting upon the charity of the public?"

Colonel Cartarette's response to this was a helpless gesture. "I'm terribly sorry," he said, "but I'm afraid that that sentiment has the advantage of sounding well and meaning nothing."

"Don't be so bloody supercilious."

"All right, George, all right."

"The more I think of this the worse it gets. Look here, Maurice, if for no other reason, in common decency . . ."

"I've tried to take common decency as my criterion."

"It'll kill my mother."

"It will distress her very deeply, I know. I've thought of her, too."

"And Mark? Ruin! A young man! My son! Starting on his career."

"There was another young man, an only son, who was starting on his career."

"He's dead!" George cried out. "He can't suffer. He's dead."

"And *his* name? And *his* father?"

"I can't chop logic with you. I'm a simple sort of bloke with, I daresay, very unfashionable standards. I believe in the loyalty of friends and in the old families sticking together."

"At whatever the cost to other friends and other old families? Come off it, George," said the Colonel.

The colour flooded back into George's face until it was empurpled. He said in an unrecognizable voice, "Give me my father's manuscript. Give me that envelope. I demand it."

"I can't, old boy. Good God, do you suppose that if I could chuck it away or burn it with anything like a clear conscience I wouldn't do it? I tell you I hate this job."

He returned the envelope to the breast pocket of his coat. "You're free, of course," he said, "to talk this over with Lady Lacklander and Mark. Your father made no reservations about that. By the way, I've brought a copy of his letter in case you decide to tell them about it. Here it is." The Colonel produced a third envelope, laid it on the desk and moved towards the door. "And George," he said, "I beg you to believe I am sorry. I'm deeply sorry. If I could see any other way, I'd thankfully take it. What?"

George Lacklander had made an inarticulate noise. He now pointed a heavy finger at the Colonel.

"After this," he said, "I needn't tell you that any question of an understanding between your girl and my boy is at an end."

The Colonel was so quiet for so long that both men became aware of the ticking of a clock on the chimney breast.

"I didn't know," he said at last, "that there was any question of an understanding. I think you must be mistaken."

"I assure you that I am not. However, we needn't discuss it. Mark . . . and Rose, I am sure . . . will both see that it is quite out of the question. No doubt you are as ready to ruin her chances as you are to destroy our happiness." For a moment he watched the Colonel's blank face. "She's head over heels in love with him," he added; "you can take my word for it."

"If Mark has told you this . . ."

"Who says Mark told me? . . . I . . . I . . ."

The full, rather florid voice faltered and petered out.

"Indeed," the Colonel said. "Then may I ask where you got your information?"

They stared at each other and, curiously, the look of startled conjecture which had appeared on George Lacklander's face was reflected on the Colonel's. "It couldn't matter less, in any case," the Colonel said. "Your informant, I am sure, is entirely mistaken. There's no point in my staying. Goodbye."

He went out. George, transfixed, saw him walk past the window. A sort of panic came over him. He dragged the telephone across his desk and with an unsteady hand dialled Colonel Cartarette's number. A woman's voice answered.

"Kitty!" he said. "Kitty, is that you?"

3

Colonel Cartarette went home by the right-of-way known as the River Path. It ran through Nunspardon from the top end of Watt's Lane skirting the Lacklander's private golf course. It wound down to Bottom Bridge and up the opposite side to the Cartarette's spinney. From thence it crossed the lower portion of Commander Syce's and Mr. Phinn's demesnes and rejoined Watt's Lane just below the crest of Watt's Hill.

The Colonel was feeling miserable. He was weighed down by his responsibility and upset by his falling out with George Lacklander, who, pompous old ass though the Colonel thought him, was a lifetime friend. Worst of all, he was wretchedly disturbed by the suggestion that Rose had fallen in love with Mark and by the inference, which he couldn't help drawing, that George Lacklander had collected this information from the Colonel's wife.

As he walked down the hillside, he looked across the little valley into the gardens of Jacob's Cottage, Uplands and Hammer Farm. There was Mr. Phinn dodging about with a cat on his shoulder: "like a blasted old warlock," thought the Colonel, who had fallen out with Mr. Phinn over the trout stream, and there was poor Syce blazing away with his bow and arrow at his padded target. And there, at Hammer, was Kitty. With a characteristic movement of her hips she had emerged from the house in skintight velvet trousers and a flame-coloured top. Her long cigarette-holder was in her hand. She seemed to look across the valley at Nuns-pardon. The Colonel felt a sickening jolt under his diaphragm. "How I could!" he thought (though subconsciously). "How I could!" Rose was at her evening employment cutting off the dead-heads in the garden. He sighed and looked up to the crest of the hill, and there plodding home-wards, pushing her bicycle up Watt's Lane, her uniform and hat ap-pearing in gaps and vanishing behind hedges, was Nurse Kettle. "In Swevenings," thought the Colonel, "she crops up like a recurring decimal."

He came to the foot of the hill and to the Bottom Bridge. The bridge divided his fishing from Mr. Danberry-Phinn's: he had the lower reaches and Mr. Phinn the upper. It was about the waters exactly under Bottom Bridge that they had fallen out. The Colonel crossed from Mr. Phinn's side to his own, folded his arms on the stone parapet and gazed into the sliding green world beneath. At first he stared absently, but after a mo-ment his attention sharpened. In the left bank of the Chyne near a broken-down boatshed where an old punt was moored, there was a hole. In its depths eddied and lurked a shadow among shadows: the Old 'Un. "Perhaps," the Colonel thought, "perhaps it would ease my mind a bit if I came down before dinner. He may stay on my side." He withdrew his gaze from the Old 'Un to find, when he looked up at Jacob's Cottage, that Mr. Phinn, motionless, with his cat still on his shoulder, was looking at him through a pair of field-glasses.

"Ah, hell!" muttered the Colonel. He crossed the bridge and passed out of sight of Jacob's Cottage and continued on his way home.

The path crossed a narrow meadow and climbed the lower reach of Watt's Hill. His own coppice and Commander Syce's spinney concealed from the Colonel the upper portions of the three demesnes. Someone was coming down the path at a heavy jog-trot. He actually heard the wheezing and puffing of this person and recognized the form of locomo-tion practised by Mr. Phinn before the latter appeared wearing an old Norfolk jacket and tweed hat which, in addition to being stuck about

with trout-fishing flies, had Mr. Phinn's reading spectacles thrust through
the band like an Irishman's pipe. He was carrying his elaborate collection of fishing impedimenta. He had the air of having got himself together in a hurry and was attended by Mrs. Thomasina Twitchett, who,
after the manner of her kind, suggested that their association was purely
coincidental.

The path was narrow. It was essential that someone should give way
and the Colonel, sick of rows with his neighbours, stood on one side.
Mr. Phinn jogged glassily down upon him. The cat suddenly cantered
ahead.

"Hullo, old girl," said the Colonel. He stooped down and snapped a
finger and thumb at her. She stared briefly and passed him with a pre-
occupied air, twitching the tip of her tail.

The Colonel straightened up and found himself face-to-face with Mr.
Phinn.

"Good evening," said the Colonel.

"Sir," said Mr. Phinn. He touched his dreadful hat with one finger,
blew out his cheeks and advanced. "Thomasina," he added, "hold your
body more seemly."

For Thomasina, waywardly taken with the Colonel, had returned and
rolled on her back at his feet.

"Nice cat," said the Colonel and added, "Good fishing to you. The
Old 'Un lies below the bridge on my side, by the way."

"Indeed?"

"As no doubt you guessed," the Colonel added against his better judgment, "when you watched me through your field-glasses."

If Mr. Phinn had contemplated a conciliatory position, he at once
abandoned it. He made a belligerent gesture with his net. "The landscape, so far as I am aware," he said, "is not under some optical interdict.
It may be viewed, I believe. To the best of my knowledge, there are no
squatter's rights over the distant prospect of the Chyne."

"None whatever. You can stare," said the Colonel, "at the Chyne, or
me, or anything else you fancy till you are black in the face, for all I care.
But if you realized . . . If you . . ." He scratched his head, a gesture that
with the Colonel denoted profound emotional disturbance. "My dear
Phinn . . ." he began again, "if you only knew . . . God bless my soul,
what *does* it matter! Good evening to you."

He encircled Mr. Phinn and hurried up the path. "And for that grotesque," he thought resentfully, "for that impossible, that almost certifi-
able buffoon I have saddled myself with a responsibility that may well
make me wretchedly uncomfortable for the rest of my life."

He mended his pace and followed the path into the Hammer coppice.

Whether summoned by maternal obligations or because she had taken an inscrutable cat's fancy to the Colonel, Thomasina Twitchett accompanied him, trilling occasionally and looking about for an evening bird. They came within view of the lawn, and there was Commander Syce, bow in hand, quiver at thigh and slightly unsteady on his feet, hunting about in the underbrush.

"Hullo, Cartarette," he said. "Lost a damned arrow. What a thing! Missed the damned target and away she went."

"Missed it by a dangerously wide margin, didn't you?" the Colonel rejoined rather testily. After all, people did use the path, he reflected, and he began to help in the search. Thomasina Twitchett, amused by the rustle of leaves, pretended to join in the hunt.

"I know," Commander Syce agreed; "rotten bad show, but I saw old Phinn and it put me off. Did you hear what happened about me and his cat? Damnedest thing you ever knew! Purest accident, but the old what-not wouldn't have it. Great grief, I told him, I *like* cats."

He thrust his hand into a heap of dead leaves. Thomasina Twitchett leapt merrily upon it and fleshed her claws in his wrist. "Perishing little bastard," said Commander Syce. He freed himself and aimed a spank at her which she easily avoided and being tired of their company, made for her home and kittens. The Colonel excused himself and turned up through the spinney into the open field below his own lawn.

His wife was in her hammock dangling a tightly encased black-velvet leg, a flame-coloured sleeve and a pair of enormous ear-rings. The cocktail tray was ready on her iron table.

"How late you are," she said, idly. "Dinner in half an hour. What have you been up to at Nunspardon?"

"I had to see George."

"What about?"

"Some business his father asked me to do."

"How illuminating."

"It was very private, my dear."

"How *is* George?"

The Colonel remembered George's empurpled face and said, "Still rather upset."

"We must ask him to dinner. I'm learning to play golf with him to-morrow, by the way. He's giving me some clubs. Nice, isn't it?"

"When did you arrange that?"

"Just now. About twenty minutes ago," she said, watching him.

"Kitty, I'd rather you didn't."

"You don't by any chance suspect me of playing you false with George, do you?"

"Well," said the Colonel after a long pause, "are you?"

"No."

"I still think it might be better not to play golf with him tomorrow."

"Why on earth?"

"Kitty, what have you said to George about Mark and Rose?"

"Nothing you couldn't have seen for yourself, darling. Rose is obviously head over heels in love with Mark."

"I don't believe you."

"My good Maurice, you don't suppose the girl is going to spend the rest of her existence doting on Daddy, do you?"

"I wouldn't have it for the world. Not for the world."

"Well, then."

"But I . . . I didn't know . . . I still don't believe . . ."

"He turned up here five minutes ago looking all churned-up, and they're closeted together in the drawing-room. Go and see. I'll excuse your changing, if you like."

"Thank you, my dear," the Colonel said miserably and went indoors.

If he hadn't been so rattled and worried he would no doubt have given some sort of warning of his approach. As it was, he crossed the heavy carpet of the hall, opened the drawing-room door and discovered his daughter locked in Mark Lacklander's arms, from which embrace she was making but ineffectual attempts to escape.

CHAPTER THREE **The Valley of the Chyne**

Rose and Mark behaved in the classic manner of surprised lovers. They released each other, Rose turned white and Mark red, and neither of them uttered a word.

The Colonel said, "I'm sorry, my dear. Forgive me," and made his daughter a little bow.

Rose, with a sort of agitated spontaneity, ran to him, linked her hands behind his head and cried, "It had to happen sometime, darling, didn't it?"

Mark said, "Sir, I want her to marry me."

"But I won't," Rose said, "I won't unless you can be happy about it. I've told him."

The Colonel, with great gentleness, freed himself and then put an arm round his daughter.

"Where have you come from, Mark?" he asked.

"From Chyning. It's my day at the hospital."

"Yes, I see." The Colonel looked from his daughter to her lover and thought how ardent and vulnerable they seemed. "Sit down, both of you," he said. "I've got to think what I'm going to say to you. Sit down."

They obeyed him with an air of bewilderment.

"When you go back to Nunspardon, Mark," he said, "you will find your father very much upset. That is because of a talk I've just had with him. I'm at liberty to repeat the substance of that talk to you, but I feel some hesitation in doing so. I think he should be allowed to break it to you himself."

"*Break* it to me?"

"It is not good news. You will find him entirely opposed to any thought of your marriage with Rose."

"I can't believe it," Mark said.

"You will, however. You may even find that you yourself (forgive me, Rose, my love, but it may be so) feel quite differently about . . ." the Colonel smiled faintly . . . "about contracting an alliance with a Cartarette."

"But, my poorest Daddy," Rose ejaculated, clinging to a note of irony, "what have you been up to?"

"The very devil and all, I'm afraid, my poppet," her father rejoined.

"Well, whatever it may be," Mark said and stood up, "I can assure you that blue murder wouldn't make me change my mind about Rose."

"O," the Colonel rejoined mildly, "this is not blue murder."

"Good." Mark turned to Rose. "Don't be fussed, darling," he said. "I'll go home and sort it out."

"By all means, go home," the Colonel agreed, "and try."

He took Mark by the arm and led him to the door.

"You won't feel very friendly towards me tomorrow, Mark," he said. "Will you try to believe that the action I've been compelled to take is one that I detest taking?"

"Compelled?" Mark repeated. "Yes, well . . . yes, of course." He stuck out the Lacklander jaw and knitted the Lacklander brows. "Look here, sir," he said, "if my father welcomes our engagement . . . and I can't conceive of his doing anything else . . . will you have any objection? I'd better tell you now that no objection on either side will make the smallest difference."

"In that case," the Colonel said, "your question is academic. And now

I'll leave you to have a word with Rose before you go home." He held out his hand. "Goodbye, Mark."

When the Colonel had gone, Mark turned to Rose and took her hands in his. "But how ridiculous," he said. "How in the world could these old boys cook up anything that would upset *us?*"

"I don't know. I don't know how they could, but it's serious. He's terribly worried, poor darling."

"Well," Mark said, "it's no good attempting a diagnosis before we've heard the history. I'll go home, see what's happened and ring you up in about fifteen minutes. The all-important, utterly bewildering and Heaven-sent joy is that you love me, Rose. Nothing," Mark continued with an air of coining a brand-new phrase, "nothing can alter that. Au revoir, darling."

He kissed Rose in a business-like manner and was gone.

She sat still for a time hugging to herself the knowledge of their feeling for each other. What had happened to all her scruples about leaving her father? She didn't even feel properly upset by her father's extraordinary behaviour, and when she realized this circumstance, she realized the extent of her enthrallment. She stood in the French window of the drawing-room and looked across the valley to Nunspardon. It was impossible to be anxious . . . her whole being ached with happiness. It was now and for the first time that Rose understood the completeness of love.

Time went by without her taking thought for it. The gong sounded for dinner and at the same moment the telephone rang. She flew to it.

"Rose," Mark said. "Say at once that you love me. At once."

"I love you."

"And on your most sacred word of honour that you'll marry me. Say it, Rose. Promise it. Solemnly promise."

"I solemnly promise."

"Good," said Mark. "I'll come back at nine."

"Do you know what's wrong?"

"Yes. It's damn' ticklish. Bless you, darling. Till nine."

"Till nine," Rose said and in a state of enthrallment went in to dinner.

2

By eight o'clock the evening depression had begun to settle over Commander Syce. At about five o'clock, when the sun was over the yard-arm, he had a brandy and soda. This raised his spirits. With its successors, up to the third or fourth, they rose still further. During this period he saw himself taking a job and making a howling success of it. From that emotional eminence he fell away with each succeeding dram, and it was during his decline that he usually took to archery. It had been in such a state of almost suicidal depression that he had suddenly shot an arrow over his coppice into Mr. Danberry-Phinn's bottom meadow and slain the mother of Thomasina Twitchett.

To-night the onset of depression was more than usually severe. Perhaps his encounter with the Colonel, whom he liked, gave point to his own loneliness. Moreover, his married couple were on their annual holiday and he had not been bothered to do anything about an evening meal. He found his arrow and limped back to the archery lawn. He no longer wanted to shoot. His gammy leg ached, but he thought he'd take a turn up the drive.

When he arrived at the top, it was to discover Nurse Kettle seated by the roadside in gloomy contemplation of her bicycle, which stood upside down on its saddle and handlebars.

"Hullo, Commander," said Nurse Kettle, "I've got a puncture."

"Evening. Really? Bore for you," Syce shot out at her.

"I can't make up me great mind to push her the three miles to Chyning, so I'm going to have a shot at running repairs. Pumping's no good," said Nurse Kettle.

She had opened a tool kit and was looking dubiously at its contents. Syce hung off and on and watched her make a pass with a lever at her tyre.

"Not like that," he shouted when he could no longer endure it. "Great grief, you'll get nowhere that fashion."

"I believe you."

"And in any case you'll want a bucket of water to find the puncture." She looked helplessly at him. "Here!" he mumbled. "Give it here."

He righted the bicycle and with a further, completely inaudible remark began to wheel it down his drive. Nurse Kettle gathered up her tool kit and followed. A look strangely compounded of compassion and amusement had settled on her face.

Commander Syce wheeled the bicycle into a gardener's shed and without the slightest attempt at any further conversation set about the removal of the tyre. Nurse Kettle hitched herself up on a bench and watched him. Presently she began to talk.

"I *am* obliged to you. I've had a bit of a day. Epidemic in the village, odd cases all over the place, and then this happens. There! Aren't you neat-fingered. I looked in at Nunspardon this evening," she continued. "Lady Lacklander's got a 'toe,' and Dr. Mark arranged for me to do the fomentations."

Commander Syce made an inarticulate noise.

"If you ask *me*, the new baronet's feeling his responsibilities. Came in just as I was leaving. Very bad colour and jumpy," Nurse Kettle gossiped cosily. She swung her short legs and interrupted herself from time to time to admire Syce's handiwork. "Pity!" she thought. "Shaky hands. Alcoholic skin. Nice chap, too. Pity!"

He repaired the puncture and replaced the tube and tyre. When he had finished and made as if to stand up, he gave a sharp cry of pain, clapped his hand to the small of his back and sank down again on his knees.

"Hul—lo!" Nurse Kettle ejaculated. "What's all this? 'Bago?"

Commander Syce swore under his breath. Between clenched teeth he implored her to go away. "Most frightfully sorry," he groaned. "Ask you to excuse me. Ach!"

It was now that Nurse Kettle showed the quality that caused people to prefer her to grander and more up-to-date nurses. She exuded dependability, resourcefulness and authority. Even the common and pitilessly breezy flavour of her remarks was comfortable. To Commander Syce's conjurations to leave him alone, followed in the extremity of his pain by furious oaths, she paid no attention. She went down on all fours beside him, enticed and aided him towards the bench, encouraged him to use it and her own person as aids to rising, and finally had him, though almost bent double, on his feet. She helped him into his house and lowered him down on a sofa in a dismal drawing-room.

"Down-a-bumps," she said. Sweating and gasping, he reclined and glared at her. "Now, what are we going to do about *you*, I wonder? Did I or did I not see a rug in the hall? Wait a bit."

She went out and came back with a rug. She called him "dear" and, taking his pain seriously, covered him up, went out again and returned with a glass of water. "Making myself at home, I suppose you're thinking. Here's a couple of aspirins to go on with," said Nurse Kettle.

He took them without looking at her. "Please don't trouble," he groaned. "Thank you. Under my own steam." She gave him a look and went out again.

In her absence, he attempted to get up but was galvanized with a monstrous jab of lumbago and subsided in agony. He began to think she had gone for good and to wonder how he was to support life while the attack lasted, when he heard her moving about in some remote part of the house. In a moment she came in with two hot-water bags.

"At this stage," she said, "heat's the ticket."

"Where did you get those things?"

"Borrowed 'em from the Cartarettes."

"My God!"

She laid them against his back.

"Dr. Mark's coming to look at you," she said.

"My God!"

"He was at the Cartarettes' and if you ask me, there's going to be some news from that quarter before any of us are much older. At least," Nurse Kettle added rather vexedly, "I *would* have said so, if it hadn't been for them all looking a bit put out." To his horror she began to take off his shoes.

"With a yo-heave-ho," said Nurse Kettle out of compliment to the navy. "Aspirin doing its stuff?"

"I . . . I think so. I *do beg* . . ."

"I suppose your bedroom's upstairs?"

"I do BEG . . ."

"We'll see what the doctor says, but I'd suggest you doss down in the housekeeper's room to save the stairs. I mean to say," Nurse Kettle added with a hearty laugh, "always provided there's no housekeeper."

She looked into his face so good-humouredly and with such an air of believing him to be glad of her help that he found himself accepting it.

"Like a cup of tea?" she asked.

"No thank you."

"Well, it won't be anything stronger unless the doctor says so."

He reddened, caught her eye and grinned.

"Come," she said, "that's better."

"I'm really ashamed to trouble you so much."

"I might have said the same about my bike, mightn't I? There's the doctor."

She bustled out again and came back with Mark Lacklander.

Mark, who was a good deal paler than his patient, took a crisp line with Syce's expostulations.

"All right," he said. "I daresay I'm entirely extraneous. This isn't a professional visit if you'd rather not."

"Great grief, my dear chap, I don't mean that. Only too grateful but . . . I mean . . . busy man . . . right itself . . ."

"Well, suppose I take a look-see," Mark suggested. "We won't move you."

The examination was brief. "If the lumbago doesn't clear up, we can do something a bit more drastic," Mark said, "but in the meantime Nurse Kettle'll get you to bed . . ."

"Good God!"

". . . and look in again to-morrow morning. So will I. You'll need one or two things; I'll ring up the hospital and get them sent out at once. All right?"

"Thank you. Thank you. You don't," said Syce, to his own surprise, "look terribly fit yourself. Sorry to have dragged you in."

"That's all right. We'll bring your bed in here and put it near the telephone. Ring up if you're in difficulties. By the way, Mrs. Cartarette offered . . ."

"NO!" shouted Commander Syce and turned purple.

". . . to send in meals," Mark added. "But of course you may be up and about again to-morrow. In the meantime I think we can safely leave you to Nurse Kettle. Good-night."

When he had gone, Nurse Kettle said cheerfully, "You'll have to put up with me, it seems, if you don't want lovely ladies all round you. Now we'll get you washed up and settled for the night."

Half an hour later when he was propped up in bed with a cup of hot milk and a plate of bread and butter and the lamp within easy reach, Nurse Kettle looked down at him with her quizzical air.

"Well," she said, "I shall now, as they say, love you and leave you. Be good and if you can't be good, be careful."

"Thank you," gabbled Commander Syce, nervously. "Thank you, thank you, thank you."

She had plodded over to the door before his voice arrested her. "I . . . ah . . . I don't suppose," he said, "that you are familiar with Aubrey's *Brief Lives*, are you?"

"No," she said. "Who was *he* when he was at home?"

"He wrote a 'brief life' of a man called Sir Jonas Moore. It begins: 'Sciatica he cured it, by boyling his buttocks.' I'm glad, at least, you don't propose to try that remedy."

"Well!" cried Nurse Kettle delightedly. "You *are* coming out of your shell, to be sure. Nighty-bye."

3

During the next three days Nurse Kettle, pedalling about her duties, had occasion to notice, and she was sharp in such matters, that something untoward was going on in the district. Wherever she went, whether it was to attend upon Lady Lacklander's toe, or upon the abscess of the gardener's child at Hammer, or upon Commander Syce's strangely persistent lumbago, she felt a kind of heightened tension in the behaviour of her patients and also in the behaviour of young Dr. Mark Lacklander. Rose Cartarette, when she encountered her in the garden, was white and jumpy; the Colonel looked strained and Mrs. Cartarette singularly excited.

"Kettle," Lady Lacklander said, on Wednesday, wincing a little as she endured the approach of a fomentation to her toe, "have you got the cure for a bad conscience?"

Nurse Kettle did not resent being addressed in this restoration-comedy fashion by Lady Lacklander, who had known her for some twenty years and used the form with an intimate and even an affectionate air much prized by Nurse Kettle.

"Ah," said the latter, "there's no mixture-as-before for *that* sort of trouble."

"No. How long," Lady Lacklander went on, "have you been looking after us in Swevenings, Kettle?"

"Thirty years if you count five in the hospital at Chyning."

"Twenty-five years of fomentations, enemas, slappings, and thumpings," mused Lady Lacklander. "And I suppose you've learnt quite a lot about us in that time. There's nothing like illness to reveal character and there's nothing like a love affair," she added unexpectedly, "to disguise it. This is agony," she ended mildly, referring to the fomentation.

"Stick it if you can, dear," Nurse Kettle advised, and Lady Lacklander for her part did not object to being addressed as "dear" by Nurse Kettle, who continued, "How do you mean, I wonder, about love disguising character?"

"When people are in love," Lady Lacklander said with a little scream as a new fomentation was applied, "they instinctively present themselves to each other in their most favourable light. They assume pleasing characteristics as unconsciously as a cock pheasant puts on his spring plumage. They display such virtues as magnanimity, charitableness and modesty and wait for them to be admired. They develop a positive genius for suppressing their least attractive points. They can't help it, you know, Kettle. It's just the behaviourism of courtship."

"Fancy."

"Now don't pretend you don't know what I'm talking about, because you most certainly do. You think straight and that's more than anybody else seems to be capable of doing in Swevenings. You're a gossip, of course," Lady Lacklander added, "but I don't think you're a malicious gossip, are you?"

"Certainly not. The idea!"

"No. Tell me, now, without any frills, what do you think of *us*?"

"Meaning, I take it," Nurse Kettle returned, "the aristocracy?"

"Meaning exactly that. Do you," asked Lady Lacklander with relish, "find us effete, ineffectual, vicious, obsolete and altogether extraneous?"

"No," said Nurse Kettle stoutly, "I don't."

"Some of us are, you know."

Nurse Kettle squatted back on her haunches retaining a firm grip on Lady Lacklander's little heel. "It's not the people so much as the idea," she said.

"Ah," said Lady Lacklander, "you're an Elizabethan, Kettle. You *believe* in degree. You're a female Ulysses, old girl. But degree is now dependent upon behaviour, I'd have you know."

Nurse Kettle gave a jolly laugh and said she didn't know what that meant. Lady Lacklander rejoined that, among other things, it meant that if people fall below something called a certain standard, they are asking for trouble. "I mean," Lady Lacklander went on, scowling with physical pain and mental concentration, "I mean we'd better behave ourselves in the admittedly few jobs that by right of heritage used to be ours. I mean, finally, that whether they think we're rubbish or whether they think we're not, people still expect that in certain situations we will give certain reactions. Don't they, Kettle?"

Nurse Kettle said she supposed they did.

"Not," Lady Lacklander said, "that I give a damn what they think. But still . . ."

She remained wrapped in moody contemplation while Nurse Kettle completed the treatment and bandaged the toe.

"In short," her formidable patient at last declaimed, "we can allow ourselves to be almost anything but shabbily behaved. That we'd better avoid. I'm extremely worried, Kettle." Nurse Kettle looked up enquiringly. "Tell me, is there any gossip in the village about my grandson? Romantic gossip?"

"A bit," Nurse Kettle said and after a pause added, "It'd be lovely, wouldn't it? She's a sweet girl. *And* an heiress into the bargain."

"Umph."

"Which is not to be sneezed at nowadays, I suppose. They tell me everything goes to the daughter."

"Entailed," Lady Lacklander said. "Mark, of course, gets nothing until he succeeds. But it's not that that bothers me."

"Whatever it is, if I were you, I should consult Dr. Mark, Lady Lacklander. An old head on young shoulders if ever I saw one."

"My dear soul, my grandson is, as you have observed, in love. He is, therefore, as I have tried to point out, extremely likely to take up a highfalutin' attitude. Besides, he's involved. No, I must take matters into my own hands, Kettle. Into my own hands. You go past Hammer on your way home, don't you?"

Nurse Kettle said she did.

"I've written a note to Colonel Cartarette. Drop it there like a good creature, will you?"

Nurse Kettle said she would and fetched it from Lady Lacklander's writing desk.

"It's a pity," Lady Lacklander muttered, as Nurse Kettle was about to leave her. "It's a pity poor George is such an ass."

4

She considered that George gave only too clear a demonstration of being an ass when she caught a glimpse of him on the following evening. He was playing a round of golf with Mrs. Cartarette. George, having attained the tricky age for Lacklanders, had fallen into a muddled, excited dotage upon Kitty Cartarette. She made him feel dangerous, and this sensation enchanted him. She told him repeatedly how chivalrous he was and so cast a glow of knight-errantry over impulses that are not usually seen in that light. She allowed him only the most meagre rewards, doling out the lesser stimulants of courtship in positively homeopathic doses. Thus on the Nunspardon golf course, he was allowed to watch, criticize and correct her swing. If his interest in this exercise was far from being purely athletic, Mrs. Cartarette gave only the slightest hint that she was aware of the fact and industriously swung and swung again while he fell back to observe, and advanced to adjust, her technique.

Lady Lacklander, tramping down River Path in the cool of the evening with a footman in attendance to carry her sketching impedimenta and her shooting-stick, observed her son and his pupil as it were in pantomime on the second tee. She noticed how George rocked on his feet, with his head on one side, while Mrs. Cartarette swung, as Lady Lacklander angrily noticed, everything that a woman could swing. Lady Lacklander looked at the two figures with distaste tempered by speculation. "Can George," she wondered, "have some notion of employing the strategy of indirect attack upon Maurice? But no, poor boy, he hasn't got the brains."

The two figures disappeared over the crest of the hill, and Lady Lacklander plodded heavily on in great distress of mind. Because of her ulcerated toe she wore a pair of her late husband's shooting boots. On her head was a battered solar topee of immense antiquity which she found convenient as an eyeshade. For the rest, her vast person was clad in baggy tweeds and a tent-like blouse. Her hands, as always, were encrusted with diamonds.

She and the footman reached Bottom Bridge, turned left and came to a halt before a group of elders and the prospect of a bend in the stream. The footman, under Lady Lacklander's direction, set up her easel, filled her water-jar at the stream, placed her camp stool and put her shooting-stick beside it. When she fell back from her work in order to observe it as a whole, Lady Lacklander was in the habit of supporting her bulk upon the shooting-stick.

The footman left her. She would reappear in her own time at Nuns-pardon and change for dinner at nine o'clock. The footman would return and collect her impedimenta. She fixed her spectacles on her nose, directed at her subject the sort of glance Nurse Kettle often bestowed on a recalcitrant patient, and set to work, massive and purposeful before her easel.

It was at half past six that she established herself there, in the meadow on the left bank of the Chyne not far below Bottom Bridge.

At seven, Mr. Danberry-Phinn, having assembled his paraphernalia for fishing, set off down Watt's Hill. He did not continue to Bottom Bridge but turned left, and made for the upper reaches of the Chyne.

At seven, Mark Lacklander, having looked in on a patient in the village, set off on foot along Watt's Lane. He carried his case of instruments, as he wished to lance the abscess of the gardener's child at Hammer, and his racket and shoes, as he proposed to play tennis with Rose Cartarette. He also hoped to have an extremely serious talk with her father.

At seven, Nurse Kettle, having delivered Lady Lacklander's note at Hammer, turned in at Commander Syce's drive and free-wheeled to his front door.

At seven, Sir George Lacklander, finding himself favourably situated in a sheltered position behind a group of trees, embraced Mrs. Cartarette with determination, fervour and an ulterior motive.

It was at this hour that the hopes, passions and fears that had slowly mounted in intensity since the death of Sir Harold Lacklander began to gather an emotional momentum and slide towards each other like so many downhill streams, influenced in their courses by accidents and detail, but destined for a common and profound agitation.

At Hammer, Rose and her father sat in his study and gazed at each other in dismay.

"When did Mark tell you?" Colonel Cartarette asked.

"On that same night . . . after you came in and . . . and found us. He went to Nunspardon and his father told him and then he came back here and told me. Of course," Rose said looking at her father with eyes as blue as periwinkles behind their black lashes, "of course it wouldn't have been any good for Mark to pretend nothing had happened. It's quite extraordinary how each of us seems to know exactly what the other one's thinking."

The Colonel leant his head on his hand and half smiled at this expression of what he regarded as one of the major fallacies of love. "My poor darling," he murmured.

"Daddy, you do understand, don't you, that theoretically Mark is absolutely on your side? Because . . . well, because the facts of any case always should be demonstrated. I mean, that's the scientific point of view."

The Colonel's half-smile twisted, but he said nothing.

"And I agree, too, absolutely," Rose said, "other things being equal."

"Ah!" said the Colonel.

"But they're not, darling," Rose cried out, "they're nothing like equal. In terms of human happiness, they're all cockeyed. Mark says his grandmother's so desperately worried that with all this coming on top of Sir Harold's death and everything she may crack up altogether."

The Colonel's study commanded a view of his own spinney and of that part of the valley that the spinney did not mask: Bottom Bridge and a small area below it on the right bank of the Chyne. Rose went to the window and looked down. "She's down there somewhere," she said, "sketching in Bottom Meadow on the far side. She only sketches when she's fussed."

"She's sent me a chit. She wants me to go down and talk to her at eight o'clock when I suppose she'll have done a sketch and hopes to feel less fussed. Damned inconvenient hour but there you are. I'll cut dinner, darling, and try the evening rise. Ask them to leave supper for me, will you, and apologise to Kitty."

"O.K.," Rose said with forced airiness. "And, of course," she added, "there's the further difficulty of Mark's papa."

"George."

"Yes, indeed, George. Well, we know he's not exactly as bright as sixpence, don't we, but all the same he is Mark's papa, and he's cutting up most awfully rough and . . ."

Rose caught back her breath, her lips trembled, and her eyes filled with tears. She launched herself into her father's arms and burst into a flood of tears. "What's the use," poor Rose sobbed, "of being a brave little woman? I'm not in the least brave. When Mark asked me to marry him, I said I wouldn't because of you and there I was, so miserable that when he asked me again I said I would. And now, when we're so desperately in love, this happens. We have to do them this really frightful injury. Mark says of course they must take it and it won't make any difference to *us*, but of course it *will*, and how can I bear to be married to Mark and know how his people feel about you when next to Mark, my darling, darling Daddy, I love you best in the world? And *his* father," Rose wept, "*his* father says that if Mark marries me, he'll never forgive him and that they'll do a sort of Montague and Capulet thing at us and, darling, it wouldn't be much fun for Mark and me, would it, to be star-crossed lovers?"

"My poor baby," murmured the agitated and sentimental Colonel, "my poor baby!" And he administered a number of unintentionally hard thumps between his daughter's shoulder blades.

"It's so many people's happiness," Rose sobbed. "It's all of us."

Her father dabbed at her eyes with his own handkerchief, kissed her and put her aside. In his turn he went over to the window and looked down at Bottom Bridge and up at the roofs of Nunspardon. There were no figures in view on the golf course.

"You know, Rose," the Colonel said in a changed voice, "I don't carry the whole responsibility. There is a final decision to be made, and mine must rest upon it. Don't hold out too many hopes, my darling, but I suppose there is a chance. I've time to get it over before I talk to Lady Lacklander, and indeed I suppose I should. There's nothing to be gained by any further delay. I'll go now."

He went to his desk, unlocked a drawer and took out an envelope. Rose said, "Does Kitty . . . ?"

"Oh, yes," the Colonel said. "She knows."

"Did you tell her, Daddy?"

The Colonel had already gone to the door. Without turning his head and with an air too casual to be convincing, he said, "O, no. No. She arranged to play a round of golf with George, and I imagine he elected to tell her. He's a fearful old gas-bag is George."

"She's playing now, isn't she?"

"Is she? Yes," said the Colonel, "I believe she is. He came to fetch her, I think. It's good for her to get out."

"Yes, rather," Rose agreed.

Her father went out to call on Mr. Octavius Danberry-Phinn. He took his fishing gear with him as he intended to go straight on to his meeting with Lady Lacklander and to ease his troubled mind afterwards with the evening rise. He also took his spaniel Skip, who was trained to good behaviour when he accompanied his master to the trout stream.

5

Lady Lacklander consulted the diamond-encrusted watch which was pinned to her tremendous bosom and discovered that it was now seven o'clock. She had been painting for half an hour and an all-too-familiar phenomenon had emerged from her efforts.

"It's a curious thing," she meditated, "that a woman of my character and determination should produce such a puny affair. However, it's got me in better trim for Maurice Cartarette, and that's a damn' good thing. An hour to go if he's punctual, and he's sure to be that."

She tilted her sketch and ran a faint green wash over the foreground. When it was partly dry, she rose from her stool, tramped some distance away to the crest of a hillock, seated herself on her shooting-stick and contemplated her work through a lorgnette tricked out with diamonds. The shooting-stick sank beneath her in the soft meadowland so that the disk which was designed to check its descent was itself imbedded to the depth of several inches. When Lady Lacklander returned to her easel, she merely abandoned her shooting-stick, which remained in a vertical position and from a distance looked a little like a giant fungoid growth. Sticking up above intervening hillocks and rushes, it was observed over the top of his glasses by the long-sighted Mr. Phinn when, accompanied by Thomasina Twitchett, he came nearer to Bottom Bridge. Keeping on the right bank, he began to cast his fly in a somewhat mannered but adroit fashion over the waters most often frequented by the Old 'Un. Lady Lacklander, whose ears were as sharp as his, heard the whirr of his reel and, remaining invisible, was perfectly able to deduce the identity and movements of the angler. At the same time, far above them on Watt's Hill, Colonel Cartarette, finding nobody but seven cats at home at Jacob's Cottage, walked round the house and looking down into the little valley at once spotted both Lady Lacklander and Mr. Phinn, like figures in Nurse Kettle's imaginary map, the one squatting on her camp stool, the other in slow motion near Bottom Bridge.

"I've time to speak to him before I see her," thought the Colonel. "But I'll leave it here in case we don't meet." He posted his long envelope in Mr. Phinn's front door, and then greatly troubled in spirit, he made for the river path and went down into the valley, the old spaniel, Skip, walking at his heels.

Nurse Kettle, looking through the drawing-room window at Uplands, caught sight of the Colonel before he disappeared beyond Commander Syce's spinney. She administered a final tattoo with the edges of her muscular hands on Commander Syce's lumbar muscles and said, "There goes the Colonel for the evening rise. You wouldn't have stood *that* amount of punishment two days ago, would you?"

"No," a submerged voice said, "I suppose not."

"Well! So that's all I get for my trouble."

"No, no! Look here, look here!" he gabbled, twisting his head in an attempt to see her. "Good heavens! What are you saying?"

"All right. I know. I was only pulling your leg. There!" she said. "That's all for to-day and I fancy it won't be long before I wash my hands of you altogether."

"Of course I can't expect to impose on your kindness any longer."

Nurse Kettle was clearing up. She appeared not to hear this remark and presently bustled away to wash her hands. When she returned, Syce was sitting on the edge of his improvised bed. He wore slacks, a shirt, a scarf and a dressing gown.

"Jolly D.," said Nurse Kettle. "Done it all yourself."

"I hope you will give me the pleasure of joining me for a drink before you go."

"On duty?"

"Isn't it off duty, now?"

"Well," said Nurse Kettle, "I'll have a drink with you, but I hope it won't mean that when I've gone on me way rejoicing, you're going to have half a dozen more with yourself."

Commander Syce turned red and muttered something about a fellah having nothing better to do.

"Get along," said Nurse Kettle, "find something better. The idea!"

They had their drinks, looking at each other with an air of comradeship. Commander Syce, using a walking-stick and holding himself at an unusual angle, got out an album of photographs taken when he was on the active list in the navy. Nurse Kettle adored photographs and was genuinely interested in a long sequence of naval vessels, odd groups of officers and views of seaports. Presently she turned a page and discovered quite a dashing water-colour of a corvette and then an illustrated menu with lively little caricatures in the margin. These she greatly admired and observing a terrified and defiant expression on the face of her host, ejaculated, "You never did these yourself! You *did!* Well, aren't you the clever one!"

Without answering, he produced a small portfolio, which he silently thrust at her. It contained many more sketches. Although Nurse Kettle knew nothing about pictures, she did, she maintained, know what she liked. And she liked these very much indeed. They were direct statements of facts, and she awarded them direct statements of approval and was about to shut the portfolio when a sketch that had faced the wrong way round caught her attention. She turned it over. It was of a woman lying on a chaise-longue smoking a cigarette in a jade holder. A bougainvillea flowered in the background.

"Why," Nurse Kettle ejaculated. "Why, that's Mrs. Cartarette!"

If Syce had made some kind of movement to snatch the sketch from her, he checked himself before it was completed. He said very rapidly, "Party. Met her Far East. Shore leave. Forgotten all about it."

"That would be before they were married, wouldn't it?" Nurse Kettle remarked with perfect simplicity. She shut the portfolio, said, "You know

I believe you could make my picture-map of Swevenings," and told him
of her great desire for one. When she got up and collected her belongings, he too rose, but with an ejaculation of distress.

"I see I haven't made a job of you yet," she remarked. "Same time
to-morrow suit you?"

"Admirably," he said. "Thank you, thank you, thank you." He gave
her one of his rare painful smiles and watched her as she walked down
the path towards his spinney. It was now a quarter to nine.

6

Nurse Kettle had left her bicycle in the village, where she was spending
the evening with the Women's Institute. She therefore took the river
path. Dusk had fallen over the valley of the Chyne, and as she descended
into it, her own footfall sounded unnaturally loud on the firm turf.
Thump, thump, thump she went, down the hillside. Once, she stopped
dead, tilted her head and listened. From behind her at Uplands came the
not unfamiliar sound of a twang followed by a sharp penetrating blow.
She smiled to herself and walked on. Only desultory rural sounds disturbed the quiet of nightfall. She could actually hear the cool voice of
the stream.

She did not cross Bottom Bridge but followed a rough path along the
right bank of the Chyne, past a group of elders and another of willows.
This second group, extending in a sickle-shaped mass from the water's
edge into Bottom Meadow, rose up vapourishly in the dusk. She could
smell willow leaves and wet soil. As sometimes happens when we are
solitary, she had the sensation of being observed, but she was not a fanciful woman and soon dismissed this feeling.

"It's turned much cooler," she thought.

A cry of mourning, intolerably loud, rose from beyond the willows and
hung on the night air. A thrush whirred out of the thicket close to her
face, and the cry broke and wavered again. It was the howl of a dog.

She pushed through the thicket into an opening by the river and found
the body of Colonel Cartarette with his spaniel Skip beside it, mourning
him.

CHAPTER FOUR

Bottom Meadow

Nurse Kettle was acquainted with death. She did not need Skip's lament to tell her that the curled figure resting its head on a turf of river grass was dead. She knelt beside it and pushed her hand under the tweed jacket and silk shirt. "Cooling," she thought. A tweed hat with fisherman's flies in the band lay over the face. Someone, she thought, might almost have dropped it there. She lifted it and remained quite still with it suspended in her hand. The Colonel's temple had been broken as if his head had come under a waxworker's hammer. The spaniel threw back his head and howled again.

"O, do be quiet!" Nurse Kettle ejaculated. She replaced the hat and stood up, knocking her head against a branch. The birds that spent the night in the willows stirred again and some of them flew out with a sharp whirring sound. The Chyne gurgled and plopped and somewhere up in Nunspardon woods an owl hooted. "He has been murdered," thought Nurse Kettle.

Through her mind hurtled all the axioms of police procedure as laid down in her chosen form of escape-literature. One must, she recollected, not touch the body, and she had touched it. One must send at once for the police, but she had nobody to send. She thought there was also something about not leaving the body, yet to telephone or to fetch Mr. Oliphant, the police-sergeant at Chyning, she would have to leave the body, and while she was away, the spaniel, she supposed, would sit beside it and howl. It was now quite darkish and the moon not yet up. She could see, however, not far from the Colonel's hands, the glint of a trout's scales in the grass and of a knife blade nearby. His rod was laid out on the lip of the bank, less than a pace from where he lay. None of these things, of course, must be disturbed. Suddenly Nurse Kettle thought of Commander Syce, whose Christian name she had discovered was Geoffrey, and wished with all her heart that he was at hand to advise her. The discovery in herself of this impulse astonished her and, in a sort of flurry, she swapped Geoffrey Syce for Mark Lacklander. "I'll find the doctor," she thought.

She patted Skip. He whimpered and scratched at her knees with his paws. "Don't howl, doggy," she said in a trembling voice. "Good boy! Don't howl." She took up her bag and turned away.

As she made her way out of the willow grove, she wondered for the first time about the identity of the being who had reduced Colonel Cartarette to the status of a broken waxwork. A twig snapped. "Suppose," she thought, "he's still about! Help, what a notion!" And as she hurried back along the path to Bottom Bridge, she tried not to think of the dense shadows and dark hollows that lay about her. Up on Watt's Hill the three houses—Jacob's Cottage, Uplands and Hammer—all had lighted windows and drawn blinds. They looked very far off to Nurse Kettle.

She crossed Bottom Bridge and climbed the zigzag path that skirted the golf course, coming finally to the Nunspardon Home Spinney. Only now did she remember that her flashlamp was in her bag. She got it out and found that she was breathless. "Too quick up the hill," she thought. "Keep your shirt on, Kettle." River Path proper ran past the spinney to the main road, but a by-path led up through the trees into the grounds of Nunspardon. This she took and presently came out into the open gardens with the impressive Georgian façade straight ahead of her.

The footman who answered the front door bell was well enough known to her. "Yes, it's me again, William," she said. "Is the doctor at home?"

"He came in about an hour ago, miss."

"I want to see him. It's urgent."

"The family's in the library, miss. I'll ascertain . . ."

"Don't bother," said Nurse Kettle. "Or, yes. Ascertain if you like, but I'll be hard on your heels. Ask him if he'll come out here and speak to me."

He looked dubiously at her, but something in her face must have impressed him. He crossed the great hall and opened the library door. He left it open and Nurse Kettle heard him say, "Miss Kettle to see Dr. Lacklander, my lady."

"Me?" said Mark's voice. "O Lord! All right, I'll come."

"Bring her in here," Lady Lacklander's voice commanded. "Talk to her in here, Mark. I want to see Kettle." Hearing this, Nurse Kettle, without waiting to be summoned, walked quickly into the library. The three Lacklanders had turned in their chairs. George and Mark got up. Mark looked sharply at her and came quickly towards her. Lady Lacklander said, "Kettle! What's happened to *you!*"

Nurse Kettle said, "Good evening, Lady Lacklander. Good evening, Sir George." She put her hands behind her back and looked full at Mark. "May I speak to you, sir?" she said. "There's been an accident."

"All right, Nurse," Mark said. "To whom?"

"To Colonel Cartarette, sir."

The expression of enquiry seemed to freeze on their faces. It was as if they retired behind newly assumed masks.

"What sort of accident?" Mark said.

He stood behind Nurse Kettle and his grandmother and father. She shaped the word "killed" with her lips and tongue.

"Come out here," he muttered and took her by the arm.

"Not at all," his grandmother said. She heaved herself out of her chair and bore down upon them. "Not at all, Mark. What has happened to Maurice Cartarette? Don't keep things from me; I am probably in better trim to meet an emergency than anyone else in this house. What has happened to Maurice?"

Mark, still holding Nurse Kettle by the arm, said, "Very well, Gar. Nurse Kettle will tell us what has happened."

"Let's have it, then. And in case it's as bad as you look, Kettle, I suggest we all sit down. What did you say, George?"

Her son had made an indeterminate noise. He now said galvanically, "Yes, of course, Mama, by all means."

Mark pushed a chair forward for Nurse Kettle, and she took it thankfully. Her knees, she discovered, were wobbling.

"Now, then, out with it," said Lady Lacklander. "He's dead, isn't he, Kettle?"

"Yes, Lady Lacklander."

"Where?" Sir George demanded. Nurse Kettle told him.

"When," Lady Lacklander said, "did you discover him?"

"I've come straight up here, Lady Lacklander."

"But why here, Kettle? Why not to Uplands?"

"I must break it to Kitty," said Sir George.

"I must go to Rose," said Mark simultaneously.

"Kettle," said Lady Lacklander, "you used the word accident. What accident?"

"He has been murdered, Lady Lacklander," said Nurse Kettle.

The thought that crossed her mind after she had made this announcement was that the three Lacklanders were, in their several generations, superficially very much alike but that whereas in Lady Lacklander and Mark the distance between the eyes and the width of mouth suggested a certain generosity, in Sir George they seemed merely to denote the naive. Sir George's jaw had dropped, and handsome though he undoubtedly was, he gaped unhandsomely. As none of them spoke, she added, "So I thought I'd better report to you, sir."

"Do you mean," Sir George said loudly, "that he's lying there in my bottom meadow, murdered?"

"Yes, Sir George," Nurse Kettle said, "I do."

"How?" Mark said.

"Injuries to the head."

"You made quite sure, of course?"

"Quite sure."

Mark looked at his father. "We must ring the Chief Constable," he said. "Would you do that, Father? I'll go down with Nurse Kettle. One of us had better stay there till the police come. If you can't get the C.C., would you ring Sergeant Oliphant at Chyning?"

Sir George's hand went to his moustache. "I think," he said, "you may take it, Mark, that I understand my responsibilities."

Lady Lacklander said, "Don't be an ass, George. The boy's quite right," and her son, scarlet in the face, went off to the telephone. "Now," Lady Lacklander continued, "what are we going to do about Rose and that wife of his?"

"Gar . . ." Mark began, but his grandmother raised a fat glittering hand.

"Yes, yes," she said. "No doubt you want to break it to Rose, Mark, but in my opinion you will do better to let me see both of them first. I shall stay there until you appear. Order the car."

Mark rang the bell. "And you needn't wait," she added. "Take Miss Kettle with you." It was characteristic of Lady Lacklander that she restricted her use of the more peremptory form of address to the second person. She now used it. "Kettle," she said, "we're grateful to you and mustn't impose. Would you rather come with me or go back with my grandson? Which is best, do you think?"

"I'll go with the doctor, thank you, Lady Lacklander. I suppose," Nurse Kettle added composedly, "that as I found the body, I'll be required to make a statement."

She had moved with Mark to the door when Lady Lacklander's voice checked her.

"And I suppose," the elderly voice said, "that as I may have been the last person to speak to him, I shall be required to make one, too."

2

In the drawing-room at Hammer there was an incongruous company assembled. Kitty Cartarette, Mark Lacklander and Nurse Kettle waited there while Lady Lacklander sat with Rose in the Colonel's study. She had arrived first at Hammer, having been driven round in her great car while Mark and Nurse Kettle waited in the valley and George rang up the police station at Chyning. George had remembered he was a Justice of the Peace and was believed to be in telephonic conference with his brethren of the bench.

So it had fallen to Lady Lacklander to break the news to Kitty, whom she had found, wearing her black-velvet tights and flame-coloured top, in the drawing-room. Lady Lacklander in the course of a long life spent in many embassies had encountered every kind of eccentricity in female attire and was pretty well informed as to the predatory tactics of women whom, in the Far East, she had been wont to describe as "light cruisers." She had made up her mind about Kitty Cartarette but had seemed to be prepared to concede her certain qualities if she showed any signs of possessing them.

She had said, "My dear, I'm the bearer of bad tidings," and noticing that Kitty at once looked very frightened, had remarked to herself, "She thinks I mean to tackle her about George."

"Are you?" Kitty had said. "What sort of tidings, please?"

"About Maurice." Lady Lacklander had waited for a moment, added, "I'm afraid it's the worst kind of news," and had then told her. Kitty stared at her. "Dead?" she said. "Maurice dead? I don't believe you. How can he be dead? He's been fishing down below there and I daresay he's looked in at the pub." Her hands with their long painted nails began to tremble. "How can he be dead?" she repeated.

Lady Lacklander became more specific, and presently Kitty broke into a harsh strangulated sobbing, twisting her fingers together and turning her head aside. She walked about the room, still, Lady Lacklander noticed, swaying her hips. Presently she fetched up by a grog tray on a small table and shakily poured herself a drink.

"That's a sensible idea," Lady Lacklander said as the neck of the decanter chattered against the glass. Kitty awkwardly offered her a drink, which she declined with perfect equanimity. "Her manner," she thought to herself, "is really too dreadful. What shall I do if George marries her?"

It was at this juncture that Nurse Kettle and Mark had appeared outside the French windows. Lady Lacklander signalled to them. "Here are my grandson and Nurse Kettle," she said to Kitty. "Shall they come in? I think it would be a good idea, don't you?"

Kitty said shakily, "Yes, please. Yes, if you like." Lady Lacklander heaved her bulk out of her chair and let them in.

"Sergeant Oliphant's there," Mark murmured. "They're going to ring Scotland Yard. Does Rose . . . ?"

"Not yet. She's out in the garden, somewhere."

Mark went across to Kitty and spoke to her with a quiet authority that his grandmother instantly approved. She noticed how Kitty steadied under it, how Mark, without fussing, got her into a chair. Nurse Kettle, as a matter of course, came forward and took the glass when Kitty had emptied it. A light and charming voice sang in the hall:

"Come away, come away, death . . ." and Mark turned sharply.

"I'll go," his grandmother said, "and I'll fetch you when she asks for you."

With a swifter movement than either her size or her age would have seemed to allow she had gone into the hall. The little song of death stopped, and the door shut behind Lady Lacklander.

Kitty Cartarette was quieter but still caught her breath now and again in a harsh sob.

"Sorry," she said looking from Nurse Kettle to Mark. "Thanks. It's just the shock."

"Yes, of course, dear," Nurse Kettle said.

"I sort of can't believe it. You know?"

"Yes, of course," Mark said.

"It seems so queer . . . Maurice!" She looked at Mark. "What was that," she said, "about somebody doing it? Is it true?"

"I'm afraid it looks very much like it."

"I'd forgotten," she muttered vaguely. "You've seen him, haven't you, and you're a doctor, of course." Her mouth trembled. She wiped the back of her hand over it. A trail of red was dragged across her cheek. It was a sufficient indication of her state of mind that she seemed to be unaware of it. She said, "No, it's no good, I can't believe it. We saw him down there, fishing." And then she suddenly demanded, "Where's George?"

Nurse Kettle saw Mark's back stiffen. "My father?" he asked.

"O, yes, of course, I'd forgotten," she said again, shaking her head. "He's your father. Silly of me."

"He's looking after one or two things that must be done. You see, the police have had to be told at once."

"Is George getting the police?"

"He's rung them up. He will, I think, come here as soon as he can."

"Yes," she said. "I expect he will."

Nurse Kettle saw George's son compress his lips. At that moment George himself walked in and the party became even less happily assorted.

Nurse Kettle had acquired a talent for retiring into whatever background presented itself, and this talent she now exercised. She moved through the open French window onto the terrace, shut the door after her and sat on a garden seat within view of the drawing-room but facing across the now completely dark valley. Mark, who would perhaps have liked to follow her, stood his ground. His father, looking extraordinarily handsome and not a little self-conscious, went straight to Kitty. She used the gesture that Mark had found embarrassing and extended her left hand to Sir George, who kissed it with an air nicely compounded of embarrassment, deference, distress and devotion.

"My dear Kitty," said Sir George in a special voice, "I'm so terribly, terribly sorry. What can one say! What can one do!"

He apparently had already said and done more than any of the others to assuage Kitty's distress, for it began perceptibly to take on a more becoming guise. She looked into his eyes and said, "How terribly good of you to come." He sat down beside her, began to pat her hand, noticed his son and said, "I'll have a word with you in a moment, old boy."

Mark was about to retire to the terrace when the door opened and his grandmother looked in. "Mark?" she said. He went quickly into the hall. "In the study," Lady Lacklander said, and in a moment he was there with Rose sobbing bitterly in his arms.

"You need pay no attention to me," Lady Lacklander said. "I am about to telephone New Scotland Yard. Your father tells me they have been called in, and I propose to send for Helena Alleyn's boy."

Mark, who was kissing Rose's hair, left off abruptly to say, "Can you mean Chief Inspector Alleyn, Gar?"

"I don't know what his rank is, but he used to be a nice boy twenty-five years ago before he left the Service to become a constable. Central? This is Hermione, Lady Lacklander. I want New Scotland Yard, London. The call is extremely urgent as it is concerned with murder. Yes, murder. You will oblige me by putting it through at once. Thank you." She glanced at Mark. "In the circumstances," she said, "I prefer to deal with a gent."

Mark had drawn Rose to a chair and was kneeling beside her, gently wiping away her tears.

"Hullo!" Lady Lacklander said after an extremely short delay. "New Scotland Yard. This is Hermione, Lady Lacklander, speaking. I wish to speak to Mr. Roderick Alleyn. If he is not on your premises, you will no doubt know where he is to be found. I don't know his rank . . ."

Her voice, aristocratic, cool, sure of itself, went steadily on. Mark dabbed at Rose's eyes. His father, alone with Kitty in the drawing-room, muttered agitatedly, ". . . I'm sorry it's hit you so hard, Kit."

Kitty looked wanly at him. "I suppose it's the shock," she said, and added without rancour, "I'm not as tough as you all think." He protested chaotically. "O," she said quite gently, "I know what they'll say about me. Not you, p'raps, but the others. They'll say it's cupboard-sorrow. 'That's what's upsetting the widow,' they'll say. I'm the outsider, George."

"Don't, Kit. Kit, listen . . ." He began to plead with her. "There's something I must ask you—if you'd just have a look for—you know—that thing—I mean—if it was found—"

She listened to him distractedly. "It's awful," George said. "I know it's awful to talk like this now, Kitty, but all the same—all the same—with so much at stake. I know you'll understand." Kitty said, "Yes. All right. Yes. But let me *think*."

Nurse Kettle out on the terrace was disturbed by the spatter of a few giant rain drops.

"There's going to be a storm," she said to herself. "A summer storm." And since she would have been out of place in the drawing-room and in the study, she took shelter in the hall. She had no sooner done so than the storm broke in a downpour over the valley of the Chyne.

3

Alleyn and Fox had worked late, tidying up the last phase of a tedious case of embezzlement. At twelve minutes to ten they had finished. Alleyn shut the file with a slap of his hand.

"Dreary fellow," he said. "I hope they give him the maximum. Damn' good riddance. Come back with me and have a drink, Br'er Fox. I'm a grass-widower and hating it. Troy and Ricky are in the country. What do you say?"

Fox drew his hand across the lower part of his face. "Well, now, Mr. Alleyn, that sounds very pleasant," he said. "I say yes and thank you."

"Good." Alleyn looked round the familiar walls of the Chief Inspector's room at New Scotland Yard. "There are occasions," he said, "when one suddenly sees one's natural habitat as if for the first time. It is a terrifying sensation. Come on. Let's go while the going's good."

They were half-way to the door when the telephone rang. Fox said, "Ah, hell!" without any particular animosity and went back to answer it.

"Chief Inspector's room," he said heavily. "Well, yes, he's here. Just." He listened for a moment, gazing blandly at his superior. "Say I'm dead," Alleyn suggested moodily. Fox laid his great palm over the receiver. "They make out it's a Lady Lacklander on call from somewhere called Swevenings," he said.

"Lady *Lacklander*? Good Lord! That's old Sir Harold Lacklander's widow," Alleyn ejaculated. "What's up with her, I wonder."

"Chief Inspector Alleyn will take the call," Fox said and held out the receiver.

Alleyn sat on his desk and put the receiver to his ear. An incisive elderly voice was saying ". . . I don't know his rank and I don't know whether he's on your premises or not, but you'll be good enough if you please to find Mr. Roderick Alleyn for me. It is Hermione, Lady Lacklander, speaking. Is that New Scotland Yard and have you heard me? I wish to speak to . . ."

Alleyn announced himself cautiously into the receiver. "Indeed!" the voice rejoined. "Why on earth couldn't you say so in the first instance? Hermione Lacklander speaking. I won't waste time reminding you about myself. You're Helena Alleyn's boy and I want an assurance from you. A friend of mine has just been murdered," the voice continued, "and I hear the local police are calling in your people. I would greatly prefer you, personally, to take charge of the whole thing. That can be arranged, I imagine?"

Alleyn, controlling his astonishment, said, "I'm afraid only if the Assistant Commissioner happens to give me the job."

"Who's he?"

Alleyn told her.

"Put me through to him," the voice commanded.

A second telephone began to ring. Fox answered it and in a moment held up a warning hand.

"Will you wait one second, Lady Lacklander?" Alleyn asked. Her voice, however, went incisively on, and he stifled it against his chest. "What the hell is it, Fox?" he asked irritably.

"Central office, sir. Orders for Swevenings. Homicide."

"Blistered apes! Us?"

"Us," said Fox stolidly.

Alleyn spoke into his own receiver. "Lady Lacklander? I *am* taking this case, it appears."

"Glad to hear it," said Lady Lacklander. "I suggest you look pretty sharp about it. Au revoir," she added with unexpected modishness, and rang off.

Fox, in the meantime, had noted down instructions. "I'll inform Mr. Alleyn," he was saying. "Yes, very good, I'll inform him. Thank you." He hung up his receiver. "It's a Colonel Cartarette," he said. "We go to a place called Chyning in Barfordshire, where the local sergeant will meet us. Matter of two hours. Everything's laid on down below."

Alleyn had already collected his hat, coat and professional case. Fox followed his example. They went out together through the never-sleeping corridors.

It was a still, hot night. Sheet-lightning played fretfully over the East End. The air smelt of petrol and dust. "Why don't we join the River Police?" Alleyn grumbled. "One long water carnival."

A car waited for them with Detective-Sergeants Bailey and Thompson and their gear already on board. As they drove out of the Yard, Big Ben struck ten.

"That's a remarkable woman, Fox," Alleyn said. "She's got a brain like a turbine and a body like a tun. My mother, who has her share of guts, was always terrified of Hermione Lacklander."

"Is that so, Mr. Alleyn? Her husband died only the other day, didn't he?"

"That's right. A quarter of a century ago he was one of my great white chiefs in the D.S. Solemn chap . . . just missed being brilliant. She was a force to be reckoned with even then. What's she doing in this party? What's the story, by the way?"

"A Colonel Maurice Cartarette found dead with head injuries by a fishing-stream. The C.C. down there says they're all tied up with the Royal Visit at Siminster and are understaffed, anyway, so they've called us in."

"Who found him?"

"A district nurse. About an hour ago."

"Fancy," said Alleyn mildly, and after a pause, "I wonder just why that old lady has come plunging in after me."

"I daresay," Fox said with great simplicity, "she has a fancy for some-one of her own class."

Alleyn replied absently, "Do you, now?" and it said something for their friendship that neither of them felt the smallest embarrassment. Alleyn continued to ruminate on the Lacklanders. "Before the war," he said, "the old boy was Chargé d'Affaires at Zlomce. The Special Branch got involved for a time, I remember. There was a very nasty bit of leak-age: a decoded message followed by the suicide of the chap concerned. He was said to have been in cahoots with known agents. I was with the Special Branch at that time and had quite a bit to do with it. Perhaps the dowager wishes to revive old memories or something. Or perhaps she merely runs the village of Swevenings, murdered colonels and all, with the same virtuosity she brought to her husband's public life. Do you know Swevenings, Br'er Fox?"

"Can't say I do, sir."

"I do. Troy did a week's painting there a summer or two ago. It's superficially pretty and fundamentally beautiful," Alleyn said. "Quaint as hell, but take a walk after dusk and you wouldn't be surprised at anything you met. It's one of the oldest in England. 'Swevenings,' mean-ing Dreams. There was some near-prehistoric set-to in the valley, I forget what, and another during Bolingbroke's rebellion and yet another in the Civil Wars. This Colonel's blood is not the first soldier's, by a long chalk, to be spilt at Swevenings."

"They *will* do it," Fox said cryptically and with resignation. For a long time they drove on in a silence broken at long intervals by the desultory conversation of old friends.

"We're running into a summer storm," Alleyn said presently. Giant drops appeared on the windscreen and were followed in seconds by a blinding downpour.

"Nice set-up for field-work," Fox grumbled.

"It may be local. Although . . . no, by gum, we're nearly there. This is Chyning. Chyning: meaning, I fancy, a yawn or yawning."

"Yawns and dreams," Fox said. "Funny sort of district! What language would that be, Mr. Alleyn?"

"Chaucerian English, only don't depend on me. The whole district is called the Vale of Traunce, or brown-study. It all sounds hellishly quaint, but that's how it goes. There's the blue lamp."

The air smelt fresher when they got out. Rain drummed on roofs and flagstones and cascaded down the sides of houses. Alleyn led the way into a typical county police-station and was greeted by a tall sandy-haired sergeant.

"Chief Inspector Alleyn, sir? Sergeant Oliphant. Very glad to see you, sir."

"Inspector Fox," Alleyn said, introducing him. There followed a solemn shaking of hands and a lament that has become increasingly common of late years in the police force. "We're that short of chaps in the county," Sergeant Oliphant said, "we don't know which way to turn if anything of this nature crops up. The Chief Constable said to me, "Can we do it, Oliphant? Suppose we call on Siminster, can we do it? And look, Mr. Alleyn, I had to say no, we can't.""

Fox said, "T'ch."

"Well, exactly, Mr. Fox," Oliphant said. "If you haven't got the chaps, it's no good blundering in, is it? I've left my one P.C. in charge of the body, and that reduces my staff to me. Shall we move off, Mr. Alleyn? You'll find it wettish."

Alleyn and Fox accompanied the sergeant in his car while Bailey, Thompson and the Yard driver followed their lead. On the way Sergeant Oliphant gave a business-like report. Sir George Lacklander had rung up Sir James Punston, the Chief Constable, who in turn had rung Oliphant at quarter past nine. Oliphant and his constable had then gone to Bottom Meadow and had found Dr. Mark Lacklander, Nurse Kettle and the body of Colonel Cartarette. They had taken a brief statement from Nurse Kettle and asked her to remain handy. Dr. Lacklander, who, in Oliphant's presence, made a very brief examination of the body, had then gone to break the news to the relatives of the deceased, taking Nurse Kettle with him. The sergeant had returned to Chyning and reported to the Chief Constable, who decided to call in the Yard. The constable had remained on guard by the body with Colonel Cartarette's spaniel, the latter having strenuously resisted all attempts to remove him.

"Did you form any opinion at all, Oliphant?" Alleyn asked. This is the most tactful remark a C.I.D. man can make to a county officer, and Oliphant coruscated under its influence.

"Not to say opinion, sir," he said. "Not to say that. One thing I did make sure of was not to disturb anything. He's lying on a patch of shingle screened in by a half-circle of willows and cut off on the open side by the stream. He's lying on his right side, kind of curled up as if he'd been bowled over from a kneeling position, like. His hat was over his face. Nurse Kettle moved it when she found him, and Dr. Lacklander moved it again when he examined the wound which is in the left temple. A dirty great puncture," the sergeant continued, easing off his official manner a point or two, "with what the doctor calls extensive fractures all round it. Quite turned my chap's stomach, drunks-in-charge and disorderly behaviour being the full extent of his experience."

Alleyn and Fox having chuckled in the right place, the sergeant continued. "No sign of the weapon, so far as we could make out, flashing our torches round. I was particular not to go hoofing over the ground."

"Admirable," said Alleyn.

"Well," said Sergeant Oliphant, "it's what we're told, sir, isn't it?"

"Notice anything at all out of the way?" Alleyn asked. The question was inspired more by kindliness than curiosity, and the sergeant's reaction surprised him. Oliphant brought his two freckled hams of hands down on the driving-wheel and made a complicated snorting noise. "Out of the way!" he shouted. "Ah, my God, I'll say we did. Out of the way! Tell me, now, sir, are you a fly-fisherman?"

"Only fair to middling to worse. I do when I get the chance. Why?"

"Now listen," Sergeant Oliphant said, quite abandoning his official position. "There's a dirty great fish in this Chyne here would turn your guts over for you. Pounds if he's an ounce, he is. Old in cunning, he is, wary and sullen and that lordly in his lurkings and slinkings he'd break your heart. Sometimes he'll rise like a monster," said Sergeant Oliphant, urging his car up Watt's Hill, "and snap, he's took it, though that's only three times. Once being the deceased's doing a matter of a fortnight ago, which he left his cast in his jaws, he being a mighty fighter. And once the late squire Sir Harold Lacklander, which he lost him through being, as the man himself frankly admitted, overzealous in the playing of him, and NOW," the sergeant shouted, "NOW, for the last and final cast, hooked, played and landed by the poor Colonel, sir, and lying there by his dead body, or I can't tell a five-pound trout from a stickleback. Well, if he had to die, he couldn't have had a more glorious end. The Colonel, I mean, Mr. Alleyn, not the Old 'Un," said Sergeant Oliphant.

They had followed Watt's Lane down into the valley and up the slope through blinding rain to the village. Oliphant pulled up at a spot opposite the Boy and Donkey. A figure in a mackintosh and tweed hat stood in the lighted doorway.

"The Chief Constable, sir," said Oliphant. "Sir James Punston. He said he'd drive over and meet you."

"I'll have a word with him, before we go on. Wait a moment."

Alleyn crossed the road and introduced himself. The Chief Constable was a weather-beaten, tough-looking man who had been a Chief Commissioner of Police in India.

"Thought I'd better come over," Sir James said, "and take a look at this show. Damn' bad show it is. Damn' nice fellow, Cartarette. Can't imagine who'd want to set about him, but no doubt you'll be able to tell us. I'll come down with you. Filthy night, isn't it?"

The Yard car had drawn up behind Oliphant's. Bailey, Thompson and the driver got out and unloaded their gear with the economic movements of long usage and a stubborn disregard of the rain. The two parties joined up and led by the Chief Constable climbed a stile and followed a rough path down a drenched hillside. Their torches flashed on rods of rain and dripping furze bushes.

"They call this River Path," the Chief Constable said. "It's a right-of-way through the Nunspardon estate and comes out at Bottom Bridge, which we have to cross. I hear the dowager rang you up."

"She did indeed," Alleyn said.

"Lucky they decided it was your pigeon anyway. She'd have raised hell if they hadn't."

"I don't see where she fits in."

"She doesn't in any ordinary sense of the phrase. She's merely taken it upon herself ever since she came to Nunspardon to run Chyning and Swevenings. For some reason they seem to like it. Survival of the feudal instinct, you might think. It does survive, you know, in isolated pockets. Swevenings is an isolated pocket and Hermione, Lady Lacklander, has got it pretty well where she wants it." Sir James continued in this local strain as they slid and squelched down the muddy hillside. He gave Alleyn an account of the Cartarette family and their neighbours with a particularly racy profile of Lady Lacklander herself.

"There's the local gossip for you," he said. "Everybody knows everybody and has done so for centuries. There have been no stockbroking overflows into Swevenings. The Lacklanders, the Phinns, the Syces and the Cartarettes have lived in their respective houses for a great many generations. They're all on terms of intimacy, except that of late years there's been, I fancy, a little coolness between the Lacklanders and old

Occy Phinn. And now I come to think of it, I fancy Maurice Cartarette fell out with Phinn over fishing or something. But then old Occy is really a bit mad. Rows with everybody. Cartarette, on the other hand, was a very pleasant, nice chap. Oddly formal and devilishly polite, though, especially with people he didn't like or had fallen out with. Not that he was a quarrelsome chap. Far from it. I have heard, by the way," Sir James gossiped, "that there's been some sort of coldness between Cartarette and that ass George Lacklander. However! And after all that, here's the bridge."

As they crossed it, they could hear the sound of rain beating on the surface of the stream. On the far side their feet sank into mud. They turned left on the rough path. Alleyn's shoes filled with water and water poured off the brim of his hat.

"Hell of a thing to happen, this bloody rain," said the Chief Constable. "Ruin the terrain."

A wet branch of willow slapped Alleyn's face. On the hill to their right they could see the lighted windows of three houses. As they walked on, however, distant groups of trees intervened and the windows were shut off.

"Can the people up there see into the actual area?" Alleyn asked.

Sergeant Oliphant said, "No, sir. Their own trees as well as this belt of willows screen it. They can see the stretch on the far side above the bridge, and a wee way below it."

"That's Mr. Danberry-Phinn's preserve, isn't it?" asked the Chief Constable. "Above the bridge?"

"Mr. *Danberry*-Phinn?" Alleyn said, sharply.

"Mr. Octavius Danberry-Phinn, to give you the complete works. The 'Danberry' isn't insisted upon. He's the local eccentric I told you about. He lives in the top house up there. We don't have a village idiot in Swevenings; we have a bloody-minded old gentleman. It's more classy," said Sir James, acidly.

"Danberry-Phinn," Alleyn repeated. "Isn't there some connection there with the Lacklanders?"

Sir James said shortly, "Both Swevenings men, of course." His voice faded uncertainly as he floundered into a patch of reeds. Somewhere close at hand a dog howled dismally and a deep voice apostrophized it, "Ah, stow it, will you." A light bobbed up ahead of them.

"Here we are," Sir James said. "That you, Gripper?"

"Yes, sir," said the deep voice. The mackintosh cape of a uniformed constable shone in the torchlight.

"Dog still at it seemingly," said the sergeant.

"That's right, Mr. Oliphant. I've got him tethered here." A torch flashed on Skip, tied by a handkerchief to a willow branch.

"Hullo, old fellow," Alleyn said.

They all waited for him to go through the thicket. The constable shoved back a dripping willow branch for him.

"You'll need to stoop a little, sir."

Alleyn pushed through the thicket. His torchlight darted about in the rain and settled almost at once on a glistening mound.

"We got some groundsheets down and covered him," the sergeant said, "when it looked like rain."

"Good."

"And we've covered up the area round the corpse as best we could. Bricks and one or two planks from the old boatshed yonder. But I daresay the water's got under just the same."

Alleyn said, "Fair enough. We couldn't ask for better. I think before we go any nearer we'll get photographs. Come through, Bailey. Do the best you can. As it stands and then uncovered, with all the details you can get, in case it washes out before morning. By Jove, though, I believe it's lifting."

They all listened. The thicket was loud with the sound of dripping foliage, but the heavy drumming of rain had stopped, and by the time Bailey had set up his camera, a waxing moon had ridden out over the valley.

When Bailey had taken his last flash-photograph of the area and the covered body, he took away the groundsheet and photographed the body again from many angles, first with the tweed hat over the face and then without it. He put his camera close to Colonel Cartarette's face and it flashed out in the night with raised eyebrows and pursed lips. Only when all this had been done, did Alleyn, walking delicately, go closer, stoop over the head and shine his torch full on the wound.

"Sharp instrument?" said Fox.

"Yes," Alleyn said, "yes, a great puncture, certainly. But could a sharp instrument do all that, Br'er Fox? No use speculating till we know what it was." His torchlight moved away from the face and found a silver glint on a patch of grass near Colonel Cartarette's hands and almost on the brink of the stream. "And this is the Old 'Un?" he murmured.

The Chief Constable and Sergeant Oliphant both broke into excited sounds of confirmation. The light moved to the hands, lying close together. One of them was clenched about a wisp of green.

"Cut grass," Alleyn said. "He was going to wrap his trout in it. There's his knife, and there's the creel beside him."

"What we reckoned, sir," said the sergeant in agreement.

"Woundy great fish, isn't it?" said the Chief Constable, and there was an involuntary note of envy in his voice.

Alleyn said, "What was the surface like before it rained?"

"Well, sir," the sergeant volunteered, "as you see, it's partly gravel. There was nothing to see in the willows where the ground was dry as a chip. There was what we reckoned were the deceased's footprints on the bank where it was soft and where he'd been fishing and one or two on the earthy bits near where he fell, but I couldn't make out anything else and we didn't try, for fear of messing up what little there was."

"Quite right. Will it rain again before morning?"

The three local men moved back into the meadow and looked up at the sky.

"All over, I reckon, sir," said the sergeant.

"Set fine," said the deep-voiced constable.

"Clearing," said Sir James Punston.

"Cover everything up again, Sergeant, and set a watch till morning. Have we any tips of any sort about times? Anybody known to have come this way?"

"Nurse Kettle, sir, who found him. Young Dr. Lacklander came back with her to look at him, and *he* says he came through the valley and over the bridge earlier in the evening. We haven't spoken to anyone else, sir."

"How deep," Alleyn asked, "is the stream just here?"

"About five foot," said Sergeant Oliphant.

"Really? And he lies on his right side roughly parallel with the stream and facing it. Not more than two feet from the brink. Head pointing down-stream, feet towards the bridge. The fish lies right on the brink by the strand of grass he was cutting to wrap it in. And the wound's in the left temple. I take it he was squatting on his heels within two feet of the brink and just about to bed his catch down in the grass. Now, if, as the heelmarks near his feet seem to indicate, he keeled straight over into the position the body still holds, one of two things must have happened, wouldn't you say, Br'er Fox?"

"Either," Fox said stolidly, "he was coshed by a left-handed person standing behind him or by a right-handed person standing in front of him and at least three feet away."

"Which would place the assailant," said Alleyn, "about twelve inches out on the surface of the stream. Which is not as absurd as it sounds when you put it that way. All right. Let's move on. What comes next?"

The Chief Constable, who had listened to all this in silence, now said, "I gather there's a cry of possible witnesses waiting for you up at Hammer. That's Cartarette's house up here on Watt's Hill. If you'll forgive me, Alleyn, I won't go up with you. Serve no useful purpose. If you want me,

I'm five miles away at Tourets. Anything I can do, delighted, but sure you'd rather be left in peace. I would in my day. By the way, I've told them at the Boy and Donkey that you'll probably want beds for what's left of the night. You'll find a room at the head of the stairs. They'll give you an early breakfast if you leave a note. Good-night."

He was gone before Alleyn could thank him.

With the sergeant as guide, Alleyn and Fox prepared to set out for Hammer. Alleyn had succeeded in persuading the spaniel Skip to accept them, and after one or two false starts and whimperings he followed at their heels. They used torches in order to make their way with as little blundering as possible through the grove. Oliphant, who was in the lead, suddenly uttered a violent oath.

"What is it?" Alleyn asked, startled.

"*Gawd!*" Oliphant said. "I thought someone was looking at me. *Gawd, d'you see that!*"

His wavering torchlight flickered on wet willow leaves. A pair of luminous disks stared out at them from the level of a short man's eyes.

"Touches of surrealism," Alleyn muttered, "in Bottom Meadow." He advanced his own torch, and they saw a pair of spectacles caught up in a broken twig.

"We'll pluck this fruit with grateful care," he said and gathered the spectacles into his handkerchief.

The moon now shone on Bottom Meadow, turning the bridge and the inky shadow it cast over the broken-down boatshed and punt into a subject for a wood engraving. A group of tall reeds showed up romantically in its light, and the Chyne took on an air of enchantment.

They climbed the river path up Watt's Hill. Skip began to whine and to wag his tail. In a moment the cause of his excitement came into view, a large tabby cat sitting on the path in the bright moonlight washing her whiskers. Skip dropped on his haunches and made a ridiculous sound in his throat. Thomasina Twitchett, for it was she, threw him an inimical glance, rolled on her back at Alleyn's feet and trilled beguilement. Alleyn liked cats. He stooped down and found that she was in the mood to be carried. He picked her up. She kneaded his chest and advanced her nose towards his.

"My good woman," Alleyn said, "you've been eating fish."

Though he was unaware of it at the time, this was an immensely significant discovery.

CHAPTER FIVE

Hammer Farm

When they approached Hammer Farm, Alleyn saw that the three demesnes on Watt's Hill ended in spinneys that separated them from the lower slopes and, as the sergeant had observed, screened them from the reaches of the Chyne below Bottom Bridge. The river path ran upwards through the trees and was met by three private paths serving the three houses. The sergeant led the way up the first of these. Thomasina Twitchett leapt from Alleyn's embrace and with an ambiguous remark darted into the shadows.

"That'll be one of Mr. Phinn's creatures, no doubt," said Sergeant Oliphant. "He's crackers on cats, is Mr. Phinn."

"Indeed," Alleyn said, sniffing at his fingers.

They emerged in full view of Hammer Farm house with its row of French windows lit behind their curtains.

"Not," said the sergeant, "that it's been a farm or anything like it, for I don't know how long. The present lady's had it done up considerable."

Skip gave a short bark and darted ahead. One of the curtains was pulled open, and Mark Lacklander came through to the terrace, followed by Rose.

"Skip?" Rose said. "Skip?"

He whined and flung himself at her. She sank to her knees crying and holding him in her arms. "Don't, darling," Mark said, "don't. He's wet and muddy. Don't."

Alleyn, Fox and Sergeant Oliphant had halted. Mark and Rose looked across the lawn and saw them standing in the moonlight with their wet clothes shining and their faces shadowed by their hatbrims. For a moment neither group moved or spoke, and then Alleyn crossed the lawn and came towards them, bareheaded. Rose stood up. The skirts of her linen house-coat were bedabbled with muddy paw marks.

"Miss Cartarette?" Alleyn said. "We are from the C.I.D. My name is Alleyn."

Rose was a well-mannered girl with more than her share of natural dignity. She shook hands with him and introduced him to Mark. Fox was summoned and Sergeant Oliphant eased up the path in an anonymous manner and waited at the end of the terrace.

"Will you come in?" Rose said, and Mark added, "My grandmother is here, Mr. Alleyn, and my father, who informed the local police."

"And Nurse Kettle, I hope?"

"And Nurse Kettle."

"Splendid. Shall we go in, Miss Cartarette?"

Alleyn and Fox took off their wet mackintoshes and hats and left them on a garden seat.

Rose led the way through the French window into the drawing-room, where Alleyn found an out-of-drawing conversation piece established. Lady Lacklander, a vast black bulk, completely filled an arm chair. Alleyn noticed that upon one of her remarkably small feet she wore a buckled velvet shoe and upon the other, a man's bath slipper. Kitty Cartarette was extended on a sofa with one black-velvet leg dangling, a cigarette in her holder, a glass in her hand and an ash tray with butts at her elbow. It was obvious that she had wept, but repairs had been effected in her make-up, and though her hands were still shaky, she was tolerably composed. Between the two oddly assorted women, poised on the hearthrug with a whisky-and-soda, looking exquisitely uncomfortable and good-looking, was Sir George Lacklander. And at a remove in a small chair perfectly at her ease sat Nurse Kettle, reclaimed from her isolation in the hall.

"Hullo," said Lady Lacklander, picking her lorgnette off her bosom and flicking it open. "Good evening to you. You're Roderick Alleyn, aren't you? We haven't met since you left the Foreign Service, and that's not yesterday nor the day before that. How many years is it? And how's your mama?"

"More than I care to remind you of and very well considering," Alleyn said, taking a hand like a pincushion in his.

"Considering what? Her age? She's five years my junior, and there's nothing but fat amiss with me. Kitty, this is Roderick Alleyn; Mrs. Cartarette. My son George."

"Hah—yoo?" George intervened coldly.

". . . and over there is Miss Kettle, our district nurse. Good evening," Lady Lacklander continued, looking at Fox.

"Good evening, my lady," said Fox placidly.

"Inspector Fox," Alleyn said.

"Now, what do you propose to do with us all? Take your time," she added kindly.

Alleyn thought to himself, "Not only must I take my time, but I must also take control. This old lady is up to something."

He turned to Kitty Cartarette. "I'm sorry," he said, "to come so hard on the heels of what must have been an appalling shock. I'm afraid that in these cases police enquiries are not the easiest ordeals to put up with. If I may, Mrs. Cartarette, I'll begin by asking you" . . . he glanced briefly round the room . . . "indeed, all of you, if you've formed any opinion at all about this affair."

There was a pause. He looked at Kitty Cartarette and then steadily, for a moment, at Rose, who was standing at the far end of the room with Mark.

Kitty said, "Somehow, I can't sort of get it. It seems so . . . so *unlikely*."

"And you, Miss Cartarette?"

"No," Rose said. "No. It's unthinkable that anyone who knew him should want to hurt him."

George Lacklander cleared his throat. Alleyn glanced at him. "I . . . ah . . ." George said, "I . . . ah . . . personally believe it must have been some tramp or other. Trespassing or something. There's nobody in the district, I mean. I mean, it's quite incredible."

"I see," Alleyn said. "The next point is: do we know of anybody who was near Colonel Cartarette within, let us say, two hours of the time . . . I believe it was five minutes to nine . . . when you, Miss Kettle, found him?"

"Exactly what," Lady Lacklander said, "do you mean by 'near'?"

"Let us say within sight or hearing of him."

"I was," said Lady Lacklander. "I made an appointment with him for eight, which he kept twenty minutes early. Our meeting took place on the river bank opposite the willow grove where I understand he was found."

Fox, unobtrusively stationed by the piano, had begun to take notes. Although her back was turned towards him, Lady Lacklander appeared to sense this activity. She shifted massively in her chair and looked at him without comment.

"Come," Alleyn said, "that's a starting point, at least. We'll return to it later if we may. Does anyone know anything about Colonel Cartarette's movements after this meeting which lasted . . . how long do you think, Lady Lacklander?"

"About ten minutes. I remember looking at my watch after Maurice Cartarette left me. He re-crossed Bottom Bridge, turned left and disappeared behind the willow grove. It was then nine minutes to eight. I packed up my things and left them to be collected and went home. I'd been sketching."

"About nine minutes to eight?" Alleyn repeated.

Kitty said, "I didn't see him, but . . . I must have been somewhere near him, I suppose, when I came back from the golf course. I got home at five past eight—I remember."

"The golf course?"

"At Nunspardon," George Lacklander said. "Mrs. Cartarette and I played a round of golf there this evening."

"Ah, yes. The course is above the stream, isn't it, and on the opposite side of the valley from where we are now?"

"Yes, but the greater part is over the crest of the hill."

"The second tee," Mark said, "overlooks the valley."

"I see. You came home by the bottom bridge, Mrs. Cartarette?"

"Yes. The river path."

"On the far side wouldn't you overlook the willow grove?"

Kitty pressed the palms of her hands against her head.

"Yes, I suppose you would. I don't think he could have been there. I'm sure I'd have seen him if he had been there. As a matter of fact," Kitty said, "I wasn't looking much in that direction. I was looking, actually, at the upper reaches to see . . ." she glanced at George Lacklander . . . "well, to see if I could spot Mr. Phinn," she said.

In the silence that followed, Alleyn was quite certain that the Lacklander wariness had been screwed up to its highest tension. All three had made slight movements that were instantly checked.

"Mr. Danberry-Phinn?" Alleyn said. "And did you see him?"

"Not then. No. He must have either gone home or moved beyond the upper bend."

"Fishing?"

"Yes."

"Poaching!" George Lacklander ejaculated. "Yes, by God, poaching!"

There were subdued ejaculations from Mark and his grandmother.

"Indeed?" Alleyn asked. "What makes you think so?"

"We saw him. No, Mama, I insist on saying so. We saw him from the second tee. He rents the upper reaches above the bridge from me, by God, and Maurice Cartarette rents . . . I'm sorry, Kitty . . . rented the lower. And there . . . damndest thing you ever saw . . . there he was on his own ground on the right bank above the bridge, casting above the bridge and letting the stream carry his cast under the bridge and below it into Cartarette's waters."

Lady Lacklander gave a short bark of laughter. George cast an incredulous and scandalized glance at her. Mark said, "Honestly! How he dared!"

"Most blackguardly thing I ever saw," George continued. "Deliberate. And the cast, damme, was carried over that hole above the punt where the Old 'Un lurks. I saw it with my own eyes! Didn't I, Kitty? Fellow like that deserves no consideration at all. *None*," he repeated with a violence that made Alleyn prick up his ears and seemed to rebound (to his embarrassment) upon George himself.

"When did this nefarious bit of trickery occur?" Alleyn asked.

"I don't know when."

"When did you begin your round?"

"At six-thirty. No!" shouted George in a hurry and turning purple. "No! Later. About seven."

"It wouldn't be later than seven-fifteen then, when you reached the second tee?"

"About then, I daresay."

"Would you say so, Mrs. Cartarette?"

Kitty said, "I should think, about then."

"Did Mr. Phinn see you?"

"Not he. Too damned taken up with his poaching," said George.

"Why didn't you tackle him?" Lady Lacklander enquired.

"I would have for tuppence, Mama, but Kitty thought better not. We walked away," George said virtuously, "in disgust."

"I saw you walking away," said Lady Lacklander, "but from where I was, you didn't look particularly disgusted, George."

Kitty opened her mouth and shut it again, and George remained empurpled.

"Of course," Alleyn said, "you were sketching, Lady Lacklander, weren't you? Whereabouts?"

"In a hollow about the length of this room below the bridge on the left bank."

"Near a clump of alders?"

"You're a sharpish observant fellow, it appears. Exactly there. I saw my son and Mrs. Cartarette in peeps," Lady Lacklander said rather grimly, "through the alders."

"But you couldn't see Mr. Phinn poaching?"

"I couldn't," Lady Lacklander said, "but somebody else could and did."

"Who was that, I wonder?"

"None other," said Lady Lacklander, "than poor Maurice Cartarette himself. He saw it and the devil of a row they had over it, I may tell you."

If the Lacklanders had been a different sort of people, Alleyn thought, they would have more clearly betrayed the emotion that he suspected had visited them all. It was, he felt sure from one or two slight manifestations, one of relief rather than surprise on Mark's part and of both elements on his father's. Rose looked troubled and Kitty merely stared. It was, surprisingly, Nurse Kettle who made the first comment.

"That old fish," she said. "Such a lot of fuss!"

Alleyn looked at her and liked what he saw. "I'll talk to her first," he thought, "when I get round to solo interviews."

He said, "How do you know, Lady Lacklander, that they had this row?"

"A: because I heard 'em, and B: because Maurice came straight to me when they parted company. That's how, my dear man."

"What happened, exactly?"

"I gathered that Maurice Cartarette came down intending to try the evening rise when I'd done with him. He came out of his own spinney and saw Occy Phinn up to no good down by the bridge. Maurice crept up behind him. He caught Occy red-handed, having just landed the Old 'Un. They didn't see *me*," Lady Lacklander went on, "because I was down in my hollow on the other bank. Upon my soul, I doubt if they'd have bridled their tongues if they had. They sounded as if they'd come to blows. I heard them tramping about on the bridge. I was debating whether I should rise up like some rather oversized deity and settle them when Occy bawled out that Maurice could have his so-and-so fish and Maurice said he wouldn't be seen dead with it." A look of absolute horror appeared for one second in Lady Lacklander's eyes. It was as if they had all shouted at her, "But he *was* seen dead with it, you know." She made a sharp movement with her hands and hurried on. "There was a thump, as if someone had thrown something wet and heavy on the ground. Maurice said he'd make a county business of it, and Occy said if he did, he, Occy, would have Maurice's dog empounded for chasing his, Occy's, cats. On that note they parted. Maurice came fuming over the hillock and saw me. Occy, as far as I know, stormed back up the hill to Jacob's Cottage."

"Had Colonel Cartarette got the fish in his hands, then?"

"Not he. I told you, he refused to touch it. He left it there, on the bridge. I saw it when I went home. For all I know, it's still lying there on the bridge."

"It's lying by Colonel Cartarette," Alleyn said, "and the question seems to be, doesn't it, who put it there?"

2

This time the silence was long and completely blank.

"He must have come back and taken it, after all," Mark said dubiously.

"No," Rose said strongly. They all turned to her. Rose's face was dimmed with tears and her voice uncertain. Since Alleyn's arrival she had scarcely spoken, and he wondered if she was so much shocked that she did not even try to listen to them.

"No?" he said gently.

"He wouldn't have done that," she said. "It's not at all the sort of thing he'd do."

"That's right," Kitty agreed. "He wasn't like that," and she caught her breath in a sob.

"I'm sorry," Mark said at once. "Stupid of me. Of course, you're right. The Colonel wasn't like that."

Rose gave him a look that told Alleyn as much as he wanted to know about their relationship. "So they're in love," he thought. "And unless I'm growing purblind, his father's got more than half an eye on her stepmother. What a very compact little party, to be sure."

He said to Lady Lacklander, "Did you stay there long after he left you?"

"No. We talked for about ten minutes and then Maurice re-crossed the bridge, as I told you, and disappeared behind the willows on the right bank."

"Which way did you go home?"

"Up through the Home Spinney to Nunspardon."

"Could you see into the willow grove at all?"

"Certainly. When I was half-way up I stopped to pant, and I looked down and there he was, casting into the willow-grove reach."

"That would be about eight."

"About eight, yes."

"I think you said you left your painting gear to be collected, didn't you?"

"I did."

"Who collected it, please?"

"One of the servants. William, the footman, probably."

"No," Mark said. "No, Gar. I did."

"You?" his grandmother said. "What were you doing . . ." and stopped short.

Mark said rapidly that after making a professional call in the village he had gone in to play tennis at Hammer and had stayed there until about ten minutes past eight. He had returned home by the river path and as he approached Bottom Bridge had seen his grandmother's shooting-stick, stool and painting gear in a deserted group on a hillock. He carried them back to Nunspardon and was just in time to prevent the footman from going down to collect them. Alleyn asked him if he had noticed a large trout lying on Bottom Bridge. Mark said that he hadn't done so, but at the same moment his grandmother gave one of her short ejaculations.

"You must have seen it, Mark," she said. "Great gaping thing lying there where Octavius Phinn must have chucked it down. On the bridge, my dear boy. You must have practically stepped over it."

"It wasn't there," Mark said. "Sorry, Gar, but it wasn't, when I went home."

"Mrs. Cartarette," Alleyn said, "you must have crossed Bottom Bridge a few minutes after Lady Lacklander had gone home, mustn't you?"

"That's right," Kitty said. "We saw her going into the Nunspardon Home Spinney as we came over the hill by the second tee."

"And Sir George, then, in his turn, went home through the Home Spinney, and you came down the hill by the river path?"

"That's right," she said drearily.

"Did you see the fabulous trout lying on Bottom Bridge?"

"Not a sign of it, I'm afraid."

"So that between about ten to eight and ten past eight the trout was removed by somebody and subsequently left in the willow grove. Are you all of the opinion that Colonel Cartarette would have been unlikely to change his mind and go back for it?" Alleyn asked.

George looked huffy and said he didn't know, he was sure, and Lady Lacklander said that judging by what Colonel Cartarette had said to her, she was persuaded that wild horses wouldn't have induced him to touch the trout. Alleyn thought to himself, "If he was disinclined to touch it, still less would he feel like wrapping it up in grass in order to stow it away in his creel, which apparently was what he had been doing when he died."

"I suppose there's no doubt about this fish being the classic Old 'Un?" Alleyn asked.

"None," Mark said. "There's not such another in the Chyne. No question."

"By the way, did you look down at the willow grove as you climbed up the hill to the Home Spinney?"

"I don't remember doing so. I was hung about with my grandmother's sketching gear and I didn't . . ."

It was at this moment that Kitty Cartarette screamed.

She did not scream very loudly; the sound was checked almost as soon as it was born, but she had half risen from her sofa and was staring at something beyond and behind Alleyn. She had clapped her hands over her mouth. Her eyes were wide open beneath their raised brows. He noticed that they were inclined to be prominent.

They all turned to discover what it was that Kitty stared at but found only an uncovered French window reflecting the lighted room and the ghosts of their own startled faces.

"There's someone out there!" Kitty whispered. "A man looked in at the window. George!"

"My dear girl," Lady Lacklander said, "you saw George's reflection. There's nobody there."

"There is."

"It's probably Sergeant Oliphant," Alleyn said. "We left him outside. Fox?"

Fox was already on his way, but before he reached the French window, the figure of a man appeared beyond its reflected images. The figure moved uncertainly, coming in from the side and halting when it was some way from the glass. Kitty make a slight retching sound. Fox's hand was on the knob of the French window when beyond it the beam of Sergeant Oliphant's torchlight shot across the dark and the man's face was illuminated. It was crowned by a tasselled smoking cap and was deadly pale.

Fox opened the French windows.

"Pray forgive an unwarrantable intrusion," said Mr. Danberry-Phinn. "I am in quest of a fish."

3

Mr. Phinn's behaviour was singular. The light from the room seemed to dazzle him. He screwed up his eyes and nose, and this gave him a supercilious look greatly at variance with his extreme pallor and unsteady hands. He squinted at Fox and then beyond him at the company in the drawing-room.

"I fear I have called at an inconvenient moment," he said. "I had no idea . . . I had hoped to see . . ." his Adam's apple bobbed furiously . . . "to see," he repeated, "in point of fact, Colonel Cartarette." He disclosed his teeth, clamped together in the oddest kind of smile.

Kitty made an indeterminate sound, and Lady Lacklander began, "My dear Octavius . . ." but before either of them could get any further, Alleyn moved in front of Mr. Phinn. "Did you say, sir," Alleyn asked, "that you are looking for a fish?"

Mr. Phinn said, "Forgive me, I don't *think* I have the pleasure . . . ?" and peered up into Alleyn's face. "*Have* I the pleasure?" he asked. He blinked away from Alleyn towards Fox. Fox was one of those, nowadays rather rare, detectives who look very much like their job. He was a large, grizzled man with extremely bright eyes.

"And in this case," Mr. Phinn continued with a breathless little laugh, "I indubitably have *not* the pleasure."

"We are police officers," Alleyn said. "Colonel Cartarette has been murdered, Mr. Phinn. You are Mr. Octavius Danberry-Phinn, I think, aren't you?"

"But how perfectly terrible!" said Mr. Phinn. "My dear Mrs. Cartarette! My dear Miss Rose! I am appalled. APPALLED!" Mr. Phinn repeated, opening his eyes as wide as they could go.

"You'd better come in, Occy," Lady Lacklander said. "They'll want to talk to you."

"To *me!*" he ejaculated. He came in and Fox shut the French window behind him.

Alleyn said, "I shall want to have a word with you, sir. In fact, I think it is time that we saw some of you individually rather than together, but before we do that, I should like Mr. Phinn to tell us about the fish he is looking for." He raised his hand. If any of his audience had felt like interjecting, they now thought better of the impulse. "If you please, Mr. Phinn?" Alleyn said.

"I'm so confused, indeed so horrified at what you have told me . . ."

"Dreadful," Alleyn said, "isn't it? About the fish?"

"The fish? The fish, my dear sir, is or was a magnificent trout. The fish is a fish of great fame. It is the trout to end all trout. A piscine emperor. And I, let me tell you, I caught him."

"Where?" Lady Lacklander demanded.

Mr. Phinn blinked twice. "Above Bottom Bridge, my dear Lady L.," he said. "Above Bottom Bridge."

"You *are* an old humbug, Occy," she said.

George suddenly roared out, "That's a bloody lie, Octavius. You poached him. You were fishing under the bridge. We saw you from the second tee."

"Dear me, George," said Mr. Phinn going white to the lips. "What a noise you do make, to be sure."

Fox had stepped unobtrusively aside and was busy with his notebook.

"To talk like that!" Mr. Phinn continued with two half bows in the direction of Kitty and Rose. "In a house of mourning! Really, George, I must say!"

"By God . . . !" George began, but Alleyn intervened.

"What," he asked Mr. Phinn, "happened to your catch?"

Mr. Phinn sucked in a deep breath and began to speak very quickly indeed. "Flushed," he said in a voice that was not quite steady, "with triumph, I resolved to try the upper reaches of the Chyne. I therefore laid my captive to rest on the very field of his defeat, *id est*, the upper, repeat upper, approach to Bottom Bridge. When I returned, much later, I cannot tell you *how* much later for I did not carry a watch, but much, *much* later, I went to the exact spot where my Prince of Piscines should have rested and . . ." he made a wide gesture during the execution of which it was apparent that his hands were tremulous . . . "Gone! Vanished! Not a sign! Lost!" he said.

"Now, look here, Occy . . ." Lady Lacklander in her turn began, and in her turn was checked by Alleyn.

"Please, Lady Lacklander," Alleyn interjected. She glared at him. "Do you mind?" he said.

She clasped her plump hands together and rested the entire system of her chins upon them. "Well," she said, "I called you in, after all. Go on."

"What did you do," Alleyn asked Mr. Phinn, "when you discovered your loss?"

Mr. Phinn looked very fixedly at him. "Do?" he repeated. "What should I do? It was growing dark. I looked about in the precincts of the bridge but to no avail. The trout was gone. I returned home, a bitterly chagrined man."

"And there you remained, it seems, for about four hours. It's now five minutes past one in the morning. Why, at such an hour, are you paying this visit, Mr. Phinn?"

Looking at Mr. Phinn, Alleyn thought, "He was ready for that one."

"Why!" Mr. Phinn exclaimed spreading his unsteady hands. "My dear sir, I will tell you why. Rendered almost suicidal by the loss of this Homeric catch, I was unable to contemplate my couch with any prospect of repose. Misery and frustration would have been my bedfellows, I assure you, had I sought it. I attempted to read, to commune with the persons of my house (I refer to my cats, sir), to listen to an indescribably tedious piece of buffoonery upon the wireless. All, I regret to say, was of no avail: my mind was wholly occupied by The Great Fish. Some three quarters of an hour or so ago, I sought the relief of fresh air and took a turn down the river path. On emerging from the ruffian Syce's spinney, I observed lights behind these windows. I heard voices. Knowing," he said with a singular gulp, "knowing that poor Cartarette's interest as a fellow angler would be aroused, I . . . my dear Lady L., why *are* you looking at me in this most disconcerting fashion?"

"Occy!" Lady Lacklander said. "Yard or no Yard, I can't contain my information for another second. I was within a stone's throw of you when you had your row with Maurice Cartarette. What's more a few minutes earlier his wife and George both saw you poaching under the bridge. I heard you or Maurice throw down the trout on the bridge and I heard you part company in a high rage. What's more Maurice came hotfoot to where I was painting and I had the whole story all over again from him. Now, my dear Roderick Alleyn, you may be as cross with me as you please, but I really could not allow this nonsensical tarradiddle to meander on for another second."

Mr. Phinn blinked and peered and fumbled with his lips. "It used to be quite a little joke between my dear wife and me," he said at last, "that one must never contradict a Lacklander."

Only Alleyn and Fox looked at him.

"Mr. Phinn," Alleyn said, "you normally wear spectacles, I think, don't you?"

Mr. Phinn made a strange little gesture with his thumb and forefinger as if he actually adjusted his glasses. Thus, momentarily, he hid the red groove across the top of his nose and the flush that had begun to spread across his face. "Not all the time," he said. "Only for reading."

Lady Lacklander suddenly clapped the palms of her hands down on the arms of her chair. "So there we are," she said. "And having said my say, George, I should like you, if you please, to take me home."

She put out her right arm and as George was a little slow in coming, Alleyn took her hand, braced himself and hauled.

"'Up she rises,'" Lady Lacklander quoted self-derisively, and up she rose. She stared for a moment at Mr. Phinn, who gaped back at her and mouthed something indistinguishable. She looked straight into Alleyn's eyes. "Do you, after all," she said, "propose to let me go home?"

Alleyn raised an eyebrow. "I shall feel a good deal safer," he said, "with you there than here, Lady Lacklander."

"Take me to my car. I have to shuffle a bit because of my damn' toe. It's no better, Kettle. George, you may join me in five minutes. I want to have a word with Roderick Alleyn."

She said goodbye to Rose, holding her for a moment in her arms. Rose clung to her and gave a shuddering sob. Lady Lacklander said, "My poor child, my poor little Rose; you must come to us as soon as possible. Get Mark to give you something to make you sleep."

Kitty had risen. "It was awfully kind of you to come," she said and held out her hand. Lady Lacklander took it and after a scarcely perceptible pause let it be known that Kitty was expected to kiss her. This Kitty did with caution.

"Come and see me to-morrow, Kettle," said Lady Lacklander, "unless they lock you up."

"Let 'em try," said Nurse Kettle, who had been entirely silent ever since Mr. Phinn's arrival. Lady Lacklander gave a short laugh. She paid no attention to Mr. Phinn but nodded to Alleyn. He hastened to open the door and followed her through a large and charmingly shaped hall to the main entrance. Outside this a vast elderly car waited.

"I'll sit in the back," she said. "George will drive. I find him an irritating companion in time of trouble."

Alleyn opened the door and switched on a light in the car.

"Now, tell me," she said, after she had heaved herself in, "tell me, not as a policeman to an octogenarian dowager but as a man of discretion to one of your mother's oldest friends, what did you think of Occy Phinn's behaviour just now?"

Alleyn said, "Octogenarian dowagers, even if they are my mother's oldest friend, shouldn't lure me out of doors at night and make improper suggestions."

"Ah," she said, "so you're not going to respond."

"Tell me, did Mr. Phinn have a son called Ludovic? Ludovic Danberry-Phinn?"

In the not very bright light he watched her face harden as if, behind its mask of fat, she had set her jaw. "Yes," she said. "Why?"

"It could hardly not be, could it, with those names?"

"I wouldn't mention the boy if I were you. He was in the Foreign Service and blotted his copybook, as I daresay you know. It was quite a tragedy. It's never mentioned."

"Is it not? What sort of a man was Colonel Cartarette?"

"Pigheaded, quixotic fellow. Obstinate as a mule. One of those pathetically conscientious people who aim so high they get a permanent crick in their conscience."

"Are you thinking of any particular incident?"

"No," Lady Lacklander said firmly, "I am not."

"Do you mind telling me what you and Colonel Cartarette talked about?"

"We talked," Lady Lacklander said coolly, "about Occy poaching and about a domestic matter that is for the moment private and can have no bearing whatever on Maurice's death. Good-night to you, Roderick. I suppose I call you Roderick, don't I?"

"When we're alone together."

"Impudent fellow!" she said and aimed a sort of dab at him. "Go back and bully those poor things in there. And tell George to hurry."

"Can you remember exactly what Mr. Phinn and Colonel Cartarette said to each other when they had their row?"

She looked hard at him, folded her jewelled hands together and said, "Not word for word. They had a row over the fish. Occy rows with everybody."

"Did they talk about anything else?"

Lady Lacklander continued to look at him and said, "No," very coolly indeed.

Alleyn made her a little bow. "Good-night," he said. "If you remember specifically anything that they said to each other, would you be terribly kind and write it down?"

"Roderick," Lady Lacklander said, "Occy Phinn is no murderer."

"Is he not?" Alleyn said. "Well, that's something to know, isn't it? Good-night."

He shut the door. The light in the car went out.

4

As he turned back to the house, Alleyn met George Lacklander. It struck him that George was remarkably ill at ease in his company and would greatly have preferred to deal exclusively with Fox.

"Oh . . . ah, hullo," George said. "I . . . ah . . . I wonder, may I have a word with you? I don't suppose you remember, by the way, but we have met a thousand years ago, ha, ha, when, I think, you were one of my father's bright young men, weren't you?"

Alleyn's twenty-five-year-old recollection of George rested solely on the late Sir Harold Lacklander's scorching comments on his son's limitations. "No damn' use expecting anything of George," Sir Harold had once confided. "Let him strike attitudes at Nunspardon and in the ripeness of time become a J.P. That is George's form." It occurred to Alleyn that this prophecy had probably been fulfilled.

He answered George's opening question and blandly disregarded its sequel. "Please do," he said.

"Fact is," George said, "I'm wondering just what the drill is. I am, by the way, and not that it makes any real difference, a Beak. So I suppose I may be said to fill my humble pigeonhole in the maintenance of the Queen's peace, what?"

"And why not?" Alleyn infuriatingly replied.

"Yes," George continued, goggling at him in the dark. "Yes. Well, now, I wanted to ask you what exactly will be the drill about poor Maurice Cartarette's—ah—about the—ah—the body. I mean, one is concerned for Kitty's sake. For their sake, I mean. His wife and daughter. One can perhaps help with the arrangements for the funeral and all that. What?"

"Yes, of course," Alleyn agreed. "Colonel Cartarette's body will remain where it is under guard until to-morrow morning. It will then be taken to the nearest mortuary and a police surgeon will make an examination and possibly an extensive autopsy. We will, of course, let Mrs. Cartarette know as soon as possible when the funeral may be held. I think we shall probably be ready to hand over in three days, but it doesn't do to be positive about these things."

"O, quite!" George said. "Quite. Quite. Quite."

Alleyn said, "Simply for the record—I shall have to put this sort of question to everybody who was in Colonel Cartarette's landscape last evening—you and Mrs. Cartarette began your round of golf, I think you said, at seven?"

"I didn't notice the exact time," George said in a hurry.

"Perhaps Mrs. Cartarette will remember. Did she meet you on the course?"

"Ah—no. No, I—ah—I called for her in the car. On my way back from Chyning."

"But you didn't drive her back?"

"No. Shorter to walk, we thought. From where we were."

"Yes, I see. . . . And Mrs. Cartarette says she arrived here at about five past eight. Perhaps you played golf, roughly, for an hour. How many holes?"

"We didn't go round the course. Mrs. Cartarette is learning. It was her first—ah—attempt. She asked me to give her a little coaching. We—ah—we only played a couple of holes. We spent the rest of the time practising some of her shots," George said, haughtily.

"Ah, yes. And you parted company at about ten to eight. Where?"

"At the top of the river path," he said and added, "as far as I remember."

"From there would you see Lady Lacklander coming up towards you? She began her ascent at ten to eight."

"I didn't look down. I didn't notice."

"Then you won't have noticed Colonel Cartarette either. Lady Lacklander says he was fishing in the willow grove at the time and that the willow grove is visible from the river path."

"I didn't look down. I . . . ah . . . I merely saw Mrs. Cartarette to the river path and went on through the Home Spinney to Nunspardon. My mother arrived a few minutes later. And now," George said, "if you'll excuse me, I really must drive my mama home. By the way, I do hope you'll make use of us. I mean, you may need a headquarters and so on. Anything one can do."

"How very kind," Alleyn rejoined. "Yes, I think we may let you go now. Afraid I shall have to ask you to stay in Swevenings for the time being."

He saw George's jaw drop.

"Of course," he added, "if you have important business elsewhere, it will be quite in order to come and tell me about it and we'll see what can be done. I shall be at the Boy and Donkey."

"Good God, my dear Alleyn . . ."

"Damn' nuisance, I know," Alleyn said, "but there you are. If they *will* turn on homicide in your bottom meadow. Good-night to you."

He circumnavigated George and returned to the drawing-room, where he found Rose, Mark and Kitty uneasily silent, Mr. Phinn biting his fingers, and Inspector Fox in brisk conversation with Nurse Kettle on the subject of learning French conversation by means of gramophone records. "I don't," Mr. Fox was saying, "make the headway I'd like to."

"I picked up more on a cycling tour in Brittany when I *had* to than I ever got out of *my* records."

"That's what they all tell me, but in our line what chance do you get?"

"You must get a holiday some time, for Heaven's sake."

"True," Fox said, sighing. "That's a fact. You do. But somehow I've never got round to spending it anywhere but Birchington. Excuse me, Miss Kettle, here's the Chief."

Alleyn gave Fox a look that both of them understood very well, and the latter rose blandly to his feet. Alleyn addressed himself to Kitty Cartarette.

"If I may," he said, "I should like to have a very short talk with Miss Kettle. Is there perhaps another room we may use? I saw one, I think, as I came across the hall. A study perhaps."

He had the feeling that Mrs. Cartarette was not overanxious for him to use the study. She hesitated, but Rose said, "Yes, of course. I'll show you."

Fox had gone to the French window and had made a majestical signal to the sergeant, who now came into the drawing-room.

"You all know Sergeant Oliphant, of course," Alleyn said. "He will be in charge of the local arrangements, Mrs. Cartarette, and I thought perhaps you would like to have a word with him. I would be grateful if you would give him the names of your husband's solicitor and bank and also of any relations who should be informed. Mr. Phinn, I will ask you to repeat the substance of your account to Sergeant Oliphant, who will take it down and get you to sign it if it is correct."

Mr. Phinn blinked at him. "I cannot," he said, with a show of spirit, "of course, be compelled."

"Of course not. But I'm afraid we shall have to trouble all of you to give us signed statements, if you are willing to do so. If you do yours first, it will leave you free to go home. I hope," Alleyn concluded, "that you will not find it too difficult without your glasses. And now, Miss Cartarette, may we indeed use the study?"

Rose led the way across the hall into the room where eight hours ago she had talked to her father about her love for Mark. Alleyn and Fox followed her. She waited for a moment and stared, as it seemed to Alleyn, with a kind of wonder at the familiar chairs and desk. Perhaps she saw a look of compassion in his face. She said, "He seems to be here, you know. The room can't go on without him, one would think. This was his place more than anywhere else." She faltered for a moment and then said, "Mr. Alleyn, he was such a darling, my father. He was as much like my child as my father, he depended on me so completely. I don't know why I'm saying this to you."

"It's sometimes a good idea to say things like that to strangers. They make uncomplicated confidants."

"Yes," she said and her voice was surprised, "that's quite true. I'm glad I told you."

Alleyn saw that she suffered from the kind of nervous ricochet that often follows a severe shock. Under its impetus the guard that people normally set over their lightest remarks is lowered and they speak spontaneously of the most surprising matters, as now when Rose suddenly added, "Mark says he couldn't have felt anything. I'm sure he's not just saying that to comfort me, because being a doctor, he wouldn't. So I suppose in a way it's what people call a release. From everything."

Alleyn asked quietly, "Was he worried about anything in particular?"

"Yes," Rose said sombrely, "he was indeed. But I can't tell you about that. It's private, and even if it wasn't, it couldn't possibly be of any use."

"You never know," he said lightly.

"You do in this case."

"When did you see him last?"

"This evening. I mean last evening, don't I? He went out soon after seven. I think it was about ten past seven."

"Where did he go?"

She hesitated and then said, "I believe to call on Mr. Phinn. He took his rod and told me he would go on down to the Chyne for the evening rise. He said he wouldn't come in for dinner, and I asked for something to be left out for him."

"Do you know why he called on Mr. Phinn?"

Rose waited for a long time and then said, "I think it had something to do with . . . with the publishing business."

"The *publishing* business?"

She pushed a strand of hair back and pressed the heels of her hands against her eyes. "I don't know who could do such a thing to him," she said. Her voice was drained of all its colour. "She's exhausted," Alleyn thought and, against his inclination, decided to keep her a little longer.

"Can you tell me, very briefly, what sort of pattern his life has taken over the last twenty years?"

Rose sat on the arm of her father's chair. Her right arm was hooked over its back and she smoothed and re-smoothed the place where his bald head had rested. She was quite calm and told Alleyn in a flat voice of the Colonel's appointments as military attaché at various embassies, of his job at Whitehall during the war, of his appointment as military secretary to a post-war commission that had been set up in Hong Kong and finally, after his second marriage, of his retirement and absorption in a history he had planned to write of his own regiment. He was a great reader, it seemed, particularly of the Elizabethan dramatists, an interest that his daughter had ardently shared. His only recreation apart from his books had been fishing. Rose's eyes, fatigued by tears, looked for a moment at a table against the wall where a tray of threads, scraps of feathers and a number of casts was set out.

"I always tied the flies. We made up a fly he nearly always fished with. I tied one this afternoon."

Her voice trembled and trailed away and she yawned suddenly like a child.

The door opened and Mark Lacklander came in looking angry.

"Ah, there you are!" he said. He walked straight over to her and put his fingers on her wrist. "You're going to bed at once," he said. "I've asked Nurse Kettle to make a hot drink for you. She's waiting for you now. I'll come and see you later and give you a nembutal. I'll have to run into Chyning for it. You don't want me again, I imagine?" he said to Alleyn.

"I do for a few minutes, I'm afraid."

"Oh!" Mark said, and after a pause, "Well, yes, of course, I suppose you do. Stupid of me."

"I don't want any dope, Mark, honestly," Rose said.

"We'll see about that when you're tucked up. Go to bed now." He glared at Alleyn. "Miss Cartarette is my patient," he said, "and those are my instructions."

"They sound altogether admirable," Alleyn rejoined. "Good-night, Miss Cartarette. We'll try to worry you as little as possible."

"You don't worry me at all," Rose said politely and gave him her hand.

"I wonder," Alleyn said to Mark, "if we may see Nurse Kettle as soon as she is free. And you, a little later, if you please, Dr. Lacklander."

"Certainly, sir," Mark said stiffly and taking Rose's arm, led her out of the room.

"And I also wonder, Br'er Fox," Alleyn said, "apart from bloody murder, what it is that's biting all these people."

"I've got a funny sort of notion," Fox said, "and mind, it's only a notion so far, that the whole thing will turn out to hang on that fish."

"And I've got a funny sort of notion you're right."

CHAPTER SIX

The Willow Grove

Nurse Kettle sat tidily on an armless chair with her feet crossed at the ankles and her hands at the wrists. Her apron was turned up in the regulation manner under her uniform coat, and her regulation hat was on her head. She had just given Alleyn a neat account of her finding of Colonel Cartarette's body, and Fox, who had taken the notes, was gazing at her with an expression of the liveliest approval.

"That's all, really," she said, "except that I had a jolly strong feeling I was being watched. There now!"

Her statement hitherto had been so positively one of fact that they both stared at her in surprise. "And now," she said, "you'll think I'm a silly hysterical female because although I thought once that I heard a twig snap and fancied that when a bird flew out of the thicket it was not me who'd disturbed it, I didn't *see* anything at all. Not a thing. And yet I thought I was watched. You get it on night duty in a ward. A patient lying awake and staring at you. You always know before you look. Now laugh that away if you like."

"Who's laughing?" Alleyn rejoined. "We're not, are we, Fox?"

"On no account," Fox said. "I've had the same sensation many a time on night beat in the old days, and it always turned out there was a party in a dark doorway having a look at you."

"Well, fancy!" said the gratified Nurse Kettle.

"I suppose," Alleyn said, "you know all these people pretty well, don't you, Miss Kettle? I always think in country districts the Queen's Nurses are rather like liaison officers."

Nurse Kettle looked pleased. "Well now," she said, "we do get to know people. Of course, our duties take us mostly to the ordinary folk, although with the present shortage we find ourselves doing quite a lot for the other sort. They pay the full fee and that helps the Association, so, as long as it's not depriving the ones who can't afford it, we take the odd upper-class case. Like me and Lady Lacklander's toe, for instance."

"Ah, yes," Alleyn said, "there's the toe." He observed with surprise the expression of enraptured interest in his colleague's elderly face.

"Septic," Nurse Kettle said cosily.

" 'T, 't, 't," said Fox.

"And then again, for example," Nurse Kettle went on, "I night-nursed the old gentleman. With him when he died, actually. Well, so was the family. And the Colonel, too, as it happens."

"Colonel Cartarette?" Alleyn asked without laying much stress on it.

"That's right. Or wait a minute. I'm telling stories. The Colonel didn't come back into the room. He stayed on the landing with the papers."

"The papers?"

"The old gentleman's memoirs they were. The Colonel was to see about publishing them, I fancy, but I don't really know. The old gentleman was very troubled about them. He couldn't be content to say good-bye and give up until he'd seen the Colonel. Mind you, Sir Harold was a great man in his day, and his memoirs'll be very important affairs, no doubt."

"No doubt. He was a distinguished ambassador."

"That's right. Not many of that sort left, I always say. Everything kept up. Quite feudal."

"Well," Alleyn said, "there aren't many families left who can afford to be feudal. Don't they call them the Lucky Lacklanders?"

"That's right. Mind, there are some who think the old gentleman over-did it."

"Indeed?" Alleyn said, keeping his mental fingers crossed. "How?"

"Well, not leaving the grandson anything. Because of him taking up medicine instead of going into the army. Of course, it'll all come to him in the end, but in the meantime, he has to make do with what he earns, though of course—but listen to me gossiping. Where was I now. Oh, the old gentleman and the memoirs. Well, no sooner had he handed them over than he took much worse and the Colonel gave the alarm. We all went in. I gave brandy. Doctor Mark gave an injection, but it was all over in a minute. 'Vic,' he said, 'Vic, Vic,' and that was all." Alleyn repeated, "Vic?" and then was silent for so long that Nurse Kettle had begun to say, "Well, if that's all I can do . . ." when he interrupted her.

"I was going to ask you," he said, "who lives in the house between this one and Mr. Phinn's?"

Nurse Kettle smiled all over her good-humoured face. "At Uplands?" she said. "Commander Syce, to be sure. He's another of my victims," she added and unaccountably turned rather pink. "Down with a bad go of 'bago, poor chap."

"Out of the picture, then, from our point of view?"

"Yes, if you're looking for . . . oh, my gracious," Nurse Kettle suddenly ejaculated, "here we are at goodness knows what hour of the morning talking away as pleasant as you please and all the time you're wondering where you're going to find a murderer. Isn't that frightful?"

"Don't let it worry you," Fox begged her.

Alleyn stared at him.

"Well, of course I'm worried. Even suppose it turns out to have been a tramp. Tramps are people just like other people," Nurse Kettle said vigorously.

"Is Mr. Phinn one of your patients?" Alleyn asked.

"Not to say patient. I nursed a carbuncle for him years ago. I wouldn't be getting ideas about him if I were you."

"In our job," Alleyn rejoined, "we have to get ideas about everybody."

"Not about *me*, I hope and trust."

Fox made a complicated soothing and scandalized noise in his throat.

Alleyn said, "Miss Kettle, you liked Colonel Cartarette, didn't you? It was clear from your manner, I thought, that you liked him very much indeed."

"Well, I did," she said emphatically. "He was one of the nicest and gentlest souls: a gentleman if ever I saw one. Devoted father. Never said an unkind word about anybody."

"Not even about Mr. Phinn?"

"Now *look* here," she began, then caught herself up. "Listen," she said; "Mr. Phinn's eccentric. No use my pretending otherwise for you've seen him for yourselves and you'll hear what others say about him. But there's no malice. No, perhaps I wouldn't say there's no *malice* exactly, but there's no real harm in him. Not a scrap. He's had this tragedy in his life, poor man, and in my opinion he's never been the same since it happened. Before the war, it was. His only son did away with himself. Shocking thing."

"Wasn't the son in the Foreign Service?"

"That's right. Ludovic was his name, poor chap. Ludovic! I ask you! Nice boy and very clever. He was in some foreign place when it happened. Broke his mother's heart, they always say, but she was a cardiac, anyway, poor thing. Mr. Phinn never really got over it. You never know, do you?"

"Never. I remember hearing about it," Alleyn said vaguely. "Wasn't he one of Sir Harold Lacklander's young men?"

"That's right. The old gentleman was a real squire. You know: the old Swevenings families and all that. I think he asked for young Phinn to be sent out to him, and I know he was very cut up when it happened. I daresay he felt responsible."

"You never know," Alleyn repeated. "So the Swevenings families," he added, "tend to gravitate towards foreign parts?"

Nurse Kettle said that they certainly seemed to do so. Apart from young Viccy Danberry-Phinn getting a job in Sir Harold's embassy, there was Commander Syce, whose ship had been based on Singapore, and the

Colonel himself, who had been attached to a number of missions in the
Far East, including one at Singapore. Nurse Kettle added, after a pause,
that she believed he had met his second wife there.

"Really?" Alleyn said with no display of interest. "At the time when
Syce was out there, do you mean?" It was the merest shot in the dark,
but it found its mark. Nurse Kettle became pink in the face and said
with excessive brightness that she believed that "the Commander and
the second Mrs. C." had known each other out in the East. She added,
with an air of cramming herself over some emotional hurdle, that she
had seen a very pretty drawing that the Commander had made of Mrs.
Cartarette. "You'd pick it out for her at once," she said. "Speaking
likeness, really, with tropical flowers behind and all."

"Did you know the first Mrs. Cartarette?"

"Well, not to say *know*. They were only married eighteen months when
she died giving birth to Miss Rose. She was an heiress, you know. The
whole fortune goes to Miss Rose. It's well known. The Colonel was
quite hard up, but he's never touched a penny of his first wife's money.
It's well known," Nurse Kettle repeated, "so I'm not talking gossip."

Alleyn skated dexterously on towards Mark Lacklander, and it was obvious that Nurse Kettle was delighted to sing Mark's praises. Fox, re-
spectfully staring at her, said there was a bit of romance going on there,
seemingly, and she at once replied that *that* was as plain as the noses on
all their faces and a splendid thing, too. A real Swevenings romance, she
added.

Alleyn said, "You *do* like to keep yourselves to yourselves in this district, don't you?"

"Well," Nurse Kettle chuckled, "I daresay we do. As I was saying to a
gentleman patient of mine, we're rather like one of those picture-maps.
Little world of our own, if you know what I mean. I was suggesting . . ."
Nurse Kettle turned bright pink and primmed up her lips. "Personally,"
she added rather obscurely, "I'm all for the old families and the old ways
of looking at things."

"Now, it strikes me," Fox said, raising his brows in bland surprise,
"and mind, I may be wrong, very likely I am, but it strikes *me* that the
present Mrs. Cartarette belongs to quite a different world. Much more
mondaine, if you'll overlook the faulty accent, Miss Kettle."

Miss Kettle muttered something that sounded like "demimondaine"
and hurried on. "Well, I daresay we're a bit stodgy in our ways in the
Vale," she said, "and she's been used to lots of gaiety and there you are."
She stood up. "If there's nothing more," she said, "I'll just have a word
with the doctor and see if there's anything I can do for Miss Rose or her
stepmother before they settle down."

"There's nothing more here. We'll ask you to sign a statement about finding the body, and, of course, you'll be called at the inquest."

"I suppose so." She got up and the two men also rose. Alleyn opened the door. She looked from one to the other.

"It won't be a Vale man," she said. "We're not a murderous lot in the Vale. You may depend upon it."

2

Alleyn and Fox contemplated each other with the absent-minded habit of long association.

"Before we see Dr. Lacklander," Alleyn said, "let's take stock, Br'er Fox. What are you thinking about?" he added.

"I was thinking," Fox said with his customary simplicity, "about Miss Kettle. A very nice woman."

Alleyn stared at him. "You are not by any chance transfixed by Dan Cupid's dart?"

"Ah," Fox said complacently, "that would be the day, wouldn't it, Mr. Alleyn? I like a nice compact woman," he added.

"Drag your fancy away from thoughts of Nurse Kettle's contours, compact or centrifugal, and consider. Colonel Cartarette left this house about ten past seven to call on Octavius Danberry-Phinn. Presumably there was no one at home, because the next we hear of him he's having a violent row with Phinn down by the bottom bridge. That's at about half past seven. At twenty to eight he and Phinn part company. The Colonel crosses the bridge and at twenty minutes to eight is having an interview with Lady Lacklander, who is sketching in a hollow on the left bank almost opposite the willow grove on the right bank. Apparently this alfresco meeting was by arrangement. It lasted about ten minutes. At ten to eight Cartarette left Lady Lacklander, re-crossed the bridge, turned left and evidently went straight into the willow grove because she saw him there as she herself panted up the hill to Nunspardon. Soon after eight Mrs. Cartarette said goodbye to that prize ass George Lacklander and came down the hill. At about a quarter past seven she and he had seen old Phinn poaching, and as she tripped down the path, she looked along his fishing to see if she could spot him anywhere. She must have just missed Lady Lacklander, who, one supposes, had by that time plunged into this Nunspardon Home Spinney they talk so much about. Kitty . . ."

Fox said, "Who?"

"Her name's Kitty, Kitty Cartarette. She came hipping and thighing down the hill with her eye on the upper reaches of the Chyne, where she expected to see Mr. Phinn. She didn't notice her husband in the willow grove, but that tells us nothing until we get a look at the landscape, and anyway, her attention, she says, was elsewhere. She continued across the bridge and so home. She saw nothing unusual on the bridge. Now Lady Lacklander saw a woundy great trout lying on the bridge where, according to Lady L., Mr. Phinn had furiously chucked it when he had his row, thirty-five minutes earlier, with Colonel Cartarette. The next thing that happens is that Mark Lacklander (who has been engaged in tennis and, one supposes, rather solemn dalliance with that charming girl Rose Cartarette) leaves this house round about the time Mrs. Cartarette returns to it and goes down to the bottom bridge, where he does *not* find a woundy great trout and is certain that there was no trout to find. He does, however, find his grandmother's sketching gear on the left bank of the Chyne and like a kind young bloke carries it back to Nunspardon, thus saving the footman a trip. He disappears into the spinney, and as far as we know, this darkling valley is left to itself until a quarter to nine when Nurse Kettle, who has been slapping Commander Syce's lumbago next door, descends into Bottom Meadow, turns off to the right, hears the dog howling and discovers the body. Those are the facts, if they are facts, arising out of information received up to date. What emerges?"

Fox dragged his palm across his jaw. "For a secluded district," he said, "there seems to have been quite a bit of traffic in the valley of the Chyne."

"Doesn't there? Down this hill. Over the bridge. Up the other hill and t'other way round. None of them meeting except the murdered man and old Phinn at half past seven and the murdered man and Lady Lacklander ten minutes later. Otherwise it seems to have been a series of near misses on all hands. I can't remember the layout of the valley with any accuracy, but it appears that from the houses on this side only the upper reaches of the Chyne and a few yards below the bridge on the right bank are visible. We'll have to do an elaborate check as soon as it's light, which is hellish soon, by the way. Unless we find signs of angry locals hiding in the underbrush or of mysterious coloured gentlemen from the East lurking in the village, it's going to look a bit like a small field of suspects."

"Meaning this lot," Fox said with a wag of his head in the direction of the drawing-room.

"There's not a damn' one among them except the nurse who isn't holding something back; I'll swear there isn't. Let's have a word with young Lacklander, shall we? Fetch him in, Foxkin, and while you're there, see how Mr. Phinn's getting on with his statement to the sergeant. I wanted an ear left in that room, the sergeant's was the only one available and the statement seemed the best excuse for planting him there. We'll have to go for dabs on those spectacles we picked up, and I swear they'll be

Mr. Phinn's. If he's got off his chest as much as he's decided to tell us, let him go home. Ask him to remain on tap, though, until further notice. Away you go."

While Fox was away, Alleyn looked more closely at Colonel Cartarette's study. He thought he found in it a number of interesting divergences from the accepted convention. True, there were leather saddleback chairs, a pipe-rack and a regimental photograph, but instead of sporting prints the Colonel had chosen half a dozen Chinese drawings, and the books that lined two of his walls, although they included army lists and military biographies, were for the greater part well-worn copies of Elizabethan and Jacobean dramatists and poets with one or two very rare items on angling. With these Alleyn was interested to find a sizable book with the title *The Scaly Breed* by Maurice Cartarette. It was a work on the habits and characteristics of fresh-water trout. On his desk was a photograph of Rose, looking shy and misty, and one of Kitty looking like an imitation of something it would be difficult to define.

Alleyn's gaze travelled over the surface of the desk and down the front. He tried the drawers. The top pair were unlocked and contained only writing paper and envelopes and a few notes written in a distinguished hand, evidently by the Colonel himself. The centre pairs on each side were locked. The bottom left-hand drawer pulled out. It was empty. His attention was sharpened. He had stooped down to look more closely at it when he heard Fox's voice in the hall. He pushed the drawer to and stood away from the desk.

Mark Lacklander came in with Fox.

Alleyn said, "I shan't keep you long; indeed I have only asked you to come in to clear up one small point and to help us with another, not so small. The first question is this: when you went home at quarter past eight last evening, did you hear a dog howling in Bottom Meadow?"

"No," Mark said. "No, I'm sure I didn't."

"Did Skip really stick close to the Colonel?"

"Not when he was fishing," Mark said at once. "The Colonel had trained him to keep a respectful distance away."

"But you didn't see Skip?"

"I didn't see or hear a dog but I remember meeting a tabby cat. One of Occy Phinn's menagerie, I imagine, on an evening stroll."

"Where was she?"

"This side of the bridge," said Mark, looking bored.

"Right. Now, you'd been playing tennis here, hadn't you, with Miss Cartarette, and you returned to Nunspardon by the bottom bridge and river path. You collected your grandmother's sketching gear on the way, didn't you?"

"I did."

"Were you carrying anything else?"

"Only my tennis things. Why?"

"I'm only trying to get a picture. Collecting these things must have taken a few moments. Did you hear or see anything at all out of the ordinary?"

"Nothing. I don't think I looked across the river at all."

"Right. And now will you tell us, as a medical man, what you make of the injuries to the head?"

Mark said very readily, "Yes, of course, for what my opinion's worth on a superficial examination."

"I gather," Alleyn said, "that you went down with Miss Kettle after she gave the alarm and that with exemplary economy you lifted up the tweed hat, looked at the injury, satisfied yourself that he was dead, replaced the hat and waited for the arrival of the police. That it?"

"Yes. I had a torch and I made as fair an examination as I could without touching him. As a matter of fact, I was able to look pretty closely at the injuries."

"Injuries," Alleyn repeated, stressing the plural. "Then you would agree that he was hit more than once?"

"I'd like to look again before giving an opinion. It seemed to me he had been hit on the temple with one instrument before he was stabbed through it with another. Although—I don't know—a sharp object striking the temple could of itself produce very complex results. It's useless to speculate. Your man will no doubt make a complete examination and what he finds may explain the appearances that to me are rather puzzling."

"But on what you saw your first reaction was to wonder if he'd been stunned before he was stabbed? Is that right?"

"Yes," Mark said readily. "That's right."

"As I saw it," Alleyn said, "there seemed to be an irregular bruised area roughly about three by two inches and inside that a circular welt that might have been made by a very big hammer with a concave striking surface, if such a thing exists. And inside that again is the actual puncture, a hole that, it seemed to me, must have been made by a sharply pointed instrument."

"Yes," Mark said, "that's an accurate descripiton of the superficial appearance. But, of course, the queerest appearances can follow cranial injuries."

"The autopsy may clear up the ambiguities," Alleyn said. He glanced at Mark's intelligent and strikingly handsome face. He decided to take a risk.

"Look here," he said, "it's no good us trying to look as if we're uninterested in Mr. Danberry-Phinn. He and Colonel Cartarette had a flaming row less than an hour, probably, before Cartarette was murdered. What do you feel about that? I don't have to tell you this is entirely off the record. What sort of a chap *is* Mr. Phinn? You must know him pretty well."

Mark thrust his hands into his pockets and scowled at the floor. "I don't know him as well as all that," he said. "I mean, I've known him all my life, of course, but he's old enough to be my father and not likely to be much interested in a medical student or a young practitioner."

"Your father would know him better, I suppose."

"As a Swevenings man and my father's elder contemporary, yes, but they hadn't much in common."

"You knew his son, Ludovic, of course?"

"Oh, yes," Mark said composedly. "Not well," he added; "he was at Eton and I'm a Wykehamist. He trained for the Diplomatic, and I left Oxford for the outer darkness of the dissecting rooms at Thomas's. Completely *déclassé*. I daresay," Mark added, with a grin, "that my grandfather thought much the same about you, sir. Didn't you desert him and the Diplomatic for Lord Trenchard and the lonely beat?"

"If you like to put it that way, which is a good deal more flattering to me than it is to either of my great white chiefs. Young Phinn, by the way, was at your grandfather's embassy in Zlomce, wasn't he?"

"He was," Mark said, and as if he realized that this reply sounded uncomfortably short, he added, "My grandfather was a terrific 'Vale Man,' as we say in these parts. He liked to go all feudal and surround himself with local people. When Viccy Phinn went into the Service, I fancy grandfather asked if he could have him with the idea of making one corner of a Zlomce field forever Swevenings. My God," Mark added, "I didn't mean to put it like that. I mean . . ."

"You've remembered, perhaps, that young Phinn blew out his brains in one corner of a Zlomce field."

"You knew about that?"

"It must have been a great shock to your grandfather."

Mark compressed his lips and turned away. "Naturally," he said. He pulled out a case and still with his back to Alleyn lit himself a cigarette. The match scraped and Fox cleared his throat.

"I believe," Alleyn said, "that Sir Harold's autobiography is to be published."

Mark said, "Did Phinn tell you that?"

"Now, why in the wide world," Alleyn asked, "should Mr. Octavius Phinn tell me?"

There was a long silence broken by Mark.

"I'm sorry, sir," Mark said. "I must decline absolutely to answer any more questions."

"You are perfectly within your rights. It's not so certain that you are wise to do so."

"After all," Mark said, "I must judge of that for myself. Is there any objection now to my driving to the dispensary?"

Alleyn hesitated for the fraction of a second. "No objection in the world," he said. "Good morning to you, Dr. Lacklander."

Mark repeated, "I'm sorry," and with a troubled look at both of them went out of the room.

"Br'er Fox," Alleyn said, "we shall snatch a couple of hours sleep at the Boy and Donkey, but before we do so, will you drag your fancy away from thoughts of District Nurses and bend it upon the bottom drawer on the left-hand side of Colonel Cartarette's desk?"

Fox raised his eyebrows, stationed himself before the desk, bent his knees, placed his spectacles across his nose and did as he was bidden.

"Forced," he said. "Recent. Chipped."

"Quite so. The chip's on the floor. The paper knife on the desk is also chipped and the missing bit is in the otherwise empty drawer. The job's been done unhandily by an amateur in a hurry. We'll seal this room and to-morrow we'll put in the camera-and-dabs boys. Miss Kettle's, Mr. Phinn's and Dr. Lacklander's prints'll be on their statements. Lacklander's and Mrs. Cartarette's grog glasses had better be rescued and locked up in here. If we want dabs from the others, we'll pick them up in the morning." He took a folded handkerchief from his pocket, put it on the desk and opened it up. A pair of cheap spectacles was revealed. "And before we go to bed," he said, "we'll discover if Mr. Danberry-Phinn has left his dabs on his reach-me-down specs. And in the morning, Foxkin, if you are a good boy, you shall be told the sad and cautionary story of Master Ludovic Phinn."

3

Kitty Cartarette lay in a great Jacobean bed. She had asked, when she was first married, to have it done over in quilted and buttoned peach velvet, but had seen at once that this would be considered an error in taste. Anxious at that time to establish her position, she had given up this idea, but the dressing-table and chairs and lamp had all been her own choice. She stared miserably at them now, and a fanciful observer might have found something valedictory in her glance. By shifting across the bed, she was able to see herself in her long glass. The pink silk sheet billowed up round her puffed and tear-stained face. "I do look a sight," she muttered. She may have then remembered that she lay in her husband's place, and if a coldness came over her at this recollection, nobody in Swevenings would have suggested that it was because she had ever really loved him. Lady Lacklander had remarked, indeed, that Kitty was one of those rare women who seem to get through life without forming a deep attachment to anybody, and Lady Lacklander would have found it difficult to say why Kitty had been weeping. It would not have occurred to her to suppose that Kitty was lonelier than she had ever been before, but merely that she suffered from shock, which, of course, was true.

There was a tap on the door and this startled Kitty. Maurice, with his queer old-fashioned delicacy, had always tapped.

"Hullo?" she said.

The door opened and Rose came in. In her muslin dressing-gown and with her hair drawn into a plait she looked like a school-girl. Her eyelids, like Kitty's, were swollen and pink, but even this disfigurement, Kitty noticed with vague resentment, didn't altogether blot out Rose's charm. Kitty supposed she ought to have done a bit more about Rose. "But I can't think of everything," she told herself distractedly.

Rose said, "Kitty, I hope you don't mind my coming in. I couldn't get to sleep and I came out and saw the light under your door. Mark's fetching me some sleeping things from Chyning and I wondered if you'd like one."

"I've got some things of my own, thanks all the same. Has everybody gone?"

"Lady Lacklander and George have and, I think, Occy Phinn. Would you like Mark to look in?"

"What for?"

"You might find him sort of helpful," Rose said in a shaky voice. "I do."

"I daresay," Kitty rejoined dryly. She saw Rose blush faintly. "It was nice of you to think of it, but I'm all right. What about the police? Are they still making themselves at home in your father's study?" Kitty asked.

"I think they must have gone. They're behaving awfully well, really, Kitty. I mean it *is* a help, Mr. Alleyn being a gent."

"I daresay," Kitty said again. "O.K., Rose," she added. "Don't worry. I know."

Her manner was good-naturedly dismissive, but Rose still hesitated. After a pause she said, "Kitty, while I've been waiting—for Mark to come back, you know—I've been thinking. About the future."

"The *future?*" Kitty repeated and stared at her. "I should have thought the present was enough!"

"I can't think about that," Rose said quickly. "Not yet. Not about

Daddy. But it came into my mind that it was going to be hard on you. Perhaps you don't realize—I don't know if he told you, but—well—"

"Oh, yes," Kitty said wearily, "I know. He did tell me. He was awfully scrupulous about anything to do with money, wasn't he?" She looked up at Rose. "O.K., Rose," she said. "Not to fuss. I'll make out. I wasn't expecting anything. My sort," she added obscurely, "don't."

"But I wanted to tell you; you needn't worry. Not from any financial point of view. I mean—it's hard to say and perhaps I should wait till we're more used to what's happened, but I *want* to help," Rose stammered. She began to speak rapidly. It was almost as if she had reached that point of emotional exhaustion that is akin to drunkenness. Her native restraint seemed to have forsaken her and to have been replaced by an urge to pour out some kind of sentiment upon somebody. She appeared scarcely to notice her stepmother as an individual. "You see," she was saying, weaving her fingers together, "I might as well tell you. I shan't need Hammer for very long. Mark and I are going to be engaged."

Kitty looked up at her, hesitated, and then said, "Well, that's fine, isn't it? I do hope you'll be awfully happy. Of course, I'm not exactly surprised."

"No," Rose agreed. "I expect we've been terribly transparent." Her voice trembled and her eyes filled with reiterant tears. "Daddy knew," she said.

"Yes," Kitty agreed with a half-smile. "I told him."

"*You* did?"

It was as if Rose was for the first time positively aware of her stepmother.

"You needn't mind," Kitty said. "It was natural enough. I couldn't help noticing."

"We told him ourselves," Rose muttered.

"Was he pleased? Look, Rose," Kitty said, still in that half-exhausted, half-good-natured manner, "don't let's bother to hedge. I know about the business over Old Man Lacklander's memoirs."

Rose made a slight distasteful movement. "I hadn't thought of it," she said. "It doesn't make any difference."

"No," Kitty agreed, "in a way, I suppose it doesn't—now. What's the matter?"

Rose's chin had gone up. "I think I hear Mark," she said.

She went to the door.

"Rose," Kitty said strongly, and Rose stopped short. "I know it's none of my business but—you're all over the place now. We all are. I wouldn't rush anything! 'Don't rush your fences,' that's what your father would have said, isn't it?"

Rose looked at Kitty with an air of dawning astonishment. "I don't know what you mean," she said. "What fences?"

She had opened the door. A well-kept hand came round it and closed over hers.

"Hallo?" Mark's voice said. "May I come in?"

Rose looked at Kitty, who again hesitated. "Why, yes," she said. "Of course. Come in, Mark."

He was really a *very* handsome young man: tall, dark and with enough emphasis in his mouth and jaw to give him the masterful air that is supposed to be so irresistible to women. He stood looking down at Kitty with Rose's hand drawn through his arm. They made what used to be known as a striking couple.

"I heard your voices," he said, "and thought I'd look in. Is there anything I can do at all? I've bought some things for Rose to help her get to sleep; if you'd like to take one, it might be quite an idea."

"I'll see," she said. "I've got something, actually, somewhere."

"Shall we leave one in case?" Mark suggested. He shook a couple of capsules from a packet onto her bedside table and fetched a glass of water. "One is enough," he said.

He was standing above Kitty and between her and Rose, who had not moved from the door at the far end of the room. Kitty looked up into his face and said loudly, "You were the first there, weren't you?"

Mark made a slight admonitory gesture and turned towards Rose. "Not actually the first," he said quietly. "Miss Kettle—"

"Oh—old Kettle," Kitty said irritably, dismissing her. "What I want to know—after all, I am his wife—what *happened*?"

"Rose," Mark said. "You run along to bed."

"No, Mark darling," Rose said, turning deadly white. "I want to know, too. Please. It's worse not to."

"Yes, much worse," Kitty agreed. "Always."

Mark waited for an appreciable time and then said quickly, "Well first of all—there's no disfigurement to his face—"

Kitty made a sharp grimace and Rose put her hands to her eyes.

"—and I don't think he felt anything at all," Mark said. He lifted a finger. "All right. It was a blow. Here. On the temple."

"That—?" Rose said. "Just that?"

"It's a very vulnerable part, darling."

"Then—might it be some sort of accident?"

"Well—no, I'm afraid not."

"O, Mark, why not?"

"It's out of the question, Rose darling."

"But why?"

"The nature of the injuries."

"More than one?" she said. He went quickly to her and took her hands in his.

"Well—yes."

"But you said—" Rose began.

"You see, there are several injuries all in that one small area. It wouldn't do any good if I let you think they might have been caused accidentally, because the—the pathologist will certainly find that they were not."

Kitty, unnoticed, said, "I see," and added abruptly, "I'm sorry, but I don't think I can take any more to-night. D'you mind?"

Mark looked at her with sharpened interest. "You should try to settle down." He lifted her wrist professionally.

"No, no," she said and drew it away. "That's unnecessary, thanks all the same. But I do think Rose ought to go to bed before she drops in her tracks."

"I quite agree," Mark said again, rather coldly, and opened the door. Rose said, "Yes, I'm going; I hope you do manage to sleep, Kitty," and went out. Mark followed her to her own door.

"Mark, darling, good-night," Rose said. She freed herself gently.

"To-morrow," he said, "I'm going to carry you off to Nunspardon."

"Oh," she said, "no—I don't think we can quite do that, do you? Why Nunspardon?"

"Because I want to look after you and because, making all due allowances, I don't think your stepmother's particularly sympathetic or congenial company for you," Mark Lacklander said, frowning.

"It's all right," Rose said. "It doesn't matter. I've learned not to notice."

4

Fox was duly acquainted with the story of Ludovic Phinn over a breakfast of ham and eggs in the parlour of the Boy and Donkey shortly after dawn. Bailey and Thompson, who had also spent the tag end of the night at the pub, were already afoot in Bottom Meadow with the tools of their trade, and the Home Office pathologist was expected from London. The day promised to be fine and warm.

"I know about young Phinn," Alleyn said, "because his debacle occurred when I was doing a spell in the Special Branch in 1937. At that time the late Sir Harold Lacklander was our Ambassador at Zlomce, and Master Danberry-Phinn was his personal secretary. It was known that the German Government was embarked on a leisurely and elaborate party with the local government over railway concessions. We picked up information to the effect that the German boys were prepared to sign an important and, to us, disastrous undertaking in the fairly distant future. Lacklander was instructed to throw a spanner in the works. He was empowered to offer the Zlomce boys certain delectable concessions, and it was fully expected that they would play. The Germans, however, learnt of his little plot and immediately pressed on their own negotiations to a successful and greatly accelerated conclusion. Our government wanted to know why. Lacklander realized that there had been a leakage of information and, since there was nobody else in a position to let the leakage occur, he tackled young Phinn, who at once broke down and admitted that it was his doing. It seems that he had not been able to assimilate his Zlomce oats too well. It's an old and regrettable story. He arrived with his alma mater's milk wet on his lips, full of sophisticated backchat and unsophisticated thinking. He made some very dubious Zlomce chums, among whom was a young gent whom we afterwards found to be a German agent of a particularly persuasive sort. He was said to have fastened on young Phinn, who became completely sold on the Nazi formula and agreed to act for the Germans. As usual, our sources of information were in themselves dubious. Phinn was judged on results, and undoubtedly he behaved like a traitor. On the night after a crucial cable had come through for his chief, he went off to the gypsies or somewhere with his Nazi friend. The decoding of the cable had been entrusted to him. It developed that he presented his Zlomce chums with the whole story. It was said afterwards that he'd taken bribes. Lacklander gave him bottled hell, and he went away and blew his brains out. We were told that he'd had a kind of hero-fixation on Lacklander, and we always thought it odd that he should have behaved as he did. But he was, I believe, a brilliant but unbalanced boy, an only child whose father, the Octavius we saw last night, expected him to retrieve the fortunes of their old and rather reduced family. His mother died a few months afterwards, I believe."

"Sad," said Mr. Fox.

"It was indeed."

"Would you say, Mr. Alleyn, now, that this Mr. Phinn, Sr., was slightly round the bend?"

"Dotty?"

"Well—eccentric."

"His behaviour in the watches of last night was certainly oddish. He was a frightened man, Fox, if ever I saw one. What do you think?"

"The *opportunity* was there," Fox said, going straight to the first principle of police investigation.

"It was. And, by the way, Bailey's done his dab-drill. The spectacles *are* Mr. Danberry-Phinn's."

"There now!" Fox ejaculated with the utmost satisfaction.

"It's not conclusive, you know. He might have lost them down there earlier in the day. He'd still be very chary of owning to them."

"Well . . ." Fox said sceptically.

"I quite agree. I've got my own idea about when and how they got there, which is this."

He propounded his idea. Fox listened with raised brows. "And as for opportunity, Fox," Alleyn went on, "as far as we've got, it was also there for his wife, all three Lacklanders and, for a matter of that, Nurse Kettle herself."

Fox opened his mouth, caught a derisive glint in his senior's eye and shut it again.

"Of course," Alleyn said, "we can't exclude the tramps or even the dark-skinned stranger from the Far East. But there's one item that emerged last night which I don't think we can afford to disregard, Fox. It seems that Colonel Cartarette was entrusted by Sir Harold Lacklander, then on his deathbed, with the Lacklander memoirs. He was to supervise their publication."

"Well, now," Fox began, "I can't say . . ."

"This item may be of no significance whatever," Alleyn rejoined. "On the other hand, isn't it just possible that it may be a link between the Lacklanders on the one hand and Mr. Octavius Phinn on the other, that link being provided by Colonel Cartarette with the memoirs in his hands."

"I take it," Fox said in his deliberate way, "that you're wondering if there's a full account of young Phinn's offence in the memoirs and if his father's got to know of it and made up his mind to stop publication."

"It sounds hellish thin when you put it like that, doesn't it? Where does such a theory land us? Cartarette goes down the hill at twenty past seven, sees Phinn poaching, and, overheard by Lady Lacklander, has a flaming row with him. They part company. Cartarette moves on to talk to Lady Lacklander, stays with her for ten minutes and then goes to the willow grove to fish. Lady L. returns home and Phinn comes back and murders Cartarette because Cartarette is going to publish old Lacklander's memoirs to the discredit of young Phinn's name. But Lady L. doesn't say a word about this to me. She doesn't say she heard them quarrel *about the memoirs*, although, if they did, there's no reason that I can see why she shouldn't. She merely says they had a row about poaching and that Cartarette talked about this to her. She adds that he and she also discussed a private and domestic business which had nothing to do with Cartarette's death. This, of course, is as it may be. Could the private and domestic business by any chance be anything to do with the publication of the memoirs? If so, why should she refuse to discuss it with me?"

"Have we any reason to think it might be about these memoirs, though?"

"No. I'm doing what I always say you shouldn't do. I'm speculating. But it was clear, wasn't it, that young Lacklander didn't like the memoirs being mentioned. He shut up like a trap over them. They crop up, Br'er Fox. They occur. They link the Cartarettes with the Lacklanders, and they may well link Mr. Phinn with both. They provide, so far, the only connecting theme in this group of apparently very conventional people."

"I wouldn't call her ladyship conventional," Fox observed.

"She's unconventional along orthodox lines, believe me. There's a car pulling up. It'll be Dr. Curtis. Let's return to the bottom field and to the question of opportunity and evidence."

But before he led the way out, he stood rubbing his nose and staring at his colleague.

"Don't forget," he said, "that old Lacklander died with what sounds like an uneasy conscience and the word 'Vic' on his lips."

"Ah. Vic."

"Yes. And Mark Lacklander referred to young Phinn as Viccy! Makes you fink, don't it? Come on."

5

By mid-summer morning light, Colonel Cartarette looked incongruous in the willow grove. His coverings had been taken away and there, close to the river's brink, he was: curled up, empty of thought and motion, wearing the badge of violence upon his temple . . . a much photographed corpse. Bailey and Thompson had repeated the work of the previous night but without, Alleyn thought, a great deal of success. Water had flooded under duct boards, seeped up through earthy places and washed over gravel. In spite of the groundsheet it had soaked into Colonel Cartarette's Harris tweeds and had collected in a pool in the palm of his right hand.

Dr. Curtis completed a superficial examination and stood up.

"That's all I want here, Alleyn," he said. "I've given Oliphant the contents of the pockets. A bundle of keys, tobacco, pipe, lighter. Fly case. Handkerchief. Pocket book with a few notes and a photograph of his daughter. That's all. As for general appearances: rigor is well established and is, I think, about to go off. I understand you've found out that he was alive up to about eight and that he was found dead at five to nine. I won't get any closer in time than that."

"The injuries?"

"I'd say, tentatively, two weapons, or possibly one weapon used in two ways. There's a clean puncture with deep penetration, there's a circular indentation with the puncture as its centre, and there's been a heavy blow over the same area that has apparently caused extensive fracturing and a lot of extravasation. It might have been made by one of those stone-breaker's hammers or even by a flat oval-shaped stone itself. I think it was the first injury he got. It would almost certainly have knocked him right out. Might have killed him. In any case it would have left him wide open to the second attack."

Alleyn had moved round the body to the edge of the stream.

"And no prints?" he said looking at Bailey.

"There's prints from the people that found him," Bailey said, "clear enough. Man and woman. Overlapping and straight forward . . . walk towards, squat down, stand, walk away. And there's his own heel marks, Mr. Alleyn, as you noticed last night. Half filled with surface drainage they were then, but you can see how he was, clear enough."

"Yes," Alleyn said. "Squatting on a bit of soft ground. Facing the stream. He'd cut several handfuls of grass with his knife and was about to wrap up that trout. There's the knife, there's the grass in his hands, and there's the trout! A whopper if ever there was one. Sergeant Oliphant says the Colonel himself hooked and lost him some days ago."

He stooped and slipped an exploratory finger into the trout's maw. "Ah, yes," he said, "it's still there. We'd better have a look at it."

His long fingers were busy for a minute. Presently they emerged from the jaws of the Old 'Un with a broken cast. "That's not a standard commercial fly," he said. "It's a beautiful home-made one. Scraps of red feather and gold cloth bound with bronze hair, and I think I've seen its mates in the Colonel's study. Rose Cartarette tied the flies for her father, and I fancy this is the one he lost when he hooked the Old 'Un on the afternoon before Sir Harold Lacklander's death."

Alleyn looked at the Colonel's broken head and blankly acquiescent face. "But you didn't hook him this time," he said, "and why in the world should you shout, at half past seven, that you wouldn't be seen dead with him, and be found dead with him at nine?"

He turned towards the stream. The willow grove sheltered a sort of miniature harbour with its curved bank going sheer down to the depth of about five feet at the top end of the little bay and running out in a stony shelf at the lower end. The stream poured into this bay with a swirling movement, turning back upon its course.

Alleyn pointed to the margin of the lower bank of the bay. It carried an indented scar running horizontally below the lip.

"Look here, Fox," Alleyn said, "and here, above it." He nodded at a group of tall daisies, strung along the edge of the bank up-stream from where the Colonel lay and perhaps a yard from his feet. They were in flower. Alleyn pointed to three leggy stems, taller than their fellows, from which the blooms had been cut away.

"You can move him," he said. "But don't tramp over the ground more than you can help. We *may* want another peer at it. And, by the way, Fox, have you noticed that inside the willow grove, near the point of entry, there's a flattened patch of grass and several broken and bent twigs? Remember that Nurse Kettle thought she was observed. Go ahead, Oliphant."

Sergeant Oliphant and P. C. Gripper came forward with a stretcher. They put it down some distance from the body, which they now raised. As they did so, a daisy head, crumpled and sodden, dropped from the coat.

"Pick it up, tenderly," Alleyn said as he did so, "and treat it with care. We must find the other two if we can. This murderer said it with flowers." He put it away in his case. Oliphant and Gripper laid the body on the stretcher and waited.

Alleyn found a second daisy on the bank below the point where Colonel Cartarette's head had lain. "The third," he said, "may have gone down-stream, but we'll see."

He now looked at Colonel Cartarette's rod, squatting beside it where it rested on the bank, its point overhanging the stream. Alleyn lifted the cast, letting it dangle from his long fingers. "The fellow of the one that the Old 'Un broke for him," he said.

He looked more closely at the cast and sniffed at it.

"He hooked a fish yesterday," he said; "there's a flake of flesh on the barb. Where, then, is this trout he caught? Too small? Did he chuck it back? Or what? Damn this ruined ground." He separated the cast from the line and put it away in his case. He sniffed into the dead curved hands. "Yes," he said, "he's handled a fish. We'll go over the hands, fingernails and clothes for any more traces. Keep that tuft of grass that's in his hand. Where's the rest of it?"

He turned back to the riverbank and gathered up every blade of grass that was scattered where the Colonel had cut it. He examined the Colonel's pocket knife and found that, in addition to having traces of grass, it smelt of fish. Then he very cautiously lifted the Old 'Un and examined the patch of stones where the great fish had lain all night.

"Traces there, all right," he said. "Are they all off this one fish, however? Look, there's a sharp flinty bit of stone with a flap of fish skin on it. Now let's see."

He turned the great trout over and searched its clamminess for a sign of a missing piece of skin and could find none. "This looks more like business," he muttered and took out his pocket lens. His subordinates coughed and shifted their feet. Fox watched him with calm approval.

"Well," Alleyn said at last, "we'll have to get an expert's opinion and it may be crucial. But it's pretty clear that he made a catch of his own, that it lay on this patch, that a bit of its skin was torn off on this stone, that the fish itself was subsequently removed and the Old 'Un put in its place. It doesn't look as if it was chucked back in the stream, does it? In that case he would have taken it off his hook and thrown it back at once. He wouldn't have laid it down on the bank. And why was a flap of its skin scraped off on the stone? And why was the Old 'Un laid over the trace of the other fish? And by whom? And when?"

Fox said, "As for when: before the rain at all events. The ground shows that."

"That doesn't help, since he was killed before the rain and found before the rain. But consider, Br'er Fox, he was killed with a tuft of cut grass in his hand. Isn't it at least possible that he was cutting his grass to wrap up his own catch? He had refused to touch the Old 'Un and had left it lying on the bridge. The people who knew him best all agree he'd stick to his word. All right. Somebody kills him. Is it that 'somebody' who takes the Colonel's fish and replaces it with the Old 'Un?"

"You'd think so, Mr. Alleyn, wouldn't you?"

"And why did he do it?"

"Gawd knows!" said Oliphant in disgust. Sergeants Bailey and Thompson and P. C. Gripper made sympathetic noises. Dr. Curtis, squatting by the stretcher, grinned to himself.

"What was the actual position of the killer at the time of the blow or blows?" Alleyn continued. "As I read it, and you'll correct me here, Curtis, Colonel Cartarette was squatting on his heels facing the stream with the cut grass in his hands. The heel marks and subsequent position suggest that when he was struck on the left temple he keeled over, away from the blow, and fell in the position in which Nurse Kettle found him. Now, he was either belted from behind by a left-hander or rammed by a sort of crouching charge from his left side or struck from the front by a swinging right-handed swipe . . . Yes, Oliphant?"

Sergeant Oliphant said, "Well, pardon me, sir, I was only going to remark, would it be, for example, something like the sort of blow a quarryman gives a wedge that is sticking out from a rock-face at the level of his knee?"

"Ah!" said P. C. Gripper appreciatively. "Or an underhand serve, like tennis."

"That kind of thing," Alleyn said, exchanging a look with Fox. "Now there wasn't enough room between the Colonel and the brink for such a blow to be delivered; which is why I suggested his assailant would have had to be three feet out on the surface of the stream. Now, take a look up-stream towards the bridge, Br'er Fox. Go roundabout, because we'll still keep the immediate vicinity unmucked up, and then come out here."

Fox joined Alleyn on the lower bank of the little bay at the point where it jutted farthest out into the stream. They looked up the Chyne past the willow grove, which hid the near end of the bridge, to the far end, which was just visible about forty feet away with the old punt moored in the hole beneath it.

Alleyn said, "Charming, isn't it? Like a lead-pencil vignette in a Victorian album. I wonder if Lady Lacklander ever sketches from this point. Have you read *The Rape of Lucrece*, Br'er Fox?"

"I can't say I have, unless it's on the police list, which it sounds as if it might be. Or would it be Shakespeare?"

"The latter. There's a bit about the eccentricities of river currents. The poem really refers to the Avon at Clopton Bridge, but it might have been written about the Chyne at this very point. Something about the stream that, coming through an arch, 'yet in the eddy boundeth in his pride back to the strait that forced him on.' Look at that twig sailing towards us now. It's got into just such a current, do you see, and instead of passing down the main stream is coming into this bay. Here it comes. Round it swirls in the eddy and back it goes towards the bridge. It's a strong and quite considerable sort of counter-current. Stay where you are, Fox, for a moment, will you. Get down on your sinful old hunkers and bow your head over an imaginary fish. Imitate the action of the angler. Don't look up and don't move till I tell you."

"Ah, what's all this, I do wonder," Mr. Fox speculated and squatted calmly at the water's edge with his great hands between his feet.

Alleyn skirted round the crucial area and disappeared into the willow grove.

"What's he up to?" Curtis asked of no one in particular and added a rude professional joke about Mr. Fox's posture. Sergeant Oliphant and P. C. Gripper exchanged scandalized glances. Bailey and Thompson grinned. They all heard Alleyn walk briskly across Bottom Bridge, though only Fox, who faithfully kept his gaze on the ground, was in a position to see him. The others waited, expecting him for some reason of his own to appear on the opposite bank.

It was quite a shock to Dr. Curtis, Bailey, Thompson, Oliphant and Gripper when round the up-stream point of the willow-grove bay the old punt came sliding with Alleyn standing in it, a wilted daisy head in his hand.

The punt was carried transversely by the current away from the far bank and across the main stream into the little willow-grove harbour. It glided silently to rest, its square prow fitting neatly into the scar Alleyn had pointed out in the down-stream bank. At the same time its bottom grated on the gravel spit and it became motionless.

"I suppose," Alleyn said, "you heard that, didn't you?"

Fox looked up.

"I heard it," he said. "But I saw and heard nothing until then."

"Cartarette must have heard it too," Alleyn said. "Which accounts, I fancy, for the daisies. Br'er Fox, do we think we know whodunit?"

Fox said, "If I take your meaning, Mr. Alleyn, I think you think *you* do."

CHAPTER SEVEN   Watt's Hill

"Things to be borne in mind," Alleyn said, still speaking from the punt. "Point one: I found the daisy head in the prow. That is to say, on the same line with the other two heads but a bit further from the point of impact. Point two: this old crock has got a spare mooring line about thirty feet long. It's still made fast at the other end and I've only got to haul myself back. I imagine the arrangement is for the convenience of Lady Lacklander, who, judging by splashes of old water-colour and a squashed tube, occasionally paints from the punt. It's a sobering thought. I should like to see her, resembling one of the more obese female deities, seated in the prow of the punt, hauling herself back to harbourage. There is also, by the way, a pale-yellow giant hairpin in close association with two or three cigarette butts, some with lipstick and some not. Been there for some considerable time, I should say, so that's another story."

"Sir G.," Fox ruminated, "and the girl-friend?"

"Trust you," Alleyn said, "for clamping down on the sex-story. To return. Point three: remember that the punt-journey would be hidden from the dwellers on Watt's Hill. Only this end of the bridge and the small area between it and the willow grove is visible to them. You can take him away now, Gripper."

Dr. Curtis covered the body with the groundsheet. P. C. Gripper and the constable-driver of the Yard car, assisted by Bailey and Thompson, carried Colonel Cartarette out of the willow grove and along the banks of his private fishing to Watt's Lane, where the Swevenings hospital van awaited him.

"He was a very pleasant gentleman," said Sergeant Oliphant. "I hope we get this chap, sir."

"Oh, we'll *get* him," Fox remarked and looked composedly at his principal.

"I suggest," Alleyn said, "that the killer saw Cartarette from the other bank, squatting over his catch. I suggest that the killer, familiar with the punt, slipped into it, let go the painter and was carried by what I'd like to call Shakespeare's current across the stream and into this bay, where the punt grounded and left the scar of its prow in the bank there. I suggest that this person was well enough acquainted with the Colonel for him merely to look up when he heard the punt grate on the gravel and not rise. You can see the punt's quite firmly grounded. Now if I stand about here, rather aft of amidships, I'm opposite the place where Cartarette squatted over his task and within striking distance of him if the blow was of the kind I think it was."

"If," said Fox.

"Yes, I know, 'if.' If you know of a better damn' theory, you can damn' well go to it," Alleyn said cheerfully.

"O.K.," Fox said. "I don't, sir. So far."

"What may at first look tiresome," Alleyn went on, "is the position of the three decapitated daisy stalks and their heads. It's true that one swipe of a suitable instrument might have beheaded all three and landed one daisy on the Colonel, a second on the bank and a third in the punt. Fair enough. But the same swipe couldn't have reached the Colonel himself."

Oliphant stared pointedly at the pole lying in the punt.

"No, Oliphant," Alleyn said. "You try standing in this punt, whirling that thing round your head, swishing it through the daisies and catching a squatting man neatly on the temple with the end. What do you think our killer is . . . a caber-tosser from Braemar?"

"Do you reckon then," Fox said, "that the daisies were beheaded by a second blow or earlier in the day? Or something?"

Sergeant Oliphant suddenly remarked, "Pardon me, but did the daisies necess*airi*ly have anything to do with the crime?"

"I think there's probably a connection," Alleyn rejoined, giving the sergeant his full attention. "The three heads are fresh enough to suggest it. One was in the Colonel's coat and one was in the punt."

"Well, pardon me, sir," the emboldened sergeant continued with a slight modulation of his theme, "but did the punt necess*airi*ly have any bearing on the crime?"

"Unless we find a left-handed suspect, I think we must accept the punt as a working hypothesis. Have a look at the area between the punt and the place where the body lay and the patch of stones between the tuft from which the grass was cut and the place where the fish lay. It would be possible to step from the punt onto that patch of stones, and you would then be standing close to the position of Colonel Cartarette's head. You would leave little or no trace of your presence. Now, on the willow-grove side of the body the ground is soft and earthy. The Colonel himself, Nurse Kettle and Dr. Lacklander have all left recognizable prints there. But there are no traces of a fourth visitor. Accept for the moment the theory that, after the Colonel had been knocked out, our assailant did step ashore onto the stony patch to deliver the final injury, or perhaps merely to make sure the victim was already dead. How would such a theory fit in with the missing trout, the punt and the daisies?"

Alleyn looked from Oliphant to Fox. The former had assumed that air of portentousness that so often waits upon utter bewilderment. The latter merely looked mildly astonished. This expression indicated that Mr. Fox had caught on.

Alleyn elaborated his theory of the trout, the punt and the daisies, building up a complete and detailed picture of one way in which Colonel Cartarette might have been murdered. "I realize," he said, "that it's all as full of 'ifs' as a passport to paradise. Produce any other theory that fits the facts and I'll embrace it with fervour."

Fox said dubiously, "Funny business if it works out that way. About the punt, now . . ."

"About the punt, yes. There are several pieces of cut grass in the bottom of the punt, and they smell of fish."

"Do they, now?" said Fox appreciatively and added, "So what we're meant to believe in is a murderer who sails up to his victim in a punt and lays him out. Not satisfied in his own mind that the man's dead, he steps ashore and has another go with another instrument. Then for reasons you've made out to sound O.K., Mr. Alleyn, though there's not much solid evidence, he swaps the Colonel's fish for the Old 'Un. To do this he has to tootle back in the punt and fetch it. And by way of a change at some time or another he swipes the heads off daisies. Where he gets his weapons and what he does with the first fish is a great big secret. Is that the story, Mr. Alleyn?"

"It is and I'm sticking to it. Moreover, I'm leaving orders, Oliphant, for a number one search for the missing fish. And meet me," Alleyn said to Fox, "on the other bank. I've something to show you."

He gathered up the long tow-rope, pulled himself easily into the counter-current and so back across forty feet of water to the boatshed. When Fox, having come round by the bridge, joined him there, he was shaking his head.

"Oliphant and his boy have been over the ground like a herd of rhinos," he said. "Getting their planks last night. Pity. Still . . . have a look here, Fox."

He led the way into a deep hollow on the left bank. Here the rain had not obliterated the characteristic scars left by Lady Lacklander's sketching stool and easel. Alleyn pointed to them. "But the really interesting exhibit is up here on the hillock. Come and see."

Fox followed him over grass that carried faint signs of having been trampled. In a moment they stood looking down at a scarcely perceptible hole in the turf. It still held water. The grass nearby showed traces of pressure.

"If you examine that hole closely," Alleyn said, "you'll see it's surrounded by a circular indentation."

"Yes," Fox said after a long pause, "yes, by God, so it is. Same as the injury, by God."

"It's the mark of the second weapon," Alleyn said. "It's the mark of a shooting-stick, Br'er Fox."

2

"Attractive house," Alleyn said as they emerged from the Home Coppice into full view of Nunspardon, "attractive house, Fox, isn't it?"

"Very fine residence," Fox said. "Georgian, would it be?"

"It would. Built on the site of the former house, which was a nunnery. Hence Nunspardon. Presented (as usual, by Henry VIII) to the Lacklanders. We'll have to go cautiously here, Br'er Fox, by gum, we shall. They'll have just about finished their breakfast. I wonder if Lady Lacklander has it downstairs or in her room. She has it downstairs," he added as Lady Lacklander herself came out of the house with half a dozen dogs at her heels.

"She's wearing men's boots!" Fox observed.

"That may be because of her ulcerated toe."

"Ah, to be sure. Lord love us!" Fox ejaculated. "She's *got* a shooting-stick on her arm."

"So she has. It may not be the one. And then again," Alleyn muttered as he removed his hat and gaily lifted it on high to the distant figure, "it may."

"Here she comes. No, she doesn't."

"Hell's boots, she's going to sit on it."

Lady Lacklander had in fact begun to tramp towards them but had evidently changed her mind. She answered Alleyn's salute by waving a heavy gardening glove at him. Then she halted, opened her shooting-stick and, with alarming empiricism, let herself down on it.

"With her weight," Alleyn said crossly, "she'll bloody well bury it. Come on."

As soon as they were within hailing distance, Lady Lacklander shouted, "Good morning to you." She then remained perfectly still and stared at them as they approached. Alleyn thought, "Old basilisk! She's being deliberately embarrassing, damn her," and he returned the stare with inoffensive interest, smiling vaguely.

"Have you been up all night?" she asked when they were at an appropriate distance. "Not that you look like it, I must say."

Alleyn said, "We're sorry to begin plaguing you so early, but we're in a bit of a jam."

"Baffled?"

"Jolly nearly. Do you mind," Alleyn went on with what his wife would have called sheer rude charm, "do you mind having your brains picked at nine o'clock in the morning?"

"What do *you* want with other people's brains, I should like to know," she said. Her eyes, screwed in between swags of flesh, glittered at him.

Alleyn embarked on a careful tarradiddle. "We begin to wonder," he said, "if Cartarette's murderer may have been lying doggo in the vicinity for some time before the assault."

"Do you?"

"Yes."

"*I* didn't see him."

"I mean really doggo. And as far as we know, which is not as far as we'd like, there's no telling exactly where the hiding place could have been. We think it might have been somewhere that commanded at any rate a partial view of the bridge and the willow grove. We also think that it may have overlooked your sketching hollow."

"You've discovered where that is, have you?"

"Simplicity itself, I promise you. You used an easel and a sketching stool."

"And with my weight to sustain," she said rocking, to his dismay, backwards and forwards on the shooting-stick, "the latter no doubt left its mark."

"The thing is," Alleyn said, "we think this person in hiding may have waited until he saw you go before coming out of cover. Did you stay down in your hollow all the time?"

"No, I had a look at my sketch several times from a distance. Anaemic beast it turned out, in the end."

"Where exactly did you stand when you looked at it?"

"On the rise between the hollow and the bridge. You can't have gone over your ground properly or you'd have found that out for yourself."

"Should I? Why?" Alleyn asked and mentally touched wood.

"Because, my good Roderick, I used this shooting-stick and drove it so far into the ground that I was able to walk away and leave it, which I did repeatedly."

"Did you leave it there when you went home?"

"Certainly. As a landmark for the boy when he came to collect my things. I dumped them beside it."

"Lady Lacklander," Alleyn said, "I want to reconstruct the crucial bit of the landscape as it was after you left it. Will you lend us your shooting-stick and your sketching gear for an hour or so? We'll take the greatest care of them."

"I don't know what you're up to," she said, "and I suppose I may as well make up my mind that I won't find out. Here you are."

She heaved herself up and, sure enough, the disk and spike of her shooting-stick had been rammed down so hard into the path that both were embedded and the shooting-stick stood up of its own accord.

Alleyn desired above all things to release it with the most delicate care, perhaps dig it up, turf and all, and let the soil dry and fall away. But there was no chance of that; Lady Lacklander turned and with a single powerful wrench tore the shooting-stick from its bondage.

"There you are," she said indifferently and gave it to him. "The sketching gear is up at the house. Come and get it?"

Alleyn thanked her and said that they would. He carried the shooting-stick by its middle and they all three went up to the house. George Lacklander was in the hall. His manner had changed overnight and he now spoke with the muted solemnity with which men of his type approach a sickroom or a church service. He made a further reference to his activities as a Justice of the Peace but otherwise was huffily reserved.

"Well, George," his mother said, and bestowed a peculiar smirk upon him, "I don't suppose they'll let me out on bail, but no doubt you'll be allowed to visit me."

"Really, Mama!"

"Roderick is demanding my sketching gear on what appears to me to be a sadly trumped-up excuse. He has not yet, however, administered what I understand to be the Usual Warning."

"Really, Mama!" George repeated with a miserable titter.

"Come along, Rory," Lady Lacklander continued and led Alleyn out of the hall into a cloakroom where umbrellas, an assortment of galoshes, boots and shoes, and a variety of rackets and clubs were assembled. "I keep them here to be handy," she said, "for garden peeps. I'm better at herbaceous borders than anything else, which just about places my prowess as a water-colourist, as, no doubt, your wife would tell you."

"She's not an aesthetic snob," Alleyn said mildly.

"She's a damn' good painter, however," Lady Lacklander continued. "There you are. Help yourself."

He lifted a canvas haversack to which were strapped an easel and an artist's umbrella. "Did you use the umbrella?" he asked.

"William, the boy, put it up. I didn't want it; the sun was gone from the valley. I left it, standing but shut, when I came home."

"We'll see if it showed above the hollow."

"Roderick," said Lady Lacklander, suddenly, "what exactly *were* the injuries?"

"Hasn't your grandson told you?"

"If he had I wouldn't ask you."

"They were cranial."

"You needn't be in a hurry to return the things. I'm not in the mood."

"It's very kind of you to lend them."

"Kettle will tell me," said Lady Lacklander, "all about it!"

"Of course she will," he agreed cheerfully, "much better than I can."

"What persuaded you to leave the Service for this unlovely trade?"

"It's a long time ago," Alleyn said, "but I seem to remember that it had something to do with a liking for facts."

"Which should never be confused with the truth."

"I still think they are the raw material of the truth. I mustn't keep you any longer. Thank you so much for helping us," Alleyn said and stood aside to let her pass.

He and Fox were aware of her great bulk, motionless on the steps, as they made their way back to the Home Coppice. Alleyn carried the shooting-stick by its middle and Fox the sketching gear. "And I don't mind betting," Alleyn said, "that from the rear we look as self-conscious as a brace of snowballs in hell."

When they were out of sight in the trees, they examined their booty. Alleyn laid the shooting-stick on a bank and squatted beside it.

"The disk," he said, "screws on above the ferrule leaving a two-inch spike. Soft earth all over it and forced up under the collar of the disk, which obviously hasn't been disengaged for weeks! All to the good. If it's the weapon, it may have been washed in the Chyne and wiped, and it has, of course, been subsequently rammed down in soft earth, but it hasn't been taken apart. There's a good chance of a blood trace under the collar. We must let Curtis have this at once. Now let's have a look at her kit."

"Which we didn't really want, did we?"

"You never know. It's a radial easel with spiked legs, and it's a jointed gamp with a spiked foot. Lots of spikes available, but the shooting-stick fits the picture best. Now for the interior. Here we are," Alleyn said, unbuckling the straps and peering inside. "Large water-colour box. Several mounted boards of not-surface paper. Case of brushes. Pencils. Bunjy. Water-jar. Sponge. Paint-rag. Paint-rag," he repeated softly and bent over the kit sniffing. He drew a length of stained cotton rag out of the kit. It was blotched with patches of watery colour and with one dark brownish-reddish stain that was broken by a number of folds as if the rag had been twisted about some object.

Alleyn looked up at his colleague.

"Smell, Fox," he said.

Fox squatted behind him and sniffed stertorously.

"Fish," he said.

3

Before returning, they visited the second tee and looked down on the valley from the Nunspardon side. They commanded a view of the far end of the bridge and the reaches of the Chyne above it. As from the other side of the valley, the willow grove, the lower reaches and the Nunspardon end of the bridge were hidden by intervening trees through which they could see part of the hollow where Lady Lacklander had worked at her sketch.

"So you see," Alleyn pointed out, "it was from here that Mrs. Cartarette and that ass George Lacklander saw Mr. Phinn poaching under the bridge, and it was from down there in the hollow that Lady Lacklander glanced up and saw them." He turned and looked back at a clump of trees on the golf course. "And I don't mind betting," he added, "that all this chat about teaching her to play golf is the cover-story for a pompous slap-and-tickle."

"Do you reckon, Mr. Alleyn?"

"Well, I wouldn't be surprised. There's Oliphant at the bridge," Alleyn said, waving his hand. "We'll get him to take this stuff straight to Curtis, who'll be in Chyning by now. He's starting his P.M. by eleven. Dr. Lacklander's arranged for him to use the hospital mortuary. I want a report, as soon as we can get it, on the rag and the shooting-stick."

"Will the young doctor attend the autopsy, do you think?"

"I wouldn't be surprised. I think our next move had better be a routine check-up on Commander Syce."

"That's the chap Miss Kettle mentioned, with lumbago, who lives in the middle house," Fox observed. "I wonder would he have seen anything."

"Depends on the position of his bed."

"It's a nasty thing, lumbago," Fox mused.

They handed over Lady Lacklander's property to Sergeant Oliphant with an explanatory note for Dr. Curtis and instructions to search the valley for the whole or part of the missing trout. They then climbed the river path to Uplands.

They passed through the Hammer Farm spinney and entered that of Commander Syce. Here they encountered a small notice nailed to a tree. It was freshly painted and bore in neatly executed letters the legend: "Beware of Archery."

"Look at that!" Fox said. "And we've forgotten our green tights."

"It may be a warning to Nurse Kettle," Alleyn said.

"I don't get you, sir?"

"Not to flirt with the Commander when she beats up his lumbago."

"Very far-fetched," Fox said stiffly.

As they emerged from Commander Syce's spinney into his garden, they heard a twang followed by a peculiar whining sound and the "tuck" of a penetrating blow.

"What the hell's that!" Fox ejaculated. "It sounded like the flight of an arrow."

"Which is not surprising," Alleyn rejoined, "as that is what it was."

He nodded at a tree not far from where they stood and there, astonishing and incongruous, was embedded an arrow prettily flighted in red and implanted in the centre of a neatly and freshly carved heart. It still quivered very slightly. "We can't say we weren't warned," Alleyn pointed out.

"Very careless!" Fox said crossly.

Alleyn pulled out the arrow and looked closely at it. "Deadly if they hit the right spot. I hope you've noticed the heart. It would appear that Commander Syce has recovered from his lumbago and fallen into love's sickness. Come on."

They emerged from the spinney to discover Commander Syce himself some fifty yards away, bow in hand, quiver at thigh, scarlet-faced and irresolute.

"Look here!" he shouted. "Damn' sorry and all that, but, great grief, how was I to know, and, damn it all, what about the notice!"

"Yes, yes," Alleyn rejoined. "We're here at our own risk."

He and Fox approached Syce, who, unlike Lady Lacklander, evidently found the interval between the first hail and, as it were, boarding distance extremely embarrassing. As they plodded up the hill, he looked anywhere but at them and when, finally, Alleyn introduced himself and Fox, he shied away from them like an unbroken colt.

"We are," Alleyn explained, "police officers."

"Good Lord!"

"I suppose you've heard of last night's tragedy?"

"What tragedy?"

"Colonel Cartarette."

"Cartarette?"

"He has been murdered."

"Great grief!"

"We're calling on his neighbours in case . . ."

"What time?"

"About nine o'clock, we think."

"How d'you know it's murder?"

"By the nature of the injuries, which are particularly savage ones, to the head."

"Who found him?"

"The District Nurse. Nurse Kettle."

Commander Syce turned scarlet. "Why didn't she get me!" he said.

"Would you expect her to?"

"No."

"Well then . . ."

"I say, come in, won't you? No good nattering out here, what!" shouted Commander Syce.

They followed him into his desolate drawing-room and noted the improvised bed, now tidily made-up, and a table set out with an orderly array of drawing materials and water-colours. A large picture-map in the early stages of composition was pinned to a drawing board. Alleyn saw that its subject was Swevenings and that a number of lively figures had already been sketched in.

"That's very pleasant," Alleyn said, looking at it.

Commander Syce made a complicated and terrified noise and interposed himself between the picture-map and their gaze. He muttered something about doing it for a friend.

"Isn't she lucky?" Alleyn remarked lightly. Commander Syce turned, if anything, deeper scarlet, and Inspector Fox looked depressed.

Alleyn said he was sure Commander Syce would understand that as a matter of routine the police were calling upon Cartarette's neighbours. "Simply," he said, "to try and get a background. When one is casting about in a case like this . . ."

"Haven't you got the fellah?"

"No. But we hope that by talking to those of the Colonel's neighbours who were anywhere near . . ."

"I wasn't. Nowhere near."

Alleyn said with a scarcely perceptible modulation of tone, "Then you know where he was found?"

"'Course I do. You say nine o'clock. Miss . . . ah . . . the . . . ah . . . lady who you tell me found him left here shortly before nine and I saw her go down into the valley. If she found him at nine, he must have been in the perishing valley, mustn't he? I watched her go down."

"From where?"

"From up here. The window. She told me she was going down the valley."

"You were on your feet, then? Not completely prostrate with lumbago?"

Commander Syce began to look wretchedly uncomfortable. "I struggled up, don't you know," he said.

"And this morning you've quite recovered?"

"It comes and goes."

"Very tricky," said Alleyn. He still had the arrow in his hand and now held it up. "Do you often loose these things off into your spinney?" he asked.

Commander Syce muttered something about a change from target shooting.

"I've often thought I'd like to have a shot at archery," Alleyn lied amiably. "One of the more blameless sports. Tell me, what weight of bow do you use?"

"A sixty-pound pull."

"Really! What's the longest . . . is clout the word? . . . that can be shot with a sixty-pounder?"

"Two hundred and forty yards."

"Is that twelve score? 'A' would have clapped i' the clout at twelve score'?"

"That's right," Commander Syce agreed and shot what might have been an appreciative glance at Alleyn.

"Quite a length. However, I mustn't keep you gossiping about archery. What I really want to ask you is this. I understand that you've known Colonel Cartarette a great many years?"

"Off and on. Neighbours. Damn' nice fellah."

"Exactly. And I believe that when Cartarette was in the Far East, you ran up against him . . . at Hong Kong, was it?" Alleyn improvised hopefully.

"Singapore."

"Oh, yes. The reason why I'm asking you is this. From the character of the crime and the apparently complete absence of motive, here, we are wondering if it can possibly be a back-kick from his work out in the East."

"Wouldn't know."

"Look here, can you tell us anything at all about his life in the East? I mean, anything that might start us off. When actually did you see him out there?"

"Last time would be four years ago. I was still on the active list. My ship was based on Singapore and he looked me up when we were in port. I was axed six months later."

"Did you see much of them out there?"

"Them?"

"The Cartarettes."

Commander Syce glared at Alleyn. "He wasn't married," he said, "then."

"So you didn't meet the second Mrs. Cartarette until you came back here, I suppose?"

Commander Syce thrust his hands into his pockets and walked over to the window. "I had met her, yes," he mumbled. "Out there."

"Before they married?"

"Yes."

"Did you bring them together?" Alleyn asked lightly and he saw the muscles in the back of Syce's neck stiffen under the reddened skin.

"I introduced them, as it happens," Syce said loudly without turning his head.

"That's always rather amusing. Or I find it so, being," Alleyn said looking fixedly at Fox, "an incorrigible match-maker."

"Good God, nothing like that!" Syce shouted. "Last thing I intended. Good God, no!"

He spoke with extraordinary vehemence and seemed to be moved equally by astonishment, shame and indignation. Alleyn wondered why on earth he himself didn't get the snub he had certainly invited and decided it was because Syce was too embarrassed to administer one. He tried to get something more about Syce's encounters with Cartarette in Singapore but was unsuccessful. He noticed the unsteady hands, moist skin and patchy colour, and the bewildered, unhappy look in the very blue eyes. "Alcoholic, poor devil," he thought.

"It's no good asking me anything," Syce abruptly announced. "Nobody tells me anything. I don't go anywhere. I'm no good to anybody."

"We're only looking for a background, and I hoped you might be able to provide a piece of it. Miss Kettle was saying last night how close the Swevenings people are to each other; it all sounded quite feudal. Even

Sir Harold Lacklander had young Phinn as his secretary. What did you say?"

"Nothing. Young perisher. Doesn't matter."

". . . and as soon as your ship comes in, Cartarette naturally looks you up. You bring about his first meeting with Miss . . . I don't know Mrs. Cartarette's maiden name."

Commander Syce mumbled unhappily.

"Perhaps you can give it to me," Alleyn said apologetically. "We have to get these details for the files. Save me bothering her."

He gazed mildly at Syce, who threw one agonized glance at him, swallowed with difficulty, and said in a strangulated voice, "De Vere."

There was a marked silence. Fox cleared his throat.

"Ah, yes," Alleyn said.

4

"Would you have thought," Fox asked as he and Alleyn made their way through Mr. Phinn's coppice to Jacob's Cottage, "that the present Mrs. Cartarette was born into the purple, Mr. Alleyn?"

"I wouldn't have said so, Br'er Fox. No."

"De Vere, though?"

"My foot."

"Perhaps," Fox speculated, reverting to the language in which he so ardently desired to become proficient, "perhaps she's . . . er . . . déclassée."

"I think, on the contrary, she's on her way up."

"Ah. The baronet, now," Fox went on; "he's sweet on her, as anyone could see. Would you think it was a strong enough attraction to incite either of them to violence?"

"I should think he was going through the silly season most men of his type experience. I must say I can't see him raising an amatory passion to the power of homicide in any woman. You never know, of course; I should think she must find life in Swevenings pretty dim. What did you collect from Syce's general behaviour, Fox?"

"Well, now, he *did* get me wondering what exactly are his feelings about this lady? I mean, they seem to be old acquaintances, don't they? Miss Kettle said he made a picture of Mrs. Cartarette before she was married. And then he didn't seem to have fancied the marriage much, did he? Practically smoked when it was mentioned, he got so hot. My idea is there was something between him and her and the magnolia bush wherever East meets West."

"You dirty old man," Alleyn said absently. "We'll have to find out, you know."

"*Crime passionnel?*"

"Again you never know. We'll ring the Yard and ask them to look him up in the Navy List. They can find out when he was in Singapore and get a confidential report."

"Say," Fox speculated, "that he was sweet on her. Say they were engaged when he introduced her to the Colonel. Say he went off in his ship and then was retired from the navy and came home and found Kitty de Vere changed into the second Mrs. Cartarette. So he takes to the bottle and gets," said Mr. Fox, "an *idée fixe*."

"So will you, if you go on speculating with such insatiable virtuosity. And what about his lumbago? Personally, I think he's having a dim fling with Nurse Kettle."

Fox looked put out.

"Very unsuitable," he said.

"Here is Mr. Phinn's spinney and here, I think, is our girl-friend of last night."

Mrs. Thomasina Twitchett was, in fact, taking a stroll. When she saw them, she wafted her tail, blinked and sat down.

"Good morning, my dear," said Alleyn.

He sat on his heels and extended his hand. Mrs. Twitchett did not advance upon it, but she broke into an extremely loud purring.

"You know," Alleyn continued severely, "if you could do a little better than purrs and mews, I rather fancy you could give us exactly the information we need. You were in the bottom meadow last night, my dear, and I'll be bound you were all eyes and ears."

Mrs. Twitchett half closed her eyes, sniffed at his extended forefinger and began to lick it.

"Thinks you're a kitten," Fox said sardonically.

Alleyn in his turn sniffed at his finger and then lowered his face almost to the level of the cat's. She saluted him with a brief dab of her nose.

"What a girl," Fox said.

"She no longer smells of raw fish. Milk and a little cooked rabbit, I fancy. Do you remember where we met her last night?"

"Soon after we began to climb the hill on this side, wasn't it?"

"Yes. We'll have a look over the terrain when we get the chance. Come on."

They climbed up through Mr. Phinn's spinney and finally emerged on the lawn before Jacob's Cottage. "Though if that's a cottage," Fox observed, "Buck House is a bungalow."

"Case of inverted snobbism, I daresay. It's a nice front, nevertheless.

Might have been the dower house to Nunspardon at one time. Rum go, couple of unattached males living side-by-side in houses that are much too big for them."

"I wonder how Mr. Phinn and the Commander hit it off."

"I wouldn't mind having a bet that they don't. Look, here he comes."

"Cripes!" Mr. Fox ejaculated. "What a menagerie!"

Mr. Phinn had, in fact, come out of his house accompanied by an escort of cats and Mrs. Twitchett's three fat kittens.

"No more!" he was saying in his curious alto voice. "All gone! Go and catch micey, you lazy lot of furs."

He set down the empty dish he had been carrying. Some object fell from his breast pocket and he replaced it in a hurry. Some of his cats pretended alarm and flounced off, the others merely stared at him. The three kittens, seeing their mother, galloped unsteadily towards her with stiff tails and a great deal of conversation. Mr. Phinn saw Alleyn and Fox. Staring at them, he clapped his hands like a mechanical toy that had not quite run down.

The tassel of his smoking cap had swung over his nose, but his sudden pallor undid its comic effect. The handle of the concealed object protruded from his breast pocket. He began to walk towards them, and his feline escort, with the exception of the Twitchetts, scattered before him.

"Good morning," Mr. Phinn fluted thickly. He swept aside his tassel with a not quite steady hand and pulled up a dingy handkerchief, thus concealing the protruding handle. "To what beneficent constabular breeze do I owe this enchanting surprise? Detectives, emerging from a grove of trees!" he exclaimed and clasped his hands. "Like fauns in pursuit of some elusive hamadryad! Armed, I perceive," he added with a malevolent glance at Commander Syce's arrow, which Alleyn had retained by the simple expedient of absent-mindedly walking away with it.

"Good morning, Mr. Phinn," Alleyn said. "I have been renewing my acquaintance with your charming cat."

"Isn't she sweet?" Mr. Phinn moistened his lips with the tip of his tongue. "Such a devoted mama, you can't think!"

Alleyn sat on his heels beside Mrs. Twitchett, who gently kicked away one of her too-greedy kittens. "Her fur's in wonderful condition for a nursing mother," he said, stroking it. "Do you give her anything special to eat?"

Mr. Phinn began to talk with the sickening extravagance of the feline-fanatic. "A balanced diet," he explained in a high-pitched voice, "of her own choosing. Fissy on Mondays and Fridays. Steaky on Tuesdays. Livvy on Wednesdays. Cooked bun on Thursdays and Sundays. Embellished," he added with a merciless smile, "by our own clever claws, with micey and birdie."

"Fish only twice a week," Alleyn mused, and Fox, suddenly feeling that something was expected of him, said, "Fancy!"

"She is looking forward to to-morrow," Mr. Phinn said, "with the devoted acquiescence of a good Catholic, although, of course, theistically, she professes the mysteries of Old Nile."

"You don't occasionally catch her dinner for her in the Chyne?"

"When I am successful," Mr. Phinn said, "we share."

"Did you," Alleyn asked, fatuously addressing himself to the cat, "did you have fresh fissy for your supper last night, my angel?" Mrs. Twitchett turned contemptuously to her kittens.

"No!" said Mr. Phinn in his natural voice.

"You made no other catch then, besides the fabulous Old 'Un?"

"No!"

"May we talk?"

Mr. Phinn, silent for once, led the way through a side door and down a passage into a sizable library.

Alleyn's eye for other people's houses unobtrusively explored the room. The Colonel's study had been pleasant, civilized and not lacking in feminine graces. Commander Syce's drawing-room was at once clean, orderly, desolate and entirely masculine. Mr. Phinn's library was disorderly, dirty, neglected and ambiguous. It exhibited confused traces of Georgian grace, Victorian pomposity and Edwardian muddle. Cushions that had once been fashionably elaborate were now stained and tarnished. There were yards of dead canvas that had once been acceptable to Burlington House, including the portrait of a fragile-looking lady with a contradictory jaw that was vaguely familiar. There were rows and rows of "gift" books about cats, cheek-by-jowl with Edwardian novels which, if opened, would be found to contain illustrations of young women in dust coats and motoring veils making haughty little *moues* at gladiators in Norfolk jackets. But there were also one or two admirable chairs, an unmistakable Lyly and a lovely, though filthy, rug. And among the decrepit novels were books of distinction and authority. It was on Mr. Phinn's shelves that Alleyn noticed an unexpected link with the Colonel. For here among a collection of books on angling he saw again *The Scaly Breed* by Maurice Cartarette. But what interested Alleyn perhaps more than all these items was a state of chaos that was to be observed on and near a very nice serpentine-fronted bureau. The choked drawers were half out, one indeed was on the floor, the top was covered with miscellaneous objects which, to a police-trained eye, had clearly been dragged out in handfuls, while the carpet nearby was littered with a further assortment. A burglar, taken by surprise, could not have left clearer evidence behind him.

"How can I serve you?" asked Mr. Phinn. "A little refreshment, by the way? A glass of sherry? Does Tio Pepe recommend himself to your notice?"

"Not quite so early in the morning, thank you, and I'm afraid this is a duty call."

"Indeed? How I wish I could be of some help. I have spent a perfectly wretched night—such of it as remained to me—fretting and speculating, you know. A murderer in the Vale! Really, if it wasn't so dreadful, there would be a kind of grotesque humour in the thought. We are so very respectable in Swevenings. Not a ripple, one would have thought, on the surface of the Chyne!"

He flinched and made the sort of grimace that is induced by a sudden twinge of toothache.

"Would one not? What," Alleyn asked, "about the Battle of the Old 'Un?"

Mr. Phinn was ready for him. He fluttered his fingers. "*Nil nisi,*" he said, with rather breathless airiness, "and all the rest of it, but really the Colonel was most exasperating as an angler. A monument of integrity in every other respect, I daresay, but as a fly-fisherman I am sorry to say there were some hideous lapses. It is an ethical paradox that so noble a sport should occasionally be wedded to such lamentable malpractices."

"Such," Alleyn suggested, "as casting under a bridge into your neighbour's preserves?"

"I will defend my action before the Judgment Seat, and the ghost of the sublime Walton himself will thunder in my defence. It was entirely permissible."

"Did you and the Colonel," Alleyn said, "speak of anything else but this . . . ah . . . this ethical paradox?"

Mr. Phinn glared at him, opened his mouth, thought perhaps of Lady Lacklander and shut it again. Alleyn for his part remembered, with exasperation, the law on extra-judicial admissions. Lady Lacklander had told him there had been a further discussion between the two men but had refused to say what it was about. If Mr. Phinn should ever come to trial for the murder of Maurice Cartarette, or even if he should merely be called to give evidence against someone else, the use by Alleyn of the first of Lady Lacklander's admissions and the concealment of the second would be held by a court of law to be improper. He decided to take a risk.

"We have been given to understand," he said, "that there was, in fact, a further discussion."

There was a long silence.

"Well, Mr. Phinn?"

"Well. I am waiting."

"For what?"

"I believe it is known as the Usual Warning," Mr. Phinn said.

"The police are only obliged to give the Usual Warning when they have decided to make an arrest."

"And you have not yet arrived at this decision?"

"Not yet."

"You, of course, have your information from the Lady Gargantua, the Mammoth Chatelaine, the Great, repeat Great, Lady of Nunspardon," said Mr. Phinn, and then surprisingly turned pink. His gaze, oddly fixed, was directed past Alleyn's elbow to some object behind him. It did not waver. "Not," Mr. Phinn added, "that, in certain respects, her worth does not correspond by a rough computation with her avoirdupois. Did she divulge the nature of my further conversation with the Colonel?"

"No."

"Then neither," said Mr. Phinn, "shall I. At least, not yet. Not unless I am obliged to do so."

The direction of his gaze had not shifted.

"Very well," Alleyn said and turned away with an air of finality.

He had been standing with his back to a desk. Presiding over an incredibly heaped-up litter were two photographs in tarnished silver frames. One was of the lady of the portrait. The other was of a young man bearing a strong resemblance to her and was inscribed in a flowing hand: "Ludovic."

It was at this photograph that Mr. Phinn had been staring.

CHAPTER EIGHT   **Jacob's Cottage**

Alleyn decided to press home what might or might not be an advantage and so did so with distaste. He had been in the police service for over twenty years. Under slow pressure his outward habit had toughened, but, like an ice cube that under warmth will yield its surface but retain its inward form, so his personality had kept its pattern intact. When an investigation led him, as this did, to take action that was distasteful to him, he imposed a discipline upon himself and went forward. It was a kind of abstinence, however, that prompted him to do so.

He said, looking at the photograph, "This is your son, sir, isn't it?"

Mr. Phinn, in a voice that was quite unlike his usual emphatic alto, said, "My son, Ludovic."

"I didn't meet him, but I was in the Special Branch in 1937. I heard about his tragedy, of course."

"He was a good boy," Mr. Phinn said. "I think I may have spoiled him. I fear I may have done so."

"One can't tell about these things."

"No. One can't tell."

"I don't ask you to forgive me for speaking of him. In a case of homicide I'm afraid no holds are barred. We have discovered that Sir Harold Lacklander died with the name 'Vic' on his lips and full of concern about the publication of his own memoirs which he had entrusted to Colonel Cartarette. We know that your son was Sir Harold's secretary during a crucial period of his administration in Zlomce and that Sir Harold could hardly avoid mention of the tragedy of your son's death if he was to write anything like a definitive record of his own career."

"You need go no further," said Mr. Phinn with a wave of his hand. "I see very clearly what is in your mind." He looked at Fox, whose notebook was in his palm. "Pray write openly, Inspector. Mr. Alleyn, you wonder, do you not, if I quarrelled with Colonel Cartarette because he proposed to make public, through Lacklander's memoirs, the ruin of my boy. Nothing could be further from the truth."

"I wonder," Alleyn said, "if the discussion, that Lady Lacklander overheard but doesn't care to reveal, was about some such matter."

Mr. Phinn suddenly beat his pudgy hands together, once. "If Lady L. does not care to tell you," he announced, "then neither for the time being do I."

"I wonder, too," Alleyn continued, "if it wouldn't be easy to misjudge completely your own motives and those of Lady Lacklander."

"Ah," Mr. Phinn said, with extraordinary complacency, "you are on dangerous ground indeed, my dear Alleyn. Peel away the layers of motive from the ethical onion and your eyes may well begin to water. It is no occupation, believe me, for a Chief Detective-Inspector."

A faint smile played conceitedly about the corners of his mouth. Alleyn might have supposed him to have completely recovered his equanimity if it had not been for the slightest possible tic in the lower lid of his right eye and a movement of the fingers of one hand across the back of the other.

"I wonder," Alleyn said, "if you'd mind showing us your fishing gear

. . . the whole equipment as you took it down yesterday to the Chyne?"

"And why not?" Mr. Phinn rejoined. "But I demand," he added loudly, "to know if you suspect me of this crime. Do you? Do you?"

"Come now," Alleyn said, "you must know very well that you can't in the same breath refuse to answer our questions and demand an answer to your own. If we may, we would like to see your fishing gear."

Mr. Phinn stared at him. "It's not here," he said. "I'll get it."

"Fox will help you."

Mr. Phinn looked as if he didn't much relish this offer but appeared to think better of refusing it. He and Fox went out together. Alleyn moved over to the book-lined wall on his left and took down Maurice Cartarette's work on *The Scaly Breed*. It was inscribed on the title page: "January 1930. For Viccy on his eighteenth birthday with good wishes for many happy castings," and was signed by the author. The Colonel, Alleyn reflected, had evidently been on better terms with young Phinn than with his father.

He riffled through the pages. The book had been published in 1929 and appeared to be a series of short and pleasantly written essays on the behaviour and eccentricities of fresh-water fish. It contained an odd mixture of folkishness, natural history, mild flights of fancy and, apparently, a certain amount of scientific fact. It was illustrated, rather charmingly, with marginal drawings. Alleyn turned back to the title page and found that they were by Geoffrey Syce: another instance, he thought, of the way the people of Swevenings stick together, and he wondered if, twenty-six years ago, the Colonel in his regiment and the Commander in his ship had written to each other about the scaly breed and about how they should fashion their book. His eye fell on a page-heading, "No Two Alike," and with astonishment he saw what at first he took to be a familiar enough kind of diagram: that of two magnified finger-prints, showing the essential dissimilarities. At first glance they might have been lifted from a manual on criminal investigation. When, however, he looked more closely, he found, written underneath: "Microphotographs. Fig. 1. Scale of Brown Trout. 6 years. 2½ lbs. Chyne River. Showing 4 years' poor growth followed by 2 years' vigorous growth. Fig. 2. Scale of Trout. 4 years. 1 lb. Chyne River. Note differences in circuli, winter bands and spawning marks." With sharpened interest he began to read the accompanying letterpress:

> It is not perhaps generally known [the Colonel had written] that the scales of no two trout are alike: I mean microscopically alike in the sense that no two sets of finger-prints correspond. It is amusing to reflect that in the watery world a rogue-trout may leave

incriminating evidence behind him in the form of what might be
called scales of justice.

For the margin Commander Syce had made a facetious picture of a roach
with meerschaum and deerstalker hat examining through a lens the
scales of a very tough-looking trout.

Alleyn had time to re-read the page. He turned back to the frontis-
piece—a drawing of the Colonel himself. Alleyn found in the face a dual
suggestion of soldier and diplomat superimposed, he fancied, on something that was pure countryman. "A nice chap, he looks. I wonder if it
would have amused him to know that he himself has put into my hands
the prize piece of information received."

He replaced the book and turned to the desk with its indescribable
litter of pamphlets, brochures, unopened and opened letters, newspapers
and magazines. Having inspected the surface, he began, gingerly, to disturb the top layer and in a moment or two had disclosed a letter addressed
to "Octavius Phinn, Esq." in the beautiful and unmistakable handwriting
of Colonel Cartarette.

Alleyn had just had time enough to discover that it contained about
thirty pages of typescript marked on the outside: "7," when he heard
Fox's voice on the stairs. He turned away and placed himself in front
of the portrait.

Mr. Phinn and Fox reappeared with the fishing gear.

"I have," Alleyn said, "been enjoying this very charming portrait."

"My wife."

"Am I imagining—perhaps I am—a likeness to Dr. Mark Lacklander?"

"There was," Mr. Phinn said shortly, "a distant connection. Here are
my toys."

He was evidently one of those anglers who cannot resist the call of the
illustrated catalogue and the lure of the gadget. His creel, his gaff, his
net, his case of flies and his superb rod were supplemented by every conceivable toy, all of them, Alleyn expected, extremely expensive. His canvas bag was slotted and pocketted to receive these mysteries, and Alleyn
drew them out one after another to discover that they were all freshly
cleaned and in wonderful order.

"With what fly," he asked Mr. Phinn, "did you hook the Old 'Un? It
must have been a Homeric struggle, surely?"

"Grant me the bridge," Mr. Phinn shouted excitedly, "grant me that,
and I'll tell you."

"Very well," Alleyn conceded with a grin, "we'll take the bridge in our
stride. I concede it. Let's have the story."

Mr. Phinn went strongly into action. It appeared that, at the mention of his prowess, the emotions that had so lately seemed to grip him were completely forgotten. Fear, if he had known fear, paternal anguish, if he had in fact experienced it, and anger, if it was indeed anger that had occasionally moved him, were all abandoned for the absolute passion of the angler. He led them out of doors, exhibited his retrospective prowess in casting, led them in again and re-enacted in the strangest pantomime his battle with the Old 'Un: how he was played, with breath-taking reverses, up through the waters under the bridge and into Mr. Phinn's indisputable preserves; how he was nearly lost, and what cunning he displayed, and how Mr. Phinn countered with even greater cunning of his own. Finally there was the great capitulation, the landing and the *coup de grâce*, this last being administered, as Mr. Phinn made clear in spirited pantomime, with a sort of angler's cosh: a short, heavily leaded rod.

Alleyn took this instrument in his hand and balanced it. "What do you call the thing?" he asked.

"A priest," Mr. Phinn said. "It is called a priest. I don't know why."

"Perhaps because of its valedictory function." He laid it on the desk and placed Commander Syce's arrow beside it. Mr. Phinn stared but said nothing.

"I really must return his arrow to Commander Syce," Alleyn said absently. "I found it in the spinney, embedded in a tree trunk."

He might have touched off a high-explosive. The colour flooded angrily into Mr. Phinn's face and he began to shout of the infamies of Commander Syce and his archery. The death of Thomasina Twitchett's mother at the hands of Commander Syce was furiously recalled. Syce, Mr. Phinn said, was a monster, an alcoholic sadist, possessed of a bloodlust. It was with malice aforethought that he had transfixed the dowager Twitchett. The plea of accident was ridiculous: the thing was an obsession. Syce would drink himself into a sagittal fury and fire arrows off madly into the landscape. Only last night, Mr. Phinn continued, when he himself was returning from the Chyne after what he now called his little *mésentente* with Colonel Cartarette, the Commander's bow was twanging away on the archery lawn and Mr. Phinn had actually heard the "tuck" of an arrow in a tree trunk dangerously near to himself. The time was a quarter past eight. He remembered hearing his clock chime at the same time.

"I think you must be mistaken," Alleyn put in mildly. "Nurse Kettle tells us that last evening Commander Syce was completely incapacitated by an acute attack of lumbago."

Mr. Phinn shouted out a rude and derisive word. "A farrago of nonsense!" he continued. "Either she is his accomplice or his paramour or possibly," he amended more charitably, "his dupe. I swear he was devilishly active last night. I swear it. I trembled lest my Thomasina, who had accompanied me to the Chyne, should share the fate of her mama. She did not join me on my return but had preferred to linger in the evening air. Indeed, the reason for my perhaps slightly dramatic entry into Hammer in the early hours of this morning was my hope of retrieving my errant Fur. The dreadful news with which you met me quite put her out of my head," Mr. Phinn concluded and did not look as if he expected to be believed.

"I see," Alleyn said and did not look as if he believed him. "Quite a chapter of accidents. Do you mind if we take possession of your fishing gear for a short time? Part of a routine check, you know."

Mr. Phinn was at a loss for words. "But how quite extraordinary!" he at last exclaimed. "My fishing gear? Well, I suppose one must not refuse."

"We shan't keep it any longer than is necessary," Alleyn assured him.

Fox put the kit in order and slung it over his massive shoulder.

"And also, I'm afraid," Alleyn said apologetically, "the shoes and suit that you wore on your fishing expedition."

"My shoes? My suit! But why, why! I don't like this. I don't like it at all."

"It may be some comfort to you to know that I shall make the same awkward demands of at least four other persons."

Mr. Phinn seemed to brighten a little. "Blood?" he asked.

"Not necessarily," Alleyn said coolly. "This and that, you know, and the other thing. May we have them?"

"A fat lot of use," Mr. Phinn muttered, "if I said no. And in any case you are perfectly welcome to every garment I possess. Homicidally speaking, they are as pure as the driven snow."

When he saw them, Alleyn reflected that although, homicidally speaking, this might be true, from any other point of view it was grossly inaccurate: Mr. Phinn's angling garments were exceedingly grubby and smelt quite strongly of fish. Alleyn saw with satisfaction a slimy deposit on the right leg of a pair of old-fashioned knickerbockers. The shoes were filthy and the stockings in holes. With a gesture of defiance, their owner flung on top of them a dilapidated tweed hat with the usual collection of flies in the band.

"Make what you like of them," he said grandly, "and see that you let me have them back in the order in which you receive them."

Alleyn gave him grave assurance to this effect and wrapped up the garments. Fox wrote out a receipt for the unlovely bundle.

"We won't keep you any longer," Alleyn said, "unless by any chance you would care to give us a true account of your ramblings in the watches of the night."

Mr. Phinn gaped at him and in doing so resembled for the moment the Old 'Un himself.

"Because," Alleyn went on, "you haven't done so yet, you know. I mean, your story of seeing lighted windows and calling to tell the Colonel of your catch was completely blown-up by Lady Lacklander. And your latest version . . . that you were on the hunt for your mother-cat . . . really won't do at all. Feline nursing mothers, and you tell us this is a particularly devoted one, do not desert their kittens for six hours on end. Moreover, we came upon Mrs. Twitchett last night on her way home about half past twelve. And why, if the Twitchett story was the true one, did you not produce it in the first instance?" Alleyn waited for some seconds. "You see," he said, "you have no answer to any of these questions."

"I shall not make any further statements. I prefer to remain silent."

"Shall I tell you what I think may have happened last night? I think that when you made your first remark as you stood in the French window at Hammer, you said something that was near the truth. I think that either then, or perhaps earlier in the evening, you had sallied out in search of your great trout. I think you regretted having flung it down on the bridge during your quarrel with Colonel Cartarette. You knew he wouldn't touch it, because he had told you so and had gone off, leaving it there. Did you not go down into the valley of the Chyne to retrieve the trout, and did you not find it gone from the bridge when you got there?"

The colour mounted in Mr. Phinn's face in uneven patches. He lowered his chin and looked quickly at Alleyn from under his meagre brows. But he said nothing.

"If this is so," Alleyn went on, "and I am encouraged by your silence to hope that it may be, I can't help wondering what you did next. Did you come straight back to Hammer and seeing the lighted windows make up your mind to accuse the Colonel of having pinched your fish after all? But no. If that had been so, your behaviour would have been different. You would not, before you were aware of his death, have trembled and gone white to the lips. Nor would you have invented your cock-and-bull story of wanting to tell the Colonel all about your catch: a story that was at once disproved when Lady Lacklander told us about your row with the Colonel over that very catch and by the fact that for a long time you have not been on visiting terms with your neighbour."

Mr. Phinn had turned aside, and Alleyn walked round him until they were again face-to-face.

"How," he said, "is one to explain your behaviour of last night? Shall I tell you what I think? I think that when you arrived at Hammer Farm at five past one this morning, you knew already that Colonel Cartarette was dead."

Still Mr. Phinn said nothing.

"Now if this is true," Alleyn said, "and again you don't deny it, you have misinformed us about your movements. You let us understand that you returned to the bottom meadow just before you came to Hammer Farm at about one o'clock. But your coat was as dry as a chip. So it must have been much earlier in the evening before the rain that you returned to the bridge in the hope of retrieving the fish and found it gone. And knowing that the Colonel was fishing his own waters not far away, would you not seek him out? Now, if you did behave as I have suggested, you did so at a time when nobody saw you. That must have been after Lady Lacklander, Mrs. Cartarette and Dr. Lacklander had all gone home. Mrs. Cartarette reached Hammer Farm at about five past eight, and Dr. Lacklander went home at quarter past eight. Neither of them saw the trout. On my working hypothesis, then, you revisited the valley after a quarter past eight and, one would also suppose, before five to nine when Nurse Kettle did so. And there, Mr. Phinn, in the willow grove you found Colonel Cartarette's dead body with your mammoth trout beside it. And didn't Nurse Kettle very nearly catch you in the willow grove?"

Mr. Phinn ejaculated, "Has she said—" and caught his voice back.

"No," Alleyn said. "Not specifically. It is I who suggest that you hid and watched her and crept away when she had gone. I suggest, moreover, that when you bolted for cover, your reading spectacles were snatched from your hat by an envious sliver and that in your panic and your terror of being seen, you dared not look for them. Possibly you did not realize they had gone until you got home. And that's why, after the rain, you stole out again—to try and find your glasses in case they were lost in a place where they might incriminate you. Then you saw the lights of Hammer Farm and dared go no further. You couldn't endure the suspense of not knowing if the Colonel had been found. You drew nearer and Sergeant Oliphant's torch-light shone in your eyes."

Alleyn turned to the window and looked down at Mr. Phinn's spinney, at the upper reaches of the Chyne and at a glimpse, between trees, of the near end of the bridge.

"That," he said, "is how I think you moved about the landscape yesterday evening and last night." Alleyn drew a pair of spectacles from the breast pocket of his coat and dangled them before Mr. Phinn. "I'm afraid I can't let you have them back just yet. But"—he extended his long finger toward Mr. Phinn's breast pocket—"isn't that a magnifying glass you have managed to unearth?"

Mr. Phinn was silent.

"Well," Alleyn said, "there's our view of your activities. It's a picture based on your own behaviour and one or two known facts. If it is accurate, believe me, you will be wise to say so."

Mr. Phinn said in an unrecognizable voice, "And if I don't choose to speak?"

"You will be within your rights, and we shall draw our own conclusions."

"You still don't give me the famous Usual Warning one hears so much about?"

"No."

"I suppose," Mr. Phinn said, "I am a timid man, but I know, in respect of this crime, that I am an innocent one."

"Well, then," Alleyn said and tried to lend the colour of freshness to an assurance he had so often given, "your innocence should cancel your timidity. You have nothing to fear."

It seemed to Alleyn as he watched Mr. Phinn that he was looking on at the superficial signs of a profound disturbance. It was as if Mr. Phinn's personality had been disrupted from below like a thermal pool and in a minute or two would begin to boil.

Some kind of climax was in fact achieved, and he began to talk very rapidly in his high voice.

"You are a very clever man. You reason from character to fact and back again. There! I have admitted everything. It's all quite true. I tiffed with Cartarette. I flung my noble Fin on the bridge. I came home but did not enter my house. I walked distractedly about my garden. I repented of my gesture and returned. The Fin had gone. I sought out my rival and because of the howl of his dog—a disagreeable canine—I—I found him—" here Mr. Phinn shut his eyes very tight—"no, really, it was too disagreeable! Even though his hat was over his face, one knew at a glance. And the dog never even looked at one. Howl! Howl! I didn't go near them, but I saw my fish! My trout! My Superfin! And then, you know, I heard *her*. Kettle. Stump, stump, stump past the willow grove. I ran, I doubled, I flung myself on my face in the undergrowth and waited until she had gone. And then I came home," said Mr. Phinn, "and as you have surmised, I discovered the loss of my reading glasses, which I frequently keep in my hatband. I was afraid. And there you are."

"Yes," Alleyn said, "there we are. How do you feel about making a signed statement to this effect?"

"Another statement. O, tedious task! But I am resigned."

"Good. We'll leave you to write it with the aid of your reading glasses. Will you begin with the actual catching of the Old 'Un?"

Mr. Phinn nodded.

"And you are still disinclined to tell us the full substance of your discussion with Colonel Cartarette?"

Mr. Phinn nodded.

He had his back to the windows and Alleyn faced them. Sergeant Oliphant had come out of the spinney and stood at the foot of the garden. Alleyn moved up to the windows. The sergeant, when he saw him, put his thumb up and turned back into the trees.

Fox picked up the parcel of clothes.

Alleyn said, "We'll call later for the statement. Or perhaps you would bring it to the police-station in Chyning this evening?"

"Very well." Mr. Phinn swallowed and his Adam's apple bobbed in his throat. "After all," he said, "I would hardly desert my Glorious Fin. Would I?"

"You did so before. Why shouldn't you do so again?"

"I am completely innocent."

"Grand. We mustn't bother you any longer. Goodbye, then, until, shall we say, five o'clock in Chyning."

They went out by a side door and down the garden to the spinney. The path wound downhill amongst trees to a stile that gave onto the river path. Here Sergeant Oliphant waited for them. Alleyn's homicide bag, which had been entrusted to the sergeant, rested on the stile. At the sound of their voices he turned, and they saw that across his palms there lay a sheet of newspaper.

On the newspaper were the dilapidated remains of a trout.

"I got 'er," said Sergeant Oliphant.

2

"She was a short piece above the bridge on this side," explained the sergeant, who had the habit of referring to inanimate but recalcitrant objects in the feminine gender. "Laying in some long grass to which I'd say she'd been dragged. Cat's work, sir, as you can see by the teeth-marks."

"As we supposed," Alleyn agreed. "Mrs. Thomasina Twitchett's work."

"A nice fish; she's been, say, two pound, but nothing to the Old 'Un," said the sergeant.

Alleyn laid the paper and its contents on a step of the stile and hung fondly over it. Mrs. Twitchett, if indeed it was she, had made short work of most of the Colonel's trout, if indeed this was his trout. The body was picked almost clean and some of the smaller bones had been chewed. The head appeared to have been ejected after a determined onslaught and the tail was semi-detached. But from the ribs there still depended some pieces of flesh and rags of skin that originally covered part of the flank and belly of the fish, and it was over an unlovely fragment of skin that Alleyn pored. He laid it out flat, using two pairs of pocket tweezers for the purpose, and with a long finger pointed to something that might have been part of an indented scar. It was about a quarter of an inch wide and had a curved margin. It was pierced in one place as if by a short spike.

"Now blow me down flat," Alleyn exulted, "if this isn't the answer to the good little investigating officer's prayer. See here, Fox, isn't this a piece of the sort of scar we would expect to find? And look here."

Very gingerly he turned the trout over and discovered, clinging to the other flank, a further rag of skin with the apex of a sharp triangular gap in it.

"Sink me if I don't have a look," Alleyn muttered.

Under Oliphant's enchanted gaze, he opened his case, took from it a flat enamel dish, which he laid on the bottom step of the stile, and a small glass jar with a screw-on lid. Using his tweezers, he spread out the piece of skin with the triangular gap on the plate. From the glass jar he took the piece of skin that had been found on the sharp stone under the Old 'Un. Muttering and whistling under his breath, and with a delicate dexterity, he laid the second fragment beside the first, opened it out and pushed and fiddled the one into the other as if they were pieces of a jigsaw puzzle. They fitted exactly.

"And that," Alleyn said, "is why Mrs. Twitchett met us last night smelling of fresh fish when she should have been stinking of liver. O, Fate! O, Nemesis! O, Something or Another!" he apostrophized. "Thy hand is here!" And in answer to Oliphant's glassy stare he added, "You've done damned handily, Sergeant, to pick this up so quickly. Now, listen, and I'll explain."

The explanation was detailed and exhaustive. Alleyn ended it with an account of the passage he had read in Colonel Cartarette's book. "We'll send out a signal to some piscatorial pundit," he said, "and get a check. But if the Colonel was right, and he seems to have been a conscientious, knowledgeable chap, our two trout cannot exhibit identical scales. The Colonel's killer, and only his killer, can have handled both fish. We do a round-up of garments, my hearties, and hope for returns."

Sergeant Oliphant cleared his throat and with an air of modest achievement stooped behind a briar bush. "There's one other matter, sir," he said. "I found this at the bottom of the hill in a bit of underbrush." He straightened up. In his hand was an arrow. "It appears," he said, "to have blood on it."

"Does it, indeed?" Alleyn said and took it. "All right, Oliphant. Damn' good show. We're getting on very prettily. And if," he summarized for the benefit of the gratified and anxious Oliphant, "if it all tallies up as I believe it must, then the pattern will indeed begin to emerge, won't it, Fox?"

"I hope so, Mr. Alleyn," Fox rejoined cheerfully.

"So off you go, Oliphant," Alleyn said. "Drive Mr. Fox to the station, where he will ring the Yard and the Natural History Museum. Deliver your treasure-trove to Dr. Curtis. I hope to have the rest of the exhibits before this evening. Come on, chaps, this case begins to ripen."

He led them back into the valley, saw Oliphant and Fox on their way with an accumulation of gear and objects of interest, and himself climbed up the hill to Nunspardon.

Here, to his surprise, he ran into a sort of party. Shaded from the noontide sun on the terrace before the great house were assembled the three Lacklanders, Kitty Cartarette and Rose. It was now half past twelve, and a cocktail tray gave an appearance of conviviality to a singularly wretched-looking assembly. Lady Lacklander seemed to have retired behind her formidable façade leaving in her wake an expression of bland inscrutability. George stood in a teapot attitude: one hand in his jacket pocket, the other on the back of a chair; one neatly knickered leg straight, one bent. Mark scowled devotedly upon Rose, who was pale, had obviously wept a great deal and seemed in addition to her grief to be desperately worried. Kitty, in a tweed suit, high heels and embroidered gloves, was talking to George. She looked exhausted and faintly sulky, as if tragedy had taken her by surprise and let her down. She lent an incongruous note to a conversation piece that seemed only to lack the attendant figures of grooms with hounds in leashes. Her voice was a high-pitched one. Before she noticed Alleyn, she had completed a sentence and he had heard it: "That's right," she had said, "Brierley and Bentwood," and then she saw him and made an abrupt movement that drew all their eyes upon him.

He wondered how many more times he would have to approach these people through their gardens and from an uncomfortable distance. In a way, he was beginning to enjoy it. He felt certain that this time, if George Lacklander could have managed it, the waiting group would have been scattered by a vigorous gesture, George himself would have retired to some manly den and Alleyn, in the ripeness of time, would have been admitted by a footman.

As it was, all of them except Lady Lacklander made involuntary movements which were immediately checked. Kitty half rose as if to beat a retreat, looked disconsolately at George and sank back in her chair.

"They've been having a council of war," thought Alleyn.

After a moment's further hesitation Mark, with an air of coming to a decision, put his chin up, said loudly, "It's Mr. Alleyn," and came to meet him. As they approached each other, Alleyn saw Rose's face, watchful and anxious, beyond Mark's advancing figure, and his momentary relish for the scene evaporated.

"Good morning," Alleyn said. "I'm sorry to reappear so soon and to make a further nuisance of myself. I won't keep you long."

"That's all right," Mark said pleasantly. "Who do you want to see?"

"Why, in point of fact, all of you, if I may. I'm lucky to find you in a group like this."

Mark had fallen into step with him and together they approached the group.

"Well, Rory," Lady Lacklander shouted as soon as he was within range, "you don't give us much peace, do you? What do you want this time? The clothes off our backs?"

"Yes," Alleyn said, "I'm afraid I do. More or less."

"And what may that mean? More or less?"

"The clothes off your yesterday-evening backs, if you please."

"Is this what my sporadic reading has led me to understand as 'a matter of routine'?"

"In a way," Alleyn said coolly, "yes. Yes, it is. Routine."

"And who," Kitty Cartarette asked in a careworn voice of nobody in particular, "said that a policeman's lot is not a happy one?"

This remark was followed by a curious little gap. It was as if her audience had awarded Kitty a point for attempting, under the circumstances, her small joke but at the same time were unable to accept her air of uncertain intimacy, which apparently even George found embarrassing. He laughed uncomfortably. Lady Lacklander raised her eyebrows, and Mark scowled at his boots.

"Do you mean," Lady Lacklander said, "the clothes that we were all wearing when Maurice Cartarette was murdered?"

"I do, yes."

"Well," she said, "you're welcome to mine. What *was* I wearing yesterday, George?"

"Really, Mama, I'm afraid I don't . . ."

"Nor do I. Mark?"

Mark grinned at her. "A green tent, I fancy, Gar darling, a solar topee and a pair of grandfather's boots."

"You're perfectly right. My green Harris, it was. I'll tell my maid, Roderick, and you shall have them."

"Thank you." Alleyn looked at George. "Your clothes and boots, please?"

"Ah, spiked shoes and stockings and plus fours," George said loudly. "Very old-fogeyish. Ha-ha."

"I think they're jolly good," Kitty said wearily. "On the right man." George's hand went to his moustache, but he didn't look at Kitty. He seemed to be exquisitely uncomfortable. "I," Kitty added, "wore a check skirt and a twin set. Madly county, you know," she added, desperately attempting another joke, "on account we played golf." She sounded near to tears.

"And your shoes?" Alleyn asked.

Kitty stuck out her feet. Her legs, Alleyn noted, were good. Her feet, which were tiny, were shod in lizard-skin shoes with immensely high heels. "Not so county," Kitty said, with the ghost of a grin, "but the best I had."

George, apparently in an agony of embarrassment, glanced at the shoes, at his mother and at the distant prospect of the Home Spinney.

Alleyn said, "If I may, I'll borrow the clothes, gloves and stockings. We'll pick them up at Hammer Farm on our way back to Chyning."

Kitty accepted this. She was looking at Alleyn with the eye, however wan, of a woman who spots a genuine Dior in a bargain basement.

"I'll hurry back," she said, "and get them ready for you."

"There's no immediate hurry."

Mark said, "I was wearing whites. I put brogues on for going home and carried my tennis shoes."

"And your racket?"

"Yes."

"And, after Bottom Bridge, Lady Lacklander's sketching gear and shooting-stick?"

"That's right."

"By the way," Alleyn asked him, "had you gone straight to your tennis party from Nunspardon?"

"I looked in on a patient in the village."

"And on the gardener's child, didn't you?" Kitty said. "They told me you'd lanced its gumboil."

"Yes. An abscess, poor kid," Mark said cheerfully.

"So you had your professional bag, too?" Alleyn suggested.

"It's not very big."

"Still, quite a load."

"It was rather."

"But Lady Lacklander had left it all tidily packed up, hadn't she?"

"Well," Mark said with a smile at his grandmother, "more or less."

"Nonsense," Lady Lacklander said; "there was no more or less about it. I'm a tidy woman and I left everything tidy."

Mark opened his mouth and shut it again.

"Your paint-rag, for instance?" Alleyn said, and Mark glanced sharply at him.

"I overlooked the rag, certainly," said Lady Lacklander rather grandly, "when I packed up. But I folded it neatly and tucked it under the strap of my haversack. Why have you put on that look, Mark?" she added crossly.

"Well, darling, when I got there, the rag, far from being neatly folded and stowed, was six yards away on a briar bush. I rescued it and put it into your haversack."

They all looked at Alleyn as if they expected him to make some comment. He was silent, however, and after a considerable pause Lady Lacklander said, "Well, it couldn't be of less significance, after all. Go indoors and ask them to get the clothes together. Fisher knows what I wore."

"Ask about mine, old boy, will you?" said George, and Alleyn wondered how many households there were left in England where orders of this sort were still given.

Lady Lacklander turned to Rose. "And what about you, child?"

But Rose stared out with unseeing eyes that had filled again with tears. She dabbed at them with her handkerchief and frowned at herself.

"Rose?" Lady Lacklander said quietly.

Still frowning, Rose turned and looked at her. "I'm sorry," she said.

"They want to know what clothes you wore, my dear."

"Tennis things, I imagine," Alleyn said.

Rose said, "Oh, yes. Of course. Tennis things."

Kitty said, "It's the day for the cleaner. I saw your tennis things in the box, didn't I, Rose?"

"I—? Yes," Rose said. "I'm sorry. Yes, I did put them in."

"Shall we go and rescue them?" Mark asked.

Rose hesitated. He looked at her for a moment and then said in a level voice, "O.K. I'll come back," and went into the house. Rose turned away and stood at some distance from the group.

"It's toughest for Rose," Kitty said, unexpectedly compassionate, and then with a return to her own self-protective mannerisms she sipped her sherry. "I wish you joy of my skirt, Mr. Alleyn," she added loudly. "You won't find it very delicious."

"No?" Alleyn said, "Why not?"

"It absolutely reeks of fish."

3

Alleyn observed the undistinguished little face and wondered if his own was equally blank. He then, under the guise of bewilderment, looked at the others. He found that Lady Lacklander seemed about as agitated as a Buddha and that George was in process of becoming startled. Rose was still turned away.

"Are you a fisherman too, then, Mrs. Cartarette?" Alleyn asked.

"God forbid!" she said with feeling. "No, I tried to take a fish away from a cat last evening." The others gaped at her.

"My dear Kitty," Lady Lacklander said, "I suggest that you consider what you say."

"Why?" Kitty countered, suddenly common and arrogant. "Why? It's the truth. What are you driving at?" she added nervously. "What's the matter with saying I've got fish on my skirt? Here," she demanded of Alleyn, "what are they getting at?"

"My good girl—" Lady Lacklander began, but Alleyn cut in. "I'm sorry, Lady Lacklander, but Mrs. Cartarette's perfectly right. There's nothing the matter, I assure you, with speaking the truth." Lady Lacklander shut her mouth with a snap. "Where did you meet your cat and fish, Mrs. Cartarette?"

"This side of the bridge," Kitty muttered resentfully.

"Did you, now?" Alleyn said with relish.

"It looked a perfectly good trout to me, and I thought the cat had no business with it. I suppose," Kitty went on, "it was one of old Occy Phinn's swarm; the cat, I mean. Anyhow, I tried to get the trout away from it. It hung on like a fury. And then when I did jerk the trout away, it turned out to be half eaten on the other side, sort of. So I let the cat have it back," Kitty said limply.

Alleyn said, "Did you notice any particular mark or scar on the trout?"

"Well, hardly. It was half eaten."

"Yes, but on the part that was left?"

"I don't think so. Here! What sort of mark?" Kitty demanded, beginning to look alarmed.

"It doesn't matter. Really."

"It was quite a nice trout. I wondered if Maurice had caught it, and then I thought old Occy Phinn must have hooked it and given it to the cat. He's crazy enough on his cats to give them anything, isn't he, George?"

"Good God, yes!" George ejaculated automatically, without looking at Kitty.

"It's a possible explanation," Alleyn said as if it didn't much matter either way.

Mark came back from the house. "The clothes," he said to Alleyn, "will be packed up and put in your car, which has arrived, by the way. I rang up Hammer and asked them to keep back the things for the cleaner."

"Thank you so much," Alleyn said. He turned to Lady Lacklander. "I know you'll understand that in a case like this we have to fuss about and try to get as complete a picture as possible of the days, sometimes even the weeks and months, before the event. It generally turns out that ninety-nine per cent of the information is quite useless, and then everybody thinks how needlessly inquisitive and impertinent the police are. Sometimes, however, there is an apparently irrelevant detail that leads, perhaps by accident, to the truth."

Lady Lacklander stared at him like a basilisk. She had a habit of blinking slowly, her rather white eyelids dropping conspicuously like shutters: a slightly reptilian habit that was disconcerting. She blinked twice in this manner at Alleyn and said, "What are you getting at, my dear Roderick? I hope you won't finesse too elaborately. Pray tell us what you want."

"Certainly. I want to know if, when I arrived, you were discussing Sir Harold Lacklander's memoirs."

He knew by their very stillness that he had scored. It struck him, not for the first time, that people who have been given a sudden fright tend to look alike: a sort of homogeneous glassiness overtakes them.

Lady Lacklander first recovered from whatever shock they had all received.

"In point of fact we were," she said. "You must have extremely sharp ears."

"I caught the name of my own publishers," Alleyn said at once. "Brierley and Bentwood. An admirable firm. I wondered if they are to do the memoirs."

"I'm glad you approve of them," she said dryly. "I believe they are."

"Colonel Cartarette was entrusted with the publication, wasn't he?"

There was a fractional pause before Mark and Rose together said, "Yes."

"I should think," Alleyn said pleasantly, "that that would have been a delightful job."

George, in a strangulated voice, said something about "responsibility" and suddenly offered Alleyn a drink.

"My good George," his mother said impatiently, "Roderick is on duty and will have none of your sherry. Don't be an ass."

George blushed angrily and glanced, possibly for encouragement, at Kitty.

"Nevertheless," Lady Lacklander said with a sort of grudging bon-homie, "you may as well sit down, Rory. One feels uncomfortable when you loom. There *is*, after all, a chair."

"Thank you," Alleyn said, taking it. "I don't want to loom any more than I can help, you know, but you can't expect me to be all smiles and prattle when you, as a group, close your ranks with such a deafening clank whenever I approach you."

"Nonsense," she rejoined briskly, but a dull colour actually appeared under her weathered skin, and for a moment there was a fleeting likeness to her son. Alleyn saw that Rose Cartarette was looking at him with a sort of anguished appeal and that Mark had taken her hand.

"Well," Alleyn said cheerfully, "if it's all nonsense, I can forget all about it and press on with the no doubt irrelevant details. About the autobiography, for instance. I'm glad Mr. Phinn is not with us at the moment because I want to ask you if Sir Harold gives a full account of young Phinn's tragedy. He could scarcely, one imagines, avoid doing so, could he?"

Alleyn looked from one blankly staring face to another. "Or could he?" he added.

Lady Lacklander said, "I haven't read my husband's memoirs. Nor, I think, has anyone else, except Maurice."

"Do you mean, Lady Lacklander, that you haven't read them in their entirety, or that you haven't read or heard a single word of them?"

"We would discuss them. Sometimes I could refresh his memory."

"Did you discuss the affair of young Ludovic Phinn?"

"Never!" she said very loudly and firmly, and George made a certain noise in his throat.

Alleyn turned to Kitty and Rose.

"Perhaps," he suggested, "Colonel Cartarette may have said something about the memoirs?"

"Not to me," Kitty said and added, "Too pukka sahib."

There was an embarrassed stirring among the others.

"Well," Alleyn said, "I'm sorry to labour the point, but I should like to know, if you please, whether either Sir Harold Lacklander or Colonel Cartarette ever said anything to any of you about the Ludovic Phinn affair in connection with the memoirs."

"Damned if I see what you're getting at!" George began, to the dismay, Alleyn felt sure, of everybody who heard him. "Damned if I see how you make out my father's memoirs can have anything to do with Maurice Cartarette's murder. Sorry, Kitty. I beg pardon, Rose. But I mean to say!"

Alleyn said, "It's eighteen years since young Ludovic Danberry-Phinn committed suicide, and a war has intervened. Many people will have forgotten his story. One among those who have remembered it . . . his father . . . must dread above all things any revival." He leant forward in his chair, and as if he had given some kind of order or exercised some mesmeric influence on his audience, each member of it imitated this movement. George Lacklander was still empurpled, the others had turned very pale, but one expression was common to them all: they looked, all of them, extremely surprised. In Kitty and George and perhaps in Lady Lacklander, Alleyn thought he sensed a kind of relief. He raised his hand. "Unless, of course," he said, "it has come about that in reviving the tragedy through the memoirs, young Phinn's name will be cleared."

It was as if out of a cloth that had apparently been wrung dry an unexpected trickle was induced. George, who seemed to be the most vulnerable of the group, shouted, "You've no right to assume . . ." and got no further. Almost simultaneously Mark and Rose, with the occasional unanimity of lovers, said, "This won't do . . ." and were checked by an imperative gesture from Lady Lacklander.

"Roderick," Lady Lacklander demanded, "have you been talking to Octavius Phinn?"

"Yes," Alleyn said. "I have come straight here from Jacob's Cottage."

"Wait a bit, Mama," George blurted out. "Wait a bit! Octavius can't have said anything. Otherwise, don't you see, Alleyn wouldn't try to find out from us."

In the now really deathly silence that followed this speech, Lady Lacklander turned and blinked at her son.

"You ninny, George," she said, "you unfathomable fool."

And Alleyn thought he now knew the truth about Mr. Phinn, Colonel Cartarette and Sir Harold Lacklander's memoirs.

CHAPTER NINE   **Chyning**

The next observation was made by Mark Lacklander.

"I hope you'll let me speak, Grandmama," he said. "And Father," he added, obviously as a polite afterthought. "Although, I must confess, most of the virtue has already gone from what I have to say."

"Then why, my dear boy, say it?"

"Well, Gar, it's really, you know, a matter of principle. Rose and I are agreed on it. We've kept quiet under your orders, but we both have felt, haven't we, Rose, that by far the best thing is to be completely frank with Mr. Alleyn. Any other course, as you've seen for yourself, just won't do."

"I have not changed my mind, Mark. Wait, a little."

"O, *yes*," Kitty said eagerly. "I *do* think so, honestly. Wait. I'm sure," she added, "it's what he would have said. Maurie, I mean." Her face quivered unexpectedly and she fumbled for her handkerchief.

Rose made one of those involuntary movements that are so much more graphic than words, and Alleyn, whom for the moment they all completely disregarded, wondered how the Colonel had enjoyed being called Maurie.

George, with a rebellious glance at his mother, said, "Exactly what I mean. Wait."

"By all means, wait," Alleyn interjected, and stood up. They all jumped slightly. "I expect," he suggested to Lady Lacklander, "you would like, before taking any further steps, to consult with Mr. Phinn. As a matter of fact, I think it highly probable that he will suggest it himself." Alleyn looked very straight at Lady Lacklander. "I suggest," he said, "that you consider just exactly what is at stake in this matter. When a capital crime is committed, you know, all sorts of long-buried secrets are apt to be discovered. It's one of those things about homicide." She made no kind of response to this, and, after a moment, he went on, "Perhaps when you have all come to a decision, you will be kind enough to let me know. They'll always take a message at the Boy and Donkey. And now, if I may, I'll get on with my job."

He bowed to Lady Lacklander and was about to move off when Mark said, "I'll see you to your car, sir. Coming, Rose?"

Rose seemed to hesitate, but she went off with him, entirely, Alleyn sensed, against the wishes of the remaining three.

Mark and Rose conducted him round the east wing of the great house to the open platform in front of it. Here Fox waited in the police car. A sports model with a doctor's sticker and a more domestic car, which Alleyn took to be the Cartarettes', waited side by side. The young footman, William, emerged with a suitcase. Alleyn watched him deliver this to Fox and return to the house.

"There goes our dirty washing," Mark said, and then looked uncomfortable.

Alleyn said, "But you carried a tennis racket, didn't you, and Sir George, I suppose, a golf bag? May we have them too?"

Mark said, "Yes, I see. Yes. All right, I'll get them."

He ran up the steps and disappeared. Alleyn turned to Rose. She stared at the doorway through which Mark had gone, and it was as if some kind of threat had overtaken her.

"I'm so frightened," she said. "I don't know why, but I'm so frightened."

"Of what?" Alleyn asked gently.

"I don't know. One of those things, I suppose. I've never felt it before. It's as if my father was the only person that I ever really knew. And now he's gone; someone's murdered him, and I feel as if I didn't properly understand anyone at all."

Mark came back with a bag of clubs and a tennis racket in a press. "This is it," he said.

"You didn't have it in one of those waterproof-cover things?"

"What? Oh, yes, actually, I did."

"May I have that too, please?"

Mark made a second trip to get it and was away rather longer. "I wasn't sure which was the one," he said, "but I think this is right."

Alleyn put it with the bag and racket in the car.

Mark had caught Rose's hand in his. She hung back a little. "Mr. Alleyn," Mark said, "Rose and I are in the hell of a spot over this. Aren't we, darling? We're engaged, by the way."

"You amaze me," Alleyn said.

"Well, we are. And, of course, wherever it's humanly possible, I'm going to see that Rose is not harried and fussed. She's had a very severe shock and . . ."

"No, don't," Rose said. "Please, Mark, don't."

Mark gazed at her, seemed to lose the thread of his subject, and then collected himself.

"It's just this," he said. "I feel strongly that as far as you and our two families are concerned, everything ought to be perfectly straightforward. We're under promise not to mention this and that, and so we can't, but we are both very worried about the way things are going. I mean, in respect of Octavius Phinn. You see, sir, we happen to know that poor old Occy Phinn had every possible reason *not* to commit this crime. Every possible reason. And if," Mark said, "you've guessed, as I rather think you may have, what I'm driving at, I can't help it."

"And you agree with all this, Miss Cartarette?" Alleyn asked.

Rose held herself a little aloof now. Tear-stained and obviously exhausted, she seemed to pull herself together and shape her answer with care and difficulty.

"Mr. Alleyn, my father would have been appalled if he could have known that because he and Octavius had a row over the trout, poor Occy might be thought to—to have a motive. They'd had rows over trout for years. It was a kind of joke—nothing. And—whatever else they had to say to each other, and as you know, there *was* something else, it would have made Octavius much more friendly. I promise you. You see, I know my father had gone to see Octavius."

Alleyn said quickly, "You mean he went to his house? Yesterday afternoon?"

"Yes. I was with him before he went and he said he was going there."

"Did he say why? I think you spoke of some publishing business."

"Yes. He—he had something he wanted to show Occy."

"What was that, can you tell us?"

"I can't tell you," Rose said looking wretchedly unhappy. "I *do* know, actually, but it's private. But I'm sure he went to Occy's because I saw him take the envelope out of the desk and put it in his pocket—" she put her hand to her eyes—"but," she said, "where is it, then?"

Alleyn said, "Where exactly was the envelope? In which drawer of his desk?"

"I think the bottom one on the left. He kept it locked, usually."

"I see. Thank you. And, of course, Mr. Phinn was not at home?"

"No. I suppose, finding him not at home, Daddy followed him down to the stream. Of course, I mustn't tell you what his errand was, but if ever," Rose said in a trembling voice, "if ever there was an errand of—well, of mercy—Daddy's was one, yesterday afternoon."

Rose had an unworldly face with a sort of Pre-Raphaelitish beauty: very unmodish in its sorrow and very touching.

Alleyn said gently, "I know. Don't worry. I can promise we won't blunder."

"How kind you are," she said. Mark muttered indistinguishably.

As Alleyn turned away towards the police car, her voice halted him. "It must be somebody mad," she said. "Nobody who wasn't mad could possibly do it. Not possibly. There's somebody demented that did it for no reason at all." She extended her hand towards him a little way, the palm turned up in a gesture of uncertainty and appeal. "Don't you think so?" she said.

Alleyn said, "I think you are very shocked and bewildered, as well you might be. Did you sleep last night?"

"Not much. I am sorry, Mark, but I didn't take the thing you gave me. I felt I mustn't. I had to wake for him. The house felt as if he was looking for me."

"I think it might be a good idea," Alleyn said to Mark, "if you drove Miss Cartarette to Hammer Farm, where perhaps she will be kind enough to hunt up her own and Mrs. Cartarette's garments of yesterday. Everything, please, shoes, stockings and all. And treat them, please, like egg-shell china."

Mark said, "As important as that?"

"The safety of several innocent persons may depend upon them."

"I'll take care," Mark said.

"Good. We'll follow you and collect them."

"Fair enough," Mark said. He smiled at Rose. "And when that's done," he said, "I'm going to bring you back to Nunspardon and put my pro-fessional foot down about nembutal. Kitty'll drive herself home. Come on."

Alleyn saw Rose make a small gesture of protest. "I think perhaps I'll stay at Hammer, Mark."

"No, you won't, darling."

"I can't leave Kitty like that."

"She'll understand. Anyway, we'll be back here before she leaves. Come on."

Rose turned as if to appeal to Alleyn and then seemed to give up. Mark took her by the elbow and led her away.

Alleyn watched them get into the sports car and shoot off down a long drive. He shook his head slightly and let himself into the front seat beside Fox.

"Follow them, Br'er Fox," he said. "But sedately. There's no hurry. We're going to Hammer Farm."

On the way he outlined the general shape of his visit to Nunspardon.

"It's clear enough, wouldn't you agree," he ended, "what has happened about the memoirs. Take the facts as we know them. The leakage of information at Zlomce was of such importance that Sir Harold Lack-lander couldn't, in what is evidently an exhaustive autobiography, ignore it. At the time of the catastrophe we learnt in the Special Branch from Lacklander himself that after confessing his treachery, young Phinn, as a result of his wigging, committed suicide. We know Lacklander died with young Phinn's name on his lips, at the same time showing the greatest anxiety about the memoirs. We know that Cartarette was entrusted with the publication. We know Cartarette took an envelope from the drawer that was subsequently broken open and went to see old Phinn on what Miss Cartarette describes as an errand of mercy. When he didn't find him at home, he followed him into the valley. Finally, we know that after they fell out over the poaching, they had a further discussion about which, although she admits she heard it, Lady Lacklander will tell us nothing. Now, my dear Br'er Fox, why should the Lacklanders or Mr. Phinn or the Cartarettes be so uncommonly touchy about all this? I don't know what you think, but I can find only one answer."

Fox turned the car sedately into the Hammer Farm drive and nodded his head.

"Seems pretty obvious when you put it like that, Mr. Alleyn, I must say. But is there sufficient motive for murder in it?"

"Who the hell's going to say what's a sufficient motive for murder? And anyway, it may be one of a bunch of motives. Probably is. Stick to *ubi, quibus, auxiliis, quomodo* and *quando,* Foxkin; let *cur* look after itself, and blow me down if *quis* won't walk in when you're least expecting it."

"So you always tell us, sir," said Fox.

"All right, all right; I grow to a dotage and repeat myself. There's the lovelorn C.P.'s car. We wait here while they hunt up the garments of the two ladies. Mrs. Cartarette's will be brand-new extra-loud tweeds smelling of Schiaparelli and, presumably, of fish."

"Must be a bit lonely," Fox mused.

"Who?"

"Mrs. Cartarette. An outsider, you might say, dumped down in a little place where they've known each other's pedigrees since the time they were *all* using bows and arrows. Bit lonely. More she tries to fit in, I daresay, the less they seem to take to her. More polite they get, the more uncomfortable they make her feel."

"Yes," Alleyn said, "true enough. You've shoved your great fat finger into the middle of one of those uncomfortable minor tragedies that the Lacklanders of this world prefer to cut dead. And I'll tell you something else, Fox. Of the whole crowd of them, *not* excluding your girl-friend, there isn't one that wouldn't feel a *kind* of relief if she turned out to have murdered her husband."

Fox looked startled. "One, surely?" he ejaculated.

"No," Alleyn insisted with a sort of violence that was very rare with him. "Not one. Not one. For all of them she's the intruder, the disturber, the outsider. The very effort some of them have tried to make on her behalf has added to their secret resentment. I bet you. How did you get on in Chyning?"

"I saw Dr. Curtis. He's fixed up very comfortably in the hospital mortuary and was well on with the P.M. Nothing new cropped up about the injuries. He says he thinks it's true enough about the fish scales and will watch out for them and do the microscope job with all the exhibits. The Yard's going to look up the late Sir Harold's will and check Commander Syce's activities in Singapore. They say it won't take long if the Navy List gives them a line on anybody in the Service who was there at the time and has a shore job now. If they strike it lucky, they may call us back in a couple of hours. I said the Boy and Donkey and the Chyning station to be sure of catching us."

"Good," Alleyn said without much show of interest. "Hullo, listen who's coming! Here we go."

He was out of the car before Fox could reply and with an abrupt change of speed began to stroll down the drive. His pipe was in his hands and he busied himself with filling it. The object of this unexpected pantomime now pedalled into Mr. Fox's ken: the village postman.

Alleyn, stuffing his pipe, waited until the postman was abreast with him.

"Good morning," said Alleyn.

"Morning, sir," said the postman, braking his bicycle.

"I'll take them, shall I?" Alleyn suggested.

The postman steadied himself with one foot on the ground. "Well, ta," he said and with a vague suggestion of condolence added, "Save the disturbance, like, won't it, sir? Only one, anyway." He fetched a long envelope from his bag and held it out. "For the deceased," he said in a special voice. "Terrible sad, if I may pass the remark."

"Indeed, yes," Alleyn said, taking, with a sense of rising excitement, the long, and to him familiar, envelope.

"Terrible thing to happen in the Vale," the postman continued. "What I mean, the crime, and the Colonel that highly respected and never a word that wasn't kindness itself. Everybody's that upset and that sorry for the ladies. Poor Miss Rose, now! Well, it's terrible."

The postman, genuinely distressed and at the same time consumed with a countryman's inquisitiveness, looked sideways at Alleyn. "You'd be a relative, I daresay, sir."

"How very kind of you," Alleyn said, blandly ignoring this assumption. "I'll tell them you sent your sympathy, shall I?"

"Ta," said the postman. "And whoever done it; what I mean, I'm sure I hope they get 'em. I hear it's reckoned to be a job for the Yard and altogether beyond the scope of Bert Oliphant, which won't surprise us in the Vale, although the man's active enough when it comes to after hours at the Boy and Donkey. Well, I'll be getting along."

When he had gone, Alleyn returned to Fox.

"Look what I've got," he said.

Fox contemplated the long envelope and, when Alleyn showed him the reverse side, read the printed legend on the flap: "From Brierley and Bentwood, St. Peter's Place, London, W. 1."

"Publishers?" said Fox.

"Yes. We've got to know what this is, Fox. The flap's very sketchily gummed down. A little tweak and—how easy it would be. Justifiable enough, too, I suppose. However, we'll go the other way round. Here comes Miss Cartarette."

She came out, followed by Mark carrying a suitcase, a tennis racket in a press and a very new golf bag and clubs.

"Here you are, sir," Mark said. "We had to fish the clothes out of the dry cleaner's box, but they're all present and correct. Rose said you might want her racket, which is absurd, but this is it."

"Thank you," Alleyn said, and Fox relieved Mark of his load and put it in the police car. Alleyn showed Rose the envelope.

He said, "This has come for your father. I'm afraid we may have to ask for all his recent correspondence and certainly for anything that comes now. They will, of course, be returned and, unless used in evidence, will be treated as strictly confidential. I'm so sorry, but that's how it is. If you wish, you may refuse to let me have this one without an official order."

He was holding it out with the typed superscription uppermost. Rose looked at it without interest.

Mark said, "Look, darling, I think perhaps you shouldn't—"

"Please take it," she said to Alleyn. "It's a pamphlet, I should think."

Alleyn thanked her and watched her go off with Mark in his car.

"Shame to take the money," said Fox.

Alleyn said, "I hope, if he knows, the Colonel doesn't think too badly of me."

He opened the envelope, drew out the enclosure and unfolded it.

Colonel M. C. V. Cartarette, M.V.O., D.S.C.
  Hammer Farm
    Swevenings

Dear Sir:
  The late Sir Harold Lacklander, three weeks before he died, called upon me for a discussion about his memoirs, which my firm is to publish. A difficulty had arisen in respect of Chapter 7, and Sir Harold informed me that he proposed to take your advice in this matter. He added that if he should not live to see the publication of his memoirs, he wished you, if you would accept the responsibility, to edit the work in toto. He asked me, in the event of his death, to communicate directly with you and with nobody else and stressed the point that your decision in every respect must be considered final.

  We have had no further instructions or communications of any kind from Sir Harold Lacklander, and I now write, in accordance with his wishes, to ask if you have, in fact, accepted the responsibility of editing the memoirs, if you have received the manuscript, and if you have arrived at a decision in the delicate and important matter of Chapter 7.

I shall be most grateful for an early reply. Perhaps you would give me the pleasure of lunching with me when next you are in London. If you would be kind enough to let me know the appropriate date, I shall keep it free.

I am, my dear sir,
Yours truly,
Timothy Bentwood

"And I'll give you two guesses, Br'er Fox," Alleyn said as he refolded the letter and returned it to its envelope, "what constitutes the delicate and important matter of Chapter 7."

2

When Mark had turned in at the Nunspardon Lodge gates, Rose asked him to stop somewhere on the drive.

"It's no use going on," she said. "There's something I've got to say. Please stop."

"Of course." Mark pulled into an open space alongside the drive. He stopped his engine and turned to look at her. "Now," he said, "tell me."

"Mark, he doesn't think it was a tramp."

"Alleyn?"

"Yes. He thinks it was—one of us. I know he does."

"What exactly, darling, do you mean by 'one of us'?"

Rose made a little faint circling movement of her hand.

"Someone that knew him. A neighbour. Or one of his own family."

"You can't tell. Honestly. Alleyn's got to do his stuff. He's got to clear the decks."

"He doesn't think it was a tramp," Rose repeated. Her voice, exhausted and drained of its colour, rose a little. "He thinks it was one of us."

Mark said after a long pause, "Well, suppose—and I don't for a moment admit it—suppose at this stage he does wonder about all of us. After all—"

"Yes," Rose said, "after all, he has cause, hasn't he?"

"What do you mean?"

"You see what's happening to us? You're pretending to misunderstand. It's clear enough he's found out about Chapter 7."

She saw the colour drain out of his face and cried out, "O! What am I doing to us both!"

"Nothing as yet," Mark said. "Let's get this straight. You think Alleyn suspects that one of us—me or my father or, I suppose, my grandmother —may have killed your father because he was going to publish the amended version of my grandfather's memoirs. That it?"

"Yes."

"I see. Well, you may be right. Alleyn may have some such idea. What I want to know now is this: You yourself, Rose—do you—can it be possible that you, too—? No," he said, "not now. I won't ask you now when you're so badly shocked. We'll wait."

"We can't wait. I can't go on like this. I can't come back to Nunspardon and pretend the only thing that matters is for me to take a nembutal and go to sleep."

"Rose, look at me. No, please. Look at me."

He took her face between his hands and turned it towards him.

"My God," he said, "you're afraid of me."

She did not try to free herself. Her tears ran down between his fingers. "No," she cried, "no, it's not true. I can't be afraid of you; I love you."

"Are you sure? Are you sure that somewhere in the back of your mind you're not remembering that your father stood between us and that I was jealous of your love for him? And that his death has made you an heiress? Because it has, hasn't it? And that the publication of the memoirs would have set my family against our marriage and brought disrepute upon my name? Are you sure you don't suspect me, Rose?"

"Not you. I promise. Not you."

"Then—who? Gar? My father? Darling, can you see how fantastic it sounds when one says it aloud?"

"I know it sounds fantastic," Rose said in despair. "It's fantastic that anyone should want to hurt my father, but all the same, somebody has killed him. I've got to learn to get used to that. Last night somebody killed my father."

She pulled his hands away from her face. "You must admit," she said, "that takes a bit of getting used to."

Mark said, "What am I to do about this!"

"Nothing; you can't do anything; that's what's so awful, isn't it? You want me to turn to you and find my comfort in you, don't you, Mark? And I want it, too. I long for it. And then, you see, I can't. I can't, because there's no knowing who killed my father."

There was a long silence. At last she heard Mark's voice. "I didn't want to say this, Rose, but now I'm afraid I've got to. There are, after all, other people. If my grandmother and my father and I fall under suspicion—O, yes, and Occy Phinn—isn't there somebody else who can't be entirely disregarded?"

Rose said, "You mean Kitty, don't you?"

"I do. Yes—equally with us."

"Don't!" Rose cried out. "Don't! I won't listen."

"You've got to. We can't stop now. Do you suppose I enjoy reminding myself—or you—that my father—"

"No! No, Mark! Please!" Rose said and burst into tears.

Sometimes there exists in people who are attached to each other a kind of ratio between the degree of attraction and the potential for irritation. Strangely, it is often the unhappiness of one that arouses an equal degree of irascibility in the other. The tear-blotted face, the obstinate misery, the knowledge that this distress is genuine and the feeling of incompetence it induces, all combine to exasperate and inflame.

Rose thought she recognized signs of this exasperation in Mark. His look darkened and he had moved away from her. "I can't help it, Mark," she stammered.

She heard his expostulations and reiterated arguments. She thought she could hear, too, a note of suppressed irritation in his voice. He kept saying that the whole thing had better be threshed out between them. "Let's face it," he said on a rising note. "Kitty's *there*, isn't she? And what about Geoffrey Syce or Nurse Kettle? We needn't concentrate exclusively on the Lacklanders, need we?" Rose turned away. Leaning her arm on the ledge of the open window and her face on her arm, she broke down completely.

"Ah, hell!" Mark shouted. He pushed open the door, got out and began to walk angrily to and fro.

It was upon this situation that Kitty appeared, driving herself home from Nunspardon. When she saw Mark's car, she pulled up. Rose made a desperate effort to collect herself. After a moment's hesitation, Kitty got out of her car and came over to Rose. Mark shoved his hands into his pockets and moved away.

"I don't want to butt in," Kitty said, "but can I do anything? I mean, just say—I'll get out if I'm no use."

Rose looked up at her and for the first time saw in her stepmother's face the signs of havoc that Kitty had been at pains to repair. For the first time it occurred to Rose that there are more ways than one of meeting sorrow, and for the first time she felt a sense of fellowship for Kitty.

"How kind of you," she said. "I'm glad you stopped."

"That's all right. I was sort of wondering," Kitty went on, with an unwonted air of hesitation; "I daresay you'd rather sort of move out. Say if you would. I'm not talking about what you said about the future but of now. I mean, I daresay Mark's suggested you stay up at Nunspardon. Do, if you'd like to. I mean, I'll be O.K."

It had never occurred to Rose that Kitty might be lonely if she herself went to Nunspardon. A stream of confused recollections and ideas flooded her thoughts. She reminded herself again that Kitty would now be quite desperately hard-up and that she had a responsibility towards her. She wondered if her stepmother's flirtations with Mark's father had not been induced by a sense of exclusion. She looked into the careworn, over-painted face and thought, "After all, we both belonged to him."

Kitty said awkwardly, "Well, anyway, I'll push off."

Suddenly Rose wanted to say, "I'll come back with you, Kitty. Let's go home." She fumbled with the handle of the door, but before she could speak or make a move, she was aware of Mark. He had come back to the car and had moved round to her side and was speaking to Kitty.

"That's what I've been telling her," he said. "In fact, as her doctor, those are my orders. She's coming to Nunspardon. I'm glad you support me."

Kitty gave him the look that she bestowed quite automatically on any presentable male. "Well, anyway, she's in good hands," she said. She gave them a little wave of her own hand and returned to her car.

With a feeling of desolation and remorse Rose watched her drive away.

3

On the way to Chyning, Alleyn propounded his theory on Chapter 7.

"Bear in mind," he said, "the character of Colonel Cartarette as it emerges from the welter of talk. With the exception of Danberry-Phinn, they are all agreed, aren't they, that Cartarette was a nice chap with uncommonly high standards and a rather tender conscience. All right. For the last time let us remind ourselves that, just before he died, old Lacklander was very much bothered by something to do with Cartarette and the memoirs and that he died with the name Vic on his lips. All right. Whenever the memoirs and/or young Viccy Phinn are mentioned, everybody behaves as if they're concealing the fact that they are about to have kittens. Fair enough. Phinn and Lady Lacklander both agree that there was further discussion, after the row, between Phinn and the Colonel. Lady Lacklander flatly refuses to divulge the subject-matter, and Phinn says if she won't, neither will he. The Colonel left his house with the intention of calling upon Phinn, with whom he had been on bad terms for a long time. Now put all those bits together, remembering the circumstances of young Phinn's death, George Lacklander's virtual admission that the memoirs exonerated young Phinn, Rose Cartarette's statement that her father's visit to old Phinn was an errand of mercy, and the contents of the publisher's letter. Put 'em together and what do you get?"

"Chapter 7 was the bit that exonerated young Phinn. Colonel Cartarette was given the responsibility of including it in this book. He couldn't decide one way or the other and took it to Mr. Phinn," Fox speculated, "to see which way he felt about it. Mr. Phinn was out fishing and the Colonel followed him up. After their dust-up the Colonel—now what does the Colonel do?"

"In effect," Alleyn said, "the Colonel says, 'All right, you unconscionable old poacher. All right. Look what I'd come to do for you?' And he tells him about Chapter 7. And since we didn't find Chapter 7 on the Colonel, we conclude that he gave it there and then to Mr. Phinn. This inference is strongly supported by the fact that I saw an envelope with a wad of typescript inside, addressed in the Colonel's hand to Mr. Phinn, on Mr. Phinn's desk. So what, my old Foxkin, are we to conclude?"

"About Chapter 7?"

"About Chapter 7."

"You tell me," said Fox with a stately smile.

Alleyn told him.

"Well, sir," Fox said, "it's possible. It's as good a motive as any for the Lacklanders to do away with the Colonel."

"Except that if we're right in our unblushing conjectures, Fox, Lady Lacklander overheard the Colonel give Chapter 7 to Mr. Phinn; in which case, if any of the Lacklanders were after blood, Mr. Phinn's would be the more logical blood to tap."

"Lady Lacklander may not have heard much of what they said."

"In which case, why is she so cagey about it all now, and what did she and the Colonel talk about afterwards?"

"Ah, blast!" said Fox in disgust. "Well, then, it may be that the memoirs and Chapter 7 and Who—Stole—the—Secret—Document—in—Zlomce haven't got anything to do with the case."

"My feeling is that they do belong but are not of the first importance."

"Well, Mr. Alleyn, holding the view you do hold, it's the only explanation that fits."

"Quite so. And I tell you what, Fox, motive, as usual, is a secondary consideration. And here is Chyning and a petrol pump and here (hold on to your hat, Fox; down, down, little flutterer) is the Jolly Kettle filling up a newly painted car which I'll swear she calls by a pet name. If you can control yourself, we'll pull in for some petrol. Good morning, Miss Kettle."

"The top of the morning to you, Chief," said Nurse Kettle turning a beaming face upon them. She slapped the back of her car as if it were a rump. "Having her elevenses," she said. "First time we've met for a fort-night on account she's been having her face lifted. And how *are* you?"

"Bearing up," Alleyn said, getting out of the car. "Inspector Fox is turning rather short-tempered."

Fox ignored him. "Very nice little car, Miss Kettle," he said.

"Araminta? She's a good steady girl on the whole," said Nurse Kettle, remorselessly jolly. "I'm just taking her out to see a case of lumbago."

"Commander Syce?" Alleyn ventured.

"That's right."

"He is completely recovered."

"You don't say," Nurse Kettle rejoined, looking rather disconcerted. "And him tied up in knots last evening. Fancy!"

"He was a cot case, I understand, when you left him round about nine o'clock last night."

"*Very* sorry for ourselves we were, yes."

"And yet," Alleyn said, "Mr. Phinn declares that at a quarter past eight Commander Syce was loosing off arrows from his sixty-pound bow."

Nurse Kettle was scarlet to the roots of her mouse-coloured hair. Alleyn heard his colleague struggling with some subterranean expression of sympathy.

"Well, fancy!" Nurse Kettle was saying in a high voice. "There's 'bago for you! Now you see it, now you don't." And she illustrated this apho-rism with sharp snaps of her finger and thumb.

Fox said in an unnatural voice, "Are you sure, Miss Kettle, that the Commander wasn't having you on? Excuse the suggestion."

Nurse Kettle threw him a glance that might perhaps be best described as uneasily roguish.

"And why not?" she asked. "Maybe he was. But not for the reason you mere men suppose."

She got into her car with alacrity and sounded her horn. "Home, John, and don't spare the horses," she cried waggishly and drove away in what was evidently an agony of self-consciousness.

"Unless you can develop a deep-seated and obstinate malady, Br'er Fox," Alleyn said, "you haven't got a hope."

"A thoroughly nice woman," Fox said and added ambiguously, "What a pity!"

They got their petrol and drove on to the police station.

Here Sergeant Oliphant awaited them with three messages from Scot-land Yard.

"Nice work," Alleyn said. "Damn' quick."

He read aloud the first message. "Information re trout scales checked with Natural History Museum, Royal Piscatorial Society, Institute for

Preservation of British Trout Streams, and Dr. S. K. K. Solomon, expert and leading authority. All confirm that microscopically your two trout cannot exhibit precisely the same characteristics in scales. Cartarette regarded as authority."

"Fine!" said Inspector Fox. "Fair enough!"

Alleyn took up the second slip of paper. "Report," he read, "on the late Sir Harold Lacklander's will." He read to himself for a minute, then looked up. "Couldn't be simpler," he said. "With the exception of the usual group of legacies to dependents the whole lot goes to the widow and to the son, upon whom most of it's entailed."

"What Miss Kettle told us."

"Exactly. Now for the third. Here we are. Report on Commander Geoffrey Syce, R.N., retired. Singapore, March 1, 195– to April 9, 195–. Serving in H. M. S. ——, based on Singapore. Shore duty. Activities, apart from duties: At first, noticeably quiet tastes and habits. Accepted usual invitations but spent considerable time alone, sketching. Later, cohabited with a so-called Miss Kitty de Vere, whom he is believed to have met at a taxi-dance. Can follow up history of de Vere if required. Have ascertained that Syce rented apartment occupied by de Vere, who subsequently met and married Colonel Maurice Cartarette, to whom she is believed to have been introduced by Syce. Sources—"

There followed a number of names, obtained from the Navy List, and a note to say that H. M. S. —— being now in port, it had been possible to obtain information through the appropriate sources at the "urgent and important" level.

Alleyn dropped the chit on Oliphant's desk.

"Poor Cartarette," he said with a change of voice, "and, if you like, poor Syce."

"Or, from the other point of view," Fox said, "poor Kitty."

4

Before they returned to Swevenings, Alleyn and Fox visited Dr. Curtis in the Chyning Hospital mortuary. It was a very small mortuary attached to a sort of pocket-hospital, and there was a ghastly cosiness in the close proximity of them all to the now irrevocably and dreadfully necrotic Colonel. Curtis, who liked to be thorough in his work, was making an extremely exhaustive autopsy and had not yet completed it. He was able to confirm that there had been an initial blow, followed, it seemed, rather than preceded by, a puncture, but that neither the blow nor the puncture quite accounted for some of the multiple injuries, which were the result, he thought, of pressure. *Contrecoup*, he said, was present in a very marked degree. He would not entirely dismiss Commander Syce's arrows nor Lady Lacklander's umbrella spike, but he thought her shooting-stick the most likely of the sharp instruments produced. The examination of the shooting-stick for blood traces might bring them nearer to a settlement of this point. The paint-rag, undoubtedly, was stained with blood, which had not yet been classified. It smelt quite strongly of fish. Alleyn handed over the rest of his treasure-trove.

"As soon as you can," he said, "do, like a good chap, get on to the fishy side of the business. Find me scales of both trout on one person's article, and only on one person's, and the rest will follow as the night the day."

"You treat me," Curtis said without malice, "like a tympanist in a jazz band perpetually dodging from one instrument to another. I'll finish my P.M., blast you, and Willy Roskill can muck about with your damned scales." Sir William Roskill was an eminent Home Office analyst.

"I'll ring him up now," Alleyn said.

"It's all right; I've rung him. He's on his way. As soon as we know anything, we'll ring the station. What's biting you about this case, Rory?" Dr. Curtis asked. "You're always slinging off at the 'expeditions' officer and raising your cry of *festina lente*. Why the fuss and hurry? The man was only killed last night."

"It's a pig of a case," Alleyn said, "and on second thoughts I'll keep the other arrow—the bloody one. If it is blood. What the hell can I carry it in? I don't want him to—" He looked at the collection of objects they had brought with them. "That'll do," he said. He slung George Lacklander's golf bag over his shoulder, wrapped up the tip of Syce's arrow and dropped it in.

"A pig of a case," he repeated; "I hate its guts."

"Why this more than another?"

But Alleyn did not answer. He was looking at the personal effects of the persons under consideration. They were laid out in neat groups along a shelf opposite the dissecting table, almost as if they were component parts of the autopsy. First came the two fish: the Old 'Un, 4 pounds of cold, defeated splendour, and beside it on a plate the bones and rags of the Colonel's catch. Then the belongings of the men who had caught them: the Colonel's and Mr. Phinn's clothes, boots, fishing gear and hat. Kitty's loud new tweed skirt and twin set. Sir George's plus fours, stockings and shoes. Mark's and Rose's tennis clothes. Lady Lacklander's tent-like garments, her sketching kit and a pair of ancient but beautifully made brogues. Alleyn stopped, stretched out a hand and lifted one of these brogues.

"Size about four," he said. "They were hand-made by the best boot-maker in London in the days when Lady Lacklander still played golf.

Here's her name sewn in. They've been cleaned, but the soles are still dampish and—" He turned the shoe over and was looking at the heel. It carried miniature spikes. Alleyn looked at Fox, who, without a word, brought from the end of the shelf a kitchen plate on which were laid out, as if for some starvation-diet, the remains of the Colonel's fish. The flap of skin with its fragment of an impression was carefully spread out. They waited in silence.

"It'll fit all right," Alleyn said. "Do your stuff, of course, but it's going to fit. And the better it fits, the less I'm going to like it."

And with this illogical observation he went out of the mortuary.

"What *is* biting him?" Dr. Curtis asked Fox.

"Ask yourself, Doctor," Fox said. "It's one of the kind that he's never got, as you might say, used to."

"Like that, is it?" Dr. Curtis, for the moment unmindful of his own terribly explicit job, muttered, "I often wonder why on earth he entered the Service."

"I've never liked to enquire," Fox said in his plain way, "but I'm sure I'm very glad he did. Well, I'll leave you with your corpse."

". . . seeing you," Dr. Curtis said absently, and Fox rejoined his principal. They returned to the police station, where Alleyn had a word with Sergeant Oliphant. "We'll leave you here, Oliphant," Alleyn said. "Sir William Roskill will probably go straight to the hospital, but as soon as there's anything to report, he or Dr. Curtis will ring you up. Here's a list of people I'm going to see. If I'm not at one of these places, I'll be at another. See about applying for a warrant; we may be making an arrest before nightfall."

"'T, 't, 't," Sergeant Oliphant clicked. "Reely? In what name, sir? Same as you thought?"

Alleyn pointed his forefinger at a name on the list he had given the sergeant, who stared at it for some seconds, his face perfectly wooden.

"It's not positive," Alleyn said, "but you'd better warn your tame J.P. about the warrant in case we need it in a hurry. We'll get along with the job now. Put a call through to Brierley and Bentwood, will you, Oliphant? Here's the number. Ask for Mr. Timothy Bentwood and give my name."

He listened while Sergeant Oliphant put the call through and noticed abstractedly that he did this in a quiet and business-like manner.

Alleyn said, "If Bentwood will play, this should mean the clearing-up of Chapter 7."

Fox raised a massive finger and they both listened to Oliphant.

"O, yerse?" Oliphant was saying. "Yerse? Will you hold the line, sir, while I enquire?"

"What is it?" Alleyn demanded sharply.

Oliphant placed the palm of his vast hand over the mouthpiece. "Mr. Bentwood, sir," he said, "is in hospital. Would you wish to speak to his secretary?"

"Damnation, blast and bloody hell!" Alleyn said. "No, I wouldn't. Thank you, Oliphant. Come on, Fox. That little game's gone cold. We'd better get moving. Oliphant, if we can spare the time, we'll get something to eat at the Boy and Donkey, but on the way, we'll make at least one call." His finger again hovered over the list. The sergeant followed its indication.

"At Uplands?" he said. "Commander Syce?"

"Yes," Alleyn said. "Have everything laid on, and if you get a signal from me, come at once with suitable assistance. It'll mean an arrest. Come on, Fox."

He was very quiet on the way back over Watt's Hill.

As they turned the summit and approached Jacob's Cottage, they saw Mr. Phinn leaning over his gate with a kitten on his shoulder.

Alleyn said, "It might as well be now as later. Let's stop."

Fox pulled up by the gate and Alleyn got out. He walked over to the gate and Mr. Phinn blinked at him.

"Dear me, Chief Inspector," he said, taking the kitten from his neck and caressing it, "how very recurrent you are. Quite decimalite, to coin an adjective."

"It's our job, you know," Alleyn said mildly. "You'll find we do tend to crop up."

Mr. Phinn blinked and gave a singular little laugh. "Am I to conclude, then, that I am the subject of your interest? Or are you on your way to fresh fields of surmise and conjecture? Nunspardon, for instance. Do you perhaps envisage my Lady Brobdignagia, the Dowager Tun, the Mammoth Matriarch, stealing a tip-toe through the daisies? Or George aflame with his newly acquired dignities, thundering through the willow grove in plus fours? Or have the injuries a clinical character? Do we suspect the young Aesculapius with scalpel or probe? You are thinking I am a person of execrable taste, but the truth is there *are* other candidates for infamy. Perhaps we should look nearer at hand. At our elderly and intemperate merryman of the shaft and quiver. Or at the interesting and mysterious widow with the dubious antecedents? Really, how very footling, if you will forgive me, it all sounds, doesn't it? What can I do for you?"

Alleyn looked at the pallid face and restless eyes. "Mr. Phinn," he said, "will you let me have your copy of Chapter 7?"

The kitten screamed, opening its mouth and showing its tongue. Mr. Phinn relaxed his fingers, kissed it and put it down.

"Forgive me, my atom," he said. "Run to Mother." He opened the gate. "Shall we go in?" he suggested, and they followed him into a garden dotted about with rustic furniture of an offensive design.

"Of course," Alleyn said, "you can refuse. I shall then have to use some other form of approach."

"If you imagine," Mr. Phinn said, wetting his lips, "that as far as I am concerned this Chapter 7, which I am to suppose you have seen on my desk but not read, is in any way incriminating, you are entirely mistaken. It constitutes, for me, what may perhaps be called a contra-motive."

"So I had supposed," Alleyn said. "But don't you think you had better let me see it?"

There was a long silence. "Without the consent of Lady Lacklander," Mr. Phinn said, "never. Not for all the sleuths in Christendom."

"Well," Alleyn said, "that's all very correct, I daresay. Would you suggest, for the sake of argument, that Chapter 7 constitutes a sort of confession on the part of the author? Does Sir Harold Lacklander, for instance, perhaps admit that he was virtually responsible for the leakage of information that tragic time in Zlomce?"

Mr. Phinn said breathlessly, "Pray, what inspires this gush of unbridled empiricism?"

"It's not altogether that," Alleyn rejoined with perfect good-humour. "As I think I told you this morning, I have some knowledge of the Zlomce affair. You tell us that the new version of Chapter 7 constitutes for you a contra-motive. If this is so, if, for instance, it provides exoneration, can you do anything but welcome its publication?"

Mr. Phinn said nothing.

"I think I must tell you," Alleyn went on, "that I shall ask the prospective publishers for the full story of Chapter 7."

"They have not been informed—"

"On the contrary, unknown to Colonel Cartarette, they were informed by the author."

"Indeed?" said Mr. Phinn, trembling slightly. "If they profess any vestige of professional rectitude, they will refuse to divulge the content."

"As you do?"

"As I do. I shall refuse any information in this affair, no matter what pressure is put upon me, Inspector Alleyn."

Mr. Phinn had already turned aside when his garden gate creaked and Alleyn said quietly, "Good morning once again, Lady Lacklander."

Mr. Phinn spun round with an inarticulate ejaculation.

She stood blinking in the sun, huge, without expression and very slightly tremulous.

"Roderick," said Lady Lacklander, "I have come to confess."

CHAPTER TEN

Return to Swevenings

Lady Lacklander advanced slowly towards them.

"If that contraption of yours will support my weight, Octavius," she said, "I'll take it."

They stood aside for her. Mr. Phinn suddenly began to gabble. "No, no, no! Not another word! I forbid it."

She let herself down on a rustic seat.

"For God's sake," Mr. Phinn implored her frantically, "hold your tongue, Lady L."

"Nonsense, Occy," she rejoined, panting slightly. "Hold yours, my good fool." She stared at him for a moment and then gave a sort of laugh.

"Good Lord, you think I did it myself, do you?"

"No, no, no. What a thing to say!"

She shifted her great torso and addressed herself to Alleyn. "I'm here, Roderick, virtually on behalf of my husband. The confession I have to offer is his."

"At last," Alleyn said. "Chapter 7."

"Precisely. I've no idea how much you think you already know or how much you may have been told."

"By me," Mr. Phinn cried out, "nothing!"

"Humph!" she said. "Uncommon generous of you, Octavius."

Mr. Phinn began to protest, threw up his hands and was silent.

"There are, however, other sources," she went on. "I understand his wife has been kept posted." She stared at Alleyn, who thought, "George has told Kitty Cartarette about Chapter 7 and Lady Lacklander has found out. She thinks Kitty has told me." He said nothing.

"You may suppose, therefore," Lady Lacklander continued, "that I am merely making a virtue of necessity."

Alleyn bowed.

"It is not altogether that. To begin with, we are, as a family, under a certain obligation to you, Octavius."

"Stop!" Mr. Phinn shouted. "Before you go on much further, before you *utter—*"

"Mr. Phinn," Alleyn cut in, breaking about three vital items of the police code in one sentence, "if you don't stop chattering, I shall take drastic steps to make you. Shut up, Mr. Phinn."

"Yes, Occy," Lady Lacklander said, "I couldn't agree more. Either shut up or take yourself off, my dear fellow." She lifted a tiny, fat hand, holding it aloft as if it was one of Mr. Phinn's kittens. "Do me the favour," she said, "of believing I have thought things over very carefully, and be quiet."

While Mr. Phinn still hesitated, eyeing Alleyn and fingering his lips, Lady Lacklander made a brief comprehensive gesture with her short arms and said, "Roderick, my husband was a traitor."

2

They made a strange group, sitting there on uncomfortable rustic benches. Fox took unobtrusive notes, Mr. Phinn held his head in his hands, Lady Lacklander, immobile behind the great façade of her fat, talked and talked. Cats came and went, gracefully indifferent to the human situation.

"That," Lady Lacklander said, "is what you will find in Chapter 7." She broke off and, after a moment, said, "This is not going to be easy and I've no wish to make a fool of myself. Will you forgive me for a moment?"

"Of course," Alleyn said, and they waited while Lady Lacklander, staring before her, beat her puff-ball palms on her knees and got her mouth under control. "That's better," she said at last. "I can manage now." And she went on steadily. "At the time of the Zlomce incident my husband was in secret negotiation with a group of Prussian fascists. The top group: the men about Hitler. They looked upon him, it appears, as their trump card: a British diplomat whose name—" her voice creaked and steadied— "was above reproach in his own country. He was absolutely and traitorously committed to the Nazi programme." Alleyn saw that her eyes were bitter with tears. "They never found that out at your M.I.5., Roderick, did they?"

"No."

"And yet this morning I thought that perhaps you knew."

"I wondered. That was all."

"So she didn't say anything."

"She?"

"Maurice's wife. Kitty."

"No."

"You never know," she muttered, "with that sort of people what they may do."

"Nor," he said, "with other sorts either, it seems."

A dark unlovely flush flooded her face.

"The extraordinary thing," Mr. Phinn said suddenly, "is *why*. *Why* did Lacklander do it?"

"The Herrenvolk heresy?" Alleyn suggested. "An aristocratic Anglo-German alliance as the only alternative to war and communism and the only hope for the survival of his own class? It was a popular heresy at that time. He wasn't alone. No doubt he was promised great things."

"You don't spare him," Lady Lacklander said under her breath.

"How can I? In the new Chapter 7, I imagine, he doesn't spare himself."

"He repented bitterly. His remorse was frightful."

"Yes," Mr. Phinn said. "That is clear enough."

"Ah, yes!" she cried out. "Ah, yes, Occy, yes. And most of all for the terrible injury he did your boy—most of all for that."

"The injury?" Alleyn repeated, cutting short an attempt on Mr. Phinn's part to intervene. "I'm sorry, Mr. Phinn. We must have it."

Lady Lacklander said, "Why do you try to stop me, Occy? You've read it. You must want to shout it from the roof-tops."

Alleyn said, "Does Sir Harold exonerate Ludovic Phinn?"

"Of everything but carelessness."

"I see."

Lady Lacklander put her little fat hands over her face. It was a gesture so out of key with the general tenor of her behaviour that it was as shocking in its way as a bout of hysteria.

Alleyn said, "I think I understand. In the business of the railway concessions in Zlomce, was Sir Harold, while apparently acting in accordance with his instructions from the British Government, about to allow the German interest to get control?"

He saw that he was right and went on, "And at the most delicate stage of these negotiations, at the very moment where he desired above all things that no breath of suspicion should be aroused, his private secretary goes out on a Central European bender and lets a German agent get hold of the contents of the vital cable which Sir Harold had left him to decode. Sir Harold is informed by his own government of the leakage. He is obliged to put up a terrific show of ambassadorial rage. He has no alternative but to send for young Phinn. He accuses him of such things and threatens him with such disastrous exposures, such disgrace and ruin, that the boy goes out and puts an end to it all. Was it like that?"

He looked from one to the other.

"It was like that," Lady Lacklander said. She raised her voice as if she repeated some intolerable lesson. "My husband writes that he drove Viccy Phinn to his death as surely as if he had killed him with his own hands. He was instructed to do so by his Nazi masters. It was then that he began to understand what he had done and to what frightful lengths his German associates could drive him. I knew, at that time, he was wretchedly unhappy, but put it down to the shock of Viccy's death and—as I, of course, thought—treachery. But the treachery, Occy, was ours, and your Viccy was only a foolish and tragically careless boy." She looked at Mr. Phinn and frowned. "Yesterday," she said, "after your row with Maurice over the trout, he came to me and told me he'd left a copy of the amended Chapter 7 at your house. Why haven't you produced it, Occy? Why just now did you try to stop me? Was it because—"

"Dear me, no," Mr. Phinn said very quietly, "not from any high-flown scruples, I assure you. It was, if you will believe me, in deference to my boy's wishes. Before he killed himself, Viccy wrote to his mother and to me. He begged us to believe him innocent. He also begged us most solemnly, whatever the future might hold, never to take any action that might injure Sir Harold Lacklander. You may not have noticed, my dear Lady L., that my foolish boy hero-worshipped your husband. We decided to respect his wishes."

Mr. Phinn stood up. He looked both old and shabby. "I am not concerned," he said, "with the Lacklander conscience, the Lacklander motive, or the Lacklander remorse. I no longer desire the Lacklanders to suffer for my dear boy's death. I do not, I think, believe any more in human expiation. Now if I may, I shall ask you to excuse me. And if you want to know what I did with Chapter 7, I burnt it to ashes, my dear Chief Inspector, half an hour ago."

He raised his dreadful smoking cap, bowed to Lady Lacklander and walked into his house, followed by his cats.

Lady Lacklander stood up. She began to move towards the gate, seemed to recollect herself and paused. "I am going to Nunspardon," she said. Alleyn opened the gate. She went out without looking at him, got into her great car and was driven away.

Fox said, "Painful business. I suppose the young fellow suspected what was up at the last interview. Unpleasant."

"Very."

"Still, as Mr. Phinn says, this Chapter 7 really puts him in the clear as far as killing Colonel Cartarette is concerned."

"Well, no," Alleyn said.

"No?"

"Not exactly. The Colonel left Chapter 7 at Jacob's Cottage. Phinn, on his own statement, didn't re-enter the house after his row with the Colonel. He returned to the willow grove, found the body and lost his spectacles. He read Chapter 7 for the first time this morning, I fancy, by the aid of a magnifying glass."

3

"Of course," Fox said, as they turned into Commander Syce's drive, "it will have been a copy. The Colonel'd never hand over the original."

"No. My guess is he locked the original in the bottom drawer of the left-hand side of his desk."

"Ah! Now!" Fox said with relish. "That might well be."

"In which case one of his own family or one of the Lacklanders or any other interested person has pinched it, and it's probably gone up in smoke like its sister-ship. On the other hand, the bottom drawer may have been empty and the original typescript in Carterette's bank. It doesn't very much matter, Fox. The publisher was evidently given a pretty sound idea of the alternative version by its author. He could always be called. We may not have to bring the actual text in evidence. I hope we won't."

"What d'you reckon is the dowager's real motive in coming so remarkably clean all of a sudden?"

Alleyn said crossly, "I've had my bellyful of motives. Take your choice, Br'er Fox."

"Of course," Fox said, "she's a very sharp old lady. She must have guessed we'd find out anyway."

Alleyn muttered obscurely, "The mixture as before. And here we go with a particularly odious little interview. Look out for squalls, Br'er Fox. Gosh! See who's here!"

It was Nurse Kettle. She had emerged from the front door, escorted by Commander Syce, who carried a napkin in his hand. She was about to enter her car, and this process was accelerated by Commander Syce, who quite obviously drew her attention to the approaching police car and then, limping to her own, opened the door and waited with some evidence of trepidation for her to get in. She did so without glancing at him and started her engine.

"She's told him," Alleyn said crossly, "that we've rumbled the 'bago."

"Acting, no doubt," Fox rejoined stiffly, "from the kindest of motives."

"No doubt." Alleyn lifted his hat as Nurse Kettle, having engaged her bottom gear with some precipitance, shot past them like a leaping eland. She was extremely red in the face.

Syce waited for them.

Fox pulled up and they both got out. Alleyn slung the golf bag over his shoulder as he addressed himself to Syce.

"May we speak to you indoors somewhere?" Alleyn asked.

Without a word Syce led the way into his living-room, where a grim little meal, half consumed, was laid out on a small table in close proximity to a very dark whisky-and-water.

The improvised bed was still in commission. A dressing-gown was folded neatly across the foot.

"Sit down?" Syce jerked out, but, as he evidently was not going to do so himself, neither Alleyn nor Fox followed his suggestion.

"What's up now?" he demanded.

Alleyn said, "I've come to ask you a number of questions, all of which you will find grossly impertinent. They concern the last occasion when you were in Singapore. The time we discussed this morning, you remember, when you told us you introduced the present Mrs. Cartarette to her husband?"

Syce didn't answer. He thrust his hands into the pockets of his coat and stared out of the window.

"I'm afraid," Alleyn said, "I shall have to press this a little further. In a word, I must ask you if you were not, in fact, on terms of the greatest intimacy with Miss de Vere, as she was then."

"Bloody impertinence."

"Well, yes. But so, when one comes to think of it, is murder."

"What the hell are you driving at?"

"Ah!" Alleyn exclaimed with one of his very rare gestures. "How footling all this is! You know damn' well what I'm driving at. Why should we stumble about like a couple of maladroit fencers? See here. I've information from the best possible sources that before she was married, you were living with Mrs. Cartarette in Singapore. You yourself have told me you introduced her to Cartarette. You came back here and found them man and wife: the last thing, so you told me, that you had intended. All right. Cartarette was murdered last night in the bottom meadow, and there's a hole in his head that might have been made by an arrow. You gave out that you were laid by with lumbago, but you were heard twanging away at your sixty-pound bow when you were supposed to be incapacitated on your bed. Now, send for your solicitor if you like and refuse to talk till he comes, but for the love of Mike don't pretend you don't know what I'm driving at."

"Great grief!" Syce exclaimed with exactly the same inflection he had used of cats. "I *liked* Cartarette."

"You may have liked Cartarette, but did you love his wife?"

" 'Love,' " Syce repeated turning purple. "What a word!"

"Well, my dear man—put it this way. Did she love you?"

"Look here, are you trying to make out that she egged me on or—or —I egged her on or any perishing rot of that sort! Thompson," Commander Syce shouted angrily, "and Bywaters, by God!"

"What put them into your head, I wonder? The coincidence that he was a seafaring man and she, poor woman, an unfaithful wife?"

"A few more cracks like that and I bloody well will send for a solicitor."

"You *are* being difficult," Alleyn said without rancour. "Will you let me have the clothes you were wearing last evening?"

"What the hell for?"

"For one thing, to see if Cartarette's blood is on them."

"How absolutely piffling."

"Well, may I have them?"

"I'm wearing them, blast it."

"Would you mind wearing something else?"

Commander Syce fixed his intensely blue and slightly bloodshot eyes on a distant point in the landscape and said, "I'll shift."

"Thank you. I see you've been using this as a bed-sitting-room during, no doubt, your attack of lumbago. Perhaps for the time being you could shift into your dressing-gown and slippers."

Syce followed this suggestion. Little gales of whisky were wafted from him, and his hands were unsteady, but he achieved his change with the economy of movement practised by sailors. He folded up the garments as they were discarded, passed a line of cord round them, made an appropriate knot and gave the bundle to Fox, who wrote out a receipt for it.

Syce tied his dressing-gown cord with a savage jerk.

"No return," Alleyn remarked, "of the ailment?"

Syce did not reply.

Alleyn said, "Why not tell me about it? You must know damn' well that I can't cut all this background stuff dead. Why the devil did you pretend to have lumbago last evening? Was it for the love of a lady?"

It would be inaccurate to say that Commander Syce blushed, since his face, throughout the interview, had been suffused. But at this juncture it certainly darkened to an alarming degree.

"Well, *was* it?" Alleyn insisted on a note of exasperation. Fox clapped the bundle of clothes down on a table.

"I know what it's like," Commander Syce began incomprehensibly. He moved his hand in the direction of Hammer Farm. "Lonely as hell. Poor little Kit. Suppose she wanted security. Natural. Ever seen that play? I believe they put it on again a year or two ago. I don't go in for poodle-faking, but it was damn' true. In the end she pitched herself out of a top window, poor thing. Frozen out. County."

"Can you mean *The Second Mrs. Tanqueray?*"

"I daresay. And they'd better change their course or she'll do the same thing. Lonely. I know what it's like."

His gaze travelled to a corner cupboard. "You have to do something," he said and then eyed the tumbler on his luncheon table. "No good offering you a drink," he mumbled.

"None in the world, worse luck."

"Well," Syce said. He added something that sounded like "luck" and suddenly drained the tumbler.

"As a matter of fact," he said, "I'm thinking of giving it up myself. Alcohol."

"It's a 'good familiar creature,'" Alleyn quoted, "'if it is well used.'"

"That's all right as far as it goes, but what sort of a perisher," Syce surprisingly observed, "took the bearings? A nasty little man and a beastly liar into the bargain."

"True enough. But we're not, after all, discussing Iago and alcohol but you and lumbago. Why—"

"All right, I heard you before. I'm just thinking what to say."

He went to the corner cupboard and returned with a half-empty bottle of whisky. "I've got to think," he said. "It's damn' ticklish, I'd have you know." He helped himself to a treble whisky.

"In that case, wouldn't you do better without that snorter you've just poured out?"

"Think so?"

Fox, with his masterly command of the totally unexpected, said, "She would."

"Who?" shouted Commander Syce looking terrified. He drank half his whisky.

"Miss Kettle."

"She would what?"

"Think you'd be better without it, sir."

"She knows what to do," he muttered, "if she wants to stop me. Or rather she doesn't. I wouldn't tell *her*," Commander Syce added in a deeper voice than Alleyn could have imagined him to produce, "I wouldn't mention it to her on any account whatsoever, never."

"I'm afraid you really are very tight."

"It's the last time so early; in future I'm going to wait till the sun's over the yard-arm. It happens to be a promise."

"To Miss Kettle?"

"Who else?" Syce said grandly. "Why not?"

"An admirable idea. Was it," Alleyn asked, "on Miss Kettle's account, by any chance, that you pretended to have lumbago last evening?"

"Who else's?" admitted Syce, who appeared to have got into one unchangeable gear. "Why not?"

"Does she know?"

Fox muttered something indistinguishable and Syce said, "She guessed." He added wretchedly, "We parted brass rags."

"You had a row about it?" Alleyn ventured.

"Not about that. About *that*." He indicated the tumbler. "So I promised. After to-day. Yard-arm."

"Good luck to it."

With the swiftest possible movement Alleyn whisked the arrow from the golf bag and held it under Syce's nose. "Do you know anything about that?" he asked.

"That's mine. You took it away."

"No. This is another of your arrows. This was found in Bottom Meadow at the foot of Watt's Hill. If you examine it, you'll see there's a difference."

Alleyn whipped the cover off the tip of the arrow. "Look," he said.

Syce stared owlishly at the point.

"Bloody," he observed.

"Looks like it. What blood? Whose blood?"

Syce thrust his fingers distractedly through his thin hair.

"Cat's blood," he said.

4

This was the selfsame arrow, Commander Syce urged, with which some weeks ago he had inadvertently slain the mother of Thomasina Twitchett. He himself had found the body and in his distress had withdrawn the arrow and cast it from him into the adjacent bushes. He had taken the body to Mr. Phinn, who had refused to accept his explanation and apologies, and they had parted, as Commander Syce again put it, brass rags.

Alleyn asked him if he did not consider it at all dangerous to fire off arrows at random into his neighbours' spinneys and over them. The reply was confused and shamefaced. More by surmise and conjecture than by any positive means, Alleyn understood Syce to suggest a close relationship between the degree of his potations and the incontinence of his archery. At this juncture he became morose, and they could get no more out of him.

"It appears," Alleyn said as they drove away, "that when he's completely plastered, he gets a sort of cupid fixation and looses off his shafts blindly into the landscape with a classic disregard for their billets. It's a terrifying thought, but I suppose his immediate neighbours have learnt to look after themselves."

"I'm afraid," Fox said heavily, "she's bitten off more than she can chew. I'm afraid so."

"My dear old Fox, there's no end to the punishment some women will take."

"Of course," Fox said dismally, "in a manner of speaking, she's trained for it. There is that."

"I rather think, you know, that she's one of the sort that has got to have somebody to cosset."

"I daresay. Whereas, barring the odd bilious turn, I'm never out of sorts. What do we do now, Mr. Alleyn?" Fox continued, dismissing the more intimate theme with an air of finality.

"We can't do anything really conclusive until we get a lead from Curtis. But we interview George Lacklander all the same, Br'er Fox, and, I hope, lay the ghost of young Ludovic Phinn. It's half past one. We may as well let them have their luncheon. Let's see what they can do for us at the Boy and Donkey."

They ate their cold meat, potato and beetroot with the concentration of men whose meals do not occur as a matter of course but are consumed precariously when chances present themselves. Before they had finished, Dr. Curtis rang up to give an interim report. He now plumped unreservedly for a blow on the temple with a blunt instrument while Colonel Cartarette squatted over his catch. Subsequent injuries had been inflicted with a pointed instrument after he lay on his side, unconscious or possibly already lifeless. The second injury had all but obliterated the first. He was unable with any certainty to name the first instrument, but the second was undoubtedly the shooting-stick. Sir William Roskill had found traces of recently shed blood under the collar of the disk. He was now checking for the blood group.

"I see," Alleyn said. "And the shooting-stick was used—?"

"My dear chap, in the normal way, one must suppose."

"Yes, one must, mustn't one? Deliberately pushed home and sat on. Horrid-awful behaviour."

"Brutal," Dr. Curtis said dispassionately.

"All the brutality in the world. Has Willy tackled the fish scales?"

"Give him time. But yes, he's begun. No report yet."

"We're going to Nunspardon. Telephone me if there's anything, Curtis, will you? You or Willy?"

"O.K."

Alleyn turned away from the telephone to discover Sergeant Bailey waiting for him with the air of morose detachment that meant he had something of interest to impart. He had, in fact, come from a further detailed overhaul of Colonel Cartarette's study. The bottom drawer on the

left of the desk carried an identifiable finger-print of Sir George Lacklander's.

"I checked it with his grog glass," Bailey said, looking at his boots.
"The drawer seems to have been wiped over, but a dab on the underside
must have been missed or something. It's his all right."

"Very useful," Alleyn said.

Fox wore that expression of bland inscrutability that always seemed
to grow upon him as a case approached its close. He would listen attentively to witnesses, suspects, colleagues or his chief and would presently glance up and move the focus of his gaze to some distant object
of complete unimportance. This mannerism had the same effect as a
change of conversation. It was as if Mr. Fox had become rather pleasurably abstracted. To his associates it was a sign of a peculiar wiliness.

"Remove your attention from the far horizon, Br'er Fox," Alleyn said,
"and bring it to bear on the immediate future. We're going to Nunspardon."

They were taken there by the Yard driver, who was now released from
his duties in Bottom Meadow.

As they drove past the long wall that marked the Nunspardon marches,
Fox began to speculate. "Do you suppose that they throw it open to the
public? They must, mustn't they? Otherwise, how do they manage these
days?"

"They manage by a freak. Within the last two generations the Lacklanders have won first prizes in world lotteries. I remember because I was
still in the Foreign Service when George Lacklander rang the bell in
the Calcutta Sweep. In addition to that, they're fantastically lucky race-
horse owners and possess one of the most spectacular collections of private jewels in England, which I suppose they could use as a sort of lucky
dip if they felt the draught. Really, they're one of the few remaining
country families who are wealthy through sheer luck."

"Is that so?" Fox observed mildly. "And Miss Kettle tells me they've
stood high in the county for something like a thousand years. Never a
scandal, she says, but then I daresay she's partial."

"I daresay. A thousand years," Alleyn said dryly, "is a tidy reach even
for the allegedly blameless Lacklanders."

"Well, to Miss Kettle's knowledge there's never been the slightest hint
of anything past or present."

"When, for the love of wonder, did you enjoy this cosy chat with
Nurse Kettle?"

"Last evening, Mr. Alleyn. When you were in the study, you know,
Miss Kettle, who was saying at the time that the Colonel was quite one
of the old sort, a real gentleman and so on, mentioned that she and her

ladyship had chatted on the subject only that afternoon!" Fox stopped, scraped his chin and became abstracted.

"What's up? What subject?"

"Well, er—class obligation and that style of thing. It didn't seem to amount to anything last night, because at that stage no connection had been established with the family."

"Come on."

"Miss Kettle mentioned in passing that her ladyship had talked about the—er—the—er—as you might say—the—er—principle of 'noblesse oblige' and had let it be known she was very worried."

"About what?"

"No particular cause was named."

"And you're wondering now if she was worried about the prospect of an imminent debunking through Chapter 7 of the blameless Lacklanders?"

"Well, it makes you think," Fox said.

"So it does," Alleyn agreed as they turned into the long drive to Nunspardon.

"She being a great lady."

"Are you reminding me of her character, her social position or what Mr. Phinn calls her avoirdupois?"

"She must be all of seventeen stone," Fox mused, "and I wouldn't mind betting the son'll be the same at her age. Very heavy-built."

"And damn' heavy-going into the bargain."

"Mrs. Cartarette doesn't seem to think so."

"My dear man, as you have already guessed, he's the only human being in the district, apart from her husband, who's sent her out any signals of any kind at all, and he's sent plenty."

"You don't reckon she's in love with him, though?"

"You never know—never. I daresay he has his ponderous attractions."

"Ah, well," Fox said and with an air of freshening himself up stared at a point some distance ahead. It was impossible to guess whether he ruminated upon the tender passion, the character of George Lacklander or the problematical gratitude of Kitty Cartarette. "You never know," he sighed, "he may even be turning it over in his mind how long he ought to wait before it'll be all right to propose to her."

"I hardly think so, and I must say I hope she's not building on it."

"You've made up your mind, of course," Fox said after a pause.

"Well, I have, Fox. I can only see one answer that will fit all the evidence, but unless we get the go-ahead sign from the experts in Chyning, we haven't a case. There we are again."

They had rounded the final bend in the drive and had come out before the now familiar façade of Nunspardon.

The butler admitted them and contrived to suggest with next to no expenditure of behaviour that Alleyn was a friend of the family and Fox completely invisible. Sir George, he said, was still at luncheon. If Alleyn would step this way, he would inform Sir George. Alleyn, followed by the unmoved Fox, was shown into George Lacklander's study: the last of the studies they were to visit. It still bore, Alleyn recognized, the imprint of Sir Harold Lacklander's personality, and he looked with interest at a framed caricature of his erstwhile chief made a quarter of a century ago when Alleyn was a promising young man in the Foreign Service. The drawing revived his memories of Sir Harold Lacklander; of his professional charm, his conformation to type, his sudden flashes of wit and his extreme sensitiveness to criticism. There was a large photograph of George on the desk, and it was strange to see in it, as Alleyn fancied he could, these elements adulterated and transformed by the addition of something that was either stupidity or indifference. Stupidity? Was George, after all, such an ass? It depended, as usual, on "what one meant" by an ass.

At this point in Alleyn's meditations, George himself, looking huffily postprandial, walked in. His expression was truculent.

"I *should* have thought, I *must* say, Alleyn," he said, "that one's luncheon hour at least might be left to one."

"I'm sorry," Alleyn said, "I thought you'd finished. Do you smoke between the courses, perhaps?"

Lacklander angrily pitched his cigarette into the fireplace. "I wasn't hungry," he said.

"In that case I am relieved that I didn't, after all, interrupt you."

"What are you driving at? I'm damned if I like your tone, Alleyn. What do you want?"

"I want," Alleyn said, "the truth. I want the truth about what you did yesterday evening. I want the truth about what you did when you went to Hammer Farm last night. I want the truth, and I think I have it, about Chapter 7 of your father's memoirs. A man has been murdered. I am a policeman and I want facts."

"None of these matters has anything to do with Cartarette's death," Lacklander said and wet his lips.

"You won't persuade me of that by refusing to discuss them."

"Have I said that I refuse to discuss them?"

"All right," Alleyn sighed. "Without more ado, then, did you expect to find a copy of Chapter 7 when you broke open the drawer in Colonel Cartarette's desk last night?"

"You're deliberately insulting me, by God!"

"Do you deny that you broke open the drawer?"

Lacklander made a small gaping movement with his lips and an ineffectual gesture with his hands. Then, with some appearance of boldness he said, "Naturally, I don't do anything of the sort. I did it by—at the desire of his family. The keys seemed to be lost and there were certain things that had to be done—people to be told and all that. She didn't even know the name of his solicitors. And there were people to ring up. They thought his address book might be there."

"In the locked drawer? The address book?"

"Yes."

"Was it there?"

He boggled for a moment and then said, "No."

"And you did this job before we arrived?"

"Yes."

"At Mrs. Cartarette's request?"

"Yes."

"And Miss Cartarette? Was she in the search party?"

"No."

"Was there, in fact, anything in the drawer?"

"No," George said hardily. "There wasn't." His face had begun to look coarse and blank.

"I put it to you that you did not break open the drawer at Mrs. Cartarette's request. It was you, I suggest, who insisted upon doing it because you were in a muck-sweat wanting to find out where the amended Chapter 7 of your father's memoirs might be. I put it to you that your relationship with Mrs. Cartarette is such that you were in a position to dictate this manoeuvre."

"No. You have no right, damn you—"

"I suggest that you are very well aware of the fact that your father wrote an amended version of Chapter 7 which was, in effect, a confession. In this version he stated firstly that he himself was responsible for young Ludovic Phinn's suicide and secondly that he himself had traitorously conspired against his own government with certain elements in the German Government. This chapter, if it were published, would throw such opprobrium upon your father's name that in order to stop its being made public, I suggest, you were prepared to go to the lengths to which you have, in fact, gone. You are an immensely vain man with a confused, indeed a fanatical sense of your family prestige. Have you anything to say to all this?"

A tremor had begun to develop in George Lacklander's hands. He glanced down at them and with an air of covering up a social blunder, thrust them into his pockets. Most unexpectedly he began to laugh, an awkward, rocketing sound made on the intake of breath, harsh as a hack-saw.

"It's ridiculous," he gasped, hunching his shoulders and bending at the waist in a spasm that parodied an ecstasy of amusement. "No, honestly, it's too much!"

"Why," Alleyn asked sedately, "are you laughing?"

Lacklander shook his head and screwed up his eyes. "I'm so sorry," he gasped. "Frightful of me, I know, but really!" Alleyn saw that through his almost sealed eyelids he was peeping out, wary and agitated. "You don't mean to say you think that I—?" He waved away his uncompleted sentence with a flap of his pink freckled hand.

"That you murdered Colonel Cartarette, were you going to say?"

"Such a notion! I mean, how? When? With what?"

Alleyn, watching his antics, found them insupportable.

"I know I shouldn't laugh," Lacklander gabbled, "but it's so fantastic. How? When? With what?" And through Alleyn's mind dodged a dis-jointed jingle. "*Quomodo? Quando? Quibus auxiliis?*"

"He was killed," Alleyn said, "by a blow and a stab. The injuries were inflicted at about five past eight last evening. The murderer stood in the old punt. As for 'with what'—"

He forced himself to look at George Lacklander, whose face, like a bad mask, was still crumpled in a false declaration of mirth.

"The puncture," Alleyn said, "was made by your mother's shooting-stick and the initial blow—" he saw the pink hands flex and stretch, flex and stretch—"by a golf-club. Probably a driver."

At that moment the desk telephone rang. It was Dr. Curtis for Alleyn.

He was still talking when the door opened and Lady Lacklander came in followed by Mark. They lined themselves up by George and all three watched Alleyn.

Curtis said, "Can I talk?"

"Ah yes," Alleyn said airily. "That's all right. I'm afraid I can't do any-thing to help you, but you can go ahead quietly on your own."

"I suppose," Dr. Curtis's voice said very softly, "You're in a nest of Lacklanders?"

"Yes, indeed."

"All right. I've rung up to tell you about the scales. Willy can't find both types on any of the clothes or gear."

"No?"

"No. Only on the rag: the paint-rag."

"Both types on that?"

"Yes. And on the punt seat."

"Yes?"

"Yes. Shall I go on?"

"Do."

Dr. Curtis went on. Alleyn and the Lacklanders watched each other.

CHAPTER ELEVEN   # Between Hammer and Nunspardon

Nurse Kettle had finished her afternoon jobs in Swevenings, but before she returned to Chyning, she thought she should visit the child with the abscess in the gardener's cottage at Hammer Farm. She felt some delicacy about this duty because of the calamity that had befallen the Cartarettes. Still, she could slip quietly round the house and down to the cottage without bothering anybody, and perhaps the gardener's wife would have a scrap or two of mournful gossip for her about when the funeral was to take place and what the police were doing and how the ladies were bearing up and whether general opinion favoured an early marriage between Miss Rose and Dr. Mark. She also wondered privately what, if anything, was being said about Mrs. Cartarette and Sir George Lacklander, though her loyalty to The Family, she told herself, would oblige her to give a good slap down to any nonsense that was talked in *that* direction.

Perhaps her recent interview with Commander Syce had a little upset her. It had been such a bitter and unexpected disappointment to find him at high noon so distinctly the worse for wear. Perhaps it was disappointment that had made her say such astonishingly snappish things to him; or, more likely, she thought, anxiety. Because, she reflected as she drove up Watt's Hill, she *was* dreadfully anxious about him. Of course, she knew very well that he had pretended to be prostrate with lumbago because he wanted her to go on visiting him, and this duplicity, she had to admit, gave her a cosy feeling under her diaphragm. But Chief Detective-Inspector Alleyn would have a very different point of view about the deception; perhaps a terrifying point of view. Well, there, she thought, turning in at the Hammer Farm drive, it was no good at her age getting the flutters. In her simple snobbishness she comforted herself with the thought that "Handsome Alleyn," as the evening papers called him, was the Right Sort, by which Nurse Kettle meant the Lacklander as opposed to the Kettle or Fox or Oliphant sort or, she was obliged to add to herself, the Kitty Cartarette sort. As this thought occurred to her, she compressed her generous lips. The memory had arisen of Commander Syce trying half-heartedly to conceal a rather exotic watercolour of Kitty Cartarette. It was a memory that, however much Nurse Kettle might try to shove it out of sight, recurred with unpleasant frequency.

By this time she was out of the car and stumping round the house by a path that ran down to the gardener's cottage. She carried her bag and looked straight before her, and she quite jumped when she heard her name called: "Hullo, there! Nurse Kettle!"

It was Kitty Cartarette sitting out on the terrace with a tea-table in front of her. "Come and have some," she called.

Nurse Kettle was dying for a good cup of tea, and what was more, she had a bone to pick with Kitty Cartarette. She accepted and presently was seated before the table.

"You pour out," Kitty said. "Help yourself."

She looked exhausted and had made the mistake of over-painting her face. Nurse Kettle asked her briefly if she had had any sleep.

"Oh, yes," she said, "doped myself up to the eyebrows last night, but you don't feel so good after it, do you?"

"You certainly do *not*. You want to be careful about that sort of thing, you know, dear."

"Ah, what the hell!" Kitty said impatiently and lit a cigarette at the stub of her old one. Her hands shook. She burnt her finger and swore distractedly.

"Now, then," Nurse Kettle said making an unwilling concession to the prompting of her professional conscience. "Steady." And thinking it might help Kitty to talk, she asked, "What have you been doing with yourself all day, I wonder?"

"Doing? God, I don't know. This morning for my sins I had to go over to Lacklanders'."

Nurse Kettle found this statement deeply offensive in two ways. Kitty had commonly referred to the Lacklanders as if they were shopkeepers. She had also suggested that they were bores.

"To Nunspardon?" Nurse Kettle said with refinement. "What a lovely old home it is! A show place if ever there was one," and she sipped her tea.

"The *place* is all right," Kitty muttered under her breath.

This scarcely veiled slight upon the Lacklanders angered Nurse Kettle still further. She began to wish that she had not accepted tea from Kitty. She replaced her cucumber sandwich on her plate and her cup and saucer on the table.

"Perhaps," she said, "you prefer Uplands."

Kitty stared at her. "*Uplands?*" she repeated, and after a moment's consideration she asked without any great display of interest, "Here! what are you getting at?"

"I thought," Nurse Kettle said with mounting colour, "you might find the company at Uplands more to your taste than the company at Nunspardon."

"Geoff Syce?" Kitty gave a short laugh. "God, that old bit of wreckage! Have a heart!"

Nurse Kettle's face was scarlet. "If the Commander isn't the man he used to be," she said, "I wonder whose fault it is."

"His own, I should think," Kitty said indifferently.

"Personally, I've found it's more often a case of *cherchez*," Nurse Kettle said carefully, "*la femme.*"

"What?"

"When a nice man takes to solitary drinking, it's generally because some woman's let him down."

Kitty looked at her guest with the momentarily deflected interest of a bitter preoccupation. "Are you suggesting I'm the woman in this case?" she asked.

"I'm not suggesting anything. But you knew him out in the East, I believe?" Nurse Kettle added with a spurious air of making polite conversation.

"Oh, yes," Kitty agreed contemptuously. "I knew him all right. Did he tell you? Here, what *has* he told you?" she demanded, and unexpectedly there was a note of something like desperation in her voice.

"Nothing, I'm sure, that you could take exception to; the Commander, whatever you like to say, *is* a gentleman."

"How can you be such a fool," Kitty said drearily.

"Well, really!"

"Don't talk to me about gentlemen. I've had them, thank you. If you ask me, it's a case of the higher you go the fewer. Look," Kitty said with savagery, "at George Lacklander."

"Tell me this," Nurse Kettle cried out; "did he love you?"

"Lacklander?"

"No." She swallowed and with dignity corrected Kitty, "I was referring to the Commander."

"You talk like a kid. Love!"

"*Honestly!*"

"Look!" Kitty said. "You don't know anything. Face it; you don't know a single damn' thing. You haven't got a clue."

"Well, I must say! You can't train for nursing, I'll have you know—"

"O, well, all right. O.K. From that point of view. But from my point of view, honestly, you have no idea."

"I don't know what we're talking about," Nurse Kettle said in a worried voice.

"I bet you don't."

"The Commander—" She stopped short and Kitty stared at her incredulously.

"Do I see," Kitty asked, "what I think I see! You don't tell me you and Geoff Syce—God, that's funny!"

Words, phrases, whole speeches suddenly began to pour out of Nurse Kettle. She had been hurt in the most sensitive part of her emotional anatomy, and her reflex action was surprising. She scarcely knew herself what she said. Every word she uttered was spoken in defence of something that she would have been unable to define. It is possible that Nurse Kettle, made vulnerable by her feeling for Commander Syce—a feeling that in her cooler moments she would have classed as "unsuitable"—found in Kitty Cartarette's contempt an implicit threat to what Lady Lacklander had called her belief in degree. In Kitty, over-painted, knowledgeable, fantastically "not-quite," Nurse Kettle felt the sting of implied criticism. It was as if, by her very existence, Kitty Cartarette challenged the hierarchy that was Nurse Kettle's symbol of perfection.

"—so you've no business," she heard herself saying, "you've no business to be where you are and behave the way you're behaving. I don't care what's happened. I don't care how *he* felt about you in Singapore or wherever it was. That was *his* business. I don't care."

Kitty had listened to this tirade without making any sign that she thought it exceptional. Indeed, she scarcely seemed to give it her whole attention but snuffed it with an air of brooding discontent. When at last Nurse Kettle ran out of words and breath, Kitty turned and stared abstractedly at her.

"I don't know why you're making such a fuss," she said. "Is he game to marry you?"

Nurse Kettle felt dreadful. "I wish I hadn't said anything," she muttered. "I'm going."

"I suppose he might like the idea of being dry-nursed. *You've* nothing to moan about. Suppose I was friends with him in Singapore? What of it? Go right ahead. Mix in with the bloody county and I hope you enjoy yourself."

"Don't talk about them like that," Nurse Kettle shouted. "Don't do it! You know nothing about them. You're ignorant. I always say they're the salt of the earth."

"Do you!" With methodical care Kitty moved the tea-tray aside as if it prevented her in some way from getting at Nurse Kettle. "Listen," she continued, holding the edges of the table and leaning forward, "listen to me. I asked you to come and sit here because I've got to talk and I thought you might be partly human. I didn't know you were a yes-girl to this gang of fossils. God! You make me sick! What have they got, except money and snob-value, that you haven't got?"

"Lots," Nurse Kettle declaimed stoutly.

"Like hell they have! No, listen. Listen! O.K., I lived with your boy-friend in Singapore. He was bloody dull, but I was in a bit of a jam and it suited us both. O.K., he introduced me to Maurice. O.K., he did it like they do: 'Look what I've found,' and sailed away in his great big boat and got the shock of his life when he came home and found me next door as Mrs. Maurice Cartarette. So what does he do? He couldn't care less what happened to *me*, of course, but could he be just ordinary-friendly and give me a leg up with these survivals from the ice-age? Not he! He shies off as if I was a nasty smell and takes to the bottle. Not that he wasn't pretty expert at that before."

Nurse Kettle made as if to rise, but Kitty stopped her with a sharp gesture. "Stay where you are," she said. "I'm talking. So here I was. Married to a—I don't know what—the sort they call a nice chap. Too damn' nice for me. I'd never have pulled it off with him in Singapore if it hadn't been he was lonely and missing Rose. He couldn't bear not to have Rose somewhere about. He was a real baby, though, about other women: more like a mother's darling than an experienced man. You had to laugh sometimes. He wasn't my cup of tea, but I was down to it, and anyway, his sort owed me something."

"O, dear!" Nurse Kettle lamented under her breath. "O, dear, dear, dear!" Kitty glanced at her and went on.

"So how did it go? We married and came here and he started writing some god-awful book and Rose and he sat in each other's pockets and the county called. Yes, they called, all right, talking one language to each other and another one to me. Old Occy Phinn, as mad as a meat-axe and doesn't even keep himself clean. The Fat Woman of Nunspardon, who took one look at me and then turned polite for the first time in history. Rose, trying so hard to be nice it's a wonder she didn't rupture something. The parson and his wife, and half a dozen women dressed in tweed sacks and felt buckets with faces like the backsides of a mule. My God, what have they *got*? They aren't fun, they aren't gay, they don't *do* anything and they look like the wreck of the schooner *Hesperus*. Talk about a living death! And me! Dumped like a sack and meant to be grateful!"

"You don't understand," Nurse Kettle began and then gave it up. Kitty had doubled her left hand into a fist and was screwing it into the palm of the right, a strangely masculine gesture at odds with her enamelled nails.

"Don't!" Nurse Kettle said sharply. "Don't do that."

"Not one of them, not a damn' one was what you might call friendly."

"Well, dear me, I must say! What about Sir George!" Nurse Kettle cried, exasperated and rattled into indiscretion.

"George! George wanted what they all want, and now things have got awkward, he doesn't want that. George! George, the umpteenth baronet, is in a muck-sweat. George can't think," Kitty said in savage mimicry, "what people might not be saying. He told me so himself! If you knew what I know about George—" Her face, abruptly, was as blank as a shuttered house. "Everything," she said, "has gone wrong. I just don't have the luck."

All sorts of notions, scarcely comprehensible to herself, writhed about in the mid-region of Nurse Kettle's thoughts. She was reminded of seaweed in the depths of a marine pool. Monstrous revelations threatened to emerge and were suppressed by a sort of creaming-over of the surface of her mind. She wanted to go away from Kitty Cartarette before any more damage was done to her innocent idolatries and yet found herself unable to make the appropriate gestures of departure. She was held in thrall by a convention. Kitty had been talking dismally for some time, and Nurse Kettle had not listened. She now caught a desultory phrase.

"Their fault!" Kitty was saying. "You can say what you like, but whatever has happened is their fault."

"No, no, no!" Miss Kettle cried out, beating her short scrubbed hands together. "How can you think that! You terrify me. What are you suggesting?"

2

"What are you suggesting?" George Lacklander demanded as Alleyn at last put down the receiver. "Who have you been speaking to? What did you mean by what you said to me just now—about—" he looked round at his mother and son—"an instrument," he said.

Lady Lacklander said, "George, I don't know what you and Roderick have been talking about, but I think it's odds on that you'd better hold your tongue."

"I'm sending for my solicitor."

She grasped the edge of the desk and let herself down into a chair. The folds of flesh under her chin began to tremble. She pointed at Alleyn.

"Well, Rory," she demanded, "what is all this? What are you suggesting?"

Alleyn hesitated for a moment and then said, "At the moment, I suggest that I see your son alone."

"No."

Mark, looking rather desperate, said, "Gar, don't you think it might be better?"

"No." She jabbed her fat finger at Alleyn. "What have you said and what were you going to say to George?"

"I told him that Colonel Cartarette was knocked out by a golf-club. I'll now add for the information of you all, since you choose to stay here, that he was finally killed by a stab through the temple made by your shooting-stick, Lady Lacklander. Your paint-rag was used to wipe the scales of two trout from the murderer's hands. The first blow was made from the punt. The murderer, in order to avoid being seen from Watt's Hill, got into the punt and slid down the stream using the long mooring rope as you probably did when you yourself sketched from the punt. The punt, borne by the current, came to rest in the little bay by the willow grove, and the murderer stood in it idly swinging a club at the daisies growing on the edge of the bank. This enemy of the Colonel's was so well known to him that he paid little attention, said something, perhaps, about the trout he had caught and went on cutting grass to wrap it in. Perhaps the last thing he saw was the shadow of the club moving swiftly across the ground. Then he was struck on the temple. We think there was a return visit with your shooting-stick, Lady Lacklander, and that the murderer quite deliberately used the shooting-stick on Colonel Cartarette as you used it this morning on your garden path. Placed it over the bruised temple and sat on it. What did you say? Nothing? It's a grotesque and horrible thought, isn't it? We think that on getting up and releasing the shooting-stick, there was literally a slip. A stumble, you know. It would take quite a bit of pulling out. There was a backward lunge. A heel came down on the Colonel's trout. The fish would have slid away, no doubt, if it had not been lying on a sharp triangular stone. It was trodden down and, as it were, transfixed on the stone. A flap of skin was torn away and the foot, instead of sliding off, sank in and left an impression. An impression of the spiked heel of a golf shoe."

George Lacklander said in an unrecognizable voice, "All this conjecture!"

"No," Alleyn said, "I assure you. Not conjecture." He looked at Lady Lacklander and Mark. "Shall I go on?"

Lady Lacklander, using strange unco-ordinated gestures, fiddled with the brooches that, as usual, were stuck about her bosom. "Yes," she said, "go on."

Mark, who throughout Alleyn's discourse had kept his gaze fixed on his father, said, "Go on. By all means. Why not?"

"Right," Alleyn said. "Now the murderer was faced with evidence of identity. One imagines the trout glistening with a clear spiked heel-mark showing on its hide. It wouldn't do to throw it into the stream or the willow grove and run away. There lay the Colonel with his hands smelling of fish and pieces of cut grass all round him. For all his murderer knew, there might have been a witness to the catch. This, of course, wouldn't matter as long as the murderer's identity was unsuspected. But there is a panic sequel to most crimes of violence, and it is under its pressure that the fatal touch of over-cleverness usually appears. I believe that while the killer stood there, fighting down terror, the memory of the Old 'Un, lying on Bottom Bridge, arose. Hadn't Danberry-Phinn and the Colonel quarrelled loudly, repeatedly and vociferously—quarrelled that very afternoon—over the Old 'Un? Why not replace the Colonel's catch with the fruits of Mr. Phinn's poaching tactics and drag, not a redherring, but a whacking great trout across the trail? Would that not draw attention towards the known enemy and away from the secret one? So there was a final trip in the punt. The Colonel's trout was removed and the Old 'Un substituted. It was at this juncture that Fate, in the person of Mrs. Thomasina Twitchett, appeared to come to the murderer's aid."

"For God's sake," George Lacklander shouted, "stop talking—" He half formed an extremely raw epithet, broke off and muttered something indistinguishable.

"Who are you talking about, Rory?" Lady Lacklander demanded. "Mrs. who?"

"Mr. Phinn's cat. You will remember, Mrs. Cartarette told us that in Bottom Meadow she came upon a cat with a half-eaten trout. We have found the remains. There is a triangular gash corresponding with the triangular flap of skin torn off by the sharp stone, and as if justice or nemesis or somebody had assuaged the cat's appetite at the crucial moment, there is also a shred of skin bearing the unmistakable mark of part of a heel and the scar of a spike."

"But can all this—" Mark began. "I mean, when you talk of correspondence—"

"Our case," Alleyn said, "will, I assure you, rest upon scientific evidence of an unusually precise character. At the moment, I'm giving you the sequence of events. The Colonel's trout was bestowed upon the cat. Lady Lacklander's paint-rag was used to clean the spike of the shooting-stick and the murderer's hands. You may remember, Dr. Lacklander, that your grandmother said she had put all her painting gear tidily away, but you, on the contrary, said you found the rag caught up in a briar bush."

"You suggest then," Mark said evenly, "that the murder was done some time between ten to eight, when my grandmother went home, and a quarter past eight, when I went home." He thought for a moment and then said, "I suppose that's quite possible. The murderer might have heard or caught sight of me, thrown down the rag in a panic and taken to the nearest cover only to emerge after I'd picked up the sketching gear and gone on my way."

Lady Lacklander said after a long pause, "I find that a horrible suggestion. Horrible."

"I daresay," Alleyn agreed dryly. "It was an abominable business, after all."

"You spoke of scientific evidence," Mark said.

Alleyn explained about the essential dissimilarities in individual fish scales. "It's all in Colonel Cartarette's book," he said and looked at George Lacklander. "You had forgotten that perhaps."

"Matter of fact, I—ah—I don't know that I ever read poor old Maurice's little book."

"It seems to me to be both charming," Alleyn said, "and instructive. In respect of the scales it is perfectly accurate. A trout's scales, the Colonel tells us, are his diary in which his whole life-history is recorded for those who can read them. Only if two fish have identical histories will their scales correspond. Our two sets of scales, luckily, are widely dissimilar. There is group A, the scales of a nine- or ten-year-old fish who has lived all his life in one environment. And there is group B, belonging to a smaller fish who, after a slow growth of four years, changed his environment, adopted possibly a sea-going habit, made a sudden spurt of growth and was very likely a newcomer to the Chyne. You will see where this leads us, of course?"

"I'm damned if I do," George Lacklander said.

"O, but yes, surely. The people who, on their own and other evidence, are known to have handled one fish or the other are Mr. Phinn, Mrs. Cartarette and the Colonel himself. Mr. Phinn caught the Old 'Un; Mrs. Cartarette tells us she tried to take a fish away from Thomasina Twitchett. The Colonel handled his own catch and refused to touch the Old 'Un. Lady Lacklander's paint-rag with the traces of both types of fish scales tells us that somebody, we believe the murderer, handled both fish. The further discovery of minute blood-stains tells us that the spike of the shooting-stick was twisted in the rag after being partially cleaned in the earth. If, therefore, with the help of the microscope we could find scales from both fish on the garments of any one of you, that one would be Colonel Cartarette's murderer. That," Alleyn said, "was our belief."

"Was?" Mark said quickly, and Fox, who had been staring at a facetious Victorian hunting print, re-focussed his gaze on his senior officer.

"Yes," Alleyn said. "The telephone conversation I have just had was with one of the Home Office men who are looking after the pathological side. It is from him that I got all this expert's stuff about scales. He tells me that on none of the garments submitted are there scales of both types."

The normal purplish colour flooded back into George Lacklander's face. "I said from the beginning," he shouted, "it was some tramp. Though why the devil you had to—to—" he seemed to hunt for a moderate word—"to put us through the hoops like this—" His voice faded. Alleyn had lifted his hand. "Well?" Lacklander cried out. "What is it? What the hell is it? I beg your pardon, Mama."

Lady Lacklander said automatically, "Don't be an ass, George."

"I'll tell you," Alleyn said, "exactly what the pathologist has found. He has found traces of scales where we expected to find them: on the Colonel's hands and the edge of one cuff, on Mr. Phinn's coat and knickerbockers and, as she warned us, on Mrs. Cartarette's skirt. The first of these traces belongs to group B and the other two to group A. Yes?" Alleyn said, looking at Mark, who had begun to speak and then stopped short.

"Nothing," Mark said. "I—no, go on."

"I've almost finished. I've said that we think the initial blow was made by a golf-club, probably a driver. I may as well tell you at once that so far none of the clubs has revealed any trace of blood. On the other hand, they have all been extremely well cleaned."

George said, "Naturally. My chap does mine."

"When it comes to shoes, however," Alleyn went on, "it's a different story. They too have been well cleaned. But in respect of the right foot of a pair of golfing shoes there is something quite definite. The pathologist is satisfied that the scar left on the Colonel's trout was undoubtedly made by the spiked heel of this shoe."

"It's a bloody lie!" George Lacklander bawled out. "Who are you accusing? Whose shoe?"

"It's a hand-made job. Size four. Made, I should think, as long as ten years ago. From a very old, entirely admirable and hideously expensive bootmaker in the Burlington Arcade. It's your shoe, Lady Lacklander."

Her face was too fat to be expressive. She seemed merely to stare at Alleyn in a meditative fashion, but she had gone very pale. At last she said without moving, "George, it's time to tell the truth."

"That," Alleyn said, "is the conclusion I hoped you would come to."

3

"What are you suggesting?" Nurse Kettle repeated and then, seeing the look in Kitty's face, she shouted, "No! Don't tell me!"

But Kitty had begun to tell her. "It's each for himself in their world," she said, "just the same as in anybody else's. If George Lacklander dreams he can make a monkey out of me, he's going to wake up in a place where he won't have any more funny ideas. What about the old family name then! Look! Do you know what he gets me to do? Break open Maurice's desk because there's something Maurie was going to make public about old Lacklander and George wants to get in first. And when it isn't there, he asks me to find out if it was on the body. No! And when I won't take that one on, what does he say?"

"I don't know. Don't tell me!"

"O, yes, I will. You listen to this and see how you like it. After all the fun and games! Teaching me how to swing—" She made a curious little retching sound in her throat and looked at Nurse Kettle with a kind of astonishment. "You know," she said, "golf. Well, so what does he do? He says, this morning, when he comes to the car with me, he says he thinks it will be better if we don't see much of each other." She suddenly flung out a string of adjectives that Nurse Kettle would have considered un-printable. "That's George Lacklander for you," Kitty Cartarette said.

"You're a wicked woman," Nurse Kettle said. "I forbid you to talk like this. Sir George may have been silly and infatuated. I daresay you've got what it takes, as they say, and he's a widower and I always say there's a trying time for gentlemen just as there is—but that's by the way. What I mean, if he's been silly, it's you that's led him on," Nurse Kettle said, falling back on the inexorable precepts of her kind. "You caught our dear Colonel and not content with that, you set your cap at poor Sir George. You don't mind who you upset or how unhappy you make other people. I know your sort. You're no good. You're no good at all. I shouldn't be surprised if you weren't responsible for what's happened. Not a scrap surprised."

"What the hell do you mean?" Kitty whispered. She curled back in her chair and staring at Nurse Kettle, she said, "You with your poor Sir George! Do you know what I think about your poor Sir George? I think he murdered your poor dear Colonel, Miss Kettle."

Nurse Kettle sprang to her feet. The wrought-iron chair rocked against the table. There was a clatter of china and a jug of milk overturned into Kitty Cartarette's lap.

"How dare you!" Nurse Kettle cried out. "Wicked! Wicked! *Wicked!*"

She heard herself grow shrill and in the very heat of her passion she remembered an important item in her code: Never Raise the Voice. So although she would have found it less difficult to scream like a train, she did contrive to speak quietly. Strangely commonplace phrases emerged, and Kitty, slant-eyed, listened to them. "I would advise you," Nurse Kettle quavered, "to choose your words. People can get into serious trouble passing remarks like that." She achieved an appalling little laugh. "Murdered the Colonel!" she said, and her voice wobbled desperately. "The idea! If it wasn't so dreadful, it'd be funny. With what, may I ask? And how?"

Kitty, too, had risen, and milk dribbled from her ruined skirt to the terrace. She was beside herself with rage.

"How?" she stammered. "I'll tell you how and I'll tell you with what. With a golf-club and his mother's shooting-stick. That's what. Just like a golf ball it was. Bald and shining. Easy to hit. Or an egg. Easy—"

Kitty drew in her breath noisily. Her gaze was fixed, not on Nurse Kettle but beyond Nurse Kettle's left shoulder. Her face was stretched and stamped with terror. It was as if she had laid back her ears. She was looking down the garden towards the spinney.

Nurse Kettle turned.

The afternoon was far advanced and the men who had come up through the spinney cast long shadows across the lawn, reaching almost to Kitty herself. For a moment she and Alleyn looked at each other and then he came forward. In his right hand he carried a pair of very small old-fashioned shoes: brogues with spikes in the heels.

"Mrs. Cartarette," Alleyn said, "I am going to ask you if when you played golf with Sir George Lacklander, he lent you his mother's shoes. Before you answer me, I must warn you—"

Nurse Kettle didn't hear the Usual Warning. She was looking at Kitty Cartarette, in whose face she saw guilt itself. Before this dreadful symptom her own indignation faltered and was replaced, as it were professionally, by a composed, reluctant and utterly useless compassion.

CHAPTER TWELVE **Epilogue**

"George," Lady Lacklander said to her son, "we shall, if you please, get this thing straightened out. There must be no reservations before Mark or—" she waved her fat hand at a singularly still figure in a distant chair—

"or Octavius. Everything will come out later on. We may as well know where we are now, among ourselves. There must be no more evasions."

George looked up and muttered, "Very well, Mama."

"I knew, of course," his mother went on, "that you were having one of your elephantine flirtations with this wretched, unhappy creature. I was afraid that you had been fool enough to tell her about your father's memoirs and all the fuss over Chapter 7. What I must know, now, is how far your affair with her may be said to have influenced her in what she did."

"My God!" George said. "I don't know."

"Did she hope to marry you, George? Did you say things like: 'If only you were free,' to her?"

"Yes," George said, "I did." He looked miserably at his mother and added, "You see, she wasn't. So it didn't seem to matter."

Lady Lacklander snorted but not with her usual brio. "And the memoirs? What did you say to her about them?"

"I just told her about that damned Chapter 7. I just said that if Maurice consulted her, I hoped she'd sort of weigh in on our side. And I—when that was no use—I—I said—that if he did publish, you know, it'd make things so awkward between the families that we—well—"

"All right. I see. Go on."

"She knew he had the copy of Chapter 7 when he went out. She told me that—afterwards—this morning. She said she couldn't ask the police about it, but she knew he'd taken it."

Lady Lacklander moved slightly. Mr. Phinn made a noise in his throat.

"Well, Occy?" she said.

Mr. Phinn, summoned by telephone and strangely acquiescent, said, "My dear Lady L., I can only repeat what I've already told you; had you all relied on my discretion, as I must acknowledge Cartarette did, there would have been no cause for anxiety on any of your parts over Chapter 7."

"You've behaved very handsomely, Occy."

"No, no," he said. "Believe me, no."

"Yes, you have. You put us to shame. Go on, George."

"I don't know that there's anything more. Except—"

"Answer me this, George. Did you suspect her?"

George put his great elderly hand across his eyes and said, "I don't know, Mama. Not at once. Not last night. But this morning. She came by herself, you know. Mark called for Rose. I came downstairs and found her in the hall. It seemed queer. As if she'd been doing something odd."

"From what Rory tells us, she'd been putting my shoes, that you'd lent her without my leave, in the downstairs cloakroom," Lady Lacklander said grimly.

"I am completely at a loss," Mr. Phinn said suddenly.

"Naturally you are, Occy." Lady Lacklander told him about the shoes. "She felt, of course, that she had to get rid of them. They're the ones I wear for sketching when I haven't got a bad toe, and my poor fool of a maid packed them up with the other things. Go on, George."

"Later on, after Alleyn had gone and you went indoors, I talked to her. She was sort of different," said poor George. "Well, damned hard. Sort of almost suggesting—well, I mean, it wasn't exactly the thing."

"I wish you would contrive to be more articulate. She suggested that it wouldn't be long before you'd pay your addresses?"

"Er—er—"

"And then?"

"I suppose I looked a bit taken aback. I don't know what I said. And then—it really was pretty frightful—she sort of began, not exactly hinting, but—well—"

"Hinting," Lady Lacklander said, "will do."

"—that if the police found Chapter 7, they'd begin to think that I—that we—that—"

"Yes, George. We understand. Motive."

"It really was frightful. I said I thought it would be better if we didn't sort of meet much. It was just that I suddenly felt I couldn't. Only that, I assure you, Mama. I assure you, Octavius."

"Yes, yes," they said. "All right, George."

"And then, when I said that, she suddenly looked—" George said this with an unexpected flash—"like a snake."

"And you, my poor boy," his mother added, "looked, no doubt, like the proverbial rabbit."

"I feel I've behaved like one, anyway," George rejoined with a unique touch of humour.

"You've behaved very badly, of course," his mother said without rancour. "You've completely muddled your values. Just like poor Maurice himself, only he went still further. You led a completely unscrupulous trollop to suppose that if she was a widow, you'd marry her. You would certainly have bored her even more than poor Maurice, but Occy will forgive me if I suggest that your title and your money and Nunspardon offered sufficient compensation. You may, on second thoughts, even have attracted her, George," his mother added. "I mustn't, I suppose, under-estimate your simple charms." She contemplated her agonized son for a few minutes and then said, "It all comes to this, and I said as much to Kettle a few days ago: we can't afford to behave shabbily, George. We've got to stick to our own standards, such as they are, and we daren't muddle our values. Let's hope Mark and Rose between them will pick up the pieces." She turned to Mr. Phinn. "If any good has come out of this dreadful affair, Occy," she said, "it is this. You have crossed the Chyne after I don't know how many years and paid a visit to Nunspardon. God knows we have no right to expect it. We can't make amends, Occy. We can't pretend to try. And there it is. It's over, as they say nowadays, to you." She held out her hand and Mr. Phinn, after a moment's hesitation, came forward to take it.

2

"You see, Oliphant," Alleyn said with his customary air of diffidence, "at the outset it tied up with what all of you told me about the Colonel himself. He was an unusually punctilious man. 'Oddly formal,' the Chief Constable said, 'and devilishly polite, especially with people he didn't like or had fallen out with.' He had fallen out with the Lacklanders. One couldn't imagine him squatting on his haunches and going on with his job if Lacklander or his mother turned up in the punt. Or old Phinn, with whom he'd had a flaring row. Then, as you and Gripper pointed out, the first injury had been the sort of blow that is struck by a quarryman on a peg projecting from a cliff-face at knee level, or by an underhand service. Or, you might have added, by a golfer. It seemed likely, too, that the murderer knew the habit of the punt and the counter-current of the Chyne and the fact that where the punt came to rest in the willow-grove bay it was completely masked by trees. You will remember that we found one of Mrs. Cartarette's distinctive yellow hairpins in the punt in close association with a number of cigarette butts, some with lipstick and some not."

"Ah," Sergeant Oliphant said. "Dalliance, no doubt."

"No doubt. When I floated down the stream into the little bay and saw how the daisy heads had been cut off and where they lay, I began to see, also, a figure in the punt idly swinging a club: a figure so familiar to the Colonel that after an upward glance and a word of greeting, he went on cutting grass for his fish. Perhaps, urged by George Lacklander, she asked her husband to suppress the alternative version to Chapter 7 and perhaps he refused. Perhaps Lacklander, in his infatuation, had told her that if she was free, he'd marry her. Perhaps anger and frustration flooded suddenly up to her savage little brain and down her arms into her hands. There was that bald head, like an immense exaggeration of the golf balls she had swiped at under Lacklander's infatuated tuition. She had been slashing idly at the daisies, now she made a complete back-swing, and in a moment her husband was curled up on the bank with the imprint of her club on his temple. From that time on she became a murderess fighting down her panic and frantically engaged in the obliteration of evidence. The print of the golf-club was completely wiped out by her nightmare performance with the shooting-stick, which she had noticed on her way downhill. She tramped on the Colonel's trout, and there was the print of her spiked heel on its hide. She grabbed up the trout and was frantic to get rid of it when she saw Mr. Phinn's cat. One can imagine her watching to see if Thomasina would eat the fish and her relief when she found that she would. She had seen the Old 'Un on the bridge. No doubt she had heard at least the fortissimo passages of Phinn's quarrel with the Colonel. Perhaps the Old 'Un would serve as false evidence. She fetched it and put it down by the body, but in handling the great trout, she let it brush against her skirt. Then she replaced the shooting-stick. Lady Lacklander's paint-rag was folded under the strap of her rucksack. Kitty Cartarette's hands were fishy. She used the rag to wipe them. Then, although she was about to thrust the shooting-stick back into the earth, she saw, probably round the collar of the spike, horrible traces of the use she had made of it. She twisted it madly about in the rag, which was, of course, already extensively stained with paint. No doubt she would have refolded the rag and replaced it, but she heard, may even have seen, Dr. Lacklander. She dropped the rag and bolted for cover. When she emerged, she found he had taken away all the painting gear." Alleyn paused and rubbed his nose. "I wonder," he said, "if it entered her head that Lady Lacklander might be implicated. I wonder exactly when she remembered that she herself was wearing Lady Lacklander's shoes."

He looked from Fox to Oliphant and the attentive Gripper.

"When she got home," he said, "no doubt she at once bathed and changed. She put out her tweed skirt to go to the cleaners. Having attended very carefully to the heel, she then polished Lady Lacklander's shoes. I think that heel must have worried her more than anything else. She guessed that Lacklander hadn't told his mother he'd borrowed the shoes. As we saw this morning, she had no suitable shoes of her own, and her feet are much smaller than her stepdaughter's. She drove herself over to Nunspardon this morning and instead of ringing, walked in and put the shoes in the downstairs cloakroom. I suppose Lady Lacklander's maid believed her mistress to have worn them and accordingly packed them up with her clothes instead of the late Sir Harold's boots which she had actually worn."

Fox said, "When you asked for everybody's clothes, Mrs. Cartarette remembered, of course, that her skirt would smell of fish."

"Yes. She'd put it in the box for the dry cleaning. When she realized we might get hold of the skirt, she remembered the great trout brushing against it. With a mixture of bravado and cunning which is, I think, very characteristic, she boldly told me it would smell of fish and had the nerve and astuteness to use Thomasina as a sort of near-the-truth explanation. She only altered one fact. She said she tried to take a fish away from a cat, whereas she had given a fish to a cat. If she'd read her murdered husband's book, she'd have known that particular cat wouldn't jump, and the story was, in fact, a bit too fishy. The scales didn't match."

Oliphant said suddenly, "It's a terrible thing to happen in the Vale. Terrible the things that'll come out! How's Sir George going to look?"

"He's going to look remarkably foolish," Alleyn said with some heat, "which is no more than he deserves. He's behaved very badly, as his mother has no doubt pointed out to him. What's more, he's made things beastly and difficult for his son, who's a good chap, and for Rose Cartarette, who's a particularly nice child. I should say Sir George Lacklander has let his side down. Of course, he was no match at all for a woman of her hardihood; he'd have been safer with a puff-adder than with Kitty Cartarette, née, Heaven help her, de Vere."

"What, sir, do you reckon—" Oliphant began, and catching sight of his superior's face, was silent.

Alleyn said harshly, "The case will rest on expert evidence of a sort never introduced before. If her counsel is clever and lucky, she'll get an acquittal. If he's not so clever and a bit unlucky, she'll get a lifer." He looked at Fox. "Shall we go?" he said.

He thanked Oliphant and Gripper for their work and went out to the car.

Oliphant said, "Has something upset the Chief, Mr. Fox?"

"Don't you worry," Fox said. "It's the kind of case he doesn't fancy. Capital charge and a woman. Gets to thinking about what he calls first causes."

"First causes?" Oliphant repeated dimly.

"Society. Civilization. Or something," Fox said. "I mustn't keep him waiting. So long."

3

"Darling, darling Rose," Mark said. "We're in for a pretty ghastly time, I know. But we're in for it together, my dearest love, and I'll watch over you and be with you, and when it's all done with, we'll have each other and love each other more than ever before. Won't we? Won't we?"

"Yes," Rose said clinging to him. "We will, won't we?"

"So that something rather wonderful will come out of it all," Mark said. "I promise it will. You'll see."

"As long as we're together."

"That's right," Mark said. "Being together is everything."

And with one of those tricks that memory sometimes plays upon us, Colonel Cartarette's face, as Mark had last seen it in life, rose up clearly in his mind. It wore a singularly compassionate smile.

Together, they drove back to Nunspardon.

4

Nurse Kettle drove in bottom gear to the top of Watt's Hill and there paused. On an impulse, or perhaps inspired by some unacknowledged bit of wishful thinking, she got out and looked down on the village of Swevening. Dusk had begun to seep discreetly into the valley. Smoke rose in cosy plumes from one or two chimneys; roofs cuddled into their surrounding greenery. It was a circumspect landscape. Nurse Kettle revived her old fancy. "As pretty as a picture," she thought wistfully and was again reminded of an illustrated map. With a sigh, she turned back to her faintly trembling car. She was about to seat herself when she heard a kind of strangulated hail. She looked back and there, limping through the dusk, came Commander Syce. The nearer he got to Nurse Kettle, the redder in the face they both became. She lost her head slightly, clambered into her car, turned her engine off and turned it on again. "Pull yourself together, Kettle," she said and leaning out shouted in an unnatural voice, "The top of the evening to you."

Commander Syce came up with her. He stood by the open driving window, and even in her flurry, she noticed that he no longer smelt of stale spirits.

"Ha, ha," he said, laughing hollowly. Sensing perhaps that this was a strange beginning, he began again. "Look here!" he shouted. "Good Lord! Only just heard. Sickening for you. Are you all right? Not too upset and all that? What a thing!"

Nurse Kettle was greatly comforted. She had feared an entirely different reaction to Kitty Cartarette's arrest in Commander Syce.

"What about yourself?" she countered. "It must be a bit of a shock to *you*, after all."

He made a peculiar dismissive gesture with the white object he carried.

"Never mind me. Or rather," Commander Syce amended, dragging feverishly at his collar, "if you can bear it for a moment—"

She now saw that the object was a rolled paper. He thrust it at her. "There you are," he said. "It's nothing, whatever. Don't say a word."

She unrolled it, peering at it in the dusk. "Oh," she cried in an ecstasy, "how lovely! How lovely! It's my picture-map! Oh, *look!* There's Lady Lacklander, sketching in Bottom Meadow. And the doctor with a stork over his head—aren't you a *trick*—and there's me, only you've been much too kind about *me.*" She leant out of the window, turning her lovely map towards the fading light. This brought her closish to Commander Syce, who made a singular little ejaculation and was motionless. Nurse Kettle traced the lively figures through the map: the landlord, the parson, various rustic celebrities. When she came to Hammer Farm, there was the gardener's cottage and his asthmatic child, and there was Rose bending gracefully in the garden. Nearer the house, one could see even in that light, Commander Syce had used thicker paint.

As if, Nurse Kettle thought with a jolt, there had been an erasure.

And down in the willow grove, the Colonel's favourite fishing haunt, there had been made a similar erasure.

"I started it," he said, "some time ago—after your—after your first visit."

She looked up, and between this oddly assorted pair a silence fell.

"Give me six months," Commander Syce said, "to make sure. It'll be all right. Will you?"

Nurse Kettle assured him that she would.

SINGING IN
THE SHROUDS

Contents

Cast of Characters

P. C. Moir
A taxi driver
A sailor
Mrs. Dillington-Blick
Her friend
Mr. Cuddy   *A draper*
Mrs. Cuddy   *His wife*
Miss Katherine Abbott   *An authority on church*
                                    music
Mr. Philip Merryman   *A retired schoolmaster*
Father Charles Jourdain   *An Anglo-Catholic priest*
His brother-cleric
Brigid Carmichael
Dr. Timothy Makepiece   *Medical officer,*
                                    Cape Farewell
Mr. Aubyn Dale   *A celebrity of commercial*
                                    television
His dearest friend
Their dearest male friend
Their dearest female friend
Mr. Donald McAngus   *A philatelist*
Dennis   *A steward*
A wireless officer
Captain Jasper Bannerman   *Master,* Cape Farewell
Superintendent Roderick Alleyn   *C.I.D., New Scotland Yard*

CHAPTER ONE   **Prologue with Corpse**

In the Pool of London and further east all through the dockyards the fog lay heavy. Lights swam like moons in their own halos. Insignificant buildings, being simplified, became dramatic. Along the Cape Line Company's stretch of wharfage the ships at anchor loomed up portentously: *Cape St. Vincent, Glasgow. Cape Horn, London. Cape Farewell, Glasgow.* The cranes that served these ships lost their heads in the fog. Their gestures as they bowed and turned became pontifical.

Beyond their illuminated places the dockyards vanished. The gang loading the *Cape Farewell* moved from light into nothingness. Noises were subdued and isolated and a man's cough close at hand was more startling than the rattle of winches.

Police Constable Moir, on duty until midnight, walked in and out of shadows. He breathed the soft cold smell of wet wood and heard the slap of the night tide against the wharves. Acres and acres of shipping and forests of cranes lay around him. Ships, he thought romantically, were, in a sort of way, like little worlds. Tied up to bollards and lying quiet enough but soon to sail over the watery globe as lonely as the planets wandering in the skies. He would have liked to travel. He solaced himself with thoughts of matrimony, promotion, and when the beat was getting him down a bit, of the Police Medal and sudden glory. At a passageway between buildings near the *Cape Farewell* he walked slower because it was livelier there. Cars drove up; in particular an impressive new sports car with a smashing redhead at the wheel and three passengers, one of whom he recognized with interest as the great television personality Aubyn Dale. It was evident that the others, a man and woman, also belonged to that mysterious world of glaring lights, trucking cameras, and fan mail. You could tell by the way they shouted "Darling" at each other as they walked through the passageway.

P. C. Moir conscientiously moved himself on. Darkness engulfed him, lights revealed him. He had reached the boundary of his beat and was walking along it. A bus had drawn up at the entry to the waterfront and he watched the passengers get out and plod, heads down and suitcases in hand, towards the *Cape Farewell*—a lush bosomy lady and her friend, two clergymen, a married couple, a benevolent-looking gentleman, a lovely young lady with a miserable expression, and a young gentleman who lagged behind and looked as if he'd like to ask her to let him carry her luggage. They walked into the fog, became phantoms, and disappeared down the passageway in the direction of the wharf.

For the next two and a half hours P. C. Moir patrolled the area. He kept an eye on occasional drunks, took a look at parked vehicles, observed ships and pubs, and had an instinctive ear open for any untoward sounds. At half-past eleven he took a turn down the waterfront and into a region of small ambiguous ships, ill-lit and silent, scarcely discernible in the fog that had stealthily accumulated about them.

"Quiet," he thought. "Very quiet, this stretch."

By a strange coincidence (as he was afterwards and repeatedly to point out) he was startled at this very moment by a harsh mewing cry.

"Funny," he thought. "You don't often seem to hear seagulls at night. I suppose they go to sleep like Christians."

The cry sounded again, but shortly, as if somebody had lifted the needle from a record. Moir couldn't really tell from what direction the sound had come, but he fancied it was from somewhere along the Cape Company's wharf. He had arrived at the farthest point of his beat and he now returned. The sounds of activity about the *Cape Farewell* grew clear again. She was still loading.

When he got back to the passageway he found a stationary taxi wreathed in fog and looking desolate. It quite surprised him on drawing nearer to see the driver motionless over the wheel. He was so still that Moir wondered if he was asleep. However, he turned his head and peered out.

"Evening, mate," Moir said. "Nice night to get lost in."

"And that's no error," the driver agreed hoarsely. " 'Ere!" he continued, leaning out and looking fixedly at the policeman. "You seen anybody?"

"How d'you mean, seen?"

"A skirt. Wiv a boxerflahs."

"No," Moir said. "Your fare, would it be?"

"Ah! My fare! 'Alf a minute at the outside, she says, and nips off lively. 'Alf a minute! 'Alf a bloody ar, more likely."

"Where'd she go? Ship?" asked Moir, jerking his head in the direction of the *Cape Farewell*.

"'Course. Works at a flah shop. Cartin' rahnd bokays to some silly bitch wot'll frow 'em to the fishes, like as not. Look at the time: arpas eleven. Flahs!"

"P'raps she couldn't find the recipient," P. C. Moir ventured, using police-court language out of habit.

"P'raps she couldn't find the flippin' ship nor yet the ruddy ocean! P'raps she's a drahned," said the taxi driver in a passion.

"Hope it's not all that serious, I'm sure."

"Where's my fare comin' from? Twelve and a tanner gone up and when do I get it? Swelp me Bob if I don't cut me losses and sling me 'ook."

"I wouldn't do that," P. C. Moir said. "Stick it a bit longer, I would. She'll be back. Tell you what, Aubyn Dale's on board that ship."

"Bloke that does the Jolyon Swimsuits session on commercial?"

"That's right. Daresay she's spotted him and can't tear herself away. They go nuts over Aubyn Dale."

"Silly cows," the taxi driver muttered. "*Telly!*"

"Why don't you stroll along to the ship and get a message up to her?"

"Why the hell should I!"

"Come on. I'll go with you. I'm heading that way."

The driver muttered indistinguishably but he clambered out of his taxi and together they walked down the passageway. It was a longish passage and very dark, but the lighted wharf showed up mistily at the far end. When they came out they were almost alongside the ship. Her stern loomed up through the fog with her name across it:

CAPE FAREWELL
GLASGOW

Her after and amidships hatches had been shut down and, forward, her last load was being taken. Above her lighted gangway stood a sailor, leaning over the rails. P. C. Moir looked up at him.

"Seen anything of a young lady who brought some flowers on board, mate?" he asked.

"Would that be about two hours back?"

"More like half an hour."

"There's been nobody like that since I first come on and that's eight bells."

"'Ere!" said the driver. "There must of."

"Well, there wasn't. I been on duty here constant. No flowers come aboard after eight bells."

P. C. Moir said, "Well, thanks, anyway. P'raps she met some one on the wharf and handed them over."

"No flowers never come aboard with nobody. Not since when I told you. Eight bells."

"Awright, awright, we 'eard," said the driver ungratefully. "*Bells!*"

"Are your passengers all aboard?" Moir asked.

"Last one come aboard five minutes back. All present and correct including Mr. Aubyn Dale. You'd never pick him, though, now he's slaughtered them whiskers. What a change! Oh, dear!" The sailor made a gesture that might have indicated his chin, or his neck. "I reckon he'd do better to grow again," he said.

"Anyone else been about? Anyone you couldn't place, at all?"

"Hullo-ullo! What's wrong, anyway?"

"Nothing so far as I know. Nothing at all."

The sailor said, "It's been quiet. The fog makes it quiet." He spat carefully overboard. "I heard some poor sod singing," he said. "Just the voice; funny sort of voice, too. Might of been a female and yet I don't reckon it was. I didn't rekkernize the chune."

Moir waited a moment and then said, "Well, thanks again, sailor, we'll be moving along."

When he had withdrawn the driver to a suitable distance he said, coughing a little because a drift of fog had caught him in the throat, "What was she like, daddy? To look at?"

The taxi driver gave him a jaundiced and confused description of his fare in which the only clear glimpse to emerge was of a flash piece with a lot of yellow hair done very fancy. Pressed further, the driver remembered pin-heels. When she left the taxi the girl had caught her foot in a gap between two planks and had paused to adjust her shoe.

Moir listened attentively. "Right you are," he said. "Now, I think I'll just take a wee look round, daddy. You go back to your cab and wait. *Wait*, see?"

This suggestion evoked a fresh spate of expostulation, but Moir became authoritative and the driver finally returned to his cab. Moir looked after him for a moment and then walked along to the forward winch, where he was received by the shore gang with a degree of guarded curiosity that in some circles is reserved for the police. He asked them if they had seen the girl and repeated the driver's description. None of them had.

As he was turning away one of the men said, "What seems to be the trouble, anyway, copper?"

"Not to say trouble," Moir called back easily.

A second voice asked derisively, "Why don't you get the Flower Murderer, Superintendent?"

Moir said good-naturedly, "We're still hoping, mate." And walked away, a man alone on his job.

He began to look for the girl from the flower shop. There were many dark places along the wharf. He moved slowly, flashing his lamp into the areas under platforms, behind packing cases, between buildings and dumps of cargo and along the dark surface of the water, where it made unsavoury but irrelevant discoveries.

It was much quieter now aboard the *Farewell*. He heard the covers go down on the forward hatch and glancing up could just see the blue peter hanging limp in the fog. The gang that had been loading the ship went off through one of the sheds and their voices faded into silence.

He arrived back at the passageway. Beyond its far end the taxi still waited. On their way through here to the wharf he and the driver had walked quickly; now he went at a snail's pace, using his flashlight. He knew that surfaces which in the dark and fog looked like unbroken walls were in fact the rear ends of sheds with gaps between them. There was an alley opening off the main passage and this was dark indeed.

It was now one minute to midnight and the *Cape Farewell*, being about to sail, gave a raucous unexpected hoot like a gargantuan belch. It jolted P. C. Moir in the pit of his stomach.

With a sudden scrabble a rat shot out and ran across his boots. He swore, stumbled, and lurched sideways. The light from his flashlamp darted eccentrically up the side alley, momentarily exhibiting a high-heeled shoe with a foot in it. The light fluttered, steadied, and returned. It crept from the foot along a leg, showing a red graze through the gap in its nylon stocking. It moved on and came to rest at last on a litter of artificial pink pearls and fresh flowers scattered over the breast of a dead girl.

CHAPTER TWO **Embarkation**

At seven o'clock on that same evening an omnibus had left Euston Station for the Royal Albert Docks.

It had carried ten passengers, seven of whom were to embark in the *Cape Farewell*, sailing at midnight for South Africa. Of the remainder, two were seeing-off friends, while the last was the ship's doctor, a young man who sat alone and did not lift his gaze from the pages of a formidable book.

After the manner of travellers, the ship's passengers had taken furtive stock of each other. Those who were escorted by friends speculated in undertones about those who were not.

"My *dear!*" Mrs. Dillington-Blick ejaculated. "*Honestly!* Not *one!*"

Her friend made a slight grimace in the direction of the doctor and raised her eyebrows. "Not bad?" she mouthed. "Noticed?"

Mrs. Dillington-Blick shifted her shoulders under their mantling of silver fox and turned her head until she was able to include the doctor in an absent-minded glance.

"I *hadn't* noticed," she confessed and added, "Rather nice? But the others! My dear! Best forgotten! Still—"

"There *are* the officers," the friend hinted slyly.

"My dear!"

They caught each other's eyes and laughed again, cosily. Mr. and Mrs. Cuddy in the seat in front of them heard their laughter. The Cuddys could smell Mrs. Dillington-Blick's expensive scent. By turning their heads slightly they could see her reflection in the window-pane, like a photomontage richly floating across street lamps and the façades of darkened buildings. They could see the ghosts of her teeth, the feather in her hat, her earrings, the orchids on her great bust, and her furs.

Mrs. Cuddy stiffened in her navy overcoat and her husband smiled thinly. They, too, exchanged glances and thought of derisive things to say to each other when they were private in their cabin.

In front of the Cuddys sat Miss Katherine Abbott—alone, neat and composed. She was a practised traveller and knew that the first impression made by fellow passengers is usually contradicted by experience. She rather liked the rich sound of Mrs. Dillington-Blick's laughter and deplored what she had heard of the Cuddy accent. But her chief concern at the moment was for her own comfort; she disliked being ruffled and had chosen her seat in the middle of the bus because people would be unlikely to brush past her and she was out of the draught when the door opened. In her mind she checked over the contents of her two immaculately packed suitcases. She travelled extremely light because she loathed what she called the "fussation" of heavy luggage. With a single exception she carried nothing that was not positively essential. She thought now of the exception, a photograph in a leather case. To her fury her eyes began to sting. "I'll throw it overboard," she thought. "That'll larn her."

The man in front of her turned a page of his newspaper and through her unshed tears Miss Abbott read a banner headline: KILLER WHO SAYS

IT WITH FLOWERS. STILL NO ARREST. She had longish sight and by casually leaning forward she was able to read the paragraph underneath.

The identity of the sex murderer who sings as he kills and leaves flowers by the bodies of his victims is still unknown. Investigations leading to hundreds of interviews have been clueless. Here is a new snapshot, exclusive to the *Evening Herald*, of piquant Beryl Cohen, found strangled ten days ago, the latest victim in this worst list of sex crimes since Jack the Ripper. Superintendent Alleyn (inset) refuses to make a statement, but says the police will welcome information about Beryl's movements during her last hours (see page 6, 2nd column).

Miss Abbott waited for the owner of the newspaper to turn to page 6 but he neglected to do so. She stared greedily at the enlarged snapshot of piquant Beryl Cohen and derisively at the inset. Superintendent Alleyn, grossly disfigured by the exigencies of reproduction in newsprint, stared dimly back at her.

The owner of the paper began to fidget. Suddenly he turned his head, obliging Miss Abbott to throw back her own and stare vaguely at the luggage rack, where she immediately spotted his suitcase with a dangling label: "P. Merryman, Passenger, S.S. *Cape Farewell*." She had an uncomfortable notion that Mr. Merryman knew she had been reading over his shoulder and in this she was perfectly right.

Mr. Philip Merryman was fifty years old and a bachelor. He was a man of learning and taught English in one of the less distinguished of the smaller public schools. His general appearance, which was highly deceptive, corresponded closely with the popular idea of a schoolmaster, while a habit of looking over the tops of his spectacles and ruffling his hair filled in the outlines of this over-familiar picture. To the casual observer Mr. Merryman was a perfect Chips. To his intimates he could be hell.

He was fond of reading about crime, whether fictitious or actual, and had dwelt at some length on the *Evening Herald's* piece about the Flower Murderer, as in its slipshod way it called this undetected killer. Mr. Merryman deplored journalese and had the poorest possible opinion of the methods of the police, but the story itself quite fascinated him. He read slowly and methodically, wincing at stylistic solecisms and bitterly resentful of Miss Abbott's trespassing glances. "Detested kite!" Mr. Merryman silently apostrophized her. "Blasts and fogs upon you! Why in the names of all the gods at once can you not buy your own disnatured newspaper!"

He turned to page 6, moved the *Evening Herald* out of Miss Abbott's line of sight, read column 2 as quickly as possible, folded the newspaper, rose, and offered it to her with a bow.

"Madam," Mr. Merryman said, "allow me. No doubt you prefer, as I confess I do, the undisputed possession of your chosen form of literature. Perhaps you have already seen it?"

"No," said Miss Abbott loudly. "I haven't and what's more, I don't want to. Thank you."

Father Charles Jourdain muttered whimsically to his brother-cleric, "Seeds of discord! Seeds of discord!" They were in the seat opposite and could scarcely escape noticing the incident.

"I do hope," the brother-cleric murmured, "that you find someone moderately congenial."

"In my experience there is always someone."

"And you *are* an experienced traveller." The other sighed, rather wistfully.

"Would you have liked the job so much, Father? I'm sorry."

"No, no, no, please don't think it for a moment, really. I would carry no weight in Durban. Father Superior, as always, has made the wisest possible choice. And you are glad to be going—I hope?"

Father Jourdain waited for a moment and then said, "Oh, yes. Yes. I'm glad to go."

"It will be so interesting. The community in Africa—"

They settled down to talk Anglo-Catholic shop.

Mrs. Cuddy, overhearing them, smelt Popery.

The remaining ship's passenger in the bus took no notice at all of her companions. She sat in the front seat with her hands thrust deep into the pockets of her camel's-hair coat. She had a black Zouave hat on the back of her head and a black belt round her waist. She was so good-looking that all the tears she had shed still left her attractive. She was not crying now. She tucked her chin into her scarf and scowled at the bus driver's back. Her name was Brigid Carmichael. She was twenty-three and had been crossed in love.

The bus lurched up Ludgate Hill. Dr. Timothy Makepiece put down his book and leaned forward, stooping, to see the last of St. Paul's. There it was, fabulous against the night sky. He experienced a sensation which he himself would have attributed, no doubt correctly, to a disturbance of the nervous ganglions but which laymen occasionally describe as a turning over of the heart. This must be, he supposed, because he was leaving London. He had come to that conclusion when he found he was no longer staring at the dome of St. Paul's but into the eyes of the girl in the front seat. She had turned, evidently with the same intention as his own, to look out and upwards.

Father Jourdain was saying, "Have you ever read that rather exciting thing of G.K.C.'s, *The Ball and the Cross?*"

Brigid carefully made her eyes blank and faced front. Dr. Makepiece returned uneasily to his book. He was filled with a kind of astonishment.

2

At about the same time as the bus passed by St. Paul's, a very smart sports car had left a very smart mews flat in Mayfair. In it were Aubyn Dale, his dearest friend (who owned the car and sat at the wheel in a mink coat) and their two dearest friends, who were entwined in the back seat. They had all enjoyed an expensive farewell dinner and were bound for the docks. "The form," the dearest friend said, "is unlimited wassail, darling, in your stateroom. Drunk, I shall be less disconsolate."

"But, *darling!*" Mr. Dale rejoined tenderly. "You shall be *plastered!* I promised! It's all laid on."

She thanked him fondly and presently turned into the Embankment, where she drove across the bows of an oncoming taxi whose driver cursed her very heartily. His fare, a Mr. Donald McAngus, peered anxiously out of the window. He also was a passenger for the *Cape Farewell.*

About two and a half hours later a taxi would leave the Green Thumb flower shop in Knightsbridge for the East End. In it would be a fair-haired girl and a box of flowers which was covered with cellophane, garnished with a huge bow of yellow ribbon and addressed to Mrs. Dillington-Blick. The taxi would head eastward. It, too, was destined for the Royal Albert Docks.

3

From the moment she came aboard the *Cape Farewell*, Mrs. Dillington-Blick had automatically begun to practise what her friends, among themselves, called her technique. She had turned her attention first upon the steward. The *Farewell* carried only nine passengers and one steward attended them all. He was a pale, extremely plump young man with blond hair that looked crimped, liquid eyes, a mole at the corner of his mouth, and a voice that was strongly cockney, strangely affected, and indescribably familiar. Mrs. Dillington-Blick took no end of trouble with him. She asked him his name (it was Dennis) and discovered that he also served in the bar. She gave him three pounds and hinted that this was merely an initial gesture. In less than no time she had discovered that he was twenty-five, played the mouth-organ, and had taken a dislike to Mr. and Mrs.

Cuddy. He showed a tendency to linger, but somehow or another, and in the pleasantest manner, she contrived to get rid of him.

"You are wonderful!" her friend exclaimed.

"My dear!" Mrs. Dillington-Blick returned. "He'll put my make-up in the refrigerator when we get to the tropics."

Her cabin was full of flowers. Dennis came back with vases for them and suggested that the orchids also should be kept in the refrigerator. The ladies exchanged glances. Mrs. Dillington-Blick unpinned the cards on her flowers and read out the names with soft little cries of appreciation. The cabin, with its demure appointments and sombre décor, seemed to be full of her—of her scent, her furs, her flowers, and herself.

"Steward!" a querulous voice at this juncture called in the passage. Dennis raised his eyebrows and went out.

"He's your slave," the friend said. "Honestly!"

"I like to be comfortable," said Mrs. Dillington-Blick.

It was Mr. Merryman who had shouted for Dennis. When it comes to separating the easygoing from the exacting passenger, stewards are not easily deceived. But Dennis had been taken in by Mr. Merryman. The spectacles, the rumpled hair, and cherubic countenance had led him to diagnose absence of mind, benevolence, and timidity. He was bitterly disappointed when Mr. Merryman now gave unmistakable signs of being a holy terror. Nothing, it seemed, was right with the cabin. Mr. Merryman had stipulated the port side and found himself on the starboard. His luggage had not been satisfactorily stowed and he wished his bed to be made up in the manner practised on land and not, he said, like an unstuck circular.

Dennis had listened to these complaints with an air of resignation, just not casting up his eyes.

"Quite a chapter of accidents," he said when Mr. Merryman paused. "Yerse. Well, we'll see what we can do for you." He added, "Sir," but not in the manner required by Mr. Merryman at his minor public school.

Mr. Merryman said, "You will carry out my instructions immediately. I am going to take a short walk. When I return I shall expect to find it done." Dennis opened his mouth. Mr. Merryman said, "That will do." Rather pointedly he then locked a case on his dressing table and walked out of the cabin.

"And I'll take me oaf," Dennis muttered pettishly, "he's T.T. into the bargain. What an old bee!"

Father Jourdain's brother-priest had helped him to bestow his modest possessions about his room. This done, they had looked at each other with the hesitant and slightly self-conscious manner of men who are about to take leave of each other.

"Well—" they both said together and Father Jourdain added, "It was good of you to come all this way. I've been glad of your company."

"Have you?" his colleague rejoined. "And I, needless to say, of yours." He hid his hands under his cloak and stood modestly before Father Jourdain. "The bus leaves at eleven," he said. "You'd like to settle down, I expect."

Father Jourdain asked, smiling, "Is there something you want to say to me?"

"Nothing of the smallest consequence. It's just—well, I've suddenly realized how very much it's meant to me having the great benefit of your example."

"My dear man!"

"No, really! You strike me, Father, as being quite tremendously sufficient (under God and our rule, of course) to yourself. All the brothers are a little in awe of you, did you know? I think we all feel that we know much less about you than we do about each other. Father Bernard said the other day that although ours is not a silent order you kept your own rule of spiritual silence."

"I don't know that I am altogether delighted by Father Bernard's aphorism."

"Aren't you? He meant it awfully nicely. But I really do chatter much too much. I should take myself in hand and do something about it, I expect. Good-bye, Father. God bless you."

"And you, my dear fellow. But I'll walk with you to the bus."

"No—please—"

"I should like to."

They found their way down to the lower deck. Father Jourdain said a word to the sailor at the head of the gangway and both priests went ashore. The sailor watched them pace along the wharf towards the passageway at the far end of which the bus waited. In their black cloaks and hats they looked fantastic. The fog swirled about them as they walked. Half an hour had gone by before Father Jourdain returned alone. It was then a quarter past eleven.

Miss Abbott's cabin was opposite Mrs. Dillington-Blick's. Dennis carried the suitcases to it. Their owner unpacked them with meticulous efficiency, laying folded garments away as if for some ceremonial robing. They were of a severe character. At the bottom of the second suitcase there was a stack of music in manuscript. In a pocket of the suitcase was the photograph. It was of a woman of about Miss Abbott's own age, moderately handsome but with a heavy dissatisfied look. Miss Abbott stared at it, and fighting back a painful sense of desolation and resentment, sat on the bed and pressed clumsy hands between large knees.

Time went by. The ship moved a little at her moorings. Miss Abbott heard Mrs. Dillington-Blick's rich laughter and was remotely and very slightly eased. There was the noise of fresh arrivals, of footsteps overhead, and of dockside activities. From a more distant part of the passengers' quarters came sounds of revelry and of a resonant male voice that was somehow familiar. Soon Miss Abbott was to know why. The cabin door had been hooked ajar, so that when Mrs. Dillington-Blick's friend came into the passage she was very clearly audible. Mrs. Dillington-Blick stood in her own open doorway and said through giggles, "Go on, then, I dare you," and the friend went creaking down the passage. She returned evidently in high excitement saying, "My dear, it is! He's shaved it off! The steward told me. It's Aubyn Dale! My dear, how perfectly gorgeous for you."

There was another burst of giggling, through which Mrs. Dillington-Blick said something about not being able to wait for the tropics to wear her Jolyon swimsuit. Their further ejaculations were cut off by the shutting of their door.

"Silly fools," Miss Abbott thought dully, having not the smallest interest in television personalities. Presently she began to wonder if she really would throw the photograph overboard when the ship was out at sea. Suppose she were to tear it up now and drop the pieces in the wastepaper basket? Or into the harbour? How lonely she would be then! The heavily knuckled fingers drummed on the bony knees and their owner began to think about things going overboard into the harbour. The water would be cold and dirty, polluted by the excreta of ships; revolting!

"Oh, *God!*" Miss Abbott said. "How hellishly unhappy I am."

Dennis knocked at her door.

"Telegram, Miss Abbott," he fluted.

"Telegram? For me? Yes?"

He unhooked the door and came in.

Miss Abbott took the telegram and shakily opened it. It fluttered between her fingers.

DARLING ABBEY SO MISERABLE DO PLEASE WRITE OR IF NOT TOO LATE TELEPHONE. F.

Dennis had lingered. Miss Abbott said shakily, "Can I send an answer?"

"Well—ye-ees. I mean to say—"

"Or telephone? Can I telephone?"

"There's a 'phone on board, but I seen a queue lined up when I passed."

"How long before we sail?"

"An hour, near enough, but the 'phone goes off earlier."

Miss Abbott said distractedly, "It's very important. Very urgent indeed."

"'Tch, 'tch."

"Wait. Didn't I see a call box on the dock? Near the place where the bus stopped?"

"That's correct," he said appreciatively. "Fancy you noticing!"

"I've time to go off, haven't I?"

"Plenty of *time*, Miss Abbott. Oodles."

"I'll do that. I'll go at once."

"There's coffee and sandwiches on in the dining-room."

"I don't want them. I'll go now."

"Cold outside. Proper freezer. Need a coat, Miss Abbott, won't you?"

"It doesn't matter. Oh, very well. Thank you."

She took her coat out of the wardrobe, snatched up her handbag, and hurried out.

"Straight ahead, down the companionway and turn right," he called after her and added, "Don't get lost in the fog, now."

Her manner had been so disturbed that it aroused his curiosity. He went out on the deck and was in time to see her running along the wharf into the fog. "Runs like a man," Dennis thought. "Well, it takes all sorts."

Mr. and Mrs. Cuddy sat on their respective beds and eyed each other with the semi-jocular family air that they reserved for intimate occasions. The blowers on the bulkhead were pouring hot air into the cabin, the porthole was sealed, the luggage was stowed, and the Cuddys were cosy.

"All right so far," Mrs. Cuddy said guardedly.

"Satisfied, dear?"

"Can't complain. Seems clean."

"Our own shower and toilet," he pointed out, jerking his head at a narrow door.

"They've all got that," she said. "I wouldn't fancy sharing."

"What did you make of the crowd, though? Funny lot, I thought."

"R. C. priests."

"Only the one. The other was seeing-off. Do you reckon R. C.?"

"Looked like it, didn't it?"

Mr. Cuddy smiled. He had a strange thin smile, very broad and knowing. "They look ridiculous to me," he said.

"We're moving in high society, it seems," Mrs. Cuddy remarked. "Notice the furs?"

"And the *perfume!* Phew!"

"I'll have to keep my eye on you, I can see that."

"Could you catch what was said?"

"Quite a bit," Mrs. Cuddy admitted. "She may talk very la-de-dah, but her ideas aren't so refined."

"Reely?"

"She's a man-eater."

Mr. Cuddy's smile broadened. "Did you get the flowers?" he asked. "Orchids. Thirty bob each, they are."

"Get on!"

"They are! It's a fact. Very nice, too," Mr. Cuddy said with a curious twist in his voice.

"Did you see what happened with the other lady reading over the elderly chap's shoulder? In the bus?"

"Did I what! Talk about a freezer! Phew!"

"He was reading about those murders. You know. The Flower Murderer. They make out he leaves flowers all scattered over the breasts of his victims. And sings."

"Before or after?"

"After, isn't it awful?" Mrs. Cuddy asked with enormous relish.

Mr. Cuddy made an indefinite noise.

His wife ruminated, "It gives me the creeps to think about. Wonder what makes him go on so crazy."

"Women."

"That's right. Put it all on the ladies," she said good-naturedly. "Just like a man."

"Well, ask yourself. Was there much in the paper?"

"I couldn't see properly, but I think so. It's on all the placards. They haven't got him, of course."

"Wish we'd got a paper. Can't think how I forgot."

"There might be one in the lounge."

"What a hope!"

"The old chap left his in the bus. I noticed."

"Did you? You know," Mr. Cuddy said, "I've got quite a fancy for the evening paper. I might stroll back and see if it's there. The bus doesn't go till eleven. I can just do it."

"Don't be long. You know what I'm like. If you missed the boat—"

"We don't sail till midnight, dear, and it's only ten to eleven now. I won't be more than a few minutes. Think I'd let you go out to sea with all these fascinatin' sailors?"

"Get along with you!"

"Won't be half a tick. I've got the fancy for it."

"I know I'm silly," Mrs. Cuddy said, "but whenever you go out—to the lodge or anything—I always get that *nervous*."

"Silly girl. I'd say come too, but it's not worth it. There's coffee on down below."

"Coffee essence, more like."

"Might as well try it when I get back. Behave yourself now."

He pulled a steel-grey felt hat down almost to his ears, put on a belted raincoat, and looking rather like the film director's idea of a private detective, he went ashore.

Mrs. Cuddy remained, anxious and upright, on her bunk.

Aubyn Dale's dearest friend, looking through the porthole, said with difficulty, "Darling, it's boiling up for a peashuper-souper. I think perhaps we ought to weep ourselves away."

"Darling, are you going to drive?"

"Naturally."

"You *will* be all right, *won't* you?"

"Sweetie," she protested, "I'm never safer than when I'm plastered. It just gives me that little something other drivers haven't got."

"How terrifying."

"To show you how completely in control I am, I suggest that it might be better to leave before we're utterly fogged down. Oh, dear! I fear I am now going into a screaming weep. Where's my hanky?"

She opened her bag. A coiled mechanical snake leaped out at her, having been secreted there by her lover, who had a taste for such drolleries. This prank, though it was received as routine procedure, a little delayed their parting. Finally, however, it was agreed that the time had come.

" 'Specially," said their dearest male friend, "as we've killed the last bottle. Sorry, old boy. Bad form. Poor show."

"Come on," said their dearest girl friend. "It's been smashing, actually. Darling Auby! But we ought to go."

They began elaborate leave-takings but Aubyn Dale said he'd walk back to the car with them.

They all went ashore, talking rather loudly, in well-trained voices, about the fog, which had grown much heavier.

It was now five past eleven. The bus had gone, the solitary taxi waited in its place. Their car was parked further along the wharf. They stood round it, still talking, for some minutes. His friends all told Dale many times how much good the voyage would do him, how nice he looked without his celebrated beard, how run down he was, and how desperately the Jolyon swimsuit programme would sag without him. Finally they drove off waving and trying to make hip-hip-hooray with their horn.

Aubyn Dale waved, shoved his hands down in the pockets of his camel's-hair coat, and walked back towards the ship. A little damp breeze lifted his hair, eddies of fog drifted past him. He thought how very photogenic the wharves looked. The funnels on some of the ships were lit from below and the effect, blurred and nebulous though it now had become, was exciting. Lights hung like globes in the murk. There were hollow indefinable sounds and a variety of smells. He pictured himself down here doing one of his special features and began to choose atmospheric phrases. He would have looked rather good, he thought, framed in the entrance to the passageway. His hand strayed to his naked chin and he shuddered. He must pull himself together.

The whole idea of the voyage was to get away from his job; not to think of it, even. Or of anything else that was at all upsetting. Such as his dearest friend, sweetie though she undoubtedly was. Immediately, he began to think about her. He ought to have given her something before she left. Flowers? No, no. Not flowers. They had an unpleasant association. He felt himself grow cold and then hot. He clenched his hands and walked into the passageway.

About two minutes later the ninth and last passenger for the *Cape Farewell* arrived by taxi at the docks. He was Mr. Donald McAngus, an elderly bachelor, who was suffering from a terrible onset of ship-fever. The fog along the Embankment had grown heavier. In the City it had been atrocious. Several times his taxi had come to a stop, twice it had gone off its course, and finally, when he was really feeling physically sick with anxiety, the driver had announced that this was as far as he cared to go. He indicated shapes, scarcely perceptible, of roofs and walls and the faint glow beyond them. That, he said, was where Mr. McAngus's ship lay. He had merely to make for the glow and he would be aboard. There ensued a terrible complication over the fare, and the tip; first Mr. McAngus undertipped and then, in a frenzy of apprehension, he overtipped. The driver adopted a pitying attitude. He put Mr. McAngus's fibre suitcases into their owner's grip and tucked his cardboard box and his brown paper parcel under his arms. Thus burdened, Mr. McAngus disappeared at a shambling trot into the fog and the taxi returned to the West End of London.

The time was now eleven-thirty. The taxi from the flower shop was waiting for his fare and P. C. Moir was about to engage him in conversation. The last hatch was covered, the *Cape Farewell* was cleared, and Captain Bannerman, master, awaited his pilot.

At one minute to twelve the siren hooted.

P. C. Moir was now at the police call box. He had been put through to the C.I.D.

"There's one other thing, sir," he was saying, "beside the flowers. There's a bit of paper clutched in the right hand, sir. It appears to be a fragment of an embarkation notice, like they give passengers. For the *Cape Farewell*."

He listened, turning his head to look across the tops of half-seen roofs at the wraith of a scarlet funnel with a white band. It slid away and vanished smoothly into the fog.

"I'm afraid I can't board her, sir," he said. "She's sailed."

CHAPTER THREE **Departure**

At regular two-minute intervals throughout the night, *Cape Farewell* sounded her siren. The passengers who slept were still, at times, conscious of this noise; as of some monster blowing monstrous raspberries through their dreams. Those who waked listened with varying degrees of nervous exasperation. Aubyn Dale, for instance, tried to count the seconds between blasts, sometimes making them come to as many as one hundred and thirty and at other times, by a deliberate tardiness, getting them down to one hundred and fifteen. He then tried counting his pulse but this excited him. His heart behaved with the greatest eccentricity. He began to think of all the things it was better not to think of, including the worst one of all—the awful debacle of the Midsummer Fair at Molton Medbury. This was just the sort of thing that his psychiatrist had sent him on the voyage to forget. He had already taken one of his sleeping pills. At two o'clock he took another and it was effective.

Mr. Cuddy also was restive. He had recovered Mr. Merryman's *Evening Herald* from the bus. It was in a somewhat dishevelled condition, but when he got into bed he read it exhaustively, particularly the pieces about the Flower Murderer. Occasionally he read aloud for Mrs. Cuddy's entertainment, but presently her energetic snores informed him that this exercise was profitless. He let the newspaper fall to the deck and began to listen to the siren. He wondered if his fellow travellers would exhibit a snobbish attitude towards Mrs. Cuddy and himself. He thought of Mrs. Dillington-Blick's orchids, heaving a little at their superb anchorage, and he gradually slipped into an uneasy doze.

Mr. Merryman, on the other hand, slept heavily. If he was visited by dreams of a familiar steward or an inquisitive spinster, they were of too deeply unconscious a nature to be recollected. Like many people of an irascible temperament, he seemed to find compensation for his troubles in the profundity of his slumber.

So, too, did Father Jourdain, who on finishing his prayers, getting into bed and putting himself through one or two pretty stiff devotional hoops, fell into a quiet oblivion that lasted until morning.

Mr. Donald McAngus took a little time to recover from the circumstances that attended his late arrival. However, he had taken coffee and sandwiches in the dining-room and had eyed his fellow passengers with circumspection and extreme curiosity. His was the not necessarily malicious but all-absorbing inquisitiveness of the Lowland Scot. He gathered facts about other people as an indiscriminate philatelist gathers stamps—merely for the sake of adding to his collection. He had found himself at the same table as the Cuddys—the passengers had not yet been given their official places—and had already discovered that they lived in Dulwich and that Mr. Cuddy was "in business," though of what nature Mr. McAngus had been unable to divine. He had told them about his trouble with the taxi. Distressed by Mrs. Cuddy's unwavering stare he had tied himself up in a tangle of parentheses and retired unsatisfied to his room and his bed.

There he lay tidily all night in his gay crimson pyjamas, occupied with thoughts so unco-ordinated and feckless that they modulated imperceptibly into dreams and were not at all disturbed by the reiterated booming of the siren.

Miss Abbott had returned from the call box on the wharf scarcely aware of the fog and with a dull effulgence under her darkish skin. The sailor at the gangway noticed and was afterwards to remember her air of suppressed excitement. She went to bed and was still wide-awake when the ship sailed. She watched blurred lights slide past the porthole and felt the throb of the engines at dead slow. At about one o'clock in the morning she fell asleep.

Brigid Carmichael hadn't paid much attention to her companions; it took all her determination and fortitude to hold back her tears. She kept telling herself angrily that crying was a voluntary physical process, entirely controllable, and in her case absolutely without justification. Lots of other people had their engagements broken off at the last minute and were none the worse for it, most of them without her chance of cutting her losses and bolting to South Africa.

It had been a mistake to peer up at St. Paul's. That particular kind of beauty always got under her emotional guard; and there she went again with the man in the opposite seat looking into her face as if he'd like to be sorry for her. From then onwards the bus journey had seemed intolerable but the walk through the fog to the ship had been better. It was almost funny that her departure should be attended by such obvious gloom. She had noticed Mrs. Dillington-Blick's high-heeled patent leather shoes tittupping ahead and had heard scraps of the Cuddys' conversation. She had also been conscious of the young man walking just behind her. When they had emerged from the passageway to the wharf he said, "Look, do let me carry that suitcase," and had taken it out of her hand before she could expostulate. "My stuff's all on board," he said. "I feel unimportant with nothing in my hand. Don't you hate feeling unimportant?"

"Well, no," Brigid said, surprised into an unconventional reply. "At the moment, I'm not minding it."

"Perhaps it's a change for you."

"Not at all," she said hurriedly.

"Or perhaps women are naturally shrinking creatures, after all. 'Such,' you may be thinking, 'is the essential vanity of the human male.' And you are perfectly right. Did you know that Aubyn Dale is to be a passenger?"

"Is he?" Brigid said without much interest. "I would have thought a luxury liner and organized fun would be more his cup of tea."

"I understand it's a rest cure. Far away from the madding camera, and I bet you anything you like that in no time he'll be missing his spotlights. I'm the doctor, by the way, and this is my first long voyage. My name's Timothy Makepiece. You must be either Miss Katherine Abbott or Miss Brigid Carmichael, and I can't help hoping it's the latter."

"You'd be in a bit of a spot if it wasn't," Brigid said.

"I risked everything on the one throw. Rightly, I perceive. Is it your first long voyage?"

"Yes."

"You don't sound as excited as I would have expected. This is the ship, looming up. It's nice to think we shall be meeting again. What is your cabin number? I'm not being fresh; I just want to put your bag in it."

"It's four. Thank you very much."

"Not at all," said Dr. Makepiece politely. He led the way to her cabin, put her suitcase into it, made her a rather diffident little bow and went away.

Brigid thought without much interest, "The funny thing is that I don't believe that young man was putting on an act," and at once stopped thinking about him.

Her own predicament came swamping over her again and she began to feel a great desolation of the spirit. She had begged her parents and her friends not to come to the ship, not to see her off at all, and already it seemed a long time ago that she had said good-bye to them. She felt very much alone.

The cabin was without personality. Brigid heard voices and the hollow sounds of footsteps on the deck overhead. She smelt the inward rubbery smell of a ship. How was she to support five weeks of the woman with the pin-heels and the couple with Clapham Common voices and that incredibly forbidding spinster? She unpacked the luggage which was already in her cabin. Dennis looked in and she thought him quite frightful. Then she took herself to task for being bloody-minded and beastly. At that moment she found in her trunk a parcel from a wonderful shop with a very smart dress in it and a message from her mother, and at this discovery she sat down on her bunk and cried like a small girl.

By the time she had got over that and finished her unpacking she was suddenly quite desperately tired and went to bed.

Brigid lay in her bed and listened to the sounds of the ship and the port. Gradually the cabin acquired an air of being her own and somewhere at the back of all the wretchedness there stirred a very slight feeling of anticipation. She heard a pleasant voice saying again, "You don't sound as excited as I would have expected," and then she was so sound asleep that she didn't hear the ship sail and was only very vaguely conscious of the fog signal, booming at two-minute intervals all night.

By half-past twelve all the passengers were in bed, even Mrs. Dillington-Blick, who had given her face a terrific workout with a new and complicated beauty treatment.

The officers of the watch went about their appointed ways and the *Cape Farewell*, sailing dead slow, moved out of the Thames estuary with a murderer on board.

2

Captain Jasper Bannerman stood on the bridge with the pilot. He would be up all night. Their job was an ancient one and though they had radar and wireless to serve them, their thoughts as they peered into the blank shiftiness of the fog were those of their remote predecessors. An emergency warning had come through with its procession of im-memorial names—Dogger, Dungeness, Outer Hebrides, Scapa Flow, Portland Bill, and the Goodwin Sands. "She's a corker," said the pilot alluding to the fog. "Proper job she's making of it."

The voices of invisible shipping, hollow and desolate, sounded at un-even distances. Time passed very slowly.

At two-thirty the wireless officer came to the bridge with two mes-sages.

"I thought I'd bring these up myself, sir," he said, referring obliquely to his cadet. "They're in code. Urgent."

Captain Bannerman said, "All right. You might wait, will you?" and went into his room. He got out his code book and deciphered the mes-sages. After a considerable interval he called out, "Sparks."

The wireless officer tucked his cap under his arm, entered the captain's cabin and shut the door.

"This is a damned perishing bloody turn-up," Captain Bannerman said. The wireless officer waited, trying not to look expectant. Captain Bannerman walked over to the starboard porthole and silently re-read the decoded messages. The first was from the managing director of the Cape Line Company:

VERY SECRET STOP DIRECTORS COMPLIMENTS STOP CONFIDENT YOU WILL SHOW EVERY COURTESY TO SUPERINTENDENT ALLEYN BOARDING YOU OFF PORTSMOUTH BY PILOT CUTTER STOP WILL TRAVEL AS PASSENGER STOP SUGGEST USES PILOTS ROOM STOP PLEASE KEEP ME PERSONALLY ADVISED ALL DEVELOPMENTS STOP YOUR COMPANY RELIES ON YOUR DIS-CRETION AND JUDGMENT STOP CAMERON STOP MESSAGE ENDS

Captain Bannerman made an indeterminate but angry noise and re-read the second message.

URGENT IMMEDIATE AND CONFIDENTIAL STOP SUPERINTENDENT R AL-LEYN WILL BOARD YOU OFF PORTSMOUTH BY PILOT CUTTER STOP HE WILL EXPLAIN NATURE OF PROBLEM STOP THIS DEPARTMENT IS IN COMMUNICATION WITH YOUR COMPANY STOP C A MAJORIEBANKS ASSISTANT COMMISSIONER CRIMINAL INVESTIGATION DEPARTMENT SCOT-LAND YARD MESSAGE ENDS

"I'll give you the replies," Captain Bannerman said, glaring at his subordinate. "Same for both! 'Instructions received and noted Bannerman.' And you'll oblige me, Sparks, by keeping the whole thing under your cap."

"Certainly, sir."

"Dead under."

"Certainly, sir."

"Very well."

"Thank you, sir."

When the wireless officer had gone Captain Bannerman remained in a sort of scandalized trance for half a minute and then returned to the bridge.

Throughout the rest of the night he gave the matter in hand, which was the pilotage of his ship through the worst fog for ten years, his sharpest attention. At the same time and on a different level, he speculated about his passengers. He had caught glimpses of them from the bridge. Like every man who so much as glanced at her, he had received a very positive impression of Mrs. Dillington-Blick. A fine woman. He had also noticed Brigid Carmichael, who came under the general heading of Sweet Young Girl and who would, as they approached the tropics, probably cause a ferment among his officers. At another level he was aware of, and disturbed by, the two radiograms. Why the suffering cats, he angrily wondered, should he have to take in at the last second a plain-clothes detective? His mind ranged through an assortment of possible reasons. Stowaway? Escaping criminal? Wanted man in the crew? Perhaps merely a last-minute assignment at Las Palmas, but if so, why didn't the fellow fly? It would be an infernal bore to have to put him up; in the pilot's room of all places, where one would be perpetually aware of his presence. At four o'clock, the time of low vitality, Captain Bannerman was visited by a premonition that this was going to be an unlucky voyage.

3

All the next morning the fog still hung over the English Channel. As she waited off Portsmouth the *Farewell* was insulated in obscurity. Her five male passengers were on deck with their collars turned up. In the cases of Messieurs Merryman, McAngus and Cuddy and Father Jourdain, they wore surprised-looking caps on their heads and wandered up and down the boat-deck or sat disconsolately on benches that would probably never be used again throughout the voyage. Before long Aubyn Dale came back to his own quarters. He had, in addition to his bed-room, a little sitting-room, an arrangement known in the company's offices as "the suite." He had asked Mrs. Dillington-Blick and Dr. Timothy Make-piece to join him there for a drink before luncheon. Mrs. Dillington-Blick had sumptuously appeared on deck at about eleven o'clock and, figuratively speaking, with one hand tied behind her back, had achieved this invitation by half-past. Dr. Makepiece had accepted, hoping that Brigid Carmichael, too, had been invited, but Brigid spent the morning walking on the boat-deck and reading in a chilly but undiscovered little shelter aft of the centrecastle.

Mr. McAngus, too, remained but a short time on deck and soon retired to the passengers' drawing-room, where, after peering doubtfully at the bookcases, he sat in a corner and fell asleep. Mrs. Cuddy was also there and also asleep. She had decided in the teeth of the weather forecast that it was going to be rough and had taken a pill. Miss Abbott was tramping up and down the narrow lower deck, having, perhaps instinctively, hit upon that part of the ship which after the first few hours is deserted by almost everyone. In the plan shown to passengers it was called the prom-enade deck.

It was Brigid who first noticed the break in the weather. A kind of thin warmth fell across the page of her book; she looked up and saw that the curtain of fog had grown threadbare and that sunlight had weakly filtered through. At the same moment the *Farewell* gave her noonday hoot and then Brigid heard the sound of an engine. She went over to the port side and there, quite close, was the pilot cutter. She watched it come alongside the rope ladder. A tall man stood amidships, looking up at the *Farewell*. Brigid was extremely critical of men's clothes and she noticed his with absent-minded approval. A sailor at the head of the ladder dropped a line to the cutter and hauled up two cases. The pilot went off and the tall man climbed the ladder very handily and was met by the cadet on duty, who took him up to the bridge.

On his way he passed Mr. Merryman and Mr. Cuddy, who looked up from their crime novels and were struck by the same vague notion, im-mediately dismissed, that they had seen the new arrival before. In this they were not altogether mistaken; on the previous evening they had both looked at his heavily distorted photograph in the *Evening Herald*. He was Superintendent R. Alleyn.

4

Captain Bannerman put his hands in his jacket pockets and surveyed his latest passenger. At the outset Alleyn had irritated Captain Banner-man by not looking like his own conception of a plain-clothes detective and by speaking with what the captain, who was an inverted snob, considered a bloody posh accent entirely unsuited to a cop. He himself had been at some pains to preserve his own Midland habits of speech.

"Well," he said. "Superintendent A'leen, is it? I take it you'll tell me what all this is in aid of and I don't mind saying I'll be glad to know."

"I suppose, sir," Alleyn said, "you've been cursing ever since you got whatever signals they sent you."

"Well—not to say cursing."

"I know damn well what a bore this must be. The only excuse I can offer is one of expedience, and I must say of extreme urgency."

Captain Bannerman, deliberately broadening his vowels, said, "Sooch a-a-s?"

"Such as murder. Multiple murder."

"Mooltipul murder? Here, you don't mean this chap that says it with flowers and sings?"

"I do, indeed."

"What the hell's he got to do with my ship?"

"I've every reason to believe," Alleyn said, "that he's aboard your ship."

"Don't talk daft."

"I daresay it does sound preposterous."

Captain Bannerman took his hands out of his pockets, walked over to a porthole and looked out. The fog had lifted and the *Farewell* was under way. He said, with a change of voice, "There you are! That's the sort of crew they sign on for you these days. Murderers!"

"My bosses," Alleyn said, "don't seem to think he's in the crew."

"The stewards have been in this ship three voyages."

"Nor among the stewards. Unless sailors or stewards carry embarkation notices."

"D'you mean to stand there and tell me we've shipped a murdering passenger?"

"It looks a bit like it at the moment."

"Here!" Captain Bannerman said with a change of voice. "Sit down. Have a drink. I might have known it'd be a passenger."

Alleyn sat down but declined a drink, a circumstance that produced the usual reaction from his companion. "Ah!" Captain Bannerman said with an air of gloomy recognition. "I suppose not. I suppose not."

His manner was so heavy that Alleyn felt impelled to say, "That doesn't mean, by the way, that I'm about to arrest you."

"I doubt if you could, you know. Not while we're at sea. I very much question it."

"Luckily, the problem doesn't at the moment arise."

"I should have to look up the regulations," sighed Captain Bannerman.

"Look here," Alleyn suggested, "may I try and give you the whole story, as far as it affects my joining your ship?"

"That's what I've been waiting for, isn't it?"

"Yes," Alleyn agreed, "I'm sure it is. Here goes, then!"

He looked full at Captain Bannerman, who seated himself, placed his hands on his knees, raised his eyebrows, and waited.

"You know about these cases, of course," Alleyn said, "as far as they're being reported in the papers. During the last thirty days up to about eleven o'clock last night there had been two homicides which we believed to have been committed by the same person. In each case the victim was a woman, and in each case she had been strangled and flowers had been left on the body. I needn't worry you with any other details at the moment."

"Last night, a few minutes before this ship sailed, a third victim was found. She was in a dark side alley off the passageway between the place where the bus and taxis put down passengers and the actual wharf where you were moored. She was a girl from a flower shop who was bringing a box of hyacinths to one of your passengers, a Mrs. Dillington-Blick. Her string of beads had been broken and the flowers had been scattered, in the usual way, over the victim."

"Any singing?"

"What? Oh, that. That's an element that has been very much played up by the press. It certainly does seem to have occurred on the first occasion. The night of the fifteenth of last month. The victim, you may remember, was Beryl Cohen, who ran a cheapjack stall in Warwick Road and did a bit of the older trade on the side. She was found in her bedsitting-room in a side street behind Paddington. The lodger in the room above seems to have heard the visitor leaving at about ten o'clock. The lodger says the visitor was singing."

"What a dreadful thing," Captain Bannerman said primly. "What sort of song, for God's sake?"

" 'The Jewel Song,' " Alleyn said, "from *Faust*. In an alto voice."

"I'm a bass-baritone, myself," the captain said absently. "Oratorio," he gloomily added.

"And it appears that the sailor on duty at the head of your gangway last night heard singing in the fog. A funny sort of voice, he said. Might mean anything, of course, or nothing. Drunken seaman. Anything. He didn't recognize the tune."

"Here! About last night. How d'you know the victim was—" Captain Bannerman began and then said, "All right. Go on."

"In her left hand, which was clenched in cadaveric spasm, was a fragment of one of the embarkation notices your company issues to passengers. I believe the actual ticket is usually pinned to this notice and torn off by the officer whose duty it is to collect it. He hands the embarkation notice back to the passenger; it has no particular value but I daresay a great many passengers think it constitutes some kind of authority and stick to it. Unfortunately this fragment only showed part of the word *Farewell* and the date."

"No name?"

"No name."

"Doesn't amount to much, in that case," said Captain Bannerman.

"It suggests that the victim, struggling with her murderer, grasped this paper, that it was torn across, and that the rest of it may have remained in the murderer's possession or may have been blown somewhere about the wharf."

"The whole thing might have been blowing about the wharf when the victim grabbed it."

"That's a possibility, of course."

"Probability, more like. What about the other half, then?"

"When I left for Portsmouth this morning, it hadn't been found."

"There you are!"

"But if all the others have kept their embarkation notices—"

"Why should they?"

"May we tackle that one a bit later? Now, the body was found by the P.C. on that beat five minutes before you sailed. He's a good chap and kept his head admirably, it seems, but he couldn't do anything about boarding you. You'd sailed. As he talked to me on the dock telephone he saw your funnel slip past into the fog. A party of us from the Yard went down and did the usual things. We got in touch with your company, who were hellishly anxious that your sailing shouldn't be delayed."

"I'll be bound!" Captain Bannerman ejaculated.

". . . And my bosses came to the conclusion that we hadn't got enough evidence to justify our keeping you back while we held a full-scale enquiry in the ship."

"My Gawd!"

"So it was decided that I should sail with you and hold it, as well as I can, under the counter."

"And what say," Captain Bannerman asked slowly and without any particular signs of bad temper, "what say I won't have it? There you are! How about that?"

"Well," Alleyn said, "I hope you don't cut up rough in that particular direction and I'm sure you won't. But suppose you did and suppose I took it quietly, which, by the way, I wouldn't, the odds are you'd have another corpse on your hands before you made your next landfall."

Captain Bannerman leaned forward, still keeping his palms on his knees, until his face was within a few inches of Alleyn's. His eyes were of that piercing, incredible blue that landsmen so correctly associate with sailors, and his face was the colour of old bricks.

"Do you mean," he asked furiously, "to tell me you think this chap's not had enoof to satisfy him for the voyage?"

"So far," Alleyn said, "he's been operating at ten-day intervals. That'll carry him, won't it, to somewhere between Las Palmas and Cape Town?"

"I don't believe it. I don't believe he's aboard."

"Don't you?"

"What sort of a chap is he? Tell me that."

Alleyn said, "You tell me. You've got just as good a chance of being right."

"Me!"

"You or anyone else. May I smoke?"

"Here—" the captain began and reached for a cigarette box.

"A pipe, if you don't mind." Alleyn pulled it out and as he talked, filled it. "These cases," he said, "are the worst of the lot from our point of view. We can pick a card-sharp or a con-man or a sneak-thief or a gunman or a dozen other bad lots by certain mannerisms and tricks of behaviour. They develop occupational habits and they generally keep company with their own kind. But not the man who, having never before been in trouble with the police, begins, perhaps latish in life, to strangle women at ten-day intervals and leave flowers on their faces. He's a job for the psychiatrist if ever there was one, and he doesn't go in for psychiatry. He's merely an example. But of what? The result of bad housing conditions or a possessive mother or a kick on the head at football or a bullying schoolmaster or a series of regrettable grandparents? Again, your guess is as good as mine. He is. He exists. He may behave with perfect propriety in every possible aspect of his life but this one. He may be, and often is, a colourless little fellow who trots to and fro upon his lawful occasions for, say, fifty years, seven months and a day. On the day after that he trots out and becomes a murderer. Probably there have been certain eccentricities of behaviour which he's been at great pains to conceal and which have suddenly become inadequate. Whatever compulsion it is that hounds him into his appointed crime, it now takes over. He lets go and becomes a monster."

"Ah!" Captain Bannerman said. "A monster. There's unnatural things turn up where you'd least expect to find them in most human souls. That I will agree to. But not in my ship."

The two men looked at each other, and Alleyn's heart sank. He knew pigheadedness when he met it.

The ship's engines, now at full speed, drove her, outward bound, upon her course. There was no more fog; a sunny seascape accepted her as its accident. Her wake opened obediently behind her and the rhythm of her normal progress established itself. England was left behind and the *Farewell*, sailing on her lawful occasions, set her course for Las Palmas.

5

"What," Captain Bannerman asked, "do you want me to do? The thing's flat-out ridiculous, but let's hear what you want. I can't say fairer than that, can I? Come on."

"No," Alleyn agreed, "that's fair enough and more than I bargained for. First of all, perhaps I ought to tell you what I don't want. Particularly, I don't want to be known for what I am."

"Is that so?"

"I gather that supercargoes are a bit out-of-date, so I'd better not be a supercargo. Could I be an employee of the company going out to their Durban office?"

Captain Bannerman stared fixedly at him and then said, "It'd have to be something very senior."

"Why? On account of age?"

"It's nothing to do with age. Or looks. Or rather," Captain Bannerman amended, "it's the general effect."

"I'm afraid I don't quite—"

"You don't look ill, either. Voyage before last, outward bound, we carried a second cousin of the managing director's. Getting over d.t.'s, he was, after taking one of these cures. You're not a bit like him. You're not a bit like a detective, either, if it comes to that," Captain Bannerman added resentfully.

"I'm sorry."

"Have you always been a 'tec?"

"Not absolutely."

"I know," Captain Bannerman said, "leave it to me. You're a cousin of the chairman and you're going out to Canberra via Durban to one of these legations or something. There's all sorts of funny jobs going in Canberra. Anybody'll believe anything, almost."

"Will they?"

"It's a fact."

"Fair enough. Who *is* your chairman?"

"Sir Graeme Harmond."

"Do you mean a little fat man with pop eyes and a stutter?"

"Well," said Captain Bannerman, staring at Alleyn, "if you care to put it that way."

"I know him."

"You don't tell me!"

"He'll do."

"Do!"

"I'd better not use my own name. There's been something in the papers. How about C. J. Roderick?"

"Roderick?"

"It happens to be the first chunk of my own name, but it's never appeared in print. When you do this sort of thing you answer more readily to a name you're used to." He thought for a moment. "No," he said. "Let's play safer and make it Broderick."

"Wasn't your picture in last night's *Herald?*"

"*Was* it? Hell!"

"Wait a bit."

The captain went into his stateroom and came back with a copy of the paper that had so intrigued Mr. Cuddy. He folded it back at the snapshot of piquant Beryl Cohen and Superintendent R. Alleyn (inset).

"Is that like me?" Alleyn said.

"No."

"Good."

"There may be a very slight resemblance. It looks as if your mouth was full."

"It was."

"I see," said Captain Bannerman heavily.

"We'll have to risk it."

"I suppose you'll want to keep very much to yourself?"

"On the contrary. I want to mix as much as possible with the passengers."

"Why?"

Alleyn waited for a moment and then asked, "Have you got a good memory for dates?"

"*Dates?*"

"Could you, for instance, provide yourself with a cast-iron alibi plus witnesses for the fifteenth of last month between ten and eleven P.M., the twenty-fifth between nine P.M. and midnight, and for last night during the half-hour before you sailed?"

Captain Bannerman breathed stertorously and whispered to himself. At last he said, "Not all three, I couldn't."

"There you are, you see."

Captain Bannerman removed his spectacles and again advanced his now empurpled face to within a short distance of Alleyn's.

"Do I look like a sex monster?" he furiously demanded.

"Don't ask *me*," Alleyn rejoined mildly. "I don't know what they look like. That's part of the trouble. I thought I'd made it clear."

As Captain Bannerman had nothing to say to this, Alleyn went on. "I've got to try and check those times with all your passengers and—please don't misunderstand me, sir—I can only hope that most of them manage to turn in solider alibis than, on the face of it, yours looks to be."

"Here! I'm clear for the fifteenth. We were berthed in Liverpool and I was aboard with visitors till two in the morning."

"If that can be proved we won't pull you in for murder."

Captain Bannerman said profoundly, "That's a queer sort of style to use when you're talking to the master of the ship."

"I mean no more than I say, and that's not much. After all, you don't come aboard your own ship clutching an embarkation notice."

Captain Bannerman said, "Not as a rule. No."

Alleyn stood up. "I know," he said, "what a bind this is for you and I really am sorry. I'll keep as quiet as I reasonably may."

"I'll bet you anything you like he hasn't shipped with us. Anything you like! Now!"

"If we'd been dead certain we'd have held you up until we got him."

"It's all some perishing mistake."

"It may be."

"Well," Captain Bannerman said grudgingly as he also rose. "I suppose we'll have to make the best of it. No doubt you'd like to see your quarters. This ship carries a pilot's cabin. On the bridge. We can give you that if it suits."

Alleyn said it would suit admirably. "And if I can just be treated as a passenger—"

"I'll tell the chief steward." He went to his desk, sat down behind it, pulled a slip of paper towards him and wrote on it, muttering as he did so, "Mr. C. J. Broderick, relative of the chairman, going out to a post at the British Embassy in Canberra. That it?"

"That's it. I don't, of course, have to tell you anything about the need for complete secrecy."

"You do not. I've no desire to make a fool of myself, talking daft to my ship's complement."

A fresh breeze had sprung up and was blowing through the starboard porthole. It caught the memorandum that the captain had just completed. The paper fluttered, turned over, and was revealed as a passenger's embarkation notice for the *Cape Farewell*.

Staring fixedly at Alleyn, the captain said, "I used it yesterday in the offices. For a memo." He produced a curiously uncomfortable laugh. "It's not been torn, anyway," he said.

"No," Alleyn said, "I noticed that."

An irresponsible tinkling on a xylophonic gong announced the first luncheon on board the *Cape Farewell*, outward bound.

CHAPTER FOUR   **Hyacinths**

Having watched Alleyn mount the companionway, Brigid Carmichael returned to her desolate little verandah aft of the centrecastle and to her book.

She had gone through the morning in a kind of trance, no longer inclined to cry or to think much of her broken engagement and the scenes that had attended it or even of her own unhappiness. It was as if the fact of departure had removed her to a spiritual distance quite out of scale with the night's journey down the estuary and along the Channel. She had walked until she was tired, tasted salt on her lips, read a little, heard gulls making their B.B.C. atmospheric noises, and watched them fly mysteriously in and out of the fog. Now in the sunshine she fell into a half-doze.

When she opened her eyes it was to find that Doctor Timothy Makepiece stood not far off, leaning over the rail with his back towards her. He had, it struck her, a pleasant nape to his neck; his brown hair grew tidily into it. He was whistling softly to himself. Brigid, still in a strange state of inertia, idly watched him. Perhaps he sensed this for he turned and smiled at her.

"Are you all right?" he asked. "Not sea-sick or anything?"

"Not at all. Only ridiculously sleepy."

"I expect that *is* the sea. They tell me it does have that effect on some people. Did you see the pilot go off and the arrival of the dark and handsome stranger?"

"Yes, I did. Had he missed the ship last night, do you suppose?"

"I've no idea. Are you going for drinks with Aubyn Dale before lunch?"

"Not I."

"I hoped you were. Haven't you met him yet?" He didn't seem to expect an answer to this question but wandered over and looked sideways at Brigid's book.

"Elizabethan verse?" he said. "So you don't despise anthologies. Which is your favourite—Bard apart?"

"Well—Michael Drayton, perhaps, if he wrote 'Since There's No Help.'"

"I'll back the Bard for that little number every time." He picked up the book, opened it at random and began to chuckle as he read aloud.

> "O yes, O yes, if any maid
> Whom leering Cupid hath betrayed . . .

"Isn't *that* a thing, now? Leering Cupid! They really were wonderful. Do you—but no," Tim Makepiece said, interrupting himself, "I'm doing the thing I said to myself I wouldn't do."

"What was that?" Brigid asked, not with any great show of interest.

"Why, forcing my attentions on you, to be sure."

"What an Edwardian expression."

"None the worse for that."

"Shouldn't you be going to your party?"

"I expect so," he agreed moodily. "I don't really like alcohol in the middle of the day and am far from being one of Mr. Aubyn Dale's fans."

"Oh."

"I've yet to meet a man who is."

"All jealous of him, I daresay," Brigid said idly.

"You may be right. And a very sound reason for disliking him. It's the greatest mistake to think that jealousy is necessarily at fault. On the contrary, it may very well sharpen the perception."

"It didn't sharpen Othello's."

"But it did. It was his *interpretation* of what he saw that was at fault. He *saw*, with an immensely sharpened perception."

"I don't agree."

"Because you don't want to."

"Now, look here—" Brigid said, for the first time giving him her full attention.

"He saw Cassio doing his sophisticated young Venetian act over Desdemona's hand. He saw him at it again after he'd blotted his copy-book. He was pathologically aware of every gallantry that Cassio showed his wife."

"Well," Brigid said, "if you're pathologically aware of every attention Aubyn Dale shows his however-many-they-may-be female fans, I must say I'm sorry for you."

"All right, smartie," Tim said amiably, "you win."

"After all, it's the interpretation that matters."

"There's great virtue in perception alone. Pure scientific observation that is content to set down observed fact after observed fact—"

"Followed by pure scientific interpretation that adds them all up and makes a nonsense."

"Why should you say that?" he asked gently. "It's you that's making a nonsense."

"Well, I must say!"

"To revert to Aubyn Dale. What about his big thing on TV? Advertising women's bathing clothes—*Pack Up Your Troubles*. In other words, 'Come to me, everybody that's got a bellyache, and I'll put you before my public and pay you for it.' If I were a religious man I'd call it blasphemy."

"I don't say I *like* what he does—"

"Still, he does make an ass of himself good and proper, on occasions. Witness the famous Molton Medbury Midsummer Muckup."

"I never heard exactly what happened."

"He was obviously plastered. He went round televising the Molton Medbury flower show with old Lady Agatha Panthing. You could see he was plastered before he spoke and when he did speak he said the first prize in the competition went to Lady Agatha's umbilicus globular. He meant," Timothy explained, "*Agapanthus umbellatus globosus*. I suppose it shattered him because after that a sort of rot set in and at intervals he broke into a recrudescence of spoonerisms. It went on for weeks. Only the other day he was going all springlike over a display of hyacinths and said that in arranging them all you really needed was a 'turdy stable.'"

"Oh, *no!* Poor chap. How too shaming for him!"

"So he shaved off his fetching little imperial and I expect he's taking a long sea voyage to forget. He's in pretty poor shape, I fancy."

"Do you? What sort of poor shape?"

"Oh, neurosis," Timothy said shortly, "of some sort. I should think."

The xylophonic gong began its inconsequent chiming on the bridge-house.

"Good Lord, that's for *eating!*" Timothy exclaimed.

"What *will* you say to your host?"

"I'll say I had an urgent case among the greasers. But I'd better just show up. Sorry to have been such a bore. Good-bye, now," said Tim attempting a brogue.

He walked rapidly away.

To her astonishment and slightly to her resentment Brigid found that she was ravenously hungry.

2

The Cape Company is a cargo line. The fact that six of its ships afford accommodation for nine passengers each does not in any way modify the essential function of the company. It merely postulates that in the case of these six ships there shall be certain accommodation. There will also be a chief steward without any second string, a bar-and-passengers steward and an anomalous offsider who may be discovered by the passengers polishing the taps in their cabins at unexpected moments. The business of housing, feeding, and within appropriate limits, entertaining the nine passengers is determined by the head office and then becomes part of the captain's many concerns.

On the whole, Captain Bannerman preferred to carry no passengers, and always regarded them as potential troublemakers. When, however, somebody of Mrs. Dillington-Blick's calibre appeared in his ship, his reaction corresponded punctually with that of ninety per cent of all other males whom she encountered. He gave orders that she should be placed at his table (which luckily was all right anyway because she carried V.I.P. letters), and until Alleyn's arrival, had looked forward to the voyage with the liveliest anticipation of pleasurable interludes. He was, he considered, a young man for his age.

Aubyn Dale he also took at his table because Dale was famous and Captain Bannerman felt that in a way he would be flattering Mrs. Dillington-Blick by presenting her with a number one personality. Now he decided, obscurely and resentfully, that Alleyn also would be an impressive addition to the table. The rest of the seating he left to his chief steward, who gave the Cuddys and Mr. Donald McAngus to the first mate, whom he disliked; Brigid Carmichael and Dr. Makepiece to the second mate and the wireless officer, of whom he approved; and Miss Abbott, Father Jourdain and Mr. Merryman to the chief engineer, towards whom his attitude was neutral.

This, the first luncheon on board, was also the first occasion at which the senior ship's officers, with the exception of those on duty, were present. At a long table in a corner sat a number of young men presenting several aspects of adolescence and all looking a trifle sheepish. These were the electrical and engineering junior officers and the cadets.

Alleyn arrived first at the table and was carefully installed by the captain's steward. The Cuddys, already seated hard by, settled down to a good long stare and so, more guardedly, did Mr. McAngus. Mrs. Cuddy's burning curiosity manifested itself in a dead-pan glare which was directed intermittently at the objects of her interest. Its mechanics might be said to resemble those of a lighthouse whose different frequencies make its signals recognizable far out at sea.

Mr. Cuddy, on the contrary, kept observation under cover of an absent-minded smile, while Mr. McAngus quietly rolled his eyes in the direction of his objective and was careful not to turn his head.

Miss Abbott, at the chief engineer's table, gave Alleyn one sharp look and no more. Mr. Merryman rumpled his hair, opened his eyes very wide and then fastened with the fiercest concentration upon the menu. Father Jourdain glanced in a civilized manner at Alleyn and turned with a pleasant smile to his companions.

At this juncture Mrs. Dillington-Blick made her entrance, rosy with achievement, buzzing with femininity, and followed by the captain, Aubyn Dale, and Timothy Makepiece.

The captain introduced Alleyn—"Mr. Broderick, who joined us today—"

The men made appropriate wary noises at each other. Mrs. Dillington-Blick, who might have been thought to be already in full flower, awarded herself a sort of bonus in effulgence. Everything about her blossomed madly. "Fun!" she seemed to be saying. "This is what I'm really good at. We're all going to like this."

She bathed Alleyn in her personality. Her eyes shone, her lips were moist, her small hands fluttered at the ends of her Rubensesque arms. "But I *watched* you!" she cried. "I watched you with my heart in my mouth! Coming on board! Nipping up that frightful thing! Do tell me. Is it as terrifying as it looks or am I being silly?"

"It's plain murder," Alleyn said, "and you're not being silly at all. I was all of a tremble."

Mrs. Dillington-Blick cascaded with laughter. She raised and lowered her eyebrows at Alleyn and flapped her hands at the captain. "There now!" she cried. "Just what I supposed. How you dared! If it was a choice of feeding the little fishes or crawling up that ladder I swear I'd pop thankfully into the shark's maw. And don't you look so superior," she chided Captain Bannerman.

This was exactly how he had hoped she would talk. A fine woman who enjoyed a bit of chaff. And troubled though he was, he swelled a little in his uniform.

"We'll have you shinning down it like an old hand," he teased, "when you go ashore at Las Palmas."

Aubyn Dale looked quizzically at Alleyn, who gave him the shadow of a wink. Mrs. Dillington-Blick was away to a magnificent start. Three men, one a celebrity, two good-looking, and all teasing her. Las Palmas?

Did they mean . . . ? Would she have to . . . ? Ah *no!* She didn't believe them.

A number of rococo images chased each other improperly through Alleyn's imagination. "Don't give it another thought," he advised. "You'll make the grade. I understand that if the sea's at all choppy they rig a safety net down below. Same as trapeze artists have when they lose their nerve."

"I won't listen."

"It's the form, though, I promise you," Alleyn said. "Isn't it, sir?"

"Certainly."

"Not true! Mr. Dale, they're being *beastly* to me!"

Dale said, "I'm on your side." It was a phrase with which he often reassured timid subjects on television. He was already talking to Mrs. Dillington-Blick as if they were lifelong friends and yet with that touch of deference that lent such distinction to his programmes and filled Alleyn, together with eighty per cent of his male viewers, with a vague desire to kick him.

There was a great deal of laughter at the captain's table. Mrs. Cuddy was moved to stare at it so fixedly that at one moment she completely missed her mouth.

A kind of restlessness was engendered in the passengers, a sense of being done out of something, and in two of the women, of resentment. Miss Abbott felt angry with Mrs. Dillington-Blick because she was being silly over three men. Mrs. Cuddy felt angry with her because three men were being silly over her and also because of a certain expression that had crept into Mr. Cuddy's wide smile. Brigid Carmichael wondered how Mrs. Dillington-Blick could be bothered and then took herself to task for being a humbug; the new passenger, she thought, was quite enough to make any girl do her stuff. She found that Dr. Makepiece was looking at her and to her great annoyance she blushed. For the rest of luncheon she made polite conversation with the second mate, who was Welsh and bashful, and with the wireless officer, who wore that wild and lonely air common to his species.

After luncheon Alleyn went to see his quarters. The pilot's cabin had a door and porthole opening on to the bridge. He could look down on the bows of the ship, thrust arrow-like into the sea, and at the sickle-shaped and watery world beyond. Under other circumstances, he thought, he would have enjoyed this trip. He unpacked his suitcases, winked at a photograph of his wife, went below, and carried out a brief inspection of the passengers' quarters. These were at the same level as the drawing-room and gave on a passage that went through from port to starboard. The doors were all shut with the exception of that opening into the cabin aft of the passage on the port side. This was open and the cabin beyond resembled an overcrowded flower shop. Here Dennis was discovered, sucking his thumb and lost in contemplation. Alleyn knew that Dennis, of whom this was his first glimpse, might very well become a person of importance. He paused by the door.

"Afternoon," he said. "Are you the steward for the pilot's cabin?"

Evidently Dennis had heard about Alleyn. He hurried to the door, smiled winsomely and said, "Not generally, but I'm going to have the pleasure of looking after *you*, Mr. Broderick."

Alleyn tipped him five pounds. Dennis said, "Oh, you shouldn't, sir, really," and pocketed the note. He indicated the flowers and said, "I just can't make up my mind, sir. Mrs. Dillington-Blick said I was to take some into the dining-room and lounge and as soon as I've finished in the bar I'm going to, but I *don't* know which to choose. Such an umberance-der-riches! What would you say for the *lounge*, sir? The décor's dirty *pink*."

Alleyn was so long answering that Dennis gave a little giggle. "Isn't it *diffy!*" he sympathized.

Alleyn pointed a long finger. "That," he said. "I should certainly make it that one," and went on his way to the passengers' lounge.

3

It was a modest combination of bar, smoking-room, and card-room and in it the passengers were assembled for coffee. Already by the curious mechanism of human attraction and repulsion they had begun to sort themselves into groups. Mr. McAngus, having found himself alongside the Cuddys at luncheon, was reappropriated by them both and seemed to be not altogether at ease in their company, perhaps because Mrs. Cuddy stared so very fixedly at his hair, which, Alleyn noticed, was of an unexpected shade of nut brown with no parting and a good deal of overhang at the back. He drew a pocket of herbal cigarettes from his pocket and lit one, explaining that he suffered from asthma. They began to chat more cosily about diseases. Mr. McAngus confided that he was but recently recovered from an operation and Mr. Cuddy returned this lead with a lively account of a suspected duodenal ulcer.

Father Jourdain and Mr. Merryman had discovered a common taste in crime fiction and smiled quite excitedly at each other over their coffee cups. Of all the men among the passengers, Alleyn thought, Father Jourdain had the most arresting appearance. He wondered what procession of events had led this man to become an Anglo-Catholic celibate priest. There was intelligence and liveliness in the face whose pallor, induced no doubt by the habit of his life, emphasized rather than concealed the opulence of the mouth and watchfulness of the dark eyes. His short white hands were muscular and his hair thick and glossy. He was infinitely more vivid than his companion, whose baby-faced petulance, Alleyn felt, was probably the outward wall of the conventional house master. He caught himself up. "Conventional?" Was Mr. Merryman the too-familiar pedant who cultivates the eccentric to compensate himself for the deadly boredom of scholastic routine? A don manqué? Alleyn took himself mildly to task for indulgence in idle speculation and looked elsewhere.

Dr. Timothy Makepiece stood over Brigid Carmichael with the slightly mulish air of a young Englishman in the early stages of an attraction. Alleyn noted the formidable lines of Dr. Makepiece's jaw and mouth, and being at the moment interested in hands, the unusual length of the fingers.

Miss Abbott sat by herself on a settee against the wall. She was reading. The hands that held her neatly covered book were large and muscular. Her face, he reflected, would have been not unhandsome if it had been only slightly less inflexible and if there had not been the suggestion of—what was it?—harshness?—about the jaw.

As for Aubyn Dale, there he was, with Mrs. Dillington-Blick, who had set herself up with him hard by the little bar. When she saw Alleyn she beckoned gaily to him. She was busy establishing a coterie. As Alleyn joined them Aubyn Dale laid a large, beautifully tended hand over hers and burst into a peal of all-too-infectious laughter. "What a perfectly marvellous person you are!" he cried boyishly and appealed to Alleyn. "Isn't she wonderful?"

Alleyn agreed fervently and offered them liqueurs.

"You take the words out of my mouth, dear boy," Dale exclaimed.

"I oughtn't to!" Mrs. Dillington-Blick protested. "I'm on an inquisitorial diet!" She awarded her opulence a downward glance and Alleyn an upward one. She raised her eyebrows. "My dear!" she cried. "You can see for yourself. I oughtn't."

"But you're going to," he rejoined and the drinks were served by the ubiquitous Dennis, who had appeared behind the bar. Mrs. Dillington-Blick, with a meaning look at Dale, said that if she put on another ounce she would never get into her Jolyon swimsuit and they began to talk about his famous session on commercial television. It appeared that when he visited America and did a specially sponsored half-hour, he had been supported by a great mass of superb models all wearing Jolyon swimsuits. His hands eloquently sketched their curves. He leaned towards Mrs. Dillington-Blick and whispered. Alleyn noticed the slight puffiness under his eyes and the blurring weight of flesh beneath the inconsiderable jaw which formerly his beard had hidden. "Is this the face," Alleyn asked himself, "that launched a thousand hips?" and wondered why.

"You haven't forgotten the flowers?" Mrs. Dillington-Blick asked Dennis and he assured her that he hadn't.

"As soon as I've a spare *sec* I'll pop away and fetch them," he promised and smiled archly at Alleyn. "They're all chosen and ready."

As Aubyn Dale's conversation with Mrs. Dillington-Blick tended to get more and more confidential Alleyn felt himself at liberty to move away. At the far end of the lounge Mr. Merryman was talking excitedly to Father Jourdain, who had begun to look uncomfortable. He caught Alleyn's eye and nodded pleasantly. Alleyn dodged round the Cuddys and Mr. McAngus and by-passed Miss Abbott. There was a settee near the far end, but as he made for it Father Jourdain said, "Do come and join us. These chairs are much more comfortable and we'd like to introduce ourselves."

Alleyn said, "I should be delighted," and introductions were made. Mr. Merryman looked sharply at him over the tops of his spectacles and said, "How do you do, sir." He added astonishingly, "I perceived that you were effecting an escape from what was no doubt an excruciating situation."

"I?" Alleyn said. "I don't quite—"

"The sight," Mr. Merryman continued in none too quiet a voice, "of yonder popinjay ruffling his dubious plumage at the bar is singularly distasteful to me and no doubt intolerable to you."

"Oh, come, now!" Father Jourdain protested.

Alleyn said, "He's not as bad as all that, is he?"

"You know who he is, of course."

"Yes, indeed."

"Yes, yes," said Father Jourdain. "We know. Ssh!"

"Have you witnessed his weekly exhibitions of indecent exposure on the television?"

"I'm not much of a viewer," Alleyn said.

"Ah! You show your good judgment. As an underpaid pedagogue it has been my hideous lot to sit on Tuesday evenings among upper-middle-class adolescents of low intelligence, 'looking in' (loathsome phrase) at this man's antics. Let me tell you what he does, sir. He advertises women's bathing clothes and to this end he incites—arrogant presumption—he incites members of the public to bring their troubles to him! And the fools do! Conceive!" Mr. Merryman invited. "Picture to yourself! A dupe is discovered, his back (or much more often hers) to the camera. Out of focus, unrecognizable, therefore. Facing this person and us, remorselessly illuminated, enthroned and elevated in blasphemous (you will appreciate that in clerical company I use the adjective advisedly) in blasphemous supremacy is or was the countenance you see before you, but garnished with a hirsute growth which lent it a wholly spurious distinction."

Alleyn glanced with amusement at Mr. Merryman and thought what bad luck it was for him that he was unable to give visual expression to his spleen. For all the world he looked like an indignant baby.

"If you will believe me," he continued angrily whispering, "a frightful process known as 'talking it over' now intervenes. The subject discloses to That Person, and to however many thousands of listening observers there may be, some intimate predicament of her (it is, I repeat, usually a woman) private life. *He* then propounds a solution, is thanked, applauded, preens himself, and is presented with a fresh sacrifice. Now! What do you think of *that!*" whispered Mr. Merryman.

"I think it all sounds very embarrassing," Alleyn said.

Father Jourdain made a comically despairing face at him. "Let's talk about something else," he suggested. "You were saying, Mr. Merryman, that the psychopathic murderer—"

"You heard of course," Mr. Merryman remorselessly interjected, "what an exhibition he made of himself at a later assignment. 'Lady Agatha's umbilicus globular,'" he quoted, and broke into a shrill laugh.

"You know," Father Jourdain remarked, "I'm on holiday and honestly don't want to start throwing my priestly weight about." Before Mr. Merryman could reply he raised his voice a little and added, "To go back, as somebody, was it Humpty Dumpty? said, to the last conversation but one, I'm immensely interested in what you were saying about criminals of the Heath type. What was the book you recommended? By an American psychiatrist, I think you said."

Mr. Merryman muttered huffily, "I don't recollect."

Alleyn asked, "Not, by any chance, *The Show of Violence*, by Frederic Wertham?"

Father Jourdain turned to him with unconcealed relief. "Ah!" he said. "You're an addict, too, and a learned one, evidently."

"Not I. The merest amateur. Why, by the way, is everybody so fascinated by crimes of violence?" He looked at Father Jourdain. "What do you think, sir?"

Father Jourdain hesitated and Mr. Merryman cut in.

"I am persuaded," he said, "that people read about murder as an alternative to committing it."

"A safety valve?" Alleyn suggested.

"A conversion. The so-called antisocial urge is fed into a socially acceptable channel; we thus commit our crimes of violence at a safe remove. We are all," Mr. Merryman said tranquilly folding his hands over his stomach, "savages at heart." He seemed to have recovered his good humour.

"Do you agree?" Alleyn asked Father Jourdain.

"I fancy," he rejoined, "that Mr. Merryman is talking about something I call original sin. If he is, I do of course agree."

An accidental silence had fallen on the little assembly. Into this silence with raised voice, as a stone into a pool, Alleyn dropped his next remark.

"Take, for instance, this strangler—the man who 'says it with'—what are they? Roses? What, do you suppose, is behind all that?"

The silence continued for perhaps five seconds.

Miss Abbott said, "Not roses. Hyacinths. Flowers of several kinds."

She had lifted her gaze from her book and fixed it on Mrs. Dillington-Blick. "Hot-house flowers," she said. "It being winter. The first time it was snowdrops, I believe."

"And the second," Mr. Merryman said, "hyacinths."

Aubyn Dale cleared his throat.

"Ah yes!" Alleyn said. "I remember now. Hyacinths."

"Isn't it awful?" Mrs. Cuddy gloated.

"Shocking," Mr. Cuddy agreed. "Hyacinths! Fancy!"

Mr. McAngus said gently, "Poor things."

Mr. Merryman with the falsely innocent air of a child that knows it's being naughty asked loudly, "Hasn't there been something on television about these flowers? Something rather ludicrous? Of what can I be thinking?"

Everybody avoided looking at Aubyn Dale, but not even Father Jourdain found anything to say.

It was at this juncture that Dennis staggered into the room with a vast basket of flowers which he set down on the central table.

"Hyacinths!" Mrs. Cuddy shrilly pointed out. "What a coincidence!"

4

It was one of those naïve arrangements which can give nothing but pleasure to the person who receives them unless, of course, that person is allergic to scented flowers. The hyacinths were rooted and blooming in a mossy bed. They trembled slightly with the motion of the ship, shook out their incongruous fragance and filled the smoking-room with reminiscences of the more expensive kinds of shops, restaurants, and women.

Dennis fell back a pace to admire them.

"Thank you, Dennis," Mrs. Dillington-Blick said.

"It's a pleasure, Mrs. Dillington-Blick," he rejoined. "Aren't they gorgeous?"

He retired behind the bar. The passengers stared at the growing flowers and the flowers, quivering, laid upon them a further burden of sweetness.

Mrs. Dillington-Blick explained hurriedly, "There isn't room for all one's flowers in one's cabin. I thought we'd enjoy them together."

Alleyn said, "But what a charming gesture." And was barely supported by a dilatory murmur.

Brigid agreed quickly, "Isn't it? Thank you so much, they're quite lovely."

Tim Makepiece murmured, "What nice manners you've got, Grandmama."

"I do hope," Mrs. Dillington-Blick said, "that nobody finds the scent too much. Me, I simply wallow in it."

She turned to Aubyn Dale. He rejoined, "But of course. You're so wonderfully exotic." Mr. Merryman snorted.

Mrs. Cuddy said loudly, "I'm afraid we're going to be spoil-sports. Mr. Cuddy can't stay in the same room with flowers that have a heavy perfume. He's allergic to them."

"Oh, I *am* so sorry," Mrs. Dillington-Blick cried. "Then, of course, they must go." She waved her hands helplessly.

"I'm sure there's no need for that," Mrs. Cuddy announced. "We don't want to make things uncomfortable. We were going to take a turn on deck anyway. Weren't we, dear?"

Alleyn asked, "Do you suffer from hay fever, Mr. Cuddy?"

Mrs. Cuddy answered for her husband. "Not exactly hay fever, is it, dear? He just comes over queer."

"Extraordinary," Alleyn murmured.

"Well, it's quite awkward sometimes."

"At weddings and funerals, for instance, it must be."

"Well, on our *silver* wedding some of the gentlemen from Mr. Cuddy's lodge brought us a gorgeous mixed booky of hot-house flowers and he had to say how much he appreciated it and all the time he was feeling peculiar and when they'd gone he said, 'I'm sorry, Mum, but it's me or the booky,' and we live opposite a hospital so he took them across and had to go for a long walk afterwards to get over it, didn't you, dear?"

"*Your* silver wedding," Alleyn said, and smiled at Mrs. Cuddy. "You're not going to tell us you've been married twenty-five years!"

"Twenty-five years and eleven days to be exact. Haven't we, dear?"

"That's correct, dear."

"He's turning colour," Mrs. Cuddy said, exhibiting her husband with an air of triumph. "Come on, love. Walky-walky."

Mr. Cuddy seemed unable to look away from Mrs. Dillington-Blick. He said, "I don't notice the perfume too heavy. It isn't affecting me."

"That's what *you* say," his wife replied, ominously bluff. "You come into the fresh air, my man." She took his arm and turned him towards the glass doors that gave on to the deck. She opened them. Cold salt air poured into the heated room, and the sound of the sea and of the ship's engines. The Cuddys went out. Mr. Cuddy shut the doors and could be seen looking back into the room. His wife removed him and they walked away, their grey hair lifting in the wind.

"They'll die of cold!" Brigid exclaimed. "No coats or hats."

"Oh, dear!" Mrs. Dillington-Blick lamented and appealed in turn to the men. "And I expect it's all my fault." They murmured severally.

Mr. McAngus, who had peeped into the passage, confided, "It's all right. They've come in by the side door and I *think* they've gone to their cabin." He sniffed timidly at the flowers, gave a small apologetic laugh and made a little bobbing movement to and from Mrs. Dillington-Blick. "*I* think we're all most awfully lucky," he ventured. He then went out into the passage, putting on his hat as he did so.

"That poor creature dyes its hair," Mr. Merryman observed calmly.

"Oh, come!" Father Jourdain protested and gave Alleyn a helpless look. "I seem," he said under his breath, "to be saying nothing but 'Oh, come.' A maddening observation."

Mrs. Dillington-Blick blossomed at Mr. Merryman: "Aren't you *naughty!*" She laughed and appealed to Aubyn Dale: "*Not* true. *Is* it?"

"I honestly can't see, you know, that if he does dye his hair, it's anybody's business but his," Dale said, and gave Mr. Merryman his celebrated smile. "Can you?" he said.

"I entirely agree with you," Mr. Merryman rejoined, grinning like a monkey. "I must apologize. In point of fact I abominate the public elucidation of private foibles."

Dale turned pale and said nothing.

"Let us talk about flowers instead," Mr. Merryman suggested and beamed through his spectacles upon the company.

Mrs. Dillington-Blick at once began to do so. She was supported, unexpectedly, by Miss Abbott. Evidently they were both experienced gardeners. Dale listened with a stationary smile. Alleyn saw him order himself a second double brandy.

"I suppose," Alleyn remarked generally, "everybody has a favourite flower."

Mrs. Dillington-Blick moved into a position from which she could see him. "Hullo, you!" she exclaimed jollily. "But of course they have. Mine's magnolias."

"What are yours?" Tim Makepiece asked Brigid.

"Distressingly obvious—roses."

"Lilies," Father Jourdain smiled, "which may also be obvious."

"Easter?" Miss Abbott barked.

"Exactly."

"What about you?" Alleyn asked Tim.

"The hop," he said cheerfully.

Alleyn grinned. "There you are. It's all a matter of association. Mine's lilac and throws back to a pleasant childhood memory. But if beer happened to make you sick or my nanny, whom I detested, had worn lilac in her nankeen bosom or Father Jourdain associated lilies with death, we'd have all hated the sight and smell of these respective flowers."

Mr. Merryman looked with pity at him. "Not," he said, "a remarkably felicitous exposition of a somewhat elementary proposition, but, as far as it goes, unexceptionable."

Alleyn bowed. "Have you, sir," he asked, "a preference?"

"None, none. The topic, I confess, does not excite me."

"I think it's a *heavenly* topic," Mrs. Dillington-Blick cried. "But then I adore finding out about People and their preferences." She turned to Dale and at once his smile reprinted itself. "Tell me your taste in flowers," she said, "and I'll tell you your type in ladies. Come clean, now. Your favourite flower? Or shall I guess?"

"Agapanthas?" Mr. Merryman loudly suggested. Dale clapped his glass down on the bar and walked out of the room.

"Now, *look* here, Mr. Merryman!" Father Jourdain said and rose to his feet.

Mr. Merryman opened his eyes very wide and pursed his lips. "What's up?" he asked.

"You know perfectly well what's up. You're an extremely naughty little man although it's none of my business I think fit to tell you so."

Far from disconcerting Mr. Merryman, this more or less public rebuke appeared to afford him enjoyment. He clapped his hands lightly, slapped them on his knees and broke into elfish laughter.

"If you'll take my advice," Father Jourdain continued, "you will apologize to Mr. Dale."

Mr. Merryman rose, bowed, and observed in an extremely highfalutin manner, "*Consilia firmiora sunt de divinis locis.*"

The priest turned red.

Alleyn, who didn't see why Mr. Merryman should be allowed to make a corner in pedantry, racked his own brains for a suitable tag. "*Consilium inveniunt multi sed docti explicant,* however," he said.

"Dear me!" Mr. Merryman observed. "How often one has cause to remark that a platitude sounds none the better for being uttered in an antique tongue. I shall now address myself to my postprandial nap."

He trotted towards the door, paused for a moment to stare at Mrs. Dillington-Blick's pearls, and then went out.

"For pity's sake!" she ejaculated. "What is all this! What's happening? What's the matter with Aubyn Dale? Why agapanthas?"

"Can it be possible," Tim Makepiece said, "that you don't know about Lady Agatha's umbilicus globular and the hyacinths on the turdy stable?" and he retold the story of Aubyn Dale's misfortunes.

"How frightful!" Mrs. Dillington-Blick exclaimed, laughing until she cried. "How too tragically frightful! And how *naughty* of Mr. Merryman."

Tim Makepiece said, "We don't 'alf look like being a happy family. What will Mr. Chips's form be, one asks oneself, when he enters the Torrid Zone?"

"He may look like Mr. Chips," Alleyn remarked. "He behaves like Thersites."

Brigid said, "I call it the rock bottom of him. You could see Aubyn Dale minded most dreadfully. He went as white as his teeth. What could have possessed Mr. Chips?"

"Schoolmaster," Miss Abbott said, scarcely glancing up from her book. "They often turn sour at his age. It's the life."

She had been quiet for so long they had forgotten her. "That's right," she continued, "isn't it, Father?"

"It may possibly, I suppose, be a reason. It's certainly not an excuse."

"I think," Mrs. Dillington-Blick lamented, "I'd better throw my lovely hyacinths overboard, don't you?" She appealed to Father Jourdain. "Wouldn't it be best? It's not only poor Mr. Dale."

"No," Brigid agreed. "Mr. Cuddy, we must remember, comes over queer at the sight of them."

"Mr. Cuddy," Miss Abbott observed, "came over queer but not, in my opinion, at the sight of the hyacinths." She lowered her book and looked steadily at Mrs. Dillington-Blick.

"My dear!" Mrs. Dillington-Blick rejoined and began to laugh again.

"Well!" Father Jourdain said with the air of a man who refuses to recognize his nose before his face. "I think I shall see what it's like on deck."

Mrs. Dillington-Blick stood between him and the double doors and he was quite close to her. She beamed up at him. His back was turned to Alleyn. He was still for a moment and then she moved aside and he went out. There was a brief silence.

Mrs. Dillington-Blick turned to Brigid.

"My dear!" she confided. "I've *got* that man. He's a reformed rake."

Mr. McAngus re-entered from the passage still wearing his hat. He smiled diffidently at his five fellow passengers.

"All settling down?" he ventured, evidently under a nervous compulsion to make some general remark.

"Like birds in their little nest," Alleyn agreed cheerfully.

"Isn't it delicious," Mr. McAngus said, heartened by this response, "to think that from now on it's going to get warmer and warmer and warmer?"

"Absolutely enchanting."

Mr. McAngus made the little chassé with which they were all to become familiar, before the basket of hyacinths.

"Quite intoxicating," he said. "They are my favourite flowers."

"Are they!" cried Mrs. Dillington-Blick. "Then do please, *please* have them. Please do. Dennis will take them to your room. Mr. McAngus, I should adore you to have them."

He gazed at her in what seemed to be a flutter of bewildered astonishment. "I?" Mr. McAngus said. "But why? I beg your pardon, but it's so very kind, and positively I can't believe you mean it."

"But I do, indeed. Please have them."

Mr. McAngus hesitated and stammered. "I'm quite overcome. Of course I should be delighted." He gave a little giggle and tilted his head over to one side. "Do you know," he said, "this is the first occasion, the *very* first, on which a lady has ever, of her own free will, offered me her flowers? And my favourites, too. Thank you. Thank you very much indeed."

Alleyn saw that Mrs. Dillington-Blick was touched by this speech. She smiled kindly and unprovocatively at him and Brigid laughed gently.

"I'll carry them myself," Mr. McAngus said. "Of course I will. I shall put them on my little table and they'll be reflected in my looking-glass."

"Lucky man!" Alleyn said lightly.

"Indeed, yes. May I, really?" he asked. Mrs. Dillington-Blick nodded gaily and he advanced to the table and grasped the enormous basket with his reddish bony hands. He was an extremely thin man and, Alleyn thought, very much older than his strange nut-brown hair would suggest.

"Let me help you," Alleyn offered.

"No, no! I'm really very strong, you know. Wiry."

He lifted the basket and staggered on bent legs with it to the door. Here he turned, a strange figure, his felt hat tilted over his nose, blinking above a welter of quivering hyacinths.

"I shall think of something to give *you*," he promised Mrs. Dillington-Blick, "after Las Palmas. There must be a reciprocal gesture."

He went groggily away.

"He may dye his hair a screaming magenta if he chooses," Mrs. Dillington-Blick said. "He's a sweetie-pie."

From behind her covered book Miss Abbott remarked in that not very musical voice, "Meanwhile we await his reciprocal gesture. After Las Palmas."

CHAPTER FIVE **Before Las Palmas**

Alleyn sat in the pilot's cabin looking at his file of the case in question. Captain Bannerman was on the bridge outside. At regular intervals he marched past Alleyn's porthole. The weather, as Mr. McAngus had predicted, was getting warmer and in two days *Cape Farewell* would sight Las Palmas. She steamed now through a heavy swell. A tendency to yawn, doze, and swap panaceas against seasickness had broken out among the passengers.

January 15th. 13 Hop Lane. Paddington [Alleyn read]. Beryl Cohen. Jewess. Cheapjack. Part-time prostitute. Showy. Handsome. About 26. Five feet 6 inches. Full figure. Red (dyed) hair. Black skirt. Red jersey. Artificial necklace (green glass). Found January 16th, 10:05 A.M., by fellow lodger. Estimated time of death: between 10 and 11 P.M. previous night. On floor, face upward. Broken necklace. Flowers (snowdrops) on face and breast. Cause: manual strangulation but necklace probably first. Lodger states she heard visitor leave about 10:45. Singing. "Jewel Song," *Faust*. High-pitched male voice.

A detailed description of the room followed. He skipped it and read on.

January 25th. Alley-way off Ladysmith Crescent, Fulham. Marguerite Slatters, of 36A Stackhouse Street, Fulham. London. Floral worker. Respectable. Quiet. Thirty-seven. Five feet 8 inches. Slight. Homely. Dark brown hair. Sallow complexion. Brown dress. Artificial pearls and teeth. Brown beret, gloves, and shoes. Returning home from St. Barnabas' Parish Church. Found 11:55 by Stanley Walker, chauffeur. Estimated time of death between 9 and 12 P.M. By doorstep of empty garage. Face upward. Broken necklace. Torn dress. Manual strangulation. Flowers (hyacinths) on face and breast. Had no flowers when last seen alive.

Alleyn sighed and looked up. Captain Bannerman bobbed past the porthole. The ship was heaved upward and forward, the horizon tilted, rose and sank.

February 4th. Passageway between sheds, Cape Company's No. 2 Wharf, Royal Albert Dock. Coralie Kraus of 16 Steep Lane, Hampstead. Assistant at Green Thumb, Knightsbridge. Eighteen. Naturalized Austrian. Lively. Well-conducted. Five feet, 4¾ inches. Fair hair. Pale complexion. Black dress, gloves, and shoes. No hat. Pink artificial jewellery. (Earrings, bracelet, necklace, clips.) Taking box of hyacinths to Mrs. Dillington-Blick, passenger, *Cape Farewell.* Found 11:48 P.M. by P. C. Martin Moir. Body warm. Death estimated between 11:15 and 11:48 P.M. Face upwards. Stocking torn. Jewellery broken. Ears torn. Manual strangulation. Fragment of embarkation notice for S.S. *Cape Farewell* in right hand. Flowers (hyacinths) on face and breast. Seaman (on duty, *Cape Farewell* gangway) mentioned hearing high male voice singing. Very foggy conditions. All passengers went ashore (ref. above seaman) except Mr. Donald McAngus, who arrived last.

Alleyn shook his head, pulled towards him a half-finished letter to his wife, and after a moment continued it.

. . . *so instead of drearily milling over these grisly, meagre, and infuriating bits of information received, I offer them, my darling, to you, together with any developments that may, as Fox says in his more esoteric flights of fancy, accrue. There they are, then, and for the first time you will have the fun, God help you, of following a case as it develops from the casebook. The form, I suppose, is to ask oneself what these three wretched young women had in common and the answer is: very nearly damn all, unless you feel inclined to pay any attention to the fact that in common with ninety per cent of their fellow females, they all wore false jewellery. Otherwise they couldn't physically, racially or morally be less like each other. On the other hand they all met their death in exactly the same fashion and each was left with her broken necklace and ghastly little floral tribute. By the way, I imagine I've spotted one point of resemblance which didn't at first jump to the eye. Wonder if you have?*

As for the fragment of embarkation notice in Miss Kraus's right hand, that's all I've got to justify my taking this pleasure cruise, and if it was blowing about the wharf and she merely happened to clutch it in her death throes, it'll be another case of public money wasted. The captain, egged on by me, got the steward (a queer little job called Dennis) to collect the embarkation notices as if it was the usual procedure. With this result:

Mrs. Dillington-Blick.	*Has lost it.*
Mr. & Mrs. Cuddy	*Joint one. Names written in. Just possible he could have fiddled in "Mr. &" when he found he'd lost his own. Room for fiddle. Can check office procedure.*
Mr. Merryman	*Had it in waistcoat pocket and now accuses steward of pinching it (!)*
Father Jourdain	*Chucked it overboard.*
Mr. McAngus	*Can't find it but says he's sure he kept it. Frantic search—fruitless.*
Dr. Makepiece	*Wasn't given one.*
Aubyn Dale	*Thinks his sweetie took it. Doesn't know why.*
Miss Abbott	*Put it in wastepaper basket. (Gone.)*
Miss Carmichael	*Has got.*

So that's not much cop. No torn embarkation notice.

I've told you about getting the D-B's hyacinths planted in the lounge. Dazzling reactions from Dale and Cuddy. Pity it was both. Explanation for Dale's megrim (spoonerism on TV) very persuasive. Note Cuddys' wedding anniversary date. Am I or am I not playing fair? Darling Troy, how very much, by the way, I love you.

On a sea voyage, you may remember, human relationships undergo a speeding-up process. People get to know each other after a fashion very quickly, and often develop a kind of intimacy. They lose their normal sense of responsibility and become suspended, like the ship, between two worlds. They succumb to infatuations. Mr. Cuddy is succumbing to an infatuation for Mrs. D-B and so, in a vague rarefied way, is Mr. McAngus. The captain belongs to the well-known nautical group "middle-aged sea-dog." High blood pressure. Probably soaks in the tropics. Amorous. (Do you remember your theory about men of a certain age?) Has also set his course for Mrs. D-B. Makepiece has got his eye on Brigid Carmichael and so have all the junior officers. She's a nice child with some sort of chip on her shoulder. The D-B is a tidy armful and knows it. Mrs. Cuddy is a network of sub-fusc complications and Miss Abbott is unlikely, on the face of it, to release the safety catch in even the most determined sex monster. But I suppose I shouldn't generalize. She shaves.

As for the men: I've told you enough about our Mr. Merryman to indicate what a cup-of-tea he is. It may help to fill in the picture if I add that he is the product of St. Chad's, Cantor, and Caius, looks a bit like Mr. Pickwick and much more like Mr. Chips and resembles neither in character. He's retired from teaching but displays every possible pedagogic eccentricity from keeping refuse in his waistcoat pocket to laying down the law in and out of season. He despises policemen, seems to have made a sort of corner in acerbity and will, I bet you, cause a real row before the journey's over.

AUBYN DALE: *Education, undivulged. ? Non-U. So like himself on TV that one catches oneself supposing him to be two-dimensional. His line is being a thoroughly nice chap and he drinks about three times as much as is good for him. For all I know, he may be a thoroughly nice chap. He has a distressing predilection for practical jokes and has made a lifelong enemy of Merryman by causing the steward to serve him with a plastic fried egg at breakfast.*

JOURDAIN: *Lancing and B.N.C. On a normal voyage would be a pleasant companion. To me, the most interesting of the men, but then I always want to find out at what point in an intelligent priest's progress P.C. Faith begins to direct the traffic. I'll swear in this one there's still a smack of the jay-walker.*

CUDDY: *Methodist school. Draper. Not very delicious. Inquisitive. Conceited. A bit mean. Might be a case for a psychiatrist.*

MAKEPIECE: *Felsted, New College, and St. Thomas's. Is a psychiatrist. The orthodox B.M.A. class. Also M.D. Wants to specialize in criminal psychiatry. Gives the impression of being a sound chap.*

MC ANGUS: *Scottish high school. Philatelist. Amiable eunuch, but I don't mean literally; a much-too-facile label. May, for all one knows, be a seething mass of "thing." Also very inquisitive. Gets in a tizzy over details. Dyes, as you will have gathered, his hair.*

Well, my dear love, there you are. The night before Las Palmas, with the connivance of Captain Bannerman, who is only joining in because he hopes I'll look silly, I am giving a little party. You have just read the list of guests. It's by way of being an experiment and may well turn out to be an unproductive bore. But what the hell, after all, am I to do? My instructions are not to dive in, boots and all, declare myself and hold a routine investigation, but to poke and peer and peep about and try to find out if any of these men has not got an alibi for one of the three vital occasions. My instruc-

tions are also to prevent any further activities, and not antagonize the master, who already turns purple with incredulity and rage at the mere suggestion of our man being aboard his ship. On the face of it the D-B and Miss C. look the likeliest candidates for strangulation, but you never know. Mrs. Cuddy may have a je ne sais quoi which has escaped me, but I fancy that as a potential victim Miss Abbott is definitely out. However that may be, you can picture me, as we approach the tropics, muscling in on any cosy little party à deux that breaks out in the more secluded corners of the boat-deck and thus becoming in my own right a likely candidate for throttling. (Not really, so don't agitate yourself.) Because the ladies must be protected. At Las Palmas there should be further reports from head-quarters, following Fox's investigations at the home end. One can only hope they'll cast a little beam. At the moment there's not a twinkle but . . .

There was a tap at the door, and on Alleyn's call, the wireless cadet, a wan youth, came in with a radiogram.

"In code, Mr. Broderick," he said.

When he had gone Alleyn decoded the message and after an interval continued his letter.

Pause indicating suspense. Signal from Fox. It appears that a young lady from the Brummagem department in Woolworth's called Bijou Browne, after thirty days' disastrous hesitation, has coyly informed the Yard that she was half-strangled near Strand-on-the-Green on January fifth. The assailant offered her a bunch of hellebore (Christmas roses to you) and told her there was a spider on her neck. He started in on her rope of beads which, being poppets, broke; was interrupted by the approach of a wayfarer and bolted. It was a dark night and all she can tell Fox about her assailant is that he too was dark, spoke very nice, and wore gloves and ever such a full dark beard.

2

Alleyn's suggestion that he should give a dinner party was made, in the first instance, to Captain Bannerman. "It may be unorthodox," Alleyn said, "but there's just a chance that it may give us a lead about these people."

"I can't say I see how you work that out."

"I hope you will, though, in a minute. And, by the bye, I'll want your collaboration, sir, if you'll agree to give it."

"Me! Now then, now then, what is all this?"

"Let me explain."

Captain Bannerman listened with an air of moody detachment. When Alleyn had finished the captain slapped his palms on his knees and said, "It's a damn crazy notion, but if it proves once and for all that you're on a wild goose chase, it'll be worth the trouble. I won't say no. Now!"

Fortified by this authority Alleyn interviewed the chief steward, who expressed astonishment. Any parties that were given aboard this ship, the chief steward explained, were traditionally cocktail parties, for which Dennis, always helpful, made very dainty little savouries and records were played over the loudspeaker.

However, before Alleyn's vast prestige as a supposed V.I.P. and relation of the managing director, objections dissolved. Dennis became flushed with excitement, the stewards were gracious, and the chef, a Portuguese whose almost moribund interest in his art revived under a whacking great tip, was enthusiastic.

Tables were run together and decorated, wine was chosen, and at the appointed hour the nine passengers, the mate, the chief engineer, Alleyn and Tim Makepiece, having first met for drinks in the lounge, were assembled in the dining-room at a much later hour than was usually observed for dinner at sea.

Alleyn sat at one end of the table with Mrs. Cuddy on his right and Miss Abbott on his left. The captain sat at the other between Mrs. Dillington-Blick and Brigid—an arrangement that broke down his last resistance to so marked a departure from routine and fortified him against the part he had undertaken to play.

Alleyn was a good host; his professional knack of getting other people to talk, coupled with the charm to which his wife never alluded without using the adjective indecent, generated an atmosphere of festivity. He was enormously helped by Mrs. Dillington-Blick, whose genuine enthusiasm and plunging neckline were, in their separate modes, provocative of jollity. She looked so dazzling that she sounded brilliant. Father Jourdain, who sat next to her, was admirable. Aubyn Dale, resplendent in a velvet dinner jacket, coruscated with bonhomie and regaled his immediate neighbours with stories of practical jokes that he had successfully inflicted upon his chums, as he called them, in the world of admass. These anecdotes met with a gay response in Mrs. Dillington-Blick.

Mr. McAngus wore a hyacinth in his buttonhole. Tim Makepiece was obviously enjoying himself and Brigid had an air of being astonished at her own gaiety. Mr. Merryman positively blossomed or, at any rate, sprouted a little under the influence of impeccably chosen wines and surprisingly good food, while Miss Abbott relaxed and barked quite jovially across the table at Mr. Cuddy. The two officers rapidly eased off their guarded good manners.

The Cuddys were the tricky ones. Mrs. Cuddy looked as if she wasn't going to give herself away if she knew it and Mr. Cuddy's smile suggested that he enjoyed secret information about something slightly discreditable to everyone else. They exchanged looks occasionally.

However, as the Montrachet was followed by Perrier-Jouet in a lordly magnum, even the Cuddys shed some of their caginess. Mrs. Cuddy, having assured Alleyn that they never touched anything but a drop of port wine on anniversaries, was persuaded to modify her austerity and did so with abandon. Mr. Cuddy cautiously sipped and asked sharp questions about the wine, pointing out with tedious iteration that it was all above his head, he being a very simple-living person and not used to posh meals. Alleyn was unable to like Mr. Cuddy very much.

Nevertheless, it was he who provided a means of introducing the topic that Alleyn had planned to exploit. There were no flowers on the table. They had been replaced by large bowls of fruit and shaded lamps, in deference, Alleyn pointed out, to Mr. Cuddy's idiosyncrasy. It was an easy step from here to the Flower Murderer. "Flowers," Alleyn suggested, "must have exactly the opposite effect on him to the one they have on you, Mr. Cuddy. A morbid attraction. Wouldn't you say so, Makepiece?"

"It might be so," Tim agreed cheerfully. "From the standpoint of clinical psychiatry there is probably an unconscious association—"

He was young enough and had drunk enough good wine to enjoy airing his shop and, it seemed, essentially modest enough to pull himself up after a sentence or two. "But really very little is known about these cases," he said apologetically. "I'm probably talking through my hat."

But he had served Alleyn's purpose, and the talk was now concentrated on the Flower Murderer. Theories were advanced. Famous cases were quoted. Arguments abounded. Everybody seemed to light up pleasurably on the subject of the death by strangulation of Beryl Cohen and Marguerite Slatters. Even Mr. Merryman became animated and launched a full-scale attack on the methods of the police, who, he said, had obviously made a complete hash of their investigation. He was about to embroider his theme when the captain withdrew his right hand from under the tablecloth without looking at Mrs. Dillington-Blick, raised his glass of champagne and proposed Alleyn's health. Mrs. Cuddy shrilly and unexpectedly shouted "Speech, speech!" and was supported by the captain, Aubyn Dale, the officers and her husband. Father Jourdain murmured, "By all means, speech." Mr. Merryman looked sardonic and the others, politely apprehensive, tapped the table.

Alleyn stood up. His great height, and the circumstance of his face being lit from below like an actor's in the days of footlights, may have given point to the silence that fell upon the room. The stewards had retired into the shadows, there was a distant rattle of crockery. The anonymous throb of the ship's progress re-established itself.

"It's very nice of you," Alleyn said, "but I'm no hand at all at speeches and would make a perfect ass of myself if I tried, particularly in this distinguished company—The Church! Television! Learning! No, no. I shall just thank you all for making this, I hope I may say, such a good party and sit down." He made as if to do so when to everybody's amazement, and judging by his extraordinary expression, his own as well, Mr. Cuddy suddenly roared out in the voice of a tone-deaf bull, "For—or—"

The sound he made was so destitute of anything remotely resembling any air that for a moment everybody was at a loss to know what ailed him. Indeed it was not until he had got as far as "jolly good fellow," that his intention became clear and an attempt was made by Mrs. Cuddy, the captain and the officers to support him. Father Jourdain then good-humouredly struck in, but even his pleasant tenor could make little headway against the deafening atonalities of Mr. Cuddy's ground swell. The tribute ended in confusion and a deadly little silence.

Alleyn hastened to fill it. He said, "Thank you very much," and caught Mr. Merryman's eye.

"You were saying," he prompted, "that the police have made a hash of their investigations. In what respect, exactly?"

"In every possible respect, my dear sir. What have they done? No doubt they have followed the procedure they bring to bear upon other cases which they imagine are in the same category. This procedure having failed they are at a loss. I have long suspected that our wonderful police methods so monotonously extolled by a too-complacent public are in reality cumbersome, inflexible, and utterly without imaginative direction. The murderer has not obliged them by distributing pawn tickets, driving licences or visiting cards about the scenes of his activities and they are left therefore gaping."

"Personally," Alleyn said, "I can't imagine how they even begin to tackle their job. I mean, what *do* they do?"

"You may well ask!" cried Mr. Merryman, now pleasurably uplifted. "No doubt they search the ground for something they call, I understand, occupational dust, in the besotted hope that their man is a bricklayer, knife-grinder, or flour-miller. Finding none, they accost numbers of blameless individuals who have been seen in the vicinity and weeks after the event ask them to produce alibis. Alibis!" Mr. Merryman exclaimed and threw up his hands.

Mrs. Dillington-Blick, opening her eyes very wide, said, "What would *you* do, Mr. Merryman, if *you* were the police?"

There was a fractional pause, after which Mr. Merryman said with hauteur that as he was not in fact a detective the question was without interest.

The captain said, "What's wrong with alibis? If a chap's got an alibi he's out of it, isn't he? So far so good."

"Alibis," Mr. Merryman said grandly, "are in the same category as statistics; in the last analysis they prove nothing."

"Oh, come now!" Father Jourdain protested. "If I'm saying compline in Kensington with the rest of my community at the time a crime is committed in Bermondsey, I'm surely incapable of having committed it."

Mr. Merryman had begun to look very put out and Alleyn came to his rescue.

"Surely," he said, "a great many people don't even remember exactly what they were doing on a specific evening at a specific time. I'm jolly certain I don't."

"Suppose, for instance, now—just for the sake of argument," Captain Bannerman said, and was perhaps a trifle too careful not to look at Alleyn, "that all of us had to produce an alibi for one of these crimes. By gum, I wonder if we could do it. I wonder."

Father Jourdain, who had been looking very steadily at Alleyn, said, "One might try."

"One might," Alleyn rejoined. "One might even have a bet on it. What do you say, Mr. Merryman?"

"Normally," Mr. Merryman declared, "I am not a betting man. However, *dissipat Evius curas edaces.* I would be prepared to wager some trifling sum upon the issue."

"Would you?" Alleyn asked. "Really? All right, then. Propose your bet, sir."

Mr. Merryman thought for a moment. "Coom on, now," urged the captain.

"Very well. Five shillings that the majority here will be unable to produce, on the spot, an acceptable alibi for any given date."

"I'll take you!" Aubyn Dale shouted. "It's a bet!"

Alleyn, Captain Bannerman and Tim Makepiece also said they would take Mr. Merryman's bet.

"And if there's any argument about the acceptability of the alibi," the captain announced, "the non-betters can vote on it. How's that?"

Mr. Merryman inclined his head.

Alleyn asked what was to be the given date and the captain held up his hand. "Let's make it," he suggested, "the first of the flower murders?"

There was a general outbreak of conversation, through which Mr. Cuddy could be heard smugly asserting that he couldn't understand anybody finding the slightest difficulty over so simple a matter. An argument developed between him and Mr. Merryman and was hotly continued over coffee and liqueurs in the lounge. Gently fanned by Alleyn, it spread through the whole party. He felt that the situation had ripened and should be harvested before anybody, particularly the captain and Aubyn Dale, had anything more to drink.

"What about this bet?" he asked in a temporary lull. "Dale has taken Mr. Merryman. We've all got to find alibis for the first flower murder. I don't even remember when it was. Does anybody remember? Mr. McAngus?"

Mr. McAngus at once launched himself upon the uncertain bosom of associated recollections. He was certain, he declared, that he read about it on the morning when his appendix, later to perforate, subjected him to a preliminary twinge. This, he was persuaded, had been on Friday, the sixteenth of January. And yet—was it? His voice sank to a whisper. He began counting on his fingers and wandered disconsolate amidst a litter of parentheses.

Father Jourdain said, "I believe, you know, that it *was* the night of the fifteenth."

". . . and only five days afterwards," Mr. McAngus could be heard droning pleasurably, "I was whisked into Saint Bartholomew's Hospital, where I hung between life and death—"

"Cohen!" Aubyn Dale shouted. "Her name was Beryl Cohen. Of course!"

"Hop Lane, Paddington," Tim Makepiece added with a grin. "Between ten and eleven."

The captain threw an altogether much too conspiratorial glance at Alleyn. "Coom on!" he said. "There you are! We're off! Ladies first."

Mrs. Dillington-Blick and Brigid at once protested that they hadn't a hope of remembering what they did on any night in question. Mrs. Cuddy said darkly and confusedly that she preferred to support her husband and refused to try.

"You see!" Mr. Merryman gleefully ejaculated. "Three failures at once." He turned to Father Jourdain. "And what can the Church produce?"

Father Jourdain said quietly that he was actually in the neighbourhood of the crime on that night. He had been giving a talk at a boys' club in Paddington. "One of the men there drove me back to the community. I remember thinking afterwards that we must have been within a stone's throw of Hop Lane."

"Fancy!" Mrs. Cuddy interposed with ridiculous emphasis. "Fred! Fancy!"

"Which would, I suppose," Father Jourdain continued, "constitute my alibi, wouldn't it?" He turned to Alleyn.

"I must say I'd have thought so."

Mr. Merryman, whose view of alibis seemed to be grounded in cantankerousness rather than logic, pointed out that it would all have to be proved and that in any case the result would be inconclusive.

"Oh," Father Jourdain said tranquilly, "I could *prove* my alibi quite comfortably. And conclusively," he added.

"More than I could," Alleyn rejoined. "I fancy I was at home that night, but I'm blowed if I could prove it."

Captain Bannerman loudly announced that he had been in Liverpool with his ship and could prove it up to the hilt.

"Now then!" he exhorted, absent-mindedly seizing Mrs. Dillington-Blick by the elbow. "What's everybody else got to say for themselves? Any murderers present?" He laughed immoderately at this pleasantry and stared at Alleyn, who became a prey to further grave misgivings. "What about you, Mr. Cuddy? You, no doubt, *can* account for yourself?"

The passengers' interest had been satisfactorily aroused. If only, Alleyn thought, Captain Bannerman would pipe down, the conversation might go according to plan. Fortunately, at this juncture, Mrs. Dillington-Blick murmured something that caught the captain's ear. He became absorbed and everybody else turned their attention upon Mr. Cuddy.

Mr. Cuddy adopted an attitude that seemed to be coloured by gratification at finding himself the centre of interest and a suspicion that in some fashion he was being got at by his fellow passengers. He was maddening but, in a backhanded sort of way, rewarding. The fifteenth of January, he said, consulting a pocketbook and grinning meaninglessly from ear to ear, was a Tuesday, and Tuesday was his lodge night. He gave the address of his lodge (Tooting), and on being asked by Mr. Merryman if he had, in fact, attended that night, appeared to take umbrage and was silent.

"Mr. Cuddy," his wife said, "hasn't missed for twenty years. They made him an Elder Bison for it and gave him ever such a nice testimonial."

Brigid and Tim Makepiece caught each other's eyes and hurriedly turned aside.

Mr. Merryman, who had listened to Mr. Cuddy with every mark of the liveliest impatience, began to question him about the time he had left his lodge, but Mr. Cuddy grew lofty and said he wasn't feeling quite the thing, which judging by his ghastly colour was true enough. He retired, accompanied by Mrs. Cuddy, to the far end of the lounge. Evidently Mr. Merryman looked upon this withdrawal as a personal triumph for himself. He straightened his shoulders and seemed to inflate.

"The discussion," he said, looking about him, "is not without interest. So far we have been presented with two allegedly provable alibis"—he made a facetious bob at the captain and Father Jourdain—"and otherwise, if the ladies are to be counted, with failures."

"Yes, but look here," Tim said, "a little further examination—"

Mr. Merryman blandly and deliberately misunderstood him. "By all means!" he ejaculated. "Precisely. Let us continue. Miss Abbott—"

"What about yourself?" Mr. Cuddy suddenly bawled from the far end of the room.

"Ah!" Mrs. Cuddy rejoined and produced a Rabelaisian laugh. "Ho, ho, ho," she said, without moving a muscle of her face. "What about yourself, Mr. Merryband?"

"Steady, Ethel," Mr. Cuddy muttered.

"Good God!" Tim muttered to Brigid. "She's tiddly!"

"She was tossing down bumpers at dinner—probably for the first time in her life."

"That's it. Tiddly. How wonderful!"

"Ho, ho, ho!" Mrs. Cuddy repeated. "Where was Merryband when the lights went out?"

"Eth!"

"Fair enough," Aubyn Dale exclaimed. "Come along, Mr. Merryman. Alibi, please."

"With all the pleasure in life," Mr. Merryman said. "I have none. I join the majority. On the evening in question," he continued didactically, as if he expected them all to start taking dictation, "I attended a suburban cinema. The Kosy, spelt (abominable vulgarism) with a 'K.' in Bounty Street, Chelsea. By a diverting coincidence the film was *The Lodger*. I am totally unable to prove it," he ended triumphantly.

"Very fishy!" Tim said, shaking his head owlishly. "Oh, very fishy indeed, I fear, sir!"

Mr. Merryman gave a little crowing laugh.

"I know!" Mr. McAngus abruptly shouted. "I have it! Tuesday! Television!" And at once added, "No, no, wait a moment. *What* did you say the date was?"

Alleyn told him and he became silent and depressed.

"What about Miss Abbott, now?" Captain Bannerman asked. "Can Miss Abbott find an alibi? Come along, Miss Abbott. January fifteenth."

She didn't answer at once but sat, unsmiling and staring straight before her. A silence fell upon the little company.

"I was in my flat," she said at last, and gave the address. There was something uncomfortable in her manner. Alleyn thought, "Damn! The unexpected. In a moment somebody will change the conversation."

Aubyn Dale was saying waggishly, "Not good enough! Proof, Miss Abbott, proof."

"Did anybody ring up or come in?" Brigid prompted with a friendly smile for Miss Abbott.

"My friend—the person I share my flat with—came in at ten-thirty-five."

"How clever to remember!" Mrs. Dillington-Blick murmured and managed to suggest that she herself was enchantingly feckless.

"And before that?" Mr. Merryman demanded.

A faint dull red settled above Miss Abbott's cheekbones. "I watched television," she said.

"Voluntarily?" Mr. Merryman asked in astonishment.

To everybody's surprise Miss Abbott shuddered. She wetted her lips. "It passed . . . it . . . sometimes helped to pass the time—"

Tim Makepiece, Father Jourdain, and Brigid, sensing her discomfiture, tried to divert Mr. Merryman's attention, but he was evidently one of those people who are unable to abandon a conversation before they have triumphed. " 'Pass the time,' " he ejaculated, casting up his eyes. "Was ever there a more damning condemnation of this bastard, this emasculate, this enervating peepshow. What was the programme?"

Miss Abbott glanced at Aubyn Dale, who was looking furiously at Mr. Merryman. "In point of fact—" she began.

Dale waved his hands. "Ah-ah! I knew it. Alas, I knew it! Nine to nine-thirty. Every Tuesday night, God help me. I knew." He leaned forward and addressed himself to Mr. Merryman. "My session, you know. The one you dislike so much. The Jolyon swimsuit programme—*Pack Up Your Troubles*, which, oddly enough, appears to create a slightly different reaction in its all-time-high viewing audience. Very reprehensible, no doubt, but there it is. They seem quite to like it."

"Hear, hear!" Mrs. Cuddy shouted vaguely from the far end of the lounge and stamped approval.

"*Pack Up Your Troubles*," Mrs. Dillington-Blick ejaculated. "Of course!"

"Madam," Mr. Merryman continued, looking severely at Miss Abbott. "Will you be good enough to describe the precise nature of the predicaments that were aired by the—really, I am at a loss for the correct term to describe these people—the protagonist will no doubt enlighten me—"

"The subjects?" Father Jourdain suggested.

"The victims?" Tim amended.

"Or the guests? I like to think of them as my guests," said Aubyn Dale.

Mrs. Cuddy said rather wildly, "That's a lovely, *lovely* way of putting it!"

("Steady, Eth!")

Miss Abbott, who had been twisting her large hands together, said, "I remember nothing about the programme. Nothing."

She half rose from her seat and then seemed to change her mind and sank back. "Mr. Merryman, you're not to badger Miss Abbott," Brigid said quickly and turned to Aubyn Dale. "You, at any rate, have got your alibi, it seems."

"Oh, yes!" he rejoined. He finished his double brandy and, in his turn, slipped his hand under Mrs. Dillington-Blick's forearm. "God, yes! I've got the entire Jolyon swimsuit admass between me and Beryl Cohen. Twenty million viewers can't be wrong! In spite of Mr. Merryman."

Alleyn said lightly, "But isn't the programme over by nine-thirty? What about the next half-hour?"

"Taking off the war-paint, dear boy, and meeting the chums in the jolly old local."

It had been generally agreed that Aubyn Dale's alibi was established when Mr. McAngus said diffidently, "Do you know—I may be quite wrong—but I had a silly notion someone said that particular session was done at another time, I mean, if of course it *was* that programme."

"Ah?" Mr. Merryman ejaculated, pointing at him as if he'd held his hand up. "Explain yourself. Filmed? Recorded?"

"Yes. But, of course I may be—"

But Mr. Merryman pounced gleefully on Aubyn Dale. "What do you say, sir? Was the session recorded?"

Dale collected everybody else's attention as if he invited them to enjoy Mr. Merryman with him. He opened his arms and enlarged his smile and he patted Mr. McAngus on the head.

"Clever boy," he said. "And I thought I'd got away with it. I couldn't resist pulling your leg, Mr. Merryman. You will forgive me, won't you?"

Mr. Merryman did not reply. He merely stared very fixedly at Aubyn Dale, and as Brigid muttered to Tim, may have been restraining himself from saying he would see him in his study after prep.

Dale added to this impression by saying with uneasy boyishness, "I swear, by the way, I was just about to come clean. Naturally."

"Then," Alleyn said, "it was not a live transmission?"

"Not that one. Usually is, but I was meant to be on my way to the States, so we filmed it."

"Indeed?" Mr. Merryman said. "And *were* you on your way to the United States, sir?"

"Actually, no. One of those things. There was a nonsense made over dates. I flew three days later. Damn nuisance. It meant I didn't get back till the day before we sailed."

"And your alibi?" Mr. Merryman continued ominously.

"Well . . . ah . . . well—don't look at me, padre. I spent the evening with my popsey. Don't ask me to elaborate, will you? No names, no packdrill."

"And no alibi," said Mr. Merryman neatly.

There was a moment's uneasy suspense during which nobody looked at anybody else and then Mr. McAngus unexpectedly surfaced. "I remember it all quite perfectly," he announced. "It *was* the evening before my first hint of trouble and I *did* watch television!"

"Programme?" Mr. Merryman snapped. Mr. McAngus smiled timidly at Aubyn Dale. "Oh," he tittered, "I'm no end of a fan, you know."

It turned out that he had, in fact, watched *Pack Up Your Troubles*. When asked if he could remember it, he said at once, "Very clearly." Alleyn saw Miss Abbott close her eyes momentarily as if she felt giddy. "There was a lady," Mr. McAngus continued, "asking, I recollect, whether she ought to get married."

"There almost always is," Dale groaned and made a face of comic despair.

"But this was very complicated because, poor thing, she felt she would be deserting her great friend and her great friend didn't know about it and would be dreadfully upset. There!" Mr. McAngus cried. "I've remembered! If only one could be sure which evening. The twenty-fifth, I ask myself? I mean the fifteenth, of course."

Dale said, "I couldn't tell you which programme but, ah, poor darling, I remember her. I think I helped her. I hope I did!"

"Perhaps," Captain Bannerman suggested, "Miss Abbott remembers now you've mentioned it. That'd fix your alibi for you."

"*Do* you, Miss Abbott?" Mr. McAngus asked anxiously.

Everybody looked at Miss Abbott and it was at once apparent to everybody but Mr. McAngus that she was greatly upset. Her lips trembled. She covered them with her hand in a rather dreadful parody of cogitation. She shook her head and her eyes overflowed.

"No?" Mr. McAngus said, wistfully oblivious and shortsightedly blinking, "Do try, Miss Abbott. She was a dark, rather *heavy* lady. I mean, of course, that was the impression one had. Because one doesn't see the face and the back of the head is rather out of focus, isn't it, Mr. Dale? But she kept saying (and I think they must distort the voice a little, too) that she knew her friend would be dreadfully hurt because apart from herself, she had so few to care for her." He made a little bob at Aubyn Dale. "You were wonderful," he said, "so tactful. About loneliness. I'm sure if you saw it, Miss Abbott, you must remember. Mr. Dale made such practical and helpful suggestions. I don't remember exactly what they were but—"

Miss Abbott rounded on him and cried out with shocking violence, "For God's sake stop talking. 'Helpful suggestions'! What 'suggestions' can help in that kind of hell!" She looked round at them all with an expression of evident despair. "For some of us," she said, "there's no escape. We are our own slaves. No escape or release."

"Nonsense!" Mr. Merryman said sharply. "There is always an escape and a release. It is a matter of courage and resolution."

Miss Abbott gave a harsh sob. "I'm sorry," she muttered. "I'm not myself. I shouldn't have had so much champagne." She turned away.

Father Jourdain said quickly, "You know, Mr. McAngus, I'm afraid you haven't quite convinced us."

"And that's the last alibi gone overboard," said the captain. "Mr. Merryman wins."

He made a great business of handing over his five shillings. Alleyn, Mr. McAngus, and Aubyn Dale followed suit.

They all began to talk at once, and with the exception of the Cuddys, avoided looking at Miss Abbott. Brigid moved in front of her and screened her from the others. It was tactfully done and Alleyn was confirmed in his view that Brigid was a nice child. Mrs. Dillington-Blick joined her and automatically a group assembled round Mrs. Dillington-Blick. So between Miss Abbott and the rest of the world there was a barrier behind which she trumpeted privately into her handkerchief.

Presently she got up, now mistress of herself, thanked Alleyn for his party and left it.

The Cuddys came forward, clearly agog, eager, by allusion and then by direct reference, to speculate upon Miss Abbott's distress. Nobody supported them. Mr. McAngus merely looked bewildered. Tim talked to Brigid and Captain Bannerman and Aubyn Dale talked to Mrs. Dillington-Blick. Mr. Merryman looked once at the Cuddys over his spectacles, rumpled his hair and said something about "*Hoc morbido cupiditatis*" in a loud voice to Alleyn and Father Jourdain. Alleyn was suddenly visited by an emotion that is unorthodox in an investigating officer; he felt a liking and warmth for these people. He respected them because they refused to gossip with the Cuddys about Miss Abbott's unhappiness and because they had behaved with decency and compassion when she broke down. He saw Brigid and Mrs. Dillington-Blick speak together and then slip out of the room and he knew they had gone to see if they could help Miss Abbott. He was very much troubled.

Father Jourdain came up to him and said, "Shall we move over here?" He led Alleyn to the far end of the room.

"That was unfortunate," he said.

"I'm sorry about it."

"You couldn't possibly know it would happen. She is a very unhappy woman. She exhales unhappiness."

"It was the reference to that damn spiritual striptease session of Dale's," Alleyn said. "I suppose something in the programme had upset her."

"Undoubtedly," Father Jourdain smiled. "That's a good description of it, a spiritual striptease. I suppose you'll think I'm lugging in my cloth, but you know I really do think it's better to leave confession to the professional."

"Dale would call himself a professional."

"What he does," Father Jourdain said, with some warmth, "is vulgar, dangerous, and altogether odious. But he's not a bad chap, of course. At least I don't think so. Not a bad sort of chap at all."

Alleyn said, "There's something else you want to say to me, isn't there?"

"There is, but I hesitate to say it. I am not sure of myself. Will you laugh at me if I tell you that, by virtue of my training perhaps, and perhaps because of some instinct, I am peculiarly sensitive to—to spiritual atmosphere?"

"I don't know that I—"

Father Jourdain interrupted him.

"I mean that when I feel there is something really out of joint spiritually —I use this word because I'm a priest, you know—with a group of people, I'm usually right."

"And do you feel it now?"

"Very strongly. I suspect it's a sense of unexpressed misery," said Father Jourdain. "But I can't hunt it home."

"Miss Abbott?"

"I don't know. I don't know."

"Even that," Alleyn said, "is not what you want to say."

"You're very perceptive yourself." Father Jourdain looked steadily at him. "When the party breaks up, will you stay behind for a moment?"

"Certainly."

Father Jourdain said so softly that Alleyn could barely hear him, "You *are* Roderick Alleyn, aren't you?"

3

The deserted lounge smelt of dead cigarettes and forgotten drinks. Alleyn opened the doors to the deck outside: the stars were careering in the sky; the ship's mast swung against them; and the night sea swept thudding and hissing past her flanks.

"I'm sorry to have kept you waiting," said Father Jourdain behind him. Alleyn shut the doors again and they sat down.

"Let me assure you at once," Father Jourdain said, "that I shall respect your—I suppose anonymity is not the right word. Your incognito, shall we say?"

"I'm not particularly bothered about the choice of words," Alleyn said dryly.

"Nor need you be bothered about my recognizing you. It's by the oddest of coincidences. Your wife may be said to have effected the introduction."

"Really?"

"I have never met her, but I admire her painting. Some time ago I went to a one-man show of hers and was very much impressed by a small portrait. It too was anonymous, but a brother-priest, Father Copeland of Winton St. Giles, who knows you both, told me it was a portrait of her husband, who was the celebrated Inspector Alleyn. I have a very long memory for faces and the likeness was striking. I felt sure I was not mistaken."

"Troy," Alleyn said, "will be enormously gratified."

"And then, that bet of Mr. Merryman's was organized, wasn't it?"

"Lord, lord! I do seem to have made an ass of myself."

"No, no. Not you. You were entirely convincing. It was the captain."

"His air of spontaneity *was* rather massive, perhaps."

"Exactly." Father Jourdain leaned forward and said, "Alleyn, why was that conversation about the Flower Murderer introduced?"

Alleyn said, "For fun. Why else?"

"So you are not going to tell me."

"At least," Alleyn said lightly, "I've got your alibi for January the fifteenth."

"You don't trust me, of course."

"It doesn't arise. As you have discovered, I am a policeman."

"I beg you to trust me. You won't regret it. You can check my alibi, can't you? And the other time, the other poor child who had been to church—when was that? The twenty-fifth. Why, on the twenty-fifth I was at a conference in Paris. You can prove it at once. No doubt you're in touch with your colleagues. Of course you can."

"I expect it can be done."

"Then do it. I urge you to do it. If you are here for the fantastic reason I half suspect, you will need someone you can trust."

"It never comes amiss."

"These women must not be left alone." Father Jourdain had arisen and was staring through the glass doors. "Look," he said.

Mrs. Dillington-Blick was taking a walk on deck. As she passed the lighted windows above the engine-rooms she paused. Her earrings and necklace twinkled, the crimson scarf she had wrapped about her head fluttered in the night breeze. A man emerged from the shadow of the centrecastle and walked towards her. He took her arm. They turned away and were lost to view. He was Aubyn Dale. "You see," Father Jourdain said. "If I'm right, that's the sort of thing we mustn't allow."

Alleyn said, "To-day is the seventh of February. These crimes have occured at ten-day intervals."

"But there have only been two."

"There was an attempt on January fifth. It was not publicized."

"Indeed! The fifth, the fifteenth and the twenty-fifth. Why, then, ten days have already passed since the last crime. If you are right (and the interval after all may be a coincidence) the danger is acute."

"On the contrary, if there's anything in the ten-day theory, Mrs. Dillington-Blick at the moment is in no danger."

"But—" Father Jourdain stared at him. "Do you mean there's been another of these crimes? Since we sailed? Why then—?"

"About half an hour before you sailed and about two hundred yards away from the ship. On the night of the fourth. He was punctual almost to the minute."

"Dear God!" said Father Jourdain.

"At the moment, of course, none of the passengers except the classic *one* knows about this, and unless anybody takes the trouble to cable the news to Las Palmas they won't hear about it there."

"The fourteenth," Father Jourdain muttered. "You think we may be safe until the fourteenth."

"One simply hopes so. All the same, shall we take the air before we turn in? I think we might." Alleyn opened the doors. Father Jourdain moved towards them.

"It occurs to me," he said, "that you may think me a busybody. It's not that. It is, quite simply, that I have a nose for evil and a duty to prevent, if I can, the commission of sin. I am a spiritual policeman, in fact. You may feel that I'm talking professional nonsense."

"I respect the point of view," Alleyn said. For a moment they looked at each other. "And, sir, I am disposed to trust you."

"That, at least, is a step forward," said Father Jourdain. "Shall we leave it like that until you have checked my alibis?"

"If you're content to do so."

"I haven't much choice," Father Jourdain observed. He added, after a moment, "And at any rate it *does* appear that we have an interval. Until February the fourteenth?"

"Only if the time theory is correct. It may not be correct."

"I suppose—a psychiatrist—?"

"Dr. Makepiece, for instance. He's one. I'm thinking of consulting him."

"But—"

"Yes?"

"He had no alibi. He said so."

"They tell us," Alleyn said, "that the guilty man in a case of this sort never says he has no alibi. They say he always produces an alibi. Of some sort. Shall we go out?"

They went out on deck. A light breeze still held but it was no longer cold. The ship, ploughing through the dark, throbbed with her own life and with small orderly noises and yet was compact of a larger quietude. As they moved along the starboard side of the well-deck a bell sounded in four groups of two.

"Midnight," Alleyn said. Sailors passed them, quiet-footed. Mrs. Dillington-Blick and Aubyn Dale appeared on the far side of the hatch, making for the passengers' quarters. They called out good-night and disappeared.

Father Jourdain peered at his watch. "And this afternoon we arrive at Las Palmas," he said.

CHAPTER SIX **Broken Doll**

Las Palmas is known to tourists for its walkie-talkie dolls. They stare out of almost every shop window, and sit in rows in the street bazaars near the wharves. They vary in size, cost and condition. Some have their garments cynically nailed to their bodies and others wear hand-sewn dresses of elaborate design. Some are bald under their bonnets, others have high Spanish wigs of real hair crowned with real lace mantillas. The most expensive of all are adorned with necklaces, bracelets and even rings, and have masses of wonderful petticoats under their flowered and braided skirts. They can be as tall as a child or as short as a woman's hand.

Two things the dolls have in common. If you hold any one of them by the arm it may be induced to jerk its legs to and fro in a parody of walking, and as it walks it also jerks its head from side to side and from within its body it squeaks, "Ma-ma." They all squeak in the same way with voices that are shockingly like those of infants. Nearly everybody who goes to Las Palmas remembers either some little girl who would like a walkie-talkie doll or, however misguidedly, some grown woman who might possibly be amused by one.

The company placed an open car at the disposal of Captain Bannerman and in it he put Mrs. Dillington-Blick, looking like a piece of Turkish delight. They drove about Las Palmas, stopping at shops where the driver had a profitable understanding with the proprietor. Mrs. Dillington-Blick bought herself a black lace near-mantilla with a good deal of metal in it, a comb to support it, some Portuguese jewellery, and a fan. Captain Bannerman bought her a lot of artificial magnolias because they didn't see any real ones. He felt proud because all the Las Palmanians obviously admired her very much indeed. They came to a shop where a wonderful dress was displayed, a full Spanish dress made of black lace and caught up to display a foam of scarlet petticoats underneath. The driver kissed his fingers over and over again and intimated that if Mrs. Dillington-Blick were to put it on she would look like the queen of heaven. Mrs. Dillington-Blick examined it with her head on one side.

"Do you know," she said, "allowing for a little Latin exaggeration, I'm inclined to agree with him."

Tim Makepiece and Brigid came along the street and joined them. Brigid said, "Do try it on. You'd look absolutely marvellous. Do. For fun."

"Shall I? Come in with me, then. Make me keep my head."

The captain said he would go to his agents' offices, where he had business to do, and return in twenty minutes. Tim, who very much wanted to buy some roses for Brigid, also said he'd come back. Greatly excited, the two ladies entered the shop.

The stifling afternoon wore into evening. Dusk was rapidly succeeded by night, palm trees rattled in an enervated breeze, and at nine o'clock, by arrangement, Captain Bannerman and Mrs. Dillington-Blick were to meet Aubyn Dale at the grandest hotel in Las Palmas for dinner.

Mrs. Dillington-Blick had been driven back to the ship, where she changed into the wonderful Spanish dress, which of course she had bought. She was excitedly assisted by Brigid. "What did I tell you!" Brigid shouted triumphantly. "You ought to be sitting in a box looking at a play by Lope de Vega with smashing caballeros all round you. It's a riot." Mrs. Dillington-Blick, who had never heard of Lope de Vega, half smiled, opened her eyes very wide, turned and turned again to watch the effect in her looking-glass and said, "Not bad. Really, it's not bad," and pinned one of the captain's artificial magnolias in her décolletage. She gave Brigid the brilliant look of a woman who knows she is successful.

"All the same," she murmured, "I can't help *rather* wishing it was the G.B. who was taking me out."

"The G.B.?"

"My dear, the Gorgeous Brute. Glamorous Broderick, if you like. I dropped hints like thunderbolts but no luck, alas."

"Never mind," Brigid said, "you'll have a terrific success, anyway. I promise you."

She ran off to effect her own change. It was when she fastened one of Tim Makepiece's red roses in her dress that it suddenly occurred to Brigid she hadn't thought of her troubles for at least six hours. After all, it *was* rather fun to be dining out in a foreign city on a strange island with a pleasant young man.

It all turned out superbly, an enchanted evening suspended like a dream between the strange intervals of a sea voyage. The streets they drove through and the food they ate, the music they danced to, the flowers, the extremely romantic lighting and the exotic people were all, Brigid told Tim, "out of this world." They sat at their table on the edge of the dance floor, talked very fast about the things that interested them, and were delighted to find how much they liked each other.

At half-past nine Mrs. Dillington-Blick arrived with the captain and Aubyn Dale. She really was, as Brigid pointed out to Tim, sensational. Everybody looked at her. A kind of religious gravity impregnated the deportment of the head waiter. Opulence and observance enveloped her like an expensive scent. She *was* terrific.

"I admire her," Brigid said, "enormously. "Don't you?"

Brigid's chin rested in the palm of her hand. Her forearm, much less opulent than Mrs. Dillington-Blick's, shone in the candlelight and her eyes were bright.

Tim said, "She's the most suffocatingly feminine job I've ever seen, I think. An all-time low in inhibitions and an all-time high in what it takes. If, of course, that happens to be your line of country. It's not mine."

Brigid found this answer satisfactory. "I like her," she said. "She's warm and uncomplicated."

"She's all of that. Hullo! Look who's here!"

Alleyn came in with Father Jourdain. They were shown to a table at some distance from Tim's and Brigid's.

" 'Distinguished visitors'!" Brigid said, gaily waving to them.

"They are rather grand-looking, aren't they? I must say I like Broderick. Nice chap, don't you think?"

"Yes, I do," Brigid said emphatically. "What about Father Jourdain?"

"I wouldn't know. Interesting face; not typically clerical."

"*Is* there a typically clerical face or are you thinking of comic curates at the Players Theatre Club?"

"No," said Tim slowly. "I'm not. But look at the mouth and the eyes. He's a celibate, isn't he? I bet it's been a bit of a hurdle."

"Suppose," Brigid said, "you wanted advice very badly and had to go to one of those two. Which would it be?"

"Oh, Broderick. Every time. *Do* you by any chance want advice?"

"No."

"If you did, I'd take it very kindly if you came to me."

"Thank you," said Brigid. "I'll bear it in mind."

"Good. Let's trip a measure."

"Nice young couple," said Father Jourdain as they danced past him and he added, "I do hope you're right in what you say."

"About—?"

"About alibis."

The band crashed and was silent. The floor cleared and two spotlights introduced a pair of tango dancers, very fierce, like game birds. They strutted and stalked, clattered their castanets, and frowned ineffably at each other. "What an angry woo," Tim said.

When they had finished they moved among the tables followed by their spotlight.

"Oh, *no!*" Father Jourdain exclaimed. "Not *another* doll!"

It was an enormous and extraordinarily realistic one, carried by the woman dancer. Evidently it was for sale. She flashed brilliant smiles and proudly showed it off, while her escort stood moodily by. "*Señores y señoras,*" announced a voice over the loud-speaker and added, they thought, something about having the honour to present "La Esmeralda," which was evidently the name of the doll.

"Curious!" Alleyn remarked.

"What?"

"It's dressed exactly like Mrs. D-B."

And so it was—in a flounced black lace dress and a mantilla. It even had a green necklace and earrings and lace gloves, and its fingers were clamped round the handle of an open fan. It was a woman-doll with a bold, handsome face and a flashing smile like the dancer's. It looked terrifyingly expensive. Alleyn watched with some amusement as it approached the table where Mrs. Dillington-Blick sat with the captain and Aubyn Dale.

The dancers had of course noticed the resemblance and so had the headwaiter. They all smiled and ejaculated and admired as the doll waddled beguilingly towards Mrs. Dillington-Blick.

"Poor old Bannerman," Alleyn said, "he's sunk, I fear. Unless Dale—"

But Aubyn Dale extended his hands in his well-known gesture, and with a smile of rueful frankness was obviously saying it was no good them looking at him, while the captain, ruby-faced, stared in front of him with an expression of acute unconcern. Mrs. Dillington-Blick shook her head and beamed and shook it again. The dancers bowed, smiled and moved on, approaching the next table. The woman stooped and with a kind of savage gaiety induced the doll to walk. "Ma-ma!" squeaked the doll. "Ma-ma!"

"Ladies and gentlemen," the loud-speaker repeated and continued, this time in English, "we have the honour to present Mees Esmeralda, Queen of Las Palmas."

From somewhere in the shadows at the back of the room a napkin fluttered. The woman snatched up the doll and swept between the tables, followed by her escort. The spotlight settled on them. Heads were turned. One or two people stood up. It was impossible to see the person at the distant table. After a short delay the dancer returned, holding the doll aloft.

"She *hasn't* sold it," Father Jourdain remarked.

"On the contrary," Alleyn rejoined, "I think she has. Look."

The doll was borne in triumph to the captain's table and with a magnificent curtsey presented to Mrs. Dillington-Blick.

At the other side of the room Tim said, "Look at that, now!"

"What a triumph!" Brigid exclaimed delightedly.

"Who's the poor fish, do you suppose?"

"I can't see. It'll be some superb grandee with flashing eyes and a crimson cummerbund. What *fun* for Mrs. Dillington-Blick."

The dancers were making gestures in the direction of their customer. Mrs. Dillington-Blick, laughing and triumphant holding the doll, strained round to see. The spotlight probed into the distant corner. Somebody stood up.

"Oh, *look!*" cried Brigid.

"Well, blow me down flat!" said Tim.

"How very surprising," observed Father Jourdain, "it's Mr. McAngus!"
"He has made his reciprocal gesture," said Alleyn.

2

The *Cape Farewell* sailed at two in the morning and the passengers
were all to be aboard by half-past one. Alleyn and Father Jourdain had
returned at midnight and Alleyn had gone to his cabin to have another
look at his mail. It included a detailed report from the Yard of the attack
that had been made upon Miss Bijou Browne on January fifth and a
letter from his senior saying nothing had developed that suggested altera-
tion in Alleyn's plan of action. Alleyn had telephoned the Yard from
police headquarters in Las Palmas and had spoken to Inspector Fox.
Following Alleyn's radiogram of the previous night, the Yard had at once
tackled the passengers' alibis. Father Jourdain was, Fox said, as good as
gold. Mr. Merryman's cinema had in fact shown *The Lodger* on the night
in question as the first half of a double bill. The name of Aubyn Dale's
sweetie so far eluded the Yard, but Fox hoped to get it before long and
would, he said, dream up some cock-and-bull story that might give him
an excuse to question her about the night of the fifteenth. The rest of
Dale's statement had been proved. Fox had got in touch with Mr. Cuddy's
lodge and had told them the police were making enquiries about a valu-
able watch. From information received they believe it had been stolen
from Mr. Cuddy near the lodge premises on the night of the fifteenth. A
record of attendances showed that Mr. Cuddy had signed in but the
secretary remembered that he left very early, feeling unwell. Apart from
Mr. McAngus having perforated his appendix four days after the date in
question, Fox dryly continued, it would be impossible to check his litter
of disjointed reminiscence. They would, however, poke about and see if
anything cropped up. An enquiry at Dr. Makepiece's hospital gave conclusive evidence that he had been on duty there until midnight.

Captain Bannerman, it appeared, had certainly been in Liverpool on
the night of the fifteenth and a routine check completely cleared the other
officers. In any case it was presumed that the ship's complement didn't
go aboard clutching passengers' embarkation notices.

The missing portion of the embarkation notice had not been found.

A number of psychiatric authorities had been consulted and all agreed
that the ten-day interval would probably be maintained and that the
fourteenth of February, therefore, might be anticipated as a deadline.
One of them added, however, that the subject's homicidal urge might
be exacerbated by an untoward event. Which meant, Inspector Fox sup-

posed dryly, that he might cut up for trouble before the fourteenth, if a bit of what he fancied turned up in the meantime and did the trick.

Fox concluded the conversation by enquiring about the weather and on being told it was semi-tropical remarked that some people had all the luck. Alleyn had rejoined that if Fox considered a long voyage with a homicidal maniac (identity unknown and boiling up for trouble) and at least two eminently suitable victims was a bit of luck, he'd be glad to swap jobs with him. On this note they rang off.

Alleyn had also received a cable from his wife which said,

LODGING PETITION FOR DESERTION DO YOU WANT ANYTHING SENT ANY-
WHERE LOVE DARLING TROY.

He put his papers away and went down to the well-deck. It was now twenty minutes past midnight but none of the passengers had gone to bed. The Cuddys were in the lounge telling Dennis, with whom they were on informal terms, about their adventures ashore. Mr. Merryman reclined in a deck-chair with his arms folded and his hat over his nose. Mr. McAngus and Father Jourdain leaned on the taffrail and stared down at the wharf below. The after-hatch was open and the winch that served it still in operation. The night was oppressively warm.

Alleyn strolled along the deck and looked down into the after-hatch, yawning black, and at the dramatically lit figures that worked it. The rattle of the winch, the occasional voices and the pulse of the engines made a not unattractive accompaniment to the gigantic fishing operation. He had watched and listened for some minutes before he became aware of another and most unexpected sound. Quite close at hand was some-one singing in Latin; an austere, strangely measured and sexless chant:

> *"Procul recedant somnia*
> *Et noctium phantasmata*
> *Hostemque nostrum comprime*
> *Ne polluantur corpora."*

Alleyn moved across the after end of the deck. In the little verandah, just visible in reflected light, sat Miss Abbott, singing. She stopped at once when she saw him. She had under her hands what appeared to be many sheets of paper; perhaps an immensely long letter.

"That was lovely," Alleyn said, "I wish you hadn't stopped. It was extraordinarily—what?—tranquil?"

She said, more it seemed to herself than to him, "Yes. Tranquil and devout. It's music designed against devils."

"What were you singing?"

She roused herself suddenly and became defensive. It seemed incredible that her speaking voice could be so harsh.

"A Vatican plainsong," she said.

"What a fool I was to blunder in and stop you. Would it be—seventh century?"

"Six-fifty-five. Printed from manuscript in the *Liver Gradualis*, eighteen-eighty-three," she barked and got up.

Alleyn said, "Don't move. I'll take myself off."

"I'm going anyway." She walked straight past him. Her eyes were dark with excitement. She strode along the deck to the lighted area where the others were congregated, sat in a deck-chair a little apart from them and began to read her letter.

After a minute or two Alleyn also returned and joined Mr. McAngus. "That was a charming gesture of yours this evening," he said.

Mr. McAngus made a little tittering sound. "I was so lucky!" he said. "Such a happy coincidence, wasn't it? And the resemblance, you know, is complete. I *promised* I'd find something and *there* it was. So very appropriate, I felt." He hesitated for a moment and added rather wistfully, "I was invited to join their party, but of course I thought better to decline. She seemed quite delighted. At the doll, I mean. The doll delighted her."

"I'm sure it did."

"Yes," Mr. McAngus said. "Yes." His voice had trailed away into a murmur. He was no longer aware of Alleyn but looked past him and down towards the wharf.

It was now twenty past one. A taxi had come along the wharf. Out of it got Brigid Carmichael and Tim Makepiece, talking busily and obviously on the best possible terms with each other and the world at large. They came up the gangway smiling all over their faces. "Oh!" Brigid exclaimed to Alleyn. "Isn't Las Palmas heaven? We *have* had such fun."

But it was not at Brigid that Mr. McAngus stared so fixedly. An open car had followed the taxi and in it were Mrs. Dillington-Blick, the captain, and Aubyn Dale. They too were gay but with a more ponderable gaiety than Tim's and Brigid's. The men's faces were darkish and their voices heavy. Mrs. Dillington-Blick still looked marvellous. Her smile, if not exactly irrepressible, was full of meaning, and if her eyes no longer actually sparkled they were still extremely expressive and the tiny pockets underneath them scarcely noticeable. The men helped her up the gangway. The captain went first. He carried the doll and held Mrs. Dillington-Blick's elbow while Aubyn Dale put his hands on her waist and made a great business of assisting her from the rear. There were jokes and a lot of suppressed laughter.

When they arrived on deck the captain went up to the bridge and Mrs. Dillington-Blick held court. Mr. McAngus was made much of, Father Jourdain appealed to, and Alleyn given a great many sidelong glances. The doll was exhibited and the Cuddys came out to see it. Mrs. Cuddy said she supposed the dolls were produced with sweated labour, but Mr. Cuddy stared at Mrs. Dillington-Blick and said, with an odd inflection, that there were some things that couldn't be copied. Alleyn was made to walk with the doll and Mrs. Dillington-Blick went behind, imitating its action, jerking her head and squeaking, "Ma-ma!"

Miss Abbott put down her letter and stared at Mrs. Dillington-Blick with a kind of hungry amazement.

"Mr. Merryman!" cried Mrs. Dillington-Blick. "Wake up! Let me introduce my twin sister Donna Esmeralda."

Mr. Merryman removed his hat, gazed at the doll with distaste and then at its owner.

"The resemblance," he said, "is too striking to arouse any emotion but one of profound misgiving."

"Ma-ma!" squeaked Mrs. Dillington-Blick.

Dennis trotted out on deck, plumply smiling, and approached her. "A night-lettergram for *you*, Mrs. Dillington-Blick. It came after you'd gone *ashore*. I've been looking out for you. Oh, mercy!" he added, eyeing the doll. "Isn't she *twee!*"

Mr. Merryman contemplated Dennis with something like horror and replaced his hat over his nose.

Mrs. Dillington-Blick gave a sharp ejaculation and fluttered her open night-lettergram.

"My dears!" she shouted. "You'll never credit this! How too frightful and murky! My dears!"

"Darling!" Aubyn Dale exclaimed. "What?"

"It's from a man, a friend of mine. You'll *never* believe it. Listen!

"SENT MASSES OF HYACINTHS TO SHIP BUT SHOP INFORMS ME YOUNG FEMALE TAKING THEM LATEST VICTIM FLOWER MURDERER STOP CARD RETURNED BY POLICE STOP WHAT A THING STOP HAVE LOVELY TRIP TONY."

3

Her fellow passengers were so excited by Mrs. Dillington-Blick's news that they scarcely noticed their ship's sailing. *Cape Farewell* separated herself from Las Palmas with an almost imperceptible gesture and moved away into the dark, taking up the rhythm of her voyage, while Mrs. Dillington-Blick held the stage.

They all gathered round her and Mr. Cuddy managed to get close enough to look sideways at the night-lettergram. Mr. Merryman, with an affectation of stretching his legs, strolled nearer, his head thrown back at an angle that enabled him to stare superciliously from under his hat brim at Mrs. Dillington-Blick. Even Miss Abbott leaned forward in her chair, grasping her crumpled letter, her large hands dangling between her knees. Captain Bannerman, who had come down from the bridge, looked much too knowing for Alleyn's peace of mind, and repeatedly attempted to catch his eye. Alleyn avoided him, plunged into the melee and was himself loud in ejaculation and comment. There was much speculation as to where and when the girl who brought the flowers could have been murdered. Out of the general conversation Mrs. Cuddy's voice rose shrilly, "And it was hyacinths again, too. Fancy! What a coincidence!"

"My dear madam," Dr. Makepiece testily pointed out, "the flowers are in season. No doubt the shops are full of them. There is no esoteric significance in the circumstance."

"Mr. Cuddy never fancied them," said Mrs. Cuddy. "Did you, dear?"

Mr. Merryman raised his hands in a gesture of despair, turned his back on her and ran slap into Mr. McAngus. There was a clash of spectacles and a loud oath from Mr. Merryman. The two gentlemen began to behave like simultaneous comedians. They stooped, crashed heads, cried out in anguish and rose clutching each other's spectacles, hats. The hyacinth Mr. McAngus had been wearing had changed hands.

"I am so very sorry," said Mr. McAngus, holding his head. "I hope you're not hurt."

"I am hurt. That is my hat, sir, and those are my glasses. Broken."

"I do trust you have a second pair."

"The existence of a second pair does not reduce the value of the first, which is, I see at a glance, irrevocably shattered," said Mr. Merryman. He flung down Mr. McAngus's hyacinth and returned to his chair.

The others still crowded about Mrs. Dillington-Blick. As they all stood there, so close together that the smell of wine on their breath mingled with Mrs. Dillington-Blick's heavy scent, there was, Alleyn thought, a classic touch, a kind of ghastly neatness in the situation if indeed one of them was the murderer they all so eagerly discussed.

Presently Brigid and Tim moved away and then Father Jourdain walked aft and leaned on the rails. Mrs. Cuddy announced that she was going to bed and took Mr. Cuddy's arm. The whole thing, she said, had given her quite a turn. Her husband seemed reluctant to follow her, but on Mrs. Dillington-Blick and Aubyn Dale going indoors the whole party broke up and disappeared severally through doors or into shadows.

Captain Bannerman came up to Alleyn. "How about that one?" he said. "Upsets your little game a bit, doesn't it?" and loudly belched. "Pardon me," he added. "It's the fancy muck we had for dinner."

"Eight of them don't know where it happened and they don't know exactly when," Alleyn pointed out. "The ninth knows everything anyway. It doesn't matter all that much."

"It matters damn all seeing the whole idea's an error." The captain made a wide gesture. "Well—look at them. I ask you. Look at the way they behave and everything."

"How do you expect him to behave? Go about in a black sombrero making loud animal noises? Heath had very nice manners. Still, you may be right. By the way, Father Jourdain and Makepiece seem to be in the clear. And you, sir. I thought you'd like to know. The Yard's been checking alibis."

"Ta," said the captain gloomily and began to count on his fingers. "That leaves Cuddy, Merryman, Dale and that funny old bastard what's-'is-name."

"McAngus."

"That's right. Well, I ask you! I'm turning in," added the captain. "I'm a wee bit plastered. She's a wonderful woman though. Good-ni'."

"Good-night, sir."

The captain moved away, paused and came back.

"I had a signal from the company," he said. "They don't want any kind of publicity and in my opinion they're right. They reckon it's all my eye. They don't want the passengers upset for nothing and n'more do I. You might 'member that."

"I'll do my best."

"At sea—master's orders."

"Sir."

"Ver' well." The captain made a vague gesture and climbed carefully up the companionway to the bridge.

Alleyn walked aft to where Father Jourdain, still leaning on the taffrail, his hands loosely folded, stared out into the night.

"I've been wondering," Alleyn said, "if you played Horatio's part just now."

"I? Horatio?"

"Observing with the very comment of your soul."

"Oh, that! If that's to be my rôle! I did, certainly, watch the men."

"So did I. How about it?"

"Nothing. Nothing at all. Unless you count Mr. Merryman keeping his hat over his face or his flying into a temper."

"Or Mr. Cuddy's overt excitement."

"Or Mr. McAngus's queer little trick of dancing backwards and forwards. No!" Father Jourdain exclaimed strongly. "No! I can't believe it of any of them. And yet—"

"Do you still smell evil?"

"I begin to ask myself if I merely imagine it."

"As well you may," Alleyn agreed. "I ask myself continually if we're building a complete fantasy round the fragment of paper clutched in that wretched girl's hand. But then—You see, you all had your embarkation notices when you came aboard. Or so it seems. Could one of the lost ones—yours, for instance—have blown through the porthole to the dock and into her hand? No. The portholes were all shut as they always are when the ship's tied up. Let's take a turn, shall we?"

They walked together down the well-deck on the port side. When they reached the little verandah aft of the engine house, they stopped while Alleyn lit his pipe. The night was still very warm, but they had run into a stiff breeze and the ship was alive with it. There was a high thrumming sound in the shrouds.

"Someone singing," Alleyn said.

"Isn't it the wind in those ropes? Shrouds, don't they call them? I wonder why."

"No. Listen. It's clearer now."

"So it is. Someone singing."

It was a high, rather sweet voice and seemed to come from the direction of the passengers' quarters.

" 'The Broken Doll,' " Alleyn said.

"A strangely old-fashioned choice."

> *"You'll be sorry some day*
> *You left behind a broken doll."*

The thin commonplace tune evaporated.

"It's stopped now," said Alleyn.

"Yes. Should these women be warned, then?" Father Jourdain asked as they continued their walk. "Before the deadline approaches?"

"The shipping company is all against it and so's the captain. My bosses tell me, as far as possible, to respect their wishes. They think the women should be protected without knowing it, which is all bloody fine for them. Makepiece, by the way, seems O.K. We'll tell him, I think. He'll be delighted to protect Miss Carmichael."

Like the captain, Father Jourdain said, "That leaves Dale, Merryman, Cuddy and McAngus." But unlike the captain he added, "I suppose it's possible. I suppose so." He put his hand on Alleyn's arm. "You'll think I'm ridiculously inconsistent; it's only that I've remembered—" He stopped for a moment, and his fingers closed over Alleyn's coatsleeve.

"Yes?" Alleyn said.

"You see, I'm a priest, an Anglo-Catholic priest. I hear confessions. It's a humbling and an astonishing duty. One never stops being dumb-founded at the unexpectedness of sin."

Alleyn said, "I suppose in a way the same observation might apply to my job."

They walked on in silence, rounded the end of the hatch and returned to the port side. The lights in the lounge were out and great pools of shadow lay about the deck.

"It's an awful thing to say," Father Jourdain observed abruptly, "but do you know, for a moment I almost found myself wishing that rather than go on in such frightful uncertainty, we knew, positively, that this murderer was on board." He turned aside to sit on the hatch. The hatch-combing cast a very deep shadow along the deck. He seemed to wade into it as if it were a ditch.

"Ma-ma!"

The voice squeaked horridly from under his feet. He made a stifled sound and lurched against the hatch.

"Good heavens, what have I done!" cried Father Jourdain.

"By the sound of it," Alleyn said, "I should say you've trodden on Esmeralda."

He stooped. His hands encountered lace, a hard dead surface and something else. "Don't move," he said. "Just a moment."

He carried a pencil-thin flashlamp in his pocket. The beam darted out like a replica in miniature of P. C. Moir's torch.

"It was already broken. Look."

It was indeed broken. The head had been twisted so far and with such violence that Esmeralda now grinned over her left shoulder at a quite impossible angle. The black lace mantilla was wound tightly round the neck and lying on the rigid bosom was a litter of emerald beads and a single crushed hyacinth.

"You've got your wish," Alleyn said. "He's on board, all right."

4

Captain Bannerman pushed his fingers through his sandy hair and rose from his sitting-room table.

"It's half-past two," he said, "and for any good the stuff I drank last night does me, I might as well have not taken it. I need a dram and I advise you gentlemen to join me."

He dumped a bottle of whisky and four glasses on the table and was careful not to touch a large object that lay there, covered with a news-paper. "Neat?" he asked. "Water? Or soda?"

Alleyn and Father Jourdain had soda and Tim Makepiece water. The captain took his neat.

"You know," Tim said. "I can't get myself geared to this situation. Really, it's jolly nearly impossible to believe it."

"I don't," said the captain. "The doll was a joke. A damn nasty, spiteful kind of joke, mind. But a joke. I'll be sugared if I think I've shipped a Jack the Ripper. Now!"

"No, no," Father Jourdain muttered. "I'm afraid I can't agree. Alleyn?"

Alleyn said, "I suppose the joke idea's just possible, given the kind of person and all the talk about these cases and the parallel circumstances."

"There you are!" Captain Bannerman said triumphantly. "And if you ask me, we haven't got far to look for the kind of chap. Dale's a great card for practical jokes. Always at it on his own confession. Bet you what you like—"

"No, no!" Father Jourdain protested. "I can't agree. He'd never per-petrate such an unlovely trick. No."

Alleyn said, "I can't agree either. In my opinion, literally it's no joke."

Tim said slowly, "I suppose you all noticed that—well, that Mr. Mc-Angus was wearing a hyacinth in his coat."

Father Jourdain and the captain exclaimed, but Alleyn said, "And that he dropped it when he clashed heads with Mr. Merryman. And that Mr. Merryman picked it up and threw it down on the deck."

"Ah!" said the captain triumphantly. "There you are! What's the good of that!"

"Where," Tim asked, "did she leave the doll?"

"On the hatch. She put it there when she got her cable and evidently forgot to take it indoors. It was just above the spot where we found it, which was about three feet away from the place where Merryman threw down the hyacinth; everything was nice and handy." He turned to Tim. "You and Miss Carmichael were the first to leave the general group. I think you walked over to the starboard side, didn't you?"

Tim, pink in the face, nodded.

"Er—yes."

"Do you mind telling me *exactly* where?"

"Er—no. No. Naturally not. It was—where was it? Well, it was sort of a bit further along than the doorway into the passengers' quarters. There's a seat."

"And you were there, would you say—for how long?"

"Well—er—"

"Until after the group of passengers on deck had dispersed?"

"Oh, Lord, yes! Yes."

"Did you notice whether any of them went in or, more importantly, came out again, by that doorway?"

"Er—no. No."

"Gentlemen of your vintage," Alleyn said mildly, "from the point of view of evidence are no damn good until you fall in love and then you're no damn good."

"Well, I must say!"

"Never mind. I think I know how they dispersed. Mr. Merryman, whose cabin is the first on the left of the passage on the starboard side and has windows looking aft and to that side, went in at the passengers' doorway near you. He was followed by Mr. McAngus, who has the cabin opposite his across the passage.

"The others all moved away in the opposite direction and presumably went in by the equivalent passengers' entrance on the port side, with the exception of Mrs. Dillington-Blick and Aubyn Dale, who used the glass doors into the lounge. Captain Bannerman and I had a short conversation and he returned to the bridge. Father Jourdain and I then walked to the after end or back or rear or whatever you call it of the deck, where there's a verandah and where we could see nothing. It must have been at that moment somebody returned and garrotted Esmeralda."

"How d'you remember all that?" Captain Bannerman demanded.

"God bless my soul, I'm on duty." Alleyn turned to Father Jourdain. "The job must have been finished before we walked back along the starboard side."

"Must it?"

"Don't you remember? We heard someone singing 'A Broken Doll.'"

Father Jourdain passed his hand across his eyes. "This is, it really is, quite beastly."

"It appears that he always sings when he's finished."

Tim said suddenly, "We heard it. Brigid and I. It wasn't far off. On the other side. We thought it was a sailor but actually it sounded rather like a choirboy."

"Oh, please!" Father Jourdain ejaculated and at once added, "Sorry. Silly remark."

"Here!" the captain interposed, jabbing a square finger at the newspaper-covered form on the table. "Can't you do any of this funny business with fingerprints? What about them?"

Alleyn said he'd try, of course, but he didn't expect there'd be any that mattered as their man was believed to wear gloves. He very gingerly removed the newspaper and there, shockingly large, smirking, with her detached head looking over her shoulder, was Esmeralda. In any case,

Alleyn pointed out, the mantilla had been wound so tightly round the neck that any fingerprints would be obliterated. "It's a right-handed job, I think," he said. "But as we've no left-handed passengers that doesn't cast a blinding light on anything." He eased away the black lace, exposing part of the pink plastic neck. "He tried the necklace first but he never has any luck with beads. They break. You can see the dents in the paint."

He dropped the newspaper over the doll and looked at Tim Makepiece. "This sort of thing's up your street, isn't it?"

Tim said, "If it wasn't for the immediacy of the problem it'd be damned interesting. It still is. It looks like a classic. The repetition, the time factor —by the way, the doll's out of step in that respect, isn't it?"

"Yes," Alleyn said. "Dead out. It's six days too soon. Would you say that made the time theory look pretty sick?"

"On the face of it—no, I don't think I would; although one shouldn't make those sorts of pronouncements. But I'd think the doll being inanimate might be—well, a kind of extra."

"A *jeu d'esprit?*"

"Yes. Like a Malcolm Campbell amusing himself with a toy speedboat. It wouldn't interfere with the normal programme. That'd be my guess. But if one could only get him to talk."

"You can try and get all of 'em to talk," said Captain Bannerman sardonically. "No harm in trying."

"It's a question, isn't it," Alleyn said, "of what we are going to do about it. It seems to me there are three courses open to us. (A) We can make the whole situation known to everybody in the ship and hold a routine enquiry, but I'm afraid that won't get us much further. I could ask if there were alibis for the other occasions, of course, but our man would certainly produce one and there would be no immediate means of checking it. We know, by the way, that Cuddy hasn't got one for the other occasion."

"Do we?" said the captain woodenly.

"Yes. He went for a walk after leaving his silver-wedding bouquet at a hospital."

"My God!" Tim said softly.

"On the other hand an enquiry would mean that my man is fully warned and at the cost of whatever anguish to himself goes to earth until the end of the voyage. So I don't make an arrest and at the other side of the world more girls are killed by strangulation. (B) We can warn the women privately and I give you two guesses as to what sort of privacy we might hope to preserve after warning Mrs. Cuddy. (C) We can take such of your senior officers as you think fit into our confidence, form ourselves into a sort of vigilance committee, and try by observation and undercover enquiry to get more information before taking action."

"Which is the only course I'm prepared to sanction," said Captain Bannerman. "And that's flat."

Alleyn looked thoughtfully at him. "Then it's just as well," he said, "that at the moment it appears to be the only one that's at all practicable."

"That makes four suspects to watch," Tim said after a pause.

"Four?" Alleyn said. "Everybody says four. You may all be right, of course. I'm almost inclined to reduce the field, tentatively, you know, very tentatively. It seems to me that at least one of your four is in the clear."

They stared at him. "Are we to know which?" Father Jourdain asked.

Alleyn told him.

"Dear me!" he said. "How excessively stupid of me. But of course."

"And then, for two of the others," Alleyn said apologetically, "there are certain indications; nothing like certainties, you might object, and yet I'm inclined to accept them as working hypotheses."

"But look here!" Tim said. "That would mean—"

He was interrupted by Captain Bannerman. "Do you mean to sit there," he roared out, "and tell us you think you know who done—damnation! Who did it?"

"I'm not sure. Not nearly sure enough, but I fancy so."

After a long pause Father Jourdain said, "Well—again, are we to know which? And why?"

Alleyn waited for a moment. He glanced at the captain's face, scarlet with incredulity, and then at the other two; dubious, perhaps a little resentful.

"I think perhaps better not," he said.

5

When at last he went to bed, Alleyn was unable to sleep. He listened to the comfortable pulse of the ship's progress and seemed to hear beyond it a thin whistle of a voice lamenting a broken doll. If he closed his eyes it was to find Captain Bannerman's face, blown with obstinacy, stupid and intractable, and Esmeralda, smirking over her shoulder. And even as he told himself that this must be the beginning of a dream, he was awake again. He searched for some exercise to discipline his thoughts and remembered Miss Abbott's plainsong chant. Suppose Mr. Merryman had ordered him to put it into English verse?

> Dismiss the dreams that sore affright,
> Phantasmagoria of the night.
> Confound our carnal enemy—
> Let not our flesh corrupted be.

"No! No! NO!" Mr. Merryman shouted, coming very close and handing him an embarkation notice. "You have completely misinterpreted the
poem. My compliments to the captain and request him to lay on six of the
best."

Mr. Merryman then opened his mouth very wide, turned into Mr.
Cuddy and jumped overboard. Alleyn began to climb a rope ladder with
Mrs. Dillington-Blick on his back and thus burdened, at last fell heavily
to sleep.

CHAPTER SEVEN   **After Las Palmas**

The passengers always met for coffee in the lounge at eleven o'clock. On
the morning after Las Palmas this ceremony marked the first appearance
of Mrs. Dillington-Blick and Aubyn Dale, neither of whom had come
down for breakfast. It was a day with an enervating faint wind and the
coffee was iced.

Alleyn had chosen this moment to present Mrs. Dillington-Blick with
the *disjecta membra* of Esmeralda. She had already sent Dennis to find
the doll and was as fretful as a good-natured woman can be when he came
back empty-handed. Alleyn told her that at a late hour he and Father Jourdain had discovered Esmeralda lying on the deck. He then indicated the
newspaper parcel that he had laid out on the end of the table.

He did this at the moment when the men of the party and Miss Abbott
were gathered round the coffee. Mrs. Cuddy, Mrs. Dillington-Blick and
Brigid always allowed themselves the little ceremony of being waited upon
by the gentlemen. Miss Abbott consistently lined herself up in the queue
and none of the men had the temerity to question this procedure.

With the connivance of Father Jourdain and Tim Makepiece, Alleyn
unveiled Esmeralda at the moment when Aubyn Dale, Mr. Merryman,
Mr. Cuddy and Mr. McAngus were hard by the table.

"Here she is," he said, "and I'm afraid she presents rather a sorry sight."

He flicked the newspaper away in one jerk. Mrs. Dillington-Blick cried
out sharply.

Esmeralda was lying on her back with her head twisted over her shoulder and the beads and dead hyacinth in position.

After its owner's one ejaculation the doll's exposure was followed by a
dead silence and then by a violent oath from Mr. Merryman.

Almost simultaneously Miss Abbott ejaculated, "Don't!"

Her iced coffee had tilted and the contents had fallen over Mr. Merry-man's hands.

Miss Abbott moistened her lips and said, "You must have jolted my arm, Mr. Merryman."

"My dear madam, I did nothing of the sort!" he contradicted and angrily flipped his hands. Particles of iced coffee flew in all directions. One alighted on Mr. Cuddy's nose. He seemed to be quite unaware of it. Half smiling, he stared at Esmeralda and with lightly clasped fingers revolved his thumbs slowly round each other.

Aubyn Dale said loudly, "Why have you done this! It looks disgusting." He reached out and with a quick movement brushed the dead hyacinth off the doll. The beads fell away with a clatter and rolled about the table. Dale straightened the flashily smiling head.

Mr. McAngus murmured gently, "She looks quite herself again, doesn't she? Perhaps she can be mended."

"I don't understand all this," Dale said angrily to Alleyn. "Why did you do it?"

"Do what, exactly?"

"Lay it out like that. Like—like—"

Mrs. Cuddy said with relish, "Like one of those poor girls. Flowers and beads and everything; giving us all such a turn."

"The doll," Alleyn said, "is exactly as Father Jourdain and I found it, hyacinth and all. I'm sorry if it's upset anyone."

Mrs. Dillington-Blick had come to the table. It was the first time, Alleyn thought, that he had seen her without so much as a flicker of a smile on her face. "Was it like that?" she asked. "Why? What happened?"

Dale said, "Don't worry, darling Ruby. Somebody must have trodden on it and broken the beads and—and the neck."

"I trod on it," Father Jourdain said. "I'm most awfully sorry, Mrs. Dillington-Blick, but it was lying on the deck in pitch-dark shadow."

"There you are!" Dale exclaimed. He caught Alleyn's eye and recovered something of his professional bonhomie. "Sorry, old boy. I didn't mean to throw a temperament. You gathered the doll up just as it was. No offense, I hope?"

"None in the wide world," Alleyn rejoined politely.

Mrs. Cuddy said, "Yes, but all the same it's funny about the flower, isn't it, dear?"

"That's right, dear. Funny."

"Being a hyacinth and all. Such a coincidence."

"That's right," smiled Mr. Cuddy. "Funny."

Mr. Merryman, who was still fretfully drying his hands on his handker-chief, suddenly cried out in anguish.

"I was mad enough to suppose," Mr. Merryman lamented, "that in undertaking this voyage I would escape, however briefly, from the egregious, the remorseless ambiguities of the lower-school urchin. Funny! Funny! Will you be so kind, my good Cuddy, as to enlighten us? In what respect do you consider droll, entertaining or amusing the discovery of a wilted hyacinth upon the bosom of this disarticulate puppet? For my part," Mr. Merryman added with some violence, "I find the obvious correlation altogether beastly. And the inescapable conclusion that I my-self was, hypothetically at least, responsible for its presence adds to my distaste. Funny!" Mr. Merryman concluded in a fury and flung up his hands.

The Cuddys eyed him with dawning resentment. Mr. McAngus said brightly, "But of course. I'd *quite* forgotten. It was *my* hyacinth. You took it, do you recollect? When we had our little collision? And threw it down."

"I did *not* 'take' it."

"Accidentally, of course. I meant accidentally." Mr. McAngus bent over the doll. His reddish knotted fingers manipulated the neck. "I'm *sure* she can be mended," he said.

Mrs. Dillington-Blick said in a constrained voice, "Do you know—I *hope* you'll forgive me, Mr. McAngus, and I expect I'm being dreadfully silly—but do you know I don't somehow think I feel quite the same about Esmeralda. I don't believe I want her mended, or at any rate not for me. Perhaps we could think of some little girl—you may have a niece." Her voice faded into an apologetic murmur.

With a kind of social readiness that consorted very ill with the look in his eyes, Mr. McAngus said, "But, of course, I quite understand." His hands were still closed round the neck of the doll. He looked at them, seemed to recollect himself, and turned aside. "I quite understand," he repeated, and helped himself to a herbal cigarette.

Mrs. Cuddy, relentless as a Greek chorus, said, "All the same it *does* seem funny." Mr. Merryman gave a strangulated cry, but she went on greedily, "the way we were all talking about those murders. You know. And then the way Mrs. Blick got that cable from her gentleman-friend about the girl being murdered who brought the flowers. And the way hyacinths keep turning up. You'd almost think it was intentional, really you would." She stared in her unwinking fashion at Mrs. Dillington-Blick. "I don't wonder you feel funny about it with the doll being dressed like you. You know. It might almost *be* you, lying there, mightn't it, Mrs. Blick?"

Miss Abbott struck her big hands together. "For God's sake!" she ejaculated. "Do we have to listen to all this? Can't someone take that thing away!"

"Of course," Alleyn said and dropped the newspaper over the doll. "I can."

He gathered up the unwieldy parcel and took it to his cabin.

2

"As usual," he wrote to his wife, "I miss you very much. I miss—" He paused and looked, without seeing them, at the objects in his cabin. He reflected on the old circumstance that although his memory had been trained for a long time to retain with scrupulous accuracy the various items of human faces, it always let him down when he wanted it to show Troy to him. Her photograph was not much good, after all. It merely reminded him of features he knew but couldn't visualize; it was only a map of her face. He put something of this down in his letter, word after careful word, and then began to write about the case in hand, setting out in detail everything that had happened since his last letter had been posted in Las Palmas.

> . . . *so you see* [he wrote], *the nature of the predicament. I'm miles away from the point where one can even begin to think of making an arrest. All I've been able to do is whittle down the field of possibles. Do you agree? Have you arrived at the predominantly possible one? I'm sure you have. I'm making a mystery about nothing, which must be the last infirmity of the police mind.*
>
> *Meanwhile we have laid a plan of action that is purely negative. The first and second mates and the chief engineer have been put wise by the captain. They all think with him that the whole idea is completely up the pole and that our man's not on board. But they'll fall in with the general scheme and at this moment are delightedly and vigilantly keeping an eye on the ladies, who, by the way, have been told that there have been thefts on board and that they'll be well advised to lock their doors, day and night. It's been made very clear that Dennis, the queer fat steward, you know, is not suspected.*
>
> *From almost every point-of-view* [Alleyn went on after a pause], *these cases are the worst of the lot. One is always hag-ridden by one's personal conviction that the law is desperately inadequate in its dealings with them. One wonders what sort of frightfulness is at work behind the unremarkable face, the more-or-less unexceptionable be-*

haviour. What is the reality? With a psychiatrist, a priest, and a policeman all present we've got the ingredients for a Pirandello play, haven't we? Jourdain and Makepiece are due here now and no doubt I shall get two completely opposed professional opinions from them. In fact—

There was a tap on the door. Alleyn hurriedly wrote, ". . . *here they are. Au revoir, darling,*" and called out, "Come in."

Father Jourdain now wore a thin light-coloured suit, a white shirt and a black tie. The change in his appearance was quite startling; it was as if a stranger had walked in.

"I really *don't* feel," he said, "that the mortification of a dog collar in the tropics is required of me. I shall put it on for dinner, and on Sunday I shall sweat in my decent cassock. The sight of you two in your gents' tropical suitings was too much for me. I bought this in Las Palmas and in happier circumstances would get a great deal of pleasure out of wearing it."

They sat down and looked at Alleyn with an air of expectancy. It occurred to him that however sincerely they might deplore the presence of a homicidal monster as their fellow traveller they were nevertheless stimulated in a way that was not entirely unpleasurable. They were both, he thought, energetic inquisitive men and each in his own mode had a professional interest in the matter in hand.

"Well," he said, when they were settled, "how do you feel about Operation Esmeralda?"

They agreed, it appeared, that nothing had happened to contradict Alleyn's theory. The reaction to the doll had been pretty well what he had predicted.

"Though the trouble is," Father Jourdain added, "that when one is looking for peculiar behaviour one seems to see it all over the place. I must confess that I found Dale's outburst, the Cuddys' really almost gloating relish, Merryman's intolerable pedantry, and McAngus's manipulations equally disturbing. Of course it doesn't arise," he added after a pause, "but even poor Miss Abbott behaved, or so it seemed to me, with a kind of extravagance. I suppose I lost my eye."

"Why," Alleyn asked, "do you call her '*poor* Miss Abbott'?"

"Oh, my dear Alleyn! I think you know very well. The problem of the unhappy spinster crops up all along the line in my job."

Tim gave an inarticulate grunt.

"Yes," Alleyn said, "she *is* obviously unhappy." He looked at Tim. "What did that knowledgeable noise mean?"

Tim said impatiently, "We're not concerned with Miss Abbott, I imagine, but it meant that I too recognize the type, though perhaps my diagnosis would not appeal to Father Jourdain."

"Would it not?" Father Jourdain said. "I should like to hear it all the same."

Tim said rapidly, "No, really. I mustn't bore you and at any rate one has no business to go by superficial impressions. It's just that on the face of it she's a textbook example of the woman without sexual attraction who hasn't succeeded in finding a satisfactory adjustment."

Alleyn looked up from his clasped hands. "From your point of view isn't that also true of the sort of homicide we're concerned with?"

"Invariably, I should say. These cases almost always point back to some childish tragedy in which the old gang—fear, frustration and jealousy—have been predominant. This is true of most psychological abnormalities. For instance, as a psychotherapist I would, if I got the chance, try to discover why hyacinths make Mr. Cuddy feel ill and I'd expect to find the answer in some incident that may have been thrust completely into his subconscious and that superficially may seem to have no direct reference to hyacinths. And with Aubyn Dale, I'd be interested to hunt down the basic reason for his love of practical jokes. While if Mr. Merryman were my patient, I'd try and find a reason for his chronic irritability."

"Dyspepsia no good?" Alleyn asked. "He's forever taking sodamints."

"All dyspeptics are not irritable woman-haters. I'd expect to find that his indigestion is associated with some very long-standing psychic disturbance."

"Such as his nurse having snatched away his favourite rattle and given it to his papa?"

"You might not be as far out as you may think you are, at that."

"What about Dale and McAngus?"

"Oh," Tim said, "I wouldn't be surprised if Dale hadn't achieved, on the whole, a fairly successful sublimation with his ghastly telly-therapy. He's an exhibitionist who thinks he's made good. That's why his two public blunders upset his applecart and gave him his 'nervous breakdown.'"

"I didn't know he'd had one," said Father Jourdain.

"He says he has. It's a term psychotherapists don't accept. As for McAngus, he really *is* interesting; all that timidity and absent-mindedness and losing his way in his own stories—very characteristic."

"Of what?" Alleyn asked.

"Of an all-too-familiar type. Completely inhibited. Riddled with anxieties and frustrations. And of course he's quite unconscious of their origins. His giving Mrs. D-B that damn doll was very suggestive. He's a bachelor."

"Oh, dear!" Father Jourdain murmured and at once added, "Pay no attention to me. Do go on."

"Then," Alleyn said, "the psychiatrist's position in respect of these crimes is that they have all developed out of some profound emotional disturbance that the criminal is quite unaware of and is unable to control?"

"That's it."

"And does it follow that he may, at the conscious level, loathe what he does, try desperately hard to fight down the compulsion, and be filled with horror each time he fails?"

"Very likely."

"Indeed, yes," Father Jourdain said with great emphasis. "Indeed, indeed!"

Alleyn turned to him. "Then you agree with Makepiece?"

Father Jourdain passed a white hand over his dark luxuriant hair. "I'm sure," he said, "that Makepiece has described the secondary cause and its subsequent results very learnedly and accurately."

"The *secondary* cause!" Tim exclaimed.

"Yes. The repressed fear, or frustration or whatever it was—I'm afraid," said Father Jourdain with a faint smile, "I haven't mastered the terminology. But I'm sure you're right about all that; indeed you *know* it all as a man of science. But you see I would look upon that early tragedy and its subsequent manifestations as the—well, as the *modus operandi* of an infinitely more terrible agent."

"I don't follow," Tim said. "A more terrible agent?"

"Yes. The devil."

"I beg your pardon?"

"I believe that this poor soul is possessed of a devil."

Tim, to Alleyn's amusement, actually blushed scarlet as if Father Jourdain had committed some frightful social solecism.

"I see," Father Jourdain observed, "that I have embarrassed you."

Tim mumbled something about everybody being entitled to his opinion.

Alleyn said, "I'm afraid I'm rather stuck for a remark, too. Forgive me, but you do mean, quite literally, exactly what you've just said? Yes, I see you do."

"Quite literally. It is a case of possession. I've seen too many to be mistaken."

There was a long pause during which Alleyn reminded himself that there were a great number of not unintelligent people in the world who managed, with some satisfaction to themselves, to believe in devils. At last he said, "I must say, in that case, I very much wish you could exorcise it."

With perfect seriousness Father Jourdain replied that there were certain difficulties. "I shall, of course, continue to pray for him," he said.

Tim shuffled his feet, lit a cigarette, and with an air of striking out rather wildly for some kind of raft, asked Alleyn for the police view of this kind of murder. "After all," he said, "you must be said to be experts."

"Not at all," Alleyn rejoined. "Very far from it. Our job, God save the mark, is first to protect society and then as a corollary to catch the criminal. These sorts of criminals are often our worst headache. They have no occupational habits. They resemble each other only in their desire to kill for gratification. In everyday life they may be anything; there are no outward signs. We generally get them but by no means always. The thing one looks for, of course, is a departure from routine. If there's no known routine, if your man is a solitary creature as Jack the Ripper was, your chances lessen considerably." Alleyn paused and then added in a changed voice: "But as to why, fundamentally, he is what he is—we are dumb. Perhaps if we knew we'd find our job intolerable."

Father Jourdain said, "You are, after all, a compassionate man, I see."

Alleyn found this remark embarrassing and inappropriate. He said quickly, "It doesn't arise. An investigating officer examining the bodies of strangled girls who have died on a crescendo of terror and physical agony is not predisposed to feel compassion for the strangler. It's not easy to remember that he may have suffered a complementary agony of the mind. In many cases he hasn't done anything of the sort. He's too far gone."

"Isn't it a question," Tim asked, "of whether something might have been done about him before his obsession reached its climax?"

"Of course it is," Alleyn agreed, very readily. "That's where you chaps come in."

Tim stood up. "It's three o'clock. I'm due for a game of deck golf," he said. "What's the form? Watchful diligence?"

"That's it."

Father Jourdain also rose. "I'm going to do a crossword with Miss Abbott. She's got the new Penguin. Mr. Merryman is Ximenes standard."

"I'm a *Times* man myself," Alleyn said.

"There's one thing about the afternoons," Father Jourdain sighed, "the ladies do tend to retire to their cabins."

"For the sake of argument only," Tim asked gloomily, "suppose Cuddy was your man. Do you think he'd be at all liable to strangle Mrs. Cuddy?"

"By thunder," Alleyn said, "if I were in his boots, *I* would. Come on."

In the afternoons there were not very many shady places on deck and a good deal of quiet manoeuvring went on among the passengers to secure them. Claims were staked. Mr. Merryman left his air ●ushion and his Panama on the nicest of the deck-chairs. The Cuddys did a certain amount of edging in and shoving aside when nobody else was about. Mr. McAngus laid his plaid along one of the wooden seats, but as nobody else cared for the seats this procedure aroused no enmity.

Aubyn Dale and Mrs. Dillington-Blick used their own luxurious chaise longues with rubber-foam appointments and had set them up in the little verandah, which they pretty well filled. Although the chaise longues were never occupied till after tea, nobody liked to use them in the meantime.

So while Tim, Brigid and two of the junior officers played deck golf, Miss Abbott and five men were grouped in a shady area cast by the centrecastle between the doors into the lounge and the amidships hatch. Mr. Cuddy slept noisily with a *Reader's Digest* over his face. Mr. McAngus dozed, Mr. Merryman and Alleyn read, Father Jourdain and Miss Abbott laboured at their crossword. It was a tranquil-looking scene. Desultory sentences and little spurts of observation drifted about with the inconsequence of a conversational poem by Verlaine.

Above their heads Captain Bannerman took his afternoon walk on the bridge, solacing the monotony with pleasurable glances at Brigid, who looked enchanting in jeans and a scarlet shirt. As he had predicted, she was evidently a howling success with his junior officers. And with his medical officer, too, reflected the captain. Sensible perhaps of his regard, Brigid looked up and gaily waved to him. In addition to being attractive she was also what he called a thoroughly nice, unspoiled little lady; just a sweet young girl, he thought. Dimly conscious, perhaps, of some not altogether appropriate train of thought aroused by this reflection, the captain decided to think instead of Mrs. Dillington-Blick—a mental exercise that came very easily to him.

Brigid took a long swipe at her opponent's disc, scuppered her own, shouted "Damn!" and burst out laughing. The junior officers, who had tried very hard to let her win, now polished off the game in an expert manner and regretfully returned to duty.

Brigid said, "Oh, Tim, I *am* sorry! You must get another partner."

"Are you sick of me?" Tim rejoined. "What shall we do now? Would you like to have a singles?"

"Not very much, thank you. I need the support of a kind and forbearing person like yourself. Perhaps some of the others would play. Mr. McAngus, for instance. His game is about on a par with mine."

"Mr. McAngus is mercifully dozing and you know jolly well you're talking nonsense."

"Well, who?" Brigid nervously pushed her hair back and said, "Perhaps it's too hot after all. Don't let's play." She looked at the little group in the shade of the centrecastle. Mr. Merryman had come out of his book and was talking to Alleyn in an admonitory fashion, shaking his finger and evidently speaking with some heat.

"Mr. Chips is at it again," Tim said. "Poor Alleyn!"

He experienced the sensation of his blood running down into his boots. Surely he, Tim Makepiece, a responsible man, a man of science, a psychiatrist, could not have slipped into so feeble, so imbecile an error. Would he have to confess to Alleyn? How could he recover himself with Brigid? Her voice recalled him.

"What did you say?" she asked.

" 'Poor Broderick.' "

"Is he called Allan? You've got down to Christian names pretty smartly. Very chummy of you."

Tim said after a pause, "I don't to his face. I like him."

"So do I. Awfully. We agreed about it before." Brigid shook her head impatiently. "At any rate," she said, "he's not the guilty one. I'm sure of that."

Tim stood very still and after a moment wetted his lips.

"What do you mean?" he said. "The guilty one?"

"Are you all right, Tim?"

"Perfectly."

"You look peculiar."

"It's the heat. Come back here, do."

He took her arm and led her to the little verandah, pushed her down on the sumptuous footrest belonging to Mrs. Dillington-Blick's chaise longue and himself sat at the end of Aubyn Dale's. "What guilty one?" he repeated.

Brigid stared at him. "There's no need, really, to take it so massively," she said. "You may not feel as I do about it."

"About *what?*"

"The business with the D-B's doll. It seems to me such a beastly thing to have done and I don't care what anyone says, it was done on purpose. Just treading on it wouldn't have produced that result. And then, putting the flower on its chest—a scurvy trick, I call it."

Tim stooped down and made a lengthy business of tying his shoelace. When he straightened up Brigid said, "You *are* all right, aren't you? You keep changing colour like a chameleon."

"Which am I now?"

"Fiery red."

"I've been stooping over. I agree with you about the doll. It was a silly unbecoming sort of thing to do. Perhaps it was a drunken sailor."

"There weren't any drunken sailors about. Do you know who I think it was?"

"Who?"

"Mr. Cuddy."

"Do you, Biddy?" Tim said. "Why?"

"He kept smiling and smiling all the time that Mr. Broderick was showing the doll."

"He's got a chronic grin. It never leaves his face."

"All the same—" Brigid looked quickly at Tim and away again. "In my opinion," she muttered, "he's a D.O.M."

"A what?"

"A dirty old man. I don't mind telling you, I'd simply hate to find myself alone on the boat-deck with him after dark."

Tim hastily said that she'd better make sure she never did. "Take me with you for safety's sake," he said. "I'm eminently trustworthy."

Brigid grinned at him absent-mindedly. She seemed to be in two minds about what she should say next.

"What is it?" he asked.

"Nothing. Nothing, really. It's just—I don't know—it's ever since Dennis brought Mrs. D-B's hyacinths into the lounge on the second day out. We don't seem to be able to get rid of those awful murders. Everybody talking about them. That alibi discussion the night before Las Palmas and Miss Abbott breaking down. Not that *her* trouble had anything to do with it, poor thing. And then the awful business of the girl that brought Mrs. D-B's flowers being a victim and now the doll being left like that. You'll think I'm completely dotty," Brigid said, "but it's sort of got me down a bit. Do you know, just now I caught myself thinking, 'Wouldn't it be awful if the Flower Murderer was on board.'"

Tim had put out a warning hand, but a man's shadow had already fallen across the deck and across Brigid.

"Dear child!" said Aubyn Dale. "What a *pathologically* morbid little notion!"

3

Tim and Brigid got up. Tim said automatically, "I'm afraid we've been trespassing on your footrests," and hoped this would account for any embarrassment they might have displayed.

"My dear old boy!" Dale cried. "Do use the whole tatty works! Whenever you like, as far as I'm concerned. And I'm sure Madame would be enchanted."

He had an armful of cushions and rugs which he began to arrange on the chaise longues. "Madame tends to emerge for a nice cuppa," he explained. He punched a cushion with all the aplomb of the manservant in *Charley's Aunt* and flung it into position. "There now!" he said. He straightened up, pulled a pipe out of his pocket, gripped it mannishly between his teeth, contrived to tower over Brigid and became avuncular.

"As for you, young woman," he said cocking his head quizzically at her. "You've been letting a particularly lively imagination run away with you. What?"

This was said with such an exact reproduction of his television manner that Tim, in spite of his own agitation, felt momentarily impelled to whistle "Pack Up Your Troubles." However, he said quickly, "It wasn't as morbid as it sounded. Brigid and I have been having an argument about the alibi bet and that led to inevitable conjectures about the flower expert."

"M-m-m," Dale rumbled understandingly, still looking at Brigid. "*I* see." He screwed his face into a whimsical grimace. "You know, Brigid, I've got an idea we've just about had that old topic. After all, it's not the prettiest one in the world, is it? What do you think? Um?"

Pink with embarrassment, Brigid said coldly, "I feel sure you're right."

"Good girl," Aubyn Dale said and patted her shoulder.

Tim muttered that it was tea-time and withdrew Brigid firmly to the starboard side. It was a relief to him to be angry.

"My God, what a frightful fellow," he fulminated. "That egregious nice-chappery! That ineffable decency! That indescribably phony good-will!"

"Never mind," Brigid said. "I daresay he has to keep in practice. And, after all, little as I relish admitting it, he was in fact right. I suppose I have been letting my imagination run away with me."

Tim stood over her, put his head on one side and achieved a quite creditable imitation of Aubyn Dale. "Good girl," he said unctuously and patted her shoulder.

Brigid made a satisfactory response to this sally and seemed to be a good deal cheered. "Of course," she said, "I didn't *really* think we'd shipped a murderer; it was just one of those things." She looked up into Tim's face.

"Brigid!" he said, and took her hands in his.

"No, don't," she said quickly. "Don't."

"I'm sorry."

"There's nothing to be sorry about. Pay no attention. Let's go and talk to Mr. Chips."

They found Mr. Merryman in full cry. He had discovered Brigid's book, *The Elizabethans*, which she had left on her deck-chair, and seemed to be giving a lecture on it. It was by an authoritative writer, but one, evidently, with whom Mr. Merryman found himself in passionate disagreement. It appeared that Alleyn, Father Jourdain and Miss Abbott had all been drawn into the discussion while Mr. McAngus and Mr. Cuddy looked on, the former with admiration and the latter with his characteristic air of uninformed disparagement.

Brigid and Tim sat on the deck and were accepted by Mr. Merryman as if they had come late for class but with valid excuses. Alleyn glanced at them and found time to hope that theirs, by some happy accident, was not merely a shipboard attraction. After all, he thought, he himself had fallen irrevocably in love during a voyage from the Antipodes. He turned his attention back to the matter in hand.

"I honestly *don't* understand," Father Jourdain was saying, "how you can put *The Duchess of Malfi* before *Hamlet* or *Macbeth*."

"Or why," Miss Abbott barked, "you should think *Othello* so much better than any of them."

Mr. Merryman groped in his waistcoat pocket for a sodamint and remarked insufferably that really it was impossible to discuss criteria of taste where the rudiments of taste were demonstrably absent. He treated his restive audience to a comprehensive de-gumming of *Hamlet* and *Macbeth*. *Hamlet*, he said, was an inconsistent, deficient and redundant *réchauffé* of some absurd German melodrama.

It was not surprising, Mr. Merryman said, that Hamlet was unable to make up his mind since his creator had himself been the victim of a still greater blight of indecision. Macbeth was merely a muddle-headed blunderer. Strip away the language and what remained? A tediously ignorant expression of defeatism. " 'What's the good of anyfink? Wy, nuffink,' " Mr. Merryman quoted in pedantic cockney and tossed his sodamint into his mouth.

"I don't know anything about Shakespeare—" Mr. Cuddy began and was at once talked down.

"It is at least something," Mr. Merryman said, "that you acknowledge your misfortune."

"All the same," Alleyn objected, "there *is* the language."

"I am not aware," Mr. Merryman countered, "that I have suggested that the fellow had no vocabulary." He went on to praise the classic structure of *Othello*, the inevitability of Webster's *The Duchess of Malfi*, and astounding, the admirable directness of *Titus Andronicus*. As an afterthought he conceded that the final scene of *Lear* was "respectable."

Mr. McAngus, who had several times made plaintive little noises, now struck in with unexpected emphasis.

"To me," he said, "*Othello* is almost spoilt by that bit near the end when Desdemona revives and speaks and then, you know, after all, dies. A woman who has been properly strangled would *not* be able to do that. It is quite ridiculous."

"What's the medical opinion?" Alleyn asked him.

"Pathological verisimilitude," Mr. Merryman interjected with more than a touch of Pooh-Bah, "is irrelevant. One accepts the convention. It is artistically proper that she should be strangled and speak again. Therefore, she speaks."

"All the same," Alleyn said, "let's have the expert's opinion." He looked at Tim.

"I wouldn't say it was utterly impossible," Tim said. "Of course, her physical condition can't be reproduced by an actress and would be unacceptable if it could. I should think it's just possible that he might not have killed her instantly and that she might momentarily revive and attempt to speak."

"But, Doctor," Mr. McAngus objected diffidently, "I *did* say properly. Properly strangled, you know."

"Doesn't the text," Miss Abbott pointed out, "say she was smothered?"

"The text!" Mr. Merryman exclaimed and spread out his hands. "What text, pray? Which text?" and launched himself into a general animadversion of Shakespearian editorship. This he followed up with an extremely dogmatic pronouncement upon the presentation of the plays. The only tolerable method, he said, was that followed by the Elizabethans themselves. The bare boards. The boy-players. It appeared that Mr. Merryman himself produced the plays in this manner at his school. He treated them to a lecture upon speechcraft, costume, and make-up. His manner was so insufferably cocksure that it robbed his discourse of any interest it might have had for his extremely mixed audience. Mr. McAngus's eyes became glazed. Father Jourdain was resigned and Miss Abbott impatient. Brigid looked at the deck and Tim looked at Brigid. Alleyn, conscious of all this, still managed to preserve the semblance of respectful attention.

He was conscious also of Mr. Cuddy, who had the air of a man balked of his legitimate prey. It was evident throughout the discussion that he had some observation to make. He now raised his voice unmelodiously and made it.

"Isn't it funny," Mr. Cuddy asked generally, "how the conversation seems to get round to the subject of ladies being throttled? Mrs. Cuddy was remarking on the same thing. Quite a coincidence, she was saying."

Mr. Merryman opened his mouth, shut it, and reopened it when Brigid cried out with some violence, "I think it's perfectly beastly. I hate it!"

Tim put his hand over hers. "Well, I'm sorry," Brigid said, "but it *is* beastly. It doesn't matter *how* Desdemona died. *Othello* isn't a clinical example. Shakespeare wasn't some scruffy existentialist, it's a tragedy of simplicity and—and greatness of heart being destroyed by a common smarty-smarty little placefinder. Well, anyway," Brigid mumbled, turning very pink, "that's what I think and I suppose one can try and say what one thinks, can't one?"

"I should damn well suppose one can," Alleyn said warmly, "and how right you are, what's more."

Brigid threw him a grateful look.

Mr. Cuddy smiled and smiled. "I'm sure," he said, "I didn't mean to upset anyone."

"Well, you have," Miss Abbott snapped, "and now you know it, don't you?"

"Thank you very much," said Mr. Cuddy.

Father Jourdain stood up. "It's tea-time," he said. "Shall we go in? And shall we decide," he smiled at Brigid, "to take the advice of the youngest and wisest among us and keep off this not very delectable subject? I propose that we do."

Everybody except Mr. Cuddy made affirmative noises and they went in to tea.

But the curious thing is [Alleyn wrote to his wife that evening], *that however much they may or may not try to avoid the subject of murder, it still crops up. I don't want to go precious about it, but really one might suppose that the presence of this expert on board generates a sort of effluvia. They are unaware of it and yet it infects them. Tonight, for instance, after the women had gone to bed, which to my great relief was early, the men got cracking again. Cuddy, Jourdain, and Merryman are all avid readers of crime fiction and of the sort of book that calls itself* Classic Cases of Detection. *As it happens there are two or three of that kind in the ship's little library, among them* The Wainwrights *in the admirable* Notable Trials *series, a very fanciful number on the Yard, and an affair called* The Thing He Loves. *The latter title derives from "The Ballad of Reading Gaol," of course, and I give you one guess as to the subject matter.*

Well, tonight, Merryman being present, there was automically a row. Without exception he's the most pugnacious, quarrelsome, arrogant chap I've ever met. It seemed that Cuddy had got The Thing

He Loves, *and was snuffling away at it in the corner of the lounge. Merryman spotted the book and at once said that he himself was already reading it. Cuddy said he'd taken the book from the shelves and that they were free for all. Neither would give in. Finally McAngus announced that he had a copy of* The Trial of Neil Cream *and actually succeeded in placating Merryman with an offer to lend it to him. It appears that Merryman is one of the fanatics who believe the story of Cream's unfinished confession. So peace was in a sense restored though once again we were treated to an interminable discussion on what Cuddy will call sex monstrosity. Dale was full of all kinds of second-hand theories. McAngus joined in with a sort of terrified relish. Makepiece talked from the psychiatric angle and Jourdain from the religious one. Merryman contradicted everybody. Of course, I'm all for these discussions. They give one an unexampled chance to listen to the man one may be going to arrest, propounding the sort of crime with which he will ultimately be charged.*

The reactions go like this:

McAngus does a great deal of tut-tuttering, protests that the subject is too horrid to dwell upon but is nevertheless quite unable to go away while it's under discussion. He gets all the facts wrong, confuses names and dates so persistently that you'd think it was deliberate, and is slapped back perpetually by Merryman.

Cuddy is utterly absorbed. He goes over the details and incessantly harks back to Jack the Ripper, describing all the ritualistic horrors and speculating about their possible significance.

Merryman, of course, is overbearing, didactic, and argumentative. He's got a much better brain than any of the others, is conversant with the cases, never muddles the known facts and never loses a chance of blackguarding the police. In his opinion they won't catch their man and he obviously glories in the notion ("Hah-hah, did he but know," sneered Hawkshaw, the detective).

Dale, like McAngus, puts up a great show of abhorrence but professes an interest in what he calls the "psychology of sadistic homicide." He talks like a signed article in one of the less responsible of of our dailies and also, of course, like a thoroughly nice chap on television. "Poor wretch!" is his cry. "Poor, poor girls, poor everybody. Sad! Sad!"

Meanwhile, being in merry pin, he has had enough misguided energy to sew up Mr. Merryman's pyjamas and put a dummy woman made from one of the D-B's tremendous nightgowns in Mr. McAngus's bed, and has thus by virtue of these hilarious pranks graduated as a potential victim himself. Merryman's reaction was to go straight to the captain and McAngus's to behave as if he was a typical example from Freud's casebook.

Well, there they are, these four precious favourites in the homicide handicap. I've told you that I fancy one in particular, and in the classic tradition, my dearest, having laid bare the facts, I leave you to your deduction; always bearing in mind that the captain and his mates may be right and there ain't no flaming murderer on board.

Good-night, darling. Don't miss our next instalment of this absorbing serial.

Alleyn put his letter away, doodled absently on his blotting paper for a few minutes, and then thought he'd stretch his legs before turning in.

He went down to the deck below and found it deserted. Having walked six times round it and had a word with the wireless officer, who sat lonely as a cloud in his cubbyhole on the starboard side, Alleyn thought he would call it a day. He passed Father Jourdain's cabin door on his way through the passengers' quarters and as he did so the handle turned and the door was opened a crack. He heard Father Jourdain's voice.

"But, of course. You must come to me whenever you want to. It's what I'm for, you know."

A woman's voice answered harshly and indistinguishably.

"I think," said Father Jourdain, "you should dismiss all that from your mind and stick to your duties. Perform your penance, come to Mass tomorrow, make the special intention I have suggested. Go along, now, and say your prayers. Bless you, my child. Good-night."

Alleyn moved quickly down the passage and had reached the stairs before Miss Abbott had time to see him.

CHAPTER EIGHT   **Sunday the Tenth**

The next day being Sunday, Father Jourdain with the captain's permission celebrated Holy Communion in the lounge at seven o'clock. The service was attended among the passengers by Miss Abbott, Brigid, Mr. McAngus, and rather surprisingly, Mr. Merryman. The third officer, the wireless officer, two of the cadets, and Dennis represented the ship's complement. Alleyn, at the back of the room, listened, watched, and not for the first time felt his own lack of acceptance to be tinged with a faint regret.

When the service was over the little group of passengers went out on deck and presently were joined by Father Jourdain, wearing, as he had promised, his "decent black cassock." He looked remarkably handsome in it with the light breeze lifting his glossy hair. Miss Abbott, standing, characteristically, a little apart from the others, watched him, Alleyn noticed, with a look of stubborn deference. There was a Sunday morning air about the scene. Even Mr. Merryman was quiet and thoughtful, while Mr. McAngus, who, with Miss Abbott, had carried out the details of Anglo-Catholic observance like an old hand, was quite giddy and uplifted. He congratulated Brigid on her looks and did his little chassé before her with his head on one side. Mr. McAngus's russet-brown hair had grown, of course, even longer at the back, and something unfortunate seemed to have happened round the brow and temples. But as he always wore his felt hat out-of-doors and quite often in the lounge, this was not particularly noticeable.

Brigid responded gaily to his blameless compliments and turned to Alleyn.

"I didn't expect to see *you* about so early," she said.

"And why not?"

"You were up late! Pacing round the deck. Wrapped in thought!" teased Brigid.

"That's all very fine," Alleyn rejoined. "But what, I might ask, were you up to yourself? From what angle of vantage did you keep all this observation?"

Brigid blushed. "Oh," she said with a great air of casualness, "I was sitting in the verandah along there. We didn't like to call out as you passed, you looked so solemn and absorbed." She turned an even brighter pink, glanced at the others, who were gathered round Father Jourdain, and added quickly, "Tim Makepiece and I were talking about Elizabethan literature."

"You were not talking very loudly about it," Alleyn observed mildly.

"Well—" Brigid looked into his face. "I'm not having a shipboard flirtation with Tim. At least—at least, I don't think I am."

"Not a flirtation?" Alleyn repeated and smiled at her.

"And not anything else. Oh, golly!" Brigid said impulsively. "I'm in such a muddle."

"Do you want to talk about your muddle?"

Brigid put her arm through his. "I've arrived at the age," Alleyn reflected, "when charming young ladies take my arm." They walked down the deck together.

"How long," Brigid asked, "have we been at sea? And, crikey!" she added. "*What* an appropriate phrase that is!"

"Six days."

"There you are! Six days! The whole thing's ridiculous. How can anybody possibly know how they feel in six days? It's out of this world."

Alleyn remarked that he had known how he felt in one day. "Shorter even than that," he added. "At once."

"*Really?* And stuck to it?"

"Like a limpet. She took much longer, though."

"But—? Did you?"

"We are *very* happily married, thank you."

"How lovely," Brigid sighed.

"However," he added hurriedly, "don't let me raise a finger to urge you into an ill-considered undertaking."

"You don't have to tell me anything about that," she rejoined with feeling. "I've made that sort of ass of myself in quite a big way, once already."

"Really?"

"Yes, indeed. The night we sailed should have been my wedding night, only he chucked me three days before. I've done a bolt from all the *brouhaha*, leaving my wretched parents to cope. Very poor show, as you don't need to tell me," said Brigid in a high uneven voice.

"I expect your parents were delighted to get rid of you. Much easier for them, I daresay, if you weren't about, throwing vapours."

They had reached the end of the well-deck and stood, looking aft, near the little verandah. Brigid remarked indistinctly that going to church always made her feel rather light-headed and talkative and she expected that was why she was being so communicative.

"Perhaps the warm weather has something to do with it, as well," Alleyn suggested.

"I daresay. One always hears that people get very unguarded in the tropics. But actually you're to blame. I was saying to Tim the other night that if I was ever in a real jam I'd feel inclined to go bawling to you about it. He quite agreed. And here, fantastically, I am. Bawling away."

"I'm enormously flattered. Are you in a jam?"

"I suppose not, really. I just need to keep my eye. And see that he keeps his. Because whatever you say, I don't see how he can possibly know in six days."

Alleyn said that people saw more of each other in six days at sea than they did in as many weeks ashore but, he was careful to add, in rather less realistic circumstances. Brigid agreed. There was no doubt, she announced owlishly, that strange things happened to one at sea. Look at her, for instance, she said with enchanting egoism. She was getting all sorts of the rummiest notions into her head. After a little hesitation, and very much with the air of a child that screws itself up to confiding a groundless fear, Brigid said rapidly, "I even started thinking the Flower Murderer was on board. Imagine!"

Among the various items of Alleyn's training as an investigating officer, the trick of wearing an impassive face in the teeth of unexpected information was not the least useful. It stood him in good stead now.

"I wonder," he said, "what in the world could have put that idea in your head."

Brigid repeated the explanation she had already given Tim yesterday afternoon. "Of course," she said, "he thought it as dotty as you do and so did the F.N.C."

"Who," Alleyn asked, "is the F.N.C.?"

"It's our name for Dale. It stands for Frightfully Nice Chap only we don't mean it frightfully nicely, I'm afraid."

"Nevertheless, you confided your fantasy to him, did you?"

"He overheard me. We were 'squatting' on his and the D-B's lush chairs and he came round the corner with cushions and went all avuncular."

"And now you've brought this bugaboo out into the light of day it's evaporated?"

Brigid swung her foot and kicked an infinitesimal object into the scuppers. "Not altogether," she muttered.

"No?"

"Well, it has, really. Only last night, after I'd gone to bed, something happened. I don't suppose it was anything much, but it got me a bit steamed up again. My cabin's on the left-hand side of the block. The porthole faces my bed. Well, you know that blissful moment when you're not sure whether you're awake or asleep but kind of floating? I'd got to that stage. My eyes were shut and I was all air-borne and drifting. Then with a jerk I was wide awake and staring at that porthole." Brigid swallowed hard. "It was moonlight outside. Before I'd shut my eyes I'd seen the moon, looking in and then swinging out of sight and leaving a procession of stars and then swinging back. Lovely! Well, when I opened my eyes and looked at the porthole—somebody outside was looking in at me."

Alleyn waited for a moment and then said, "You're quite sure, I suppose?"

"Oh, yes. There he was, blotting out the stars and the moon and filling up my porthole with his head."

"Do you know who it was?"

"I haven't a notion. Somebody in a hat, but I could only see the outline.

And it was only for a second. I called out—it was not a startlingly original remark—'Hullo! Who's there?' and at once it—went down. I mean it sank in a flash. He must have ducked and then bolted. The moon came whooping back and there was I, all of a dither and thinking 'Suppose the Flower Murderer is on board and suppose after everyone else has gone to bed, he prowls and prowls around like the hosts of Midian'—or is it Gideon, in that blissful hymn? So you see, I haven't quite got over my nonsense, have I?"

"Have you told Makepiece about this?"

"I haven't seen him. He doesn't go to church."

"No, of course you haven't. Perhaps," Alleyn said, "it was Aubyn Dale being puckish."

"I must say I never thought of that. Could he hit quite such an all-time low for unfunniness, do you suppose?"

"I would have expected him to follow it up with a dummy spider on your pillow. You do lock your door at night, don't you? And in the day-time?"

"Yes. There was that warning about things having been pinched. Oh, Lord!" Brigid ejaculated. "Do you suppose that's who it was? The petty larcener? Why on earth didn't I remember before! Hoping he could fish something out through the porthole, would you think?"

"It wouldn't be the first time," Alleyn said.

The warning gong for breakfast began to tinkle. Brigid remarked cheerfully, "Well, that's *that*, anyway."

Alleyn waited for a moment and then said, "Look. In view of what you've just told me, I'd keep your curtains over your port at night. And as there evidently is a not-too-desirable character in the ship's complement, I don't think, if I were you, I'd go out walking after dark by yourself. He might come along and make a bit of a nuisance of himself."

Brigid said, "O.K., but what a *bore*. And, by the way, you'd better hand on that piece of advice to Mrs. D-B. She's the one to go out walking —or dancing, rather—by the light of the moon." Brigid smiled reminiscently. "I do think she's marvellous," she said. "All that *joie de vivre* at her age. Superb."

Alleyn found time to wonder how much Mrs. Dillington-Blick would relish this tribute and also how many surprises Brigid was liable to spring on him at one sitting.

He said, "*Does* she dance by the light of the moon? Who with?"

"By herself."

"You don't tell me she goes all pixy-wixy on the boat-deck? Carrying that weight?"

"On the other deck, the bottom one, nearer the sharp end. I've seen her. The weight doesn't seem to matter."

"Do explain yourself."

"Well, I'm afraid you're in for another night-piece—in point of fact the night before last. It was awfully hot; Tim and I had sat up rather late, *not,* I'd have you know again, for amorous dalliance but for a long muddly argument. And when I went to my cabin it was stuffy and I knew I wouldn't sleep for thinking about the argument. So I went along to the windows that look down on the lower deck—it's called the forrard well-deck, isn't it?—and wondered if I could be bothered climbing down and then along and up to the bows where I rather like to go. And while I was wondering and looking down into the forrard well-deck, which was full of black shadows, a door opened underneath me and a square patch of light was thrown across the deck."

Brigid's face, vivid and gay with the anticipation of her narrative, clouded a little.

"In point of fact," she said, "for a second or two it was a trifle grisly. You see, a shadow appeared on the lighted square. And—well—it was exactly as if the doll, Esmeralda, had come to life. Mantilla, fan, wide lace skirt. Everything. I daresay it contributed to my 'thing' about the flower murders. Anyway it gave me quite a jolt."

"It would," Alleyn agreed. "What next?"

"Well, somebody shut the door and the light patch vanished. And I knew, of course, who it was. There she stood, all by herself. I was looking down on her head. And then it happened. The moon was up and just at that moment it got high enough to shine into the deck. All those lumps of covered machinery cast their inky-black shadows, but there were patches of moonshine and it was exciting to see. She ran out and flirted her fan and did little pirouettes and curtseys and even two or three of those sliding backsteps they do with castanets in *The Gondoliers.* I think she was holding her mantilla across her face. It was the strangest sight."

"Very rum, indeed. You're sure it was the D-B?"

"But, of course. Who else? And, do you know, I found it rather touching. Don't you agree? She only stayed for a few moments and then ran back. The door opened and her shadow flashed across the patch of light. I heard men's voices, laughing, and then it was all blanked out. But wasn't it gay and surprising of Mrs. Dillington-Blick? Aren't you astonished?" asked Brigid.

"Flabbergasted. Although one does hear, of course, of elephant dances in the seclusion of the jungle."

Brigid said indignantly, "She's as light as a feather on her pins. Fat people are, you know. They dance like fairies. Still, perhaps you'd better warn her not to on account of the petty larcener. Only please don't say I told you about her moonlight party. In a funny sort of way I felt like an interloper."

"I won't," he promised. "And in the meantime don't take any solitary walks yourself. Tell Makepiece about it, and see if he doesn't agree with me."

"Oh," Brigid assured him. "He'll agree all right." And a dimple appeared near the corner of her mouth.

The group round Father Jourdain had moved nearer. Mr. McAngus called out, "Breakfast!" and Brigid said, "Coming!" She joined them, turned, crinkled her eyes at Alleyn and called out, "You *have* been nice. Thank you—Allan."

Before he could reply she had made off with the others in search of breakfast.

2

During breakfast Tim kept trying to catch Alleyn's eye and got but little response for his pains. He was waiting in the passage when Alleyn came out and said with artificial heartiness, "I've found those books I was telling you about. Would you like to come along to my room, or shall I bring them up to yours?"

"Bring them," Alleyn said, "to mine."

He went straight upstairs. In five minutes there was a knock on his door and Tim came in, burdened with unwanted textbooks. "I've got something I think I ought to tell you," he said.

"Brigid Carmichael wonders if the Flower Murderer is on board and Aubyn Dale knows she does."

"How the hell did you find out!" Tim ejaculated.

"She told me."

"Oh."

"And I'm rather wondering why you didn't."

"I didn't get a chance before dinner. I was going to after dinner, but you were boxed up with the D-B and Dale in the lounge and later on— well—"

"You were discussing Elizabethan literature on the verandah?"

"Exactly."

"Very well. At what stage did you inform Miss Carmichael of my name?"

"Damn it, it's not as bad as you think. Look—did she tell you that too?"

"She merely called it out before the whole lot of them as we came down to breakfast."

"She thinks it's your Christian name—Allan."

"Why?"

Tim told him. "I really am ashamed of myself," he said. "It just slipped out. I wouldn't have believed I could be such a *bloody* fool."

"Nor would I. I suppose it comes of all this poodle-faking nonsense. Calling oneself by a false name! Next door to wearing false whiskers, I've always thought, but sometimes it can't be avoided."

"She's not a notion who you are, of course."

"That, at least, is something. And, by the way, she'll be telling you about an incident that occurred last night. I think you'll agree that it's serious. I've suggested the mythical sneak-thief as the culprit. You'd better take the same line."

"But what's happened?"

"A Peeping Tom's happened. She'll tell you. She may also tell you how Mrs. Dillington-Blick goes fey among the derricks by moonlight."

"*What!*"

"I'm going to see the captain. Father Jourdain's joining me there; you'd better come too, I think. You might as well know about it."

"Of course. If I'm not confined to outer darkness."

"Oh," Alleyn said, "we'll give you another chance."

Tim said, "I'm sorry about my *gaffe*, Alleyn."

"The name is Broderick."

"I'm sorry."

"She's a nice child. None of my business but I hope you're not making a nonsense. She's had one bad knock and she'd better not be dealt another."

"She seems," Tim observed, "to confide in you a damn sight more freely than in me."

"Advanced years carry their own compensation."

"For me, this is *it*."

"Certain?"

"Absolutely. I wish I was as certain about her."

"Well—look after her."

"I've every intention of doing so," Tim said, and on that note they found Father Jourdain and went to visit Captain Bannerman.

It was not an easy interview.

Alleyn would have recognized Captain Bannerman for an obstinate man even if he had not been told as much by members of the Cape Line Company before he left. "He's a pigheaded old b.," one of these officials had remarked. "And if you get up against him he'll make things very uncomfortable for you. He drinks pretty hard and is reported to be bloody-minded in his cups. Keep on the right side of him and he'll be O.K."

So far, Alleyn thought, he had managed to follow this suggestion, but when he described the episode of the moonlit figure seen by Brigid on Friday night, he knew he was in for trouble. He gave his own interpretation of this story and he suggested that steps should be taken to ensure that there was no repetition. He met with a flat refusal. He then went on to tell them of the man outside Brigid's porthole. The captain said at once that he would detail the officer of the watch, who would take appropriate steps to ensure that this episode was not repeated. He added that it was of no particular significance and that very often people behaved oddly in the tropics—an observation that Alleyn was getting a little tired of hearing. He attempted to suggest a more serious interpretation and met with blank incredulity.

As for the Dillington-Blick episode, the captain said he would take no action either to investigate it or prevent a repetition. He treated them to a lecture on the diminishing powers of a ship's master at sea and grew quite hot on the subject. There were limitations. There were unions. Even passengers nowadays had their rights, he added regretfully. What had occurred was in no way an infringement of any of the regulations, he didn't propose to do anything about it and he must request Alleyn to follow suit. And that, he said finally, was flat.

He stood with his hands in his jacket pockets and glared through his porthole at the horizon. Even the back of his neck looked mulish. The other three men exchanged glances.

"The chap's not aboard my ship," the captain loudly announced without turning his head. "I know that as well as I know you *are*. I've been master under the Cape Company's charter for twenty years and I know as soon as I look at him whether a chap'll blow up for trouble at sea. I had a murderer shipped fireman aboard me, once. Soon as I clapped eyes on him I knew he was no good. Never failed yet. And I've been observing this lot. Observing them closely. There's not a murdering look on one of their faces, not a sign of it." He turned slowly and advanced upon Alleyn. His own face, lobster-red, wore an expression of childish complacency. "You're on a wild goose chase," he said blowing out gusts of whisky. Then with quite astonishing violence he drew his mottled hirsute fist from his pocket and crashed it down on his desk. "That sort of thing," said Captain Bannerman, "doesn't happen in *my ship!*"

"May I say just this?" Alleyn ventured. "I wouldn't come to you with the suggestion unless I thought it most urgently necessary. You may, indeed, be perfectly right. Our man may not, after all, be aboard. But

suppose, sir, that in the teeth of all you feel about it, he *is* in this ship."
Alleyn pointed to the captain's desk calendar. "Sunday the tenth of February," he said. "If he's here we've got four days before his supposed deadline. Shouldn't we take every possible step to prevent him going into action? I know very well that what I've suggested sounds farfetched, cockeyed, and altogether preposterous. It's a precautionary measure against a threat that may not exist. But isn't it better—" He looked at that unyielding front and very nearly threw up his hands. "Isn't it better, in fact, to be sure than sorry?" said Alleyn in despair. Father Jourdain and Tim murmured agreement but the captain shouted them down.

"Ah! So it is and it's a remark I often pass myself. But in this case it doesn't apply. What you've suggested is dead against my principles as master and I won't have it. I don't believe it's necessary and I won't have it."

Father Jourdain said, "If I might just say one word—"

"You may spare yourself the trouble. I'm set."

Alleyn said, "Very good, sir, I hope you're right. Of course we'll respect your wishes."

"I won't have that lady put-about by any interference or—or criticism."

"I wasn't suggesting—"

"It'd look like criticism," the captain mumbled cryptically and added, "A touch of high spirits never did anyone any harm."

This comment, from Alleyn's point of view, was such a masterpiece of meiosis that he could find no answer to it.

He said, "Thank you, sir," in what he hoped was the regulation manner and made for the door. The others followed him.

"Here!" Captain Bannerman ejaculated and they stopped. "Have a drink," said the captain.

"Not for me at the moment, thank you very much," said Alleyn.

"Why not?"

"Oh, I generally hold off till the sun's over the yardarm if that's the right way of putting it."

"You don't take overmuch then, I've noticed."

"Well," Alleyn said apologetically, "I'm by the way of being on duty."

"Ah! And nothing to show for it when it's all washed up. Not that I don't appreciate the general idea. You're following orders, I daresay, like all the rest of us, never mind if it's a waste of time and the public's money."

"That's the general idea."

"Well—what about you two gentlemen?"

"No thank you, sir," said Tim.

"Nor I, thank you very much," said Father Jourdain.

"No offense, is there?"

They hurriedly assured him there was none, waited for a moment and then went to the door. The last glimpse they had of the captain was of a square, slightly wooden figure making for the corner cupboard where he kept his liquor.

3

The rest of Sunday passed by quietly enough. It was the hottest day the passengers had experienced and they were all subdued. Mrs. Dillington-Blick wore white and so did Aubyn Dale. They lay on their chaise longues in the verandah and smiled languidly at passers-by. Sometimes they were observed to have their hands limply engaged; occasionally Mrs. Dillington-Blick's rich laughter would be heard.

Tim and Brigid spent most of the day in or near a canvas bathing pool that had been built on the after well-deck. They were watched closely by the Cuddys, who had set themselves up in a place of vantage at the shady end of the promenade deck, just under the verandah. Late in the afternoon Mr. Cuddy himself took to the water clad in a rather grisly little pair of puce-coloured drawers. He developed a vein of aquatic playfulness that soon drove Brigid out of the pool and Tim into a state of extreme irritation.

Mr. Merryman sat in his usual place and devoted himself to Neil Cream, and when that category of horrors had reached its appointed end, to the revolting fate that met an assortment of ladies who graced the pages of *The Thing He Loves*. From time to time he commented unfavourably on the literary style of this work and also on the police methods it described. As Alleyn was the nearest target he found himself at the receiving end of these strictures. Inevitably, Mr. Merryman was moved to enlarge once again on the flower murders. Alleyn had the fun of hearing himself described as "some plodding Dogberry drest in a little brief authority. One Alleyn," Mr. Merryman snorted, "whose photograph was reproduced in the evening newssheets—a countenance of abysmal foolishness, I thought."

"Really?"

"Oh, shocking, I assure you," said Mr. Merryman with immense relish. "I imagine, if the unknown criminal saw it, he must have been greatly consoled. I should have been, I promise you."

"Do you believe, then," Alleyn asked, "that there is after all an 'art to find the mind's construction in the face'?"

Mr. Merryman shot an almost approving glance at him "Source?" he demanded sharply. "And context?"

"*Macbeth*, one, four. Duncan on Cawdor," Alleyn replied, feeling like Alice in Wonderland.

"Very well. You know your way about that essentially second-rate melodrama, I perceive. Yes," Mr. Merryman went on with pedagogic condescension, "unquestionably, there are certain facial evidences which serve as pointers to the informed observer. I will undertake for example to distinguish at first sight a bright boy among a multitude of dullards, and believe me," Mr. Merryman added dryly, "the opportunity does not often present itself."

Alleyn asked him if he would extend this theory to include a general classification. Did Mr. Merryman, for instance, consider that there was such a thing as a criminal type of face? "I've read somewhere, I fancy, that the police say there isn't," he ventured. Mr. Merryman rejoined tartly that for once the police had achieved a glimpse of the obvious. "If you ask me whether there are facial types indicative of brutality and low intelligence I must answer yes. But the sort of person we have been considering"—he held up his book—"need not be exhibited in the countenance. The fact that he is possessed by his own particular devil is not written across his face that all who run may read."

"That's an expression that Father Jourdain used in the same context," Alleyn said. "He considers this man must be possessed of a devil."

"Indeed?" Mr. Merryman remarked. "That is of course the accepted view of the Church. Does he postulate the cloven hoof and toasting-fork?"

"I have no idea."

A shadow fell across the deck and there was Miss Abbott.

"I believe," she said, "in a personal devil. Firmly."

She stood above them, her back to the setting sun, her face dark and miserable. Alleyn began to get up from his deck-chair, but she stopped him with a brusque movement of her hand. She jerked herself up on the hatch, where she sat bolt upright, her large feet in tennis shoes dangling awkwardly.

"How else," she demanded, "can you explain the cruelties? God permits the devil to torment us for His own inscrutable purposes."

"Dear me!" observed Mr. Merryman, quite mildly for him. "We find ourselves in a positive hive of orthodoxy, do we not?"

"You're a churchman," Miss Abbott said, "aren't you? You came to Mass. Why do you laugh at the devil?"

Mr. Merryman contemplated her over his spectacles and after a long pause said, "My dear Miss Abbott, if you can persuade me of his existence I assure you I shall not treat the Evil One as a laughing matter. Far from it."

"*I'm* no good," she said impatiently. "Talk to Father Jourdain. He's full of knowledge and wisdom and will meet you on your own ground. I suppose you think it very uncouth of me to butt in and shove my faith down your throats, but when—" She set her dark jaw and went on with a kind of obstinacy, "When I hear people laugh at the devil it raises him in me. I *know* him."

The others found nothing to say to her. She passed her hand heavily across her eyes. "I'm sorry," she said. "I don't usually throw my weight about like this. It must be the heat."

Aubyn Dale came along the deck, spectacular in sharkskin shorts, crimson pullover, and a pair of exotic espadrilles he had bought in Las Palmas. He wore enormous sunglasses and his hair was handsomely ruffled.

"I'm going to have a dip," he said. "Just time before dinner and the water's absolutely superb. Madame won't hear of it, though. Any takers here?"

Mr. Merryman merely stared at him. Alleyn said he'd think about it. Miss Abbott got down from the hatch and walked away. Dale looked after her and wagged his head. "Poor soul!" he said. "I couldn't be sorrier for her. Honestly, life's hell for some women, isn't it?"

He looked at the other two men. Mr. Merryman ostentatiously picked up his book and Alleyn made a non-committal noise. "I see a lot of that sort of thing," Dale went on, "in my fantastic job. The Lonely Legion, I call them. Only to myself, of course."

"Quite," Alleyn murmured.

"Well, let's face it. What the hell is there for them to do—looking like that? Religion? Exploring Central Africa? Or—ask yourself. *I* dunno," said Dale, whimsically philosophical. "One of those things."

He pulled out his pipe, shook his head over it, said, "Ah, well!" and meeting perhaps with less response than he had expected, walked off, trolling a stylish catch.

Mr. Merryman said something quite unprintable into his book and Alleyn went in search of Mrs. Dillington-Blick.

He found her, still reclining on the verandah and fanning herself, enormous but delectable. Alleyn caught himself wondering what Henry Moore would have made of her. She welcomed him with enthusiasm and a helpless flapping gesture to show how hot she was. But her white dress was uncreased. A lace handkerchief protruded crisply from her décolletage and her hair was perfectly in order.

"You look as cool as a cucumber," Alleyn said and sat down on Aubyn Dale's footrest. "What an enchanting dress."

She made comic eyes at him. "My dear!" she said.

"But then all your clothes are enchanting. You dress quite beautifully, don't you?"

"How sweet of you to think so," she cried delightedly.

"Ah!" Alleyn said, leaning towards her. "You don't know how big a compliment you're being paid. I'm extremely critical of women's clothes."

"*Are* you, indeed. And what do you like about mine, may I ask?"

"I like them because they are clever enough to express the charm of their wearer," Alleyn said with a mental reservation to tell that one to Troy.

"Now, I do call that a *perfect* remark! In future I shall dress 'specially for you. There now!" promised Mrs. Dillington-Blick.

"Will you? Then I must think about what I should like you to wear. Tonight, for instance. Shall I choose that wonderful Spanish dress you bought in Las Palmas. May I?"

There was quite a long pause during which she looked sideways at him. "I think perhaps that'd be a little too much, don't you?" she said at last. "Sunday night, remember."

"Well, then, tomorrow?"

"Do you know," she said, "I've gone off that dress. You'll think me a frightful silly-billy, but all the rather murky business with poor *sweet* Mr. McAngus's doll has sort of set me against it. Isn't it queer?"

"*Oh!*" Alleyn exclaimed with a great show of disappointment. "*What* a pity! And what a waste!"

"I know. All the same, that's how it is. I just *see* Esmeralda looking so like those murdered girls and all I want to do with my lovely, lovely dress is drop it overboard."

"You haven't done that!"

Mrs. Dillington-Blick gave a little giggle. "No," she said. "I haven't done that."

"Or given it away?"

"Brigid would swim in it and I can't quite see Miss Abbott or Mrs. Cuddy going al flamenco, can you?"

Dale came by on his way to the bathing pool, now wearing Palm Beach trunks and looking like a piece of superb publicity for a luxury liner. "*You're* a couple of slackers," he said heartily and shinned nimbly down to the lower deck.

"I shall go and change," sighed Mrs. Dillington-Blick.

"But not into the Spanish dress?"

"I'm afraid not. Sorry to disappoint you." She held out her luxurious little hands and Alleyn dutifully hauled her up. "It's too sad," he said, "to think we are never to see it."

"Oh, I shouldn't be absolutely sure of that," she said and giggled again. "I may change my mind and get inspired all over again."

"To dance by the light of the moon?"

She stood quite still for a few seconds and then gave him her most ravishing smile. "You never know, do you?" said Mrs. Dillington-Blick.

Alleyn watched her stroll along the deck and go through the doors into the lounge.

". . . *and I expect you will agree,*" he wrote to his wife that evening, "*that in a subsidiary sort of way, this was a thoroughly disquieting bit of information.*"

4

Steaming down the west coast of Africa, *Cape Farewell* ran into the sort of weather that is apt to sap the resources of people who are not accustomed to it. The air through which she moved was of the land—enervated and loaded with vague impurities. A thin greyness that resembled dust rather than cloud obscured the sun but scarcely modified its potency. Mr. Merryman got a "touch" of it and looked as if he was running a temperature but refused to do anything about it. Dysentery broke out among the crew and also afflicted Mr. Cuddy, who endlessly consulted Tim and, with unattractive candour, anybody else who would listen to him.

Aubyn Dale drank a little more and began to look it and so, to Alleyn's concern, did Captain Bannerman. The captain was a heavy, steady drinker, who grew less and less tractable as his potations increased. He now resented any attempt Alleyn might make to discuss the case in hand and angrily reiterated his statement that there were no homicidal lunatics on board his ship. He became morose, unapproachable, and entirely pigheaded.

Mr. McAngus on the other hand grew increasingly loquacious and continually lost himself in a maze of *non sequiturs.* "He suffers," Tim said, "from verbal dysentery."

"With Mr. McAngus," Alleyn remarked, "the condition appears to be endemic. We mustn't blame the tropics."

"They seem to have exacerbated it, however," observed Father Jourdain wearily. "Did you know that he had a row with Merryman last night?"

"What about?" Alleyn asked.

"Those filthy medicated cigarettes he smokes. Merryman says the smell makes him feel sick."

"He's got something there," Tim said. "God knows what muck they're made of."

"They stink like a wet haystack."

"Ah, well," Alleyn said, "to our tasks, gentlemen. To our unwelcome tasks."

Since their failure with the captain they had agreed among themselves upon a plan of campaign. As soon as night fell each of them was to "mark" one of the women passengers. Tim said flatly that he would take Brigid and that arrangement was generally allowed to be only fair. Father Jourdain said he thought perhaps Alleyn had better have Mrs. Dillington-Blick. "She alarms me," he remarked. "I have a feeling that she thinks I'm a wolf in priest's clothing. If I begin following her about after dark she will be sure of it."

Tim grinned at Alleyn, "She's got her eye on you. It'd be quite a thing if you cut the Telly King out."

"Don't confuse me," Alleyn said dryly, and turned to Father Jourdain. "You can handle the double, then," he said. "Mrs. Cuddy never leaves Cuddy for a second and—" He paused.

"And poor Miss Abbott is not, you feel, in any great danger."

"What do you suppose is the matter with her?" Alleyn asked and remembered what he had heard her saying as she left Father Jourdain on Saturday night. The priest's eyes were expressionless. "We are not really concerned," he said, "with Miss Abbott's unhappiness, I think."

"Oh," Alleyn said, "it's a sort of reflex action for me to wonder why people behave as they do. When we had the discussion about alibis, her distress over the Aubyn Dale programme of the night of January the fifteenth was illuminating, I thought."

"I thought it damn puzzling," said Tim. "D'you know, I actually found myself wondering, I can't think why, if she was the victim and not the viewer that night."

"I think she was the viewer."

Father Jourdain looked sharply at Alleyn and then walked over to the porthole and stared out.

"As for the victim—" Alleyn went on, "the woman, do you remember, who told Dale she didn't like to announce her engagement because it would upset her great friend?—" He broke off and Tim said, "You're not going to suggest that Miss Abbott was the great friend?"

"At least it would explain her reactions to the programme."

After a short silence Tim said idly, "What does she do? Has she a job, do you know?"

Without turning his head Father Jourdain said, "She works for a firm of music publishers. She is quite an authority on early church music, particularly the Gregorian chants."

Tim said involuntarily, "I imagine, with that voice, she doesn't sing them herself."

"On the contrary," Alleyn rejoined, "she does. Very pleasantly. I heard her on the night we sailed from Las Palmas."

"She has a most unusual voice," Father Jourdain said. "If she were a man it would be a counter tenor. She represented her firm at a conference on church music three weeks ago in Paris. I went over for it and saw her there. She was evidently a person of importance."

"Was she indeed?" Alleyn murmured and then, briskly: "Well, as you say, we are not immediately concerned with Miss Abbott. The sun's going down. It's time we went on duty."

On the evenings of the eleventh and twelfth, according to plan, Alleyn devoted himself exclusively to Mrs. Dillington-Blick. This manoeuvre brought about the evident chagrin of Aubyn Dale, the amusement of Tim, the surprise of Brigid, and the greedy observance of Mrs. Cuddy. Mrs. Dillington-Blick was herself delighted. "My dear!" she wrote to her friend. "I've nobbled the Gorgeous Brute!! My dear, too gratifying! Nothing, to coin a phrase, *tangible*. As yet! But *marked* attention! And with the tropical moon being what it is, I feel something *rather* nice may eventuate. In the meantime, I promise you, I've only to wander off after dinner to my so suitable little verandah and he's after me in a flash. A.D., my dear, rapidly becoming pea green, which is always so gratifying. Aren't I hopeless—but what fun!!!"

On the night of the thirteenth, when they were all having coffee, Aubyn Dale suddenly decided to give a supper-party in his private sitting-room. It was equipped with a phonograph on which he proposed to play some of his own records.

"Everybody invited," he said largely, waving his brandy glass. "I won't take no for an answer." And indeed it would have been difficult under the circumstances for anybody to attempt to refuse, though Mr. Merryman and Tim looked as if they would have liked to do so.

The "suite" turned out to be quite a grand affair. There were a great many signed photographs of Aubyn Dale's poppet and of several celebrities and one of Aubyn Dale himself, bowing before the grandest celebrity of all. There was a pigskin writing-case and a pigskin record-carrier. There were actually some monogrammed Turkish cigarettes, a present, Dale explained with boyish ruefulness, from a potentate who was one of his most ardent fans. And almost at once there was a great deal to drink. Mr. McAngus was given a trick glass that poured his drink over his chin and was not quite as amused as the captain, the Cuddys, and Mrs. Dillington-Blick, though he took it quite quietly. Aubyn Dale apologized with the air of a chidden child and did several very accurate imitations of his fellow celebrities in television. Then they listened to four records, including one of Dale himself doing an Empire Day talk on how to be broadminded though British, in which he laid a good deal of stress on the national trait of being able to laugh at ourselves.

"*How* proud we are of it, too," Tim muttered crossly to Brigid.

After the fourth record most of the guests began to be overtaken by the drowsiness of the tropics. Miss Abbott was the first to excuse herself and everybody else except Mrs. Dillington-Blick and the captain followed her lead. Brigid had developed a headache in the overcrowded room and was glad to get out into the fresh air. She and Tim sat on the starboard side under Mr. McAngus's porthole. There was a small ship's lamp in the deckhead above them.

"Only five minutes," Brigid said. "I'm for bed after that. My head's behaving like a piano accordion."

"Have you got any aspirins?"

"I can't be bothered hunting them out."

"I'll get you something. Don't move, will you?" Tim said, noting that the light from Mr. McAngus's porthole and from the ship's lamp fell across her chair. He could hear Mr. McAngus humming to himself in a reedy falsetto as he prepared for bed. "You will stay put," Tim said, "won't you?"

"Why shouldn't I? I don't feel at all like shinning up the rigging or going for a strapping walk. Couldn't we have that overhead light off? Not," Brigid said hurriedly, "in order to create a romantic gloom, I assure you, Tim. It shines in one's eyes, rather; that's all."

"The switch is down at the other end. I'll turn it off when I come back," he said. "I shan't be half a tick."

When he had gone, Brigid lay back and shut her eyes. She listened to the ship's engines and to the sound of the sea and to Mr. McAngus's droning. This stopped after a moment and through her closed lids she was aware of a lessening of light. "He's turned his lamp off," she thought gratefully, "and has tucked his poor dithering old self up in his virtuous couch." She opened her eyes and saw the dim light in the deckhead above her.

The next moment, it, too, went out.

"That's Tim coming back," she thought. "He *has* been quick."

She was now in almost complete darkness. A faint breeze lifted her hair. She heard no footfall but she was conscious that someone had approached from behind her.

"Tim?" she said.

Hands came down on her shoulders. She gave a little cry: "Oh, *don't!* You made me jump."

The hands shifted towards her neck and she felt her chain of pearls move and twist and break. She snatched at the hands and they were not Tim's.

"No," she cried out. "*No! Tim!*"

There was a rapid thud of retreating feet. Brigid struggled out of her chair and ran down the dark tunnel of the covered deck into someone's arms.

"It's all right," Alleyn said. "You're all right. It's me."

5

A few seconds later, Tim Makepiece came back.

Alleyn still held Brigid in his arms. She quivered and stammered and clutched at him like a frightened child.

"What the hell—" Tim began but Alleyn stopped him.

"Did you turn out the deckhead lights?"

"No. Biddy, darling—"

"Did you meet anyone?"

"No. Biddy—!"

"All right. Take over, will you? She'll tell you when she's got her second wind."

He disengaged her arms. "You're in clover," he said. "Here's your medical adviser."

She bolted into Tim's arms and Alleyn ran down the deck.

He switched on the overhead lights and followed round the centre-castle. He looked up and down companionways, along hatch combings, behind piles of folded chairs and into recesses. He knew, as he hunted, he was too late. He found nothing but the old blankness of a ship's decks at night. On the excuse that he had lost his pocketbook with his passport and letters of credit, he aroused all the men, including Mr. Cuddy. Dale was still dressed and in his sitting-room. The others were in pyjamas and varying degrees of ill temper. He told Father Jourdain, briefly, what had happened and arranged that they would go, with Tim, to the captain.

Then he returned to Brigid's chair. Her pearls were scattered on the deck and in the loose seat. He collected them and thought at first that otherwise he had drawn a blank. But at the last he found, clinging to the back of the chair, discoloured and crushed, a scrap of something which, when he took it to the light, declared itself plainly enough. It was a tiny fragment of a flower petal.

It still retained, very faintly, the scent of hyacinth.

CHAPTER NINE   **Thursday the Fourteenth**

"Now," Alleyn demanded, standing over Captain Bannerman. "Now do you believe this murderer's on board? Do you?"

But as he said it he knew he was up against the unassailable opponent: the elderly man who has made up his mind and is temperamentally incapable of admitting he has made it up the wrong way.

"I'll be damned if I do," said Captain Bannerman.

"I am appalled to hear you say so."

The captain swallowed the end of his drink and clapped the glass down on the table. He looked from Alleyn to Father Jourdain, wiped his mouth with the back of his hand and said, "You've got this blasted notion into your heads and every footling little thing that takes place you make out is something to do with it. What takes place?

Little Miss Brigid is sitting all alone in her deck-chair. Some chap comes up and puts his hands on her shoulders. Playful, like. And what's unnatural in that? By gum, I wouldn't blame—" He pulled himself up, turned a darker shade of brick red and continued, "On your own statement, she's got ideas into her head about these murders. Natural enough, I daresay, seeing how the lot of you can't let the matter alone but never stop talking about it. She's startled, like, and jumps up and runs away. Again—natural enough. But you come blustering up here and try to tell me she was nigh-on murdered. You won't get anywhere with me, that road. Someone's got to hang on to his common sense in this ship and, by gum, that's going to be the master."

Father Jourdain said, "But it's not the one incident, it's the whole sequence, as Alleyn has shown us only too clearly. An embarkation paper in the hand of the girl on the wharf. The incident of the doll. The fact that singing was heard. The Peeping Tom at Miss Carmichael's porthole. Now this. What man among us, knowing these crimes are in all our minds, would play such a trick on her?"

"And what man among you would murder her—tell me that!"

Tim had been sitting with his head between his hands. He now looked up and said, "Sir, even if you do think there's nothing in it, surely there can be no harm in taking every possible precaution—?"

"What the hell have you all been doing if you haven't been taking precautions? Haven't I said just that, all along? Didn't I"—he pointed his stubby finger at Alleyn—"get them all jabbering about alibis because you asked me to? Haven't I found out for you that the whole boiling went ashore the night we sailed, never mind if my own deckhand thought I was balmy? Haven't I given out there's an undesirable character in my ship's company, which there isn't, and ordered the ladies to lock their doors? What the suffering cats more could I have done? Tell me that!"

Alleyn said instantly, "You could, you know, do something to ensure that there's no more wandering about deserted decks at night in Spanish dresses."

"I've told you. I won't have any interference with the rights of the individual in my ship."

"Will you let me say something unofficially about it?"

"No."

"Will you consider a complete showdown? Will you tell the passengers who I am and why I'm here? It'll mean no arrest, of course," Alleyn said, "but with the kind of threat that I believe hangs over this ship I'm prepared to admit defeat. Will you do this?"

"No."

"You realize that tomorrow is the night when, according to the considered opinion of experts, this man may be expected to go into action again?"

"He's not aboard my ship."

"And that Miss Carmichael," Father Jourdain intervened, "naturally will speak of her fears to the other ladies."

Tim said, "No."

"No?"

"No," Alleyn said. "She's not going to talk about it. She agrees that it might lead to a panic. She's a courageous child."

"She's been given a shock," Tim said angrily to the captain, "that may very easily have extremely serious results. I can't allow—"

"Dr. Makepiece, you'll be good enough to recollect you have signed on as a member of my ship's company."

"Certainly, sir."

The captain stared resentfully about him, made a petulant ejaculation and roared out, "Damn it, you can tell her to stay in bed all day tomorrow and the next day too, can't you? Suffering from shock? All right. That gets *her* out of the way, doesn't it? Where is she now?"

"I've given her a Nembutal. She's asleep in bed. The door's locked and I've got the key."

"Well, keep it and let her stay there. The steward can take her meals. Unless you think *he's* the sex monster," said the captain with an angry laugh.

"Not in the sense you mean," Alleyn said.

"That's enough of that!" the captain shouted.

"Where," Father Jourdain asked wearily, "is Mrs. Dillington-Blick?"

"In bed," the captain said at once, and added in a hurry, "She left Dale's suite when I did. I saw her to her cabin."

"They do lock their doors, don't they?"

"She did," said the captain morosely.

Father Jourdain got up. "If I may be excused," he said. "It's very late. Past midnight."

"Yes," Alleyn said and he also rose. "It's February the fourteenth. Good-night, Captain Bannerman."

He had a brief session with Father Jourdain and Tim. The latter was in a rage. "That *bloody* old man," he kept saying. "Did you ever know such a *bloody* old man!"

"All right, all right," Alleyn said. "We'll just have to go on under our own steam. The suggestion, by the way, to keep Miss Carmichael in bed for twenty-four hours has its points."

Tim said grandly that he'd consider it. Father Jourdain asked if they were to do anything about the other women. Could they not emphasize that as Brigid had had an unpleasant experience it might be as well if the ladies were particularly careful not to wander about the deck at night without an escort.

Alleyn said, "We've done that already. But think a minute. Suppose one of them chose the wrong escort."

"You know, it's an extraordinary thing," Father Jourdain said after a moment, "but I keep forgetting it's one of us. I almost believe in the legend of the unsavoury deckhand."

"I think it might be a good idea if you suggest a four of bridge or canasta. Mrs. Dillington-Blick plays both, doesn't she? Get Mrs. Cuddy and Miss Abbott to come in. Or if Dale and the other men will play you might get two fours going. Makepiece will look after Miss Carmichael."

"What'll you do?" Tim asked.

"I?" Alleyn asked. "Look on. Look round. Just look. Of course they may refuse to play. In which case we'll have to use our wits, Heaven help us, and improvise. In the meantime, you probably both want to go to bed."

"And you, no doubt," said Father Jourdain.

"Oh," Alleyn said, "I'm an owl by habit. See you in the morning. Good-night."

He was indeed trained to put up with long stretches of sleeplessness and faced the rest of the short night with equanimity. He changed into slacks, a dark shirt and rope-soled shoes and then began a systematic beat. Into the deserted lounge. Out on to the well-deck, past the little verandah where the two chaise longues stood deserted. Round the hatch, and then to the cabin quarters and their two covered decks.

The portholes were all open. He listened outside each of them. The first cabin, facing aft and to the starboard side, was Mr. Merryman's. It appeared to be in darkness, but after a moment he saw that a blue point glowed somewhere inside. It was the little night light above the bed. Alleyn stood near the porthole and was just able to make out Mr. Merryman's tousled head on the pillow. Next came the doorway into the passage bisecting the cabin-quarters and then further along on the starboard side was Mr. McAngus, who could be heard whistling in his sleep. The Cuddys, in the adjoining cabin, the last on the starboard side, snored antiphonally. He turned left and moved along the forward face of the block, past Miss Abbott's dark and silent cabin and then on to Father Jourdain's. His light still shone and as the porthole was uncovered Alleyn thought he would have a word with him.

He looked in. Father Jourdain was on his knees before a crucifix, his joined hands pressed edgeways to his lips. Alleyn turned away and walked on to the "suite." Dale's light was still up in his sitting-room. Alleyn stood a little to one side of the forward porthole. The curtain across it fluttered and blew out. He caught a brief glimpse of Dale in brilliant pyjamas with a glass in his hand. He turned left past Brigid's porthole with its carefully drawn curtain and then moved aft to Mrs. Dillington-Blick's cabin. Her light too was still on. He paused with his back to the bulkhead and close to her porthole and became aware of a rhythmic slapping noise and a faint whiff of some aromatic scent. "She's coping with her neckline," he thought.

He moved on past the darkened lounge. He had completed his round and was back at Mr. Merryman's cabin.

He approached the iron ladder leading to the forward well-deck and climbed down it. When he had reached the bottom he waited for a moment in the shadow of the centrecastle. On his left was the door through which the figure in the Spanish dress had come on Friday night. It led into a narrow passage by the chief steward's quarters. Above him toward the centrecastle. He knew if he walked out into the moonlight, the second officer, keeping his watch far above on the bridge, would see him. He did walk out. His shadow, black as ink, splayed across the deck and up the hatch combing.

On the fo'castle two bells sounded. Alleyn watched the seaman who had rung them come down and cross the deck towards him.

"Good-night," he said.

"Good-night, sir," the man replied and sounded surprised.

Alleyn said, "I thought I'd go up into the bows and see if I could find a cap-full of cool air."

"That's right, sir. A bit fresher up there."

The man passed him and disappeared into shadow. Alleyn climbed up to the fo'castle and stood in the bows. For a moment or two he faced the emptiness of the night. Beneath him, in a pother of phosphorescence, the waters were divided. "There is nothing more lonely in the world," he thought, "than a ship at sea."

He turned and looked at the ship, purposeful and throbbing with her own life. Up on the bridge he could see the second officer. He waved with a broad gesture of his arm and after a moment the second officer replied, slightly, perhaps ironically.

Alleyn returned to the lower deck. As he climbed down the ladder, a door beneath him, leading into the seamen's quarters in the fo'castle, opened and somebody came out. Alleyn looked down over his shoulder. The newcomer, barefooted and clad only in pyjama trousers, moved out, seemed to sense that he was observed and stopped short.

It was Dennis. When he saw Alleyn he made as if to return.

Alleyn said, "You keep late hours, steward."

"Oh, it's *you*, Mr. Broderick. You quite startled me. Yes, *don't* I? I've been playing poker with the boys," Dennis explained. "Fancy you being up there, sir, at this time of night."

Alleyn completed his descent. "I couldn't sleep," he said. "It's the heat, I suppose."

Dennis giggled. "I *know*. Isn't it terrific!"

He edged away slightly.

"What's it like in your part of the world?" Alleyn asked. "Where are your quarters?"

"I'm in the glory-hole, sir. Down below. It's *frightful*."

"All the same, I fancy it's healthier indoors."

Dennis said nothing.

"You want to be careful what you wear in the tropics. Particularly at night."

Dennis looked at his plump torso and smirked.

Alleyn waited for a moment and then said, "Well, I shall take my own advice and go back to bed. Good-night to you."

"Good *morning,* sir," said Dennis pertly.

Alleyn climbed up to the bridge deck. When he got there he looked back. Dennis still stood where he had left him but after a moment turned away and went back into the fo'castle.

At intervals through the rest of the night Alleyn walked round his beat but he met nobody. When the dawn came up he went to bed and slept until Dennis, pallid, glistening, and silent, brought in his morning tea.

2

That day was the hottest the passengers had experienced. For Alleyn it began with a radioed report in code from Inspector Fox, who was still sweating away with his checks on alibis. Apart from routine confirmations of Mr. McAngus's appendicial adventure and Aubyn Dale's departure for America, nothing new had come to hand. The Yard, Fox intimated, would await instructions, which meant, Alleyn sourly and unfairly reflected, that if he made an arrest before Cape Town, somebody would be flown over with a spare pair of handcuffs or something. He made his way, disgruntled, to continue observation on the passengers.

They were all on the lower deck. Brigid, who was still rather white, had flatly refused to stay in bed and spent most of the day in or near the bathing pool, where an awning had been erected and deck-chairs set out. Here she was joined by Tim and at intervals by one or two of the others. Only Miss Abbott, Mr. McAngus and Mrs. Cuddy refrained from bathing, but they too sat under the awning and looked on.

At noon Mrs. Dillington-Blick took to the water and the appearance was in the nature of a star turn. She wore a sort of bathing negligée which Aubyn Dale, who escorted her, called a "bewilderment of nonsense." It was all compact of crisp cotton frills and black ribbons, and under it Mrs. Dillington-Blick was encased in her Jolyon swimsuit which belonged to a group advertised as being "for the Queenly Woman." She had high-heeled thonged sandals on her feet and had to be supported down the companion-ladder by Aubyn Dale, who carried her towel and sun-shade. At this juncture only Brigid, Tim, Alleyn and Mr. Cuddy were bathing. The others were assembled under the awning and provided an audience for Mrs. Dillington-Blick. She laughed a great deal and made deprecatory *moues.* "My dears!" she said. "*Look* at me!"

"You know," Brigid said to Tim, "I really *do* admire her. She actually cashes in on her size. I call that brilliant."

"It's fascinating," Tim agreed. "Do look! She's standing there like a piece of baroque, waiting to be unveiled."

Dale performed this ceremony. Alleyn, who was perched on the edge of the pool near the steps that led down into it, watched the reaction. It would have been untrue to say that anybody gasped when Mrs. Dillington-Blick relinquished her bathing-robe. Rather, a kind of trance overtook her fellow passengers. Mr. Cuddy, who had been frisking in the waters, grasped the rim of the pool and grinned horridly through his wet fringe. Mr. Merryman, who wore an old-fashioned gown and an equally old-fashioned bathing-dress and whose hair had gone into a damp fuzz like a baby's, stared over his spectacles, as startled as Mr. Pickwick in the Maiden Lady's four-poster. Mr. McAngus, who had been dozing, opened his eyes and his mouth at the same time and turned dark red in the face. On the bridge, Captain Bannerman was transfixed. Two deckhands stood idle for several seconds round a can of red lead and then self-consciously fell to work with their heads together.

Mrs. Cuddy tried to catch somebody's eye but, failing to do so, stared in amazement at her infatuated husband.

Miss Abbott looked up from the letter she was writing, blinked twice and looked down again.

Father Jourdain, who had been reading, made a slight movement with his right hand. Alleyn told himself it was absurd to suppose that Father Jourdain had been visited by an impulse to cross himself.

Brigid broke the silence. She called out, "Jolly good! Come in, it's heaven."

Mrs. Dillington-Blick put on a bathing cap, removed her sandals, precariously climbed the ladder up to the rim of the pool, avoided looking at Mr. Cuddy and held out her hands to Alleyn.

"Launch me," she invited winningly and at the same moment lost her balance and fell like an avalanche into the brimming pool. The water she displaced surged over the edges. Alleyn, Mr. Cuddy, Brigid and Tim bobbed about like flotsam and jetsam. Aubyn Dale was drenched. Mrs. Dillington-Blick surfaced, gasping and astounded, and struck out for the nearest handhold.

"Ruby!" Aubyn Dale cried anxiously, as he dashed the sea-water from his face. "What have you done?"

For the first time in the voyage Mr. Merryman burst into peals of ungovernable laughter.

This incident had a serio-comic sequel. While Mrs. Dillington-Blick floated in a corner of the pool, clinging to the edges, Mr. Cuddy swam slily alongside and with a quick grab pulled her under. There was a struggle from which she emerged furious and half-suffocated. Her face was streaked with mascara, her nose was running and her bathing cap was askew. She was a terrible sight. Alleyn helped her up the submerged steps. Dale received her on the far side and got her down to deck level.

"That horrible man!" she choked out. "That horrible man!"

Mr. McAngus also hurried to her side while Mr. Cuddy leered over the rim of the pool.

A ridiculous and rather alarming scene ensued. Mr. McAngus, in an unrecognizably shrill voice, apostrophized Mr. Cuddy. "You're an un-mitigated bounder, sir," he screamed and actually shook his fist in Mr. Cuddy's wet face.

"I must say, Cuddy!" Dale said, all restraint and seemly indignation. "You've got an extraordinary idea of humour."

Mr. Cuddy still leered and blinked. Mrs. Cuddy from her deck-chair cried anxiously, "Dear! You're forgetting yourself."

"You're an ape, sir!" Mr. McAngus added and he and Dale simulta-neously each placed an arm round Mrs. Dillington-Blick.

"I'll look after her," said Dale coldly.

"Let me help you," said Mr. McAngus. "Come and sit down."

"Leave her alone. Ruby, darling—"

"Oh, shut up, both of you!" said Mrs. Dillington-Blick. She snatched up her robe and made off—a mountain of defaced femininity.

Mr. Merryman continued to laugh, the other gentlemen separated and Mr. Cuddy swam quietly about the pool by himself.

It was the only incident of note in an otherwise torpid day. After luncheon all the passengers went to their respective cabins and Alleyn allowed himself a couple of hours' sleep. He woke, as he had arranged with himself to wake, at four o'clock and went down to tea. Everybody was limp and disinclined to talk. Dale, Mr. McAngus, and Mr. Cuddy had evidently decided to calm down. Mr. Merryman's venture into the pool had brought on his "touch of the sun" again. He looked feverish and anxious and actually didn't seem to have the energy to argue with anyone. Brigid came over to him. She very prettily knelt by his chair, and begged him to let her find Tim and ask him to prescribe. "Or at least take some aspirin," she said. "I'll get some for you. Will you?" She put her hand on his but he drew it away quickly.

"I think I may have a slight infection," he said in explanation and positively added, "But thank you, my dear."

"You're terribly hot." She went away and returned with the aspirin and water. He consented to take three tablets and said he would lie down for a little while. When he went out they all noticed that he was quite shaky.

"Well," Mr. Cuddy said, "I'm sure I hope it's nothing catching."

"It's not very considerate," Mrs. Cuddy said, "to sit round with every-body if it is. How are you feeling, dear?"

"Good, thanks, dear. My little trouble," Mr. Cuddy said to everybody, "has cleared up nicely. I'm a box of birds. I really quite enjoy the heat, something a bit intoxicating about the tropics, to my way of thinking."

He himself was not urgently intoxicating. His shirt had unlovely dark areas about it, the insides of his knees were raddled with prickly heat and his enormous hands left wet patches on everything they touched. "I'm a very free perspirer," he said proudly, "and that's a healthy sign, I'm told."

This observation met with a kind of awed silence, broken by Mr. McAngus.

"Has everybody seen?" he asked, turning his back on Mr. Cuddy. "There's going to be a film tonight. They've just put up a notice. On the boat-deck, it's going to be."

There was a stir of languid interest. Father Jourdain muttered to Alleyn, "That disposes of our canasta party."

"How lovely!" Mrs. Dillington-Blick said. "Where do we sit?"

"I *think*," Mr. McAngus fluted, at once tripping up to her, "that we all sit on deck-chairs on the top of the hatch. Such a good idea! You must lie on your chaise longue, you know. You'll look quite wonderful," he added with his timid little laugh. "Like Cleopatra in her barge with all her slaves round her. Pagan, almost."

"My dear!"

"What's the film?" Dale asked.

"*Othello*. With that large American actor."

"Oh, God!"

"Mr. Merryman *will* be pleased," said Brigid. "It's his favourite. If he approves, of course."

"Well, *I* don't think he ought to come," Mrs. Cuddy at once objected. "He should consider other people."

"It'll be in the open air," Miss Abbott countered, "and there's no need, I imagine, for you to sit next to Mr. Merryman."

Mrs. Cuddy smiled meaningly at her husband.

Brigid said, "But how exciting! Orson Welles and everything! I couldn't be better pleased."

"We'd rather have a nice musical," said Mrs. Cuddy. "But then we're not arty, are we, dear?"

Mr. Cuddy said nothing. He was looking at Mrs. Dillington-Blick.

3

The film version of *Othello* began to wind up its remarkable course. Mr. Merryman could be heard softly invoking the retribution of the gods upon the head of Mr. Orson Welles.

In the front row Captain Bannerman sighed windily, Mrs. Dillington-Blick's jaw quivered, and Dale periodically muttered, "Oh, *no!*" Alleyn, who was flabbergasted by the film, was able to give it only a fraction of his attention.

Behind the captain's party sat the rest of the passengers, while a number of ship's officers were grouped together at one side. Dennis and his fellow stewards watched from the back.

The sea was perfectly calm, stars glittered with explosive brilliance. The cinema screen, an incongruous accident, with a sterile life of its own, glowed and gestured in the surrounding darkness.

> "*Put out the light, and then put out the light:*
> *If I quench thee, thou flaming minister,*
> *I can again thy former light restore,*
> *Should I repent me . . ."*

Brigid caught her breath and Tim reached for her hand. They were moved by a single impulse and by one thought—that it was superbly right for them to listen together to this music.

> "*I know not where is that Promethean heat*
> *That can thy light relume . . ."*

"*Promethean heat,*" Father Jourdain murmured appreciatively.

The final movement emerged not entirely obscured by the treatment that had been accorded it. A huge face loomed out of the screen.

> "*Kill me tomorrow; let me live tonight!*
> *. . . But half an hour!*"
> "*Being done, there is no pause.*"
> "*But while I say one prayer!*"
> "*It is too late.*"

A white cloth closed like a shroud about Desdemona's face and tightened horridly.

The screen was no longer there. At their moment of climax Othello and Desdemona were gone and their audience was in darkness. The pulse of the ship's engines emerged and the chief engineer's voice saying that a fuse had blown somewhere. Matches were struck. There was a group of men round the projector. Alleyn produced his torch, slipped out of his seat, which was at the end of the row, and walked slowly along the hatch. None of the passengers had stirred but there was a certain amount of movement among the stewards, some of whom, including Dennis, had already left.

"The circuit's gone," a voice near the projector said and another added,

"That's the story. Hold everything." One of the figures disentangled itself and hurried away.

"'Put out the light,'" a junior officer quoted derisively, "'and then put out the light.'" There was a little gust of laughter. Mrs. Cuddy, in the middle of the third row, tittered. "He stifles her, doesn't he, dear? Same thing again! We don't seem to be able to get away from it, do we?"

Miss Abbott said furiously, "Oh, for pity's *sake!*"

Alleyn had reached the edge of the hatch. He stood there, watching the backs of the passengers' chairs, now clearly discernible. Immediately in front of him were Tim and Brigid, their hands enlaced, leaning a little towards each other. Brigid was saying, "I don't want to pull it to pieces yet. After all there *are* the words."

A figure rose up from the chair in the middle of the row. It was Mr. Merryman.

"I'm off," he announced.

"Are you all right, Mr. Merryman?" Brigid asked.

"I am nauseated," Mr. Merryman rejoined, "but not for the reason you suppose. I can stomach no more of this slaughterous—this impertinent travesty—Pray excuse me."

He edged past them and past Father Jourdain, moved round the end of the row and thus approached Alleyn.

"Had enough?" Alleyn asked.

"A bellyful, thank you."

He sat on the edge of the hatch, his back ostentatiously presented to the invisible screen. He was breathing hard. His hand which had brushed against Alleyn's was hot and dry.

"I'm afraid you've still got a touch of your bug, whatever it is," Alleyn said. "Why don't you turn in?"

But Mr. Merryman was implacable. "I do not believe," he said, "in subjecting myself to the tyranny of indisposition. I do not, like our Scottish acquaintance, surrender to hypochondriacal speculations. On the contrary, I fight back. Besides," he added, "in this Stygian gloom, where is the escape? There is none. *J'y suis, et j'y reste.*"

And so in fact he remained. The fuse was repaired, the film drew to its close. An anonymous choir roared its anguish and, without benefit of authorship, ended the play. The lights went up and the passengers moved to the lounge for supper. Mr. Merryman alone remained outside, seated in a deck-chair by the open doors and refusing sustenance.

Alleyn, and indeed all of them, were to remember that little gathering very vividly. Mrs. Dillington-Blick had recovered her usual form and was brilliant. Dressed in black lace, though not that of her Spanish dress, and wreathed in the effulgence of an expensive scent that had by now acquired the authority of a signature tune, she held her customary court. She discussed the film—it had, she said, *really* upset her. "My dear! That ominous man! Terrifying! But all the same—there's *something*. One could quite see why she married him."

"I thought it disgusting," Mrs. Cuddy said. "A black man. She deserved all she got."

Mrs. Dillington-Blick laughed. She and Aubyn Dale, Alleyn noticed, kept catching each other's eye and quickly looking away again. Neither Mr. Cuddy nor Mr. McAngus could remove his gaze from her. The captain hung over her; even Miss Abbott watched her with a kind of brooding appreciation while Mrs. Cuddy resentfully stared and stared. Only Brigid and Tim, bent on their common voyage of discovery, were unmindful of Mrs. Dillington-Blick.

Presently she yawned, and she even managed to yawn quite fetchingly. "I'm for my little bed," she announced.

"Not even a stroll round the deck?" asked the captain.

"I *don't* think so, really."

"Or a cigarette on the verandah?" Dale suggested loudly.

"I might."

She laughed and walked over to the open doors. Mr. Merryman struggled up from his deck-chair. She wished him good-night, looked back into the lounge and smiled intimately and brilliantly at Mr. McAngus. "Goodnight," she repeated softly and went out on the deserted deck.

Father Jourdain caught his breath. "All right," Alleyn muttered. "You carry on here."

Tim glanced at Alleyn and nodded. The captain had been buttonholed by Mr. McAngus and looked restive. Brigid was talking to Mr. Merryman, who half rose, bestowed on her an old-fashioned bow and sank groggily back into his chair. Aubyn Dale was drinking and Mr. Cuddy was in the grasp of his wife, who now removed him.

Alleyn said, "Good-night, everybody." He followed the Cuddys into the passageway, turned left and went out to the deck by the port side door. He was just in time to see Mrs. Dillington-Blick disappear round the verandah corner of the engine house. Before he could reach it she returned, paused for a second when she saw him and then swam gaily towards him.

"Just one gulp of fresh air," she said rather breathlessly. She slipped her arm through his and quite deliberately leaned against him.

"Help me negotiate that frightful ladder, will you? I want to go down to the lower deck."

He glanced back at the lounge. There they all were, lit up like a distant peep show.

"Why the lower deck?"

"I don't know. A whim." She giggled. "Nobody will find me for one thing."

The companion ladder was close to where they stood. She led him towards it, turned and gave him her hands.

"I'll go backwards. You follow."

He was obliged to do so. When they reached the promenade deck she took his arm again.

"Let's see if there are ghost fires tonight."

She looked over the side still holding him.

Alleyn said, "You're much too dangerous a person for me, you know."

"Do you really think so?"

"I do indeed. Right out of my class. I'm a dull dog."

"I don't find you so."

"How enchanting of you," Alleyn said. "I must tell my wife. That'll larn her."

"Is she very attractive?"

Suddenly, in place of the plushy, the abundant, the superbly tended charms now set before him, Alleyn saw his wife's head with its clearly defined planes, its delicate bone and short, not very tidy hair.

He said, "I must leave you, I'm afraid. I've got work to do."

"Work? What sort of work, for heaven's sake?"

"Business letters. Reports."

"I don't believe you. In mid-ocean!"

"It's true."

"Look! There *are* ghost fires."

"And I don't think you'd better stay down here by yourself. Come along. I'll see you to your cabin."

He put his hand over hers. "Come along," he repeated. She stared at him, her lips parted.

"All right!" she agreed suddenly. "Let's."

They returned by the inside stairway and he took her to her door.

"You're *rather* nice," she whispered.

"Lock your door, won't you?"

"Oh, good *heavens!*" said Mrs. Dillington-Blick and bounced into her cabin. He heard her shoot her bolt and he returned quickly to the lounge.

Only Father Jourdain, Tim and Captain Bannerman were there. Miss Abbott came in by the double doors as Alleyn arrived. Tim furtively signalled "thumbs up," and Father Jourdain said "Everybody seems to be going to bed early tonight."

"It's not all that early," Captain Bannerman rejoined, staring resentfully at Miss Abbott.

She stopped dead in the middle of the room and with her eyes down-cast seemed to take in the measure of her own unwantedness.

"Good-night," she said grudgingly and went out.

Father Jourdain followed her to the landing. "By the way," Alleyn heard him say, "I got that word in the Ximenes. It's 'holocaust.' "

"How brilliant!" she said. "That should be a great help."

"I think so. Good-night."

"Good-night."

Father Jourdain came back: " 'Safely stowed,' " he quoted and smiled at Alleyn.

Alleyn asked sharply, "Where's everybody else?"

"It's O.K.," Tim rejoined. "The women are all in their cabins; at least I suppose you've accounted for the D-B, haven't you?"

"And the men?"

"Does it matter? Cuddy went off with his wife and McAngus, very properly, by himself. Merryman toddled off some time after that."

"And Dale?"

"He left after the Cuddys," Tim said.

"I think," Father Jourdain observed, "that someone must have gone out on deck?"

"Why?"

"Only because I thought I heard someone singing." His voice faded and his face blanched. "But there's nothing in that!" Father Jourdain ejaculated. "We can't panic every time somebody sings."

"I can!" Alleyn said grimly.

"With the women all in their cabins? Why?"

Captain Bannerman interjected, loudly scoffing, "You may well ask why! Because Mr. Ah-leen's got a bee in his bonnet. That's why!"

"What had McAngus got to say to you?" Alleyn asked him.

The captain glowered at him. "He reckons someone's been interfering with his hyacinths."

"Interfering?"

"Pinching them."

"Damnation!" Alleyn said and turned to go out.

Before he could do so, however, he was arrested by the sound of thud-ding feet.

It came from the deck outside and was accompanied by torturous breathing. For a moment the brilliant square cast by the light in the lounge was empty. Then into it ran an outlandish figure, half-naked, wet, ugly, gasping.

It was Cuddy. When he saw Alleyn he fetched up short, grinning abominably. Water ran from his hair into his open mouth.

"Well?" Alleyn demanded. "What is it?"

Cuddy gestured meaninglessly. His arm quivered like a branch.

"What is it? Speak up! Quickly."

Cuddy lunged forward. His wet hands closed like clamps on Alleyn's arms.

"Mrs. Dillington-Blick," he stuttered and the syllables dribbled out with the water from his mouth. He nodded two or three times, came close to Alleyn and then threw back his head and broke into sobbing laughter.

"The verandah?"

"What the bloody hell are you talking about?" the captain shouted.

Cuddy nodded and nodded.

Alleyn said, "Captain Bannerman, will you come with me, if you please? And Dr. Makepiece." He struck up Cuddy's wet arms and thrust him aside. He started off down the deck with them both at his heels.

They had gone only a few paces when a fresh rumpus broke out behind them. Cuddy's hysterical laughter had mounted to a scream.

Father Jourdain shouted, "Dr. Makepiece! Come back!"

There was a soft thud and silence.

Captain Bannerman said, "Wait a bit. He's fainted."

"Let him faint."

"But—"

"All right. *All right.*"

He strode on down the deck. There was a light in the deckhead over the verandah. Alleyn switched it on.

The Spanish dress was spread out wide, falling in black cascades on both sides of the chaise longue. Its wearer lay back, luxuriously, each gloved hand trailing on the deck. The head was impossibly twisted over the left shoulder. The face was covered down to the tip of the nose by part of the mantilla which had been dragged down like a blind. The exposed area was livid and patched almost to the colour of the mole at the corner of the mouth. The tongue protruded, the plump throat already was discoloured. Artificial pearls from a broken necklace lay scattered across the décolletage, into which had been thrust a white hyacinth.

"All right," Alleyn said without turning. "It's too late, of course, but you'd better see if there's anything you can do."

Tim had come up with Captain Bannerman behind him. Alleyn stood aside. "Only Dr. Makepiece, please," he said. "I want as little traffic as possible."

Tim stooped over the body.

In a moment he had straightened up.

"But, look here!" he said. "It's not—it's—it's—"

"Exactly. But our immediate concern is with the chances of recovery. Are there any?"

"None."

"Sure?"

"None."

"Very well. Now, this is what we do—"

4

Captain Bannerman and Tim Makepiece stood side by side exactly where Alleyn had placed them. The light in the deckhead shone down on the area round the chaise longue. It was dappled with irregular wet patches, most of which had been made by large naked feet. Alleyn found that they were overlaid by his own prints and Tim's and by others which he examined closely.

"Espadrilles," he said, "size nine."

The wearer had approached the chaise longue, stood beside it, turned and made off round the starboard side.

"Running," Alleyn said, following the damp prints. "Running along the deck, then stopping as he got into the light, then turning and stopping by the hatch and then carrying on round the centrecastle to the port side. Not much doubt about that one."

He turned back towards the verandah, pausing by a tall locker near its starboard corner. He shone his torch behind this. "Cigarette ash and a butt."

He collected the butt and found it was monogrammed and Turkish.

"How corny can you get?" he muttered, showing it to Tim, and returned to the verandah, from where he pursued the trace of the wet naked feet. Their owner had come to the port side companion-ladder from the lower deck and the swimming pool. On the fifth step from the top there was a large wet patch.

He returned to Captain Bannerman.

"In this atmosphere," he said, "I can't afford to wait. I'm going to take photographs. After that we'll have to seal off the verandah. I suggest, sir, that you give orders to that effect."

Captain Bannerman stood lowering at him. "This sort of thing," he said at last, "couldn't have been anticipated. It's against common sense."

"On the contrary," Alleyn rejoined, "it's precisely what was to be expected."

CHAPTER TEN   **Aftermath**

The passengers sat at one end of the lounge behind shut doors and drawn blinds. Out of force of habit each had gone to his or her accustomed place and the scene thus was given a distorted semblance of normality. Only Mr. Merryman was absent. And, of course, Mrs. Dillington-Blick.

Alleyn himself had visited the unattached men in their cabins. Mr. Merryman had been peacefully and very soundly asleep, his face blank and rosy, his lips parted and his hair ruffled in a cockscomb. Alleyn decided for the moment to leave him undisturbed. Shutting the door quietly, he crossed the passage. Mr. McAngus in vivid pyjamas had been doing something with a small brush to his hair, which was parted in the middle and hung in dark elf locks over his ears. He had hastily slammed down the lid of an open box on his dressing-table and turned his back on it. Aubyn Dale, fully dressed, was in his sitting-room. He had a drink in his hand and apparently he had been standing close to his door, which was not quite shut. His manner was extraordinary—at once defiant, terrified, and expectant. It was obvious also that he was extremely drunk. Alleyn looked at him for a moment and then said, "What have you been up to?"

"I? Have a drink, dear boy? No? What d'you mean, up to?" He swallowed the remains of his drink and poured out another.

"Where have you been since you left the lounge?"

"What the devil's that got to do with you?" He lurched towards Alleyn and peered into his face. "Who the bloody hell," he asked indistinctly, "do you think you are?"

Alleyn took him in the regulation grip. "Come along," he said, "and find out."

He marched Dale into the lounge and deposited him in the nearest chair.

Tim Makepiece had fetched Brigid and Mrs. Cuddy. Mr. Cuddy, recovered from his faint, had been allowed to change into pyjamas and dressing-gown, and looked ghastly.

Captain Bannerman, lowering and on the defensive, stood beside Alleyn.

He said, "Something's happened tonight that I never thought to see in my ship and a course of action has to be set to deal with it."

He jerked his head at Alleyn. "This gentleman will give the details. He's a Scotland Yard man and his name's A'leen not Broderick and he's got my authority to proceed."

Nobody questioned or exclaimed at this announcement. It was merely accorded a general look of worried bewilderment. The captain nodded morosely at Alleyn and then sat down and folded his arms.

Alleyn said, "Thank you, sir." He was filled with anger against Captain Bannerman, an anger not unmixed with compassion and no more tolerable for that. At least half the passengers were scarcely less irritating. They were irresponsible, they were helpless, two of them were profoundly silly, and one of them was a murderer. He took himself sharply to task and began to talk to them.

He said, "I shan't, at the moment, elaborate or explain the statement you've just heard. You will, if you please, accept it. I'm a police officer. A murder has been committed and one of the passengers in this ship, almost certainly, is responsible."

Mr. Cuddy's smile, an incredible phenomenon, was stamped across his face like a postmark. His lips moved. He said with a kind of terrified and incredulous jocosity, "Oh, go on!" His fellow passengers looked appalled, but Mrs. Cuddy dreadfully and incredibly tossed her head and said, "Mrs. Blick, isn't it? I suppose it's a remark I shouldn't pass, but I must say that with that type of behaviour—"

"No!" Father Jourdain interposed very strongly. "You must stop. Be quiet, Mrs. Cuddy!"

"Well, I must say!" she gasped and turned to her husband. "It *is* Mrs. Blick, Fred, isn't it?"

"Yes, dear."

Alleyn said, "It will become quite apparent before we've gone very much further who it is. The victim was found a few minutes ago by Mr. Cuddy. I am going to take statements from most of you. I'm sorry I can't confine the whole business to the men only and I hope to do so before long. Possibly it's less distressing for the ladies, who are obviously not under suspicion, to hear the preliminary examination than it would be for them to be kept completely in the dark."

He glanced at Brigid, white and quiet, sitting by Tim and looking very young in a cotton dressing-gown and with her hair tied back. Tim, when he fetched her from her cabin, had said, "Biddy, something rather bad has happened to somebody in the ship. It's going to shock you, my dear."

She had answered, "You're using the doctor's voice that means somebody has died." And after looking into his face for a moment: "Tim—? *Tim*, can it be the thing I've been afraid of? Is it that?"

He told her that it was and that he was not able just then to say anything more. "I've promised not," he had said. "But don't be frightened. It's not as bad as you'll think at first. You'll know all about it in a few minutes and—I'm here, Biddy."

So he had taken her to join the others and she sat beside him, watching and listening to Alleyn.

He turned to her now. "Perhaps," he said, "Miss Carmichael will tell me at once when she went to her cabin."

"Yes, of course," she said. "It was just after you left. I went straight to bed."

"I saw her to her door," Tim said, "and heard her lock it. It was still locked when I returned just now."

"Did you hear or see anything that seemed out of the way?" Alleyn asked her.

"I heard—I heard voices in here and—somebody laughed and then screamed, and there were other voices shouting. Nothing else."

"Would you like to go back to your cabin now? You may if you'd rather."

She looked at Tim. "I think I'd rather be here."

"Then stay. Miss Abbott, I remember that you came in here from outside, on your way to your cabin. Where had you been?"

"I walked once round the deck," she said, "and then I leaned over the rails on the, I think, starboard side. Then I came in for a few minutes."

"Did you meet or see or hear anyone?"

"Nobody."

"Was there anything at all, however slight, that you noticed?"

"I think not. Except—"

"Yes."

"When I'd passed the verandah and turned, I thought I smelt cigarette smoke. Turkish. But there was nobody about."

"Thank you. When you left here I think Father Jourdain walked to your door with you?"

"Yes. He saw me go in, I suppose. Didn't you, Father?"

"I did," said Father Jourdain. "And I heard you lock it. It's the same story, I imagine."

"Yes, and I'd rather stay here, too," said Miss Abbott.

"Are you sure?" Father Jourdain asked. "It's not going to be very pleasant, you know. I can't help feeling, Alleyn, that the ladies—"

"It would be much less pleasant for the ladies," Miss Abbott said grimly, "to swelter in their cabins in a state of terrified ignorance." Alleyn gave her an appreciative look.

"Very well," he said. "Now, Mrs. Cuddy, if you please. Your cabin faces forward and to the starboard side and is next to Mr. McAngus's. You and your husband went to it together. Is that right?" Mrs. Cuddy, who, unlike her husband, never smiled, turned her customary fixed stare upon Alleyn. "I don't see that it matters," she said, "but I retired with Mr. Cuddy, didn't I, dear?"

"That's right, dear."

"And went to bed?"

"I did," she said in an affronted voice.

"But your husband evidently did not go to bed?"

Mrs. Cuddy said after a pause and with some constraint, "He fancied a dip."

"That's right. I fancied it. The prickly heat was troubling me."

"I told you," Mrs. Cuddy said without looking at him, "it's unwholesome in the night air and now see what's happened. Fainting. I wouldn't be surprised if you hadn't caught an internal chill and with the trouble you've been having—"

Alleyn said, "So you changed into bathing trunks?"

"I don't usually go in fully dressed," Mr. Cuddy rejoined. His wife laughed shortly and they both looked triumphant.

"Which way did you go to the pool?"

"Downstairs, from here, and along the lower deck."

"On the starboard side?"

"I don't know what they call it," Mr. Cuddy said contemptuously. "Same side as our cabin."

"Did you see anything of Miss Abbott?"

"I did not," Mr. Cuddy said and managed to suggest that there might be something fishy about it.

Miss Abbott raised her hand.

"Yes, Miss Abbott?"

"I'm sorry, but I do remember now that I noticed someone was in the pool. That was when I walked round the deck. It's a good way off and down below; I didn't see who it was. I'd forgotten."

"Never mind. Mr. Cuddy, did you go straight into the pool?"

"It's what I was there for, isn't it?"

"You must have come out almost at once."

There was a long pause. Mr. Cuddy said, "That's right. Just a cooler and out."

"Please tell me exactly what happened next."

He ran the tip of his tongue round his lips. "I want to know where I stand. I've had a shock. I don't want to go letting myself in for unpleasantness."

"Mr. Cuddy's very sensitive."

"There's been things said here that I don't fancy. I know what the police are like. I'm not going to talk regardless. Pretending you was a cousin of the company's!"

Alleyn said, "Did you commit this crime?"

"There you are! Asking me a thing like that."

Mrs. Cuddy said, "The idea!"

"Because if you didn't you'll do well to speak frankly and truthfully."

"I've got nothing to conceal."

"Very well, then," Alleyn said patiently, "don't behave as if you had. You found the body. After a fashion you reported your discovery. Now, I want the details. I suppose you've heard of the usual warning. If I was thinking of charging you I'd be obliged to give it."

"Don't be a fool, man," Captain Bannerman suddenly roared out. "Behave yourself and speak up."

"I'm ill. I've had a shock."

"My dear Cuddy," Father Jourdain said, "I'm sure we all realize that you've had a shock. Why not get your story over and free yourself of responsibility?"

"That's right, dear. Tell them and get it over. It's all they deserve," said Mrs. Cuddy mysteriously.

"Come along," Alleyn said. "You left the pool and you started back. Presumably you didn't return by the lower deck but by one of the two companion-ladders up to this deck. Which one?"

"Left hand."

"Port side," the captain muttered irritably.

"That would bring you to within a few feet of the verandah and a little to one side of it. Now, Mr. Cuddy, do go on like a sensible man and tell me what followed."

But Mr. Cuddy was reluctant and evasive. He reiterated that he had had a shock, wasn't sure if he could exactly recall the sequence of events and knew better than to let himself in for a grilling.

His was the sort of behaviour that is a commonplace in the experience of any investigating officer, but in this instance, Alleyn was persuaded, it arose from a specific cause. He thought that Mr. Cuddy hedged, not because he mistrusted the police on general grounds but because there was something he urgently wished to conceal. It became increasingly obvious that Mrs. Cuddy, too, was prickly with misgivings.

"All right," Alleyn said. "You are on the ladder. You climb up it and your head is above the level of the upper deck. To your right, quite close and facing you, is the verandah. Can you see into the verandah?"

Mr. Cuddy shook his head.

"Not at all?"

He shook his head.

"It was in darkness? Right. You stay there for some time. Long enough to leave quite a large wet patch on the steps. It was still there some minutes later when I looked at them. I think you actually may have sat down on a higher step, which would bring your head below the level of the upper deck. Did you do this?"

A strange and unlovely look had crept into Mr. Cuddy's face, a look at once furtive and—the word flashed up in Alleyn's thoughts—salacious.

"I do hope," Alleyn went on, "that you will tell me if this is in fact what happened. Surely there can be no reason why you shouldn't."

"Go on, Fred," Mrs. Cuddy urged. "They'll only get thinking things."

"Exactly," Alleyn agreed and she looked furious.

"All right, then," Mr. Cuddy said angrily. "I did. Now!"

"Why? Was it because of something you saw? No? Or heard?"

"Heard's more like it," he said and actually, after a fashion, began to smile again.

"Voices?"

"Sort of."

"What the hell," Captain Bannerman broke out, "do you mean, sort of! You heard someone talking or you didn't."

"Not to say talking."

"Well, what *were* they doing. Singing?" Captain Bannerman demanded and then looked horrified.

"That," said Mr. Cuddy, "came later."

There was a deadly little silence.

Alleyn said, "The first time was it one voice? Or two?"

"Sounded to me like one. Sounded to me—" he looked sidelong at his wife—"like hers. You know. Mrs. Blick." He squeezed his hands together and added, "I thought at the time it was, well—just a bit of fun."

Mrs. Cuddy said, "Disgusting. Absolutely disgusting."

"Steady, Ethel."

Father Jourdain made a small sound of distress. Brigid thought, "This is the worst thing yet," and couldn't look at the Cuddys. But Miss Abbott watched them with hatred and Mr. McAngus, who had not uttered a word since he was summoned, murmured, "Must we! Oh, must we!"

"I *so* agree," Aubyn Dale began with an alcoholic travesty of his noblest manner. "Indeed, *indeed*, must we?"

Alleyn lifted a hand and said, "The answer, I'm afraid, is that indeed,

indeed, we must. Without interruption, if possible." He waited for a moment and then turned again to Cuddy. "So you sat on the steps and listened. For how long?"

"I don't know how long. Until I heard the other thing."

"The singing?"

He nodded. "It sort of faded out. In the distance. So I knew he'd gone."

"Did you form any idea," Alleyn asked him, "who it was?"

They had all sat quietly enough until now. But at this moment, as if all their small unnoticeable movements had been disciplined under some imperative stricture, an excessive stillness fell upon them.

Mr. Cuddy said loudly, "Yes. I did."

"Well?"

"Well, it was what he was singing. You know. The chune," said Mr. Cuddy.

"What was it?"

He turned his head and looked at Aubyn Dale. Like automata the others repeated this movement. Dale got slowly to his feet.

"You couldn't fail to pick it. It's an old favourite. 'Pack Up Your Troubles.' After all," Cuddy said, grinning mirthlessly at Aubyn Dale, "it *is* your theme song, Mr. Dale, isn't it?"

2

There was no outcry from any of the onlookers, not even from Aubyn Dale himself. He merely stared at Cuddy as if at some unidentifiable monster. He then turned slowly, looked at Alleyn and wetted his lips.

"You can't pay any attention to this," he said with difficulty, running his words together. "It's pure fantasy. I went to my cabin, didn't go out on deck." He passed his hand across his eyes. "I don't know that I can prove it. I—can't think of anything. But it's true, all the same. Must be some way of proving it. Because it's true."

Alleyn said, "Shall we tackle that one a bit later? Mr. Cuddy hasn't finished his statement. I should like to know, Mr. Cuddy, what you did next. At once, without evasions, if you please. What did you do?"

Cuddy gave his wife one of his sidelong glances, and then slid his gaze over to Alleyn. "I haven't got anything to conceal," he said. "I went up and I thought—I mean it seemed kind of quiet. I mean—you don't want to get fanciful, Eth—I got the idea I'd see if she was O.K. So I—so I went into that place and she didn't move. So I put out my hand in the dark. And she didn't move and I touched *her* hand. She had gloves on. When I touched it, it sort of slid sideways like it wasn't anything belonging to anybody and I heard it thump on the deck. And I thought, she's fainted. So, in the dark, I felt around and I touched her face and—and—then I knew and—Gawd, Eth, it was ghastly!"

"Never mind, Fred."

"I don't know what I did. I got out of it. I suppose I ran round the side. I wasn't myself. Next thing I knew I was in the doorway there and—well, I come over faint and I passed out. That's all. I never did anything else, I swear I didn't. Gawd's my judge, I didn't."

Alleyn looked thoughtfully at him for a moment and said: "That, then, is an account of the discovery by the man who made it. So far, of course, there's no way of checking, but in the meantime we shall use it as a working hypothesis. Now. Mr. McAngus."

Mr. McAngus sat in a corner. The skirts of his dressing-gown, an unsuitably heavy one, were pulled tight over his legs and clenched between his knees. His arms were crossed over his chest and his hands buried in his armpits. He seemed to be trying to protect himself from anything anybody might feel inclined to say to him. He gazed dolorously at Alleyn as the likeliest source of assault.

"Mr. McAngus," Alleyn began, "when did you leave this room?"

"I don't remember."

"You were still here when I left. That was after Mrs. Dillington-Blick had gone. Did you leave before or after Mr. And Mrs. Cuddy?" He added, "I would rather Mr. McAngus was not prompted." Several of Mr. McAngus's fellow passengers who had opened their mouths shut them again.

Mr. McAngus did not embark on his usual round of periphrases. He blinked twice at Alleyn and said, "I am too upset to remember. If I tried I should only muddle myself and you. A dreadful tragedy has happened; I cannot begin to think of anything else."

Alleyn, his hands in his coat pockets, said dryly, "Perhaps, after all, a little help is called for. May we go back to a complaint you made to Captain Bannerman before you went to bed. You said, I think, that somebody had been taking the hyacinths that Mrs. Dillington-Blick gave you."

"Oh, *yes*. Two. I noticed the second had gone this morning. I was *very* much distressed. And now, of course, even more so."

"The hyacinths are growing, aren't they, in a basket which I think is underneath your porthole?"

"I keep them there for the fresh air."

"Have you any idea who was responsible?"

Mr. McAngus drew down his upper lip. "I am very much averse," he said, "to making unwarranted accusations, but I confess I *have* wondered about the steward. He is always admiring them. Or, then again, he might have knocked one off by accident. But he denies it, you see. He denies it."

"What colour was it?"

"White, a handsome spike. I believe the name is Virgin Queen."

Alleyn withdrew his hand from his pocket, extended and opened it. His handkerchief was folded about an irregular object. He laid it on the table and opened it. A white hyacinth, scarcely wilted, was disclosed.

Mr. McAngus gave a stifled cry, Brigid felt Tim's hand close on hers. She saw again in an instantaneous muddle the mangled doll, the paragraphs in the newspapers, and the basket of hyacinths that Dennis had brought in on their first morning at sea. She heard Miss Abbott say, "I *beg* you not to speak, Mrs. Cuddy," and Mrs. Cuddy's inevitable cry of "Hyacinths! Fred!" And then she saw Mr. McAngus rise, holding his lower lip between his thumb and forefinger.

"Is that it?" Alleyn asked.

Mr. McAngus moved slowly to the table and stopped.

"Don't touch it, if you please."

"It—it looks like it."

Mrs. Cuddy said shrilly, "Wherever did you find it?"

Mr. Cuddy said, "Never mind, Eth," but Mrs. Cuddy's deductive capacity was under a hard drive. She stared, entranced, at the hyacinth. Everyone knew what she was about to say, no one was able to forestall it.

"My Gawd!" said Mrs. Cuddy. "You never found it on the corpse! My Gawd, Fred, it's the Flower Murderer's done it. He's on the ship, Fred, and we can't get orf!"

Miss Abbott raised her large hands and brought them down heavily on her knees. "We've been asked to keep quiet," she cried out. "Can't you, for pity's sake, hold your tongue!"

"Gently, my child," Father Jourdain murmured.

"I'm not feeling gentle."

Alleyn said, "It will be obvious to all of you before long that this crime has been committed by the so-called Flower Murderer. At the moment, however, that's a matter which need not concern us. Now, Mr. McAngus. You left this room immediately after Mr. and Mrs. Cuddy. Did you go straight to your cabin?"

After a great deal of painstaking elucidation it was at last collected from Mr. McAngus that he had strayed out through the double doors of the lounge to the deck, had walked round the passengers' block to the port side, had gazed into the heavens for a few addled minutes, and had re-entered by the door into the interior passageway and thus arrived at his own quarters. "My thoughts," he said, "were occupied by the film. I found it *very* moving. Not, perhaps, what one would have expected but nevertheless *exceedingly* disturbing."

As he had not been seen by anybody else after he had left the lounge, his statement could only be set down for what it was worth and left to simmer.

Alleyn turned to Aubyn Dale.

Dale was slumped in his chair. He presented a sort of travesty of the splendid figure they had grown accustomed to. His white dinner-jacket was unbuttoned. His tie was crooked, his rope-soled shoes were unlatched, his hair was disordered and his eyes were imperfectly focussed. His face was deadly pale.

Alleyn said, "Now, Mr. Dale, are you capable of giving me an account of yourself?"

Dale crossed his legs and with some difficulty joined the tips of his fingers. It was a sketch of his customary position before the cameras.

"Captain Bannerman," he said, "I think you realize I'm ver' close friend of the general manager of y'r company. He's going to hear juss how I've been treated in this ship and he's *not* going to be pleased about it."

Captain Bannerman said, "You won't get anywhere that road, Mr. Dale. Not with me nor with anyone else."

Dale threw up his hands in an unco-ordinated gesture. "*All* right. On y'own head!"

Alleyn crossed the room and stood over him. "You're drunk," he said, "and I'd very much rather you were sober. I'm going to ask you a question that may have a direct bearing on a charge of murder. This is not a threat, it is a statement of fact. In your own interest you'd better pull yourself together if you can and answer me. Can you do that?"

Dale said, "I know I'm plastered. It's not fair. Doc, I'm plastered, aren't I?"

Alleyn looked at Tim. "Can you do anything?"

"I can give him something, yes. It'll take a little time."

"I don't want anything," Dale said. He pressed the palms of his hands against his eyes, held them there for some seconds and then shook his head sharply. "I'll be O.K.," he muttered and actually did seem to have taken some sort of hold over himself. "Go on," he added with an air of heroic fortitude. "I can take it."

"Very well. After you left this room tonight you went out on deck. You went to the verandah. You stood beside the chaise longue where the body was found. What were you doing there?"

Dale's face softened as if it had been struck. He said, "You don't know what you're talking about."

"Do you deny that you were there?"

"Refuse to answer."

Alleyn glanced at Tim, who went out.

"If you're capable of thinking," Alleyn said, "you must know where that attitude will take you. I'll give you a minute."

"Tell you, I refuse."

Dale looked from one of his fellow passengers to the other—the Cuddys, Brigid, Miss Abbott, Father Jourdain, Mr. McAngus—and he found no comfort anywhere.

"You'll be saying presently," he said with a sort of laugh, "that I had something to do with it."

"I'm saying now that I've found indisputable evidence that you stood beside the body. In your own interest don't you think you'd be well advised to tell me why you didn't at once report what you saw?"

"Suppose I deny it?"

"In your boots," Alleyn said dryly, "I wouldn't." He pointed to Dale's rope-soled shoes. "They're still damp," he said.

Dale drew his feet back as if he'd scorched them.

"Well, Mr. Dale?"

"I—I didn't know—I didn't know there was anything the matter. I didn't know he—I mean she—was dead."

"Really? Did you not say anything? Did you just stand there meekly and then run away?"

He didn't answer.

"I suggest that you had come into the verandah from the starboard side—the side opposite to that used by Mr. Cuddy. I also suggest that you had been hiding by the end of the locker near the verandah corner."

Unexpectedly Dale behaved in a manner that was incongruously, almost embarrassingly theatrical. He crossed his wrists, palms outward, before his face and then made a violent gesture of dismissal. "No!" he protested. "You don't understand. You frighten me. No!"

The door opened and Tim Makepiece returned. He stood, keeping it open and looking at Alleyn.

Alleyn nodded and Tim, turning his head to the passage, also nodded.

A familiar scent drifted into the stifled room. There was a tap of high heels in the passage. Through the door, dressed in a wonderful negligée, came Mrs. Dillington-Blick.

Mrs. Cuddy made a noise that was not loud but strangulated. Her husband and McAngus got to their feet, the latter looking as if he had seen a phantom and the former as if he was going to faint again. But if, in fact, they were about to say or do anything more they were forestalled. Brigid gave a shout of astonishment and relief and gratitude. She ran across the room and took Mrs. Dillington-Blick's hands in hers and kissed her. She was half crying, half laughing. "It wasn't you!" she stammered. "You're all right. I'm so glad. I'm so terribly glad."

Mrs. Dillington-Blick gazed at her in amazement.

"You don't even know what's happened, do you?" Brigid went on. "Something quite dreadful but—"

She stopped short. Tim had come to her and put his arm round her. "Wait a moment, my darling," he said and she turned to him. "Wait a moment," he repeated and drew her away.

Mrs. Dillington-Blick looked in bewilderment at Aubyn Dale.

"What's all the fuss?" she asked. "Have they found out?"

He floundered across the room and seized Mrs. Dillington-Blick by the arms, shaking and threatening her.

"Ruby, don't speak!" he said. "Don't say anything. Don't tell them. Don't you dare!"

"Has everybody gone mad?" asked Mrs. Dillington-Blick. She wrenched herself out of Dale's grip. "Don't!" she said and pushed away the hand that he actually tried to lay across her mouth. "What's happened? *Have* they found out?" And after a moment, with a change of voice: "Where's Dennis?"

"Dennis," Alleyn said, "has been murdered."

3

It was, apparently, Mr. Cuddy who was most disturbed by the news of Dennis's death but his was an inarticulate agitation. He merely stopped smiling, opened his mouth, developed a slight tremor of the hands and continued to gape incredulously at Mrs. Dillington-Blick. His wife, always predictable, put her hand over his and was heard to say that someone was trying to be funny. Mr. McAngus kept repeating, "Thank God. I thank God!" in an unnatural voice. Miss Abbott said loudly, "Why have we been misled! An abominable trick!" while Aubyn Dale crumpled back into his chair and buried his face in his hands.

Mrs. Dillington-Blick herself, Alleyn thought, was bewildered and frightened. She looked once at Aubyn Dale and away again, quickly. She turned helplessly towards Captain Bannerman, who went to her and patted her shoulder.

"Never you fret," he said and glared uneasily at Alleyn. "You ought to have had it broken to you decently, not sprung on you without a word of warning. Never mind. No need to upset yourself."

She turned from him to Alleyn and held out her hands. "You make me nervous," she said. "It's not true, is it? Why are you behaving like this? You're angry, aren't you? Why have you brought me here?"

"If you'll sit down," he said, "I'll tell you." She tried to take his hands. "No, just sit down, please, and listen."

Father Jourdain went to her. "Come along," he said and led her to a chair.

"He's a plain-clothes detective, Mrs. Blick," Mrs. Cuddy announced with a kind of angry triumph. "We've all been spied upon and made mock of and put in danger of our lives and now there's a murderer loose in the ship and he says it's one of us. In my opinion—"

"Mrs. Cuddy," Alleyn said, "I must ask you for the moment to be quiet."

Mr. Cuddy, automatically and for the last time on the voyage, said, "Steady, Ethel."

"Indeed," Alleyn went on, "I must ask you all to be quiet and to listen carefully. You will understand that a state of emergency exists and that I have the authority to deal with it. The steward, Dennis, has been killed in the manner you have all discussed so often. He was clad in the Spanish dress Mrs. Dillington-Blick bought in Las Palmas and the inference is that he was killed in mistake for her. He was lying in the chair in the unlit verandah. The upper part of his face was veiled and it was much too dark to see the mole at the corner of his mouth. In the hearing of all of the men in this room Mrs. Dillington-Blick had said she was going to the verandah. She did go thère. I met her there and went with her to the lower deck and from thence to her cabin door. She was wearing a black lace dress, not unlike the Spanish one. I returned here and almost immediately Mr. Cuddy arrived announcing that he had discovered her and that she was dead. Apparently he had been deceived by the dress. Dr. Makepiece examined the body and says death had occurred no more than a few minutes before he did so. For reasons which I shall give you when we have time for them, there can be no question of his having been murdered by some member of the ship's complement. His death is the fourth in the series that you have so often discussed and one of the passengers is, in my opinion, undoubtedly responsible for all of them. For the moment you'll have to accept that."

He waited. Aubyn Dale raised his head and suddenly demanded, "Where's Merryman?"

There were exclamations from the Cuddys.

"That's right!" Mr. Cuddy said. "Where is he! All this humbugging the rest of us about. Insinuations here and questions there! And Mr. Know-all Merryman mustn't be troubled, I suppose!"

"Personally," Mrs. Cuddy added, "I wouldn't trust him. I've always said there was something. Haven't I, dear?"

"Mr. Merryman," Alleyn said, "is asleep in bed. He's been very unwell and I decided to leave him there until we actually needed him as, of course, we shall. I have not forgotten him."

"He was well enough to go to the pictures," Mrs. Cuddy pointed out. "I think the whole thing looks very funny. Very funny indeed."

Brigid suddenly found herself exclaiming indignantly, "Why do you say it looks 'funny'? Mr. Merryman has already pointed out what a maddeningly incorrect expression it is and he *is* ill and he only came to the pictures because he's naughty and obstinate and I think he's a poppet and certainly not a murderer and I'm sorry to interrupt but I do."

Alleyn said, almost as Father Jourdain might have said, "All right, my child. All right," and Tim put his arm round Brigid.

"It will be obvious to you all," Alleyn went on exactly as if there had been no interruption, "that I must find out why the steward was there and why he was dressed in this manner. It is here that you, Mrs. Dillington-Blick, can help us."

"Ruby!" Dale whispered, but she was not looking at him.

"It was only a joke," she said. "We did it for a joke. How could we possibly know—?"

"We? You mean you and Mr. Dale, don't you?"

"And Dennis. Yes. It's no good, Aubyn. I can't not say."

"Did you give Dennis the dress?"

"Yes."

"After Las Palmas?"

"Yes. He'd been awfully obliging and he said—you know what an odd little creature he was—he admired it awfully and I, I told you, I took against it after the doll business. So I gave it to him. He said he wanted to dress up for a joke at some sort of birthday party the stewards were having."

"On Friday night?"

"Yes. He wanted me not to say anything. That was why, when you asked me about the dress, I didn't tell you. I wondered if you knew. Did you?"

Alleyn was careful not to look at Captain Bannerman. "It doesn't arise at the moment," he said.

The captain made an indeterminate rumbling noise that culminated in utterance.

"Yes, it does!" he roared. "Fair's fair and little though I may fancy the idea, I'm not a man to shirk my responsibilities." He jerked his head at Alleyn. "The superintendent," he said, "came to me and told me somebody had been seen fooling about the forrard well-deck in that damned dress. He said he hadn't seen it himself and whoever did see it reckoned it was Mrs. Dillington-Blick. And why not, I thought? Her dress, and why wouldn't she be wearing it? He asked me to make enquiries and stop a repetition. I didn't see my way to interfering and I wouldn't give my consent to him doing it on his own. All my time as master, I've observed a certain attitude towards my passengers. I didn't see fit to change it. I was wrong. I didn't believe I'd shipped a murderer. Wrong again. Dead wrong. I don't want it overlooked or made light of. I was wrong."

Alleyn said, "That's a very generous statement," and thought it best to carry on. "I had not seen the figure in the Spanish dress," he said. "I had been told it was Mrs. Dillington-Blick and there was no reason that anybody would accept to suppose it wasn't. I merely had a notion, unsupported by evidence, that the behaviour as reported was uncharacteristic."

Brigid said, "It was I who told about it. Mr. Alleyn asked me if I was sure it was Mrs. Dillington-Blick and I said I was."

Mrs. Dillington-Blick said, "Dennis told me what he'd done. He said he'd always wanted to be a dancer." She looked at Alleyn. "When you asked me if I would wear the dress to dance by the light of the moon, I thought you'd seen him and mistaken him for me. I didn't tell you. I pretended it *was* me, because—" her face crumpled and she began to cry —"because we were planning the joke."

"Well," Alleyn said, "there it was. And now I shall tell you what I think happened. I think, Mr. Dale, that with your fondness for practical jokes, you suggested that it would be amusing to get the steward to dress up tonight and go to the verandah and that you arranged with Mrs. Dillington-Blick to let it be understood that she herself was going to be there. Is that right?"

Aubyn Dale had sobered up considerably. Something of his old air of conventional decency had reappeared. He exhibited all the troubled concern of a good chap who is overwhelmed with self-reproach.

"Of course," he said, "I'll never forgive myself for this. It's going to haunt me for the rest of my life. But how could I know? How *could* I know! We—I mean, I—I take the whole responsibility—" he threw a glance, perhaps slightly reproachful, at Mrs. Dillington-Blick—"I just thought it would be rather amusing to do it. The idea was that this poor little devil should—" he hesitated and stole a look at Mr. McAngus and Mr. Cuddy—"well, should go to the verandah, as you say, and if anybody turned up he was just to sort of string them along a bit. I mean, putting it like that in cold blood after what's happened, it may sound rather poor but—"

He stopped and waved his hands.

Miss Abbott broke her self-imposed silence. She said, "It sounds common, cheap, and detestable."

"I resent that, Miss Abbott."

"You can resent it till you're purple in the face but the fact remains. To plot with the steward! To make a vulgar practical joke out of what may have been the wretched little creature's tragedy—his own private, inexorable weakness—his devil!"

"My child!" Father Jourdain said. "You must stop." But she pointed wildly and clumsily at Cuddy. "To trick that man! To use his idiotic, hopeless infatuation! And the other—"

"No, no. Please!" Mr. McAngus cried out. "It doesn't matter. Please!"

Miss Abbott looked at him with what might have been a kind of compassion and turned on Mrs. Dillington-Blick. "And you," she said, "with your beauty and fascination, with everything that unhappy women long for, to lend yourself to such a thing! To give him your lovely dress, to allow him to so much as touch it! What were you thinking of!" She ground her heavy hands together. "Beauty is sacred!" she said. "It is sacred in its own right; you have committed sacrilege."

"Katherine, you must come away. As your priest, I insist. You will do yourself irreparable harm. Come with me."

For the first time she seemed to hear him. The familiar look of mulish withdrawal returned and she got up.

"Alleyn?" Father Jourdain asked.

"Yes, of course."

"Come along," he said, and Miss Abbott let him take her away.

4

"That woman's upset me," Mrs. Dillington-Blick said, angrily sobbing. "I don't feel at all well. I feel awful."

"Ruby, darling!"

"No! No, Aubyn, don't paw me. We shouldn't have done it. You shouldn't have started it. I feel ghastly."

Captain Bannerman squared his shoulders and approached her. "Nor you!" she said, and, perhaps for the first time in her adult life, she appealed to someone of her own sex. "Brigid!" she said. "Tell me I needn't feel like this. It's not fair. I'm hating it."

Brigid went to her. "I can't tell you, you needn't," she said, "but we all know you do and that's much better than not minding at all. At least—" she appealed to Alleyn—"isn't it?"

"Of course it is."

Mr. McAngus, tying himself up in a sort of agonized knot of sympathy, said, "You mustn't think about it. You mustn't reproach yourself. You are goodness itself. Oh, don't!"

Mrs. Cuddy sniffed piercingly.

"It's this awful heat," Mrs. Dillington-Blick moaned. "One can't *think*." She had, in fact, gone very white. "I—I feel faint."

Alleyn opened the double doors. "I was going to suggest," he said, "that we let a little air in." Brigid put her arm round Mrs. Dillington-Blick and Tim went over to her. "Can you manage?" he asked. "Come outside."

They helped her through the doors. Alleyn moved Mr. Merryman's chair so that its back was turned to the lounge and Mrs. Dillington-Blick sank out of sight. "Will you stay here?" Alleyn asked. "When you feel more like it I should be glad of another word with you. I'll ask Dr. Makepiece to come and see how you are. Perhaps, Miss Carmichael, you'd stay with Mrs. Dillington-Blick. Would you?"

"Yes, of course."

"All right?" Tim asked her.

"Perfectly."

Alleyn had a further word with Tim and then the two men went back into the room.

Alleyn said, "I'm afraid I must press on. I shall need all the men, but if you, Mrs. Cuddy, would rather go to your cabin, you may."

"I prefer to stay with Mr. Cuddy, thank you."

Mr. Cuddy moistened his lips and said, "Look, Eth, you toddle off. It's not suitable for ladies."

"I wouldn't fancy being there by myself."

"You'll be O.K., dear."

"What about you, though?"

He didn't look at her. "I'll be O.K.," he said.

She was staring at him, expressionless as always. It was odd to see that her eyes were masked in tears.

"Oh, Fred," Mrs. Cuddy said, "why did you do it?"

CHAPTER ELEVEN   **Arrest**

The four men in the lounge behaved exactly as if Mrs. Cuddy had uttered an indecency. They looked anywhere but at the Cuddys, they said nothing, and then after a moment eyed Alleyn surreptitiously, as if they expected him to take drastic action.

His voice broke across the little void of silence.

"Why did he do what, Mrs. Cuddy?"

"Eth," Mr. Cuddy said, "for God's sake choose your words. They'll be thinking things, Eth. Be careful."

She didn't take her eyes off him, and though she seemed to disregard completely what he had said to her, Alleyn thought that she was scarcely aware of anybody else in the room. Mr. Cuddy returned her gaze with a look of terror.

"You know how I feel about it," she said, "and yet you go on. Making an exhibition of yourself. I blame her, mind, more than I do you; she's a wicked woman, Fred. She's poking fun at you. I've seen her laughing behind your back with the others. I don't care," Mrs. Cuddy went on, raising her voice and indicating the inarticulate back of Mrs. Dillington-Blick's deck-chair, "if she hears what I say. What's happened is her fault; she's as good as responsible for it. And you had to go and chase after her and get yourself mixed up with a corpse. I hope it'll be a lesson to you." A kind of spasm twitched at her mouth and her eyes overflowed. She ended as she had begun. "Oh, Fred," Mrs. Cuddy said again, "why did you do it!"

"I'm sorry, dear. It was just a bit of fun."

"Fun!" Her voice broke. She went up to him and made a curious gesture, a travesty of playfulness, shaking her fist at him. "You old fool!" she said and without a word to anyone else bolted out of the room.

Mr. Cuddy made a slight move as if to follow her but found himself confronted by Alleyn. He stood in the middle of the room, half smiling, scanning the faces of the other men.

"You don't want to misunderstand Mrs. Cuddy," he ventured. "I'm not a violent man. I'm quiet."

Captain Bannerman cleared his throat. "It looks to me," he said, "as if you'll have to prove that." He glanced at the open doors to the deck, at the back of Mrs. Dillington-Blick's chair and at Brigid, who sat on the edge of the hatch with her chin in her hands.

"This is a man's job," he said to Alleyn. "For God's sake, keep the women out of it," and with some emphasis shut the doors.

Alleyn had been speaking to Tim. He said, "Very well. For the moment."

The captain pulled chairs up to the biggest table in the room, motioning Alleyn to sit at one end and himself taking the other. "I like to see things done shipshape," he muttered and his longing for a boardroom could be sensed. Aubyn Dale and Mr. McAngus at once took chairs. Tim, after a moment's hesitation, followed suit. Mr. Cuddy hung off, winding the cord of his dressing-gown round his spatulate fingers. Mr. McAngus, with trembling fingers, lit one of his medicated cigarettes.

Father Jourdain came back and, in response to a gesture from the captain, also sat at the table.

"That's more like it," sighed Captain Bannerman and made a clumsy ducking movement at Alleyn.

"Carry on, if you please, Mr. A'leen," he said.

But Aubyn Dale, who for some time had been casting fretful glances at the bar, cut in. "Look, I need a drink. Is there anything against my ringing for the steward?"

"Which steward?" Captain Bannerman asked, and Dale said, "God, I forgot."

"We'll do our drinking," the captain pronounced, "later. Mr. Cuddy, I'll thank you to take a seat."

Mr. Cuddy said, "That's all right, Captain. Don't rush us. I'd still like to know why we don't send for Merryman," and he pulled out his chair, sat back in it with an affectation of ease, and stared, nervously impertinent, at Alleyn.

Aubyn Dale said, "I must say, seeing this gets more like a board meeting every second, I don't see why Merryman should have leave of absence. Unless—" He paused and the others stirred, suddenly alert and eager. "Unless—"

Alleyn walked to the head of the table and surveyed its occupants. "If this were a normal investigation," he said, "I would see each of you separately while the others were kept under observation. In these circumstances I can't do that; I am taking each of your statements now in the presence of you all. That being done I shall send for Mr. Merryman."

"Why the hell should he be the kingpin?" Dale demanded and then took the plunge. "Unless, by God, he did it!"

"Mr. Merryman," Alleyn rejoined, "sat in the deck-chair now occupied by Mrs. Dillington-Blick. He was still there when the men left this room. He commanded a view of the deck, each side of it. He could see both approaches to the verandah. He is, therefore, the key witness. His temperament is not complaisant. If he were here he'd try to run the whole show. I therefore prefer to let you account for yourselves now and bring him in a little later."

"That's all very well," Mr. Cuddy said. "But suppose he did it. Suppose he's the Flower Murderer. How about that?"

"In that case, being ignorant of what you have all told me, he may offer a statement that one of you can disprove."

"So it'll be our word," Dale said, "against his?"

"With this reservation. That he was in a position to see you all, and none of you, it seems, was able to see him or each other. He can speak about you all, I hope. Each of you can only speak for himself."

Mr. McAngus said, "I don't know why you all want him; he makes *me* feel uncomfortable and silly."

"Ah, for God's sake!" Dale ejaculated. "Can't we get on with it!"

Alleyn, still standing, put his hands on the back of his chair and said, "By all means. This is the position as far as we've gone. I suggest that you consider it."

They were at once silent and uneasily attentive.

"Three of you," Alleyn said, "have given me statements about your movements during the crucial time—the time, a matter of perhaps eight minutes, between the moment when Mrs. Dillington-Blick left this room and the moment when Mr. Cuddy came back with an account of his discovery of the body. During those eight minutes the steward Dennis was strangled, I believe in mistake for Mrs. Dillington-Blick. None of the three statements corroborates either of the other two. We have a picture of three individuals all moving about, out there in the semi-dark, without catching sight of each other. For myself, I was the first to go. I met Mrs. Dillington-Blick by the verandah to which she went—I'm sorry to put it like this but there's no time for polite evasions—as a decoy. No doubt she assured herself that Dennis was there and she was about to take cover when I appeared. To get rid of me she asked me to help her down the port side companion-ladder to the lower deck. I did so and then saw her to her cabin and returned here. Mr. Cuddy, in the meantime, had changed, gone below and then to the pool by way of the starboard side on the lower deck. Miss Abbott, who left after he did, walked round this deck and stood for some minutes on the starboard side. She remembers that she saw somebody in the pool.

"Mr. McAngus says he left by these double doors, stood for a time by the passengers' quarters on the port side and then went to his cabin and to bed. Nobody appeared to have noticed him.

"Mr. Dale, I imagine, will now admit that his first statement, to the effect that he went straight to his cabin, was untrue. On the contrary, he was on deck. He hid behind a locker on the starboard side near the verandah corner hoping to overhear some cruelly ludicrous scene of mistaken identity. He afterwards went into the verandah, presumably discovered the body, returned to his cabin and drank himself into the state from which he has at least partially recovered."

"I resent the tone—" Dale began.

"You'll have to lump the tone, I'm afraid. I now want to know what, if anything, you heard from your hiding place and exactly what you did and saw when you went into the verandah. Do you propose to tell me?"

"Captain Bannerman—"

"No good coming at me," said the captain. "You're in a tight spot, Mr. Dale, and truth had better be your master."

Dale smacked the palm of his hand down on the table. "*All right!* Turn on me. The whole gang of you and much good may it do you. You badger and threaten and get a man tied up in knots until he doesn't know what he's saying. I'm as anxious as anyone for this bloody murderer to be caught. If I could tell you anything that'd bring him to book I would. All right. I did what you say. I sat behind the locker. I heard Miss Abbott go past. Tramp, tramp. She walks like a man. I couldn't see her, but I knew it was Miss Abbott because she was humming a churchy tune. I've heard her before. And then, it was quiet. And then, after a bit, somebody else went by. Going towards the verandah. Tip-toe. Furtive. I heard him turn the corner and I heard somebody—Dennis, I suppose—it was rather high-pitched—make a little sound. And then—" He wiped his hand across his mouth. "Then there were other sounds. The chair legs scraped. Somebody cried out. Only once and it was cut short. Then there was another sort of bumping and scraping. Then nothing. I don't know for how long. Then the tip-toe footsteps passed again. A bit faster but not running and somebody singing, as Cuddy said. 'Pack Up Your Troubles.' In a head-voice. Falsetto. Only a phrase of it and then nothing."

"In tune?" Alleyn asked.

"I beg your pardon?"

"Was the voice in tune?"

Dale said, "Well, really! Oh, yes. Yes. Perfectly in tune," and gave a half laugh.

"Thank you. Go on. What did you do next?"

"I was going to come out but I heard another voice."

He screwed round in his chair and jerked his head at Cuddy. "You," he said. "It was your voice. Unmistakably. You said, 'All alone?'" He aped a mellifluous, arch enquiry. "I heard you go in. Wet feet on the deck. And then, after a pause, you made a sort of retching noise and you ran out, and I suppose you bolted down the deck."

"I've explained everything," Mr. Cuddy said. "I've told them. I've concealed nothing."

"Very well," Alleyn said. "Keep quiet. And then, Mr. Dale?"

"I waited. Then I thought I'd just go round and ask what had happened. I must have had some sort of idea there was something wrong; I realize that now. It was—it was so deadly quiet."

"Yes?"

"So I did. I went in. I said something, I don't remember what, and there was no answer. So I—I got out my cigarette lighter and flashed it on—Oh, God, *God!*"

"Well?"

"I couldn't see much at first. It seemed funny he didn't say anything. I put the flame nearer and then I saw. It was hell. Like that doll. Broken. And the flowers. The deck was wet and slippery. I thought, 'I've done this; it's my fault. I arranged it and she'll say I did. Let somebody else discover it!' Something like that. I'd had one or two drinks over the eight and I suppose that's why I panicked. I ran out and round the deck, past the locker. I heard Cuddy's voice and I saw him by the doors here. I ducked down behind the hatch and heard him tell you. Then I heard you walk past on the other side and I knew that you'd gone to look. I thought, 'It's too late for me to tell them. I'm here. I'll be involved.' So I made for the forward end of the deck."

"Father Jourdain," Alleyn said, "I think you must at that time have been by the entrance to this room looking after Mr. Cuddy, who had fainted. Did you see Mr. Dale?"

"No. But, as you say, I was stooping over Mr. Cuddy. I think my back was turned to the hatch."

"Yes," Dale said. "Yes, it was. I watched you. I don't remember much else except—my God, yes!"

"What have you remembered?"

Dale had been staring at his hands clasped before him on the table. He now raised his head. Mr. McAngus sat opposite him. They seemed to be moved by some common resentment.

"Go on," Alleyn said.

"It was when I'd gone round the passengers' block to the port side. I wanted a drink damn badly, and I wanted to be by myself. I'd got as far as the entrance into the passage and waited for a bit to make sure nobody was about. Ruby—Mrs. Dillington-Blick—was in her cabin. I could hear her slapping her face. I wondered if I'd tell her and then—then I smelt it."

"Smelt what?"

Dale pointed at Mr. McAngus. "That. One of those filthy things he smokes. It was quite close."

Mr. McAngus said, "I have already stated that I waited for a little on deck before I went to my cabin. I have said so."

"Yes. But *where? Where* were you? I couldn't see you and yet you must have been quite close. I actually saw the smoke."

"Well, Mr. McAngus?" Alleyn asked.

"I—don't exactly remember where I stood. Why should I?" He ground out his cigarette. A little malodorous spiral rose from the butt.

Dale said excitedly, "But the deck's open and there was the light from her porthole. Why couldn't I see him!"

"The door giving on the passage opens back on the outside bulkhead," Alleyn said. "Close to Mrs. Dillington-Blick's porthole. Were you standing behind that door, Mr. McAngus?"

"Hiding behind it, more like," Mr. Cuddy eagerly exclaimed.

"Well, Mr. McAngus?"

The long indeterminate face under the dyed hair was unevenly pallid. "I admit nothing," said Mr. McAngus. "Nothing."

"Are you sure?"

"Nothing."

"Do you think he might have been there, Mr. Dale?"

"Yes. Yes, I do. You see, I thought he must be in the passage and I waited and then I thought: 'I've *had* this!' And I looked and there was nobody there. So I went straight in. My door's just on the left. I had a Scotch neat and I daresay it was a snorter. Then I had another. I was all anyhow. My nerves are shot to pieces. I've had a breakdown. I'm supposed," Dale said in a trembling voice, "to be on a rest cure. This has set me all back to hell."

"Mr. McAngus, did you hear Mr. Cuddy when he came and told us of his discovery? He was hysterical and made a great noise. Did you hear him?"

Mr. McAngus said, "I heard something. It didn't matter."

"Didn't matter?"

"I knew where she was."

"Mrs. Dillington-Blick?"

"I cannot answer you, sir."

"You have yourself told us that you left this room by the deck doors, walked round the centrecastle block and then waited for some time on the port side. Do you stick to that statement?"

Mr. McAngus, holding to the edge of the table as if for support, did not take his eyes off Alleyn. He had compressed his mouth so ruthlessly that drops of saliva oozed out of the corners. He inclined his head slightly.

"Very well then—"

"No! No, no!" Mr. McAngus suddenly shouted. "I refuse! What I have done, I have done under compulsion. I cannot discuss it. Never!"

"In that case," Alleyn said, "we have reached an impasse. Dr. Makepiece, will you be so kind as to ask Mr. Merryman if he will join us?"

2

Mr. Merryman could be heard coming down the passage. His sharp voice was raised to its familiar pitch of indignation.

"I should have been informed of this," he was saying, "at once. Immediately. I demand an explanation. *Who* did you say the man is?"

An indistinguishable murmur from Tim.

"Indeed? *Indeed!* Then he has no doubt enjoyed the salutary experience popularly assigned to eavesdroppers. This is an opportunity," the voice continued as its owner drew nearer, "that I have long wished for. If I had been consulted at the outset, the typical, the all-too-familiar pattern of official ineptitude might have—nay, would have been anticipated. But, of course, that was too much to hope for. I—"

The door was opened by Tim, who came in, pulled an eloquent grimace at Alleyn and stood aside.

Mr. Merryman made a not ineffective entrance. He was girded into his dressing-gown. His cockscomb was erect and his eyes glittered with the light of battle. He surveyed the party round the table with a Napoleonic eye.

Captain Bannerman half rose and said, "Come in, Mr. Merryman. Hope you're feeling well enough to join us. Take a chair." He indicated the only vacant chair, which faced the glass doors leading to the deck. Mr. Merryman made a slight acknowledgment but no move. He was glaring at Alleyn. "I daresay," the captain went on, "that it's in order, under the circumstances, for me to make an introduction. This gentleman is in charge of the meeting. Superintendent A'leen."

"The name," Mr. Merryman said at once, "is Alleyn. *All*eyn, my good sir. Al-*lane* is permissible. A'leen, never. It is, presumably, too much to expect that you should have so much as heard of the founder of Dulwich College, an Elizabethan actor who was unsurpassed in his day, Edward Alleyn. Or, less acceptably in my poor opinion, Al-*lane*. Good evening, sir," Mr. Merryman concluded, nodding angrily at Alleyn.

"Over to you," the captain muttered woodenly, "Mr. Allan."

"*No!*" Mr. Merryman objected on a rising inflexion.

"It's of no consequence," Alleyn hastily intervened. "Will you sit down, Mr. Merryman?"

"Why not?" Mr. Merryman said and did so.

"I believe," Alleyn went on, "that Dr. Makepiece has told you what has happened."

"I have been informed in the baldest manner conceivable that a felony has been committed. I assume that I am about to be introduced to the insupportable *longueurs* of a police investigation."

"I'm afraid so," Alleyn said cheerfully.

"Then perhaps you will be good enough to advise me of the nature of the crime and the circumstances under which it was committed and discovered. Unless, of course," Mr. Merryman added, throwing back his head and glaring at Alleyn from under his spectacles, "you regard me as a suspect, in which case you will no doubt attempt some elephantine piece of finesse. *Do* you, in fact, regard me as a suspect?"

"Yes," Alleyn said coolly. "Together with sundry others. I do. Why not?"

"Upon my word!" he said after a pause. "It does not astonish me. And pray what am I supposed to have done? And to whom? And where? Enlighten me, I beg you."

"You are supposed at this juncture to answer questions, and not to ask them. You will be good enough not to be troublesome, Mr. Merryman. "No," Alleyn said as Mr. Merryman opened his mouth, "I really can't do with any more tantrums. This case is in the hands of the police. I am a policeman. Whatever you may think of the procedure, you've no choice but to put up with it. And we'll all get along a great deal faster if you can contrive to do so gracefully. Behave yourself, Mr. Merryman."

Mr. Merryman put on an expression of mild astonishment. He appeared to take thought. He folded his arms, flung himself back in his chair and stared at the ceiling. "Very well," he said. "Let us plumb the depths. Continue."

Alleyn did so. Without giving any indication whatever of the nature or locale of the crime, an omission which at once appeared to throw Mr. Merryman into an extremity of annoyance, he merely asked for an account in detail of anything Mr. Merryman might have seen from his vantage point in the deck-chair, facing the hatch.

"*May* I ask," Mr. Merryman said, still looking superciliously at the ceiling, "*why* you adopt this insufferable attitude? *Why* you elect to withhold the nature of your little problem? Do I detect a note of professional jealousy?"

"Let us assume that you do," said Alleyn with perfect good nature.

"Ah! You are afraid—"

"I am afraid that if you were told what has happened you would try to run the show, and I don't choose to let you. What did you see from your deck-chair, Mr. Merryman?"

A faint, an ineffably complaisant smile played about Mr. Merryman's lips. He closed his eyes.

"What did I see?" he ruminated, and as if they had joined the tips of their fingers and thumbs round the table, his listeners were involved in a current of heightened tension. Alleyn saw Aubyn Dale wet his lips. Cuddy yawned nervously and McAngus again hid his hands in his armpits. Captain Bannerman was glassy-eyed. Father Jourdain's head was inclined as if to hear a confession. Only Tim Makepiece kept his eyes on Alleyn rather than on Mr. Merryman.

"What did I see?" Mr. Merryman repeated. He hummed a meditative air and looked slyly round the table and said loudly, "Nothing. Nothing at all."

"Nothing?"

"For a very good reason. I was sound asleep."

He broke into a triumphant cackle of laughter. Alleyn nodded to Tim, who again went out.

McAngus, rather shockingly, joined in Mr. Merryman's laughter. "The key witness!" he choked out, hugging himself. "The one who was to prove us all right or wrong. Fast asleep! What a farce!"

"It doesn't affect you," Dale pointed out. "He wouldn't have seen you anyway. You've still got to account for yourself."

"That's right. That's dead right," Mr. Cuddy cried out.

"Mr. Merryman," Alleyn said, "when did you wake up and go to your room?"

"I have no idea."

"Which way did you go?"

"The direct way. To the entrance on the starboard side."

"Who was in the lounge at that time?"

"I didn't look."

"Did you meet anyone?"

"No."

"May I just remind you of your position out there?"

Alleyn went to the double doors. He jerked the spring blinds and they flew up with a sharp rattle.

The lights were out on deck. In the glass doors only the reflection of the room and of the occupants appeared—faint, hollow-eyed, and cadaverous as phantoms, their own faces stared back at them.

From a region of darkness there emerged, through these images, another. It moved towards the doors, gaining substance. Mrs. Dillington-Blick was outside. Her hands were pressed against the glass. She looked in.

Mr. Merryman screamed like a ferret in a trap.

His chair overturned. He was round the table before anyone could stop him. His hands scrabbled at the glass pane.

"No. No! Go away. Go away! Don't speak. If you speak I'll do it again. I'll kill you if you speak."

Alleyn held him. It was quite clear to everybody that Mr. Merryman's hands, starving against the glass like fish in an aquarium, were ravenous for Mrs. Dillington-Blick's throat.

CHAPTER TWELVE   **Cape Town**

Cape Farewell steamed into Table Bay at dawn and hove to awaiting the arrival of her pilot cutter and the police launch from Cape Town. Like all ships coming in to port she had begun to withdraw into herself, conserving her personality against the assaults that would be made upon it. She had been prepared. Her derricks were uncovered, her decks broken by orderly litter. Her servants, at their appointed stations, were ready to support her.

Alleyn looked across neatly scalloped waters at the butt-end of a continent and thought how unlikely it was that he would ever take such another voyage. At Captain Bannerman's invitation, he was on the bridge. Down on the dismantled boat-deck eight of the nine passengers were already assembled. They wore their shore-going clothes because *Cape Farewell* was to be at anchor for two days. Their deck-chairs had been stowed away, the hatch was uncovered and there was nowhere for them to sit. Sea-gulls, always a little too true to type, squawked and dived, squabbled and swooped about the bilgewater of which *Cape Farewell* blandly relieved herself.

Two black accents appeared distantly on the surface of the Bay.

"There we are," Captain Bannerman said, handing Alleyn his binoculars.

Alleyn said, "If you don't mind I'm going to ask for the passengers to be sent to their sitting-room."

"Do you expect any trouble?"

"None."

"He won't—" Captain Bannerman began and hesitated. "You don't reckon he'll cut up rough?"

"He is longing," Alleyn said, "to be taken away."

"Bloody monster," the captain muttered uneasily. He took a turn round the bridge, and came back to Alleyn.

"There's something I ought to say to you," he said. "It doesn't come easy and for that reason, I suppose, I haven't managed to get it out. But it's got to be said. I'm responsible for that boy's death. I know it. I should have let you act like you wanted."

"I might just as easily have been wrong."

"Ah! But you weren't, and there's the trouble." The captain fixed his gaze on the approaching black accents. "Whisky," he said, "affects different men in different ways. Some it makes affable, some it makes glum. Me, it makes pigheaded. When I'm on the whisky I can't stomach any man's notions but my own. How do you reckon we'd better handle this job?"

"Could we get it over before the pilot comes on board? My colleague from the Yard has flown here and will be with the Cape police. They'll take charge for the time being."

"I'll have a signal sent."

"Thank you, sir," Alleyn said and went below.

A seaman was on guard outside the little hospital. When he saw Alleyn he unlocked the door and Alleyn went in.

Sitting on the unmade-up bed with its sharp mattress and smartly folded blankets, Mr. Merryman had adopted an attitude quite unlike the one to which his fellow passengers had become accustomed. His spine curved forward and his head depended from it as if his whole structure had wilted. Only the hands, firmly padded and sinewed, clasped between the knees, retained their eloquence. When Alleyn came in, Mr. Merryman looked up at him over the tops of his spectacles but said nothing.

"The police launch," Alleyn said, "is sighted. I've come to tell you that I have packed your cases and will have the things you need sent with you. I shall not be coming in the launch but will see you later today. You will be given every opportunity to take legal advice in Cape Town or to cable instructions to your solicitors. You will return to England as soon as transport is available, probably by air. If you have changed your mind and wish to make a statement—"

Alleyn stopped. The lips had moved. After a moment, the voice, remotely tinged with arrogance, said, ". . . not in the habit of rescinding decisions—tedium of repetition. No."

"Very well."

He turned to go and was arrested by the voice.

"—a few observations. Now. No witnesses and without prejudice. Now."

Alleyn said, "I must warn you, the absence of witnesses doesn't mean that what you may tell me will not be given in evidence. It may be given in evidence. You understand that," he added, as Mr. Merryman raised his head and stared blankly at him, "don't you?" He took out his notebook and opened it. "You see, I shall write down anything that you say."

Mr. Merryman said with a vigour that a moment ago would have seemed impossible, "Esmeralda. Ruby. Beryl. Bijou. Coralie. Marguerite."

He was still feverishly repeating these names when Inspector Fox from the Yard, with members of the Cape Town police force, came to take him off.

2

For a little while Alleyn watched the police launch dip and buck across the bay. Soon the group of figures aboard her lost definition and she herself became no more than a receding dot. The pilot cutter was already alongside. He turned away and for the last time opened the familiar doors into the sitting-room.

They were all there, looking strange in their shore-going clothes.

Alleyn said, "In about ten minutes we shall be alongside. I'm afraid I shall have to ask you all to come to the nearest police-station to make your depositions. Later on you will no doubt be summoned to give evidence, and if that means an earlier return, arrangements will be made for transport. I'm sorry but that's how it is. In the meantime I feel that I owe you an explanation, and perhaps something of an apology." He paused for a moment.

Brigid said, "It seems to me the boot's on the other foot."

"And to me," said Tim.

"I'm not so sure," Mrs. Cuddy remarked. "We've been treated in a very peculiar manner."

Alleyn said, "When I boarded this ship at Portsmouth I did so on the strength of as slight a piece of information as ever sent an investigating officer to sea. It consisted of the fragment of an embarkation notice for this ship and it was clutched in the hand of the girl who was killed on the wharf the night you sailed. It was at least arguable that this paper had been blown ashore or dropped or had come by some irrelevant means into the girl's hand. I didn't think so, your statements didn't suggest it, but it was quite possible. My superior officers ordered me to conceal my identity, to make what enquiries I could, entirely under cover, to take no action that did not meet with the captain's approval, and to prevent any further catastrophe. This last, of course, I have failed to do. If you consider them, these conditions may help to explain the events that followed. If the Flower Murderer was aboard, the obvious procedure was to discover which of you had an acceptable alibi for any of the times when these crimes were committed. I took the occasion of the fifteenth of January, when Beryl Cohen was murdered. With Captain Bannerman's assistance I staged the alibi conversation."

"Good Lord!" Miss Abbott exclaimed. She turned dark red and added, "Go on. Sorry."

"The results were sent by radio to London and my colleagues there were able to confirm the alibis of Father Jourdain and Dr. Makepiece. Mr. Cuddy's and Mr. McAngus's were unconfirmed, but in the course of the conversation it transpired that Mr. McAngus had been operated upon for a perforated appendix on the nineteenth of January, which made him incapable of committing the crime of the twenty-fifth, when Marguerite Slatters was murdered. If, of course, he was speaking the truth. Mr. Cuddy, unless he was foxing, appeared to be unable to sing in tune, and one of the few things we did know about our man was his ability to sing."

Mrs. Cuddy, who was holding her husband's hand, said, "Well, really, Mr. Cuddy would be the last to pretend he was a performer! Wouldn't you, dear?"

"That's right, dear."

"Mr. Dale," Alleyn went on, "had no alibi for the fifteenth, but it turned out that on the twenty-fifth he was in New York. That disposed of him as a suspect."

"Then why the hell," Dale demanded, "couldn't you tell me what was up?"

"I'm afraid it was because I formed the opinion that you were not to be relied upon. You're a heavy drinker and you have been suffering from nervous strain. It would, I felt, be unsafe to trust to your discretion."

"I must say!" Dale began angrily but Alleyn went on.

"It has never been supposed that a woman was responsible for these crimes, but"—he smiled at Miss Abbott—"one of the ladies, at least, had an alibi. She was in Paris on the twenty-fifth, at the same conference, incidentally, as Father Jourdain, who was thus doubly cleared. Until I could hear that the remaining alibis were proved, I couldn't take any of the passengers except Father Jourdain and Dr. Makepiece into my confidence. I should like to say, now, that they have given me every possible help and I'm grateful as can be to both of them."

Father Jourdain, who was very pale and withdrawn, raised his hand and let it fall again. Tim said they both felt they had failed at the crucial time. "We were sceptical," he said, "about Mr. Alleyn's interpretation of Biddy's glimpse of the figure in the Spanish dress. We thought it must have been Mrs. Dillington-Blick. We thought that with all the women accounted for, there was nothing to worry about."

"I saw it," Brigid said, "and I told Mr. Alleyn I was sure it was Mrs. Dillington-Blick. That was my blunder."

"I even heard the singing," Father Jourdain said. "How could I have been so tragically stupid!"

"I gave Dennis the dress and pretended I didn't," Mrs. Dillington-Blick lamented.

Aubyn Dale looked with something like horror at Mr. Cuddy. "And you and I, Cuddy," he pointed out, "listened to a murder and did nothing about it."

Mr. Cuddy, for once, was not smiling. He turned to his wife and said, "Eth, I'm sorry. I'm cured, Eth. It won't occur again."

Everybody tried to look as if they didn't know what he was talking about, especially Mrs. Dillington-Blick.

"O.K., dear," said Mrs. Cuddy, and actually smiled.

Mr. McAngus leaned forward and said very earnestly, "I can, of course, see that I have not behaved at all helpfully. Indeed, now I come to think of it, I almost ask myself if I haven't been suffering from some complaint." He looked wistfully at Mrs. Dillington-Blick. "A touch of the sun perhaps," he murmured and made a little bob at her. "It is," he added after a moment's added reflection, "very fussing to consider how one's actions go on and on having the most distressing results. For instance, when I ventured to buy the doll I never intended—"

A steamer hooted and there, outside, was a funnel sliding past and beyond it a confusion of shipping and the wharves themselves.

"I never intended," Mr. McAngus repeated, but he had lost the attention of his audience and did not complete his sentence.

Miss Abbott said in her harsh way, "It's no good any of us bemoaning our intentions. I daresay we've all behaved stupidly one way or another. I know I have. I started this trip in a stupid temper. I've made stupid scenes. If it's done nothing else it's shown me what a fool I was. Control!" announced Miss Abbott. "And common sense! Complete lack of both leads to murder, it seems."

"And of charity," Father Jourdain added rather wearily.

"That's right. And of charity," Miss Abbott agreed snappishly. "And of proportion and I daresay of a hundred other things we'd be the better for observing."

"How right you are!" Brigid said so sombrely that Tim felt obliged to put his arm round her.

Alleyn moved over to the glass doors and looked out. "We're alongside," he said. "I don't think there's anything more to say. I hope, when you go ashore, you still manage to find some sort of—what? compensation? —for all that has happened."

Mrs. Dillington-Blick approached him. She offered him her hand, and when he took it leaned towards him and murmured, "I've had a blow to my vanity."

"Surely not."

"Were all your pretty ways purely professional?"

Alleyn suppressed a mad desire to reply, "As surely as yours were not," and merely said, "Alas, I have no pretty ways. You're much too kind." He shook her hand crisply and released it to find that Brigid and Tim were waiting for him.

Brigid said, "I just wanted to tell you that I've discovered you haven't got it all your own way."

"What does that mean?"

"You're not the only one to find the real thing on a sea voyage."

"Really?"

"Really. *Dead* sure."

"I'm so glad," Alleyn said and shook hands with them.

After that the Cuddys and Mr. McAngus came and made their odd little valedictions. Mr. Cuddy said that he supposed it took all sorts to make a world and Mrs. Cuddy said she'd always known there was something. Mr. McAngus, scarlet and inextricably confused, made several false starts. He then advanced his long anxious face to within a few inches of Alleyn's and said in a rapid undertone, "You were perfectly right, of course. But I didn't look in. No, No! I just stood with my back to the wall behind the door. It was something to be near her. Misleading, of course. That I *do* see. Good-bye."

Aubyn Dale let Mr. McAngus drift away and then pulled in his waist and with his frankest air came up to Alleyn and extended his hand.

"No hard thoughts, I hope, old boy?"

"Never a one."

"Good man. Jolly good." He shook Alleyn's hand with manly emphasis. "All the same," he said, "dumb though it may be of me, I still can*not* see why, at the end, you couldn't warn us men. Before you fetched him in."

"A., because you were all lying like flatfish. As long as you thought he was the innocent observer who could prove you lied, I had a chance of forcing the truth from you. And B., because one or more of you would undoubtedly have given the show away if you'd known he was guilty. He's extremely observant."

Dale said, "Well, I never pretended to be a diplomatic type," and made it sound noble. Then, unexpectedly, he reddened. "You're right about the drinks," he said. "I'm a fool. I'm going to lay off. If I can. See you later." He went out. Miss Abbott marched up to Alleyn.

She said, "I suppose what I'd like to say couldn't be of less importance. However, you'll just have to put up with it. Did you guess what was wrong with me, the night of the alibi conversation?"

"I fancied I did," he said.

"So I supposed. Well, if it's any consolation, I'm cured. It's a mistake for a lonely woman to form an engrossing friendship. One should have the courage of one's loneliness. This ghastly business has at least taught me that."

"Then," Alleyn said gently, "you may give thanks, mayn't you? In a Gregorian chant?"

"Well, good-bye," she said, and she too went out.

The others having all gone, Father Jourdain and Tim, who had both waited at the far end of the room, came up to Alleyn.

Father Jourdain said, "Alleyn, may I go to him? Will you let me see him?"

Alleyn said that of course he would but added, as gently as he could, that he didn't think Mr. Merryman would respond graciously to the visit.

"No, no. But I must go. He received Mass from me in a state of deadly sin. I must go."

"He was struggling with—" Alleyn hesitated. "With his devil. He thought it might help."

"I must tell him. He must be brought to a realization," Father Jourdain said. He went out on deck and stared, without seeing it, at Table Mountain. Alleyn saw his hand go to his breast.

Tim said, "Am I wanted?"

"I'm afraid you are. He's talked to me. It's pretty obvious that the defence will call psychiatric opinions and yours may be crucial. I'll tell you what he has said and then ask you to see him. If you can get him to speak, it may go some way in his favour."

"You talk," Tim said, "as if you weren't a policeman."

3

So the priest and the psychiatrist are to do what they can [Alleyn wrote to his wife]. *Makepiece, of course, says he would need weeks to arrive at a full report. He's professionally all steamed up over Merryman's readiness to describe an incident that no doubt will be advanced as the key to his obsession and is a sort of textbook shining example of the Oedipus complex and the whole blasted job. Do you remember there was one curious link in all these wretched crimes? It was the women's names. All jewels. Marguerite, of course, means pearl, and the doll's name Esmeralda, emerald. The necklaces were always twisted and broken. And, of course, there were the flowers. This is his story. When he was just seven years old, his mother, a stupid woman whom he adored, had a birthday. It was in the early spring and he spent the contents of his money-box on a handful of hyacinths. He gave them to her, but at the same time his father brought her a necklace. He fastened it round her neck with a display of uxoriousness which Merryman describes through his teeth. In raising her hands to him she dropped the hyacinths and in the subsequent embrace trod on them. Makepiece says the pattern, from his point of view, is perfect—jewels, flowers, neck, amorousness, and fury. The boy flew into a blind rage and went for her like a demon, twisted and broke the necklace, and was dragged away and given a hiding by his father. This incident was followed at ten-day intervals by a series of something he calls faint-ing fits. Makepiece suspects petit mal. Here Merryman's story ends.*

It's as if the fact of his arrest had blown the stopper off a life-long reticence, and as if, having once spoken, he can't stop, but with extraordinary vehemence is obliged to go through with it again and and again. But he won't carry his history an inch further and re-fuses to speak if any attempt is made to discuss the cases in hand. Makepiece thinks his mistaking Dennis for the woman has had a profound effect.

There's no doubt that for years he has fought a lonely, frantic battle with his obsession, and to some extent may have beaten it off by segregating himself in a boys' school. Perhaps by substituting the lesser crime for the greater. He may have bought and destroyed necklaces and flowers for all one knows. But when his climacteric was reached and he retired from his school, the thing may have suddenly become malignant. I believe he took this voyage in an attempt to escape from it and might have done so if he hadn't en-countered on the wharf a girl with flowers, and those the most dan-gerous for him. The fact that her name was Coralie finished it. As for the earlier cases, I imagine that when his ten-day devil arose, he put on his false beard, went out on the hunt, buying flowers for the purpose, and picked up women with whom he got into conver-sation. He probably discarded many who didn't fit in with the pattern.

He exhibits, to a marked degree, the murderer's vanity. I doubt if he has made one statement that was untrue throughout the voy-age. He was eager to discuss these cases and others of their kind.

Makepiece says he's a schizophrenic; I'm never absolutely certain what that means, but no doubt it will be advanced at the trial and I hope to God it succeeds.

Of course, almost from the beginning, I thought he was my man, if my man was aboard. If the others' alibis stood up, he was the only one left. But there were signs. His preferences in literature, for instance. Any Elizabethan play that concerned the murder of a woman was better than any that didn't. The Duchess of Malfi and Othello were the best because of the way in which the heroines are killed. He resented any suggestion that "sex monsters" might be unpleasant to look at. He carried bits of paper and sodamints in his waistcoat pocket. He spilt coffee all over himself when I uncovered the doll, and blamed Miss Abbott for it. He had been to a choir school and could therefore sing. He is an expert in make-up and no doubt bearded himself for the encounters. The beard, of course, went overboard after the event.

But it was one thing to realize all this and a hell of another to sheet it home. When I saw him, as sound asleep as if he'd expiated a deadly crime instead of committing one, I realized there was only one chance of getting him. He had no doubt decided on the line he would take after the body had been found; I would have to give him the kind of shock that would jerk him off it. I fixed it up with Makepiece. When the right moment presented itself, we would confront Merryman with Mrs. Dillington-Blick. He knew he'd made his kill and of course believed her to be his victim. He was relaxed, eased of his fever and immensely enjoying his act. She loomed up on the other side of the window and—it worked.

The fact of the D-B being in her own style a femme fatale muddled the issues, since she quite deliberately went gunning for any male in sight and thus stirred up Cuddy and McAngus to the dizziest heights of middle-aged fatuity. Dale, of course, had merely settled down to a routine shipboard affair. She's a pretty consistent job of work, I must say, and I don't mind betting that when she's got over her vapours she'll take the whole thing as a sort of backhanded tribute.

For my part, having from the outset been hamstrung by captain's orders, I hope never to be given such a job again. I can even allow myself one brief bellyache, which is this: Why the hell did the D-B have to dress up a queer steward and put him in the verandah? And conversely, why the hell couldn't she tell me about it? It could have been turned without harm to advantage. Well, there it is; by his death he brought about a denouement grotesquely out-of-drawing to anything in his life.

Well, my darling, an air mail goes out at noon and will bring you this great wad of a letter. I'm staying in the ship until she sails and will return with the official party. In the meantime—

He finished his letter and went out on the bridge.

Cape Farewell was discharging cargo. At midnight, having got rid of a bull-dozer, four cars, three tons of unbleached calico, and a murderer, she would continue her voyage to Durban.

He supposed he was unlikely ever to travel in her again.